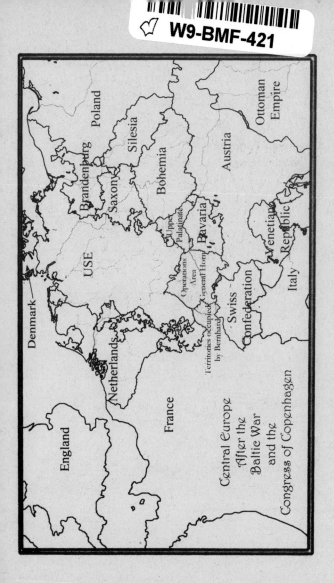

Central Europe
After the
Baltic War
and the
Congress of Copenhagen

England

Denmark

Netherlands

France

USE

Brandenburg

Poland

Saxony

Silesia

Bohemia

Upper Palatinate

Bavaria

Operations Area

Vienna Home

Austria

Ottoman Empire

Swiss Confederation

Venetian Republic

Italy

Territories occupied by Bernhard

IN CASE OF EMERGENCY ...

The take-off wasn't too bad, actually. Lannie would have been in the air force except Jesse Wood didn't want any part of his drinking habits. But he did know how to fly, as such.

Denise suspected that "as such" probably didn't cover all that a pilot needed. But it was a done deal now, so there was no point fretting over it.

"That way," she said, pointing. "It's called 'southeast.'"

"You don't gotta be so sarcastic."

Fortunately, she'd thought to make sure they had a map before they took off. Lannie and Keenan, naturally, hadn't thought of that. Apparently, they thought Denise could navigate by feminine instinct or something.

Printed on the top of the map, the ink a little smeared, was a notice that read: *Property of Kelly Aviation. Unauthorized Use Will Be Prosecuted.*

"How'd you talk Bob into letting you use the plane whenever you wanted?"

"Well," said Lannie.

Behind her, Keenan cleared his throat. "It's an emergency, you know."

"Oh, perfect," said Denise. "The first recorded instance since the Ring of Fire of plane-stealing. I betcha that's a hanging offense."

Lannie looked smug. "Nope. I checked once. Seems nobody's ever thought to getting around to making it a crime yet."

Amazing. Did the jerks really think that somewhere in the books there wasn't a provision for prosecuting *Grand Theft, Whatever We Overlooked?*

But . . . this was kinda fun, actually, except for having to help Keenan attach the two bombs underneath. The bombs weren't all that big, just fifty-pounders, but they were still a little scary. . . .

—from "The Austro-Hungarian Connection"

OTHER BOOKS IN THIS SERIES

EDITED BY ERIC FLINT

RING
OF FIRE II

EDITED BY
Eric Flint

RING OF FIRE II

This is a work of fiction. All the characters and events portrayed in this book are fictional, and any resemblance to real people or incidents is purely coincidental.

Copyright © 2008 by Eric Flint

A Baen Books Original

Baen Publishing Enterprises
P.O. Box 1403
Riverdale, NY 10471
www.baen.com

ISBN 10: 1-4165-9144-3
ISBN 13: 978-1-4165-9144-3

Cover art by Tom Kidd
Maps by Gorg Huff

First Baen paperback printing, February 2009

Distributed by Simon & Schuster
1230 Avenue of the Americas
New York, NY 10020

Library of Congress Cataloging-in-Publication Data:
2007042362

Printed in the United States of America

10 9 8 7 6 5 4 3 2

To Hank Landau,
Ken Diamond, and
Matthew Diamond

Contents

Preface

This is the second of the *Ring of Fire* anthologies, following the one that came out four years ago, in January of 2004. As was the case with the original *Ring of Fire*, the stories in this anthology are all part of the 1632 series which I began in 2000 with the founding novel, *1632*, and have since continued with the following novels:

1633
1634: The Baltic War
1634: The Galileo Affair
1634: The Bavarian Crisis
1635: The Cannon Law

In addition to the six novels so far published in the series and the two *Ring of Fire* anthologies, other stories in the 1632 setting have been published in the part-anthology/part-novel titled *1634: The Ram Rebellion*, as well as the *Grantville Gazette*. The *Gazette* is an electronic magazine devoted to the 1632 series which I began publishing in 2003, the fifteenth issue of which has just come out. Beginning in the summer of last year, the *Gazette* is published on a regular bi-monthly basis. The first three volumes of the magazine were published by Baen Books in a paper edition, and the fourth volume is coming out in paper in June of this year.

(For information on how to subscribe to the Gazette, see the end of this preface.)

To put it another way, short fiction is as integral a part of this series as novel length stories. "Integral," not simply in the sense that the stories are part of the setting, but that they often play a major role in shaping the series. They are not simply, as is usually the case with spin-off anthologies attached to a popular series, stories "off to the side." What happens in these stories very often lays the basis for major developments in the novels, as well as either introducing important characters or developing them still further.

That's especially true of the stories which appear in the *Ring of Fire* anthologies. There is no sharp and clear dividing line between stories that appear in the *Gazette* and stories that appear in the RoF anthologies. The distinction is certainly not one of literary quality in the abstract. But, as much as possible, I try to select stories for the *Ring of Fire* anthologies which connect more directly with the series as a whole than do most of the stories in the *Gazette*.

That was true for the first *Ring of Fire* anthology, as I explained in some detail in my preface to that volume. It is true of this second one, as well. To give some examples:

Andrew Dennis' "Lucky at Cards" is an integral part of the story line which he and I began in *1634: The Galileo Affair,* developed further in *1635: The Cannon Law,* and will be continuing in novels to come. It depicts an episode in the career of Giulio Mazarini—now Jules Mazarin, having taken service with Cardinal Richelieu's France.

Gorg Huff and Paula Goodlett's "A Trip to Amsterdam," along with Iver Cooper's "The Chase," develop further the adventures of a group of young American entrepreneurs whose story was begun by Gorg as far back as the first volume of the *Gazette* (see "The Sewing Circle") and has continued in a number of stories published in later issues of the magazine. So far, those characters and their activities have only received incidental mention in the novels, but that will be changing in the future. These kids are not about to go away, to say the least.

David Carrico's "Command Performance" is one of several stories he's written, the first of which appeared in the *Gazette,* that depicts the impact of the time-transplanted Americans on seventeenth-century music and musicians. These same characters will figure prominently in a murder mystery novel he and I are co-authoring titled *1635: Symphony for the Devil.*

K.D. Wentworth's "Eddie and the King's Daughter" tells the story of how the romance between Eddie Cantrell and the Danish king's daughter Anne Cathrine, which figured prominently in *1634: The Baltic War*, got started in the first place.

Virginia's DeMarce's "Second Thoughts" continues the story of Noelle Murphy, one of the central characters in *1634: The Ram Rebellion*, and serves as a preface to the final story in this anthology.

That's my own short novel, "The Austro-Hungarian Connection," which ties the development of Noelle as a character to major changes taking place in political and military developments in Austria and Hungary with the accession to the throne of a new emperor. The story also features Denise Beasley, one of the major characters in a new novel I've co-authored with Virginia entitled *1635: The Dreeson Incident*, which will be coming out within a year.

And this preface is probably long enough. I hope you enjoy the book.

Eric Flint
July, 2007

Those of you interested in subscribing to the *Grantville Gazette* can find it at the following URL: http://www.grantvillegazette.com.

Horse Thieves

Karen Bergstralh

Fall 1633

The rain pelted down solidly, stirring up the puddles in the road's many ruts. Four men and a boy slowly rode along, huddled in misery. This stretch of road passed through several still-abandoned villages and the nearest inn lay several miles down it.

"Why does it always rain when the four of us travel together? Twice I've gone with Herr Parker and it only rained a little. It didn't rain at all when we went to Magdeburg and Jena with Fraulein Parker. Why does it do so now? If we had brought them, would they keep the rain from falling?" The soft tenor grumble came from Reichard Blucher, a huge man with a cheerful smile not reflected in his voice.

"It rained plenty when Rob was with us," Dieter replied. "I think it is just France telling us it is time to go home."

"We've been out of France for a week," Wilfram Jones muttered back. A trickle of cold water traced down the back of his neck and he tried fruitlessly to adjust the collar of his rain slicker. The battered old Stetson he wore directed the rain away from the back of his neck better than any other headgear he'd worn, yet some cold water always got through. The true miracle was the slicker. It shed water better than any oiled wool cloak and was far lighter.

"Papa, will it rain all the way home?" Jacques asked. The thirteen-year-old boy had been adopted the previous year. Some of the former mercenaries had stumbled into Jacques' village and found only two women and four children alive. Christian was now married to one of the women and had adopted the surviving children. This horse-buying trip was the first time Jacques had come along.

"No, son," Christian replied, smiling at the boy. That gentle smile on Christian's face always surprised the other men. Christian du Champ generally looked like a priest about to launch into a three-hour sermon on mortal sin.

Despite the rain, it had been a good trip. The results, forty large horses, followed quietly on lead ropes behind the men. On this trip they had gone to Le Perche in their search for draft horses. The mercenaries-turned-horsetraders had gotten a good selection of young mares and two yearling colts. The animals were slated for Ev Parker's heavy horse breeding program, but only the colts belonged to Herr Parker. All the rest belonged to them.

A sense of satisfaction settled on Wilf. Two years before they had all been mercenaries in one of Tilly's tercios, marching on Badenburg. The tercio had found out that the rumors of "wizards" nearby were true, as up-time guns had shattered it. Taken prisoner, the men had been saved by Gretchen Richter. It still amazed him, to have gone from mercenary to prisoner to hired farm help and now to partner in Herr Parker's draft horse breeding operation—all in the space of those two years. Give them another year like the last, and they would be rich men. A better end, he thought, than his father had predicted years before. Maybe next spring he would travel back to England and see if his father still lived.

Lightning bloomed overhead followed immediately by thunder, making several of the horses dance. When eyes and ears had adjusted, Wilf signaled his companions to silence. He had caught the sounds of someone else swearing. Christian moved his horse ahead of Jacques, giving Dieter the lead rope of his string of horses. Reichard swung his mount alongside Wilf's and handed over his string also. Hands now free, the two men moved slightly ahead of the rest.

Out of the darkness and rain emerged two sodden men on horseback—men dressed in uniforms with muskets at the ready. Wilf had just enough time to see Reichard's lifted eyebrow and nod before one of the soldiers spoke.

The order for them to halt was no surprise. What had caught their attention was the uniforms and the muskets—flintlock muskets.

Complying with the soldiers' orders, the group stopped and waited. After a brief consultation that looked more like a whispered argument, one soldier remained in front of them. The other rode past, peering intently at them as he passed. Having inspected them, the second soldier then rode back to join his companion. Another whispered argument followed with much gesturing.

Reichard leaned toward Wilf and muttered under his breath, his eyes on the two soldiers. "They want our horses, from what I make out."

"Aye," Wilf replied, "and they'll not care about any objections from us."

Wilf turned his head and caught Dieter Wiesskamp's eye. Dieter smiled tightly and quickly tucked one of his lead ropes under his thigh. His free hand dipped into his slicker pocket. That pocket now contained an up-time revolver.

At Reichard's side, Christian frowned blackly, nodding also. In his right hand, hidden by his slicker, would be one of those lovely small swords the up-timers called a "Bowie knife." In Christian's hands, blades had a deadly elegance.

Turning back to face the soldiers, Wilf dallied both lead ropes around the saddle's horn with a quickly muttered prayer that the draft horses would remain calm and docile. Wilf's hand slipped through his own slicker pocket and the slit behind it to find the pistol at his waist.

Easing it out of the holster, he snuggled it down in the raincoat's pocket.

"They're going to split up, one riding next to me, the other next to Christian. Think we're the merchants." Reichard whispered. "Leave them to Christian and me. We can do it quietly and if we miss . . ."

Wilf nodded in agreement. Gunshots from up-time guns sounded distinct to the trained ear. He had no wish to announce the group's connections with Grantville if it could be avoided. Soldiers like these wouldn't be alone. More would be somewhere nearby. If Reichard and Christian could dispose of these without having to shoot them, there was one less risk of bringing unwanted attention to them.

Finally the two soldiers reached a decision. "You will come with us. Do not argue or we will kill you. If you try to escape, we will kill you." With that the speaker turned his horse and motioned for Reichard to join him. The second soldier moved to the side of the road and took up station alongside Christian.

"You," growled the second soldier, his musket pointed at Christian, "will ride at the back." When Christian nodded in agreement, the first soldier motioned for the group to move out.

The first soldier rode just to one side. His musket was aimed at Reichard but he was trying to watch all of them. Turned awkwardly, the soldier didn't see the tree branch looming ahead. Although it was barely more than a large twig, the slap of the branch against the side of his head distracted him. That was all Reichard needed. He reached out with one huge hand and wrapped it around the soldier's neck. A quick jerk dragged the man from his saddle to dangle over the road. Reichard's other hand grabbed a shoulder and twisted. The sound of the soldier's neck breaking was almost hidden by the splatter of the rain. Reichard dropped the limp body and spun his horse around.

Behind them, Christian saw Reichard's first movement. Slamming his horse hard against the second soldier's, Christian's hand snaked out with the Bowie knife. The nearly headless body slumped down and slid off onto the muddy road.

"Papa, weren't you afraid he would shoot you?" asked Jacques in a quivering voice.

"No, son. Flintlocks aren't worth spit in heavy rain; wet powder won't fire. He wasn't a very good soldier, either. He rode too close to me. You did well, Jacques, for your first fight. Now, take the horses over there, under that tree, and wait."

"Yes, Papa." The boy smiled, proud of his stepfather's praise.

"We can make a soldier out of him," Dieter commented. "Now, what should we do with this one?"

"Pray God he never becomes a soldier. I'll not have that life for him." Christian spat and shot a sour look at Dieter. "As for this piece of filth . . . " He dismounted and approached the dead soldier. "Haul him into the woods and let the wolves deal with him."

"Did you notice their horses and how the beasts move?" asked Dieter.

"Like they were on their last legs. See, this one just stands here." Working gently Christian slipped a rope over the horse's head and unbuckled the bridle. "Ever seen a bit like this before?"

"In several books—the same books that showed uniforms like they were wearing and saddles like that one," Reichard replied, bringing up the other loose horse.

"Up-time books?" Wilf asked.

"Yes, those ones on the Americans' civil war. Rob Clark loaned them to me, when my leg was broken. He thought I'd like it because it was about soldiers. The cavalry used this kind of saddle. Some Scotsman made them, I think. I've even seen one, at Herr Parker's."

"Aye, Herr Parker has one of these saddles. 'McClellans,' they are called. Miserable things to ride, but they are lightweight and are supposed to fit horses better than ours. It appears someone else has been reading the same books."

"Well, this saddle doesn't fit this horse very well. I've never seen such sores before." Christian cursed as he eased the saddle off. "As large as my fist, this one is—and another on the other side just as big."

"We need to get off this road before some of their friends come looking for them." Wilf chewed his lip for a moment, then shrugged. "Tie the bodies up on their horses. We shouldn't be too far from that meadow we've camped at before. Then we need to find out where the rest of them are. God grant they are not between us and home."

"Aye, we can dump the bodies deep in the woods and let the pigs deal with them," Reichard stated matter-of-factly. "After a day or so there won't be enough left for their mothers to recognize them if they are found. Once that's done, let me do a little scouting. If the rest of these soldiers are close, I'll find them."

The rain had ceased some time ago, but here under the trees water still dripped. The ground beneath gave up water like a squeezed sponge whenever Wilf moved. At least it wasn't as cold here where the wind didn't reach. He looked at the men on each side, gauging their discomfort. Reichard Blucher lay quietly, only his eyes moving. Reichard's size should have made him clumsy in the woods but he moved like a wolf. Wilf had heard the tales Reichard told of his forester father and grandfather. Now, hunkered down in these sopping woods he found himself believing them. On his other side, Christian du Champ stretched full length in the wet turf, his body still, his hands holding a pair of treasured up-time binoculars to his eyes.

"What do you think?" Wilf hissed.

"Just what I thought last evening," Christian replied, his voice irritated. "They number about a hundred and show no signs of breaking camp. And they are blocking our road home."

"Waiting for someone or something." The soft tenor voice was always a surprise from the burly Reichard. "They're the oddest cavalry I've ever seen."

"Aye, all of them have rifles—flintlock muskets. Pistols, too. Even the camp is laid out strangely."

The slightest of rustling noises behind him caught Wilf's attention. He turned his head and saw it was Sam O'Reilly crawling cautiously up the slope. Slithering into place beside Christian, Sam held a hand out for the binoculars. The previous night, when Reichard had returned from his scout, Sam O'Reilly and Klaus Goltz had been with him.

"Found them messing about in the woods, making enough noise to frighten a deaf old woman. I thought it better to bring them here than have them blunder into our new friends," was all Reichard said. O'Reilly and Klaus had explained that they were tracking a group of horse thieves who had hit a village near Grantville.

"Looks like the bastards got ahold of an old U.S. Cavalry manual," Sam whispered. "Damn camp is laid out like something from the Civil War. Even got themselves uniforms."

"Yes," Reichard replied softly. "You are right. This camp does have the look of something from that manual. Good book, lots of good ideas there."

"Where'd you see it?" Sam asked suspiciously.

"One of you Americans. He saw me reading a book on your civil war and loaned me a copy. Very good book. He's one of those who play act as soldiers."

"Oh, one of the reenactors. Shouldn't have let you see it; your people get enough ideas without our folks helping." Resentment heavily laced Sam's voice.

"Ah, but we are on your side now. We are all citizens of Grantville. This, my friend, is not a good place to argue—those soldiers may hear us." Reichard's voice was barely audible.

"Aye, well they might," Wilf whispered. "Sam, have you any idea why these troops are just sitting here?"

"Guarding the road?"

"H'mm, I think not. This is hardly a major road, after all—which is why we were using it. We're nowhere near a crossroad or ford. They haven't been pillaging, save for your missing horses. The officers are holding the men in camp."

Wilf sighed. "Why are they here? This road only leads to . . . Ah! To the Badenburg road. Clever bastards. Sneak along this road—" Wilf took a twig and sketched a rough map in the mud "—until you are in position to drop down on the main road. Wonder what their target is? What about guards?"

"Sheltering out of the wet under trees there, there, and there." Reichard pointed, a feral grin spreading across his face. "Poor bastards will catch hell if their captain finds them, but they've left a couple of nice gaps for us. It would seem some old habits die hard. None of the officers have ventured out of their tents except to go into that big tent. No one is checking the scouts. The officers are lazy pigs."

"Probably noble-born sons," Christian whispered hoarsely. "Useless sots. This lot could use someone like Captain von Schorlemer."

"Or Captain Ramos." Wilf snorted. The other mercenaries laughed silently at old memories.

"No sergeants, then. No one keeping them on their toes." Sam finally handed the binoculars back to Christian.

"Oh, they've got sergeants. They are the men sitting around that nice big fire on the edge of the camp. It is old habits, bad old habits, which this new cavalry troop hasn't lost. The weather's too bad for battle so everyone huddles down and waits. I thought your army people were crazy at first. Your sergeants work very hard all the time. Now, sitting up here and looking down on these, I understand."

Reichard nodded at Sam. "I do not think one of your army units would be so easily spied on."

"Don't count on it," Wilf replied thoughtfully. "All men get lazy and careless. I think that too often you up-timers believe rate-of-fire is all there is to war. Your manuals warn repeatedly about getting careless—as do your sergeants."

"Yeah, Little Big Horn syndrome. Just because you got better guns doesn't mean the enemy can't kill you," Sam agreed. "Guess you Limeys had some problems that way with the Zulus, someplace called Rorke's Drift."

"Ah, yes. I've seen that movie, too. The English hold out in that one. I think the one you mean is *Zulu Dawn*. A few brave English soldiers attempt to stand up to thousands of spear carrying natives with predictable results. The lesson is: don't get cocky and don't get careless and don't assume better arms mean you will win. General Jackson and others say such things often. Which is why I think we should depart this hill before continuing our discussion. Sam, you go first, Christian next, then me, and Reichard will tidy up after us."

"Ha! Those guards, should they move from their dry spots, will never know we were here." Reichard smiled. "And when the time comes, they will not know they are dead until they try to get up. I have some new tricks I want to try." His smile grew wider and fiercer.

The horse traders were camped in a small valley a little distance from the cavalry camp. Unless one looked very carefully it was hard to spot the three small shelters tucked under some tall bushes. What did draw attention was the large number of horses grazing along the tiny creek. When Sam approached, one horse, a big, ugly roan, looked up and snorted. Dieter Wiesskamp stepped into visibility, an up-time rifle cradled in his arms. Nodding at Sam, Dieter whistled two short bursts and Jacques du Champ stood up from a low spot in the meadow, proudly holding a .22 rifle.

"Where are Wilf and Reichard?" Dieter asked.

"Scouting to see if we've drawn any unwanted attention." Sam tried not to show his dismay at not having spotted either Dieter or Jacques. Damn, when had they gotten so good?

"So what's the verdict? Are we going to sneak back to Grantville?"

"So impatient, Dieter, always you are so impatient," Christian chided, coming out of the woods and crossing the meadow behind Sam.

"I want to get somewhere dry," Sam groused and resumed walking. The idea that his down-time companions might be better woodsmen irritated him.

"Aye, and I wouldn't turn down a warm meal." Christian angled off to admire his adopted son's clever hiding spot.

"So my best guess is that whoever these men are they are waiting for someone or something. What their target is, I wish I could guess." Wilf spoke around the stem of his pipe.

"Might be looking for targets of opportunity. A hundred men aren't that large a force. Especially armed with flintlocks in this weather." Sam gestured at the rain, again bucketing down outside their shelter.

"A hundred men . . . . From the two we met up with they might be Bavarians. I can't see them being Spanish but maybe good old John George has grown a backbone.

Whoever, they appear to be copying an up-time manual so this would be a company, correct?" Reichard poked at the fire, flipping a piece of burning wood back into the center.

"Depends on how they're organized," Sam replied. "Might be, I don't know. I've never run around in my great-granddaddy's long johns pretending to be a soldier. Had enough of soldiering when I was in the army. This bunch of foreign bastards isn't big enough to be a serious threat to Badenburg or Grantville."

"Mayhap the target is not Badenburg. The war is heating up again. Troops and supplies might well be found moving along that road. A hundred men could do damage there." Dieter's voice was thoughtful.

"A hundred men could destroy villages and set fire to farms," Klaus agreed. "To a village a hundred such men is a very big threat."

"Sherman's March to the Sea. Terrorize the farmers, burn what they can't steal and generally create havoc. But would they think of that?" Sam sat cross-legged, field stripping and cleaning his .30-06.

"It appears they have a cavalry manual so they probably have several histories." Reichard shook his head. "I've read about Sherman's march in different books. There are lots of ideas in those books, especially for fast raids with cavalry. If they have something about General Forrest . . . that could give them very nasty ideas. As it is, they seem to have obtained flintlock muskets in some numbers."

His huge hands caressed one of the soldier's muskets. A sack at his side contained the uniforms and other items the two dead soldiers had carried. "Not rifled, and they are not using cartridges. This pattern doesn't look like any I've seen in Grantville."

"Might be from Suhl. There've been rumors of Suhl selling flintlocks in great numbers." Christian peered closely at the other musket. "No, none of the marks are from Suhl. There are people in Grantville who should see these."

"Agreed, see them and soon," Wilf stated, puffing on his pipe. "We need to decide what we will do. Grantville and Badenburg must be warned about these fine gentlemen camped in the woods. You two have found your horse thieves; mayhap you should give the warning. Whatever else, we have horses to deliver."

"I think someone needs keep a watch on them and, perhaps, discomfort them somewhat." Reichard's voice had a rough edge. He tossed the musket and sack across the fire to Dieter.

"Aye, watch them indeed," Wilf agreed amiably. "There are too many friends here about for me to find comfort in either these soldiers' presence or the thought of losing sight of them. The odds are poor, though. A hundred against six . . . best not stir them."

"I'm with Reichard," Dieter said. "The army may not have any troops close enough to get here before these move off. Besides, we all are members of the army. Reservists to be sure, but still . . . " He examined the musket he now held. "Piss poor flint on this one. Is the other any better?"

Wilf smiled. "And some of us are getting a bit soft with all this fine living we've been doing. I agree, watch them. But watch only. If you do your usual throat cutting, they'll know we are here."

Christian frowned. "This powder is poor. Badly milled." He sniffed at it and touched his tongue lightly to the small pile in his hand. "Bah! I think someone's let sand get into this powder. The other man's powder was better. Do they each supply their own?" Shrugging, Christian dusted his hands.

"Maybe they do have a bigger target in mind. Maybe they are waiting for more companies to join them. Say they broke their regiment up to sneak them in this close." Sam finished cleaning his rifle and began reassembling it. "Damned sneaky, foreign bastards."

"Oh, aye. A warning must get to Grantville. Our horses must be gotten away from here or else they give away our presence. So many gray horses are difficult to hide. Besides, fresh horses might be what the soldiers are awaiting. Their own appear to be in bad shape. Christian, I think it best if you and Jacques go with the horses and the warning."

Wilf pointed his pipe at the sleepy boy leaning against Christian. "Sam and Klaus should go, also. They are family men and should our friends discover us . . . " Wilf shrugged and smiled grimly. "Dieter, you'll be needed to help with the horses. Your woodcraft is not as good as mine is. Reichard and I will stay and keep watch on the camp."

Christian nodded. "Best we leave before dawn. Reichard, if we take that path you showed us, don't we hit the Badenburg road?"

"Yes, but well enough down it that you should miss any stray patrols. The trail is narrow in spots, only one horse wide, so don't think you can hurry along it. I'll get you started on it come morning."

"Come on, Jacques, you need to get some sleep." Standing, Christian looked around the group. "I will pray for your safety as I will not be there to keep you out of trouble. Do not get too fancy with your plans lest they tangle you up—as usual."

Wilf grinned back at the thin mercenary. It was Christian who usually got tangled up, especially when the wine or beer had been freely flowing.

"I'm staying." The flat statement came from Sam.

"Three men cannot handle all the horses on that trail," came the equally flat reply from Dieter. "The boy is not strong enough if there is trouble."

"Then Wilf should go in my place." Sam's response was forceful and final.

"Why should I go in place of you?" Wilf asked, surprised at Sam's attitude.

There had been trouble with the man the previous spring. A matter of inheritance, or lack of it. In addition, O'Reilly was one of the few up-timers who never seemed comfortable working with down-timers. Sam was often found at Club 250, drinking and cursing all "foreigners." When the final blow up occurred over the disputed inheritance, the man had gotten massively drunk, beaten up his wife and stolen several horses and guns. Quickly caught and as quickly convicted, Sam O'Reilly had served a year of hard labor. After that, he had appeared to calm down. He did his work but he continued to complain if he thought some down-timer was given an easier job.

In short, sneaking around in a wet forest keeping watch on a hundred soldiers was hardly a task Wilf expected Sam O'Reilly to volunteer for.

"Why should you stay?" Dieter asked.

"Because I've got this." Sam slapped his hand against the butt of the .30-06. "And this." He drew a huge pistol; one Wilf thought was a .357 Magnum.

"If things get dicey I can off more foreign bastards faster and from farther away than that little popgun of yours." The light from the fire played across Sam's face, giving his eyes a red and feral glint.

Glancing at Reichard, Wilf caught a thoughtful look and gesture of agreement from the big mercenary. Dieter and Klaus remained silent but had their hands near their own guns. They both remembered Sam's blow-up the previous year.

Sighing, Wilf nodded. "Aye, nearly a cannon that gun is. Should blow great holes in our friends if needed. Agreed. I'll go back with the rest and leave you and Reichard to entertain yourselves watching yon miserable excuses for soldiers sitting in the rain. Give the sack to me, Dieter. I'll see it delivered."

"You should take these fake McClellans back with you, too." Sam spat into the fire. "There are a couple of guys, reenactors, who should see 'em. Look like damn poor imitations to me, but these guys will know. Might be someone in Grantville has been selling old saddles to the enemy. If they have . . . well, leave it to these guys."

"I think you are right in calling them imitations." Reichard picked up one of the saddles and turned it over. "From the way they are made the saddler had only a picture or sketch. Look here, how narrow the bars are. I've seen Herr Parker's saddle. Its bars are wider and smoother. This leather is thin and soft. See how it has wrinkled here? The real one, it is covered with rawhide."

"Yeah, the tree should be covered in rawhide," Sam replied. "Then the seat gets covered in saddle leather. Damned trees aren't even from side to side and the two saddles don't match, either. Crappy workmanship."

"Hurried, and working without a true model to show how it should be. Still, as you say, the poor workmanship surprises me. Someone wasn't paying proper attention to the work."

Reichard's large hands stroked the underside of the saddle. "Saddlemakers know well enough that the leather must be smooth. Wonder if some saddlemaker isn't too fond of the man buying these saddles."

Dieter shook his head skeptically. "And what happens when that man notices the problem and takes his complaints back to the saddlemaker? Chance there would be one less saddlemaker alive."

Normally silent, Klaus spoke up. "I think it is either a case of bad workmanship or very clever sabotage. See, on this saddle the leather is not wrinkled. The tree is still uneven but the stitching is better. Yet, be the poor work deliberate, the false saddlemaker may live. There are no maker's marks on either saddle. So how is anyone to know which saddlemaker did this work?"

"Crappy work or sabotage, what does it matter? We've got that bunch of foreign bastards to keep an eye on come morning." With that final comment Sam picked up his rifle and moved off to the shelter where his sleeping bag awaited him.

"He may have the right of it. For now it matters little. Rest well, gentlemen." Wilf nodded to his companions and pondered Sam's motives. Very quietly he whispered to Reichard, "Watch yourself. Yon man is too eager to kill foreigners, any foreigners."

"I understand. I'll be careful."

"Jesus! What the hell did you do to him?" Sam choked out, his face going pale and green. "Looks like a panther chewed him up and spit him out."

"Softly, softly, my friend. There are four other guards about." Reichard looked up. "Should any of them wander over here and find him, I think they will be confused. Lynx do not usually attack humans."

"Yeah, yeah. Maybe they'll think the cat was rabid. But how did you manage to make it look so real?" Swallowing, Sam peered down at the body.

"These." Reichard held up a necklace of five claws strung together with a number of teeth. "Made it when I was ten years old. I'd just killed an old lynx that was bothering the sheep and Papa let me keep the teeth and claws. It was a silly, childish thing to do. I don't know why I keep it."

Sam gave a grim chuckle. "I've got the claws from the first bear I shot. Strung 'em just about the same way, too. I was just turned twelve when Pa took me on that bear hunt. Won't his friends wonder why there was no noise?"

"That, my friend, depends. If any among them are foresters the deception will not hold. If luck is with us, they are all city scum. I was going to just cut his throat, but even a city scum understands that means some enemy is nearby. Come. This one's on his way to damnation and we need to avoid the rest."

"Hey, I've got an idea. Two of these jerks are down that gully—" Sam pointed back the way he had come "—and they're arguing something fierce."

"Ah, let us go along carefully and see. Perhaps they can be pushed into a duel. But first, any changes in the camp?"

"No. Saw the night road patrols come in and the morning ones go out. Took 'em half an hour to switch off. Only one sergeant was involved in the shift change. He sent three patrols out, two headed east and one west."

"What about their horses?" As they backed away from the body, Reichard carefully removed any traces of their presence.

"Oh, yeah. You were right. Looks like they've only got maybe ten horses still in good enough shape to ride patrol. That piebald and the little dun went out again but not with the same troopers. Those two they stole from us. That same guy was out again plastering mud on the sores. Damn good way to get 'em infected. If we have to scoot, these boys can't put up much of a pursuit."

"We cannot count on that. If they are stirred up enough they will come after us no matter how bad the horses' condition. We must remain careful. Let them be cold, wet, and afraid. Waiting in these conditions is hard."

"Hey, man, they get a look at that poor sucker and they're going to be having nightmares. Hell, he's enough to give me nightmares."

Reichard laughed. "Aye, nightmares are what we shall give them. Strange happenings, odd noises—such will have the most hardened soldier looking over his shoulder. Perhaps some will decide to flee."

"And how about we pick off the saps that flee? Let the rest know they'll meet uncanny fates within this wood?"

Reichard chuckled and smiled. "Aye, aye. Then the rest are less eager to continue. They must know they are near Grantville. Everyone knows the minions of Satan protect Grantville. Ah, my man, you give me ideas!" Reichard sighed and looked at Sam. "But it must be done carefully."

Two hours later and the score stood at five dead cavalrymen. One soldier had the bad luck of deciding to urinate from the top of a boulder. Reichard snapped that one's neck and tossed him down onto the rocks below. Sam garroted the third and used a piece of rope to hang the body from a handy tree branch. Reichard carefully marked the ground beneath the body.

"Now," the big man commented, "It looks properly like he hung himself. When the neck doesn't break it takes a bit for one to strangle to death."

The two guards Sam had seen arguing were easily provoked from words to knives by a couple of well-thrown rocks. The surviving guard, as he stood swaying over his dead companion, never saw Sam looming behind him.

"Ah, good work." Reichard chuckled grimly. "One more cut will not be noticed on this one."

"Yeah, and nobody's likely to notice the bump on the back of his head, either." Sam shook his head. "Wonder what the hell they were arguing over."

"I think a woman. At least a woman's name was being thrown back and forth. Now, we must leave this place.

They will be missed and their sergeant will come looking."

"Damn, but it would be easy to pick off those officers." O'Reilly caressed the stock of his rifle. "I'm getting tired of all this sneaking around."

"How many bullets do you have?"

"About thirty rounds for my rifle and twenty-four for the magnum. Why?"

"I have twelve for my pistol," Reichard said. "If we both shoot like Julie Sims, never missing, we will have forty left alive. Those forty will be very, very upset with us. Those are not odds I like."

"Shit! We shoot a few of the officers and the rest will tuck their tails and run!"

"Ah, like our tercio did at the Battle of the Crapper?"

Sam stared into the distance. Reichard could see the man was remembering that day. The tercio had just kept coming and coming and coming—right up the muzzles of the Grantville Army's rifles. And with Frank Jackson's M-60 hammering them from the side. Reichard had been in those ranks and had taken a machine gun round himself.

Shaking his head, Sam finally replied. "Okay. Guess you've got a point there."

Reichard exhaled slowly. The crisis was over for now. O'Reilly might be tired of skulking about in the woods, but Reichard was tired of dealing with Sam's inclination for blind violence. Very tired. The up-timer had some woodcraft but he had no patience, and no subtlety.

Gunfire awoke Reichard. Rolling out of his blankets, he knelt and listened. The sound of several rifles boomed raggedly in the distance. Above those was the rhythmic crack-pause-crack-pause of an up-time rifle. Reichard gave a low, sharp whistle, his hands busy picking up the small amount of camping gear and stuffing it into a pair of sacks. At the sound of the whistle, the two horses grazing in the meadow lifted their heads. The larger of the two began to trot toward Reichard. The other, smaller horse grabbed another mouthful of grass and then trailed after his companion. Troll, a massive, ugly, half-Clydesdale gelding, had become Reichard's horse the year before. In that time the big roan horse had learned that such a whistle meant 'oats.' Sam's horse, Travy, appeared to be making the same connection.

Seeing the horses were coming, Reichard again listened. The shooting had decreased somewhat. There was a long pause in the up-time rifle, then it started up again. When the horses arrived, Reichard poured a handful of oats into the feedbags and tied the bags over their noses. While the animals munched on their oats, he quickly brushed their backs and bellies, then threw their saddles on. Troll rubbed his head against Reichard's back, nearly knocking him over.

"Sorry, boy, but we've no time for a leisurely breakfast this morning." He slapped the big horse's neck affectionately. It took only a minute or so more to bridle the horses and tie the sacks of camping supplies behind the saddles.

"Now we are ready to leave this place in a hurry." Reichard snapped lead ropes to the halters he'd left on under the bridles. "So we will go and get that crazy man out of trouble. Trouble I've no doubt he started himself."

Leading the horses through the woods, Reichard came to a spot just below the ridge where they had first spied on the soldiers' camp. The shooting had quieted some.

The first response from the camp, disorganized by the surprise attack, was coming under control. The officers and sergeants were back in charge. The lack of smoke from O'Reilly's rifle would keep the soldiers from pin-pointing Sam's exact position. But soon, very soon, some bright man would figure out that the firing was coming from one place on the ridge. Reichard tied the horses to a sapling. He double-checked that both knots would release with a quick pull. When beating a hasty retreat, not being able to untie your horse was not a good idea.

Sam's fire had also slackened. That meant that the easy targets had gone to ground. Reichard eased up the slope in a crouch, his eyes watching for movement on either side of him. Near the top he dropped to his belly and started to crawl toward the rocks where O'Reilly hid.

"Sam, it's time to get out of here," Reichard whispered.

Startled, Sam half-turned, his rifle almost lining up on Reichard's head. "Oh, it's you. About time you showed up. Get up here and give me a hand. Got 'em dancing! Bet they think it's the whole U.S. Army up here!" Turning back, Sam sent a pair of shots down into the camp.

Reichard watched Sam's face carefully. The man's expression seemed unnaturally gleeful. "If we're going to play like we're the Army, we need to change positions. You've been in this spot too long."

"What? Whaddaya mean?" Confusion chased suspicion across Sam's face.

"You've been firing from this spot all along. To make them think we are an army we need to fire from several different positions." Reichard was close enough now to smell Sam's breath and the whiskey on it. Connecting that with the empty bottle now residing behind Travy's saddle, Reichard had an explanation for Sam's behavior.

"I gotta good spot here. Can see all of the camp. You go someplace else and shoot at 'em." Rearing up, Sam took aim at a running man. He fired and missed, fired again and whooped as the man fell and rolled out of sight. "Got the bastard! Why the hell should I move?"

In point of fact, Reichard knew he'd missed the man. That roll had been a controlled one, not the flopping of a man killed or badly wounded.

A movement caught Reichard's eye and he looked to his left. Two more cavalrymen were slipping through the trees, muskets ready.

"Because we are being flanked." Reichard shot at them before he finished the sentence. One man dropped with the loose boned look of death, the other dodged behind a large tree. A shot slammed into the rocks, coming from Sam's right.

"Damn! They should be running by now! I've killed twenty, twenty-two of 'em! The damned bastards should be panicked and running!"

"Well, they aren't," Reichard growled. He left off adding that O'Reilly's estimate of the men he'd killed was wildly exaggerated. A superb marksman such as Julie Sims might be able to kill that many men in such a situation, but there was no chance at all that O'Reilly had done so—or could have, even if he'd been sober.

"If we are to keep fighting them we need to get away from this spot," he repeated urgently.

"I can't see anyone over there . . . guess you're right. Let's boogie!" O'Reilly rose, fired a couple of shots into the woods to the right and started walking down the hill.

"Stay down!"

"Hell, man, Americans don't run and we sure as hell don't crawl!" Sam stopped, turned deliberately, and sent another shot into the trees before resuming his walk. .

"The horses are over there." The remaining soldier on the left stepped away from a tree, his musket aimed and ready. Reichard snapped a shot that way and saw the soldier duck back. Fumbling a bit, he reloaded as he followed Sam down the hill.

When they reached the horses Reichard was relieved to find them still there and alone. He ground his teeth in frustration as Sam took time to check Travy over and readjust the saddle.

"Ain't one of you foreigners can saddle a horse right." Sam finally swung up in the saddle. "Won't see me . . . "

He paused as several shots came from the top of the ridge. " . . . soring any of my horses' backs." Grunting, he shook his head, then slid the rifle into the saddle scabbard. Unsnapping his holster, Sam pulled the .357 out and emptied the cylinder at the men now coming down the slope. Not one of the shots came close to any of the approaching enemy, so far as Reichard could see.

"Getting a bit warm around here!" Sam grinned, spun Travy around and set the horse off at a run.

"Just a bit warm," agreed Reichard, relieved that O'Reilly was no longer arguing to stay and fight. He sent Troll in pursuit of the smaller horse. As they galloped out into the sunshine of the meadow, Reichard saw the stain spreading just below Sam's right armpit. It wasn't sweat.

When Travy half-jumped the little stream, Sam wavered. He took the reins in his right hand and wrapped his left around the saddle horn. The horse, aware something was wrong, slowed. Reichard caught up and saw the paleness in Sam's face.

"Can you hold on until we've hit the path? Once back in woods we'll stop and tend your wound."

"Bastards!" Disbelief edged out pain in Sam's reply. "Can't believe some stupid foreign bastards waving old-fashioned smoke poles managed to hit me. Can't hit a barn door with one at fifty yards. Everybody knows none of you can hit what you shoot at. That's why all the foreigners in the army got our shotguns."

Unwilling to argue with the wounded man, Reichard only replied, "Put enough lead into the air and some of it is certain to find flesh. The one who shot you may have been aiming at me."

"Oh, yeah, you make a bigger target." Sam moaned and slumped as they entered the woods on the far side of the meadow.

When Reichard brought his horse to a stop, Sam's horse stopped also. Gently Reichard plucked the smaller man off his saddle and laid him on the ground. Sam moaned and tried to say something. Even before he lifted the bloody shirt Reichard knew the wound was fatal. Blood foamed from Sam's lips and bubbled out the hole under his arm.

" 'S not in my back . . . didn't get shot in the back?" O'Reilly managed.

"No, Herr O'Reilly," Reichard replied. "One of the flankers shot you. I'll bandage it." He felt O'Reilly go limp.

Glancing across the meadow he saw several soldiers moving on foot. One was pointing toward the trees and shouting at the others. Reichard moved swiftly, wrapping Sam's body in his rain slicker and tying it across Travy's saddle. Finished, he checked the meadow again. The tracker was now trotting along their tracks. Ten or so horsemen appeared on the far side, muskets ready across saddles. It was time to go.

Reichard came out of the last patch of woods and onto the Badenburg road. He couldn't hear his pursuers but, considering the determination that they had shown so far, he was certain that they were still following him.

He started trotting along the road toward Grantville. A quarter of a mile later he realized that there was no other traffic.

"Ah, boys," he told the horses, "this is good. Our friends got through. I'll bet they sent Jacques ahead on his fast little pony. Come on now, Troll, step lively."

Ahead the road bent around a half-rebuilt mill and crossed the mill creek bridge. Something about the scene bothered Reichard and he stopped his horse.

"You wouldn't shoot a friend, would you?" a familiar voice called softly from the rubble.

Reichard chuckled. "No," he replied. "Especially not when that friend is behind a nice big wall and I can't see him. Hold on for a few minutes and you will have some targets you can shoot at with my blessings. It would be nice to discourage them."

Major Stieff stepped out into the open, an up-time
rifle cradled in his arms. He gestured toward a pile of
downed trees across the road. "We've enough to do that,
I hope." He smiled. "Four of us on this side and four
more over there. How many are we waiting for?"

"Eight, maybe nine. I think I wounded a couple."

"Ah, so you didn't manage to bring the entire bunch
after you. Eight or nine we can handle. There's an army
unit headed down from above Badenburg. We'll leave
the main body to them. Your horses look like they could
use a breather. They can join ours in the trees while we
see if we can discourage your pursuers." Stieff faded
back to his place behind the mill's walls.

Reichard dismounted and led the horses into the trees.
The pile of tree trunks, he noticed, made a solid, U-shaped
wall. Each tree had the nice, clean cuts of a chainsaw.
He grinned in approval when he saw that someone had
plastered mud over the newly sawn wood. The soldiers
chasing him should see a pile of cut trees and not realize
it was a freshly made fort. Afterward, the mill owner's
lawyers would have something to say about those trees.

One of the figures behind the wooden wall stepped
forward and took Travy's lead rope. "Sam did something
stupid, didn't he?" Lannie Parker's voice had a disgusted tone.

"Ah, well."

"Was he drinking, again? Forget it. Of course he was
drinking. Poor Maggie."

"Fraulein Parker, he's at peace now, however he found
it," Reichard said.

Reichard looped Troll's lead around a branch and loos-
ened the cinch on his saddle. Lannie stripped the bridle

off Travy, leaving the halter. She gave the horses a quick drink from a canvas bucket before escorting Reichard into the fort.

"Hey, Reichard. How the heck did they miss a target your size?" Rob Clark slapped the big man on the back. "Glad to see you made it this far."

"Of course I made it. I'm too mean to die. What is that saying your aunt had?"

"Heaven won't have me and Satan's afraid I'll take over hell."

"That's me, Rob. That's me. Put your hat on, boy. These men aren't blind, and that red hair of yours is a wonderful target."

Lannie sighed. "Thanks, Reichard. I've been telling him that for that last fifteen minutes. He doesn't listen to me."

"Fraulein, it is ever that way between men and their women." Reichard bowed to Lannie and winked. "A man cannot openly take his woman's advice without feeling that his friends will mock him."

The other men behind the improvised fort were up-timers whose names he didn't remember. The younger up-timer glanced toward Sam's body and gestured up the trail.

"Did you kill him or did they?"

Reichard grunted at the insult. Rob laid a hand on Reichard's arm and Lannie rounded on the man.

"Doggie, you dumbass. You're still the dumbest guy I know. You sure haven't eaten any smart pills since high school."

"Hey, Lannie. Back down. Why're you mad at me? Sam's your cousin, not mine," Doggie whined. "I was just asking. Gotta watch ourselves around these krauts, you know."

Lannie glared at him. "Sam's had a death wish for a long time. He knew Grandpa would shoot him if he raised a hand against Maggie or the girls again. That was if I didn't get to him first."

Reichard smiled down at the red-faced up-timer. "He wasn't shot by me." He tapped his up-time pistol. "Go dig the ball out and see for yourself."

Lannie Parker's defense of Reichard or the offer of an on-the-spot autopsy quieted Doggie. The young man turned back to watch the road. The other man said nothing, only nodding toward the road.

"Didn't hear what you told the major. How many we waiting for?" he asked politely.

"Eight or nine."

"Riding or walking?"

"Riding, the last time I saw them."

"Doggie," the older man addressed the younger, "aim for the middle of the chest."

"Why you telling just me?"

"Because the rest of us have been in a fire fight before. Shut up, Doggie. Or I gotta figure Lannie's got the right take on your brains."

Doggie looked offended but said nothing.

Reichard examined the wooden fort with a critical eye.

He nodded and spoke to Rob and Lannie. "This will do nicely. You've moved fast to block the road and get this ambush set up."

"Yeah." Rob replied. "Jacques had sense enough to come to my place. He knew I'd take his message seriously. I got on the phone to Major Stieff and he sent out the call-up. We were ready soonest and headed up here with the major. Got a couple of regular army units headed this way but it will take time for them to arrive. We're just supposed to slow your 'friends' down if they come this way and then fade back into town."

Lannie added. "Wilf and guys came through late last night. The rest of the militia is mustering in town. Just in case it's another raid."

Reichard shook his head. "I do not think it is a raid on Grantville." He grinned. "If I'm wrong we will treat them rudely and send the remnants running home."

"You and Sam stirred things up." Rob said. He pointed down the road and continued in a whisper. "Here comes your tail. Is that all of them?"

Reichard peered over the logs. "Yes. They've bunched up. The one on the gray seems to be their leader."

Rob pulled out a child's walkie-talkie and conveyed Reichard's words to Major Stieff.

"Wait until the last man passes the dead tree." The major's voice hissed scratchily in return.

Rob pointed out the tree in question and Reichard quickly settled himself. He broke open his pistol to reload and stopped. The only bullets he had were the two left in the gun. Lannie clucked and dug into her fanny pack. "Here. You're using .38's, right?" She dropped a box of bullets into his hands. "Thank God Rob's dad stocked up for Y2K—or was it World War III?"

"Y2K followed by the complete disintegration of civilization," Rob replied, his eyes on the approaching horsemen. "Dad suffered from having been both a Boy

Scout and a Marine. 'Be Prepared for Anything' was his motto."

His pistol reloaded, Reichard turned his attention back on the road. The soldiers on the road had stopped. He counted seven of them. He must have hit a couple in that last exchange of shots before reaching the Badenburg road. The soldiers' horses stood still, heads drooping with fatigue while the men argued.

"They've spotted us." Doggie whispered. "Told you they would."

"Shut up, Doggie." Rob whispered back. "They're arguing about tracks. The guy with the corporal's stripes thinks Reichard went the other way. None of them are trackers if they can't pick out Troll's size thirteens."

The argument resolved itself and the soldiers kicked their horses into motion toward the bridge. The last man, the corporal, rode past the dead tree and the ambush was sprung.

Reichard emptied his pistol into the body of men and bent to reload. Beside him Rob's rifle cracked out, followed by Lannie's and the older up-timer's. The major's up-time rifle snapped from the mill along with the bass booms of flintlocks. Reichard straightened up in time to see two of the soldiers turning their horses and trying to flee. Lannie's and Rob's rifles cracked, and the two were down. Over the ringing in his ears, Reichard heard men and horses screaming. Lannie and Rob fired together and the screaming horse was silent.

Doggie was on his knees, white faced and vomiting.

Hans Buchen came out from the mill and cautiously approached the dead and wounded soldiers. Major Stieff followed, his rifle at the ready.

Reichard moved to join them.

"Hang on, Reichard." Lannie spoke quietly. "We're supposed to stay here and keep guard."

Hans checked each body, tossing any weapons he found away from unfriendly hands. Five of the bodies were too still for life. Satisfied that neither of the wounded was a danger, Hans whistled and a two-horse wagon creaked out from behind the mill. Buchen and the driver loaded the dead on first and then, more gently, lifted the wounded aboard. The second man climbed into the wagon bed and began bandaging the wounded.

Major Stieff walked across the road. His eyes continued to stray up the road. "Is that the lot, Blucher?"

"They're the ones I saw following me." Reichard answered. "Could be others. The rest may come along, too."

"Of course. That is why we will stay here and watch. How many did you and Sam kill?"

"Somewhere between five and seven that I'm certain about. Perhaps another five wounded too badly to ride," Reichard replied.

The major turned toward the others. "I want to keep Georg here." He gestured toward the wagon driver. "We may need our other medic. That means I need someone to drive the wagon while Peter tends to the wounded. I'd like to have at least one of them get to Grantville alive."

Doggie stepped forward. In a shaky voice the young man volunteered as a wagon driver. Major Stieff looked him over and nodded, then turned back to Reichard. "Go with the wagon, Blucher. See that everyone gets back safely. Then get a good meal and some rest."

"Yes, sir. I should take Herr O'Reilly's body to his wife. She should know how he died."

"Yes, yes, by all means!" the major said. "Please extend my condolences to the good lady."

"A toast to a job well done." Ev Parker lifted his stein. "Your mares are beauties. I don't think I could have done any better myself. Those colts look to grow up into good studs."

Wilf lifted his stein in response. "Herr Parker, without your guidance—without your friendship, we would still be but a gang of poor mercenaries."

The other ex-mercenaries nodded in agreement.

"You have, Herr Parker," Christian said, "given us lives, livelihoods, and a home."

Wilf refilled the steins. "Nay, good Christian. Not just a home but a home and family. 'Tis not something mercenaries often find at the end of their soldiering." He looked around for a barmaid. It was a quiet time at the Thuringen Gardens, midway between the last of the lunch crowd and the beginnings of the dinner crowd. Most of the staff were taking their well-deserved breaks.

"Before Grantville's arrival," Wilf continued, "the best we could hope for was to be killed quickly in battle. Else we'd end our days begging for drinking money in some village until death claimed us." One of the barmaids was approaching the table at last.

"Yes." Reichard picked up the conversation. "Surviving as the village drunk and filling young boys' heads with tales of the loot and glory of a war company. Little wonder some of those boys run off and join the first company they find."

"Some of us," Christian chimed in, "found ourselves, ah, encouraged to leave home. When one has no home, no family, and no craft, the mercenary companies offer food, companionship, and a craft."

Wilf noticed the look on the barmaid's face as she came closer. "Methinks we have trouble brewing, boys." He stood and shoved his chair back.

"Herren," the barmaid whispered. Her face was white with fright. "The men, the no-kraut men, they are looking for you. They say you murdered a man."

"Damn bunch of rednecked idiots!" Ev swore. "Damn that Sam O'Reilly—still kicking up trouble even when he's dead."

"I think that trouble wears the name of Doggie this time." Reichard said. "He accused me of murder at the mill."

"Doggie's dumber than a pail full of rocks," Ev replied. "Unfortunately he's got a overly-healthy imagination fueled by too much beer and weed. He's also got a big mouth on him."

They were all standing when the front doors slammed open and twenty some men pushed in. Seeing their targets standing calmly, the mob halted in confusion. A few taunts were shouted at the ex-mercenaries but more were aimed at getting the mob organized for its attack.

"Shit, man, get your skinny ass over here and stop trying to bash Win's head in. Save it for the krauts!" shouted a skinny man in a John Deere gimme cap.

"BB, you dumbass, you poke me once more with that thing and I'll wrap it around your fat neck," a voice yelled over the general uproar.

Reichard faced toward the mob and the others lined up on either side of him. Wilf leaned over and whispered, "Herr Parker, if you don't mind, it would be better if you moved aside. We'll be the ones these fools are after."

"I've a mind to join in but it's been fifty years since my last bar fight." Ev grinned briefly.

Wilf was relieved when the old man moved to the back of the room. He turned his attention to the mob milling around just inside the door. They would have to cross thirty feet to reach his group. Thirty feet full of heavy tables, chairs and benches. Good. They had to either move those tables and chairs out of the way or split up. The sound of wood scraping on wood behind him brought a savage grin. Klaus was moving tables to block anyone trying to get at their backs.

"Break bones but let's try to avoid killing." Wilf said.

Christian barked a laugh. "Ah, but their blood is too hot and some of them need a medicinal bloodletting. Look at that one in the red shirt. His face is the same shade."

Dieter chuckled. "Aye. The one in the green cap also has that look."

"That's the old way," Reichard stated pontifically. "The new doctors suggest rest. A little tap on the head and he'll go to sleep."

"Keep the bloodletting down." Wilf growled. "We don't want a massacre."

The men took notice that the mob was armed mostly with baseball bats. A couple of them had lengths of motorcycle drive chain and one fellow sported a golf club. Two men at the back had ropes in their hands—ropes with hangman's nooses tied in them.

"They're looking for a lynching," Dieter said. "Do you think that they believe we will quietly cooperate with their plans?"

The mob had finally sorted itself out and began its charge. Their tight group split up as they wove between tables and chairs. The first man to reach them planted himself and swung a length of chain at Wilf's head.

Wilf grinned, ducked and slammed his fist into the chain wielder's stomach. Things got a bit busy then. Wilf caught occasional glimpses of his friends. He saw Reichard pluck a baseball bat out of a man's hands and slam it back into that man's ribs.

Wilf braced himself for the next attacker. The man in the green cap pushed forward, swinging his golf club. Wilf stepped inside the swing and swept the man's feet out from under him. When the man was on the floor, Wilf stomped on his hand. A blow took him across the back and he turned to deal with it.

A high-pitched scream cut above the general noise. Wilf risked a glance. One of the mob was clutching his stomach with both hands, trying to keep his intestines in. At his feet lay a rusty machete. The sight of serious blood gave the mob pause. Six other combatants lay on the floor, two writhing in pain from broken bones.

Most of the mob turned and fled. Four did not. The man in the red shirt screamed, "You fucker! You fucker! You killed him!" and pulled a pistol from his waistband. His hand shaking with fury, he pointed it at Christian. "I'm going to blow your fucking brains out!"

Christian's Bowie knife swept up, knocked the pistol aside and almost separated the man's hand from his arm.

A shot deafened them all. Wilf's attention snapped
back to the remaining attackers. One was down; his body
completely limp, head resting at an impossible angle.
The dead man's hand was wrapped around a revolver.
Reichard stood over him, blood seeping from his forearm. The last two attackers looked at each other in horror
and ran for the door.

"I'm not out here to arrest anyone, Ev," Dan Frost
explained. "I just need to finish my paperwork on that
brawl."

"The boys," Ev Parker replied, "have already paid the
Gardens for cleaning up and the broken furniture. Which
was generous of them, I'd say. Especially as they only
defended themselves. Reichard's arm is busted, Klaus
has cracked ribs, Dieter's got broken toes and a couple
of broken fingers, and Wilf's probably got a cracked
shoulder blade. Christian needed some stitches in his
thigh."

Dan snorted. "I've got Austin O'Meara dead. The doctors had BB Baldwin in surgery for eight hours and
they're not giving him good odds to last the week. Winston Beattie's got a fractured skull to go with having his
right hand nearly amputated. His odds aren't great,
either. The other injuries run to broken ribs and arms
with lots of cuts and bruises mixed in. One sorry speci-
men may be singing tenor. He's hospitalized and, for
once in his life, praying mightily."

"Yeah, heard about him." Ev grinned. "I also hear that
his wife is praying his voice change is permanent."

"There aren't going to be any charges pressed against
any of your 'boys.' We've got plenty of witnesses for self

defense." Frost leaned back in his chair. He sat silently for a minute, sipping his coffee and thinking.

"You know, Ev, everything considered, I'm kind of surprised that only one man is dead. Even if BB and Winston die, that's not the result I'd have expected. Your boys pulled their punches. It wasn't a fair fight. More like a bunch of junkyard dogs trying to take on a pack of wolves. No, that isn't quite right."

It was Ev's turn to snort. "Twenty drunken amateurs going up against five professional soldiers. Try 'a bunch of junkyard dogs taking on five grizzlies.' "

"Now that sounds right, Ev."

Second Issue?

Bradley H. Sinor

The back door of the *Grantville Times* printing plant flew open with a bang. An icy blast of January air came rushing in, whipping the flames of several candles placed around Paul Kindred's work table, scattering the numerous sheets of paper that he had spread out on it.

He muttered a comment about idiots, in this case himself, who forgot to lock doors at night. The middle of January, especially in northern Germany in the year of our Lord 1633, was not the time you left a door standing wide open.

Before he could get out of his chair, Paul caught a glimpse out of the corner of his eye of someone coming through that door. Who he saw was enough to know that this was no chance gust of wind, even though Paul realized he definitely hadn't locked the door.

"Yuri Andreovich, would you shut that damn door!"

When Yuri Andreovich Kuryakin heard Paul's voice he turned with a start, looking around for the source of the voice. With his small frame and twitchy on-the-move manner, he gave the impression of being younger than his twenty some years, not to mention of being frightened by his own shadow.

"Oh, there you are, Paul," the young Russian said, letting a small sigh escape. "I'm glad to find you working late."

"Never mind that, just shut the damn door; in case you haven't looked at the calendar, it's January!"

"I know it's January!" he replied. "Just wait until it gets really cold, like in Mother Russia!"

"Unless you have a cord of wood with you, shut the damn door!"

Yuri made a big show of checking the pockets of his down jacket and thick leather chaps, in the processes of which he managed to push the door closed.

"Nope, no extra wood here," he said with a grin.

It wasn't that he was stupid, far from it. That much Paul had realized within five minutes of meeting Yuri. He just tended to be so enthusiastic that when he got an idea it pushed everything else, including common sense, out the back door.

This was not the first time Yuri had shown up unexpectedly. It had become a regular habit since he had come striding into the *Times'* office and asked for a job as a reporter. He claimed to have worked for several "local papers" in other parts of Germany, Russia and farther south in the Balkans.

Paul's father hadn't been that enthusiastic about hiring him, but Paul had convinced him to hire the young Russian anyway. As his father's chief of staff, and managing editor of the *Times*, he had some say in who was on the staff. There was something in Yuri's intensity, his willingness to follow a story no matter what, that reminded Paul of himself just a few years ago.

Though there were moments, like this one, where he would have cheerfully strangled Yuri or taken a two-by-four to him, depending on what was handiest.

"So why the late night visit?" asked Paul, picking up the papers from his table. They showed designs for a fountain pen that local craftsmen could make. Paul shoved them into a box and guessed he wouldn't get any more work done on them tonight. He was a newspaperman at heart, but it never hurt to have several money-making enterprises going.

Yuri began to pace back and forth, occasionally glancing toward the windows as if expecting someone to be looking back at him.

"I've got a story, a big one. Okay, this goes back a few weeks," he said, "to the Christmas party at the high school."

That party had been a brilliant stroke, if Paul did say so himself. It had helped improve the morale of all of Grantville; some of the up-timers had been having major problems coming to terms with their "new reality."

"Yeah, Nina and I were there."

"I saw you." Yuri grinned. He stopped, again, staring out the window. "But I also saw something else that apparently you missed entirely."

"Such as?"

Yuri turned to face Paul, the smile on his face a little too self-satisfied for the older man's liking. "How about General Pappenheim himself there in the school."

"Gottfried Heinrich Pappenheim? You've got to be joking."

"I wish I was. When that man shows up there is trouble. It was him, of that I'm sure; the birthmark on his face marks him. Besides, I stood a dozen feet away from him a couple of years ago and got a good look at the man," said Yuri.

"Wallenstein's chief general, here? Now that might just be a story."

"It gets better. I spotted him going into the, what do you call it, men's room. He came out dressed all in red. Julie Mackay made him start giving out presents to everyone."

Santa? Pappenheim had been Santa? Try as he might, Paul couldn't recall the man's face; that red suit dominated everything.

"Remember when 'Santa' disappeared down the hallway? I was in one of the classrooms and saw what happened. There was some altercation involving two men and a barrel of gunpowder. A few minutes later, I saw Pappenheim talking to Julie Mackay and President Stearns. I couldn't hear worth a damn, but I saw everything. I would swear on my mother's grave that the two of them knew who he was."

This story sounded so fantastic that Paul wasn't sure if he should kick Yuri out or take him seriously. Not that Paul trusted the government. Oh, Mike Stearns and the rest, individually, were good men and he had no doubt that they were working for the general good. They were still politicians and that meant you had to keep your eye on them.

Yuri pulled out several sheets of paper and passed them to Paul. "I've got it all written up. It can go in the next edition!"

One thing you could say about Yuri, he did have easily read handwriting and knew how to put an article together. The story covered everything he had seen, plus a lot of speculation.

"No, Yuri Andreovich. We can't run this story, not as it stands now," Paul said. "You cannot accuse the government of a secret conspiracy without proof."

"I've spent the last week asking questions! All it's gotten me is a lot of blank stares and denials. Though I think Lefferts suspects something; I've been followed everywhere I go." Lefferts was Captain Harry Lefferts; he was part of the army but he also functioned as the head of Mike Stearns' special security unit that was directly under the President's authority.

"I didn't say we wouldn't publish it, but before I will—Proof, we will need proof before we could even consider going to press with this," said Paul.

Yuri stared at Paul for a long time. "Very well, I will get proof." His voice suggested that his idea of getting proof would look something akin to a bull in a china shop. Yuri pulled his jacket tight about him and headed out the door without a word. A moment later he opened it again and leaned part way in.

"My byline, above the fold. *Da*?"

"Of course. I wouldn't have it any other way."

Yuri would not wait long, that much Paul knew. While the reporter was long on talent, he was at times short on patience, and Paul had a gut feeling that *this* could very well be one of those times.

Pappenheim playing Santa at the Christmas party was just so bizarre that it could have happened. Now if Yuri had suggested it had been Wallenstein, that would have been too much. It wasn't that Stearns wasn't capable of making a deal with Pappenheim, Paul was fairly certain he would, if it were necessary. Like all the other up-timers, Stearns had been forced to adapt to political realities in the seventeenth century.

Paul needed information, fast.

That meant Mirari Sesma.

Mirari was Basque. She had turned up in Grantville three months after the Ring of Fire. Just exactly why she had left the Pyrenees was a bit unclear; a few dropped hints suggested something about a vendetta, but she had never been forthcoming with details.

Mirari had taken over one of the empty buildings in town and had set up a small café that turned out to be extremely popular. People came, they ate, they drank, they talked, and, most importantly, Mirari listened. Her dark hair and dark eyes gave her an exotic appearance, but her manner was such that people just trusted her. It wasn't long before Mirari seemed to know everything that was going on in town, and if she didn't know it, she could find it out.

Paul found her in the back of her shop, just after closing at midnight. She was pouring a dark liquid into a cup. Before he could say anything she offered it to him and poured herself another.

"Chocolate?" he asked, savoring the familiar taste.

"I just got a supply in. I'll be saving it for special occasions," answered Mirari. "How is Nina?"

"She's almost over the cold. That herb tea you left certainly helped." Mirari and Nina, Paul's wife, had met weeks before he had been introduced to her. By that time the two of them were like long lost sisters.

"Besides drinking up my chocolate, what brings you out and about this late at night?"

"You always did know how to cut to the point." Paul wrapped his hands around the cup, enjoying the warmth. "I've picked up a rumor that General Pappenheim has been seen in the area, the night of the Christmas party?"

Mirari was hard pressed to keep from laughing. "You've got to be joking. He's not stupid enough to come anywhere near here, not without a very large army at his back. Have you seen the reward for his head?"

Paul was very familiar with the reward. The *Times* had bid on and gotten the job of printing wanted posters of both Pappenheim and Wallenstein.

"And you're serious about this?" asked Mirari.

"Just see what you can find out, as soon as possible."

"There is something going on," said Mirari. She had shown up at Paul's front door just after six the next evening. She seemed more than a bit unhappy. "Since noon I've had the feeling I was being followed, though I saw no one. It's not a feeling that I like."

Nina had been as pleased to see her as Paul was. The two women hugged and began talking about a half a dozen different subjects as the three of them sat down on the couch.

Among other things that Paul discovered in the next few minutes was that Nina and Mirari were working on setting up some new classes at the high school and were even talking about going into business together. This was the first time that he had heard anything about that.

"Hey, even the *Times* doesn't get every story." Nina laughed.

"We can try," he told his wife.

Mirari picked up a small glass vase from the coffee table and began to turn it over and over in her hand. "I've not been able to find anyone who might have seen Pappenheim the night of the Christmas party. Of course, there are the usual sorts of rumors about what he is doing, but none of them put him anywhere near Grantville.

"One thing I did put together; it may be related to this, it may not, but some of Harry Leffert's men have been hanging around at all hours of the day and night near Edith Wild's house."

"You're stumbling over Harry Lefferts' men, Yuri was sure they were after him. I am beginning to wonder if Lefferts might be the story, not Pappenheim," muttered Paul, leaning back in his chair and staring up at the ceiling. "And what does Edith Wild have to do with it?"

Edith Wild was a nurse, and a force of nature in the minds of many Grantville residents. She was a volunteer on the Red Cross Sanitation Squad, a job that required that type of personality to get the job done. She definitely took her duties seriously and would brook no interference in performing them.

"I hadn't heard anything about Harry seeing Edith, and I'm not sure if even he could stand up to her should the situation arise," Nina said as she came back from the kitchen with a plate of cookies. "But I suppose it's possible."

"I wouldn't lay odds on his surviving." Paul chuckled.

"Are you sure you know the way?"

Paul didn't bother answering the question, as he hadn't the last four times that Yuri had asked it. His companion did seem to have sense enough to keep his voice down to a whisper, though.

They had been walking for the better part of two hours, gradually working their way through the forest toward the far end of Grantville. Edith Wild's house was less than a half hour's walk from the *Times* offices, but just walking over and knocking on her door was not going to get the answers that Paul and Yuri wanted. Paul still wasn't sure that he believed Yuri's story, but he had the definite feeling that something might just be going on.

Paul had made a point of not going anywhere near Edith's house during the day, not that he normally did anyway. There wasn't that much to see anyway, beyond the home that Wild had occupied for more than half her life.

There were enough other matters on his plate concerning the *Times* and several other business projects that his family had in the works to take up Paul's time as he waited at the office for Yuri. A note to Yuri had told him to show up at midnight. The Russian was there at 10 p.m., champing at the bit to get on with it. Paul had considered taking Mirari along, but she had made it clear that she was not interested. Besides, Yuri and she usually ended up arguing about some damn thing or another and they didn't need that tonight.

"I still think that we should have gone this morning to the President's office and confronted him, in front of everyone. That way he couldn't have squirmed out of it," said Yuri.

"That isn't the way the *Times* does things. We need proof, Yuri Andreovich. There may be something going on, there may not; it may just be a lot of things taken out of context. If you don't like it, you can take your story somewhere else," Paul said.

Yuri muttered something, but it was in Russian and Paul couldn't be sure of exactly what he said.

In the just over twenty-four hours since Yuri had come sneaking in the back of the *Times*, the weather had not changed, beyond adding a fresh layer of snow. It was still bitterly cold. The two men's breaths hung in the air, and the ground was frozen, grass crackling under their feet with every step.

In spite of the weather, Paul did not feel safe in taking a direct route to Edith Wild's house. There was a chance that Yuri could be right, so they doubled back, crossing and recrossing their own trail, watching for any signs that they were not alone in the darkness.

At one point, Yuri almost tripped over a pair of foxes who were prowling the bushes, looking for food and, no doubt, a warm place to spend the night. It was a sentiment that Paul had come to identify with in the last few hours.

"We're alone," said Yuri. "Let's get on with it."

As they neared the house there was a movement a dozen yards ahead of them. Paul tried to focus on it.

Before he could say anything or point out the guard to Yuri, half a dozen figures came on them from three different directions. Voices and fists flew and chaos drew Paul in. There were no faces, just colors and shapes and sound.

Yuri kept moving, dodging the attackers, until he reached the house. He boosted himself up toward a window, using a snow-covered box, hanging on the sill for only a matter of a heartbeat or two.

Paul had little time to watch Yuri. He managed to land several good punches, his fists connecting with bare flesh and clothing. As he turned, Paul felt a sharp pain in the lower part of his back and then a matching one at the base of his neck that sent him crashing to the ground and into darkness.

Paul opened blurry eyes and found himself staring at the business end of a double-barreled shotgun about eight inches from his face. A million miles away, at the other end of the weapon, Paul could just make out the face of a man he did not recognize.

"Can I interest you in a subscription to the *Times*? Makes a great after Christmas gift for yourself." He gulped. In the back of his mind he was envisioning what the shotgun would do to his face. Of course, he also knew that he would not be alive to see it. He figured flippancy could be the only way to go right now; it wasn't as if he had a whole lot of options right then.

Mike Stearns stepped out of the shadows. He looked at Paul for a moment, shook his head, softly chuckled and waved the shotgun wielding man back.

"On your feet." Mike extended his hand to help Paul get to his feet. "What the hell are you doing prowling around in the woods tonight? And before you ask, I already am a *Times* subscriber."

"I would say that shows your good taste, but I happen to know you subscribe to the *Daily News* and the *Street* as well," said Paul.

Another man came up to Mike. It took Paul a moment to recognize Harry Lefferts. "There were two of them," he told Mike. "We lost the trail of the other one, down by the creek. I'm fairly certain that it was a pain-in-the-butt reporter named Kuryakin. My men have been watching him for the last couple of days."

"Bloody great," muttered Mike. "So, Paul, you never answered my question."

Paul struggled to his feet, wiped himself off and pulled his notebook and a pencil out. "I'm doing my job, reporting. I've come to interview your visitor."

"Visitor? Visitor? I'm not sure what you're talking about," said Mike.

"Mike, let's cut the crap. You and those playmates of yours wouldn't be prowling around the woods at three in the morning any more than I would, unless something important was going on. You can deny it, but I'd know you were lying." This wasn't the first time Paul had run a bluff to get a story, though in the pit of his stomach he felt it wasn't a bluff. "The *Times* is going to run a story, speculating on just who that visitor might be and why you're going to all this trouble to hide him. Now, you can help me make this story as accurate as possible, or live with the consequences of not bringing me in on it."

Mike went immobile for a moment. The only sound, beyond those drifting in from the woods, was their breathing. It was almost two full minutes before he spoke.

"All right, come inside. There's someone that you need to meet."

The "visitor" was awake. It was not who Paul had expected.

Wallenstein was sitting up in bed, with several pillows behind him. He looked pale, even in the light from the single candle next to his bed. The man's lower jaw was wrapped in bandages. There was a bulge under the blanket that Paul suspected might be a loaded pistol.

Harry Lefferts stood in one corner of the room, an unhappy expression on his face.

"You, sir, present me with a moral dilemma," Paul said after Mike had introduced him. "You know I came here to get a story for my newspaper. But if I write it, I cause major problems not only for my government, which I don't mind doing, but possibly for all of Grantville."

Wallenstein picked up a pad and wrote quickly:

MORALS ARE FOR CHURCHMEN;
STATESMEN CANNOT AFFORD THEM.

"Thank you, Señor Machiavelli."

Wallenstein looked at Paul oddly but wrote nothing.

"We got word that he had survived Alte Veste through General Pappenheim, who came to us with a most unusual offer of alliance."

"Ah yes, Pappenheim. Or should we also be calling him Santa Claus?"

Mike smiled. "Not bad, not bad at all. He offered an alliance to help stir up a revolt in Bohemia plus a few other little political actions that could work to our advantage. The deal was he wanted our dentists to reconstruct the damage that Julie's bullet did. Then there is also the matter of Chmielnicki."

Paul didn't recognize the name, but then he had never been good with European history. He waited for an explanation.

"It's a massacre of ten thousand Polish Jews in 1648. Wallenstein says that if we help him he may be able to stop it."

Wallenstein handed a hastily scribbled note to Mike, who in turn offered it to Paul.

NO MAY. I WILL STOP IT.
BUT ONLY IF YOU HELP ME.

"You want me to sit on the story," Paul said. "That much is obvious."

His first impulse was to say to hell with this, publish the story and expose the whole deal. He wasn't fond of secret government plots, but he could see the logic implicit in what Mike seemed to be doing. It still didn't feel right to him.

"If I was to agree with what you're doing, and I am not saying I will, there is one other problem. Yuri may or may not have seen Wallenstein, but he knows that you were involved with Pappenheim. That can cause a lot of problems in and of itself."

"Then he has to be dealt with," said Lefferts, his voice quiet and without emotion.

"I hope you're not going to try to arrange an accident for him," said Paul.

"Paul, please. There are certain levels I won't stoop to," said Mike. "You know he's going to want to get that story published and he can do it. It's just a matter of time." There were newspapers outside of Grantville, some good, some bad. "We both know there are more than a few places that would be willing to publish it."

"If I agree to go along with you on keeping this quiet, I want an exclusive on it when you do go public," said Paul.

"Provided we haven't been exposed and strung up over this whole thing, you've got a deal," Mike said. "Seriously, I wish I were handing you an easy story to deal with, like a secret squad of ninjas setting up operations in Grantville, but I can't."

"Ninjas, yeah, I've heard those rumors, as well as the ones about aliens. You're sounding like you think I run the *Weekly World News* rather than the *Grantville Times*. Not that a fine upstanding gentleman like yourself would know anything about the *Weekly World News*."

"At least with *Playboy* you could claim that you were reading it for the articles." Mike laughed.

Paul nodded, only half listening. Later he could not say when the idea had hit him. It was just suddenly there.

"I know exactly what I'm going to do. I think you will like the idea."

"And that is?" said Mike.

"I'm going to do what I always do. I'm going to write the story about Wallenstein being alive and see it published." Paul grinned.

"Now, stop me if I've got this wrong, but isn't that exactly what we don't want to have happen?"

"Trust me."

Paul slid into a booth in the far corner of the inn's greatroom. The place was virtually empty at just after three in the afternoon. That was just fine with him; he could use a little down time. The beer and sandwich that sat in front of him looked very good.

From a chair near the booth he had picked up a copy of the latest sensation to sweep Grantville, the *National Inquisitor*. The paper had made its appearance five days earlier, turning up in bundles at taverns, stores and any place else that a crowd could gather. There was nothing in it to indicate who had published it; the only bylines on stories were obvious pseudonyms such as Sarah Bellum and Noah Ward.

With its glaring headlines and outrageous woodcuts, it was definitely distinguishable from the *Times*, the *Daily News* and, most certainly, the *Street*. The seventy-five point headline WALLENSTEIN ALIVE, LIVING IN SECRET WITH BIGFOOT said it all. A second story announced PAPPENHEIM BUYS CONDO IN GRANTVILLE.

Paul's experienced eye slid over the pages, checking the text, the layout and the content. Not that he needed to; he was quite familiar with every column inch of it. He had written most of it; and what he hadn't done had been penned by Mirari and a few others they had enlisted. The entire matter had been done in a dozen intense hours after his return from Edith Wild's house.

That this had been done without anyone apparently being the wiser still astonished Paul. In the back of his mind he had been convinced that someone would spot them and put two and two together, especially when they were distributing the papers.

But that didn't happen.

The lead story told how Wallenstein had survived the battle of Alte Veste with help from that legendary humanoid creature. There were not going to be many people who would put any stock in stories published in other papers that the man was alive, or that Pappenheim was anywhere near Grantville, at least for the next few months.

"Checking out the competition, now are we? Or is it just admiring your own work?" said Mirari as she came up and sat down across the table from him.

"I just hope a few other people are 'admiring' it," said Paul.

"That is something you don't have to worry about." Mirari laughed and motioned for a beer. "I've been keeping my ears open, and it is fairly obvious that you've got yourself a runaway hit. The up-timers are laughing their heads off about it. I heard some of them saying it reminds them of something called the *National Enquirer*, whatever that is. Down-timers aren't quite sure what to make of the *Inquisitor*, but they like it. I even saw a couple of priests reading it and giggling."

That was a relief. Mike Stearns had expressed considerable doubts when Paul had suggested the idea. Hell, even Paul hadn't been that sure it would work.

Short of sending killers after Yuri, it was the only idea they could come up with in a hurry that had even a glimmer of a chance of succeeding. Revealing the truth was out of the question; Wallenstein still needed weeks of recuperation and the political repercussions would have been devastating.

"I heard some talk that Yuri has been kicked out of three newspaper offices in other towns. He can't seem to give his story away," said Mirari.

"Good." Paul reached down and tapped the copy of the *Inquisitor*. "It was kind of fun, but I am glad it's over."

Mirari leaned her head back, letting her eyes roll toward the ceiling. "Lord, please help me. The man is as slow and unthinking as a churchman who hasn't been bribed!"

"Woman, what in the hell are you talking about?"

"Okay, let's put this in simple terms. The *Inquisitor* is a success. Everyone wants to know when the second issue will be coming out."

Second issue? Second issue? That was something that had never even been discussed, that he had never even thought of. The whole concept seemed utterly ridiculous. There wasn't going to be a second issue!

"I know what you are going to say," said Mirari. "There was never supposed to be a second issue. But this thing is popular; people are eating it up and demanding more."

"Yeah, what does that do to the *Times'* credibility with me editing the *Inquisitor*?"

"You don't have to." Mirari smiled in a way that warned Paul that the woman had some ideas of her own.

"I suppose you know someone who could become the editor." He already knew the answer.

"Of course. Me. I'll have a second issue out in no time."

There was that phrase, second issue. Mirari would make a good editor; that much he had learned during their marathon session putting the *Inquisitor* together.

As he mulled it over he kept remembering a lot of the more outrageous rumors that had escaped into the world since the Ring of Fire; a hidden battalion of twenty-first century Marines who just happened to be passing through town when it was transported back in time was only one of many.

"A second issue," Paul muttered. "I suppose it might be fun."

Diving Belle

Gunnar Dahlin and Dave Freer

Stockholm

"Where to, sweetling?" the old woman at the oars asked
with a cheerful grin. "For a copper I'll row you anywhere
in Stockholm."

Ginny Cochran hesitated for a moment, then flung
her duffel bag across her shoulder and clambered down
the ship's side. "American Consulate please," she said.
"I'm told it's in the city."

"You are American?" The old woman beamed and said
in broken English, "I thought you didn't look German."
She grinned again. "Besides, I never saw a German
woman travel alone."

"My company was diverted elsewhere. But yes, I am American. I'm Ginny, by the way," she said, impulsively holding out her hand.

"Later, sweetling," The woman shook her head. "You'll make me miss my stroke. I'm Toke-Karin. Best rower in these here waters."

Ginny looked around. The boat was small and worn but lovingly maintained, and the old woman rowed with sure and certain ease. Suddenly something touched Ginny's foot, and she pulled it up with startled exclamation. From the recess under her seat, a small boy clutching a piglet looked up at her.

"Gustav!" the old woman's voice was suddenly sharp, and although Ginny spoke next to no Swedish it was clear that the boy had become the recipient of a ferocious scolding.

"He didn't hurt me," Ginny said. "I was just startled."

"Bad for business," Toke-Karin grumbled. "He's named after His Majesty, but barring God's hand, he'll come to a bad end." She huffed noisily. "Frighten the customers like that and they'll never come back." Then she threw a glance over her shoulder and slewed the small craft around to alight against a wooden pier.

"Here you are, sweetling. Köpmangatan. Just walk up the street and turn right at the first crossing." She grinned. "You can't miss the flag."

"Thank you," Ginny handed over a silver coin. "I'll be sure to call on you in the future."

"Bless you, child," Toke-Karin exclaimed. "That's a princely pay, but don't wave that much money around. Times are hard."

Ginny nodded, waved at Gustav and clambered onto the ladder. Then, without a backward glance, she began to walk up the narrow street. "Crossing" was such an arbitrary word. Had the old woman really meant this noisome alley? And there would be no flag after sundown, surely?

Off an alley near the Köpmangatan, in the tap room of the Silver Eel, the arm-wrestling match had been going on for quite some time now, and Per Lennartson had begun to worry. Not about his brother at the table, but at the tension in the room. The atmosphere was so thick that you could cut the air with a wooden knife. Per glanced at his younger brother. Lars didn't look half as strong as he was, but he held the burly boatswain at bay with seeming ease. Occasionally he took a pull from his mug and grinned as he strained against the other man.

"I raise," a corporal shouted hoarsely. "Twenty-five on the soldier boy."

Per shuddered. He had seen games like this get out of hand before. He scanned the tap room for his other brothers. Olof was sulking in a corner, and Karl . . .

Per groaned. Karl was chatting up the serving girl, quite oblivious to her father's dark looks. Per groaned again, the sound going unheard in the terrible din. What was it about Karl that made every girl take one look at him and fall instantly in love? The wench had put her tankards on a shelf and was preening herself avidly, her thirsty customers momentarily forgotten. Per looked back to the struggling contestants. The boatswain was built like a tree-stump with gnarled roots for arms.

Beside him, the lanky Lars with his shock of brown hair looked like a sapling.

The alehouse door swung open abruptly. Per jerked around to see if it was yet another problem.

The first thing he saw was naked steel.

Bloody naked steel.

The girl with the bloody knife in her hand looked terrified, but there was something about her expression that said: "I'll cut at least half of you before I go down."

Ginny clutched her bloody penknife as if her life depended on it. It probably did. This place looked like no refuge either. It looked like a whole tavern full of the same kind of men who had attacked her in the alley. Two minutes earlier, she'd been trying to decide whether to go back, either to the road or even to the quayside, when her adventure had turned into a horror story.

Papa hadn't wanted his little girl to go. That was more than half of why she'd decided to do it. She hadn't expected him to be right. . . .

The four of them had rounded the corner in front of her. She'd nearly turned and run. But this was supposed to be the safest city in Europe, outside of Grantville itself. She'd kept walking.

Then one of them had said, in German, "Fresh meat!"

It had gone downhill very fast from there. And now the door under the green bush that she'd run to had led her to worse.

One of the street-thugs swaggered his way in. He looked right at home here. He probably was. His two companions were just behind him. One was bleeding. They looked like sharks, closing for the kill.

Then a big hand reached out of the shadows next to the door and took hold of the thug's jacket front, and lifted him off his feet.

Per wasn't ever sure just what made him intervene. Maybe it was her expression. Maybe her clothes—this was no dockyard tramp. Maybe it was just that in Delsbo you didn't treat women like that. Besides, he didn't like the fellow's looks. "And what are you looking for, mister?" Per said. "Besides trouble, *ja*.."

Karl instantly left off his flirtation. "Maybe they are lost," he said, cracking his knuckles.

"That slut cut Heinrich and Wolf and tried to stick me . . ."

Per's eyes narrowed. He spoke quietly. Most patrons were still focused on the arm wrestling. If the crowd got involved, this could turn very ugly. "*Ja*. So maybe your friends don't know a slut from a respectable woman. This one looks like gentry. You get caught taking liberties with one of those and the justices will see you get cut, too. Cut off."

The sailor's eyes widened. But his blood was up. "There's only two of you."

"Three," said Olof.

And then things happened quite fast. The second fellow should never have decided that it was a good time to try and grab Karl. The ruffians were a lot more than half-drunk. That probably messed up their judgment. It certainly wrecked their chances in the fight. The easiest and most peaceful solution was to toss them into the alley, so Per started by doing that. That got his man out of the brawl, and neatly knocked the fourth fellow, who had just arrived, right back into the wall of the house on the far side of the alley. Karl placed his fist on the jaw, and his foot in the belly, of the falling man, and Olof threw his opponent over his hip. Per assisted his departure with a foot on his backside, as he staggered to his feet.

Then it was just a case of closing the door.

The girl stood there, white-faced, knife in hand. She'd stepped forward to help. Per found himself smiling at her. A courageous little sparrow, this one. He ducked his head in a bow. "You're very brave, fraulein," he said reassuringly. "But you don't need the knife anymore."

Ginny, still shivering, turned to look at him. She didn't feel brave in the least, but the young man with the huge hands smiled encouragingly.

"Very brave," he repeated. "Four against you, and you only armed with that itty-bitty knife. But you can put it away now. Really."

Ginny took a deep breath and studied her rescuer. From his looks and accented German she guessed he was Swedish. "Please," she said. "I'm looking for the American Consulate. I must have taken the wrong turn."

"I don't know about this 'Consulate,' " he said, shaking his head, "We only came here yesterday. But be easy. We will help you. American, eh!" He bobbed his head. "My name is Per, fraulein, and this is my brother Karl . . . " The handsome youngster smiled and interrupted in Swedish.

"He wants to know your name," Per said.

"I'm Ginny," Ginny said. "Ginny Cochran."

Karl bowed, as her third rescuer scowled and muttered something. Per chuckled. "I get there. You are not forgotten, Olof. Fraulein Cochran, this is Olof, my youngest brother."

The scowling face smoothed out for a moment as the tall youth gave a minute nod.

"Don't mind him," Per said. "Olof was born angry." Then he grinned at Ginny. "I'll introduce my other brother in a moment." He turned toward the crowd thronging around the arm-wrestlers and shouted something.

"Stop playing with him, Lars. I want you to meet someone." Per Lennartson's shout cut through the din like a clarion call and Lars Lennartson grinned wryly. "Sorry pal," he said, "This was fun, but my big brother calls." He twisted his hand minutely and then slowly, inexorably, began to really push. The boatswain struggled like a man possessed, but Lars just pushed, adding leverage to force to increase the descent, and when the twinned hands hit the table, the sound was drowned by the roars of the crowd. Lars bowed to his opponent before bounding across the room to stop beside Per. He stopped with comic abruptness and bowed awkwardly before Ginny. "Pleased to meet you," he said in Swedish.

The reaction set in. Ginny, surrounded by tall smiling Swedes, found her legs decidedly wobbly. "I really need to sit down," she said. "Can I share your table?"

"We don't have a table." For a moment Per floundered, looking so out of his depth that Ginny felt sorry for him despite her situation. He rallied gallantly. "But

Karl will get us all a round of beer." He turned to Karl. "Beer for all of us," he said royally. He looked at Ginny. "And a seat for the lady. First. And some aquavit for her. We will find this consulate of yours."

It was, Ginny decided later, probably a mistake to have accepted the aquavit. She hadn't drunk paint stripper before, but the vile stuff still did nothing for your common sense and judgment. Well. If Ginny was going to be honest with herself, she didn't always have a lot of common sense. She did rush into things. Like applying for and accepting this job. It had seemed better than staying in her father's house after the last argument. Now that she had some physical distance, she could see that it was just that he loved her and wanted to protect her, but at the time . . . Well, added to the awkwardness about the stolen books from the library . . . No one said it was exactly her fault, but she had helped Fermin Mazalet with his research into the *Vasa*.

The aquavit had warmed her up though, and she stopped shaking. From there it had seemed quite sensible to have bought the boys who had helped her another beer, and to have turned to talking about what they were doing here, and then to her own dreams.

Ginny hadn't got very far into her story before Per's translation was interrupted. She'd plainly stirred them up badly with something she'd said.

"She's a Häxa, a witch!" burst out Olof—whose German was rudimentary at best. "I say we kill her before she turns us to her purpose." His freckled young face was hard, and he stared warily at the woman.

"Don't be an idiot, Olof!" Lars Lennartson grinned. "She doesn't want to raise the king's father. She's talking about the ship. You know. That big galley that sits in the bay with only the top of her masts above the water-line."

"How do you know that's what she means?" Karl looked from one brother to the next. His German was the next best. "She said 'raise the Vasa.' We saw good King Gustav's own grave in Uppsala, didn't we?"

Per drained his mug of ale and put it down with an air of finality. "*We* did?" he said with calculated cruelty. "As I recall it, brother mine, you stole off into some nook to kiss Bishop Kenicius' granddaughter. We saw the grave. Big heavy coffin made from marble. It would take some strong men just to lift that lid."

"That's why she wants us." Olof looked torn between pride and anger. "Since we're strong, I mean."

"Delsbo boys are the strongest," Lars agreed, "But it is plain for anyone with eyes in their heads that we couldn't be tricked into robbing graves. We are both too smart and too God-fearing to do such a bad thing. If this lady was a witch, she'd be the first to see that."

◊   ◊   ◊

It was obvious, thought Ginny, that she'd put her foot in it. Why would a shipwreck be so important to them? They were, by their own admission, upcountry farm boys who had never been in a place as big and magnificent—to them—as this town—which they knew not at all. It was a naval botch, sure, having the pride of your fleet sink in channel out of the harbor. But even the aristocrat-ruled navy had tried to raise it before. Yet—except for

Per—the big Swedes were now leaning away. Looking slightly worried. "What did I say?" she asked.

Per smiled. "There was some misunderstanding," he said. "My brother," he nodded towards Olof, "thought that you wanted to raise old King Gustav. He is often spoken of as 'Vasa.' He is afraid you are witch, looking to recruit good strong Delsbo boys to haul the lid off the coffin."

Sometimes, you forgot the kind of superstition that had ruled. Correction, Ginny amended herself, the kind of superstition that *still* ruled. In the old world, Ginny knew, more than three hundred Swedish women would burn at the stake, victims of both vicious courts and frightened lynch mobs. Up to now, it had been a rather dry fact in the back of her mind. Seeing Olof's cold eyes made it a very different thing indeed.

"I meant the ship," Ginny said rather forcefully. "And I'm no witch."

"What are you then, lady?" asked filmstar-faced Karl in awkward German.

"I'm an assistant librarian. Or I was. I've taken a job to be aide to the new American consul."

By the looks on their faces "witch" was at least something her rescuers understood. But they were prepared to listen. And to marvel. And they were the first down-time people she'd ever spoken to who didn't think that her idea was just the craziest thing that a twenty-year-old woman could ever think of. Perhaps it was back country ignorance, or beer. But they seemed to think that it could be done. By them. On Lars' back.

They had more beer. She should have asked them to take her back to the ship. At least she could find that, if not the consulate. Instead they got to talking about America and up-timers. And the fact that the boys were supposed to be on a boat to Germany as conscripts. And about American women.

"I knew straight away you were from Grantville," said Per.

"Oh, and how?"

He looked thoughtful. "The way you speak, to start." Per shrugged. "You're not a native German, rather you sound a bit like the Scots mercenary I served with, except for not swearing so much, but you pick your words like someone with lots of learning. Your clothes mark you as rich, but no woman from the nobility would have come down this alley." He smiled. "Not without two stout footmen, anyway. Also, you are very direct, like a man almost."

"And is that bad in a woman?" Ginny almost bit her tongue. She had loved debate class, but down-timers had strong views on a woman's place, and this was maybe not quite the right time to tell them how wrong they were.

The big Swede just smiled, however. "No, and most of the women back home are quite forthright, even more than the men sometimes, but usually not at first meeting. It's just here in the city they're different. But no. It is the way you treat people like us. You act a little as if everyone was an old friend. A noble woman would not treat us with any kind of courtesy, and a burgher's daughter would not be sitting here drinking ale with four penniless peasants." He chuckled. "And neither would attempt to salvage the biggest warship in Swedish history. They should have got a peasant to design her. Then she would not have been so toplofty, eh."

Somehow, he had taken it from "dream" to something she was going to try to do. She'd been furious enough at Mazalet's trickery to dream of trying. To take it as another reason for coming here. This man seemed to assume she'd do it. That was . . . neat.

Per took a long pull from his mug before continuing. "It will take a little bit convincing Olof though. My brothers are honest men, but we come from a small village. It is easier to believe in witchcraft than in people from the future. As our employer you might want to remember that."

"Your employer?" Ginny blurted.

"Yes. Wasn't that what you had in mind when you told us of this? You will need strong backs for this job. It's a big ship." Per shrugged. "I'm sorry if I misspoke."

Ginny drank some of the beer herself. "I hadn't thought that far, to be honest. And I don't have the money to pay you. I'd need partners, not employees, anyway."

He looked puzzled. "What?"

"A share of the ship's salvage."

Now it was Per's turn to look surprised. "You mean as equals?"

She nodded. "That's the best I could do."

There was a long silence. "It's too good." Per shrugged again. "We couldn't make it stick. As soon as we were successful at the salvage, some nobleman would muscle in and grab the lion's share for himself."

"Damn that! Not if I can stop them," said Ginny, lifting her chin.

That was as far as it all got because a stool flew across the room and hit the far wall, announcing the start of a brawl. It was not a very large alehouse, so inevitably to some extent they were involved when the city watch arrived a little later. Patrons who had not fled found themselves escorted off to a night in the cells.

"She demanded to speak to you, sir," said the watchman. The officer of the watch was rather taken aback to discover that the somewhat disheveled woman had addressed him first in an unfamiliar tongue and then in accented German. Taking stock, he realised she was rather well dressed for dockside trollop. She also seemed angry, rather than either jaded or afraid. "This is a fine welcome to Stockholm!" she said. "What the hell do you think you're doing?"

Just after she'd said it, Ginny realised it was probably not the most tactful approach to have taken. But her night, so far, hadn't left her feeling tactful.

"My job," said the watch-officer, his back stiffening.

"It's a pity you weren't doing it when I was attacked and nearly raped and murdered earlier. Those men you've just hauled away had to save my life."

The officer blinked. "Just who are you, fraulein? And what are you doing here? Where are you from?"

"Grantville."

It seemed that this man had also heard of American women. And that he did not approve. "It is normal for your women to drink in low taverns with the scaff and raff?"

"It's not normal for us to get attacked when we get lost," said Ginny, icily. "Several of the men in the tavern saved my life, or at least my virtue. If they had not, you would be answering very awkward questions tomorrow.

They were very kind to me and got me somewhere to sit while I recovered." Ginny conveniently omitted that that had been several hours ago. "They were just about to escort me to the home of Herr Boelcke, the new American consul. I am due to start work there, as his assistant. As it is, I suggest you let them and me go. They weren't part of that fight. They were just in the tavern."

"Lothar Boelcke?" The officer seemed a little taken aback. But he was not ready to back down . . . yet. "Corporal Petzel. Run to his home and ask if Herr Boelcke can come and confirm this young lady's story." He shook his head in bemusement. *Not taking part. Half my squad won't walk for a week, and most of it was those northerners' doing.*

"I could hardly think of a worse way to begin your work at my consulate." Lothar Boelcke, the Grantville consul in Stockholm looked furious. "I questioned your appointment, Fraulein Cochran," Boelcke continued with icy precision, "and it seems I stand vindicated."

"I'm really sorry," Ginny began, but Consul Boelcke cut her short.

"Fraulein, I'm a great admirer of the American way, but fighting the city guards does nothing to enhance our status here."

"I'm sorry," Ginny repeated, "but I got lost. The directions to the consulate were all wrong, or this place is very confusing to strangers."

"Well, there is that." Boelcke looked at the ceiling for a moment. "But Colonel Harvärja should have helped you out then. He was supposed to escort you."

Ginny sighed. "Lady Harvärja went into labor six weeks early. They chose to stay with relatives in Kalmar."

"I see. Still, it was inadvisable to go walking alone so late." Boelcke shrugged. "Brave, but foolish."

Ginny frowned. "I was given to believe that Stockholm was a safe place."

Boelcke nodded. "Generally speaking, yes," he said. "It's heaven compared to anything south of the Baltic Sea." Suddenly he smiled. "Swedes are nice people as a rule. Sober, hard-working, Lutherans, the lot of them, but Stockholm is both a port town and a naval wharf. On top of the soldiers, sailors and workers from all over Europe come here, and, well . . . " Boelcke's smile thinned. "You saw for yourself what might happen."

"I did indeed," Ginny said with feeling. "However, I want to set a few things straight."

An arched eye-brow. "Such as?"

"I was assaulted by foreigners," Ginny said forcefully. "Germans or Poles." The Swedish men, boys really, saved my ass . . . uh, my virtue. They are peasants from a small town in the north and mistook the guards for the thug's reinforcements. If you'd be so kind as to intercede with the authorities, I'll gladly pay their fines."

Boelcke beamed. "The American way! You honor your obligations. That's why I agreed to associate myself with this new nation of yours, in spite of them sending you here."

"Hogwash."

The snort was so explosive and so unexpected that Ginny jumped. The consul chuckled ruefully and bowed towards the short woman striding through the side door.

Lothar Boelcke smiled. "Allow me to introduce Anna, my wife. She has one very bad habit. She always listens at doors."

The new entrant to the room—dressed in silk and still beautiful in early middle-age—shook her finger at the consul and then turned to smile at Ginny. "Don't let my husband fool you." She spoke good German, but with a strong accent. "Lothar was so happy about his appointment that he couldn't talk about anything else for weeks." She then curtsied to Ginny. "I am Anna Hansdotter, Fraulein Cochran. I just wish your first day in Stockholm had been better." She spoke formally, as if meeting royalty at a levee.

"Please, call me Ginny," Ginny said, floundering with Swedish protocol, wondering if she should extend a hand or curtsey in return. She did both, which didn't work too well. But it did break the ice. "How do I address you?"

"Anna, of course." The older woman winked mischievously. "Although Lothar prefers Herr Consul. It makes him feel important."

"Herr Consul." Ginny bowed. "But it is important, you know. I'm just a young girl, but I've studied history. Only an important nation would bother with a consul. Your presence here, Consul Boelcke, gives us a certain prestige. The more accustomed they become to your title, the more the idea of the United States will take hold."

This plainly pleased Lothar. "Broadly speaking yes." He nodded. "Some of my neighbors will insist that I've delusions of grandeur."

"And rightly so," Frau Anna murmured with a wicked dimple. Ginny decided she was going to like Anna.

The consul didn't deign to notice his wife's comment. Instead he looked at Ginny. "Now, Fraulein Cochran, would you be so kind as to tell me what you are planning to do in Stockholm? I was just informed you had been appointed to my staff."

Ginny tried hard not to swallow. Despite his initial fury and fussy manner, she had decided Lothar Boelcke was no one's fool. Part of what she was supposed to do here, was to report back . . . about him. Boelcke had been recommended to the powers-that-be in Grantville. He was known to be scrupulously honest in his business dealings with the fledgling state, and was apparently very supportive of American up-timer ideals. Stockholm didn't warrant an ambassador yet . . . but a consul, even if he was a local, could help with matters, principally with the burgeoning trade. But . . . an up-timer-born like herself could tell the authorities if the man was really a good choice. "I was an assistant librarian," she said calmly. "I can handle writing, filing and other secretarial duties. I'm also fluent in English and Spanish and by now fairly conversant in German."

"Your German is certainly good enough," the consul allowed. "But most of my ledgers are in Swedish." Boelcke nodded thoughtfully, and looked directly at Ginny. "Let me ask that question again, Fraulein Cochran. What do you want to do in Stockholm?"

"I think the first answer is to become fully fluent in Swedish," she said with a smile. "And as time goes on we will get more English-speaking up-timers here. I could be useful dealing with them."

"It still, at this stage, is work that will not take up much of your time. You need, fraulein, a project to allow you to mix with Swedish people. Something with a good, popular profile, *ja*?"

"I think," said Ginny, "I may have just the thing. But let me think about it, please." She had a feeling "raising the *Vasa*" was not quite what he had in mind.

"Indeed, Lothar. Let her find her feet for a day or two," said Anna.

"Thank you." Ginny smiled tiredly. "But I do need to liberate those poor men. They got into trouble for my sake. And they seemed good, honest fellows. Upcountry farmers."

Boelcke nodded. "They mock them here in the capital, but they're the bedrock of the country."

"Mother was right." Olof Lennartson's punch sent fractured mortar spurting across the cell. Olof sucked his knuckles and grimaced "She always said Karl would come to a bad end over a girl."

"I doubt she meant it this way though," Lars said with a grin. "She didn't expect him to ever defend a German lady's virtue against foreign ruffians. Anyway, it wasn't Karl. It was Per."

"More fool you." Karl sighed. "If you're serious about it, defending virtues must be the most thankless job in the world."

"I'm not so sure about that," Per interjected. "That foreign lass was no ordinary girl."

"Indeed." Lars quipped. "For starters she looked at you and not at Karl."

"There is that, too," Per allowed, "but mainly she didn't act like the women I met in Germany." He was about to say something else when the door opened and

a turnkey followed by two guards motioned the brothers
to step outside.

"I'd rather see you hung," the turnkey said sourly,
"But some foreign woman conned the boss into letting
you out."

"Told you so," Per said. "That's no ordinary girl."

Gods, but they are big, Ginny thought. She had seen
larger men, but taken together in a good light the Lennartson brothers loomed like trees and boulders on a
steep slope . . . right before the avalanche. They all
looked expectantly at her, too. Ginny hesitated for a
moment, and then she turned towards the oldest one.

"Please translate for your brothers," Ginny said. "I
came to thank you."

"You got us free," Karl blurted. "Just like that."

"Well," Ginny answered, "I had to talk for a while and
part with some silver, but you are free to go."

"Then we're in your debt." Per said something in
Swedish, and as one, the brothers bowed.

"Of course not," Ginny said. "You helped me. Paying
your fine was the least I could do for you."

"You paid it for us?" Per's face was a study in wonder-
ment, and Ginny found herself nodding. The brothers
went into a huddle and then Per spoke again.

"We thank you, lady." For a moment, Per looked
uncertain, but then he went on. "We fought those who
attacked you because that's our way. For that, you owe
us nothing. We fought the guards because of a misunderstanding. Again, you owe us nothing. Now you've paid
for our freedom with both your word and your silver.
We're in your debt today and for all future." The other

brothers nodded, at once crossing their hearts like Catholics.

Like something out of the Dark Ages, Ginny thought. Then she checked herself. *I guess these boys never heard about the Renaissance.* There was no mistaking their heartfelt sincerity however, and Ginny swallowed a lump in her throat.

"Well, you could do something for me."

"Surely."

"When it is light tomorrow, go and look from the dockside at the masts of the *Vasa* sticking out of the water. Then we'll talk. Where can I find you?"

Per grimaced. "We will send a message. The place we will be sleeping is not for well-bred ladies. It is not safe."

"Not unless they are lady rats," said Karl, grinning.

Things were going well indeed, Fermin Mazalet reflected as he sat waiting in Admiral Fleming's opulent antechamber. Although there was no one else in the room, the Frenchman hid his smile. His bronze-into-gold-scheme had succeeded beyond his wildest imagination. The suckers, silly aristocrats all of them, hadn't even realized they'd been duped, and most of them would be ready to back his claims of scientific and engineering expertise. Mazalet snorted. Useful fools the lot of them. Swedish aristocrats were more hidebound than those of his country were, and they really believed that knowledge of anything save war would stain their precious honor. A nobleman neither traded nor tilled the earth, and that created enormous possibilities for a man like Fermin Mazalet. Being a foreigner was the key of course; a Swedish go-between would never be anything but a servant.

Being seen as outside the system, but with exquisite manners and commercial shrewdness, was a real door-opener with the more hypocritical among the nobility.

"Can't swindle an honest man, Fermin," he thought. *"Let's find out what kind of man Admiral Fleming really is."* He leaned back on the marble bench about to make himself comfortable for a long wait when a young officer opened the door. Mazalet rose and bowed floridly. The officer just stared.

"The admiral will listen to your proposal, Monsieur Mazalet," he said coldly. "Please follow me."

Arrogant. Mazalet hid his disdain behind a friendly smile. *I would keep an armed unknown in front of me if I were he. Treville would have him drubbed out of service in the wink of an eye.*

The reason for the officer's seeming nonchalance became evident soon enough. As Mazalet crossed the threshold into the admiral's office, a huge wolfhound rose from the floor and padded towards across the flagstones. The beast pinned Mazalet with its stare as it sniffed loudly. Suddenly it growled, a deep thrumming sound emanating from the large chest. Mazalet stood still, looking intently at the admiral who remained behind his desk. Mazalet did not bow. The admiral was in control of the situation, and he would get to the point eventually. Mazalet just waited.

Finally, Admiral Fleming rose from his chair. "It seems that my dog has taken a dislike to you, Monsieur Mazalet," he said and whistled softly. Immediately the big dog walked backwards to his master's side, all the time pinning Mazalet with a baleful gaze.

"Can't imagine why," Mazalet said lightly. "I'm most grateful for this opportunity to present my suggestion to the admiralty, and I'm quite certain that Your Grace will find that my plan has no inconsiderable merit."

"Get to the point." The admiral sat down behind his desk. "My time is short, and even if I enjoyed your company, I would not have the time to procrastinate over every flowery phrase you strew about you. Besides, your reputation precedes you, Monsieur Mazalet. A nephew of mine invested in your alchemical shenanigan. He's an idiot, granted, but outside warfare a gentleman does not take advantage of idiocy."

Not counting your peasants and servants, of course. Mazalet bowed again. "I was not aware that someone of your peerage could engage in any industrial endeavour," he said blandly. "But if Your Grace prefers to question my honor. I'd be more than willing to give satisfaction." He glanced at the prone dog. "No animals in the salle, of course."

"Heh! You don't lack for guts." The admiral smiled suddenly. "I don't trust you of course, but my nephew probably had it coming, anyway." He waved for Mazalet to proceed.

"Is the salvage contract for *Vasa* still open?" Mazalet asked. "If so, I want to take a crack at it."

The admiral started. "You want the reward for the salvage?" he asked incredulously. "What makes you think you can succeed where Ian Bulmer failed?"

"I've just returned from a trip to Thuringia," Mazalet said. "And yes, the knowledge and expertise residing with those newcomers is nothing less than miraculous. I didn't spend nearly enough time there, but with the knowledge I've acquired, I'm convinced that the salvage is possible."

"The contract is open." Admiral Fleming leaned back in his chair, and steepled his fingers. "I suppose it doesn't cost me anything to let you try." He turned toward the short officer. "Sparre, please go outside and call for a drop of wine. I'm afraid the discussion will take longer than I expected." He gestured with his hand. "Don't stand there man. I doubt Herr Mazalet will try to hurt the hand that might feed him."

"It's a matter of vast embarrassment to us," said Lothar Boelcke, sipping his wine. "I mean, with the masts sticking out of the water for every trading vessel to see and laugh at. If it could be raised . . . well it would do the prestige of those involved a great deal of good—besides the monetary value of the salvage, that is. But this Monsieur Fermin Mazalet d'Angouleme . . . well, his reputation is a little stained. I would be very careful doing business with him. I think, perhaps, Fleming is being clever with him. If he fails . . . well he had better leave the country fast and forever or he will end up rotting in a jail—which would please Fleming and a number of other highly placed people. If—as seems unlikely—he succeeds . . . Fleming will get the credit."

"There is the third scenario. He tricks a fair number of people into investing in it . . . and leaves with the money," said Ginny, thoughtfully. "My father is a good, solid man. But he invested a part of his savings into some scheme to pump water out of very profitable coal mines. It was a scam."

"A what?"

She explained.

Boelcke nodded. "He has a glib tongue. And he deals well with aristocrats. Not . . . " He smiled. " . . . with business people like me."

Anna smothered a laugh. "Yes, dear. Because you told me about his last scheme, and I said if it sounded too good to be true, it probably was. So tell us, Ginny. Just what is your plan?"

"I'm not very glib or good at raising money. I couldn't do that in a million years. But I have read and researched enough to know how the *Vasa* really could be salvaged, if not brought to the surface. I'd like Mazalet to raise the money . . . and trick him into setting things up so we can actually do it. As long as we get to the stage of bringing up the first salvage, he probably won't cut and run."

"It sounds very good," said Boelcke. "But how do you plan to do this?"

Ginny's eyes were narrowed. "Because I have read the same books from the Grantville library—and a few more—that Mazalet has, I know what he needs and what I think he intends to do. He came here by way of Finland. But he came alone. I've made a friend among the ferry women . . . ."

"You have a happy knack of making friends here in Sweden. Maybe you can raise money easier than you think," said Anna. "So what did the ferry woman tell you, dear? They hear all the gossip of Stockholm sooner or later."

"He had hired some Karelians. Just like Bulmer. But there was fight over money and the equipment he wished to use. They went back."

"Karelians?"

"Divers," said Anna briskly.

"Really, my dear," the consul began, but his wife cut him short.

"Divers," she repeated. "Men that walk under water. There were quite a few Karelians in Bulmer's crew."

"I was just about to say that," Boelcke said evenly. "Bulmer kept a savage bunch that swaggered around town raising all kinds of hell. Not our kind of people by any means, and I don't suppose they did a lot for Bulmer either, since he lost his contract. Diving like that is not something I can say I ever heard of Swedes doing."

"That means," said Ginny slowly, "that manpower is his real bottle neck." She nodded. "With the books he stole, Mazalet might be able to build the equipment, but he will struggle to find divers who will trust him. And I have four of those at my call."

"Those two-fisted northerners?" Boelcke smiled. "They'd certainly be hard to stop if you managed to line them up in the right direction. The question is if they're glib enough to approach Mazalet on their own? He'd be suspicious if you were there."

Ginny nodded. "I think we can arrange it, with me in the background. Then all we need is to catch him."

"And keep him," said Anna. "He is not an honest man."

"I have an idea there, too. I don't think he'd worry about breaking an agreement with ordinary yeoman farmers. He'll expect to run off with the money from the investors and leave the peasants swinging in the wind. I am not too sure of Swedish law, Consul . . . "

Boelcke rubbed his hands in pleasure. "Just leave it to me, fraulein. He'll be happy to agree to a deal with them—not realizing that they have the right to sell their shares to a third party. You."

Ginny nodded. "Part of them, anyway."

Stockholm: Three days later

He was being watched. Fermin Mazalet had the native instincts of both predator and prey, and he had never found reason to distrust those instincts. Although he stopped at the quay and looked back up the street, he saw no discernible threat. Still, it was with relief he clambered down into a cockleshell boat held flush against the water stairs.

"The naval wharf," Mazalet told the old woman who sat at the oars. "No hurry though." He paused and smiled. "As a matter of fact, I could enjoy a round trip along the quays. The weather is good and I'll pay double."

The woman grinned. "For money like that, I can wait until you're done out there." She nodded towards the wharf. "It's a slow day anyway, my lord."

"Never tell that to the customer," Mazalet said lightly. "and I'm no lord. I just dress that way so that noblemen will take me seriously."

The crone chuckled as she rowed her small craft. "Your secret's safe with me." She chuckled again. "As long as you pay like a lord."

"Get up, dear." Toke-Karin looked after Mazalet's departing form and tapped the pile of tarps. Instantly a tow-headed urchin sat up and jumped onto the wharf. The boy made fast and dropped back into the boat, nimble as a shrew. "Go to the end of the quay and wave to our lady. You know the signal."

"The boy is waving," Ginny lowered her binoculars, "That means Mazalet will return by boat."

"Good," said Per. "With a little luck your Frenchman will see our little show. Lars will complain if he swims for nothing in this water. Even if we have some side bets for a small profit."

"He isn't my Frenchman." Ginny muttered. "But I think he'll bite."

"*Sacre Bleu*." Mazalet almost fell out of the little boat. "Look at that man."

"Where?" The old woman swivelled her head around vaguely.

"There!" Mazalet pointed. "Up on that bowsprit. It looks like he's going to jump."

"Crossed love!" The old woman cackled. "It happens, it happens. Ah, there he goes."

"Turn that way!" Mazalet shouted as the body plunged headfirst into the water. "We must pick him up."

"I don't want a madman in my boat," the woman said stolidly. She had turned toward the scene anyway.

"We need to help him, by God." Mazalet grasped his rapier. "Don't worry, madam. I can handle a half-drowned fool."

She snorted and bent to her oars.

"Is he coming up?" she asked a little later.

"No." Mazalet scanned the surface. "Yes. There he is. A little bit to port, if you please. No! *Pardonnez-moi*. Make that starboard and hurry now!"

The old crone muttered darkly, but steered the boat as if by magic, without a backwards glance. Within seconds, however, Mazalet could see that the man in the water had no trouble staying afloat. His arms moved in lazy circles and he smiled and shouted something in accented Swedish. Several young men on the quay shouted encouragement while a bunch of sailors on the ship looked sulkily on.

"Can I be of assistance?" Mazalet asked with a faint smile, as they drew close. This fellow might be exactly what he was looking for. A madman. And one who could swim.

"No," the man turned in the water revealing a young face under a mop of wet brown hair. "Begging my lord's pardon," he said with a strange slow accent, "but we're so close to land that I could walk on the bottom and still get there." The swimmer leaned backwards and began to paddle with his feet as he used his arms to keep the face above water. To Mazalet it looked as the lad was merely resting in the water.

"Crazy boy." The rowing madam spat in the water. "You gave us quite a fright."

"I'm sorry, Grandmother," the boy said. "But winning that bet means I won't starve tonight."

"Do you know this fellow?" Mazalet asked her politely.

"Never seen him before." The old woman spat again. "I know his type. Crazy northerner, nothing but trouble. They trounce our boys and make free with the maidens."

Mazalet ignored her. "You swim well, boy."

"Not as well as my brothers, my lord." The lad rose from the water, standing on the submerged stairs. "It was nice talking to you," he said as casually as if they had met walking along a street, "But I have to go collect my wagers."

"Wait," Mazalet shouted. The Frenchman pulled out a large coin and flipped it towards the crone. "Thanks for the service, madam. I'll be sure to recommend you to my friends." Then he jumped onto the sea-stairs looking wildly for the departing northerner.

"Hey you! You there!" called the Frenchman from behind him.

Lars Lennartson grinned like a fox. It seemed as if their target had swallowed the bait. He ignored the call and stalked towards the group of scowling sailors. "All right, friends," he said. "I braved your bowsprit and I made it ashore. You better cough up the money."

"Why?" A rough-looking sailor said, bunching his shoulders.

"Because I have you outnumbered." Lars pointed with his chin, signalling to Karl, Per and Olof to move in, crowding the sailors from all directions. "There four of us to your six. We're a peaceful bunch," Lars continued, "but you put your money on the line just as we did." His grin would have sent a wolf scurrying for shelter. "Now, will you hand over our winnings or should we pry it from your mangled fingers?"

Slowly, sullenly, with studied nonchalance the sailor handed over a small purse. Lars stuck it inside his belt without bothering to count.

"We trust you." He grinned. "And we know where to find you. Now scoot." Then he turned and bowed clumsily before the speechless Mazalet.

"Did you want to speak to me, milord?"

"Yes." Mazalet smiled winningly. "If you can spare the time."

"Yes, milord," Lars answered. "We have nothing to do anyway. I've some dry clothes to put on, but then we'd be free."

"Let me treat you to a mug of ale then," Mazalet said. "Wine if you prefer. Invite your friends, too. They look like good people to me."

"The best." Lars nodded happily. "Delsbo boys all of them, just like me. My brothers, in fact." He paused. "Can I really have wine? I don't think I ever had that outside of communion."

"Wine it is, then," Mazalet said with another smile. "Please collect your brothers while I go inside and order for all of us." Without waiting for an answer, the Frenchman walked across the quay and disappeared inside a tavern. Lars looked at the retreating back and grinned again.

"She was right. There are more ways than one to skin a bear," he mumbled as he motioned his brothers to join him.

"I must confess to be curious," Mazalet said. "My travels have taken me all around Europe and I thought swimming was a dead art. Where did you learn it?"

"Back home of course," Lars answered. "In Delsbo the smallest child knows how to swim. Of course, the water is not as warm as this place."

His brothers nodded assent.

"So all of you," Mazalet asked shrewdly, "know how to swim?"

"Yes," Per answered. "Olof is the best, but since he's a tad afraid of heights, Lars volunteered to jump from the bow sprit."

"Am not," Olof grunted. "I'm not afraid of anything."

Mazalet smiled. "I quite believe you, young master. But I'm still curious. How come the people of Delsbo are such proficient swimmers?"

"Well," Olof said in an awkward manner. "Lars will tell you it's because Delsbo people are the best, but really it's on account of Good King Gustav and the church bells." He paused, looking around helplessly.

"Go on," Per said. "It will do you good to use your voice for anything but muttered curses."

"I don't curse," Olof muttered. Then he took a deep breath.

"As Grandpa told the story," he said, "Good King Gustav wasn't so good after all. No, he was greedy and wanted our church bells. As Lars would tell you, our church bells were the largest and their tolls carried on even to Norway."

"They had to be," Lars interjected hotly, "since our church steeple reaches the sky."

"As I said," Olof continued. "The old men of Delsbo decided to hide the bells in the lake. Lars will tell you, Lake Dellen is the deepest lake in the world, and they thought the bells would be secure there."

"I see," Mazalet said. "What happened?"

"Well, the old men tied the bells together and put them in the largest church boat. Even that boat was hard pressed to hold the bells, but they were all good sailors so they reached the middle of Lake Dellen. There they cut a notch in the side of the boat and heaved the bells over the side."

"A notch?" Mazalet asked. "Why?"

"To mark the place of course," Olof said. "That's what Grandpa told me anyway," he ended truculently.

"But then you couldn't find the bells again?" Mazalet said.

"That's right," Olof nodded. " 'Cause the boat with the notch in the side got burned in a cattle raid. Anyway, since then all the boys in our village go into the lake during summer. To look for the bells, I mean."

"Amazing," Mazalet took a gulp of wine. "Can you actually look under water?"

"Sure," Karl said. "It stings the eyes a little at first and you can't see that far, but fish have eyes too, don't they?"

"Most certainly," Mazalet averred. "And a man should have better eyes than a fish. Anything else would be against God's design."

"Wouldn't know about that," Olof said. "The priest threw me out for snoring. Bloody Lutheran."

"Olof!" Per did not raise his voice, "Why don't the three of you go outside for a while?"

Olof nodded, drained his ale and stood up in one fluid movement. Quickly, his brothers followed suit. Mazalet looked at their retreating backs and smiled.

"Monsieur Treville would have loved your brothers," he said.

"Who?" Per asked.

"An old acquaintance of mine, a leader of soldiers."

"I doubt Karl or Lars would make good soldiers," Per said with a rueful shrug. "I've tried it and I don't want any of us to join the army. Soldiers die."

"It happens." Mazalet's answering shrug was pure Gallic. "It happens. However, I might have a proposition for you later, but I can't contain my curiosity. Was your brother pulling my leg about those bells?"

Per smiled. "Not really. But he was just six years old when Grandpa died. As I understand it, they put the bells on a barge and tied them to a rope with a sealed keg at the other end."

"And that notch? It sounds like a nobleman's joke about stupid peasants."

"Nothing stupid about it," Per said. "The village elders held the barge just so and cut several grooves aimed at different landmarks. You could only see those landmarks through the grooves when the barge was in the right spot. Fishermen do it all the time when they find a good spot. This was a little more precise, and with a little rowing and shouting they would have found the bells after the tax collectors went home."

"But the barge burned?" Mazalet asked.

"I don't rightly know." Per shrugged again. "It is nowhere to be found, and by now the rope and keg must have rotted or sunk and so the bells are lost. Looking for them is a tradition in Delsbo."

"I see," Mazalet said, waving for the serving wench. "In fact, I believe that together, we could bring back those bells." He smiled as he watched the young woman pour. "After all, the highest church steeple in the world deserves the best bells."

◇   ◇   ◇

"He swallowed the bait," Per said.

Ginny grinned. "Hook, line and sinker," she said. "If you understand the expression?"

"Of course." Per smiled faintly. "I see what you mean about him being a good liar and cheat though. He agreed to us each getting an equal share without batting an eyelid. With two shares for himself, and, of course, expenses. He even agreed to write it down and signed it with a fine pen. I made a show of being barely able to read, and struggling with figures, just as you told me."

"He believed that?" asked Ginny.

Per nodded. "Just as he believed we were great swimmers. He didn't guess you had half killed us these last few days teaching us more than just to stay afloat."

"Still, to agree to your starting position . . . "

Per shrugged. "He intends to cheat us, but he needs divers to persuade people that he really will raise the ship. He would sign anything. He doesn't know that I got the innkeeper and the consul to sign as witnesses. In those old peasant clothes he wore, I wouldn't have recognized Herr Consul myself." Per shook his head admiringly. "He was the perfect fat peasant burgher. Anyway, Mazalet said he didn't care, as it was really the honor of salvaging the ship that he was after."

"He's lying," Ginny said flatly. "Did I tell you what the ship is worth?"

"You did," Per said, "but I didn't understand all of it. That GNP business was a bit beyond me."

"You and most people," Ginny said. "It's been estimated that the *Vasa* was worth one twentieth of everything that was produced in Sweden that year."

"I still don't understand that," Per complained. "The wharf is big, but even among the locals, not even one man in twenty works there. And most people are farmers in the countryside, anyway.

"All those farmers are taxed," Ginny said, "Are they not?"

"Of course," Per said. "Nobody likes it, but just about everyone outside Delsbo pays."

"Right." Ginny spread her hands. "And much of that money goes into building ships and guns. Believe me, if we succeed, Mazalet will be richer than all but the dukes. My only doubt is whether Mazalet intends us to succeed or just to look like we may. But if it looks like it is working, he will stay."

"And he isn't the sharing kind?" Per asked.

"No," Ginny said. "Definitely not. He'd go back on that deal in an instant."

"Not anymore," said Lothar Boelcke, emerging dressed in his own clothes once more. "That contract is binding."

Per nodded. "We will need you to make over the shares to Fraulein Cochran, Herr Boelcke."

"I see we're going to argue again," said Ginny.

Per shook his head. "No. Without you, lady, we would be worrying about being conscripted, let alone working for a bright future for four penniless farm boys. As it is we can claim to be working on a project sanctioned by the admiral himself. You will pay us fairly," he said with finality.

Lothar Boelcke shook his head. "To save having the argument again. I asked Anna. She said four shares—two for you brothers, two for Ginny here, *ja*. She has all the knowledge and all the planning, but she needs you for diving, for courage and strength, and one third is fair for Mazalet having to swindle up the money for the barge and equipment." His eyes twinkled. "And Anna is always right. Ask Ginny. Ask me. I have thirty years' experience of it."

Per looked at his brothers. Nodded. "Very well. Now we just need to explain this to Mazalet."

"Let's wait a little," said Ginny.

Lars nodded. "Always make sure that the crayfish is in the trap first, before you haul it out of the water. Now, lady, explain again how this 'diving bell' works?"

"*Ja.* I want to understand what I drown in," said Olof, in broken German.

A little later, they were sitting in a salle at the consulate, as Ginny demonstrated with Anna's largest preserving bowl and a glass and small piece of thin bent copper pipe. She pushed the glass—mouth down—into the water. "It still holds air. Now watch how the water pressure pushes at it. The air cannot escape, but water now fills the bottom half of the glass." She handed the J-shaped tube to Olof. "Now, put your finger over this end, and the other end into the bottom of the glass."

"I have it!" he said, delightedly. "We sit inside the glass and breathe through the tube!"

Ginny shook her head. "It won't work. Trust me, please. I will show what would happen."

He did as he was told. "Now take your finger off. The air will come out. And if you tried your way, it would even suck the air out of your lungs. Even if you pumped air down . . . you need a good non-return valve to stop that happening."

"What is a non-return valve?"

Ginny explained. And then explained again. The Lennartson brothers were sharp, but she did have a few centuries to bridge. "But there one simple solution. Air always rises in water. If you can pass me that other tube over there, Per." The tube had a wire framework soldered to its end—a framework that held the end of the pipe below the glass. "Now, Olof. You blow down that pipe. We will have a pump on the surface that does that. Air bubbles up into the glass. Air comes out under the bottom lip. But unless the glass turns over, there is always air trapped inside for the diver to breathe. The diver inside the bell uses oxygen—but new air is constantly pumped down from the surface."

It took some more explaining and repetition, but they had it eventually. They were, in their way, shrewd farm boys, used to contriving when there was no money to buy. "Now all we need is strong enough and big enough glass—with very heavy bottom edges. We do not wish it to turn upside down," said Lars.

"It doesn't have to be glass. Metal or even a barrel with many iron hoops will do. Do better, actually."

Ginny nodded. "Now we will have to persuade Mazalet to do it this way. He had some very strange ideas. Another thing. It will be cold and dark down there. You're going to get wet. You need wetsuits or something that will keep water in to get warm."

"Wool. Wool to the skin," said Olof, whose German was improving as fast as Ginny's Swedish. "Mama always said that."

"Wool, and tight-weave linen over it. With tight cuffs, collars and ankles. Maybe even belts to keep them tight. It will still be cold and miserable."

"It is the job, *ja*," said Lars. "We Delsbo boys are not afraid of a little cold. Besides they can haul us up quickly to get warm."

"NO. Um. Look, believe me on this . . . Decompression will kill you. You will have to come up slowly. I've got decompression tables."

"She knows what she's talking about, boys," said Per, calmly. "But we can take some dry clothes. The divers can get dry and have a drink when they come out of the water, even if they are in a big barrel. Look at the glass. There is still some room to sit above the water level."

Ginny nodded again. "You will have to take some kind of lantern down there. As long as air keeps coming from the surface, you'll be fine. Look, Mazalet was full of wild ideas about making up-time devices to dive with. I spent a lot of time explaining that the diving bell was simple, relatively easy to make and did not require some kind of non-return valve, because air is lighter than water."

Per held up the glass. "Will this work?" he asked. "The secret is that the air-pipe from the surface must bubble into the water right? Otherwise this, how do say, pressure, will push the air out of the bell. So we attach the pipe to the bottom of the bell, but we drill little holes, here—about one third of the way up from the lip. The water will always go as high as the holes, because the air is only trapped in the upper two thirds of the bell. The bubbling-in air comes in at the bottom. The trapped air can never meet."

Ginny smiled. He was the quickest of the four brothers. "Yes. And you can pump air to a diver with a helmet down a pipe—so long as the air is pumped from the air that is trapped inside the bell, and the diver is working at nearly the same depth. But to be safe if the bell is at ten fathoms, the diver probably should not go more than say another two fathoms to twelve fathoms. So we could pump air to a diver from the surface, but only if he is not more than two fathoms down."

"And what is the use of that?" asked Lars. "We can swim from the surface to two fathoms."

"But if we are at twenty fathoms, we can go to twenty-two—provided the pumping is done from inside the bell," said Olof thoughtfully. "The air is thick in the bell from the heaviness of the water. So the water cannot push it so easily."

It wasn't perhaps a text-book explanation, but he did have some of the idea of pressure, which considering his background was amazing. "Normally, the deeper the diver goes the more risk that the pressure, that heaviness, pushing back air—even the air in his lungs—up the hose to the surface. With the system we are using if the pump fails, only the air inside the hose will flow back because the canvas hose will collapse. And there is no air connection to air in his lungs or the bell. If it sucks anything it will suck water. We'll test the pumps for their ability to push air to various depths, but I have some plans for a simple double cylinder rotary one that ought to work."

She had to start explaining again and drawing pictures.

Fermin Mazalet shook his head. "This is more complex than I thought. The barge, yes. But the barrel? All those iron hoops? And the reinforcing to the top of the thing? It's more like a battering ram than something for going under the sea. And the weight of it . . . I'm not sure we'll get it to work. . . ."

"Look at it from the bright side," Lars quipped. "Even if it doesn't work, our treasure sits in plain sight. We could even lash ourselves to the mainmast if there is a storm."

"Lash ourselves to the mainmast?" Per shook his head. "What would be the point of that?"

"It's the done thing," said Lars, with a seriousness only betrayed by a tiny twitch. "In all the best stories."

Mazalet shook his head in bemusement. The Lennartson brothers were unlike any other Swedes he knew. The common people in Stockholm were a solid and dependable lot. They were not exactly dull, but not given to much frivolity either. His divers were different. They were inventing commercial diving on an ad hoc basis, solving problems at a frightening rate, and with an incongruously off-hand manner. Sometimes they even came up with solutions to problems that Mazalet had not even been aware of. Despite the summer heat, the Frenchman shuddered. Mazalet was honest enough, with himself at least, to realize that his contributions had become increasingly irrelevant. Some of his own half-baked solutions would probably have killed the crew, and Mazalet had come to look forward to Per's explanations with a sort of dreadful fascination. He'd perchance found men who would, if not salvage the bronze cannon, at least make it look very tempting to investors. He swayed between belief and the warm and cozy feel of a good scam coming together. "If you weren't so clever . . . If that piglet you used had not lived for a good twenty minutes beneath the water surface inside the barrel, I would be tempted to have you all committed as madmen."

"The piglet was mad enough when we untied it," said Lars. "I think all Stockholm heard it. That nosy Norwegian certainly did. Good thing you sent him away."

"He looks like a pirate and is most certainly a spy. But I heard you filling him with tales of men walking to the deepest depths with our pumps."

"He was buying the drinks. And we know that cannot work like that. You cannot pump air to very deep without a very good non-return valve. That is not that easy to make. Our system works. That will not."

Mazalet looked suspiciously at him. "How do you know? I have seen pictures."

"We know," said Per smiling. "You see . . . we must introduce you to our partner. At the workshed."

It was barely ten yards away from the quayside where they had been talking, and Fermin Mazalet found himself being led out of the sun and into the half dark where Karl and Olof were working on the windlass, with a pair of local carpenters . . . and a familiar face.

"Monsieur Mazalet. Perhaps you have some books you would like to return?" said someone he thought safely in Grantville Library.

Mazalet's eyes nearly started out of his head. Then he started to laugh. "I have always said you could not cheat an honest man. Now I have proved it to myself, on myself. You out-thought me, mam'zelle. Well done."

"You don't seem angry, monsieur," said Ginny. "I expected trouble, to be honest. Until we brought you to your senses, that is."

Mazalet shrugged. "What would be the point? I have a project now that may well even succeed . . . and shares which have become vastly valuable. The local wealthy folk may not trust Fermin Mazalet. But they do believe in the technological advantages of Grantville. And you need me for my connections at least. But I wonder why you came out of hiding now."

Per answered. "Because tomorrow we do our first test and she wants to be there. And this afternoon would be too late, because you have arranged for us to see *Nya Nyckeln*."

"Good afternoon, fellows. I'm Lieutenant Sparre, the admiral's aide." The smallish officer looked none too pleased with his task, but there was no scorn in his voice. "Word's come down from on high that you boys need a guided tour to one of our largest ships."

"The largest," Lars answered. "Or the one that looks most like *Vasa* anyway."

Sparre made a *tch*ing sound. "Another attempt at a salvage!"

"Is there a problem?" Per asked.

"Well, yes." The young officer looked uncomfortable. "I trust I can rely on your discretion?"

"Of course," Lars said gaily. "All Delsbo boys like to talk."

"He means you should keep your mouth shut," Karl said.

"No problem," Lars said. "We're real good at that, too."

Lieutenant Sparre tugged his jaw. "Several of my peers lost friends and family when *Vasa* sank and there has been a lot of bad feeling about the whole thing."

"Yeah," Lars said, "Like the ship not being sea-worthy."

"Shut up!" Per snapped. "I'll do the talking from now on." He pushed forward towards Sparre and bowed from the waist. "My brothers are fresh from the north," he said. "Please, forgive them some naive bluntness."

"No matter," Sparre said stiffly. "*Nya Nyckeln* is waiting. Please follow me." He turned abruptly and walked down towards the half-finished hulls still propped up on their slipways.

"*Nya Nyckeln*," Sparre said half proud, half sad. "Maybe the last of her kind."

"Almost as big as a church boat back home," Lars murmured.

Per stared. *Nya Nyckeln*, the New Key, was huge, almost twice the size of most naval ships, and sitting on her slipway, her entire hull towered over the group of people, reducing them into insignificance.

"She's the size of *Vasa*?" he asked in a quiet voice.

"Yes," Sparre said. "Somewhat broader of beam and with a little more draft, but close enough."

"That's a tall order," Karl said. "Lifting her in one piece I mean."

"It can't be done," a nasal voice interjected. "It was tried and nothing good came out of it."

Per turned and looked into a florid face made no prettier by being drawn into a supercilious sneer.

"Fellows," Lieutenant Sparre said formally. "This is Captain Stolpeskott." He shrugged. "Sorry, Captain, but I am acting on orders from the admiral himself."

"Letting unlettered peasants aboard his majesty's ships," Stolpeskott sneered. "Well, I heard that it was that slimy frog Mazalet who's got the contract, so I probably shouldn't be too surprised. Drinking and whoring is all those papists are good for." He turned abruptly and disappeared toward the administrative buildings.

"I'd ask you to forgive the captain," Sparre said quietly. "His brother was on the *Vasa*."

"Of course," Per said looking along the stupendous hull. "Are those the gun ports?"

"Why, yes." Sparre smiled. "Of course, the guns are added last, usually with a crane after the ship is already in the water."

"Could we see a gun like those on *Vasa*?" Per asked. "One of those cranes would be interesting, too."

"Certainly." Sparre motioned towards another building. "We'll get there in a moment." He smiled in an odd way. "Maybe I should ask to be assigned as the naval liaison." He shrugged in an eloquent way. "Anything to get away from Stolpeskott."

It was an unusually quiet group of northerners that left the naval dockyard some hours later. Finally the enormity of their task had actually dented the confidence of Delsbo. Dented, but not broken. They were all there the next morning when the barge was towed out to the mast tops sticking out above the water.

It appeared to be getting to the Frenchman, too. He might be a swindler, but Fermin Mazalet was no cold-blooded murderer. "Are you certain about this?" he asked, looking at the bell. "Shouldn't we test her somewhere else first?"

"Where?" Per asked. "All shipping avoids this site. No one wants to run afoul of a sunken spar. That makes it a perfect spot." He grinned. "Also, as you've explained, it pays to advertise. No matter how it goes, people will know we've come this far, at least. The admiralty will see us out here."

"There is that," Mazalet said with a quick nod. "Funding might become less of a problem."

"Are we strapped for cash?" Karl asked.

"Not really," Mazalet said, "but it never hurts to spread the risk. I plan to sell a few shares in the salvage project."

Karl frowned. "Won't that decrease our share?"

"Not really." Mazalet repeated. "To my knowledge, it never has, anyway."

"All anchors are in place," Captain Sigismund reported. "We might drift a foot or two but hardly more."

"Very good." Per nodded. "Start pumping air."

"Is that really necessary?" Mazalet asked. "I mean, they'll be tired long before the bell even hits the water."

"That's why we have replacements." Per lowered his voice. "It's my brothers going down there, and we're taking enough chances as it is already. Pumps start before anyone goes inside the bell and don't stop until the last diver is back on deck. Any man who forgets that will go along for the next dive. Outside the bell.

"Divers to the bell," he shouted. "Check the air and keep your feet up." He waited as Lars and Olof ducked to get through the little port in the weighted edge of the bell and scrambled inside. The port was below the air-bleed holes, and if they wished to exit it once they were down, they would have to swim.

Olof's voice sounded strange, coming from inside the bell. "We're ready to go."

"Good." Per shouted. "Remember, we'll only lower you a few feet at a time so if something happens, you just go outside and swim to the surface." He turned around and signalled to Karl. "All right, remove the planks and go ahead with the crane when you're ready. Remember, just a few feet at a time."

Karl grinned. "Don't worry, big brother. By now I can do this in my sleep." He watched as the last plank was pulled aside, and motioned his men towards the windlass.

"Everyone got a hold? Good." Karl nodded. "Good. Can you feel the weight? My brothers' lives are hanging on your shoulders. Don't make me regret picking you for this job." There were tight grins from the men, but no one looked strained. "On my mark," Karl said, "you will all take one step backwards. Ready, steady, go."

"Here we go," Lars said gleefully as the diving bell rose from the deck. "The first lads since Jonah to walk the bottom of the sea."

"Don't tell our boss," Olof complained. "Thanks to you he really believes we've done this for generations. Don't make him change his mind."

Lars face hardened in the gloom. "Don't you think we can do it?" he challenged. "There is nothing we can't do if we really try."

"We can't fly," Olof said.

"Of course we can." Lars grinned. "You just wait and see. With all the money from *Vasa*, we can build some other machine."

"One that flies?"

"Why not," Lars said serenely. "We're from Delsbo, and Per is really clever. Nothing is impossible."

Olof stood up on his seat. "The pump is still working anyway; I can feel the air coming in."

"Told you so." Lars looked down into the water. "The counterweight is barely under the surface yet," he muttered. "What's taking Karl so long?"

"He's being careful, Brother."

"It's something he should try with women. Ah. That's more like it!" Lars chuckled as the bottom of the bell slid into the water. "It gets dark fast though," he noted.

"Get used to it," said Olof gloomily. "Miss Ginny says it will be pitch black down there."

"Good thing we have a lamp, then."

"*Ja.*" There was silence, only disturbed by the bubbling air coming up from the hose. The bell slowly sank, with the pressure increasing. "We will only go to five fathoms," said Lars, comforting himself. "We could swim up from that."

"We could, but we are not going to," said Olof.

"No," said Lars, "But I am going to swim outside, little brother."

"But we are not supposed to. This is a test." As if to emphasise that the little bell connected by wire to the surface tinged. Olof tugged the reply ringer.

"*Ja.* But I am just a little scared, brother. If I don't do it now, I will never do it. And we are promised to the enterprise." He took a coil of rope and tied himself to the end. "You can haul me back in if I get into trouble. I will tug hard, twice, if I need you to do that." He smiled ruefully, and pointed at the surface. "Besides, the Frenchman wanted something to prove we'd been down here. Let me see what I can find."

"Does Per know of this plan?"

Lars shook his head. "He probably guesses I will by now. He knows me. And I think he was planning to do the same thing if he had won at the drawing of the straws."

Olof bit his lip "You have your knife? You remember Ginny said the greatest danger was from becoming entangled."

Lars patted it. The bell's descent had stopped and he slipped down into the water. Olof also knew his older brother. For Lars to have admitted fear was unheard of. Olof knew nothing would stop him defeating it. So he held the rope and prayed.

After what seemed a long, long time, just as he was ready to start hauling rope anyway, it went slack. He took in. He breathed a sigh of relief when his brother's head popped up. And then he screamed.

"Ach. It's just the poor fellow's skull. It came loose when I started to cut him free of the rigging. He should have taken Ginny's advice and had a sharp knife with him."

Olof shuddered and refused to take the skull. "What have you done with the body?"

"Still out there. I will tie him on to the other end of the rope. His uniform is holding him together."

There was a silence. Then Olof reached out and took the skull with its tatters of hair. "He needs a Christian burial," he said, "whoever he was."

"*Ja.* Besides, this is exactly the kind of evidence Mazalet was looking for."

Olof giggled suddenly.

"What?" Lars asked.

"I can't wait to see Karl's face when he first puts his eyes on the skull."

"There is that, too," Lars admitted with a grin. "Wish me luck."

"You don't need any," Olof said. "You'll be doing the Lord's work out there."

"Then I wish that he made water just a little warmer." Lars sucked in a huge breath and slid down into the water. Working his way along the spar, he wrapped a rope around the corpse and pulled himself back into the bell.

"A boat hook would work," he muttered, as he hung from the rungs taking huge gulps of air. "This bell hangs lightly in the water."

Lars dived back outside and worked his way back to the corpse. It was harder this time. As Ginny had said, the water had turned misty with silt and Lars had to touch the body far more than he was comfortable with to make sure it was secured. Finally, after four trips, he climbed inside and, with Olof's help, pulled off his clothes. Shivering, he dried himself. "I've had my fill of water for one day. I need to feel the sun on my skin."

Olof nodded fervently.

◇   ◇   ◇

Fermin Mazalet looked around his crew and bowed deeply.

"Gentlemen, lady", he said. "Today, we've made history. Tonight the beer is on me."

"And tomorrow?" Lars Lennartson called out.

"Tomorrow," Mazalet said slowly. "Tomorrow we'll follow that unfortunate sailor to his last rest. We'll probably never know who he was, but the Lord almighty knows his own and Lieutenant Sparre agrees that a member of the Swedish Navy deserves a proper burial."

The small liaison officer nodded briefly. "I do so think," he said stiffly. "And I'll so inform the admiral." Then he smiled slightly. "Don't let that dampen your spirits tonight. My preliminary report will cite your exemplary conduct, and I do look forward to see what new miracles you can bring about."

They were the toast of the town. Per flinched as yet another roaring reveller threw him a hearty backslap. Unlike his own free-living neighbours from the north, the people of Stockholm were staid and sober people, but tonight they had abandoned their usual reserve. *Vasa's* shipwreck had deeply affected many families, and Lars' spur of the moment decision to retrieve the drowned lookout had struck exactly the right chord with the whole town. The funeral, originally to be held at the naval yard, had been postponed until Sunday and would take place in Stockholm's largest church.

Per winced again. The festivity was all very nice, but the sun had burnt his back and shoulders to flaking cinder and every movement hurt. Adding insult to injury, the locals had a real penchant for bracing backslaps, delivered with calloused hands and serious good cheer. Per had spent most of the evening with his back against the wall. He drained his mug and looked around. The tavern was packed to the rafters and there was more than the usual share of gold and lace about. Lars, slightly drunk, told tall tales of his underwater adventures, while Olof sat at a table talking earnestly to Lieutenant Sparre. Karl was nowhere to be seen, and Per made yet another mental note to investigate his handsome sibling's current love life. The brothers had the chance of several lifetimes, rising in society almost as fast as the bell sank towards the bottom. This was no time for indiscriminate dallying.

Then a sudden current in the sea of people caught his eye. People moved aside as the tall and sombre Admiral Fleming strode into the room. Before Per could move, Mazalet disengaged himself from his company and bowed deeply before the admiral. Per could not hear what was said, but suddenly Fleming smiled and made his way toward him. Per groaned and steeled himself. Braving the pain, he bowed deeply, even as Mazalet waved him forward.

"Your Grace. This is Master Per Lennartson, my chief diver," said the Frenchman.

"Ah. The divers from famous Delsbo," Admiral Fleming said with an almost straight face, betrayed only by an irrepressible twitch of the lips. "You are fortunate to have found such experienced men, Mazalet. I hear you plan to go down with them yourself tomorrow?"

Mazalet nodded. "I was just telling Captain Stolpeskott."

"Well. You must take care, monsieur." Fleming held out a hand to Per. Slowly, hesitantly, not really believing his eyes, Per stretched forth his own hand. The admiral showed no hesitation. He grasped Per's hand in his own big paw and shook heartily. Then he turned back to Mazalet. "Tell the innkeeper to bring up some of his best. The crown pays."

"Of course, Your Grace." Mazalet said. "I'll go look for the man myself."

The admiral watched the departing Frenchman for a moment, and then he turned back to Per. "I met the last member of your partnership at a levee two nights ago," he said with a broad wink. "She told me how Mazalet obtained his books, and of the great divers of Delsbo." He started to chuckle. "It makes a pleasant change for us Swedes to enjoy a private joke at the expense of these oh-so-sophisticated foreigners. And I have obtained copies of the agreement from Consul Boelcke. The crown is in your debt, boy. I shall see it is honored."

"Thank you, Your Grace."

Fleming patted him on the shoulder. "I have my own reasons," he said with a hint of sadness, "and we'll speak more in the future. Good evening to you, Master Per." And with that he turned to leave.

Per stood a movement clearing his head. For reasons of his own, Sweden's highest naval officer had just given a promise to a rural nobody. They were fishing in deep waters indeed. He just wished Ginny was here to consult with. She'd spent part of every day with them now for the last month . . . and yes, he was a rural nobody, but one with whom Admiral Fleming had personally spoken. Even a nobody in that position could dream a little.

"Perhaps next time," Per said shaking his head firmly. "You are good at money matters, Herr Mazalet. But you do not swim as well as we men of Delsbo. And this is early days yet. Today we bring up a deck cannon from the main deck." And with that he and Lars climbed into the bell.

Ginny watched as the clumsy thing was swung into the water. She wondered just how hard you trailed a lure for Per to notice it . . . and her. Well, it was improving her Swedish. And Consul Boelcke was right. There really wasn't enough for a full day's work at the consulate. She would just watch the bell sink and then Toke-Karin would row her to the foundry to see how well they were coming along with the dive helmets.

Ginny watched as the bell sank down, with the comforting stream of life-giving bubbles rushing upward. And then she yelled, "STOP! Lift the bell. Now!"

"Raise it," said Karl firmly to his team. And then he ran over to her on the edge of the barge. "What is it?"

She pointed. "Air is coming out of the hose. Not the escape holes on the edge of the bell."

"My God! The canvas must have broken. Thank heaven, you spotted it!"

But the sturdy canvas tube was not broken.

It had been slashed.

"But who would try to kill us?" said Lars, for about the fifth time.

"I have enemies," said Mazalet.

"So does Sweden," said Captain Stolpeskott, sneering at him. "Enemies who would be glad to see this fail. And you'd take money from anyone."

Mazalet stood up slowly. "Captain. At least Lieutenant Sparre has manners. Yours more closely resemble those of a pig. And you are nearly as clever as one, too. I was planning to go down with the bell. Now, would you like to name your seconds, sir?"

"There will be none of this," said Per firmly. "Lars. Cut the damaged section out, and you and Olof reattach the hose. Captain Stolpeskott, Mazalet. You two are coming down with us. You may wish to change your clothes."

Stolpeskott looked at Per incredulously. "Are you mad?"

"Probably," said Per. "But you Navy people were here before us this morning, and you've shown your contempt for Herr Mazalet. If Mazalet is with us, he can hardly be engaged in sabotage. If someone wished us to fail—the best thing we can do is to succeed. Today. And if you fight down there, Lars and I will deal with you. You will have no swords and no pistols. Of course if you are too scared . . . "

Stolpeskott stood up straight. "Scared, you peasant? I am an officer of the Swedish Navy."

"Good," said Mazalet, taking off his shoes. "As we're about to go onto the deck of a royal ship, you should be with us."

"You are going down?" asked Stolpeskott, shaking his head.

Mazalet nodded. "I am not afraid."

Stolpeskott plainly was, but was left with no way out. "Pull my boots off," he said stiffly to Per.

"Get one of your men to do it," said Per shortly. "I am going to check the equipment very carefully. You want me to do that, don't you?"

Ginny got the helmet maker to come to her. She decided she wasn't leaving the barge until Per . . . and the others came up. After an eternity . . . something did. It was a messenger buoy. Whatever else was happening in the cramped lamplight down there, they had also managed to get a rope onto a cannon. The brass barrel was hauled to the surface a few minutes later. Ginny had to comfort herself that they were at least alive. Then Karl began the slow haul, following the tables that Ginny had written out for him. They eventually swung the bell out as well. Stolpeskott was the first out, looking both pale and relieved. And deflated from his normal bombastic self. He staggered across to a bench.

Then came Karl and Per, grinning. "Did you get the cannon up?"

Ginny found herself unable to speak. She pointed to it, as Mazalet climbed out of the bell. He walked over to her, as the others went to admire the first booty, with the lion embossing still crisp on it. Mazalet mopped his brow. "I will never admit this to them, but they earn too small a share in this venture. I braved the swim a little. The water is barely above freezing and it is not very much warmer in that bell. And you can wring the air out. But it took the bravado out of our captain. He plans to complain to the admiral." Mazalet looked at the cannon. "Let him. When Fleming sees those come up, he's more likely to order the idiot to accompany us. The boys want to try for another now. They're stronger men than I."

"What would you have done," Ginny asked, "if Stolpeskott had wanted a duel?"

"It would have been unfortunate." A Gallic shrug. "I gave lessons in swordfighting."

Mazalet's prediction proved accurate. Admiral Fleming was indeed more than happy to have some of his officers take part in the exercise, and willing to have the

bell guarded night and day. It was just a little more difficult to find officers keen to do this. Only Lieutenant
Sparre was regularly willing. It was equally difficult to
get Mazalet back into the bell until the deck cannons
were up. But, a few weeks later, with the new helmet
system working—with air pumped from those in the
bell—the Frenchman decided to do so. Admiral Fleming
had requested that the divers try to retrieve the log—if it
was still in one piece, and the astrolabe from the captain's
chamber. "The captain's widow has asked for it for her
son," said Fleming quietly. "The request has the blessing
of His Majesty himself."

Naturally, as the admiral was going to be aboard,
Mazalet wanted to go down. Well, as Lars remarked, at
least he could be relied on to keep the helmet pump
working.

But on his way back the air stopped bubbling. "Lord
and saints!" Per swore inside his helmet. "What are they
doing back there?" Trying to remain calm he began
heading back to the bell. The water around it was still
murky and stirred up. With relief Per pulled himself into
the port and up the ladder, breaking the surface . . . face
to muzzle with a huge cavalry pistol.

"Please stay where you are," Lieutenant Sparre said.
"I haven't hurt your brother, but that will change if you
do something rash." Slowly, Per lowered himself into
the water.

"What are you doing?" Per asked.

Sparre wiped water from his brow. The lieutenant was
soaking wet, evidently he, too, had been outside the bell.

"I've cut away the messengers and the air hose," he said. "That way you won't be able to inform the surface."

"They'll still know something is wrong," Per said. "But what are you up to, Lieutenant? You're the last one I'd have pegged for a traitor."

Sparre smiled sadly. "It's not about treason, Master Per. I'm loyal to the king, but this is a personal matter." His smile twisted into a rictus of hate. He pointed a shaking finger at Mazalet. "This man ruined my uncle," he snarled. "He spun tales of alchemy and industry, and my uncle lost most of the family money chasing moonbeams. He ruined my life, my family and my chances of marriage."

"I tricked Fleming's nephew, too," Mazalet murmured groggily, blood oozing from his scalp. "Is the admiral in on this?"

"Of course not," Sparre spat. "This is about the honor of my family."

"I'm an idiot," Per mumbled. "From the first accident I thought it was Stolpeskott."

"Hans has nothing to do with it either," Sparre said. "I doubt he'll shed any tears, but he's quite innocent."

"It was you who slit the hose then?" Per asked.

Sparre nodded. "This bastard of a Frenchman was supposed to go down that day."

"So what will you do?" Per asked. "You can kill us all, I suppose, but you'll look very strange coming up all alone."

"I won't be coming up," Sparre said, that sad smile back on his face. "You're such an honorable man, Master Per, that I sometimes forget you're a peasant at heart. To a nobleman the answer would be obvious. I've detached the shackle. Replaced it with a broken one. I have cut the air hose. We will all die down here. The salvage project will die too . . . "

"For which," said Mazalet, "The French will pay handsomely." Sparre stared at him.

Mazalet shrugged. "The offer was made to me. But I don't even rob honest men, let alone kill them."

"Heavens above," Ginny breathed looking into the water. "It's the hose. It's the air hose!" she shouted, but Karl was there already, his face pale under the tan.

"Keep pumping!" he roared waving to the crew. "Are they dead?" he asked.

"No way to know," Ginny said, trying hard to stay calm. "Start to raise the bell. At least we won't have to get the hose down very far. Even for Per and Olof—they haven't been much deeper than fifty-five feet on this dive. They've been down about ninety-three minutes. We'll need fourteen minutes at the ten foot mark."

The windlass began to turn. "There is no weight on it, Karl," yelled a horrified sailor.

"Stop!" shouted Lars. "Lower slowly. To the same depth and three feet."

"Why?" demanded Karl.

"They can reattach it. They can't if we have it here."

"Not if they don't have air. Or something is wrong . . . "

"So we get the air hose down. If they have air, they can solve any problems. Right now they don't have very long."

"How do we do that?" Karl asked looking at the hose.

"We sink it," Lars said. "The hose looks good, it moves like a snake with every spurt of air. We don't need to replace it, and that should save us time."

"Good." Karl said. "We tie the hose to a weight and send it down along the main hawser."

Ginny nodded. "That would work as far as it goes, but how will they get the hose inside? How will they know it is down?"

"We could rig something," Lars voice trailed off.

Ginny took a deep breath. "I'll go down," she said. "I swim far better than all of you. They're on the aftercastle. That stood sixty-five feet high. It shouldn't be more than forty feet down. None of you could swim that, but I can. I'll go down and then inside. As soon as I'm in, one of the others can go out with a helmet and reattach the hose and the hawser. We don't even need the shackle, a big knot will do."

"You can't do that!" Karl flared. "Per wouldn't allow that. Come to think of it, neither would Monsieur Mazalet."

"There isn't much they can do about it." Ginny said. "And I doubt they'll kick me out on principle."

"Too dangerous," Lars said. "I'll do it."

"No. You work well under water, but I am a far, far better swimmer." Ginny smiled and pulled a thin book from her pocket. "Here are the dive tables. They are in Swedish, and Boelcke has the original info in his safe."

Lars looked at her slowly and thoughtfully "Besides," he said, "you didn't come back three centuries in time just to lose your love to the water."

"Mazalet?" Karl asked, gaping.

"No, dummy," Lars said, "Per."

Ginny nodded ruefully. "Pull the hose towards the ship, but don't wind it up. Keep the loops separated."

"You want the hose or a rope?" Lars asked, while Karl still goggled.

"A rope, I think." Ginny said. "The hose might snag and break. Pulling the hose down will be heavy with all the air but there are five of us. We'll manage. I'll want a dive weight."

Karl shook his head in disbelief. Then he walked across the deck, bent down and grabbed a small cannon. "Think this one will work?" he asked.

"No," Ginny said. "Or rather, it might hole the bell. A cannon ball—smallish. In a sack."

"Right." Lars said. "I'll loop a short piece of rope around the hawser so that you stay close to the bell. You hold that in one hand, the bag in the other, and the rope around your waist. One tug to attach the air hose, two for a bit more rope." He took his belt and knife off. "In case of snags, *ja*. Anything else?"

Admiral Fleming had walked over with two of his men. Ginny nodded. Blushed. "I can't do this in a skirt. Admiral, will you have your men turn their backs while I jump over?"

It was Fleming's turn to gape. "What? What is happening?"

"The hose has come adrift. We need to get it back to the bell," said Ginny calmly. "Now please tell your men to turn around. Now. We don't have much time to get the air down." She knew that the rush was not quite so dire, but she couldn't bear not knowing. She didn't even wait for a reply, just unbuttoned her skirt. Hyperventilated. And jumped.

The water was not too bad at the surface . . . but it grew colder as she passed through the thermocline and down, pulled by the cannon ball. She'd dived to thirty feet before . . . once. She equalized. Visibility was not great but she could see—to her relief—the shape of the bell, slightly off to one side. She equalized again, and reached the deck . . . Now she had to somehow not let go of her weight, or she would have simply begun to ascend. And, burning to breathe, she had to cross the few yards to the bell . . . and her limbs were quite weak with the bitter cold.

Somehow she did it, letting her breath out as she grasped the lowest rung. If there was no air within she was dead, long before she could reach the surface again.

Per had been weighing options. Both Olof and Mazalet were tied up. Should he duck underwater and try and swim for the surface? He knew what the consequences would be. He still tensed to do it. But Lieutenant Sparre must have read his intentions. "If you do, I will shoot your brother. Come out of the water."

Per moved slowly. First, he was very cold. Second, he needed to think. And third . . . well, there was no third. Sparre was going to at very least hit them on the head. All he needed was a distraction.

He was at the top of the ladder when he got it.

Bubbles.

It nearly stopped him in his tracks.

It didn't stop his younger brother kicking Sparre. The gun boomed—incredibly loud in the confined space. Per launched himself, feeling the bullet burn his ribs. Mazalet had used his head and butted the lantern, which went out. Per grappled in the darkness.

Ginny's head burst into the bell to a deafening explosion and sudden darkness. But there was air. Thick, moist and stale. Air . . . And the sound of fighting.

"Per?" she called, feeling for Lars' knife. Had Mazalet gone mad?

The little lieutenant was insanely strong. Well, he probably was insane. And he had a knife. He'd managed to cut Per's face. And then, suddenly there was a voice Per had only expected to hear in heaven again. Perhaps he was dead. Well, if Ginny was here . . . He'd better deal with this madman. He grabbed hair and hit the fellow's head against the oak so hard that the bell rang. Then he did it again. "Ginny?" he said shakily.

"Are you all right?"

"I think so. Or am I dead? How did you get here?"

"I swam down."

Per's heart sank. He couldn't say anything.

"With a rope to haul the air hose down."

"Dear God!" said Mazalet.

"Brother," said Olof. "Stop fooling around and go see to our lady. Then you can cut us free."

So Per felt his way to the ladder, still unable to speak. But he could feel her arms around him.

Olof coughed. "Now, can you cut us free and we can haul the airhose down, light the lantern and see what Sparre hit with that pistol shot."

It took a little time to achieve all that. The ball was lodged in the four-inch-thick planks. Per had pushed Sparre's head nearly as deep into the wood. And the bubbling air was the sweetest thing Per had ever felt, except for Ginny's fingers twined in his.

On the surface, Karl timed. He did not look away. He'd seen enough women nearer naked than that. When the count reached one eighty he stopped just sweating and went cold. The rope stopped moving.

Karl prayed. He knew he did not pray alone.

And then . . . two tugs. "Get that airhose attached," he yelled, tears starting in his eyes. "Now, Lars!" In the city they must be wondering what the cheering was for this time. Karl sat down, weak-kneed with relief, as Lars tied on the hose, and it slipped away into the water.

By the time the bell was raised—and, with allowing for decompression that was a good while—the barge was in danger of sinking with the people crowded onto her. Toke-Karin and the other rowers had never had such a day. The water around the barge was full of boats packed with onlookers. The story had crossed the city like wildfire. It wasn't just the admiral and Consul Boelcke and his wife waiting, anxious and hoping.

Then the bell broke the surface and the real cheering started. Olof was first out. Dragging a near-naked lieutenant.

Then came Mazalet, then, as Karl and Lars held their breath, their oldest brother, bandaged and bloody but smiling—giving a hand to Ginny.

And the cheering reached a new crescendo.

Admiral Fleming stepped forward . . . and bowed respectfully. "Stockholm never raised a greater treasure, nor a braver lady, from the deep, " he said, kissing her hand.

Ginny smiled, not letting go of Per.

Per hugged her hard. "We'll bring more treasures up." he said. "We'll bring the whole ship up in time. Still, Herr Admiral, I agree with you."

A Gift from the Duchess

Virginia DeMarce

"3. 'If I have to live through a revolution I would rather make it than suffer from it.' What did Bismarck mean by this statement and what was the character of the revolution he helped make?"
>—Matt Trelli's vague recollection
> of an essay exam question
> once formulated by Miss Mailey.

Bozen, Tirol
October 1633

"Tell me again. Why I should send the three best plague doctors in the pay of the government of Tyrol and Upper Austria to Franconia? One of whom is the personal physician for my children and myself? And keep on paying them while they are there? Our budget . . . "

Claudia de Medici, twenty-nine years old and twice widowed, regent for her five-year-old son of the particular, specific, and independent-from-Austria-proper Habsburg duchy called Tirol, leaned back in her chair and looked at the board of medical consultants, gently tapping the end of the wonderful new fountain pen that the merchant Vignelli had brought back from his latest trip into the United States of Europe against her bracelet.

Vignelli had purchased a dozen. He had given one to her and one to the chancellor, Dr. Bienner. A half dozen to his most important business contacts in Bozen and Venice. The others, presumably, were being taken apart by the artisans in his employ, with a plan to expand the profits that were rolling in from his "duplicating machines" by adding "mechanical pens" to his product line. Already, he had changed the name of his enterprise to "Vignelli's European Office Supplies." All of which was good for Tirol's tax base, of course. It would be even better if Vignelli's people could make a better typewriter and adding machine than the ones coming out of Magdeburg. The man had spent an exorbitant amount to obtain prototypes. Still . . .

She returned her attention to the three men standing at the other end of the conference table.

Paul Weinhart, the personal physician in question, had been watching his ruler. Her auburn curls were threatening to burst out of the clips and pins that were supposed to be restraining them. Her brown eyes were snapping. On mornings such as this, it was best to proceed carefully. He cleared his throat. "We all do have practical experience in controlling plague outbreaks ..." he began. For twenty minutes, he continued. "Of course, my lady, you may say that it is absurd of us to undertake such a thing at our ages," he finished.

"I have not said so."

"If I had a qualified son ..." Weinhart's voice trailed off. "But my wife and the boys born in my first marriage all died in the plague of 1610–1611 in Innsbruck. Perhaps if we had these up-time devices then, the DDT, the medicaments ... But that is irrelevant. The children of my second marriage are still young. Ignaz, the oldest boy, is only seventeen. Franz sixteen. Paul and Caspar are just starting Latin school."

"Do you need to go now?"

Weinhart shook his head. "The up-timers have quarantined Kronach, of course. In addition to the fact that the commander has closed the city gates from the inside. Quarantine is really the only way to control spread of plague. Total quarantine. But it's hard on the people inside the lines if there's no decent hospital and no enforcement of destroying the bedding and clothing. If it were summer, it would be a public health emergency already, but winter is coming. The plague almost always becomes less fierce in cold weather. Kronach should survive the winter."

Guarinoni intervened. His early education by the Jesuits was never very far from his mind. Next to medicine, perhaps even above medicine, returning the lapsed peoples of Europe to the Catholic faith was his passion. "If we don't go, there won't be any Catholics left in Kronach for us to assist. In the spring and summer of 1634, if they have not opened the walls, a Catholic city, the fiercest Catholic city in Franconia, may die. There is time to prepare. Time for us to learn more about Grantville and time for them to learn more about our capabilities. We can assist these up-timers in Bamberg with the outbreak at Kronach, Your Grace, but we can also learn from them at the same time. While serving God and the Church. But it must be soon."

Claudia de Medici continued to tap her fountain pen on her bracelet for quite some time after she dismissed them. Then she pulled the written proposal toward her and started to read. After a few moments, she picked it up and walked to the window.

Wilhelm Bienner, watching the regent, wondered if Dr. Weinhart, also, had noted the restlessness that the regent's self-discipline was barely keeping leashed these last few months. The duchess was tired of merely sending an occasional merchant who could double as a researcher to Grantville, no matter how fascinating the music and other information they brought back. Was Weinhart perceptive enough to be offering a route by which she could take a larger part on the stage of Europe? He untied a packet of the unending paperwork that made government function, rolled up the red tape that had tied it neatly, and started to scribble marginal comments.

Two hours later, Duchess Claudia returned to the table. He looked up, waiting.

"Let's send them to Franconia. But not only them and not only to Franconia. There must be something to toss to Leopold's brother in Vienna, as one tosses a bone to a dog. Let Vienna have the musicians. And the music. Ferdinand's spirits are in need of cheering, I hear. So. A harmless distraction. What trouble can this sentimental play about a pious up-time Austrian girl who married a baron possibly cause?"

Outside the Walls of Kronach, Franconia
October 1633

Winter was setting in hard, already. It had snowed five or six inches overnight—hard to tell exactly how much, with the wind whipping it around—but cleared off at dawn. Matt Trelli stood with his binoculars fixed on the Rosenberg fortress at Kronach.

The old commander must have died. Or be sick, at least. He hadn't been out on the walls for—Matt thought a minute—not for a couple of weeks now.

A gust whipped around the corner of his lookout. Up-time, Matt Trelli figured, he'd been as pious as most Catholics. At least, as pious as most Catholics with divorced parents and a remarried father with whom he wanted to stay on reasonably good terms. Mr. Piazza had never complained in CCD classes.

Here, though, down-time . . . he remembered to thank God for some of the weirdest things. This morning, the topic was "thermal underwear, sincere gratitude for."

With a postscript concerning "down parkas, sincere gratitude for." So he wasn't in uniform. What the hell? He was warm. And he had a uniform around somewhere if Cliff Priest or Scott Blackwell should happen to show up.

No real way to tell who had succeeded Neustetter in command. There were two choices.

The first possibility was Francesco de Melon, the Bavarian officer—*military adviser* Matt thought—whom Maximilian of Bavaria had sent to assist old Neustetter when the war moved into Franconia in 1631. Really, given that any practical assistance was far more likely to come from Maximilian of Bavaria than from the Austrians, Melon had probably been Neustetter's boss, for all practical purposes.

Or the new commander might turn out to be one of the bishop's relatives, a canon in the Bamberg cathedral chapter: Wolf Philipp Fuchs von Dornheim.

Matt hoped it was de Melon. He'd sent off a request to the Research Center in Grantville for anything they could find out about either of the men. Nothing had turned up about Dornheim. Melon, though . . .

It had taken them a long time. Finally they'd figured out they were supposed to be looking for a Portuguese name instead of the French-sounding one that Vince's informants had given the NUS people in Bamberg. All they had finally come up with was some stuff in a Spanish history book that Mrs. Hernandez at the high school had. Spanish as in—written in Spanish. That's what Mrs. Hernandez taught. Mr. Hernandez too, for that matter. The guy was in the book because he wrote poetry and history. It just mentioned as a sort of afterthought that he'd won some pretty important battles. But lost the last one, which was what military historians seemed to think counted most. Those were a real bunch of "what have you done for me lately" guys. Not that Gustavus Adolphus wasn't.

Don Francisco Manuel de Mello, count of Azumar and marques of Torrelaguna. Not an old guy. He was born in 1611, in Lisbon. Hell—he was five years younger than Matt. But only eighteen months younger than the cardinal-infante up in the Netherlands, and being young hadn't exactly stopped that guy.

Plus. In that other world, when the time came . . . This kid had succeeded Don Fernando as Spanish regent in the Netherlands. Succeeded the brother of the king of Spain. Preceded the brother of the Holy Roman Emperor. Compared to them, a Portuguese count was just an ordinary guy. So he was likely no nincompoop. It would be . . . well, it *ought* to be . . . easier to negotiate with someone who had smarts than with a dope. Easier to negotiate with someone who didn't want to die by being cooped up in a city suffering from the plague. Not if someone else could somehow get the news across the wall that he had a great career ahead of him.

Assuming that the bishop's relative hadn't come out ahead in the politicking, of course.

Matt swung his binoculars slowly. As the sun rose higher, the light reflecting off the new snow was practically blinding, but it was hard to use the things in combination with sunglasses. There . . . he focused.

A man on the wall where the old commander used to stand. *Magnify*. Matt adjusted the lenses.

Young. Straight black hair, dark eyes. Not overweight, but a little jowly. Heavy eyebrows, prominent nose, mustache. Melon, then. Matt grinned. *Hi, Bro!* He'd fit right in at a Trelli family reunion.

Which cousin are you? He could almost hear Marcie's old maid great-aunts quizzing the guy. What a pair they'd been. Too bad they were up-time if they were still alive. They hadn't been spring chickens, either of them.

Impulsively, he stepped out of the blind and waved.

After only a short pause, the man on the walls of Rosenberg waved back.

Because the great-aunts had wandered through his mind, Matt added another postscript to his prayers. "Abruzzo, Laura Marcella, gratitude for." Marcie was loyal right down to her bone marrow. Whatever other problems he might have, a "Dear John" letter from his fiancee wouldn't ever be one of them.

Marcie was stubborn, maybe. Well, she was stubborn, definitely. But that had its okay side. Once she made up her mind about something, she stuck with it, right to the bitter end.

Bozen, Tirol
November 1633

"So the duchess-regent has approved our proposal." Guarinoni was nearly incoherent with joy.

"How can we get there?" Gatterer asked practically. "Not all of us are as enthusiastic about mountain climbing as you are, Hippolyt."

Weinhart stroked his beard. "It still remains to be seen whether or not the Swede's administrators will accept our presence."

Bamberg, Franconia
December 1633

Vince Marcantonio shook his head. "The duchess-regent of Tyrol is offering the services of these physicians as a free gift. She's paying them herself. It's a matter of hospitality, she says in the letter. It's only gracious for hosts to welcome their guests and thus far seventeenth-century Europe has been remiss in making Grantville properly welcome."

"*Timeo Danaos, et dona ferentes.*"

Wade Jackson scowled. "Can the Latin, Janie."

"Virgil said it because it was a wise thing to say."

Stewart Hawker was sharpening his pencil with a knife. "What *does* it say?"

"I fear the Greeks, even when they come bearing gifts."

"What was that about?"

"The Trojan horse."

"Oh."

Vince rapped on the table. "What do we know about the duchess?"

Janie Kacere nodded at her husband, who was the economic liaison. He grinned. "Mainly, that as nobles go, she's a savvy businesswoman with an eye to the bottom line. Hell, as corporate sharks go, she's a savvy businesswoman with an eye to the bottom line."

Wade Jackson scowled again. "That Virgil of Janie's could have had a point."

Bamberg, Franconia
February 1634

"Do we know *anything* about these guys?" Vince Marcantonio asked. "The only thing they seem to have in common is that they all studied medicine at Padua."

"Out of up-time books? Not one damned word about any of them anywhere in Grantville, according to the Research Center."

"So it looks like we'll have to rely on their letters of introduction."

"With a grain of salt."

"A shovel full of rock salt would probably be better. According to the duchess-regent, they practically walk on water. There's something else in common, maybe, which is some connection to the Fugger. Weinhart was born in Augsburg and Gatterer's medical education was partly paid for by a guy in the Tyrol government who married into those bankers. And Guarinoni is a physician for the mines in Schwaz, among a lot of other things."

Janie Kacere picked up the letter. "Guarinoni—that's Guarinonius in Latin—got a job as physician for the royal *Damenstift* in Hall in Tyrol in 1598." She looked up. "I thought they only had *Damenstifte* in places like Quedlinburg, where the ladies are Lutherans. Shouldn't they still be nuns in Catholic countries? Anyway . . . " She kept going. " . . . he's still got that job. He's also the city physician for Hall, and the physician for the salt springs—I guess that's a kind of health spa—there. Schwaz—that's pretty close to Hall. He also has what looks like a half dozen various honorary memberships. What's the Order of the Golden Fleece? He's set up a specialized botanical garden for Alpine plants. He's a member of the duchess' board of medical consultants— he's been on it since 1617, which is well before the time of the duchess. And he's interested in 'practical hygiene,' whatever they understand by that. She's also sent a couple of his books along for us to read."

"Just a couple."

"There are more than a couple?"

"Quite a few more. Not just Latin, but German, too. Apparently, he's something of a popularizer. One of them is practical advice on dealing with plague, published in Ingolstadt in 1612, *Pestilentz Guardien, für allerley Stands Personen*, which would be "Plague Guardian for People of all Ranks," I guess. There's a vernacular book by Weinhart in the pile, too. *Short but Comprehensive Instructions on What to Do in the Current Difficult Times*. Published in Innsbruck in 1611, so I guess that's on dealing with plague, too. I haven't had time to look at it yet. She's got a lot less to say about Gatterer."

"Okay," Vince said. "Stew, you have your Hearts and Minds people take a look at these books, will you, ASAP. And get a summary back to me."

Bozen, Tirol
February 1634

"Look." Paul Weinhart was waving a newspaper over his head. "The USE has sent its greatest chemist to Venice to teach their secrets to those capable of understanding them. Stone, his name is. The *pharmaceuticals* man. To Venice, the paper says. Which, of course, means Padua. Perhaps they have some sense after all, these up-timers, to know that Padua is the greatest medical school on the continent."

Gatterer poured each of them a glass of wine. It was rewarding to see proper recognition given to one's *alma mater*.

Bamberg, Franconia
March 1634

Stewart Hawker winked. "Guarinoni is opposed to pre-mature death. His motto is, "Let's all be *gesondt*." He wrote a book about it. The title's *Grewel der Verwüstung Menschlichen Geschlechts*. That's something like *The Horror of the Decay of the Human Race*, if you translate it into English. It's been in print for a quarter-century or more, I think. Not very systematic. We've used bits and pieces of it for the Hearts and Minds pamphlets, some of them. Yeah, that's plagiarism by up-time stan-dards, but whatever works. He's the one who came up with GESONDT." He tossed a Hearts and Minds pam-phlet on the table.

"What in hell does that acronym mean, anyway?" Wade Jackson looked at his colleagues in annoyance.

"Well, *gesondt* is *gesund* in modern German. Healthy. I've tried to put it into English. Some lines use the same letters in both languages and some don't. For the ones that do, I've got:

"God as the source of all good;

"Eating and drinking—moderately, that is;

"Sleeping and waking—at the proper times and a proper amount of each;

"The next couple don't use the same letters. Or at least, I can't think of any English words that will work, like:

"O—that's *Oede*, or leisure time, and he talks about avoidance of excess during it. It's a sort of 'you ought not to pig out on junk food or get drunk' for the seventeenth century;

"N—that's *Nutzung*, or use and exercise of the body. Maybe I could use 'Nuts about exercise,' because he really is.

"Then we're back to something I got English for:

"D—daily fresh air; and

"T—trustful attitude. That seems to involve being up-beat.

"Or maybe, I guess, for that last, an up-timer would be more likely to say 'optimism' or 'confidence.' But for Guarinoni, it really comes back to *Trost*—'consolation' or 'relying on God,' so he's back where he started."

Janie made a face. "I could have gotten that out of just about any women's magazine on the grocery store shelves up-time."

Stew nodded. "Yup. High school health classes, too. Except that he thinks that being healthy and being holy are pretty much interchangeable, so it's closer to the stuff that the Fellowship of Christian Athletes used to hand out on campus. The body is the temple of the holy spirit and all that stuff. On the other hand, the health advice can't hurt anyone. Good diet, regular exercise, plenty of fresh air. He wrote a whole book on the importance of watering down your wine. Given how drunk people get around here, watering down your wine is probably a good idea."

Stew shuffled through the pile of books the duchess had sent. "And he's absolutely convinced that premarital chastity and post-marital fidelity prevent VD and thus produce healthier children. Which a person has got to admit is perfectly true in a world that doesn't have much in the way of antibiotics. Hey, here's his manual of advice for Christian married couples. *The Joy of Sex* for the here and now. Right down your alley, Janie." He slid it down the table.

"I took a look at it. It's more on the order of a pre-Cana manual."

"Ah. Well, too bad."

Vince got the meeting back on track. Or tried, at least. "What makes the duchess think that Kronach will let them in? Can we head them off?"

Cliff Priest shook his head. "Telling Duchess Claudia not to send them isn't an option. They're already on their way."

"Right through the middle of a peasant revolt?" Wade Jackson sounded skeptical.

"Well, it hasn't started yet, really. We're just expecting it. They'll probably get here before April."

"They've probably all been through peasant revolts before, anyhow," Stewart Hawker said mildly.

"Yeah. I sort of keep forgetting that they're all over the place."

"The doctors?"

"Naw. Peasant revolts."

Vince could hardly wait for Matt Trelli to arrive. He'd been to Grantville for his first R&R in over a year. They'd sent Tom O'Brien up to Kronach to sub for him. When he came through, he would escort the doctors up to Kronach so Tom could come back and contribute his bit to handling the peasant revolt. However a munitions specialist chose to do that.

Vince could hardly wait for the day that the three doctors departed hence into another place. Ever since they set foot in town, Dr. Guarinoni had treated the entire Bamberg administration, up-time and down-time, to large free helpings of his health advice. Bennett Norris would have called it "patented health advice" if they had patents.

He never stopped. Stacey O'Brien told Janie that if the man had been born up-time, he would have found his calling as a motivational speaker holding success seminars at the Holiday Inn for twenty-five dollars a head.

From Stacey, this didn't count as a compliment. She'd said it after Guarinoni gave a critique of her child-rearing methods.

He didn't limit his efforts to the administration, either. He got out and around in the streets of the city. He even—since he turned out to be really and truly pretty famous in this time and place—got an invitation to address the city council.

According to Else Kronacher, the Bamberg Committee of Correspondence had no particular objection to the health component of his message, but wasn't reacting well to the intransigence with which he wrapped it up in Catholic dogma.

As long as they avoided theology, though, he got along great with Willard and Emma Thornton. Most of his practical policies—applied health practices, Vince supposed—fit right in with Mormon ideas about what was good for you.

Weinhart and Gatterer spent their time following Matewski around, observing both his military medicine and his volunteer efforts at the orphanages and city hospital. He didn't seem to mind them. He might have minded Guarinoni, he said honestly to Wade Jackson, but that guy was too busy blowharding to hassle a man who had work to do.

Matt made pretty good time coming up from Würzburg. Vince sent him and the doctors on their way on a really fast turnaround. In spite of the tension, nobody bothered them, neither the peasants nor the imperial knights. That might be, Matt thought, because there were a lot more peasants than knights, and Vince had a kind of . . . understanding . . . with the Ram.

On the Road to Kronach, Franconia
April 1634

Gatterer turned out to be a chatterer. Matt was just as pleased. Kronach was more than a little out of the loop, so he hadn't seen anywhere near as much data on these guys as Vince's inner circle had gotten.

"Dr. Weinhart was a student of Mercurialis, you know."

"Of who? I mean, of whom?"

"A professor at Padua. He is dead, now, for a quarter century, but he was very famous for what up-time you call 'sports medicine.' He wrote *De arte gymnastica* which isn't about what you call gymnastics, though. It's about caring for the body during exercising it. Mostly, though, Dr. Weinhart writes about diseases of the eyes. He is mostly here because he is, as you say, *committed* to fighting the plague. And, of course, because he has enough influence with the duchess to get the project approved."

Matt wondered vaguely just how Gatterer had come to hear of sports medicine. Then he thought of various reports about the number of down-time researchers combing through Grantville's books and encyclopedias and pushed it off into the category of *not a problem*. Of course there was stuff about sports medicine in the high school library and even if there hadn't been, Dr. Daoud, the chiropractor, loved to give classes and seminars.

"Please try to be tactful with Dr. Guarinoni," Gatterer said.

"Why?"

"You must understand. His father, the late Dr. Bartolomeo Guarinoni, was the emperor's personal physician. Logically, one would assume, our Dr. Guarinoni would have started life in a position of advantage. Unfortunately, ah, his parents were not married to one another. Although his father acknowledged him and provided him with an excellent education . . . "

"Narrow-minded folks talk."

"Precisely. He accompanied his father to the imperial courts—that of Maximilian II and Vienna and that of Rudolf II in Prague. He studied at the University of Padua. Still, every now and then, there is a certain . . . condescension . . . that he must cope with. Therefore, if, sometimes, he seems a bit . . . excessive . . . "

"Excessive? How?"

"Not everyone appreciates the comedy skits with which he attempted to enliven his book on practical health. Many of them are taken from stage routines. Directly adapted from them, even. But when he tries to get people who have come to him for advice to stand up and act them out . . . . "

"I always hated that when my teachers made us do it. Both when I had to do it myself and when I had to watch other kids."

"But it is a good technique for embedding a concept in the memory. Excellent." Gatterer nodded sagely.

Near the Walls of Kronach
May 1634

Matt pointed down at the figure on the walls of the Rosenberg. The three doctors were taking fascinated turns with his up-time binoculars. "That's de Melon. Actually, he's expecting you. Inside the city, I mean."

"How do you know?"

"Well, we've set up the drop point. We keep the quarantine hard. No meetings with their people. No letting parties outside the walls to bury the dead. But . . . I'll show you. Over there—see? We've got that table in the middle of this field outside the walls. It's where their militia drills in normal times. We leave things on it and back off about the length of a football field. They come out and pick them up. They leave things on it and go inside again. We come down and pick them up."

"Things?"

"Information, mostly. Negotiations over this and that. So they know you're coming. We gave them a copy of the letters that came from your Duchess Claudia. And both of your books, Dr. Guarinoni and Dr. Weinhart."

"De Melon will receive us?"

"That's not the problem."

Matt smiled at Dr. Weinhart, who shuddered.

"There are two sides to this, you know. Not just 'will he receive you' but 'will good old Matt here let you go.' "

"How can you make conditions? People's lives are at stake."

"They've been at stake here ever since we came down to Franconia. If I don't finally get some kind of cooperation out of these stiff-assed . . . ."

"What conditions are you imposing on them?"

"That if the three of you come into the city, I come too."

Guarinoni gaped at him. Very few people, other than physicians and clergy, voluntarily walked into plague sites.

"And then the quarantine comes down again. My guys don't lift it until they get a plain signal from me that we have an 'all clear.' Or . . . Look, I'm a realist. A plain signal from someone. The instructions are in my wallet."

Bamberg, Franconia
May 1634

"Weinhart was right. Kronach let the doctors in." Vince Marcantonio's expression didn't match what should have been good news.

"There's a catch." Bennett Morris made the obvious diagnosis.

"Bound to be," Wade Jackson said. "What is it, Vince?"

"Matt went in with them. Turned the command at Kronach over to Bachhausen, the lieutenant from Coburg, and went in with them. Without so much as a 'by your leave' to Cliff Priest or to me."

"Well." Wade flipped his pencil around his thumb. "That much makes sense, at least. He must have known perfectly well that you wouldn't 'leave' him."

"Yeah, he knew. He admits it straight out in the letter he sent us. And points out that this way we're spared from having to court-martial him for disobeying an order."

"What got them in?"

"Matt softened up de Melon and the city council with a lot of propaganda. Guarinoni's an author, too, beyond being a health nut. And a real religious bigot. Poetry. Lives of saints, real and imaginary. Steve Salatto's tame printer down in Würzburg ordered some of his titles that the duchess-regent didn't send us so Stew Hawker's people could look at them. And an architect. He's designing and building a church dedicated to Saint Charles Borromeo. He's paying for it himself. Duchess Claudia was right about that much. The doctors are the kind of people who are heartily welcome in Kronach. Aside from this plague medicine stuff, all three of them are more Catholic than the pope."

Bamberg, Franconia
late June 1634

"Vince, remember what you said about those doctors we sent up to Kronach being more Catholic than the pope?"

"Yeah." Vince Marcantonio yawned. "God, I'm tired."

"Given some of the news that's come in this week, that might not be hard right now." Cliff Priest read out the latest bulletin that Scott Blackwell had just sent up from Würzburg.

The meeting paused a moment in honor of the disconcerting notion that Larry Mazzare, the parish priest of most of the members of the administration, was now, unexpectedly, Lawrence Cardinal Mazzare, Cardinal Protector of the United States of Europe.

Then, since there was nothing that any of them could do about it, they went back to work. Joe Matewski got together a batch of pamphlets and stuff to send up to Kronach. He looked at the latest arrival. In Amberg, down in the Upper Palatinate, Bill Hudson had been dealing with a diphtheria epidemic for the last six weeks or so. He'd sent an SOS to Grantville, where the doctors had said, basically, "chloramphenicol doesn't work." They'd also said, "we won't be making DPT vaccines or vaccines for any part of DPT for several years." So much for that, which took up the first two pages. The boiled-down message was that they didn't have anything to help a field medic who was faced with a diphtheria outbreak right now.

The rest of the pamphlet was full of information, mostly from the retired docs, old Sims and McDonnell, on stuff that might help during diphtheria outbreaks if only they had the tools to make tools. Lots of woodcuts and illustrations of syringes and hypodermic needles. Diagrams of just what the problems were. Irrelevant. Whoever might have the tools to make tools, it wasn't him and it wouldn't happen in Bamberg. The plague doctors handled other epidemics, too. Maybe they'd be interested. He could always get another copy if he needed one. He tossed it into the pile for Matt.

Kronach, Franconia
July-August 1634

Matt stopped just outside the door. It was one thing to have heard "sometimes you have to be cruel to be kind" as a proverb. Grandma Geraldine used to say it all the time before she died last winter.

It was another thing to watch it in action. The segregation of entire families, the healthy members with the infected. The closing of markets and trade, with the unemployment that came from that. Not that Kronach had been trading anyhow, since it was under siege. Burning the furnishings and goods when an infected house was finally opened up again. Dealing with the kind of people for whom reopening plague-infected houses and burning the contents was an economic and social step up in the world. Maintaining enough oversight to keep that kind of people from stealing the infected stuff and selling it on the black market, where it would start the cycle again.

The *Pesthaus*, the quarantine hospital for the sick, was obviously a good idea, if not exactly a new one. Pious Catholics didn't always think that something like requisitioning monasteries to serve as plague hospitals was such a wonderful idea, but as Weinhart had pointed out, one could hardly use the municipal hospital for plague victims, since it was, as usual, full of orphaned children, crippled people, various elderly who had no family members to care for them, the epileptic, the languid, and the lunatic.

The "languid" had turned out to be those mentally ill who just sat there. Who'dathunkit?

Getting DDT into all of Kronach's houses, rich and poor alike, hadn't been too much of a challenge, once the authorities swung into action. With the doctors from Padua there to direct things, the council had set up a Magistracy of Public Health on the Venetian model. Which didn't exactly involve separation of powers. The Health Board could legislate action to be taken, it could order the action carried out, and it was the judicial authority that heard noncompliance cases. Given the level of down-time medical knowledge, it was no surprise that, according to Dr. Guarinoni, the motto of plague doctors was, "prevention is much more noble and more necessary than therapy."

It wasn't hard to get enough DDT. Matt had brought some with him when he came back from Grantville. They'd found an ample supplementary supply at the drop point within two weeks of asking for it.

Yeah. While they were stuck in Kronach, the three doctors had absorbed the up-time medical knowledge about transmission vectors, so they'd directed a lot of their efforts toward persuading de Melon and the city council that the rats had to be eradicated. It hadn't been all that hard for Matewski to persuade them that the transmission vector was little bugs in the blood rather than nasty, sticky, bad-smelling, poisonous, atoms that emanated from infected sources such as stinking garbage in alleys and stuck to inanimate objects, animals, and people when the air was corrupted, or miasmic, rather than salubrious.

After all, a person couldn't see either one. Matewski had promised them that after this was over, he'd somehow get hold of an up-time microscope from Grantville and let them take a look at plague bacilli. They were looking forward to this, particularly since he told them that up-time science had confirmed the existence of atoms, even if they were too small to see through a microscope.

The doctors were particularly happy to hear that plague bacilli were made up of atoms, ultimately. Probably nasty, poisonous, ones. So maybe that wasn't the way Nichols or Adams or Shipley would have explained it to them, but Matewski had never claimed to be a doctor.

They were also happy to hear that almost the first enterprise of every Italian health board when the plague struck—namely, cleaning up the smelly garbage—had been a good idea, even if the underlying theory was inaccurate. So was the custom of having the men from lay sodalities visit all the poor houses in the town, clean them thoroughly, and give them a fresh coat of whitewash, inside and out.

At any rate, if Grantville had any luck at all, it was luck that it had made an ally of Venice. And not enemies, really, of Florence and Genoa. Those cities had developed plague-fighting as far as it could go with the knowledge and techniques that the seventeenth century had available. They'd had the organization, already. What they knew about medicine hadn't matched up to it, but . . . In Kronach, now, they were combining what Grantville knew about medicine with what plenty of Italians already knew about handling the, uh, bureaucracy of the thing. If it worked here, the new USE would put it into force in all the towns and cities.

What the USE really needed was some sort of . . . pipeline . . . for hiring more Italians. It really did.

Yeah, they'd gotten exemplary military and civilian cooperation on the rat eradication project.

Even if that meant that the fleas went looking for other hosts—human hosts—faster than would ordinarily have been the case. At least they hadn't done the old-fashioned thing of killing off the dogs and cats. Dogs and cats not only caught rats, but gave the fleas a few more options. And Kronach wasn't starving. He'd seen to that himself. So the Kronacher weren't eating the cats and dogs. Much less plague-infected rats.

The city had food. He was making the council pay for it, but it came in regular deliveries. He also made sure that the city council let the people know that the food was arriving because of his benevolent magnanimity. Or Vince's. Or Steve Salatto's. Or Grantville's. Or by sufferance of Mike Stearns and Gustavus Adolphus.

Think nice thoughts about us, folks. After all, one of my jobs is to incorporate this town into a happy, democratic, tolerant, Franconia when the time comes. Sure. That's gonna work. Kronach and Coburg. The ranchers and the farmers should be friends. Yippee.

He looked down at himself. In a world without latex, you did what you could, even if that meant that you swathed and robed yourself in waxed linen, with a breath mask over your face. The down-time theory was that it was harder for the nasty atoms to stick to waxed cloth. According to Gatterer, a slippery silk ought to work, too, but it cost too much. Guarinoni had admitted that he had never previously had much faith in the usefulness of the waxed linen robes, thinking that they were a Frenchified affectation and that all they really did was keep most of the fleas that tended to infest pest houses off the physicians. Then he'd thought again about transmission vectors and added, "Well . . . Maybe there is some point to them, after all."

They waxed the fabric on the stretchers that the attendants used to carry patients to the *Pesthaus*, too.

That brought his mind back to the current state of the *Pesthaus*. Bursting at the seams. Grandma Geraldine had another saying. "The hotter the battle, the shorter the war." She'd gotten that from her own mother. With the help of a set of twins, Great-Grandma Anna had managed to have seven children in eight years before she stopped cold at age thirty.

He hoped his great-grandmother was right.

So he opened the door and went in. It always took him a pause and some thought before he managed to walk up and open that door.

De Melon had become accustomed to the smoke. Something was always burning. When the Health Board had sent members of the council and the lay sodalities out to make a survey of the city, they had found many uninfected families sleeping on straw pallets that were filthy and fetid. That was scarcely surprising. That the poor had pallets at all was a sign of the comparative prosperity of the Germanies as compared to Spain.

The Health Board had ordered them all confiscated and burned. Ordinarily, that would have left the poor sleeping on the ground. Not that this was a terrible hardship in the summer. De Melon had slept on the ground more than once.

The order for a couple thousand clean, uninfected replacement pallets to be delivered to the drop-off point had put a big dent in his budget. Luckily, he hadn't had to pay cash. He had used bank drafts, duly countersigned by two members of the Magistracy for Health and payable in Würzburg. If fortune smiled, he would be reimbursed. By someone. Given the events of the summer, it no longer seemed probable that Duke Maximilian of Bavaria would reimburse him. He was far from sure that the duke was still his employer.

Maybe the bishop of Bamberg? Then, again, probably not, with Dornheim dead in Carinthia and the cathedral chapter not yet having elected a successor. It would be Hatzfeld, probably, but no telling how long it would take the pope to confirm him. It wasn't likely that a suffragan would be willing to authorize large, unexpected, expenditures.

The Health Board had given the fresh pallets to households that had already been cleaned and whitewashed, in return for a promise by the housewife that she would continue to use DDT.

It cost a lot. Probably less than burning corpses, though. Because of the siege, it was not feasible to establish a plague cemetery without continuing to reinfect the city. No way to make burials outside the walls. The church frowned on cremation except in the direst emergency. However . . . Surely the up-time understanding of atoms would lead to a change in policy. Logically, it should not be any more difficult for God to reassemble atoms dispersed in the air than those dispersed in the earth. So . . . Corpses were remarkably hard to burn, even if one saved on fuel by using old pallets and the rags and furnishings taken from infected houses as much as possible. One could regard the new pallets as a good use of limited funds. One would certainly interpret the new pallets as such a good use when reporting the condition of one's budget to one's employer.

There were other savings to be attributed to the siege, also. He did not have to deal with preventive quarantine of possibly infected individuals coming into the town from elsewhere. That tended to be expensive because of the need for posting guards outside the quarantine barracks. Merchants and other travelers often resented having their journeys interrupted, not to mention taking exception to being charged a reasonable amount for board and room during their period of isolation.

Of course, the siege also meant that the Health Board had not been able, thus far, to expel all transients, vagrants, mountebanks, and other undesirable elements who had been in the city when the plague broke out. So the authorities were having to feed them.

He would have to talk to Herr Trelli about that. Expulsion was pretty standard procedure. It was Herr Trelli who had forbidden the council to follow that procedure, on the grounds that they would starve to death between the city walls and the siege lines, or attempt to escape through the siege lines and possibly spread the plague into the countryside.

If Kronach offered to surrender in return for the SoTF's absorbing all the costs of coping with the plague as a starting point for negotiations . . . At the very least, by the time the negotiations ended, Herr Marcantonio in Bamberg should certainly reimburse de Melon for feeding those noncitizens all summer. That was only reasonable. This epidemic was eating up about forty percent of his budget and he wasn't really in the best position to float loans at the moment. No banker worth his salt was going to finance a military entrepreneur who was probably unemployed. Or if employed, employed by the wrong side.

He wonder how much ransom the USE would ask for him if he surrendered.

He was pretty sure that Duke Maximilian would not be in a mood to pay it.

Matt wasn't sure just how much he was in a position to promise, but de Melon was in a mood to dicker.

"Let me draw up a proposal. Everything we've talked about. I think that this is even way beyond Steve Salatto's pay grade, though."

They paused for an explanation of pay grades.

"Vince can radio it to him. He can radio it to the prime minister and emperor."

De Melon nodded agreement.

◊   ◊   ◊

Matt spent the whole evening writing. He figured that he had an ace up his sleeve. Now he needed to finish up what he'd leave for Bachhausen at the drop-off point tomorrow morning—well, later this morning, given the time—in a thoroughly sealed envelope.

"So de Melon is worried about Duke Maximilian and pretty sure the Bavarians won't ransom him if he surrenders the city. We can open the gates. The plague has tapered off and the doctors from Padua did pretty good. They're congratulating themselves pretty hard that only a fifth of the people died instead of two thirds."

Which really was something for them to be proud of, all things considered. But anyway . . .

"Now what we know, and what de Melon doesn't, is this stuff about Don Fernando and what de Melon did later in the Netherlands."

He started a new page. "So I was sort of thinking, and I know it's no business of mine to be suggesting foreign policy, but still, I've been stuck here at Kronach a long time and I'd really like to see the end of the siege."

He crossed that out. Nobody up at the level of Stearns was going to care that one up-time lieutenant was to the point that he'd be happy to cast himself down on a sword if that would just finish up the siege of Kronach.

"My recommendation, based on the current local situation, is that the State Department ought to make a copy of what the Research Center found out about de Melon and send it to Don Fernando. It makes de Melon look like a good enough catch that maybe he'll reimburse him for his expenses here. I don't know whether the USE is doing ransoms or not. If it is, Don Fernando might even ransom him and ask to have him come to Belgium."

Matt crossed that out. *Damn. I know it isn't Belgium down-time. I'm up way too late.*

" . . . to the Spanish Netherlands, which would get him out of Franconia."

Matt crossed that out, too.

" . . . which would . . . " *Well, what would it?*

" . . . to the Spanish Netherlands, where he might find a useful and constructive outlet for his undeniable talents."

Bingo! Mr. Piazza and Ms. Mailey would be proud of him. Mr. Piazza and Ms. Mailey had spent a lot of time talking to him about useful and constructive outlets back in his high school days.

He pulled out another sheet of paper and started on the clean copy.

Kronach, Franconia
September 1634

"There's not going to be any real fall-out from the Ram Rebellion for Kronach, one way or the other, directly," Matt pointed out to Cliff Priest. "Since the whole city was closed up by the quarantine for the crucial months, they weren't really involved on either side. Except . . . ".

"Except?" Scott Blackwell raised his eyebrows. His expression said that the worst was yet to come. Just because it always was.

"They've come out to find out that their peasant 'subjects' in the hinterland have taken severe exception to being 'subjects' and have acted upon their convictions. Never mind. They'll just have to learn to live with it. I've told Bachhausen that if they try to use their militia to restore the old order, it's his job to stand up for the citizens of the State of Thuringia-Franconia."

"One could say that the Kronacher are SoTF citizens, too."

Matt grinned. "Not till they take the oath of allegiance, they aren't. Which they missed last winter because of the siege and this summer because of the quarantine. Which I somehow just haven't gotten around to administering yet. The farmers, on the other hand . . . "

"You didn't used to be like this," Stew Hawker said.

The grin turned a little bleak. "Let's just say that Kronach's been an educational experience and leave it at that. Okay?"

Cliff looked at his former high school student and said, "Okay."

Bamberg, Franconia
September 1634

Matt was sitting on the floor of the Real Estate Titles office. "So that's the plan. I'm going to Padua as soon as I finish up here in Franconia. Marcie and me . . ."

Janie winced.

"—okay, Marcie and I—are getting married in December. She's coming down to Würzburg and we'll leave from there."

"Padua? Why on earth?"

"First of all, Stoner's there. Stoner's what I'm looking for. I've got to learn everything the man knows. If Kronach taught me anything, it taught me that. I'm no boy genius or anything, but I did have basic chemistry and stuff at Fairmont State before I had to quit to save up some more money. I'd have gone back and finished up-time, so why not here?"

"There's always Jena. And the new med school. It's a lot closer to home."

"Well, yeah." Matt looked a little uncomfortable. "But it's still just a start-up, really. As the doctors put it to me, the only reason that Beulah MacDonald and her people have had any success at all getting their ideas across in Jena is that the med school dean, Rolfinck his name is, is a Padua man himself. Guarinoni said that if the dean there had been the product of a university like Wittenberg or Paris, the folks from Leahy would have been dead in the water. And Gatterer asked why should I get Padua second-hand when I can have the real thing. In a lot more words, but that's what it boiled down to."

Janie looked at him. She'd heard all about Steve Salatto's explosion at Johnnie F. Haun—that the point of Hearts and Minds was for Us to convert Them rather than vice versa. "It sounds sort of like you've swallowed their viewpoint."

Matt wriggled. "Well, I figure things this way. They have a lot more experience living in the seventeenth century than we do. It seems a little silly not to take advantage of it."

"I hate to be crass, but how are you planning to pay for it? Living in Padua and sitting at the foot of the master and all that?" Janie waved her hand vaguely. "That could be years. Do they take transfer credits? Universities in this day and age, I mean?"

"Our three doctors will write recommendations, since they're all alumni. And, yeah, they do accept transfer credits in a way. You can take your exams as soon as you're up to them. Nobody really cares where you took the courses as long as you can pass the exams. The Latin will be the big thing, but Weinhart has been tutoring me while we were in Kronach."

"Well, you show up at our place in the evenings and I'll keep on tutoring you here. Nothing like a head start, especially when it comes for free."

"We talked about it, Marcie and me. Well, we wrote letters about it. We haven't really talked much for two years. I've only gotten up to Grantville that one time since we came down here after the Gustavus/Stearns detente in '32. Her folks were so sure that talking wasn't what we had on our minds that we scarcely got to see each other at all. If you've ever got a job here that requires privacy minimization, consider hiring Rosemary."

"People have been reacting to the Ring of Fire in all sorts of ways. We have Father Mazzare—Cardinal Mazzare, now—pulling and tugging to bring the Church into a post-Vatican II frame of mind, and Catholics in Grantville like Rosemary who would just as soon sink back into a comfortable pre-Vatican II world." She tapped her toe on the footstool that she used to boost herself up to the pedestal desk. "Rosemary's close to five years older than I am. She probably was confirmed before Vatican II had any effect on the catechism or anything."

Matt leaned forward, his hand on his chin. "What the hell does Rosemary think we did back when we were dating in college? Or after we got engaged, before I got sent down to Franconia? Not that Marcie was in a mood to push it. We were almost like strangers again. We thought about putting off getting married indefinitely. Partly because of the money thing, but that's not most of it. We think we can make it, that way. She's a fully qualified engineer, now. She had three years of college before the Ring of Fire—one more than me because she didn't have to work so many hours—and she's trained at USE Steel ever since it started up. Stoner has the clout to get her a good job, even in the Most Serene Republic of Venice, where female engineers aren't exactly a dime a dozen. So she can support me. As long as she doesn't get pregnant. Which, as far as we're concerned, she won't."

"She's going to Padua with you?"

"Not much point in getting married and then having me in Padua and her in Grantville. That wouldn't be any different from the last couple of years. Why bother to get married at all, if we did it that way? Joe and Rosemary are having kittens, of course. She's their baby girl. Leaving home for foreign parts. Rosemary's being a drama queen."

Janie winced. "Your folks?"

"Well, Mom would just like me to come home, of course. Even after so many changes, she's not that crazy about the idea of my hanging around Stoner. She hoped that we'd settle down right in Grantville after I got out of the army. That Marcie would come be an engineer in town and I'd find a job of some kind and we'd provide grandchildren. It's hard for her, especially. Dad just ignored the church and got married again even before the Ring of Fire, so he has Abby and the little kids. But Mom's stuck in limbo, there at the Curl and Tan. She's sort of given up. First she was sure I'd get killed on this posting to Bamberg and now she's sure that I'll die of some awful disease in Italy."

Janie snorted. "If Rosemary's five years older than I am, then Amy's ten years younger. She doesn't have any excuse. It's a gumption issue with her, if you ask me. Pardon my French, since she's your mother and all."

"Herr Matewski, you do have it all?"

Joe Matewski looked up. "Yes, I have it all."

"The addresses of the professors in Padua, and the others who have been hearing the lectures of Professor Stone?"

"Yeah."

"The glassblowers whom we are recommending?"

"Yeah?"

"Our new addresses?"

"Yeah."

"Our letters to Dr. Sims and Dr. McDonnell."

"Yeah."

"I am most anxious to enter into correspondence with both of them."

"I'm sure."

"It is the gold that is important. Remember that. It is the gold. If indeed they can draw brass fine enough to make these hypodermic needles for drawing blood to make this 'serum-based antitoxin' and one of the main problems is that blood corrodes the needles so quickly, it is the gold that is important. They must coat these brass needles with gold."

"Yeah," Joe Matewski said. "I've got it. Really I do. I figure that this is really important to you. The medical types in Grantville and Jena will get the short version over the radio tonight and this"—he held up several hundred pages of closely written paper—"just as soon as I can get it there. A couple of weeks, at most."

Gatterer expressed profuse gratitude.

"I'll radio the short version to Venice for Stoner, too. Express-courier the second copy to him."

Gatterer grasped his head and kissed him on both cheeks.

Matewski thought that a friendly handshake would have been just plenty, but he managed to keep from backing off.

He didn't enjoy going to those Hearts and Minds lectures, but maybe they did some good, after all.

**Bamberg, Franconia
October 1634**

"What do you think, Vince?" Janie Kacere turned a couple of pieces of paper over and then turned them back again. "Were they a Trojan horse that we sent into Kronach? Successfully, I have to admit, the way Matt"—she waved toward him down at the end of the table—"pulled things off. Or . . . "

" . . . were they a Trojan horse that the Duchess Claudia de Medici planted on us?" Cliff Priest finished her sentence. "And if she did, why?"

Vince Marcantonio shook his head. "I don't know which one. Not yet. Maybe we won't know for years." He grinned suddenly. "But she's damned determined that they're going to see Bernhard of Saxe-Weimar next, whether they want to or not, so I've gotten the better of Guarinoni's complaints that their 'old bones' wouldn't stand a trip over to Swabia at his age."

"Vince." Stewart Hawker looked apprehensive. "What have you done? They are over sixty, after all. Guarinoni and Weinhart both. And Gatterer's no spring chicken, either. He got his M.D. more than thirty years ago. They were pretty wiped out when they came in from Innsbruck last March, even though the duchess paid for a carriage so they didn't have to ride out in the weather. The trip from here up to Kronach wasn't easy for them, either. And the summer didn't exactly count as a vacation, either."

"I asked him if he was open to new experiences. Of course he's so full of himself that he had to say 'yes.'

And what with the fact that there's a landing field at Rheinfelden now . . . "

"You got hold of a *plane*?" Stew spilled his coffee on the flagstone floor.

"Yep. A Gustav is coming to drop a couple of high-ranking diplomats off in Bayreuth. The pilot will transport the good doctors and deposit them right on Bernhard of Saxe-Weimar's doorstep. Bernhard isn't going to let our medical people from Fulda into his territory, I don't think. We have to live with that. But he seems to be willing to take these men from the Duchess Claudia. Don't know why. Maybe parts of the Catholic and Austrian territories that he's scooped up aren't as docile as he had hoped."

"Nobody's ever as docile as a person hopes." Bennett Norris spoke in the world-weary voice of anyone who has ever parented a teenager. Vince ignored him. Bennett was starting to succumb to short-timer-itis. As soon as the national election was over and done with, in February, Ed Piazza was transferring him and Marian to Mainz.

"They're the best that this time and place has to offer, and they can take some of our tricks with them. Maybe they can contain the plague that's scheduled to sweep up through Swabia and Wuerttemberg into the USE in the next couple of years. Maybe Bernhard's just self-interested enough not to want half the population of his new sandbox dead. God, I hope so. And even if they can't pull it off . . . "

It didn't look like Vince was going to finish the sentence.

Janie looked up at the cherubs on the ceiling. " . . . there's always the possibility that we've sent a secret weapon."

"What?"

"Guarinoni may bore Duke Bernhard to death with extended lectures on a healthful lifestyle. Replete with mnemonic tricks and pompous admonitions."

Together, most of the SoTF administrative staff in Bamberg chanted, "Let's all be *gesondt.*"

Bozen, Tirol
October 1634

"God rest his soul," Duchess Claudia said. She was referring to her late brother-in-law Ferdinand, the Holy Roman Emperor.

Dr. Bienner crossed himself.

"Ferdinand was never seriously interested in the Austrian holdings in Swabia."

Bienner nodded cautiously.

"Our nephew Ferdinand is not likely to make them his primary concern, either. He worries about Hungary. And the Turks."

"As well he should."

"The Austro-Hungarian Empire?"

"Premature, perhaps. But not unreasonable, given the situation in the Germanies."

"Which leaves Tyrol to worry about Duke Bernhard of Saxe-Weimar. If, of course, the Swede does not manage to *smash* him." The duchess-regent smashed her hand down on the table. "I like that English word. It has such a satisfying sound."

"General Horn is not given to smashing."

"So I have heard. Duke Bernhard accepted Our physicians?"

"And, apparently, their advice. There is the whole winter to prepare for what we may, according to the up-timers' encyclopedias, expect next spring. They will work with the up-time 'nurse.' "

"Perhaps our agents in the Vorarlberg should initiate diplomatic relations with him?"

Dr. Bienner stroked his beard without replying.

Duchess Claudia walked to the window. "We are well matched in age. I am only thirty and proven fertile."

Dr. Bienner nodded. Her first marriage, little over a year in duration, had produced a child who still lived. Female, unfortunately. The second, five children in eight years, four of them still alive and healthy and two of them boys. Claudia de Medici was a woman to gladden any ambitious dynast's heart.

While his mind wandered, she had continued talking. "Perhaps it was prescient that Leopold and I chose to name our first daughter Isabella Clara. Two years before this 'Ring of Fire.' If the king in the Low Countries and Maria Anna have a son right away, the age gap will not be too great. A boy is old enough to beget years before a woman has matured enough to give birth with maximum safety. And the symbolism should appeal to them."

Dr. Bienner nodded silently.

"Duke Bernhard is a heretic, but that is no insuperable obstacle. After all, the pope granted a dispensation for the French king's sister to marry that stupid Englishman. Lutherans are no more heretical than Anglicans."

She tapped her fingernails, one by one, on the window pane. "I am scarcely in Vienna's confidence, of course. But if it should happen that Our cousins are too preoccupied to think seriously about the, um, 'challenges and opportunities' presented by the situation in *Vorderoesterreich* and the Breisgau . . . ah, not to mention Alsace and the Franche Comte . . . "

She turned around from the window, leaning forward. "Tyrol is not."

Dr. Bienner nodded again. "May your generosity be rewarded, Your Grace."

Lucky at Cards

Andrew Dennis

"So, how do we play this game?" Richelieu's manner was open, inquiring, almost naive.

Smirks passed around the table. The business of state had finished hours ago and the guests who had remained in the Louvre to drink and gamble the night away were somewhat relaxed from the formality of occasions of state.

"Armand, you are *impossible*." Abel Servien, marquis de Sable, was a little more relaxed than most, laughing out loud as he spoke. Louder than most, too. It was all Mazarin could do not to wince at the way the man boomed. He actually liked the fellow, but it was a lot easier to picture him riding to hounds or spearing a boar than haggling the fine provisions of a treaty or partaking of a detailed academic correspondence. He did both of the latter, to the mild puzzlement of many, who looked at the big, hearty, beefy fellow with the loud voice and the bombastic manner and assumed he was, at best, an uncomplicated soul. The missing eye, lost in a hunting accident in his youth, did nothing to detract from the image of a simple brawler from the rural nobility.

Which he was. Simply a highly intelligent, supremely educated one whose achievements off the hunting field had just won him election to the newly-formed *Academie Francaise*, an accolade that paled somewhat beside being regarded by Richelieu as a smart man. Mazarin also had a high opinion of his talents: he had thrashed out the Peace of Cherasco with Servien, what seemed now like a lifetime ago, and both of them had done well as a result. Mazarin had made a name that now saw him in good odor in Paris and Rome both, and Servien had ended up minister of war and able to place any number of his relatives in the cardinal's service. His fourth cousin, Etienne, was one of the more notorious of the special *intendants* who did the cardinal's more surreptitious work.

"*Impossible*, Abel?" Richelieu smiled back.

"Impossible." Servien gestured for the cardinal to be included in the deal. "If Etienne hasn't already furnished you with a complete set of rules, some other of your army of sneaks has done so, and I can't imagine it took you more than, oh, an hour or so to learn them fully and devise seventeen winning stratagems."

Richelieu quirked an eyebrow. "Why would you think I might do such a thing? A churchman, studying so disreputable an activity as cards?"

"Hah!" Servien barked. "It would be an improvement from all those grubby actors and playwrights you throw money at. And it's not as if we don't already have a cardinal taking us for every ecu in our pockets. Clearly it is an entirely reputable activity if we now have two princes of the church at table, although it will not be long before we have a beggar in my chair."

"Come, Abel," Mazarin said, "you can afford it. Can I help it if you're not as good at cards as you are at diplomacy?"

"I remain to be convinced that this 'Texas hold 'em' is quite the game of skill you claim it is." Servien grumped. "I have been dealt nothing but excrement since the evening began, and nothing seems to answer for making good the execrable luck I'm having."

At that he was doing better than Leon Bouthillier, who was to Mazarin's left; the fortunes of the comte de Chavigny were being heavily depleted and much of it had ended up in Mazarin's gratifyingly large stack of ecus. Alas, the poor fellow had learned to play poker from Harry Lefferts, and both men did not have a tell so much as consist entirely of one; one simply had to judge *how* excited the fellow was. Neither was much concerned to consider the odds, and had a basic instinct for unrestrained aggression. Harry did it a good deal better than Leon, but the principle was the same in either case—audacity, audacity and more audacity. Unfortunately, Bouthillier couldn't quite manage the same level of sheer single-minded sanguinity and would occasionally back down from a truly insane bluff; against Harry one played the probabilities and over time, wore him down. Against Leon, a show of force on a moderately strong hand would occasionally see him off.

The cards were going around again and this time Richelieu was being dealt in. "Could we have the door closed for some few moments?" he asked as he briefly examined his hole cards and arranged them neatly before him.

"Certainly," de Sable said, and waved at a servant to attend to the matter.

"And a moment of privacy?" Richelieu asked, prompting another wave for the assorted servants—including the fellow who was serving up the cards, at another nod and quirk of the eyebrow from the cardinal—to withdraw for the moment.

Mazarin noted the company. Himself, de Sable, Bouthillier, and Richelieu. And, now that the last of the servants had left, Etienne Servien pulling the door closed and standing by it to ensure their privacy, he raised an eyebrow.

"Yes, Your Eminence," Richelieu said, noting the gesture, "I am afraid I must interrupt you at cards with business. Tiresome, but necessary, and I do apologize."

"There is no need for Your Eminence to apologize," Mazarin said, "Since I am now fully employed here, my time is Your Eminence's."

"Can we drop the formality, please?" de Sable said. "Things were pleasantly relaxed, Jules, before you started Eminencing all over the place."

"Please excuse me, Abel," Mazarin said, realizing that he was actually at fault and grateful to the irascible war minister for the correction, "I still have a little trouble thinking of myself as a cardinal. A habit I am working on, I assure you."

"Work swiftly, if you would," Bouthillier said, speaking for the first time since Richelieu had entered. "The sense I have among Gaston's circle is that they would as soon not give you any time at all for that."

"Really?" It was Richelieu's turn to raise an eyebrow. "And how do they propose to arrange the dismissal of a cardinal who has His Holiness' favor so firmly in hand?"

Mazarin wondered too. He had successfully smoothed over the ripples that the Galileo Affair had caused, tidied up the loose ends from what had been, potentially, one of the most major upsets arising from the Ring of Fire. It hadn't been easy—the Venetian Committee of Correspondence had managed to set a record for bad luck *and* bad management that looked unlikely to be beaten—but it had just about been possible to maneuver the thing so that everyone got something and no one was left empty-handed. Spain was unhappy about it, but they were perennially unhappy about everything, so that wasn't much of a loss. It had taken all of Mazarin's skill as a lawyer and diplomat and, there at the end when he had to sell the thing to a sceptical curia, outright bare-faced cheek. What Harry Lefferts would call 'bafflin' 'em with bullshit.' The bluff had carried the day, and with Rome's political factions baffled into immobility and the damage to France—D'Avaux, the French ambassador to Venice, had managed to outdo himself for sheer fatheaded incompetence—was neatly contained.

Leon shrugged. "I don't think anyone has got quite so far as actual planning, although perhaps Giulio, or Jules rather—" he turned to Mazarin "—I do apologize, I've known you as Giulio for so long I keep forgetting—"

Mazarin waved it aside. If truth be told, he'd only had the new name for a couple of months and wasn't quite used to his new signature himself. Still, it did not do to take one's naturalization by half-measures.

"As I was saying before I put my foot so firmly in my mouth," Leon continued, "Jules will likely be seeing himself slandered in pamphlets before long."

Richelieu's grin was disarming. "The *mazarinades* are starting early, then," he said.

Mazarin couldn't help but be sarcastic. "I had *so* been looking forward to that," he said, "perhaps I should write a few memoirs of my time as a student in Madrid, so they can have some of the more noteworthy items to print."

"Really?" Abel asked, grinning broadly, "not quite the serious fellow I thought, are you?"

"Of course he is," Richelieu said, deadpan. "Would a prince of the church have spent his student years raising absolute hell in Madrid?"

"I didn't know I was entering the church then," Mazarin said, blushing slightly. He had, in fact, taken full advantage of his time as an undergraduate to make a perfect beast of himself and honed the skills of fast talking and persuasion he had later parlayed into a career in diplomacy. Watching Harry Lefferts in action in Rome had brought back some very pleasant memories indeed. And, although wild horses would not drag the admission out of him in this company, made him wish rubber had been invented back then. Those things were a *marvellous* invention.

"Be that as it may," Richelieu said, before Mazarin could wander off into pleasant remembrances, "if Gaston is minded to make trouble I think we should take him seriously. We have nothing specific as yet, but there is suggestion that he has been meeting with more Spaniards lately."

"And His Majesty still won't have his brother executed?" Abel Servien's tone was arch and sneering in a way that would have surprised anyone who didn't know him well.

"Please, Abel," Richelieu said, "until His Majesty is blessed with an heir, Monsieur Gaston has to remain alive."

"I am very carefully not commenting on His Majesty's practice in that regard," Servien said, suddenly absolutely without tone or affect in his voice.

"Her Majesty has been pregnant several times, as you know, Abel," Richelieu said, his tone chiding.

Servien simply harrumphed.

Richelieu waved the issue of royal issue aside. "Perhaps something might be done to warn off Monsieur Gaston?" He opened the question to general debate with his tone and a glance around the table. "While we consider it, may I ask to whom falls the honor of opening the betting?"

The business of betting occupied everyone for a few moments; by ironclad convention there was no gossip while a hand was in play, a rule that held as well for primero and baccarat as it did for Texas hold 'em. Unfortunately, Mazarin was holding a rather nice pair of fours that turned in to three of a kind on the flop, so the preoccupation of the other three men at the table made for disappointing betting. The river gave him a full house, nines over fours, but Leon had had the other two nines, so perhaps the rather light betting had been a mercy. He would cheerfully have called Leon's bluff all the way to the hilt, and probably reversed their relative positions. As it was, Leon made a dent in the stack of ecus he'd lost to Mazarin.

"Keep playing like that, Jules," he said, "and the dark rumors Gaston's crowd want to spread about your gaming debts will come true."

"Rumors?" Mazarin felt the beginnings of a chill at that. If it got about that he wasn't good for his notes of hand, the sudden loss of welcome at Paris's gaming tables would only be the start of his troubles. A man who couldn't pay his card debts wasn't a gentleman, and therefore unfit to take his place in polite society. As such, he would be politically useless, practically and as a matter of correct protocol both.

"That you've gambled away every benefice you've had, and our patron here has hold of your 'leash' because he's settling your debts for you, or so they say. And His Eminence knows he will have you under control forever because you keep getting in trouble no matter how many times you are dragged out of the hole. I wish you'd stop it, Jules," Leon said, grinning broadly, "as the constant calls of debt-collectors grow most tiresome."

Mazarin grinned back. "What can I do? I keep losing so badly, but one day my luck will change, I am sure of it. I have a *foolproof* system." In fact, the only callers on Mazarin's lodgings at the Maison Chavigny were those delivering his winnings, usually with rueful notes from the assorted notables who hadn't had the sense to stop playing against him when they exhausted what they had at table and had to resort to notes of hand. He'd lost more than he sat down with exactly once in the last two months, when he'd written a note to cover the last call of the night, for the princely sum of five hundred ecus—slightly less than a week's income from the larger of his two benefices. The only delay in redeeming his note had been because he'd slept in the next day. His foolproof system was simply that he was very, very good at any game that depended on bluff; primero and, lately, poker. He would play basset, faro and baccarat to be sociable, but he had grown out of pure gambling long ago.

Everyone around the table knew it, and his remark raised a round of chuckles. "I could take it very amiss, you know, that Monsieur Gaston thinks me stupid enough to keep playing when I'm losing."

"Now, now, Jules," Richelieu said, wagging a finger, "Cardinals aren't allowed affairs of honor. And if you think you are embarrassed to learn that Gaston's crowd thinks little of you, imagine how embarrassed I should be to have you imprisoned for duelling and for killing the king's brother."

"Shame," Abel said, into the thoughtful silence that followed that. "He's given me cause a couple of times."

"Perhaps some other kind of contest," Leon added, suddenly with a 'butter wouldn't melt' expression on his face.

Servien erupted. "Arm-wrestling!" he choked out between guffaws, "Bowling! Duels will be transformed! A new fashion!"

Leon grinned. "I was thinking of, perhaps, something a little more in keeping with the spirit of the slander. Jules, Gaston has taken to playing primero rather a lot."

"Really? I had thought him a basset man, and baccarat when he feels like an intellectual challenge." Mazarin had been at Monsieur Gaston's table a couple of times, but had never found the company truly congenial. The man was perennially unhappy at not being his elder brother, and tended to attract the like-minded to his circle. They were not marked so much by a lack of talent as an inability to use it because they flatly refused to believe the world was as it was, insisting that it was as they would like it to be.

"Until recently, yes," Leon said, "but the new fashion for poker affronts him, and thus his entire circle. Apparently it is a foreign game that no true Frenchman would be seen playing."

"What patriotism." Richelieu's drawl was dry and deadpan. The regularity with which Gaston took foreign support for his schemes was notorious. Had he not been the king's brother he would have gone to the headsman along with his conspirators. "Perhaps you can show him how a foreigner plays the game, Jules? If that is what Leon is driving at?"

"How could a naturalized Frenchman teach so senior a Frenchman as Monsieur Gaston how to play a game that was invented in Italy?" It was too good to resist, Mazarin thought. Gaston, a serial traitor who frequently colluded with foreign powers was flouting his Frenchness by playing an Italian game? If that was the defining standard, Jules could prove himself easily. He'd been beating his relatives at it when he was twelve.

"The idea has merit," Richelieu said. "He will think himself presented with an opportunity to ruin you financially—what little I know tells me that over time the player with deepest pockets can win. And—forgive me Jules, but it was necessary to know—I understand that you rarely lose over the long term. The worst that will happen is that you will rise from the table with some trifling loss, and we might well see Monsieur Gaston subsidizing your new estate."

"I cannot simply walk in to his circle," Mazarin observed, "unless you want the gesture to be theatrical in the extreme."

"No, no," Richelieu said, "an outright challenge would be counterproductive for the moment. If Leon would procure you an entree, you should work your way toward playing cards with the fellow for high stakes, somewhere very public. And then, Jules, forget the rules of protocol. You rank before him as a prince of the church. You are entirely permitted, encouraged even, to take him for everything you can."

The opportunity came shortly after Christmas, at the kind of levee that Mazarin had come to look forward to immensely. Her Majesty, whatever the king thought of her, was a thoroughly charming lady and one whose company he could not get enough of. She, too, liked him. He could see Richelieu's purpose in bringing them together as much as was possible—Anne of Austria, despite the name, was quite thoroughly Spanish, despite the best efforts of her court ladies. She also corresponded frequently with her brother, Philip of Spain, and while the correspondence could not be practically intercepted,

Richelieu had deep suspicions that it went beyond simple matters of family gossip. Although, for the Habsburgs, politics, statecraft and warfare *were* simple matters of family gossip. And Philip of Spain, faced with separations between his own throne and those of Austria and the Netherlands—the United States of Europe had not just messed things up in the Germanies—would be scrabbling for any connection he could get his hands on. And it was only a matter of time before she got drawn into the machinations of another de Chalais—Richelieu had had that one executed but there seemed to be an inexhaustible supply of traitors.

So—as far as Mazarin could reconstruct Richelieu's thinking—best to get Anne firmly attached to someone in his own party to shield her from the troublemakers. Mazarin felt fairly sure that Richelieu wasn't so cold-blooded that he would even suggest, let alone order, something so outrageous as a seduction. Not that he would say no, it had to be said, but there were limits and a prince of the church conducting an affair with the queen of France was pretty certain to be beyond them. Probably. The domestic situation of His Most Christian Majesty, Louis of France, was odder even than most monarchs.

The Louvre was host to a levee for the Feast of the Epiphany. His Majesty was away at Saint-Maur, leaving most of the court luminaries to celebrate in his absence, with the queen as hostess for the evening. And Monsieur Gaston, Duc D'Orleans, comte de Blois and comte d'Anjou was there as well.

Mazarin had wandered along with Leon Bouthillier several times to levees and soirees that Gaston had thrown over the preceding few weeks. From time to time, he had even let the man inveigle him into a game of baccarat or basset, at which Mazarin had been careful to bet injudiciously and badly, losing a modest amount each time. That had grated, somewhat. The benefices Richelieu had settled on him were handsome, and entirely adequate for his modest living expenses and to get him a seat at Paris' better card tables. The rest—and after he brought home his winnings, it was a substantial rest—was going into procuring the nucleus of a fine, fine collection of books and art. He begrudged the money he had hurled at Gaston instead of at that.

Oh, he could understand the necessity. The man was important, virtually untouchable provided he had the sense to spend occasional periods out of the country, and, within his sphere, powerful. Cultivating him was necessary, and that was part of why Richelieu ensured he had the likes of Bouthillier to act as liaison, for all that the senior de Chavigny couldn't abide Gaston. But he had to be cultivated. Flattered even.

For now, though, there was a card game in the offing. Gaston had got back to his love of primero. "Is there room for another?" Mazarin asked as he walked into the room Gaston had selected.

"But of course," Gaston said, waving to a free spot. A spot where he would have to open the betting if Gaston kept the deal, a prerogative he could claim if he so chose. Leon Bouthillier was already in the game, and had a respectable stack of coin in front of him. Clearly this was company in which Leon could win. There were four others, none of whom Mazarin more than vaguely recognized.

A servant brought a chair and Mazarin sat down. "How is this game played, then?" he asked, provoking a round of cultured titters.

"If you sit down needing the rules explained, Your Eminence," Gaston drawled, "you deserve all you get."

Mazarin nodded to acknowledge the sally. If Gaston thought that that was cutting wit, he was welcome to it. "Do deal me in," he said, "and I shall answer for my own losses, such as they are." He grinned. This was a game he *knew*.

Gaston crooked an eyebrow and began. Mazarin's first two cards were perfectly ordinary, and yet a surprise. The Grantville patterns, similar to the Rouen cards, were becoming widespread. What was unusual was to see Gaston using them after his public prating about the whole business not being sufficiently French. The hand itself was a four and a five of hearts and clubs respectively, worth a low *numero* bid at best, and neatly removing temptation to start aggressively. "*Numero* thirty," he said, beginning with a half-dozen or so ecus simply to bait the field, and bidding a hand he could make with just two cards. Indeed, it would be hard to manage a hand that couldn't make that with a couple of draws. Playing like an old woman for the first couple of rounds was generally worthwhile, especially if there were pigeons at table. And, nobility being what they were—basset stakes were limited by law for anyone but the nobility for a *reason*—there was bound to be one or two. Being able to laugh off massive gaming losses was practically a badge of nobility.

Betting started out suitably extravagant following Mazarin's lead, none of the nobility wanting to look like they couldn't afford to plunge, and plunge hard. Mazarin felt a warm, warm glow somewhere begin somewhere in his belly. Now, if he could just persuade them to start trying to *take* him . . .

Gaston completed the deal once there were something like four hundred ecus on the table between six players, and already a *supremo* bid. Mazarin had seen the bets, joking that he was already in over his head despite the fact that he knew at least two of the men around the table had seen him play before. And, when the bids and the raises got hard, he let himself look a little worried and confined himself to seeing them. With his hand complete, Mazarin had his own bid in hand—a five and a six of hearts, but the bid was *supremo*. He folded without further ado.

"A little rich for your blood, Your Eminence?" Gaston asked, a minor barb whose sheer crudity meant that Mazarin could do little other than ignore it.

"A little, monsieur," Mazarin allowed, nodding his deference. His acting was not entirely thespian; conceding defeat in the first rounds made good tactical sense but he hated to do it. Letting his feelings show at this stage was sensible, if distasteful. "Perhaps I will be more fortunate in the next round?"

"Perhaps."

After that, Mazarin had to sit and be calm while the pot rose over two thousand ecus on one hand, which was frankly ludicrous. It was all he could do not to get up and demand to know what the hell these clowns thought they were playing at—most of the bids were flat-out impossible. And, sure enough, no one made his bid at the end of the game.

Time to conduct a little raid, he thought. If there were two thousand on the table, it was worth a little aggressive play. He got the six and seven of spades on the opening deal, and bid a supremo on the first round, running the bidding up handsomely, with fluxus bids that there was no chance of the table beating by the end of the first round, which he raised with a blithe smile. There was actually a slightly better chance of his making a fluxus than a supremo, assuming an honest deal.

He put up his best annoying smile when the deal was completed, and to his amusement he actually got the ace he needed for a supremo. From here on in it was a simple business of keeping the bets and draws going until he had that fourth spade without running the fluxus bids up so high—it was all of fifty right now—that he was faced with a lot of folding before he could make his hand. He grinned broadly. "Supremo," he said, tossing in the useless heart and setting down the three cards of his hand. He didn't even trouble to look at the card Gaston dealt him. The bidding suddenly became conservative.

So I am the kind of news that gets around, he thought. It was a gratifying consideration. A quick glance showed him that everyone was watching him carefully. Just because aristocracy likes to spend heavily, one should not assume they like to lose, and he was the best prospect for that just at the moment. The bids came back to him with a modest raise to match. He checked his draw card. Two of spades, giving him a fluxus and fifty-seven points on a supremo bid; he was bust. He considered, and rejected, the possibility of bidding the plain and naked truth. "I'll see that and vie for my supremo," he said, "all in." Not, strictly speaking, a good bid. Unless someone chose to raise him with a real fluxus.

Everyone folded. Even Gaston. "I should really have seen that hand," Gaston said as he shuffled and cut for the next hand. "I think we were bluffed."

"I had a fluxus and fifty-seven," Mazarin said, deadpan. "You were."

Gaston laughed. "You know, that was very convincing? You could as well have told everyone you had forty-two and no hand."

Mazarin kept his tone exactly the same. "I did."

That got a round of laughs. *I have all of you now,* he thought.

The next two hands passed off without incident, and the table talk was subdued. Mazarin made conservative bids and then folded when the deal was complete, risking only a little of the money he had taken with that early coup. That Gaston was not passing the deal around made things a little more difficult. Mazarin considered his cards. Two coats in clubs. A rather small numero right there, maybe a fluxus on the deal. He'd have to see if he could provoke a raise. "Numerus, forty," he said, tossing in a vie that was frankly far too large for the hand he was bidding.

The round of chuckles was what he had been hoping for. "Surely you may bluff better than that?" Gaston observed, "I had heard you had problems, Your Eminence, but I had ascribed them to ill-fortune."

"My fortunes are as God grants they should be, monsieur," Mazarin countered, "and the run of play is how I help myself. Let us see what problems arise in this hand."

Gaston nodded for the bidding to continue. The first four—the specimens of fungible nobility of the kind that clustered around whichever of Gaston or the king happened to be most readily available—all saw his bet, content to wait and see what the second round brought up. Leon Bouthillier considered for a moment. "I shall see that," he said, pushing forward his stake, "and re-vie another hundred ecus—numerus fifty-four."

Not a serious bid, Mazarin thought, *one point short of supremo.* It seemed young Leon had guessed what Mazarin was up to and was deliberately provoking the table. Which was helpful in its way, but—

"Supremo," Gaston said, matter-of-factly, seeing Leon's raise and adding a couple of hundred ecus of his own. "This game is starting to get interesting."

"Monsieur always did play for high stakes," Leon said, provoking a moment of silence around the table and a few worried frowns.

"Indeed," Gaston said, "all true Frenchmen should. Do you see?"

Mazarin loved moments such as these. The play at cards was thrill enough by itself—he had his play, to simply see the raises and watch whether the other players folded. A supremo bid was a tough one to make but easy enough to beat, especially if he managed to make his fluxus. The table talk, though, was growing delightfully heated. Leon—and Mazarin wished there was some way to warn him not to prejudice his valuable position in Gaston's circle—had made a sally at Gaston's unfortunate record in committing treason, and Gaston was, apparently, counting on Mazarin's clerical status and his own royal blood to avoid being called out to answer for his insult.

"I am told our newest cardinal has made a coup?" Everyone turned around to see who had spoken, and it was Her Majesty, Anne of Austria. The existing tension dissipated and a whole new kind arose. There was no love lost between her and her brother-in-law after he had entangled her in his last, disastrous, plot.

"I have had some small success, Your Majesty," Mazarin said, rising first to kiss her hand. "And I have some hope that Your Majesty's presence will bring me more luck."

"I shall remain and watch the play, then," she said. "Pray continue, my lords, Your Eminence." She took up a position behind Mazarin, her ladies attending in her wake like a small flotilla behind a graceful ship of the line.

"Your Majesty is most gracious," Gaston said, "and I recall the action is with His Eminence?"

"Indeed, monsieur," Mazarin agreed, "and I will see the three hundred that are bid and be content to await the completion of the deal."

The four nobles—Mazarin still couldn't recall any names—all saw the raise as well, taking six fresh cards between them. Floundering for a better hand, all of them, but unwilling to back down in a sensible manner now that Gaston had raised the moral temperature of the table.

Leon stayed in as well, smiling faintly and throwing off tells in all directions. Nothing useful, knowing Leon as well as he had come to. He was simply an excitable fellow.

Gaston completed the deal without comment. Mazarin checked his cards. Seven of clubs and the four of hearts. That was his original bid made; a pity the bid was supremo. And also a pity Gaston hadn't chosen to play the English version of primero—the pirates' version of the game where bidding was not troubled with and the strongest hand won. Much more like the American's poker and a far better game for bluffing since there was so much less information passing around the table. A fellow had to be able to truly *read* his table mates.

"The action is with you, again, Your Eminence," Gaston said.

"I shall pass for the moment and take another card," he said, flicking the four out of his hand with a negligent gesture.

"Not riding full tilt in to the action on this round, Your Eminence?" Gaston asked, an eyebrow raised as he dealt the card. "I seem to recall Your Eminence acquired some fame for that in your youth. In Italy."

"There is a right time and a wrong time to risk all, monsieur," Mazarin said, checking his card—*Ace of Clubs, yes!*—"as monsieur well knows."

Gaston's face went carefully blank. Mazarin had seen Leon's allusion to Gaston's habit of treason and raised with an allusion to Gaston's incompetence in his treason. The angrier Gaston got, the better, and Gaston was fighting with both hands behind his back in a needling contest. Gaston had a truly remarkable record of stupidity and vice to hint at, whereas Mazarin could sit and listen to allusions to his own personal history all day without being upset. So he was not a natural-born Frenchman? As well insult him over the size of his shoes.

It was a fact about him, nothing more. Reminding Gaston
he was a known traitor when Spain was massing its
armies to the south, that would *sting*. Nor would anyone
be much surprised if Gaston transpired to have some
role to play in Spain's plans.

"Is it favorable?" Her Majesty asked.

"Very much so," Mazarin said, turning in his seat to
address her, which was permissible now that she herself
was seated. "The game is convivial and the company has
become so."

The queen's dimples deepened as she suppressed a
laugh. She had a wicked and impious sense of humor
among her confidants, and jokes with a sting of sarcasm
always pleased her. Clearly she could sit and listen to
Gaston being the butt of humorous sallies all night long.
"I hope the company brings you luck?" she said, and her
expression added a new layer of meaning to the simple
remark. "His Eminence Cardinal Richelieu suggested I
come to the table in the hope of bringing you luck."

Mazarin frankly grinned. It was a terrible quirk of fate
that had left this woman married to a man with King
Louis' . . . proclivities. "I am sure Monsieur Gaston will
not insult Your Majesty by trying to deal me another
queen."

There was a slight intake of breath around the table
at that. Never mind that he had given Gaston his back,
however obliquely and however permissible it was when
the queen was the object of his attentions, he had made
sure his remark was loud enough that everyone heard
him publicly suggest he was planning *lese-majesté* and
cheating at cards. Mazarin excused himself from the
queen and turned back to the table to see that Gaston's

face was perfectly still, two of the disposable nobles were growing red-faced on his behalf while the other two were as closed-faced as their patron and Leon was visibly trying to control a smirk. "Where is the action?" he asked brightly, "Please excuse my inattention, but a royal lady comes before the ladies of the cards."

"Quite," Gaston said, "it is with my lord Bouthillier de Chavigny—"

"Your pardon, Monsieur," Leon said, "I will vie for supremo, four hundred ecus." Clearly the disposables had all passed. Leon took his compulsory draw, one card only, doing nothing to give the lie to his claim.

A bold bid, Mazarin thought, *I wonder if he's really holding one*. He'd never actually seen Leon play primero, only poker, and so had no idea if he was as bullish at the old game as he was at the new. There was one way to find out, and hopefully Leon was not going to be mulish about getting his stake back if he was good enough to run the betting up as high as he hoped it would get.

Gaston played right to form. "Supremo," he said, "I see your four hundred and re-vie one thousand." That provoked intakes of breath from those present.

Mazarin thought briefly about which of his tells to use, and settled on smiling faintly. "I shall see the fourteen hundred on the table and vie for fluxus, forty." He stared right into Gaston's eyes as he pushed a stack of ecus forward. Gaston stared right back.

"I do believe you are showing off for me, Your Eminence," the queen whispered, her lips thrillingly close to his ear.

He leaned back over his shoulder. "If a gentleman cannot show off in front of a queen, he cannot show off in front of any lady."

She sat back, and from the whispers and giggles it sounded as if the remark was being passed around the ladies.

The first three disposables folded, having passed already. Even half their stakes were a nice addition to the pot, though. The fourth exercised his privilege of passing once after the vie, and took another card. There was a possibility the fellow had a good hand building but he had none of the tells of a good hand or even a solid bluff.

Leon was grinning. Either he had a flux of his own—about one in four of the compulsory draws on a supremo bid would bust the hand with a fluxus—making Mazarin's bid a godsend, or he was simply enjoying the spectacle of Gaston's stony-faced anger. So—"I shall see that fluxus bid and re-vie for a fluxus of forty-five. A raise of a thousand ecu of my own." Leon was not far short of all-in with that. And, clearly, simply raising the temperature. If he was holding a busted supremo the least he would have would be a fluxus and sixty-five, and a genuine play to win would start just short of that. He was leaving the bid where he could be certain Mazarin could raise it to something he could make. *Well done, Leon*, Mazarin thought. Richelieu had selected a good man for the work he did.

Gaston was silent when the action passed to him. Silent for a long, long moment. He could assume that Mazarin and Bouthillier were bluffing, which was all well and good and he could simply stand with his supremo bid, or he could vie with another fluxus and see if he could call their bluff. He could raise a little and see if he could break their collective nerve, or he could raise a lot and simply dump the pot with a bid that no one could make, hoping to take it in the next hand. Or he could take the sensible move and see the bet, draw in the hope he could bust the supremo he was blatantly holding, and pray the one remaining interchangeable vicomte de wherever was sensible enough to make the right bid depending on what Mazarin did. "I shall see these bets, and draw one card," Gaston said, at length. In truth, it was all he could do. Anything else was either outright cowardice or likely to result in him losing.

Mazarin smiled serenely. "Fluxus, fifty, and a raise of another thousand." He stole a glance at Leon, who was grinning broadly. It would be interesting to see if Leon stayed in at this point.

The one disposable who had stayed in saw the bet, raised to fluxus fifty-one and another hundred ecus. He drew a card and was clearly trying to stay in long enough to build the hand; if he stayed in two rounds of betting the odds shifted in his favor. Mazarin wondered if the man felt foolish making raises of a hundred ecus in a game where at least two of the other players had three months' income staked on a single hand. Certainly his fellow hangers-on were giving him pitying looks, they having had the sense to get out of the way once it became obvious that this was a grudge match.

"I'll have fluxus, fifty-two," Leon said, covering the bet. "Will the table indulge me with a note of hand for the raise?" With the bet covered, he had only a few dozen ecu in front of him.

"I'll stand for it," came Abel Servien's booming voice.

Mazarin jumped slightly. Servien was a big man, a loud man, and ought not to be able to move that quietly, he reflected. Still, the man was a dedicated huntsman, or had been in his youth, and so ought to have *some* skill in the stalk. And if the whispering hangers-on around the room had done their job correctly he'd have heard there was a kill to be in at.

Servien's intervention left Gaston with no choice. He might legitimately express concern for the comte de Chavigny's finances if his son Leon was writing notes on his allowance, but he could not publicly insult the marquis de Sable who had plenty of hunting estates to back his note. "Certainly, if my lord the marquis is guarantor. How much was monsieur proposing to raise?"

"Five thousand," Leon said, grinning broadly as a footman set a small writing desk in front of him and he scratched a note for the sum.

The vicomte de whoever dropped his cards with an expression of disgust on his face. There was no way he could stay in and cover that long enough to make his flux, clearly, and was going to have to fold when the action came back to him.

Gaston's face was pale. A whispered exchange with a manservant brought him more money to the table, and he saw the bet without comment. Tellingly, he drew another card. Mazarin watched him intently. Was he relieved? Terrified? Even for such as Gaston, this was insane betting.

"I am afraid to say that the best I can do is go all-in," Mazarin said, beaming cheerfully back at Leon, as he pushed his ecus forward "unless the table will indulge me as it has M. Bouthillier?"

"Only fair," Servien barked, looking steadily at Gaston the while.

Gaston waved his assent, wordlessly. Fortunately, the footman had not gone far with the writing set.

Gaston looked pleadingly at the last of his cronies. If the fellow would stay in, there was a chance of keeping the play going long enough for him to build a flux while the two maniacs from Richelieu's party raised the stakes through the roof. Shaking his head regretfully, the fellow folded.

"Then," Leon said, relish in his voice, "it is time to see whether I or His Eminence has the better flux, not so? Or whether Monsieur Gaston is able to surprise us both?"

Mazarin smiled back. "Can you beat a fifty-seven with that flux that made you grin so widely?" he said, laying his cards down.

"Alas, no," Leon said, "I had fifty-six. The supremo bid was the bluff, and I did not make it."

Gaston tossed his supremo in with a noise of disgust. "I grow weary," he said, "and shall retire." Without saying more he gave everyone, including the queen, his back and left. His cronies followed him in short order.

With them out of the room, Servien leaned on the back of Leon's chair, his eyes screwed up and shaking in silent mirth.

Leon leaned over the table. "My note, Your Eminence," he said, proffering the thing while the footman raked Mazarin's winnings over to him. Leon was grinning awfully broadly for a man who was handing over that much money.

"Really, Leon, that isn't necessary," Mazarin protested. They had, between them, stung Gaston and his cronies for better than twenty thousand on one hand, "I was morally all-in on that last, and you have the second hand. Keep it as your share."

"A noble gesture," Servien said, aloud. "Keep it as a souvenir, young Leon."

"As the marquis says," Leon demurred, accepting the face-saving formula to avoid having to redeem his note in cash.

Mazarin turned to Her Majesty, who was smiling broadly, her eyes glinting. "Your Majesty brought me luck tonight," he said. "Allow me to share it with the royal lady who brought me the boon." He grabbed a double handful of coins, worth a couple of thousand at a guess since most of the coins were livres tournois, and offered them. He was flushed with the win, and it simply seemed—right.

"Handsomely done, Your Eminence," she said, "But your winning hand—I see a king and a knave. You did not play a queen?" Her smile turned impish.

"The night is yet young, Your Majesty."

A Trip to Amsterdam

Gorg Huff and Paula Goodlett

When the news that Haarlem had fallen and Amsterdam would be under siege inside a week reached Henry Dreeson, the first thing he did was insist that the news not be leaked for as long as possible. The second thing he did was call in Horace Bolender of the Department of Economic Resources, Treasury Secretary Tony Adducci and Coleman Walker at the Fed to ask them what they thought the effect would be.

"The guilder will go through the floor," Tony answered. "The dollar will go through the roof. Remember the bubble in February? Well, this will be worse. We could hit a dollar per guilder. If that happens, we can just kiss the boom goodbye, because no one in Germany will have enough money to buy anything we sell."

"So we put more dollars out," Horace said. "Besides, the dollar rising isn't all bad. Imports would be a lot cheaper that way."

"Until something happens to threaten the faith the down-time Germans have in the miraculous American dollar," Coleman answered, coming to his feet. "Damn it, Horace, we have to have at least something approaching enough product to support the dollar or we're just another corrupt principality minting money to pay our debts. The Germans aren't dumb, for God's sake. They give us some trust because of the Ring of Fire, but that trust won't last through even slight inflation of the dollar. You can measure the amount of silver in a German coin, but you can't measure faith. It's either there or it ain't."

"All right, Coleman," Dreeson said, trying to calm everyone. "We'll get though this. What do we need to keep the worst from happening?"

"Someone is going to have to buy guilders, a whole lot of guilders. It will have to be enough guilders to keep the price up, and it can't be the bank that does it," Coleman answered, falling back into his chair. "Under these circumstances, if the bank started buying them, people would assume that we're trying to hold the price up and the selling frenzy would just increase. People would be afraid they would still have guilders when I put on the brakes and let the guilder fall. They'd be right, too. We can't buy all the guilders in Grantville and we certainly can't buy all the guilders in Germany. It has to be someone, preferably several people, we can trust.

They have to have the money, and they need to be people known for doing well. Other people need to believe that they're buying guilders because they believe that the guilder will come back."

"Fine," Henry answered. "Who do you think it should be?"

"I can think of maybe fifty people that either have enough money or have control of enough money. Unfortunately, I don't trust most of them."

Horace snorted at that. It was a well known fact that Coleman Walker didn't trust anyone.

"Get David Bartley to do it," Tony suggested. "Sarah Wendell would work too, 'cept her dad works for us. The down-timers think the Sewing Circle have some sort of a magic touch."

"He won't do it," Coleman said. "The Bartley boy refused to use OPM funds to bail out his grandma and every one knows it. There is no way he would use OPM funds for this. It's too risky. I can't fault his fiduciary responsibility, but in this case it makes him useless."

"What about having him use our money?" Henry asked.

"Maybe, but if we do that, the Fed will probably take a loss this year," Coleman answered. "Can the government afford the loss of thirty million or more dollars? For this? Especially considering that it may not work."

Henry Dreeson was silent for almost a minute. Then he said, "I'll set it up. Expect a call this evening with the details."

The guilder was falling from the opening bell. That was expected but it was falling a bit faster than it should have. David wondered if the news had leaked to certain people ahead of time. He spent the morning watching the market, doing school assignments at a table near the trading floor, and quietly drinking cocoa. He hadn't developed a taste for coffee. When the guilder hit $45, he would start buying. He had to wait to make it look like he was buying guilders because he wanted them, not because he was trying to save them. He had to sell people on the idea that guilders were still worth something.

The news hit the floor around noon. Amsterdam was either under siege now, or would be within days. The evidence was fairly good that, at least for the present, Amsterdam was unlikely to be taken. On the other hand, who would have believed a month ago that the Dutch fleet would be routed and mostly destroyed? The money on deposit in the Wisselbank was safe, for the moment, but how long would it remain safe?

The guilder started to drop faster. Just a little at first, as the news filtered onto the floor. Then, it really started to fall. $53 to the guilder was not followed by $52.90 but by $52.00. Next, the price was $50 to the guilder.

Then a surprising thing happened. Prince Karl Eusebius von Liechtenstein started buying guilders. True, he was buying them with Ferdinand's new silver-backed bank notes, but considering that Amsterdam was under siege, those notes were starting to look like a good deal to a lot of people.

The price of the guilders started to drop a little slower and, oddly enough, the Holy Roman notes started to rise a bit. There was something the notes could buy outside of the Holy Roman Empire, after all. This would have been fine with David, except that the guilder was still dropping against the dollar.

When the guilder hit $45, David stood up. Over the last couple of years David Bartley had gone from short and skinny to tall and skinny. His new height made him noticeable, but he still felt like he looked like a geek. Here in this room, though, people were judged by their bank balances more than by anything else. Here, David Bartley was imposing.

Trading continued. The guilder continued to drop, but people were watching him. He could see and feel it. As he stepped to the floor he made a "come here" gesture. The gesture meant "I'm buying at the last offer." The last offer had been $39 to the guilder. David was mobbed, but he kept making the gesture.

For almost an hour people sold guilders and he and Karl bought them. The price hit $37.50 to the guilder. Finally, slowly, people began to hesitate.

Why were they buying? What did they know? David could hear the murmurs. The price was holding.

David made a bid on some of the Wisselbank notes that Karl had bought, but he shook his head. David was buying, but Karl wasn't selling. Some of the players noticed. The price of guilders started to rise. David kept buying, so did Karl.

David Bartley spent twenty-seven million dollars in the space of about two hours. It was twenty-seven million dollars that wasn't his, but very few people knew that. Still, the guilder closed at $47.50 to the dollar. Smiling like he knew something no one else knew, David went back to his table and finished his cocoa.

Karl walked over to David and asked, "I know why I was buying, but why were you?"

"Maybe we ought to have a talk," said David, and led Karl to the room Sarah was using to watch the show. They had not wanted people to think that the government was exerting influence through Sarah's parents. From the prince's expression, keeping Sarah out of sight had been the right move.

Sarah grinned like a Cheshire cat when she noticed his expression. "No, you've read it at least partially wrong," she said. "Neither I nor my parents attempted to exert any influence on David. It wouldn't have worked anyway. You've forgotten that I am the CFO of OPM. While we do want to avoid the collapse of the guilder, David wouldn't have put OPM resources into it unless it was a good risk."

"So what do you know? What makes it a good risk?"

"We're gambling," David answered. "Did you know that Brent Partow is a student of military history, and his brother Caleb even more of one?" This was a total bluff. Brent Partow had been interested in all things military for about a month after the Ring of Fire. David had no real idea how deep Brent's older brother's interest went.

"You don't think Don Fernando can take Amsterdam, do you?"

"No, we don't. If he takes Amsterdam at all, it certainly won't happen very quickly. Unfortunately, that may not matter that much. The issue with the bank money is going to be availability, not silver, which will hurt you as much as us." David had dealt with Prince Karl before and knew that the prince was bright, capable and conscientious, but he had a weakness, one that David was prepared to use. Karl believed in taking care of number one, and he preferred to assume everyone else felt the same way. David was pretty sure that Karl wasn't truly incapable of non-self-centered acts, but his bias did color his vision a bit.

"So, I ask again, why?" Karl wasn't thrown off that easily.

Sarah came to the rescue. "Why did you? If Don Fernando doesn't win quickly, you're looking at having that money tied up in Amsterdam behind siege lines. That's going to make it rather harder to get to than the HRE gilders you traded for them. Unless something is done, they are going to lose more and more value. The trade through Amsterdam will die. It will take years to grow back elsewhere. Why did you buy guilders?"

Karl discovered suddenly that he was sitting in one of the chairs in the conference room. He must have sat down, he was clearly seated. He just didn't remember moving. He had had several reasons for buying guilders. First, he figured that with his connections, they were worth more to him than to a German merchant. He had also wanted to bring up the price of the Holy Roman Empire guilder in the Grantville market, largely because that's what much of his money was. He had some financial obligations that were best handled in bank money, or would have been, before the siege.

The real reason, though, was that he had seen a bargain and gotten carried away. He had been buying, David started buying and, well, face it . . . he had been caught up in the moment. He didn't really need that much bank money. At this point, that didn't matter much. If he, or David, started selling, the guilder would collapse in the Grantville market. Karl was so stunned that he didn't notice that David never answered his question.

"Well, it's stopped for now, Tony," Coleman Walker said on the phone that night to Tony Adducci.

"You think it will hold?"

"I'm not sure. The way I heard it, David Bartley and that prince from the HRE were cooperating to corner the market in Dutch guilders. I'm starting to wonder if we got took."

"The way I got it from Fletcher Wendell is that Prince Karl was trying to get Wisselbank notes because he figured that Don Fernando would honor them for him even if he wouldn't for a bunch of Dutch merchants. He is an allied prince, after all, or at least his uncles are. David saw an opportunity to make it look like they were trying to sew up the market and took it," Tony defended David. "So how much is the bank out?"

"Nothing yet," Tony could hear the dissatisfaction in Coleman's voice. "The Bartley boy pointed out that if he just acted as an agent for the bank there would be another run as soon as the word got out. To make it work, the guilders would have to appear on the OPM books. So he proposed that we give OPM a low interest loan and a guarantee to buy the guilders at cost. He got Franz Kunze to go along with it. We probably should have gone to Herr Kunze in the first place. Anyway, for now, OPM is sitting on the guilders and the bank is just showing a loan. We won't have a loss on the books till the loan comes due and we have to take Amsterdam's waste paper at cost."

"That's great, isn't it? From what I hear, Frederik Hendrik figures that he can hold. We may come out of this all right."

"Maybe, but the longer the siege goes on the worse it's going to get."

Tony was convinced that Coleman Walker made pessimism into an art form. "The dollar has been going up against the guilder right along. By the time the siege is over, confidence in the guilder could be so low that they won't be worth what the Bartley boy paid for them during today's panic. The only way that we could prevent that from happening would be to increase the number of American dollars. We could probably manage that, but while the dollar has deflated over the last two years there has been inflation in German currencies to compensate."

"You've mentioned that before, Coleman," Tony Adducci agreed, while thinking *Over and over again, you've mentioned it.*

"Why would the up-timers want to save the guilder? It makes no sense. If the guilder collapses their American dollars will be worth more and they will be richer," Josef Gandelmo, Prince Karl's tutor, wondered aloud later that evening. A little more than a year earlier, Karl had called Richelieu a dotard in this room. Josef looked at financial matters in terms of what they accomplished. What David had done was stop the Dutch guilder from collapsing. To Josef, that probably meant that David had *meant* to prevent the Dutch guilder from collapsing. The question

became: why a strong guilder? It seemed to him to be
to the up-timers' disadvantage.

"It does make sense in a way, Josef. Remember the
lecture series we attended. One was about exchange
rates. Having an overpriced currency can price you out
of the export market. High value money makes import
cheaper but export more difficult. If most of your spending is local, you want a low value currency because the
people you buying from are using the same money, so
the lower the value of your money, the less you're paying.

"If you're buying more stuff from far away, then you
want a high value so that less of your money buys more
of theirs. The up-timers have been running a trade sur-
plus since the day they arrived. They apparently wish to
keep doing so. Wait . . . " Karl had apparently just realized what Josef was getting at. "Do you think that David
was trying to prop up the Dutch guilder?"

"It seems so. He certainly, with your help, managed
to do so," Josef offered. "Now you've provided a reason
for it."

"No. If he had gotten a personal loan, then that would
be a possibility, but to use OPM funds? I don't think
so." Karl shook his head. "Some of the up-timers are
fanatical about their reputations, you know, and David
more than most. Fiduciary responsibility and all that,
they take it very seriously. If David used OPM funds to
save the guilder at the expense of the fund stockholders,
it would destroy his reputation." Karl paused in thought.
"Could he have some arrangement that protected the
stockholders?"

"That's possible. If he does, then we should not bandy
it about. OPM has a bit over half a million Dutch guilders. As of now, Your Highness, we have more invested

in saving the Dutch guilder than OPM does. Almost twice as much."

Karl and Josef paused to listen to the evening news on the up-time radio. Radio, in Karl's opinion, was a marvelous thing, as important to him as indoor plumbing, frankly. The nightly news program helped him project what might or might not happen in the surrounding area, keep up with events, and determine where to place his investments. He was shocked, though, to hear his own name mentioned.

"This is Hans Günter, reporting for Voice of America. Today was an interesting day in the money market here in Grantville. With the siege closing in around Amsterdam, the famed bank money of Amsterdam started what at first appeared to be a fatal plunge. Then Prince Karl Eusebius von Liechtenstein and Master David Bartley unaccountably began buying. The Wisselbank money finished the day at an impressive $47.50 to the dollar. The market is asking itself: what do these two young men know? We have with us tonight Karl Gottlieb, of the *Street*.

"Karl is an expert in the histories and psychology of the financial movers and shakers who affect the market. Karl, just how much of a surprise was today's play by these two relatively young men?"

"Very," the financial expert answered. "Neither one of them has a reputation for this sort of risk taking, though for very different reasons . . . "

Karl was a bit miffed to hear this Gottlieb person discuss his motivations for all to hear. Publicity was rapidly becoming extremely distasteful to him. Private business shouldn't be dispersed over the airways for anyone to hear, in his opinion.

The news program, had he only known, went farther and faster than he expected. It was heard in cities and hamlets within a footprint of over thirty thousand square miles. The effect of the interview was to prop up the bank money of Amsterdam throughout the CPE, an effect he was grateful for over the coming weeks.

Franz Kunze, director of OPM, first suggested it in the Exchange Coffee Shop. "Perhaps a visit to the cardinal-infante might help. Don Fernando seems to be dealing with his conquered territory gently." Quite a number of financial movers and shakers found the Exchange Coffee Shop to be a convenient place to grab a quick bite to eat. It was often full of people who played the markets and seemed to be becoming an adjunct to the stock exchange.

"That's a possibility. What should we ask of him though?" Prince Karl asked.

"Perhaps a public statement that he won't loot the Wisselbank," suggested Sarah Wendell.

"Do you think he would actually agree to something like that?" Kaspar Heesters asked, caught between hope and doubt. His father was in Amsterdam. Herr David Heesters had apparently had an opportunity to get out of the city. Kaspar had chosen to stay in order to watch over the family's business interests there.

"It's possible," Don Alfredo de Aguilera said. "He's not obligated to, you understand. Wisselbank silver would clearly be the just spoils of war and the campaign has to be stretching his finances to the limit. He might do it though, if given adequate reason."

"To keep every market in Europe from collapsing! To keep millions of people from losing everything, that's a reason," Kaspar replied, exaggerating more than a little. "You know as well as I do what will happen if the Wissel-bank is looted by Don Fernando and the Dutch guilder is rendered valueless."

"Don't overstate the case," Don Alfredo corrected, waving to the waiter for another cup of coffee. "The economy of Europe is not dependent on the Dutch guil-der. At most there will be a minor correction in the money markets. Some will lose, some will gain." Don Alfredo was understating the case just as much as Kaspar had overstated it.

"Don't make light of either," Prince Karl said in turn. "Yes, the markets will correct themselves but not that quickly and not without damage."

David considered the suggestions for a moment. "I think Herr Kunze and Sarah have come up with an excel-lent approach. We go see Don Fernando and explain what the consequences of his looting the bank would be and ask for his public assurance that he won't. How would we arrange a visit?"

"However we arrange it, David," Karl Schmidt, his stepfather, interrupted. "You won't be going. Amsterdam is still a war zone. I doubt Delia would agree and I know your mother wouldn't. I prefer a reasonable amount of peace and quiet in my household. Besides, if you plan on graduating with your class there is only so much school you can afford to miss."

David got a stubborn look on his face. "Karl, I decided to invest in the guilders. I'm obligated to see it through. And I'm far enough ahead that a couple of months away wouldn't hurt me at school. If anyone goes, I'm going."

Don Alfredo accepted a glass of wine from one of the von Liechtenstein servants. "I do not know if it will help or not. But, I think we must try to speak to him," Don Alfredo finally agreed. "A delegation, do you think? You, me, some of the others, Franz Kunze, particularly, I think."

Prince Karl nodded in agreement, pleased by this development. It had taken some days to get Don Alfredo on board. "Yes. I also believe we must. David will be coming, you know. Having invested OPM's money, he will insist on it. We need an adult up-timer, though."

"Why?" Don Alfredo asked. "Are we not men of substance ourselves? Up-timers are not the only people of knowledge in the world."

"To look after David." Karl grinned. "Sarah Wendell suggested it. No, Alfredo, I am not seriously suggesting we take along a nanny for David Bartley or that we lack substance. Still an up-timer will add weight to our arguments and answer technical points that are still new to us."

For the second time in less than three years Mike Stearns was busy forging a new government out of bits and pieces of whatever he could find. This time it was in Magdeburg. He had more pieces now, but it was a bigger government. "What is it now, Francisco?" he asked, with a tired-sounding sigh.

"Apparently Horace Bolender wants to send Fletcher Wendell to Amsterdam. A bunch of merchants want to have a little chat with the cardinal-infante and they want him to go along. Prince Karl Eusebius thinks Fletcher, with his knowledge of the way economies work, will be a good addition to their delegation."

"Why do a bunch of merchants want to talk to Don Fernando?" Mike asked. "What good will that do?"

"There was an aborted panic about the Dutch guilder when the siege of Amsterdam was closing in, Mike," Don Francisco explained. "It seems like these people think they can talk the cardinal-infante out of looting the Wisselbank. They think, and I stress think, that if he promises not to loot the bank it will help keep the economy stable. Anyway, Horace has Tony and Coleman signing off on the request. It seems Mr. Wendell is fairly good at economic theory and making it understandable to others."

Normally, Mike would have paid a bit more attention to such a plan. Now however, he was in the process of forcing the USE down the throats of a whole bunch of nobles. Most of these nobles wouldn't have agreed to the measures Gustav had planned for the CPE two weeks earlier, much less the program Mike had in mind.

The relatively minor matter of several merchants going to have a chat with Don Fernando of Spain was given about five minutes of his time. Then, he turned the matter over to Francisco Nasi.

"Fine, if Fletcher's willing to go and you think it's wise. Make sure they don't do anything to upset Rebecca's apple cart, Francisco. Very sure! Oh, and try to keep them from getting themselves killed."

Francisco Nasi was rather busy himself these days. Still, he was a bit more involved with the markets in Grantville than Mike was. For now he tentatively approved the plan. He would leave whether Fletcher Wendell went up to Mr. Wendell. If Fletcher did decide to go, Francisco would have a chat with him when they came through Magdeburg on their way to Amsterdam. He sent a message to that effect and turned his attention to the many other matters he was concerned with. One of those concerns was to send notification to the Amsterdam diplomatic mission, and prepare Rebecca Stearns for the arrival of the trade delegation.

In the Wendell kitchen, back in Grantville, the trip was of more immediate concern. "Judy, I really think I ought to go." Fletcher went to give her a hug. "I don't think I'll be gone more than a couple of months at the most."

"I wish I could go," Sarah muttered, flopping down into her favorite chair. "It was my idea, partly, anyway."

"I know the school is being fairly understanding about absences due to work, Sarah," Fletcher responded. "But your education is more important, as far as I'm concerned. David's going, that's all the teenager I want to have to deal with."

"Sarah, you'll get your chance to travel," Judy the Elder noted. "Just not right now. It's bad enough that your dad is going. Yes, Fletcher, I know you need to do it. I'm not that crazy about it, considering you're going to be traveling through a war zone, but I understand. Just try not to get hurt."

Fletcher circled Judy the Elder with his arms and placed a kiss on her cheek. "Have I ever mentioned what a good little wife you are?"

Fletcher hadn't thought it out. He'd hugged Judy from behind. Her elbow met his midriff with some force. "Omff."

Judy the Elder turned around and frowned at him. "Don't get any ideas, buster. I'm not that happy about being left to deal with two girls on my own. Still, I understand. If you can keep the European economy stable, well, you need to."

Outside Amsterdam, in Vredenhof, the villa Don Fernando was using for a headquarters, Miguel de Manrique held up a sheet of paper. "I have an interesting letter here, Your Highness."

"Yes?"

"It's from Prince Karl Eusebius von Liechtenstein and a group of merchants. They would like to visit to discuss the economic effects of the siege. They request 'a little of your time if it would be convenient.' A Spaniard, Don Alfredo de Aguilera, will be coming, too, as well as several German merchants of generally good reputations and large purses, and an up-timer financial expert."

"Well, merchants generally show up at a siege. This is a rather unusual group, though. What do we know about the prince and the up-timer?"

"I'll find out."

Some days later Miguel had an answer. "Your Highness," Miguel spoke quietly, "I have that report you asked for."

Don Fernando looked up with a sigh, "Which report, Miguel? I seem to fill my days with one report after another. Please tell me this one is at least amusing."

Miguel shrugged. "Not amusing, then, Miguel?" Don Fernando asked. "What is it then? More supply problems? The fleet wants to move a few more miles out to sea just to be safe? The Inquisition has gone on a rampage?"

"I doubt the inquisitors would dare, Your Highness. I believe we were fairly firm with them. No, this is about the people who want to visit you, Prince von Liechtenstein and his party of merchants."

"Ah, yes . . . that report. I don't suppose the up-timers are here to sell me a marvelous siege engine, one that will reduce Amsterdam's walls to gravel?"

"Not at this time, I fear. I have quite a bit of information, though. One visitor is the 'chairman of the board of directors' of a very wealthy entity called 'Other People's Money.' It is a mutual fund, I'm told. Another is called a 'financial expert' from up-time. I have a prospectus here, and an annual report from this OPM, as well." Miguel passed the papers over to Don Fernando and waited patiently as the prince read through them.

"Is this true, Miguel? Does this OPM truly have this kind of money?"

"Of that, I am not sure, Your Highness. It will take some time to confirm. I do have some information on Prince Karl, also. It seems that his father was in business with the traitor, Wallenstein, a number of years ago. A bit later in their lives, he tried to have Wallenstein executed for treason, which, you must admit, is fairly standard for Ferdinand's court. A very wealthy young man, and, unlike his uncles, Gundaker and Maximilian, who support His Majesty, Ferdinand II, it appears that young Karl is making certain overtures to Wallenstein."

"Yet another traitor, Miguel?"

Miguel shifted a bit uncomfortably. "His lands, many of them, are now in the territory claimed by Wallenstein. I'm forced to admit, were I in his position, I might have to do the same."

"All right, set up a meeting. It might prove to be amusing after all."

They had arrived at the siege of Amsterdam almost a week before. Now they were seated around a large table in the dining room of the estate Don Fernando was using as his headquarters. It was the third day of talks between Don Fernando and the Grantville merchants. The group had made their request and Don Fernando had agreed to it without hesitation. However, simply assuring the world that he would not loot the Wisselbank didn't strike him as all that good a solution. He wanted more information on effects of the siege. Now, finally, they were getting down to the reasons the merchants felt this action had been necessary.

"If the Dutch guilder disappears or is drastically devalued, more money must be introduced into the economies of the nations that that use the guilder as currency for large-scale transactions," Fletcher Wendell explained. He knew he was being too technical, but he didn't want to sound like he was talking down to Don Fernando. "In the United States of Europe, the guilder represents a small but significant percentage of the money supply because of its consistent value. New United States dollars were initially set at a price in guilders. After their intro-duction, the dollars have been allowed to float, but we still use the guilder as the primary currency they are compared to. The sudden . . . "

"I am interested in how your American money works," Don Fernando interrupted. "This dollar, it is not backed by anything, no gold, no silver. You seem to print it at need. Yet, from what I'm told, it is generally accepted in the German states. Why?"

"The dollar is backed by the full faith and credit of the New United States, Your Highness," Fletcher said, "And we don't print it as we need it. We print just enough to keep the economy running."

" 'Full faith and credit'? Those are just words. Why could I not start printing money?" Don Fernando demanded.

It was immediately apparent to Don Fernando that he had said something silly or perhaps offensive. The clear desire of everyone in the room was to have someone else explain his gaffe to him, just so they wouldn't have to. People were looking at one another with that "you tell him" look that he had occasionally seen in his tutors when he brought up an indelicate subject. "Prince Karl, it appears I am in need of correction and my other guests are not anxious to provide it. Would you kindly explain?"

"Ah, it is a somewhat delicate subject, Your Highness. Forgive me, please, for being blunt. The question becomes 'whose words can be believed'? The Spanish crown has found it necessary some three times in the last century to default on its loans. That experience has . . . ah, weakened the faith placed in the Spanish crown and somewhat limited its credit."

Don Fernando nearly asked what printing money had to do with getting credit, but the up-timer, Fletcher Wendell, stepped in. "At heart, at the most basic level, money is a loan. It's a loan from the people who use the money. The same things that cause a government to default on a loan cause them to inflate the currency. If a country defaults on a loan, people lose faith in that currency."

Don Fernando looked at Karl and Fletcher, somewhat startled. The prince had indeed been blunt. On the other hand, Don Fernando had not himself been involved in those defaults, so was prepared to listen. "Very well, you have explained why I can't but not why the up-timers can. Why can they print money and have it accepted?"

"Not once in the history of the United States has it ever defaulted on a loan. Not once. Not back in the up-time U.S., and not here in the down-time," Fletcher answered. "Not through revolution, economic boom or bust, wars and world wars, and not even now, after having a small part of the nation transported through time to the middle of a war."

"More than that," Karl added, "you can't look at the cliffs left by the Ring of Fire and not know that it must be the work of God. That gives the up-timers, ah, well, a certain amount of credence to start with. They arrived with good references." He held up his hand when it looked like Don Fernando was about to explain why the origins of the Ring of Fire didn't matter.

"I am no theologian, and I make no pretense of knowing God's intent in placing them amongst us. Still, after seeing the Ring Wall, as it's called, the question isn't why should we trust them, but why shouldn't we. So far they have not given anyone reason to doubt the value of their currency. Nor do I think it likely that they will."

"Yet, what you ask me for is simply my public word, my word, that I will not loot the Wisselbank. I won't break my word if I give it, but why do you believe that I won't?"

"The guilder has not collapsed, not yet," Franz Kunze answered. "It's fallen but not collapsed. How far it falls depends in part on how likely most observers think you are to actually take Amsterdam. If you give your public word not to loot the Wisselbank, that is one more bit of assurance that the money is safe, still good. Some people will trust the guilder because they don't think you'll take Amsterdam. Others will trust the guilder because you have given your word and they believe it. Some of the trust will be partly for one reason and partly for the other.

"It really isn't a question of whether we," Franz waved to include the delegation in his statement and continued, "trust you. It's a question of whether merchants all over Europe trust you. To be quite blunt, some will and some won't. We are hoping that enough will to restore some of the confidence in the guilder.

"If you, having publicly given your word not to loot the Wisselbank, break your pledge, it will be like Spain has again defaulted on your loans. Quite frankly, if Spain defaults on its loans for a fourth time, it's unlikely, maybe even impossible that it will ever get another one. There are just too many other places for people to put their money; places where they can invest it and watch it grow. They'll put their money in those safer places, places that offer more profit, like Amsterdam was, before the siege. Places like Grantville, Magdeburg or Hamburg."

Don Fernando gazed out over the bay. He had never wanted to be a cardinal. He had certainly never wanted to deal with the sort of religious complications brought up by the Ring of Fire. What did God mean by placing a small piece of a future in the middle of the Germanies? Don Fernando didn't know, and wasn't sure that he wanted to.

It was evening and he was tired after the day's meetings. The sun was setting red across the bay. The sleeping garden was tinted by the evening light. Don Fernando knew what Richelieu claimed was the reason for the Ring of Fire. He also knew why Richelieu had said it. The up-timers, on the other hand, didn't claim to know why the Ring of Fire happened. They said, by their actions and in their words "you must decide for yourself." There were quite a few things the up-timers could have said that would have been greatly to their advantage. They hadn't said those things. *Why not?* Don Fernando wondered.

Miguel de Manrique interrupted his thoughts. "How did your meeting go, Your Highness?"

"I'm honestly not sure, Miguel," Don Fernando said. "We got onto the subject of why the American dollars are accepted in the Germanies. From there we went on to discuss the Ring of Fire and what it means."

"Did the up-timers claim the authority of God then?"

"The up-timers were unwilling to say what the Ring of Fire means. That, in itself, says something about them. How many princes do you know, Miguel, who, having such miraculous origins, would not claim divine authority? Cortez claimed to be a god, but these people don't even claim to speak for Him.

"Prince Karl pointed out that, whatever the good Lord intended, one effect was to at least start the up-timers out with a good reputation. A truly monumental understatement, I suspect. I have been standing here looking out at the sunset wondering what it means." Don Fernando shook himself. "One thing is clear; I am a better soldier than I am a cardinal."

"They are right about one thing, Your Highness," Don Alfredo said. "There will be real consequences to the economies of several states if the Wisselbank is looted." They were in Don Fernando's private study, going over the day's discussions.

"You have used that term, economy, several times. You use it in what seems to me an unusual way. How would gaining the silver in the Wisselbank damage the Spanish crown's household management?"

"It's an up-timer usage of the word, Your Highness. Their idea of the economy is somewhat larger than even the broadest sense we have for that word. To an up-timer, the economy of Spain includes every peasant gathering wood, every merchant, every item he buys or sells, every housewife buying needles, all of it, summed up together. The economy of Spain is a part of the economy of Europe. The Spanish economy affects, and is affected by, the economies of France and the CPE, ah—United States of Europe, as well as by every little state in Italy. They are all interconnected and each one affects all the others, to one degree or another.

"It is the economy of the Netherlands that would be most affected by the looting of the Wisselbank, but it would spread from there to every nation in Europe. Merchants who found some part of their money worthless would no longer be in a position to buy cork or Spanish wool. That inability, in turn, would bring down the price of that wool or cork. Then, if the price is lower, that would decrease the taxes paid to the crown. The point is—it's all interconnected."

"The point is," His Highness, Don Fernando, corrected in a cool voice, "if this siege lasts as long as it looks to, I won't gain a rich province but a broken one. The Netherlands are rich, but from what you and your friends have said, they won't stay that way if trade is interrupted for long. What can be done about that, I wonder? The wealth of Amsterdam is trade and an interruption of that trade could well destroy it.

"When I take Amsterdam I want a city of wealth, a jewel to add to the Spanish crown, not a broken wreck. So tell me, Don Alfredo, with your friends and your uptimer expert, how am I to do that?"

De Aguilera looked at him in shock. "I don't know, Your Highness."

"Well, go find out." Don Fernando waved him out.

◊   ◊   ◊

"Don Fernando wants his omelet without as much as a cracked egg. Now all we need is a transporter to move . . . " Fletcher paused. "Move the bank. For that matter, move as much as we can of the bank's auxiliary institutions to some other city. It would work if we could do it." Fletcher gazed, unseeing, at the lovely wall hangings the room was furnished with.

"I don't see how we can," Franz said. "Why would Frederik Hendrik agree? Or the Amsterdam city council, for that matter. The Wisselbank is a city-owned institution."

"We simply need to find something that they want in exchange," Karl said.

"And what would that be?" Don Alfredo asked. "Remember that it must be something that Don Fernando is willing to give."

"I have no idea," Karl answered. "Perhaps we should ask them? First we will need to get Don Fernando's agreement in principle."

"I think Brussels would be an excellent place for the Wisselbank," Miguel suggested with a sly grin. "It's your capital, after all, and the Wisselbank deserves a prestigious location."

"I quite agree, Miguel. Brussels would be an ideal location." Don Fernando laughed. "But I suspect that Frederik Hendrik will disagree."

"Actually, I tend to agree with Don Miguel's suggestion, Highness, at least as an opening position," Don Alfredo remarked. He was getting almost used to being in the prince's private study. "Start with Brussels, at any rate. He must have some room to negotiate, after all. There will be a problem, though. The Wisselbank managers and the Amsterdam city council, they are the ones that chartered the bank, not Frederik Hendrik or the states general. The managers and the city council will not want the bank moved out of Amsterdam. They will especially not want it put under Spain's control."

"Then you and your friends will have some negotiating to do, will you not?" Don Fernando smiled.

Don Alfredo shrugged with the arrogance of a hidalgo born. "We'll try, Your Highness."

Frederik Hendrik was waiting as Rebecca was ushered into his private chambers. He had heard about the delegation from Grantville. He had been halfway hoping that Don Fernando would clap them in irons and perhaps offend the USE enough to produce a relieving force. Then Rebecca outlined the Spanish prince's proposal. Apparently, it was to be Spanish cleverness, not Spanish arrogance that would rule the day.

"They want me to give the Wisselbank to Don Fernando? That is ridiculous. Besides, I can't do it. The Wisselbank, the Lombard Bank and the exchange are chartered by the city of Amsterdam, not by me."

Rebecca just looked at him. They had gotten to know each other a bit over the last month or so. Rebecca knew full well that the offer wasn't ridiculous, but rather a first offer to begin the bargaining. She knew that he knew it, too. Rebecca also knew that even though the Wisselbank was chartered by the city of Amsterdam, under the current circumstances whatever Frederik Hendrik agreed to was going to happen.

"All right, Rebecca," Frederik muttered unhappily. "So Don Fernando is proving to be clever. I had almost hoped . . . Well, no matter."

"I understand how you feel, but it's still better this way. Just as things are better without another Alva," Rebecca commented. "Now, we must counteroffer, as well you know. What would Don Fernando agree to?"

"He's not getting the Wisselbank in Brussels. I'll not agree to that. Neither will the members of the city council who are still in town. In fact, getting them to agree to move it at all will not be easy. They will have to get something for it, something substantial."

"That seems like a reasonable assumption. I'm sure we can eventually find a compromise," Rebecca agreed.

Rebecca had performed the introductions and Frederik Hendrik had been very gracious, offering everyone a seat in the meeting room and listening carefully to their explanations. Andries Bicker, the representative of the city council, was obviously disturbed. Bicker wanted the bank open, but he wanted it kept in Amsterdam. His attitude came across as a sort of groveling resentment.

"What brings you through a siege to visit Amsterdam?" Frederik Hendrik asked. "I know the outline of what you have done but not really the why of it."

Looks were passed among the group and ended up on Fletcher. "We want the Dutch guilder to survive as a viable currency, especially the bank money. It facilitates trade and allows a fairly constant money for other currencies, including the New U.S. dollar and probably soon the USE dollar, to trade against."

"Why? The failure of the Wisselbank and the loss of bank money would seem to be an advantage to you."

"We want to limit the number of New U.S. dollars to those supported by the product of New U.S. industry. On the other hand, we want enough good dependable money to allow the economy to grow. If we do the first, we can't do the second, not with our own money. So, we suggest that the Wisselbank be moved. Don Fernando offers Brussels as a suitable location."

"Brussels?" Andries Bicker squeaked. "What good does the Wisselbank do Amsterdam in Brussels? Is this the sort of aid you bring us after all the money the citizens of Amsterdam . . ."

"Calmly, Herr Bicker," Frederik Hendrik instructed. He then turned to Fletcher. "I would likely make the same suggestion if I were Don Fernando. If I agree with this, he can sit back, relax and let the besieged city cart all its wealth to his treasury without having to actually take the city to get it. And, at the same time, he would receive the praise of Europe's merchants. At least, they will praise him until his brother needs some extra cash. Then the merchants of Europe may not be so pleased. The Spanish Habsburgs don't have the best reputation where money is concerned, you understand."

"Yes, sir, that is true," Prince Karl agreed. "However, Don Fernando is not his brother."

"He is his brother's subject," Frederik Hendrik insisted. "To place the Wisselbank in his capital is to place the key to the vault in the hands of King Philip of Spain. Olivares will talk Philip into looting the bank because Gaspar Olivares thinks he can restore the glory of Spain if he hires enough mercenaries. I won't put the Wisselbank into Olivares' control, not even indirectly."

"Yet if the Wisselbank remains here it does neither Europe nor your nation any good," Don Alfredo pointed out. "Not unless you are prepared to loot the Wisselbank yourself. What is the benefit to Europe if you do so, rather than His Majesty, the king of Spain?"

"I would pay it back," was Frederik Hendrik's quick response, "assuming it became necessary to use the funds at all."

"Granted," Franz Kunze gave Frederik Hendrik a respectful nod. "Miss Wendell, the daughter of Herr Wendell here," Franz indicated Fletcher, "had the excellent notion of seeing if things could be settled peacefully through negotiations. When we had the notion of moving the bank, Don Fernando offered Brussels as a possible site. I don't expect you to agree to it, nor do I believe that Don Fernando does. It was an opening bid. The question now is: what is your counter offer?"

Frederik Hendrik sat quietly for a moment. "I see," he finally answered. "I must have some time to consider. Perhaps you will attend me tomorrow?"

As the party left his reception room, Frederik Hendrik motioned for Rebecca to stay behind. When he was sure that no one could overhear his remarks, he turned to Rebecca, with a grin on his face. "That went quite well, I think. What do you think, Rebecca?"

"It went moderately well, yes." Rebecca responded with her own grin. "What will you tell them at tomorrow's meeting?"

"The truth, Rebecca. And the truth is that I will not allow the Wisselbank to be moved to Brussels. Whatever they may say, or even believe, that would be too much of a temptation for Philip, and I cannot trust that Don Fernando will not comply with his wishes. I will suggest Groningen, I think. We won't get an agreement for that, and it's a stupid place to put the Wisselbank, anyway. Still it may encourage my young opponent to make a serious offer."

Frederik Hendrik smiled thoughtfully. "It will do us no harm, in the long run, for Don Fernando to realize that his word is not in question. I do not question his word, myself, even. But, as long he is under his brother's orders and cannot guarantee his brother's actions, any agreement we make with him might be overridden."

"Just how good a point does Frederik Hendrik have about King Philip and Olivares?" Fletcher asked Don Alfredo, when the servants had left the room.

Don Alfredo hesitated. "His Majesty came to the throne when he was very young, just sixteen. His advisors felt that at such a young age he was not ready to assume the duties of the king of Spain." Don Alfredo looked around at his companions, but they were nodding in agreement. "Olivares is an honest man and was chosen to run things until the king came of age. Olivares did, in fact, do a great deal to remove corruption from the court.

"However," he continued, "Philip wasn't encouraged to study or prepare to take on his royal duties. Instead, he was encouraged to enjoy the privileges of his birth. His Majesty is now twenty-eight years old, but Olivares is still mostly running things."

"Sounds like what I've heard," Fletcher agreed. "How are relations between Don Fernando and Philip?"

"Not good," Don Alfredo conceded. "Olivares has encouraged, shall we say, a certain, ah . . . distrust. Don Fernando is generally sent to posts as far from Castile as Olivares can manage. Don Fernando and his brother have never been allowed to become close."

"All of which means that Frederik Hendrik has an excellent point," Prince Karl said.

Franz Kunze nodded his agreement. "Olivares will want the silver and not just because it's a lot of money. He will want it because he won't want Don Fernando to have it. For that matter, the credit rating and popularity that Don Fernando will get out of this if everything goes well will likely give Olivares pause. It's likely to become a test of loyalty."

"Test of loyalty?" David asked, confused. "How could it be a test of loyalty?"

"Perhaps, a surety of loyalty," Karl explained. "Try to look at this situation from Philip's point of view, or the point of view of Olivares. Here is Don Fernando, a successful general and competent administrator. Why should he not want the throne? To turn the silver over weakens Don Fernando and strengthens the king. If they demand the silver and Don Fernando refuses them, they will take it to mean that he is no longer loyal. Even if he's loyal at the moment, they will feel that that could change as Don Fernando falls under the influence of others. Olivares, and Phillip, for that matter, will feel that the only sure safety is to keep Don Fernando weak."

Karl grinned as some of the delegation members looked at him in horror. "Actually, no, my family is not like that, not at all. I have seen this, though, in the court of Ferdinand, in Austria. Anyway, Olivares and Phillip will start with the presumption that Don Fernando is disloyal and look at every thing he does in that light. Anything Don Fernando does that makes him stronger or more popular will be seen as a step toward taking the throne. Putting the bank in Brussels is going to make them almost as nervous as it makes Frederik Hendrik. They will feel that they must get the silver out of there—partly to get the silver, true, but to keep Don Fernando weak as well."

The bargaining began in Don Fernando's headquarters. "No. Not Groningen," Don Fernando mused. "That is not acceptable. Perhaps Rotterdam."

In Amsterdam the next day, Frederik Hendrik laughed without merriment. "Rotterdam would be excellent," he agreed, "once I have forced the prince of Spain from my territory, and control my capital again. In the mean time, however, there is still the problem of his older brother. Besides, in the event of a peaceful settlement, having the Wisselbank in Rotterdam would make it rather harder for Don Fernando to return my capital. Not Rotterdam."

Negotiations continued, back and forth for several days.

Karl was beginning to feel like the "rubber ball" in the song he had heard at the coffee shop one day. "Brussels, Groningen, Rotterdam, good grief! Can't these two agree on a location for the Wisselbank?"

"It's not really about the location, and you know it. It's about who controls the location. Neither one wants to cede that control to the other. Do you suppose the two of them would agree to a suggestion from us?" Fletcher asked. "How would they feel about Hamburg? That would be convenient for us, and it would take the bank out of both their territories. I'd like to get home before Christmas, you know. It seems like we've been stuck here forever."

"I don't believe that either one will agree to Hamburg," Karl countered. "And it's nowhere near Christmas. You exaggerate. Still, we can try it. It might even give them the impetus they need to agree on a place."

The Hamburg suggestion received such a resounding *no* from both parties, that Don Alfredo and Karl felt like their ears were ringing. They sat at the table, resting from the ordeal of dealing with two very clever princes, each determined to get the best deal he could.

"See, David, the concept of 'nobility' is not entirely without merit." Karl grinned. "They are both amazingly clever and capable men." The delegation was staying at the inn in Amsterdam that night.

"Philip." David held up one finger. "Charles." He held up another. "Louis." He held up a third.

"I said 'not entirely,'?" Karl muttered.

Fletcher snorted. The on-going discussion, well, friendly argument, over the merits of democracy versus royalty had provided entertainment and some irritation for the rest of the group.

"Okay," Franz mused, bringing everyone back to the point. "What do we have? So far, we've eliminated Brussels, Groningen, Rotterdam, Haarlem and Hamburg. Neither one of them is willing to let loose of the Wisselbank, it seems. What if they split it? Keep part in Amsterdam and part of it in a city controlled by Don Fernando? After the siege is settled, I mean. Until the siege is settled, they'll have to use one of Don Fernando's cities. Frederik Hendrik doesn't have a city that's suitable, and I'm sure he knows it."

Karl and Don Alfredo considered the suggestion for a moment. "That might work," Karl remarked. "It just might. They would both have it that way, at least eventually."

"Wait a minute," David said. "Why wait for the end of the siege to split the bank? What about this . . . the Wisselbank is a full reserve bank, and all the reserves are in one place. About a block and a half over that way." David pointed vaguely, and, Karl noticed with amusement, waved in the wrong direction.

"Suppose the reserves were split now," David continued. "It would remain a full reserve bank. The reserves would simply be split between two locations. Part of the reserves stay in Amsterdam and the rest gets moved to a town controlled by Don Fernando. Say Antwerp. That might solve part of the problem."

"True," Karl said. "If all of the reserve goes to Don Fernando's territory, Philip is going to get greedy and demand the silver. Don Fernando would have to either give him the silver or go into open revolt. If all the reserves stay here, people can't get at their silver. That would cause the guilder to collapse, exactly what we're trying to prevent."

"That's just it," Franz said. "If we only move part of it—if we move, say, a third of the reserve, there will still be two-thirds safe here in Amsterdam. With Don Fernando's promise that he won't loot the Wisselbank if he takes Amsterdam, and Frederik Hendrik's promise that Don Fernando won't take Amsterdam, well, the bank will be protected by two armies for as long as the siege lasts. There will be absolutely no way that Philip can get at the silver that remains in Amsterdam. If he grabs the silver in Don Fernando's territory, he'll hurt himself badly. His reputation will suffer just as much as if he'd grabbed the whole lot, but he'll have a lot less cash to gain."

"In fact," Fletcher added, "if Philip takes the silver in Don Fernando's territory, it's the sort of thing that could push Don Fernando into rebelling. Especially since the whole pile won't be in Philip's hands. The silver that stays in Amsterdam will act as a guarantee of the good faith of Don Fernando and his brother."

"Be careful, gentlemen," Don Alfredo advised. "You're coming perilously close to advocating or accusing or something . . . Well, never mind. But, please, let's keep our speculation to financial matters. For my peace of mind, if for no other reason."

"Certainly," Fletcher agreed and continued. "A chunk of the silver will be in one of Don Fernando's cities and be available for anyone with bank money to withdraw. I think that there should be another part of the agreement, too. There should be an arrangement to move more silver if the Antwerp reserves run low. For that matter, there ought to be an arrangement to shift reserves to Amsterdam if the bank gets a lot of deposits in Antwerp. That would restore most of the confidence in the Dutch guilder, don't you think? The same thing can be done with the lending bank."

"It looks to be the best we can do," Don Alfredo agreed.

Rebecca continued to sit quietly, hands folded in her lap, waiting for Frederik Hendrik to finish thinking. The delegation had made their proposal of a split silver reserve.

Frederik Hendrik looked up, smiling. "I will move the Wisselbank to Antwerp. I'll do it in spite of Herr Gunthor's objections. It is the best choice, given the sureties the merchants suggest. It is a symbolic victory for Don Fernando that doesn't really hurt us, at least not any more than any other city he controls does. Best if I offer it, I think. Your merchants have done a dangerous thing, Rebecca Abrabanel. They have given me a hope to cling to.

"I told you at our first meeting that I would win the siege but lose the war. I wasn't just talking about the war of armies, as you know. Amsterdam can hold out for at least a year. With the warehouses and their contents, we could probably hold out much longer. A year, though, that will be long enough for Don Fernando to see the wisdom of a negotiated settlement. I knew that before the siege closed in. My biggest concern all along has been what would be left of the Dutch Netherlands after the war is over. A siege would not destroy Amsterdam, not really. A year in which all the business that was done in Amsterdam had to be done somewhere else—that would be different. A year in which the bank and the exchange are closed and the merchants have to take their business elsewhere, what effects will that have?

"I'm the leader of a nation of merchants, Rebecca." There was a glistening in Frederik Hendrik's eyes. "Fifty years, at least, is what it would take before Amsterdam recovered, if it ever did. Now, though, if we can reach agreement, it will not be so bad. If the Wisselbank can reopen its doors and the exchange can resume its functions, Amsterdam could recover in a decade, possibly less. For that . . . I'll throw the dice, Rebecca. For that, I will risk it all.

"I will only allow it if I am provided with concessions in return and not all of those concessions will be from Don Fernando. From him, well, raw materials will be running out soon, and a tradesman must have supplies. The tradesmen also need customers. Perhaps Don Fernando would see his way clear to allow the import of certain items.

"I'm sure he won't allow food to be imported, but with the amount of grain that is stored in the city's warehouses, I am not greatly worried about food. Leather, though, leather for the boot makers and saddle makers, perhaps that might be allowed, I hope, as well as a few other requirements."

Rebecca nodded, heart pounding with hope. Maybe the Spanish prince would see reason.

Frederik Hendrik continued. "I will also need some solid assurance that the bank will not be looted. The splitting of the reserves, it will help, but I will need more. So from you, Rebecca, I need your miraculous radio between here and Antwerp, so that the merchants of Amsterdam may keep in contact and arrange deals and do business. The radio, it will also be a way to confirm that any more silver shipped from Amsterdam does indeed represent silver that has been legally withdrawn from the Wisselbank and not a loan coerced by Philip."

Rebecca found herself holding her breath.

"I am serious, Rebecca. I will not let it go, not without this concession." Frederik Hendrik slapped his hand on his thigh for emphasis, the sound causing her to start a bit and begin breathing again. "I will not."

"I shall see what can be arranged," Rebecca agreed. "I cannot make a promise, you understand. There are many things to be considered."

"I understand." Frederik Hendrik nodded. "But I will not allow this move unless I get what I asked for. Without some point of contact with the rest of the world, Amsterdam's business community will die."

Back in the embassy the news was good. "This is *so* not a problem, Rebecca." Jimmy Andersen laughed.

"It really isn't," Jeff agreed. "Radio isn't a secret. Long distance communications without great, big towers is the secret. We can get radio for Amsterdam and Antwerp, no prob."

"Not even," Jimmy enthused. "We'll set up a station here and one in Antwerp. We'll put great, big, hulking cables in both places. It'll be neat."

"A CW link," Jeff added, "forty or so words a minute . . ."

Rebecca felt her eyes begin to glaze over. Techno-geek was a specialized language, one she didn't under-stand. She escaped as quickly as she could, and let Jeff and Jimmy indulge their preference without her presence.

"Antwerp?" Don Fernando asked, as they walked along. "That is surprisingly generous of Frederik Hen-drik. I agree to Antwerp and I appreciate Frederik Hen-drik's offering it. Actually, and just between the two of us, I like the idea of split reserves as well. It has political consequences that could prove useful. Now, about these trading concessions, what does that Dutch merchant want?"

Miguel stifled a guffaw. "Sire, is it really the proper thing to call another prince a merchant? I'm quite sure he would be offended by this." The garden was mostly dormant at this time of year but it was well-arranged. It was a pleasant place to walk and think, even in winter.

"The man deals like a merchant. If he acts like a merchant, I'll call him a merchant. We are not—and you may tell him so—we are absolutely not, going to allow foodstuffs to be transported into the city, if that's what he wants. Nor will we open our lines while he ships in cannon or shot. Gunpowder is out, too."

"He doesn't ask for that, and I don't believe he would think for a moment that you would agree to it, either. However, he does ask that raw materials, like leather for the boot makers, clay for the potters, be allowed through the lines. And he asks that goods, finished goods, be allowed out."

Don Fernando grasped his head between his own hands and pretended to tear his own hair. "Gah! What did I call him? A merchant, wasn't it? This is a military operation, is it not? We are here to take the city, are we not? And yet Frederik Hendrik wants to continue to do business, even through a siege? I am astounded, truly astounded."

Miguel couldn't hold the guffaw back any longer. He broke into laughter, and laughed until the tears ran down his face. Don Fernando, after one amazed look at his usually serious aide, began to laugh also. At first, it was only a small snicker, but it grew and grew, until he, too, was laughing uproariously.

Don Alfredo, who most definitely was a merchant, and quite a good one, waited patiently for the mirth to subside. Eventually, Don Fernando wiped his eyes and calmed down a bit. Still trying to repress more laughter, he said, "Well, Don Alfredo, what do you say to the merchant of Amsterdam's latest proposal?"

"I can't speak to the military effect, Your Highness, but speaking as a merchant, I would think it a very good idea. I will go further, even. What do you want when you have taken Amsterdam? Do you wish a denuded city that will take decades to recover from the siege, like Antwerp? Or would you prefer a prosperous city, one that has not been destroyed?"

"Very well." Don Fernando sighed. "I will allow raw materials through the lines, after the wagons have been thoroughly inspected, and I will allow goods to be exported, as well. However, I will allow export only if my army is allowed to purchase goods as well. After all, equipment does wear out, you know. I, myself, could use a new pair of boots. Why not allow it, after all?"

Don Alfredo looked a bit pained, like he wanted to say something or perhaps use the toilet. "What is it, Don Alfredo? You think I ask too much?"

"You do not ask enough, Your Highness, not nearly enough. Remember . . . taxes. Taxes on everything that goes in," Don Alfredo waved his hand one way, "and taxes on everything that comes out," he waved his hand the other. "You are the rightful prince, Your Highness. It's only your due. And since you are a good and gracious prince, you don't want your subjects to suffer under a harsh or usurious double tax.

"I believe you should suggest that Frederik Hendrik must stop taxing imports and exports from Amsterdam. He will not agree to this, of course, so a compromise must be reached. A compromise that will insure that the taxes are fair and reasonable, I hope. Your Highness will receive some needed revenue. True, Frederik Hendrik will receive some revenue, but he is trapped in Amsterdam."

No one was laughing now, but slowly Don Fernando and Miguel began to smile. Most of Don Fernando's advance into the Dutch Netherlands had been stopped not by lack of arms but by lack of money and supplies.

"I will consider this proposal. Of course, we will have to make some arrangements for the future, after I have succeeded with this siege." Don Fernando nodded. "You have served Spain very well this day, Don Alfredo. Now I want you to tell me what the results of this agreement will be."

"The Wisselbank is still the Wisselbank," Don Alfredo said. "Now, though, it will have offices in Antwerp and an extra army in defense of most of its reserves. Antwerp already has an exchange, true. The addition of the Wisselbank and the lending bank will go a long way toward helping Antwerp in its recovery. With the trade agreements, the small merchants and tradesmen of Amsterdam will stay in business.

"The taxes both to you and to Frederik Hendrik will continue supporting your armies. Eventually, you will take Amsterdam or reach an agreement with Frederik Hendrik and, through it all, business will go on. The people of the Low Countries, Spanish and Dutch, will suffer less than in most wars. Probably much less."

Don Alfredo got a thoughtful look and seemed to be more thinking out loud than speaking to the prince. "I think someday there will be a statue in Amsterdam, of you and Frederik Hendrik shaking hands. Something like that, anyway. I believe that someday the history books will call you 'the wise.'"

◇   ◇   ◇

"As I said, Rebecca." Frederik Hendrik smirked. "I knew that Antwerp would be accepted. What is your answer to my requirement?"

"It turns out that it will be no problem at all. We will use 'great, big, hulking cables' as Jimmy Andersen describes them. They will be attached to already standing towers here and in Antwerp. That way, even the presumption that we need obvious means to transmit over long distances will be preserved. It will be expensive and you and Don Fernando will have to bear the cost. On the other hand, you will make back the cost of introduction in no more than a year of regular use. Or so I am compellingly informed by Fletcher Wendell and David Bartley."

Frederik Hendrik smirked some more. "Marvelous." He rubbed his hands together in anticipation. Every agreement he could make now was a step toward the larger agreement that would end the siege. Further, each agreement made the siege less damaging to Amsterdam and the Dutch Netherlands in general.

Then Rebecca told him about the taxes Don Fernando had suggested. "Who is advising that pup, Rebecca?

Whoever it is I want him assassinated. No, even better, I want to hire him." He laughed.

The counteroffer was subtle. If he agreed, the siege of Amsterdam would become much less of a drain on Don Fernando's resources, a result that Frederik Hendrik preferred to avoid. Unfortunately, he knew he had to agree to this compromise. It was a good one, and would allow Amsterdam's craftsmen to continue their work. They would be able to keep their shops open, and do more than just survive the siege. The merchants would come out of the siege whole, or at least close to it. Amsterdam produced a lot of finished goods, and would now be able to continue to sell them.

Frederik Hendrik was almost sure now that when the siege of Amsterdam ended it would be through negotiations, not combat. Don Fernando was someone he could negotiate with. "We will be haggling over the amount of tax to go to each prince for some time. We will also haggle over who will collect the taxes and where, I expect. When do you expect the radio equipment from Grantville? The Wisselbank and the lending bank need to reopen their doors to merchants outside of Amsterdam."

"Messages have already been sent to Grantville and the messengers will find the providers unusually prepared, I'm told. All by chance, of course." Rebecca smiled. "There will be supplies that have been collected for other uses available. Fortunately, they'll be ready to go.

"I warn you, this will not be cheap," Rebecca continued. "The radios must be made from expensive up-time parts and involve long steel cables. Then there are the batteries and a generator for power and regular maintenance. All these things will cost money, and a good bit of it. Once it is done; however, communication between Amsterdam and Antwerp will be nearly instantaneous."

"It depends on what you're ordering," David Bartley told David Heesters. He had been meeting regularly with Amsterdam's factor for OPM since the party had first been allowed access to Amsterdam. "If it's local items, you're probably going to have to order it through the Spaniards. Anything else will have to go through Antwerp."

"Antwerp?"

"That's where they've decided to establish a branch of the Wisselbank."

"There will be people who won't like that," Herr Heesters pointed out. "Much of Amsterdam's success was, in a sense, stolen from Antwerp. People will be afraid Antwerp will steal it back." They were sitting in Herr Heesters' office in his townhouse. There was a Van Dyck on the wall, David noticed.

"You see, at the beginning of the war, the Spanish were very hard on anyone who was not Catholic and unpaid Spanish troops sacked the city. Many of the merchants of Antwerp escaped to Amsterdam. They came here, where it was safer to practice their faith and where they could do business without the Spanish inquisition poking its nose where it didn't belong. Later, Antwerp was blockaded by our fleet as part of the war for independence. Our stock exchange was actually copied from theirs, as well.

"Now it looks like things are going full circle. We are besieged and the Wisselbank is opening a branch in Antwerp. God has an interesting sense of humor, don't you think?"

"Yes," David answered, all the while thinking about airplanes, fast food and the Internet. "The Ring of Fire and its consequences are proving to be quite . . . unusual."

"Damn it," Fletcher exploded. "I have a wife and two daughters back in Grantville, not to mention a job. Why is it us that have to go to Antwerp?"

"We're the people they can agree on," Don Alfredo answered. "Frederik Hendrik has few people he can trust and he needs most of them where they are. Most of the city council fled when the siege began. Don Fernando is not allowing just anyone to leave Amsterdam, but we can go. This is only reasonable in a siege, as you know, since the point of a siege is to keep people in. We have freedom of movement, citizens of Amsterdam do not."

"Coleman, have you heard the latest?" Henry Dreeson asked. "The guilder is going up again. It seems like the mission to Amsterdam has been a success, at least so far. We're hearing good things."

"I've heard all sorts of things, Henry," Coleman answered. "I've heard that orders for the Higgins machines are coming in. Trust that group to take care of themselves, all right."

"You're being a little uncharitable, aren't you, Coleman? Of course, David Bartley and Franz Kunze are going to take care of the HSMC and OPM. He's a businessman and that's what people in business do. The guilder is going up, that's the important thing," Henry pointed out. "It was only, what, a few months ago that we were worried about it falling forever?"

"This one will do, I think," Karl remarked. "It's tall enough, and it has the space we need. What do you think, Don Alfredo, Herr Kunze?"

"It will be well enough," Franz answered, looking at the building. "We must see these managers and have a meeting. I wish someone from Amsterdam could have come with us, to make recommendations. How do we know that the men Don Fernando agreed to will actually do their best for the bank, and not merely the best for themselves?"

"I'll have to check my figures," Jimmy Anderson advised. "We'll need to consider structural stress. Also we'll want to talk to whoever knows the most about the building, what it was constructed from, whether the builder took any short cuts. We don't need internal space in the radio tower, so we can rig a wire connection from the tower to the bank and the Antwerp exchange. How is the city council reacting?" Jimmy Anderson had been borrowed from the USE embassy because the merchants had failed to bring a radio-head along.

"Rubbing their hands together and chortling a lot," Don Alfredo answered. "They aren't fond of Amsterdam. I think the biggest problem is going to be that Antwerp will try to 'rip off' Amsterdam rather more than His Majesty."

"I wouldn't count on that," Franz said. "From what I hear Philip is already upset about the way Don Fernando is handling the campaign here. He isn't being the 'defender of the faith' that Philip wanted and he is not nearly unpopular enough to suit either Philip or Frederik Hendrik."

"Do you think the Antwerp city council will be a problem?" Fletcher wondered.

He was answered with an eloquent Gallic shrug.

The building would do, Jimmy decided, after spending a week taking measurements and doing tests. He'd done the same thing in Amsterdam. Sometimes being the designated genius was a pain in the tail, as far as he was concerned.

The radio tower needed a tall building, partly for appearances' sake, and one that could take the stress from the cables and the wind blowing through them. It needed to have anchorages for the antenna cables and probably some balancing cables. Even Don Fernando was getting into the act, making an additional request that they find a building where he might make future connections to other cities someday.

Don Alfredo de Aguilera was thinking too. He had come to Grantville from Madrid the first time he visited. He was a subject of the Spanish crown, but now he had met His Highness, Don Fernando, and knew that was where his loyalty lay. More and more it was looking like the Spanish empire was going to break apart in this world before it had in the other one that the up-timer books described.

At first Don Alfredo had hoped that the shock of the future knowledge would weld the empire back together. It didn't look like that was going to happen. Castile was even more set in its ways and more determined to have its own way by force of arms, in spite of the evidence that this method would not work. On the other hand, the people of the provinces were heartened by the knowledge of eventual liberation and anxious to hurry it along.

◊   ◊   ◊

It was done. The months spent in Amsterdam had borne really big fruit. The guilder was recovering nicely throughout the USE, and OPM's guilders had been spent on products in Amsterdam and Antwerp where they were worth considerably more. David conservatively estimated that those products were worth a bit over a hundred million New U.S. Dollars. "So, David, you never did tell me why you bought the guilders," Karl said.

"No, I didn't." And David said no more. Karl probably knew by now and the option to sell the guilders at cost would not be used now anyway. Still, Fletcher Wendell had some reservations about Prince Karl Eusibus von Liechtenstein. It was true that Karl had been quite helpful, but he had had a lot to lose. How helpful he would have been if he hadn't been heavily invested in the guilders was another question. David didn't exactly disagree with Mr. Wendell's assessment of Karl. He just figured it was the way people were.

"So what are your plans now that you have seen a bit of the world?" Karl let the question of buying guilders drop.

David looked out the window of the train that was taking them the last miles to Grantville and considered. Right after the Ring of Fire he had figured he would be going into the army when he finished high school. He still figured that he would be in the reserves. After OPM got started, he had been told that he would not be accepted into the regular service. He was doing a crucial job, according to the government. He guessed it was, in a way. "I don't know. The factories going up in Magdeburg are impressive as all get out."

"True enough. But most of them are at least partially owned from Grantville and Grantville still has the phones and computers," Karl said. "Unless you're going to settle down to run a single factory, I think Grantville is the place to be, at least, for the next few years."

"Back in a few hours, eh, David?" Fletcher smiled, joining them. "I'm about ready to get back home."

"Same here," David agreed, as Fletcher sat down. "I'm glad things got worked out, but it took a while longer than we planned, didn't it?"

"Yes it did, indeed," Fletcher nodded. "I'll be glad to see all my girls."

"We were discussing the future," Karl said, "I'm going to have to come to some understanding with Wallenstein, somehow. But I'm keeping my place in Grantville. I suspect that much of the business of the USE and Europe will be conducted there for some time to come."

"I don't know about that," Fletcher said politely enough. "Magdeburg is the capital of the USE and rapidly turning into an industrial center. I imagine that the treasury and the USE Fed will be located there, probably sometime soon. A lot of the banking will have to be conducted there. The switch from the New U.S. dollar to the USE dollar is going to keep the bank hopping for a while."

"David, I'm glad you're back," Sarah bubbled. This was kind of unusual for Sarah. She wasn't a bubbly girl, normally. The train station was packed with a welcoming crowd.

Brent and Trent enthusiastically agreed. "Nice to have you back," Trent said. "You've got to tell us all about it."

"I will," David said. "I will. We've got a couple of months before graduation, so there's plenty of time to talk. After that, we're probably not going to have much time."

"Why not?" Brent asked. "We get out of school; we'll have more time to work together."

"That's something we need to think about, you guys. What are we going to do once we get out of school? Sarah's Dad and I talked about this a lot, and Karl joined in those conversations. We really need to think about plans."

"What sort of plans?" Sarah asked.

"The army, for one. We'll be in the reserves, I imagine. And business, for another. Karl thinks Grantville is going to stay the financial center of the USE but your dad isn't so sure, Sarah," David said. "It's certainly going to stay the intellectual and research capital for a while. Brent and Trent will mostly be here, probably, but we need to think about OPM. Is staying in Grantville the right thing for OPM?"

"I hadn't really thought about it," Sarah said. "We're doing okay."

"OPM will do all right this year," David said. "Herr Kunze and I were able to spend the guilders in Amsterdam and Antwerp and made a nice profit. But we may be missing a bet, trying to stay in Grantville when the Fed is probably going to move to Magdeburg. We'll probably need to think about that."

"Large fortunes to be made there?" Trent guessed.

"Seriously large fortunes," David agreed. "Look, we made a lot of money. But Karl made even more; and it's all his."

Sarah thought for a moment. "We probably ought to think about it. I'm not sure I want to, but you're right. We have a responsibility to the shareholders to do the best we can."

"David," Coleman Walker said, "I need to talk to you about paying back that loan. I've been trying to for three days now."

"Well, I've been busy," David answered. "But you're right. We need to talk about a lot of things. You'll be glad to know we won't be exercising our sales option on the guilders."

"I know that. I'm mostly concerned about that loan, David," Coleman said. "The bank would like you to pay it back just as soon as you can."

"Why?"

"Because I had to loan Fed money to the bank of Grantville to issue it."

David thought for a moment. Coleman meant that the Fed had created the money to make the loan and it would disappear again as soon as it was paid back.

"As a citizen of Grantville, one who is now more than ever concerned over the overvaluation of the American dollar in the USE, I really can't see any benefit to that loan being paid off early," David pointed out. "OPM accepted that loan and the condition that it would be used to prevent a dangerous monetary fluctuation. It was used for that."

"Why, you . . . " Coleman began.

"Do you realize how overpriced American dollars are becoming?" David interrupted before Coleman could work up a head of steam. "I'm convinced that the dollar needs to drop against the Dutch guilder, the HRE guilder and the ducat. The reason they're so overpriced is the artificial shortage you've insisted on. You're stifling industrial growth, Mr. Walker. I'm not going to help you do that. OPM has the best part of a year to pay the money back, and we're going to use every minute of it.

"That twenty-seven million is in the economy, Mr. Walker," David insisted. "And that's where it's going to stay. It's barely a drop in the bucket compared to what's needed. Besides, we need the liquidity."

◇   ◇   ◇

"Hello, Leonhard," David said as he walked into his office. "How have things been going?"

"Rather slowly," Leonhard admitted. "With most of the officers away in Amsterdam, there was no one to make some of the decisions that needed to be made."

"I figured that." David sighed. With his hand on the door knob to his office, he turned to Leonhard and asked, "Just how high is the stack of paper in my inbox?"

"Quite high," Leonhard answered with an evil gleam in his eyes. "Quite high."

"You enjoyed that, didn't you?" David asked.

"Me? Oh, no, Master David." Leonhard smirked. "I couldn't possibly."

"Right," David said. "I'm sure. Before I get started on it, I've got a little project for you. Herr Kunze says Don Fernando wants to buy a lot of stuff from the USE. We'll need to check with the government on some of it. Here's his wish list. Look into it, will you?"

David felt his own smirk beginning as he watched Leonhard gape at Don Fernando's wish list. David decided to let Leonhard deal with the government's response to Don Fernando's desire for long distance radios. It would keep him busy.

Overloaded inbox or not, David was happy to be back in his office. Even the tower of paper was going to be easier to deal with than the last few months of high school. Latin was giving him fits. Calculus was even worse. He'd managed to stay caught up in his other classes, but those two were a torment. With finals no farther away than they were, it was going to take a lot of work.

David sat down and began to go through all the proposals that had been forwarded to his desk. "Brent, have a look at this," he wrote on one, then reached for the next.

David read through it then read through it again. "Leonhard! What the hell is this?"

Leonhard didn't look up. "Mrs. Simpson has invited OPM to become a corporate sponsor of the Magdeburg Opera House. She points out that corporate sponsorship is a tax deductible charitable contribution. According to our attorney, we may actually save more in taxes than we contribute. Something about corporate tax brackets, he said. We are in the highest one at the moment."

David continued to read while Leonhard spoke and noted the details of the sponsorship request. In addition to the Opera House there were plans to sponsor a library, a museum, a theater and a college. All good causes he thought, and began to calculate the totals.

All together the bill would come to something close to thirty million dollars over the next three years. From the proposal's details, OPM was not the only corporate sponsor being solicited. Several other businesses were already listed as sponsors.

David checked the approved box and tossed the request into his outbox. Business as usual, he thought, and began to smile.

This'll Be the Day . . .

Walt Boyes

"I'm looking for Father Friedrich Spee von Langenfeld," the well-dressed man said as he crowded the doorway. "I'm told he has his office here." The man was dressed in black, mostly velvet, with white at the neck and the cuffs.

He was clearly a down-timer, thought Josef, the Jesuit brother who served as doorman for the Spee household. Up-timers habitually referred to Father Friedrich as "von Spee" because that was the way their up-time histories listed him. Down-timers usually called him by his correct territorial name, "von Langenfeld."

"May I say who is asking?"

"I am Father Goswin Nickel."

"Father Provincial!" Josef's eyes grew very wide. "We weren't expecting you . . . I didn't recognize you . . . Please come in! Come in, come in!"

"Cease your babbling, my son," Father Nickel said, smiling, as he entered the house. "Please tell me if Father Friedrich is within."

"He is not, Father," Brother Josef said, "He is at the cathedral rehearsing the choir. He has some new *Kirchenlieder,* some hymns, that he has written for them to sing."

"Please have someone send for him, then, and also, if you would be so kind, have someone see to my horse."

"At once, Father."

The Jesuit provincial allowed himself to be led to the sitting room, where he sat down to wait for Spee. "*Spes fuerat, spes Fridericus erat,*" he recited to himself softly. "In Spee they placed hope, Friedrich was their hope." Perhaps yet again, he thought.

The drum set looked incongruous in the apse of the cathedral, thought Friedrich Spee, even though he'd written the music that required it. The young man who played it was dressed in the style known as *lefferto* after the up-timer, Harry Lefferts, and he even sported a patch over one eye. The patch, as Friedrich knew, was entirely for show. The young man, whose name was Franz, had told him so, and that he only wore it because he thought it made him look "bad." It appeared that "bad" was somehow good in the new cant of these up-timer-aping youth. Friedrich smiled, and shook his head, ruefully.

Up-timer-aping, indeed. For was not what he had written for the cathedral choir here in Magdeburg up-timer-aping as well? A work for rock band and choir. At least, since he was now on the staff of the up-timer Cardinal Mazzare, he'd had no problem with the *nihil obstat* and the *imprimatur* necessary to be able to print the work and get it performed by the cathedral choir. He'd had more problems trying to figure out how to work around the "electric guitar" and the "electric piano" he'd heard in the recording that Cardinal Larry's friend the Methodist minister in Grantville had let him listen to, something called *Godspell*. He had substituted a massed section of Spanish guittarrones, all played in the up-timer style by a band of surly *lefferti*, and the cathedral organ. He was sure it was not rock and roll, but it sounded good to him.

What do they say in Grantville, "It's not rock and roll, but I like it?" He laughed out loud at the thought, causing the nearer members of the choir to stare at him strangely.

"All right, then," Friedrich said, tapping his baton on the lectern. "From the start, if you will, please."

Just as the band and choir swung into the first part of the chorale, Friedrich heard a commotion at the back of the cathedral. He swung around, to see several people running up the aisle. They were armed, and one had a huge wheel-lock *pistole*. The man with the *pistole* stopped and aimed it at Friedrich. It went off with a thunderous boom, but the ball, thankfully, missed and lodged itself with a great spray of splinters into the pulpit in front of which Friedrich had placed his conductor's lectern.

"Ow, *scheiss!*" One of the splinters had found a target in the lead guittarrone player. Friedrich turned, but the young *lefferto* waved him off. "I'm fine, Father. I'm fine."

The cathedral guards had by now caught up with the assassins, if that's what they were, and they were clubbing them down in the narthex of the cathedral. Friedrich strode quickly up to them in a half-run hampered by his cassock.

"Stop it, you!" he shouted. "They are down! Stop it!"

He began to pull the cathedral guards off the small group of intruders, and managed to get the beatings to stop.

"Who are you?" he asked the quondam shooter.

"You are a witch! And a helper of witches!" the man shouted, and was whacked by the end of one of the guards' staves for his pains. "Father del Rio says you are no true Jesuit! He says you are demon-inspired. He says you and your demon friends from the future will deliver us all to the Devil!"

One of the others pulled a knife from his doublet but a guard was faster, and knocked it out of his hand before he could throw.

"Father Friedrich," the chief of the guard detachment began, "I think it would be better—"

"If I were not so close to them until you see who else has weapons?" Friedrich finished for him.

"Yes, Father."

"Fine, take them to the prison, but no more beatings!"

"Yes, Father."

Friedrich turned, and slowly walked back to the altar. He was not surprised to find himself shaking. "I think we've practiced enough for one day," he said. "Let us get back together in the morning after Mass."

Friedrich was just coming down the steps of the cathedral, his unbuttoned cassock skirts flapping behind him when his secretary, Pieter van Donck, rushed up to him. Van Donck was a Flemish seminarian from the Jesuit college and seminary at Douai. He was short and stout where Spee was tall and slender. "Mutt *und* Jeff," Cardinal Mazzare had called them when he first met van Donck in Spee's company. Of course he had had to explain the up-timer reference, Spee thought wryly.

"Father Friedrich," the young Jesuit scholastic began, panting.

"Slowly, friend Pieter," Spee said, as the young man hyperventilated. "Take a moment, and then tell me what has you all out of breath." Spee ran his fingers through his unruly mop of hair, then put his hand down. A nervous tic, he thought. Mustn't do that. He stroked his short, curly black beard instead, then put his hands down at his sides.

The seminarian gathered himself together. "The provincial, Father. The provincial is in your rooms, waiting for you! He sent me to find you right away!"

Friedrich was still, thinking of all the things that the provincial's unannounced arrival could mean, most of them bad.

"Well, Pieter," Friedrich said, smiling, and holding in all his fears, "we must go to him then, and see what has brought him all this way in such a hurry. Did he bring an entourage?"

"No, Father, he came himself alone."

Friedrich stopped in mid step. "He what?"

"He is by himself, so Brother Josef said, and he arrived on horseback."

Friedrich turned and began to quickly stride up the street to his lodgings. As van Donck tried to keep up with him, Spee broke into a jog. The little fat youth tried valiantly to keep step, but fell steadily behind. Friedrich didn't seem to notice and quickly outdistanced his secretary.

When he reached his door, Spee pushed it open.

"Brother Josef," he said to the doorman, "please tell me where Father Provincial is."

"He is in your sitting room, Father," the Jesuit brother replied, "I provided him with bread and some beer."

"Fine," Spee said. "Now when Pieter comes, please send him along to us there."

"Yes, Father." The brother said it to Spee's back, as the Jesuit swept quickly along the hallway to the sitting room, opened the door and passed inside.

"Father Provincial," he began, going to one knee.

"No need, Friedrich," Nickel said, rising to greet him. "Please, sit down. We have to talk, and there may not be much time."

"Does this have to do with the people who just tried to kill me in the cathedral?"

"Thank God! I was not in time to warn you, but it seems you were able to foil their aim anyway," the provincial said, sinking back into his chair.

"I think that it was not I but the Lord who foiled their aim, or at least made their pistoleer a bad shot," Spee said, smiling and taking a chair. "This has happened before, as you know, and I was spared then as well."

"For this we can thank God, then," Nickel said.

"I came straightaway, Father," Spee said, "so I have no idea who they were. They are under guard at the cathedral prison now."

"I know who they are. Or at least who sent them," Nickel said.

"They shouted the name of del Rio," Spee said quietly, hands in his lap.

"I rather thought they might," the Provincial said. "For three years now, you have been very publicly identified as the author of the *Cautio Criminalis*. Not only do you not deny it, most have seen the up-timer history books that say it as well."

"You know that I wrote it."

"Yes, and you have done the penance I and Father General Vitelleschi deemed appropriate for writing it contrary to the directions we gave you," Nickel said. "It is done, and it is, for the most part, well done. I agree with you that witchcraft may or may not be real, but these witch trials are hideous perversions of justice and God's law." The provincial's jaw worked.

"Unfortunately," he said, "there are those, both within the Society and without, who do not agree with us."

Spee was silent.

"It has not helped that the general has given you to Cardinal Mazzare to be 'his' Jesuit, along with Heinzerling," Nickel continued. "For those opposed to your view on witchcraft, this only further compounds your sin. You are in league with the Grantville demons who are perverting our Society, so they are saying."

"I see the fine hand of some of our Spanish brothers in this," Spee said, neutrally.

"Of course," Nickel said. "Since the pontiff has allied himself with Grantville, the Spanish crown and those of the church under its control have begun a whispering campaign, not only among the laity but among the religious as well. It seems that the pope has perhaps made league with the devil, and among the most active of his Satan-inspired associates is always the Father General Vitelleschi. Even some of our brethren in the Society have taken this point of view."

"Let me guess," Friedrich responded. "Our brother del Rio."

"Of course. Not only del Rio, but also your old friend and my predecessor as provincial, Hermann Baving. Baving appears to be the center of the campaign. Hermann still hates you, believes in witch trials as a way to rout out Protestants and unbelievers, and has many friends in our order."

"It is likely," Friedrich said, "that even with clear instructions from the father general, we might have a schism in the order over this."

"Yes. And so Father General Vitelleschi has radioed me to come to Magdeburg both for safety, and to confer with Cardinal Mazzare, and with yourself."

"Radioed?" Friedrich was rather surprised.

"Of course, radioed. Did you think the Society of Jesus so backward that we could not figure out how to design and build a radio?"

"Well, I . . ."

"What? Did you think that Father Kircher would not be able to tell us that you don't need a huge antenna?"

"I suppose not."

"Now you know. The radio is at Paderborn, in my rooms at the college. If you should ever need to use it, you must take somebody who knows the Code of Morse."

Nickel ran his hands through his thinning hair. "The news from Rome continues to be grim, since the Spanish attacked the Holy See. Father General Vitelleschi believes that Cardinal Borja will seek to become pope. He expects this to happen any day, and he does not believe that he, Vitelleschi, will be able to stop it. Especially since it is likely that if Borja's people catch him, or the pope, for that matter, that they'll be killed."

"We shall have a schism, then, for certain."

"Yes," Nickel said. "It is almost upon us. That is why I have come to see the cardinal. Vitelleschi is not sure what will happen, or whether he or the pope will be killed. I am to call a general assembly of the Society here in Magdeburg if he is killed, and we are to elect a successor."

"You will, of course, wish to be housed in the episcopal palace with the cardinal," Spee started.

"I will not."

"What?"

"I expect you may have an extra room here, Friedrich?"

"Well, yes, of course, Father," Spee said, "but . . . "

"I would rather not broadcast my presence quite yet," the provincial said. "I would rather see what happens, first."

"Your wish, Father," Spee bowed his head and sighed. And it was not yet noon, he thought.

"I need to see the cardinal," Nickel went on. "But I don't want it advertised that I am here. Can you send someone to ask for an audience?"

Young van Donck had come in the room some time before, and had quietly stood inside the door.

"Pieter will go," Spee said. Van Donck looked alert.

"Pieter, go quickly but quietly to the episcopal palace, and see if you can find Father Heinzerling. I believe he is there. Find him, and ask him to come to us, quietly please."

"Of course, Father." Van Donck gave a quick nod to Spee, and bowed his head to the provincial of the Order, and vanished out the door. He could be heard running down the hallway, and the outside door slammed with a great thud.

Spee and the provincial smiled at each other. "Ah, youth!" Nickel said.

"Shall we find something to eat while we wait?" Spee asked.

"Why not? And we can talk about better times, Friedrich," Nickel said as they went out the door and turned toward the kitchens.

"And so I have been studying the music of Grantville," Spee said. "Not just the holy music but the popular tunes. And I have written a work of *Kirchenlieder*, church songs, that I was rehearsing this morning in the cathedral."

"Their music is sometimes too strange for me," Nickel said. "Rock and roll, for example. Baving says it is the devil's own music, and I am not sure he is wrong, Friedrich."

The kitchen door burst open, revealing young van Donck puffing as if he were one of the new steam engines. With him were two of the cardinal's guard.

"Cardinal Mazzare says you are to come to him now!" van Donck said. "There are new messages from Rome!"

Nickel and Spee hurried to the door. There was a carriage waiting in the alley. They climbed in, followed by the guards and van Donck. As they shut the door, they were jolted back into their seats when the carriage moved.

Van Donck started to pull open the window curtain.

"Don't." Spee put out his hand in warning. "It would not be wise for Father Nickel to be seen."

Within minutes the carriage pulled up to the back entrance of the episcopal palace. The guards hustled the three Jesuits out of the carriage and up the steps into the building. Waiting for them inside the entrance was Father Heinzerling. The normally jovial Jesuit was solemn to the point of tears.

"Come quickly," he said, turning and ushering them down a long corridor.

"Come in, Father Provincial," the cardinal said.

"Your Eminence," Nickel knelt and kissed Mazzare's ring. Spee and van Donck did likewise.

"There, now that's over with," Mazzare said, brushing back his sleeves. "Please sit down."

There was a long conference table littered with maps and papers in the room. At one end, a fireplace, cold and dark in the heat of summer in the Germanies. Above the mantel, a painting of the pope, Urban VIII. At the other end of the room, as if staring the pope down, was a painting of King Gustav, the emperor of the United States of Europe.

They took chairs at one end of the table. Mazzare sat at the head.

"Why are you here, Father Nickel?" the cardinal asked.

"I have been in contact with Father General Vitelleschi, Eminence," Nickel said, "by radio."

"Aha!" The cardinal slapped the table. "I knew it. Mike Stearns owes me money. I told him the Jebbies would be able to figure out how to build radios on the q.t., given enough time. He didn't believe me, but now he will have to." He looked across the table at Nickel. "And what does the father general say?"

"Much the same as he told me when I left Rome in May. And of course, what he predicted," Nickel paused, "has sadly come to pass."

Mazzare grimaced. "And what does the Black Pope think, now that he's been on the run for two months?"

"That he believed that Borja's conclave would elect him pope very soon, and that he, Vitelleschi, and Pope Urban would have prices on their heads."

"That much we know," Mazzare said. "I've just come from a meeting with Piazza, Stearns and Nasi . . . the Spaniards have consolidated their hold on Rome and the Campania. We think Borja will be declared pope shortly."

"So the general believed two days ago when he radioed me," Nickel agreed. "He sent me to you with some advice for you, and instructions for me."

"Go on," Mazzare said.

"He believes that the pope may be assassinated, like many of the cardinals loyal to the house of Barberini have already been. Father General Vitelleschi told me to tell you that if the pope dies, you may want to think about holding a rival conclave here." Nickel stared at the

Grantviller. "And if we find that he is also dead, I am to hold a general assembly of the order under your authority to elect a new superior general."

"Did Vitelleschi say who he recommended as his successor?"

"Me."

"Well, then we must both pray to be spared these cups, don't you think?" Mazzare smiled, a wintry smile.

"Indeed, Eminence, indeed." Nickel matched Mazzare's bitter smile.

"Shall we have an anti-pope, then?" Spee asked quietly.

"It looks like we already do, Friedrich," Mazzare said. "And his name is Borja."

"While we wait for news," Nickel said, "I must be about the tasks that the father general set me. I have his commission as his deputy while he is out of touch, and I think I should begin to draw the reins of the society in before our brothers in Spain begin to do it instead."

"Wise move," Mazzare said.

"Friedrich," Nickel said, "would you be willing to be my secretary for a while this evening? And Meester van Donck as well?"

"Of course, Father," Spee quickly agreed. Van Donck nodded his agreement as well.

"Then, with Your Eminence's permission, might we use this room as our offices for the evening?"

"Yes, of course," Mazzare said. "I will send somebody with refreshments while you work. And now, if you will forgive me, I must see the prime minister." Mazzare swept out of the room.

Friedrich marveled at how different his friend from Grantville had become. Well, not different, exactly, he mused, but the cardinal's hat sat well on him.

Nickel's cough brought him out of his reverie. "So Friedrich, we need to write to Baving, and to the other senior members of the order, and tell them that it is the father general's orders that the Society of Jesus will support the properly elected pope, and that is Pope Urban VIII. You know what to say. Van Donck, come with me, I have other writing for you to do." Nickel moved down the table a ways.

Spee pulled out a piece of paper, and got one of the new metal pens from the inkstand. As always, he began his first letter the same way.

"A. M. D. G," he wrote.

Ad Maiorem Dei Gloriam—to the greater glory of God . . .

"Friedrich Spee von Langenfeld, priest of the Society of Jesus, this seventh day of August, in the year of our Lord 1635 . . ." he wrote.

Suddenly, he felt a chill. August the seventh, 1635. His mind raced back to his first morning in Grantville, over three years ago, now. He remembered standing in the kitchen of Larry Mazzare's rectory, with the Catholic Encyclopedia in his hands. Standing, trembling, almost unable to read the words on the pages open before him. After three years, he found he could recite them verbatim. "A poet, opponent of trials for witchcraft, born at Kaiserswerth on the Rhine, 25 February, 1591; died at Trier 7 August, 1635."

He could not believe he had forgotten. His pen dropped to the table.

"What is wrong, Friedrich?" Father Nickel asked, hurrying back up the table.

"Ah . . . nothing, really, Father," Friedrich gave a huge sigh. "Just a personal realization."

"And what was it?" Nickel pressed.

"In the original time line, before Grantville came to us," Spee said heavily, and then paused. "In the original time line, today I would have died in Trier of some plague contracted from nursing soldiers in the hospital. I had forgotten the date."

"Ah," the provincial said. "It must be a shock. To know what might have been."

"I am sure you know about yourself, too, Father," Spee said, looking Nickel in the eyes.

"Yes, and I sincerely hope that I do not become general of the society twenty years before I did, eh, before I would have . . . ach, there are not the right tenses to discuss this time travel!" Nickel grimaced.

"Friedrich," he said, gently, "this is why I believe that we are not inspired by the devil, no matter what Borja and Baving and del Rio would like the world to believe. Because Grantville exists, Trier has not been overrun, and one of our great hymnists can still write to the greater glory of God. And you were spared yet again, in the cathedral this morning. Now write, for we have an important task, and you have been spared by God to do it."

Friedrich Spee von Langenfeld walked back from the cathedral after the Sunday mass where he had conducted the premiere of his new music. He had noticed that there were many smiling faces, and he'd noticed that the cardinal's foot was tapping in time to the music during the performance.

Spee started whistling as he walked down the heavily graveled street to his lodgings. American music certainly was strange. He'd had the cardinal explain the lyrics of many songs to him, but he still was puzzled, especially by one song in particular. It was beginning to drive him crazy, because the melody was so hard to get out of his head. Like right now, for instance.

He found himself whistling the chorus over and over. *"Singin' this'll be the day that I die."*

Command Performance

David Carrico

**Magdeburg
Friday, October 14, 1633**

Franz knocked on the door, and waited impatiently for someone to answer. Marla made a slight grunt, and her hold on his arm became a fierce clutch. He leaned over to her bowed head, and said, "But a moment more, and you will be out of the rain and able to sit." She nodded her head slightly, and he straightened.

At that moment, the door opened and a young woman looked out at them. "Yes?" she said in accented English.

"Fraulein Marla Linder, come at Frau Simpson's invitation," Franz replied.

The young woman opened the door wide. "Please, come in. *Wilkommen.*"

Franz led Marla into the house. The comparative warmth of the sitting room was a very welcome change from the liquid ice of the October rain, and he heard her sigh. Another woman swept into the room from a side door as the maid shut the front door behind them.

"Miss Linder, I am so glad to finally meet you face to face," the newcomer exclaimed.

Franz was in no doubt as to who this was, although he had never seen her before in his life. Even in Grantville they had begun to hear of Mary Simpson, the Dame of Magdeburg, whose grace and courtesy had charmed even the young myrmidons of the Committees of Correspondence.

Marla's fingers clenched on his arm again. "Your pardon, Frau Simpson," Franz hastily interjected, "but it would be a kindness if Marla could sit down."

Mrs. Simpson's beaming smile shifted to an expression of concern, and her eyes widened as she took Marla's hands. "Dear, your hands are like ice! You poor thing." Mary released Marla's hand and began unfastening buttons. "At the end of a long journey, and you're soaking wet and cold. Hilde, help take her coat." With the maid's help, the drenched coat was removed and hung up. "Come with us, and we'll get you warm and dry."

The serving woman led Marla out of the sitting room as Mary turned to Franz. "Please, make yourself at home, while we take care of Miss Linder. Tell me, Mr. . . . ." she looked at him in inquiry.

"Franz Sylwester, Frau Simpson," he responded with a slight bow.

Mary smiled. "Oh, good, I was hoping to meet you. We'll talk later, but for right now, do you know if Marla gets like this often? How long has she been hurting?"

"Never have I seen her like this," Franz said, his worry coming to the fore. "She has been suffering for over two days now, since after the rain started."

Mary nodded. "As I thought. If we get her dry and warm, it should ease up. Please, Franz, be seated, and we'll be back with you before long." She turned and hurried out of the room.

Franz took his violin in its bag and Marla's flute in its case from the plastic bags that had protected them from the rain. He set the instruments on a nearby table, then hung the precious bags to dry on a peg next to Marla's coat near the door. He stopped for a moment to look at the bags, and marvel at the stuff they were made from. How plastic was made still seemed like magic to him, but there was no denying how useful the stuff was. Take these bags—they weighed next to nothing, could be folded and stuck into a pocket, yet at a moment's notice they could be taken out and used to shield anything they would contain from moisture. Truly, the future must be a marvelous place if it could produce Marla, the music he was coming to love so strongly, and plastic.

With a smile he started on his own buttons, and moments later his own very wet coat was hung on the next peg in the wall. Finally shed of his various burdens, he took a seat in one of the most comfortable chairs it had ever been his pleasure to sit in. The warmth radiating from the stove soaked into him and the chill left his own extremities. He felt his body relaxing for the first time since the trip from Grantville had begun.

Traveling in Thuringia in the late fall and early winter was unpleasant at best, and arduous at worst. Rain or early snow could turn what roads there were into muddy bogs. Shepherding a grand piano from Grantville to Magdeburg in early October had been ... interesting, Franz mused.

The process began when Marla accepted Mary Simpson's invitation to come to Magdeburg and bring 'modern' music with her. The day the letter from Mrs. Simpson arrived, Franz saw a rare mixture of emotions in Marla. She was very excited, which was to be expected; but for the first time in their relationship, Franz saw Marla experiencing uncertainty. It had taken the combined support of Marcus Wendell, Marla's old high school band director, Ingram Bledsoe, her instrument maker friend, and her entire circle of down-time musician friends to convince her that she should take up this opportunity.

Once Marla decided to come to Magdeburg, however, her self-confidence came rolling back like a river flooding over its banks. The metaphor, Franz smiled as he recalled those days, was an apt one; she was as relentless in her focus as a flash flood. The days that followed were very intense, as she gathered music and supplies. Her biggest need, however, was a piano—a good one.

That need for a piano caused a whirlwind inventory of instruments in Grantville. The results surprised every up-timer except Ingram, who was Grantville's resident piano tuner. For such a small town, there were a surprising number of pianos. They found nearly one hundred upright, console and spinet pianos in various states of repair with ages ranging from pre-World War I instruments to one that had been delivered only a few weeks before the Ring of Fire. A fair quantity of the older and more dilapidated instruments were now located in the warehouse-cum-workshop of Bledsoe & Riebeck, the new piano manufacturing firm formed by Ingram and Hans Riebeck, the father-in-law of one of Franz's downtimer friends. They all made jokes about the graveyard of old pianos, but actually the craftsmen were mining the instruments for hardware to make new pianos for down-timers.

Marla didn't even consider selecting one of the smaller pianos, though it would have been easier to move. She focused her attention on the larger grand and baby grand instruments. Franz remembered going with her on her rounds of various houses and churches. There were over half a dozen baby grands in Grantville, and she played each one extensively. He also remembered their conversation as they left the last house.

"Well, that was disappointing," she said, as they walked down the sidewalk from the house. "I haven't heard a baby grand yet that I really liked, but that one was just bad."

"So what will you do?" Franz asked.

"I don't have any choice. I have to have one of the big grands."

"Tell me again where they are."

"First Baptist Church has a Baldwin, the Methodist church has a recent model Steinway, and Marcus Wendell tells me there's an old Steinway in the High Street Mansion," Marla said.

"Do you know them well?"

"The ones in the churches I do. I haven't seen or played the old Steinway, but from what Marcus tells me, it needs some pretty extensive work done to it."

"So which one do you want?"

"I don't have time to wait on the mansion's piano to get fixed. Besides, Girolamo Zenti is having a bidding war with Bledsoe and Riebeck for it, and who knows how long it will take to settle that. It will have to be one of the church pianos. I'll take whichever one I can get," Marla answered, "but I want the Steinway. The Baldwin's tone is too dark, and although it's a lot newer than the mansion's piano, it's still old enough that I'm a little afraid to move it very far. No, it has to be the Methodist Steinway. It's going to put a big hole in the church's music program though," she said in a worried tone, concerned about her home church. "I hope that Reverend Jones will forgive me."

Ingram had once warned Franz that when Marla 'shifted into high gear,' she was hard to keep up with. Franz learned exactly what the older man had meant over the next three days, his recollection of which was a little blurred. He moved in Marla's wake, watching mostly in silence from behind her shoulder as she went from office to office and person to person, asking, pleading, demanding and negotiating. Her concern about the effect of this requisition on her home church didn't stop her from making it all the same.

At the end of it, Marla had forged an agreement between several parties wherein the Methodist church agreed to release their grand piano for shipment to Magdeburg. In exchange, the church was to receive some compensation from Mary Simpson's arts league, the use of the best of the baby grand pianos (which happened to be owned by a member of the church, who was also to be compensated), and an option to purchase a new grand from Bledsoe & Riebeck at cost when their new company was able to begin manufacturing them. The arts league agreed to pay the costs to transport the requisitioned instrument to Magdeburg, and the government agreed to give Bledsoe & Riebeck a tax deduction for the difference between the cost of the replacement piano and the price for which they would normally have sold it.

It was the piano that dictated when they would leave for Magdeburg. Their friends Ingram Bledsoe and Friedrich Braun first had to build a shipping crate for it. And of course, Marla was hovering at their shoulders while they were doing so, anxious that it should be perfect so that no harm should come to her beloved Steinway. It was well designed, well constructed and definitely well padded. She finally agreed it was time to encase the piano and prepare to leave. At that point Ingram, for the first time since Franz had become acquainted with him, became firm with her. His words were, "Marla, if you're here, you will drive us all batty. Even if you don't say anything, you'll make us so nervous there will be an accident. Now, be a good girl and go with Franz, and let us pack your baby up for you."

Franz smiled as he remembered the expression on Marla's face. She was surprised more than anything that a man she considered to be like a favorite uncle would speak so to her, but she did understand the sense of it, and reluctantly—very reluctantly—came away with Franz.

The next morning they went to the church to find that the piano was packed, wrapped in one of those marvelous sheets of plastic—Ingram called it a "tarp"—and sealed with some also marvelous sticky stuff. When he asked Ingram what it was, he thought he didn't hear the answer correctly. "Duck tape?" It gave rise to a number of interesting mental images.

"Duct tape. Duct with a 't,'?" Ingram said. "The late-twentieth century's answer to twine and baling wire." And then Ingram had to explain what baling wire was.

Several large and brawny men had been recruited to remove the crate from the church and load it onto the wagon that was going to carry it to the river. Franz remembered his surprise at the size of the crate. He had expected it to be quite large, but it was only about eight or nine feet long, about six feet wide and about four feet high. When he remarked on this, Friedrich looked at him with a supercilious expression—"Of course, the legs come off"—as if Franz were a dunce. Before Franz could hit him, the call came to lift the crate, so his sarcastic friend escaped without lumps.

The crate was lifted with a great deal of heaving, straining and grunting; and with a great deal more it was walked out the doors of the church meeting hall, through the entry and out into the daylight. It had to be lifted even higher to place it into the bed of the wagon, so along with the heaving and grunting, Franz remembered hearing words muttered that properly should not be spoken near a church. It took all their strength, but it was finally loaded onto the wagon and on its way to the riverside.

The River Saale was not very wide or deep at the place where they were to embark, and those who had arranged for the barges had told Marla of the trouble they had in finding one that was large enough to carry the piano yet small enough to navigate the course of the river that far upstream. There were actually two barges awaiting them when they arrived at the riverside—one to carry the piano, and one to carry Marla and her friends and their bags and instruments. When she saw the barges, Marla almost had an apoplectic fit. The larger of the two was for the piano. It seemed as though it almost touched the banks on both sides of the river, yet when she looked at the crate it appeared to be wider than the barge. Ingram and Friedrich consulted with the barge master, then Ingram took out his . . . "tape measure," Franz thought it was called—another marvelous device—and measured the width of the barge cargo space, then measured the crate, and pronounced a judgment that it would fit. That calmed Marla to some extent, but she was still nervous as they wrapped the harness around the crate and attached the hoisting tackle.

Franz still had a bruise from where Marla's long, strong pianist's fingers clamped on his arm while the crate with the almost invaluable and definitely irreplaceable Steinway was swayed up and out and eventually lowered to the deck of the first barge. She relaxed finally as the deck hands lashed down the crate. Piano and crate together only weighed about a thousand up-time pounds, so the barge didn't settle much in the water, which was a good thing—the river was not only narrow at this place, it was also shallow. In any event, the crate filled the craft from side to side. There might have been room for someone to step between it and the side of the barge, but that someone would have needed a very small foot.

That was actually the most exciting part of the trip. The people were loaded on the second barge in a matter of minutes. Marla, of course, wanted to ride on the first barge with her "baby," but the barge master refused. He said that with the cargo area so full there was only room for his crew. He was right. There might have been five feet between the bow and the crate, and maybe a little more than that between the crate and the stern, which truly was barely enough room for himself, his brother and his two sons to work in. He offered to let her ride on top of the crate. Franz still wasn't sure if the barge master was jesting or not, the man's craggy face was so sober. He thought that Marla actually considered it, but she finally refused, to Franz's relief.

"Well," Marla had said, "here we go." Their bags were being tossed from the dock to the deck of the second barge, so she led the way down the gangplank, followed by Franz and the rest of those who were traveling with them, all clutching precious instrument cases under their arms. The mooring ropes were untied and thrown on deck, and the bargemen leaned into their poles to shove off into the river's current and begin the journey downstream to Magdeburg.

Then the rain began.

Franz's train of thought stopped abruptly when Mary Simpson returned. He shot to his feet.

"Frau Simpson, how is Marla?" The worry in his tone matched the expression on his face. Mary settled into a nearby chair, crossed her legs and waved him back to his own seat.

"Marla is just fine," she said, smiling. "She's changed into dry clothing and is getting warm. She was already starting to feel better when I left her."

"But will she be all right?" he persisted.

"Franz, she is fine." Mary's voice had a soothing note, and Franz finally relaxed back into the embrace of his chair.

Now that his mind was easing, Franz became very aware of the presence of Mary Simpson. She reminded him of Marla. It wasn't a physical resemblance. Neither woman was classically beautiful; Mary's nose was somewhat aquiline, and Marla's chin was a shade too strong. Physically, Mary was a small woman, slightly built, whereas most down-timer men, including Franz himself, had to look up to meet Marla's eyes. And when it came to eyes, Marla's were blue and set in a pale complexion, while Mary's were gray and framed by slightly olive skin. At the moment, Mary's eyes were warm and smiling, but Franz could easily guess that if she became angry they would be storm cloud gray, to match the ice that could sometimes come to Marla's gaze. They both had black hair, but Marla's was glossy, long and straight, while Mary had short wavy black hair turning gray at the temples. That gray hair and the small wrinkles at the outside corners of her eyes were the only things that indicated that Mary was perhaps older than she appeared to be at first glance.

Though there wasn't a strong likeness in appearance, the two women were even so similar in poise and grace.

Just now, despite the fact that Mary was wearing trousers, Franz still felt an impression that earlier she had been gracefully moving in formal attire. Marla could move with sufficient poise at times that one would ignore the jeans and sweater that she might be wearing. Both women had a smile that could light a room and serve as a beacon of warmth. Right now Mrs. Simpson's smile was focused on him.

"So, since you're here, Franz, I assume that the piano made the trip safely?"

"Yes, Frau Simpson . . ."

"Call me Mary, please."

"Mary," Franz smiled a little, recalling his comparison of Mary and Marla, and how frequently he had heard another voice saying, "Call me Marla." Recollecting the question he had been asked, he continued, "Yes, the piano arrived safely. Even in her pain, Marla would not move from the docks until she saw it taken from the barge and loaded safely on a wagon."

"Good." Mary nodded. "I really wanted it to unload at the naval docks, but I couldn't get John to agree." Franz realized she was referring to her husband, John Simpson, admiral of the USE Navy. "He said that things were too tightly scheduled right now for him to spare that much time at one of their docks." She frowned a little, then shrugged. "He did agree that he would send one of his men to the civilian docks to oversee the unloading there and make sure that everything went well."

"There was a Navy man at the dock, and he did indeed watch all the unloading," Franz said. "But everyone on the dock, including the Navy man, was watching another man out of the corners of their eyes. I do not know him. He did nothing but stand there in the rain, hands in pockets, and watch the unloading. He was not dressed well, but all the dockmen and bargemen acted as if he was an angel of the Lord. They walked wide circles around him, would not face him, and they worked at the unloading like men possessed. The crate was off its barge and on the wagon almost before we could climb up the gangplank from our barge to the dock. He did not introduce himself the whole time, even when the Navy man was telling the wagon driver where to take the crate and me how to find your house."

"That must have been Gunther," Mary replied. In response to Franz's raised eyebrow she continued, "Gunther Achterhof, the head of the local Committee of Correspondence."

Now both of Franz's eyebrows climbed to meet his hairline, and he gave a low whistle. Gunther Achterhof was building a reputation among the Committees of Correspondence. If Gretchen Higgins was the Moses of the CoC and Spartacus was Aaron the spokesman, then Gunther was reputed to be another Caleb, the fierce old man who at the age of eighty had told Joshua, "Give me the mountain with the wildest tribes to conquer," and then had gone out and done it. Remembering the stony face he had seen at the dock, Franz had no trouble believing everything he had heard about him.

"Oh, yes," Mary smiled slightly, "right now John and I are in very good favor with the Committees, partly because of the Navy and partly because of some other things."

Franz knew she referred to the events of the previous two weeks, where Magdeburg—indeed, much of northern Germany—seethed on the edge of open rebellion after the Battle of Wismar and the revelation of the self-sacrifice of Hans Richter. The actions of Admiral and Mrs. Simpson had been part of the lid that had kept that particular political pot from boiling over.

"Right now, anything that either of us finds important," Mary continued, "the Committees take an interest in. I imagine Hilde, our housekeeper, told him about the piano." In response to Franz's quizzical expression, she laughed a little. "Oh, yes, Hilde keeps them informed. I don't mind. John doesn't bring anything secret home from work, and since they have appointed themselves to see to our security, better that they get their information straight from the house rather than from rumors or from having to guess." She uncrossed her legs and leaned forward a little. "Now, tell me how the trip went. The last word I had was from a week ago, where Marla said she had the Steinway—which was great news—and that she would be coming by barge and would be arriving sometime around now."

Hilde had appeared with a tray carrying a coffee service while Mary was speaking. She poured two large cups of coffee as Mary finished and handed them to Franz and her mistress. She then took the wet coats from the hooks near the door and carried them away; to the kitchen Franz supposed, where they would be hopefully dried and warmed. Franz cradled the cup in his hands for a long moment, soaking up the warmth, especially in his crippled left hand, which was still aching from the cold. Finally, he took a sip and let it seep down his throat.

"Aaah."

Mary smiled over the rim of her own cup. "Yes, when you're cold and wet, a big cup of coffee is a good thing to have."

Franz nodded agreement, took another long sip, then leaned back in his chair again. He briefly recounted everything that had occurred in requisitioning the piano and preparing it for shipment. Taking another sip of coffee, he continued with, "We unmoored and pushed away somewhat before noon, and the rain began not long afterward. The bargemen put up a canvas shelter in the middle of the barge where we were able to sit and stay mostly dry. Marla, however, constantly fretted over the piano, so she spent most of her time up near the bow, watching the other barge like a mother whose only child is marching off to battle. From time to time I would bring her back to the shelter, but before long she would be back up leaning on the bow rail, watching her beloved piano. She spent most of the trip there, even at night."

"So how long did the trip take?"

"Three days from the time the barges pushed away from their moorings near Grantville to the time we touched the dock here in Magdeburg," Franz replied. "The barge masters had their crews poling during the first few hours. Gerd Eugenson, the master on our barge, told me that they wanted to get along as fast as they could while the rain was keeping the water high. He warned me that if either barge ran aground on a shallow bottom we would all have to get in the water and help pull it free. God be praised that was not required.

"Once we reached a place where the river was wider and deeper, they stowed the poles and we floated with the current. We only pulled to shore one morning when fog arose, as the barge masters were concerned about running into objects they could not see. The rest of the time we floated, even at night. They would light lanterns and hang them on the prow and stern, and keep a lookout ahead. When I asked why, Master Gerd laughed and said that they were being paid by the trip, not the number of days.

"We arrived at Magdeburg at last, and made our way past the activity of the Navy yard to the comparative quiet of the city docks, where we moored fast and unloaded. And so, we are here, safe and sound."

"And when did Marla start having trouble?" Mary asked.

"Yesterday," Franz answered. "She is, as you are no doubt aware, somewhat strong-willed." He chuckled. "And as I said, would not stay in the shelter. She kept going out on the prow in the rain, so she was cold and wet all the time. By this morning she was as you saw her when we arrived."

"I should have known you'd be talking about me," another voice said, and Franz's head whipped around to see Marla standing in the doorway at the back of the room, dressed in a thick robe and with a large shawl wrapped around her.

In the next moment, he was at her side and guiding her to a chair near the stove. "You should be resting," he scolded, worry in his eyes.

"I'm fine, Franz," she said, a little of her normal fire returning to her face and voice. "Once I got dry and started to get warm, I began to feel better."

"Are you sure?"

"Franz . . ." with a warning tone.

Marla's face was still somewhat drawn, but the color was returning, and she was smiling. A knot of worry in Franz's mind released, and he sighed in response. "All right, if you insist. But you are not going outside again today, maybe not tomorrow."

"I promise," she said. "But . . . "

"But what?"

"I want to know about the Steinway."

"Marla . . . " with exasperation.

"Franz . . . " sweetly.

He gazed into her eyes, and sighed. "All right, if I go and bring word to you, will you stay here?"

"Yes."

"Promise?"

She raised a hand to his face. "I promise." He captured her hand and brought it around to kiss the fingertips.

"Then I will go forth and return with word of your precious Steinway." Franz straightened, then looked down at her with a grin. "You know, if that piano was a man, I would be very jealous."

"You!" She slapped his leg. "Get, and find out what's happening with my piano!"

"As you command," he intoned. Hilde appeared with his coat, which, if not totally dry, was at least drier than it had been, and considerably warmer to boot.

"By your leave, Frau Simpson," he said with a slight bow.

"Go, Franz." She laughed. "She won't rest until you do."

He stepped to the door, raised a hand in farewell, and was gone.

Franz closed the door behind him and turned to face the street. Immediately he noticed that the rain had almost stopped. Casting a quizzical eye to the sky, he muttered, "You could have answered my prayer to stop the rain a little earlier than this, and spared Marla." He looked back at the street, and started down the steps. "I know, I know, 'The Lord giveth and the Lord taketh away, blessed be the Name of the Lord.'"

When he reached the bottom, he turned and began walking toward the docks. At the end of the row of houses, he stopped a merchant's apprentice hurrying by and asked for directions to the Weavers' Guildhall. Slipping and sliding through the mud, he dodged wagons, horses and other people and finally arrived at the guildhall without injury. The wagon that had been hired to carry the piano from the docks to the hall was still waiting in front of it.

Like the rest of Magdeburg, the building had been built anew after the fires from Tilly's sack had destroyed the original hall. It was a rather large structure that had much of the raw look of the newer construction, but he could see where some friezes and a few small statues had been added to the original plain exterior. The weavers were a wealthy guild, and no doubt would continue to ornament their hall until it reflected what they felt to be their position in Magdeburg's society.

Franz walked up the main steps to the portico, paused at the top to scrape his boots on the tool provided for that purpose, then faced a pair of large but plain doors. No doubt the guild would have them replaced with ornately carved panels at their earliest convenience. He passed through them and entered a foyer of sorts: a couple of offices on each side, then a cross hallway, and on the other side a large pair of doors flanked by stairways. The guild had already spent some money here, for these doors had glass panes in them.

One of the office doors was open, so Franz stuck his head in the doorway. He spied a clerk hard at work at a ledger book. "Where is the ballroom?"

The clerk didn't even look up, just jabbed with the quill in his hand toward his left. "Through the glass doors." Dipping his quill in his ink, he continued his hasty scribbling.

The first thing Franz noticed as he opened the doors was Friedrich Braun's voice. "No, you idiot! Do not start lifting until I tell you to!"

Franz entered the room at the far end from where Friedrich was rolling out from under the piano to glare at someone Franz didn't know. Several of the men standing around the piano looked around as he approached. He saw Hermann Katzberg, Isaac Fremdling and Josef and Rupert Tuchman standing together, watching as Friedrich worked at uncrating the piano. Several Magdeburg locals, obviously drafted to provide muscle power, were grouped together on the other side of the piano. It was one of them that Friedrich was glaring at. The man started to bristle, but something caught his attention, and he paled and backed away to mingle with his companions. Franz followed his eyes, to see Gunther Achterhof leaning against the side wall and directing a very piercing gaze at the offender.

Franz's footsteps sounded in the suddenly quiet room, and Friedrich turned to spy him. "Franz! How is Marla?"

All of his friends looked at him with concern written on their faces, expressions which lightened as they saw the smile on his own face.

"She is feeling better," he responded as he joined their rank. "Getting her inside where she could be warm and dry has made much difference. In a day or two, we will have her amongst us again, belaboring us with directions and criticisms, and assuring us that we will grow used to the dissonance."

They all laughed in relief as Franz squatted to bring himself down to Friedrich's level. "So what happens here, oh greatest of all journeymen?"

"Have a care how you speak to one who holds tools in his hands," Friedrich retorted, "lest you find them applied to your skull instead of this crate." He rolled back under the piano. "As you can see, the bottom of the shipping crate is resting on trestles. Master Ingram, who is indeed worthy of that accolade, designed the crate in such a manner that while it rests on the trestles, we can remove part of the bottom and reattach the legs and pedals to the piano. Thus we do not have to tilt it onto its side, nor have many men attempt to hold it in the air whilst I scurry around like a beetle underneath it, striving to attach the legs before it is dropped upon me. That is, if a certain lackwit can be restrained from attempting to lift one side of it until I am finished!" Friedrich's voice at that moment dripped acid. The man he referred to shuffled his feet and moved to the rear of the group of locals.

"So the liberating of the Steinway from its crate proceeds well, then?" Franz asked lightly.

"Aye, well indeed, thanks to the artifice of those unknown craftsmen who made the Steinway. 'Tis a miracle of design, Franz. So spare in features, so well crafted, so few tools needed to disassemble and reassemble it. There is an elegance in their work that I despair of ever attaining. And in its own way, Master Ingram's design of the crate is almost as elegant, allowing the piano to be enveloped by the crate's assembly around it, rather than forcing the instrument to be jostled around and eventually placed inside the crate. Much less risk of damage in his way. There!" he exclaimed, rolling out from under the piano again.

Climbing to his feet, Friedrich said, "All right, you lot, space yourselves around the piano, but leave the curved side open for the moment." He waited for the locals and Isaac, Johann and Rupert to take their places. "Do not grasp the packing crate, but the bottom of the instrument itself. Take a good grasp, so that the blanket wrapping it does not slip in your hands. And do not lift until I say the word!" with an indiscriminate glare for everyone involved. "Franz, Hermann, when we lift, gently pull the trestles and the remaining portion of the crate from under the piano. I remind you all, if anyone mars the beauty of this creation, he will answer to Mistress Marla, and I would not be in his shoes for all the silver in Amsterdam." Franz took his coat off and tossed it to the floor some distance away.

Friedrich took his place at the keyboard end between two of the locals, took his grip and looked around at them all. "Lift!" The piano elevated, and Hermann dove under it to support the bottom of the case and guide it as Franz carefully pulled the first trestle from under the small end of the piano. After what seemed like an eternity, but was probably no more than a very few of the up-timers' minutes, it was accomplished.

Hermann came out from under the instrument with a sour look on his face. Guessing that the expression came from his being apparently relegated to the easy work because of his short stature, Franz caught his eye and held up his damaged left hand, not saying a word. It took a moment for Hermann to catch his meaning, but catch it he did, and he acknowledged it with a nod and a wry twist of his mouth. As much as they might wish otherwise, Franz thought, they both had to acknowledge their limitations.

Friedrich handed a purse to Isaac, asking him to pay the locals, then rolled back under the piano. Franz heard Friedrich muttering, so he squatted again. "Now what occurs, oh wonder in the firmaments of craftsmanship?"

"What occurs is that a certain flap-tongued sawyer of strings is treading the steps of a dangerous dance, and may well find himself dancing with the devil if he continues." Friedrich muttered again, and this time Franz caught a mention of matter that was typically shoveled out of stable stalls.

Given that his friend normally took seriously the scriptural instruction to avoid vulgarity, Franz therefore knew that he was indeed frustrated about something underneath the Steinway. "Is there aught I can do?" he asked in a sober tone.

"Nay. The blanket that enwraps the piano is laced together underneath," Friedrich's voice sounded strained. "The knots will not release their hold."

"And who tied these knots?"

Silence, for a moment, then a surly, "I did."

Franz looked up at his other friends, to see grins that matched his own.

"Aha!" came from under the piano, and they could hear the sound of cords being drawn through holes, evidence that the knots had finally given way. In a few moments, Friedrich rolled out from underneath with two fists full of cords. The blanket edges now hung down straight from the sides of the piano. Friedrich pulled the blanket off, then opened the lid and took out the blanket that had been padding the props and the edge of the opening. Propping the lid open, he then unlocked the keyboard cover and removed the padding that had been inserted underneath it. "Hermann," he said, pulling over the bench that had been set to one side, "you are the best of us at this in Marla's absence. Play, so that we can hear if it has suffered some hidden injury."

Hermann sat down and began to play something contrapuntal, something Franz knew he had heard before. After a moment, he recognized it as one of the *Three-Part Inventions* by J. S. Bach, one of the pieces that Marla had used early in their discussions about the future of music to demonstrate the final glories of the contrapuntal style of composition. Hermann played it well. After he brought the work to its conclusion, he looked at Friedrich, then at Franz, saying, "To my ear, it rings true."

"To me as well." Friedrich nodded. "Marla will probably want to tune it, but I think it has survived its travels without injury."

"Good," Franz replied, picking up his coat and shrugging it on. "That is the word that Marla sent me to obtain.

Now I can take that to her, and she will at last be at her ease." His fingers busy with buttons, he asked, "Where are we sleeping tonight? Have you found word of an inn where we can stay until we can find rooms?"

Before anyone could respond, Gunther Achterhof pushed off from the wall where he had been leaning, forgotten all this time. The friends turned to face him, and Franz forced himself to not step back from the man's presence. "No need for an inn," the CoC leader said. "Mistress Linder will be staying with Admiral and Frau Simpson, and rooms for all of you have been provided by Mr. Wilhelm Wettin."

Franz knew that name, but it took him a moment to remember why he knew it. Then his eyes opened wide—the former duke of Saxe-Weimar! That was who was providing them accommodations! He glanced around, and the others were as stunned as he was. From the slight smile on Gunther's face, he found their reactions humorous.

"Umm," Franz hemmed, "are you certain?"

"Oh, yes," Gunther replied, still smiling that slight smile, "the former duke of Saxe-Weimar, now the commoner Wilhelm Wettin, has offered to 'put you up,' as the Americans say. I think it would be rude to refuse." They all assured him they were in agreement with him. "And besides, your bags have already been delivered there," Gunther concluded, which left them with nothing at all to say.

"Good. Now, Herr Sylwester, let me walk with you back to Admiral Simpson's house." And with that, Franz found himself waving goodbye to his friends as Gunther urged him out the door.

He looked over at the Committee man's face as they walked down the street, wondering what Gunther's desire to walk with him foreboded. Gunther caught him at it and smiled his slight smile again. "Do not worry, Herr Sylwester. I simply wanted a little privacy to tell you something."

"Tell me something?" Franz almost stuttered.

"Yes." The smile disappeared. "We will be watching over you."

"Over us?" Franz knew he sounded stupid, but he was almost struck dumb over the notion of the Committees of Correspondence keeping watch on Marla and himself.

"Yes. Magdeburg is not as . . . civilized . . . as Grantville. You will be protected, much as we protect the admiral and his lady."

Moments of silence as they walked along, then, "Why?" from Franz.

"Partly because Fraulein Linder is American, and you are hers; partly because she is here under the wing of the admiral's lady; and partly because of who she is." Gunther paced quietly for several steps. "I heard her sing once, at the Gardens. Almost I forgot who I was." More silent steps, then, "Will she sing for us here?" There was a tone in his voice, one that Franz could not recognize, but something more than the usual gruffness.

"I cannot speak for her, but it would not surprise me," Franz responded.

"Good."

They stopped at an intersection of streets, where Gunther clapped Franz on his shoulder, staggering him slightly. "The admiral's street is the second corner after this one. You should make it with no problems from here. And remember, we are watching. If you need anything, just look around. You will find us." Whistling tunelessly between his teeth, he turned up the cross street. Franz stared after him.

Marla reached up and undid her ponytail holder as the door closed behind Franz, allowing her coal black hair to settle around her shoulders and flow down her back. She leaned back in the embrace of the chair, resting her head against the upholstery.

"So how do you really feel, Marla?" she heard Mary ask.

Opening her eyes, she said, "I think I've felt worse than this in my life, but I can't really remember when." She raised her head with a tired smile, receiving a smile in return.

"Probably a combination of stress and being thoroughly chilled," Mary said.

"Is there any coffee left in that pot, Mrs. Simpson?" She leaned her head back against the chair again.

"Call me Mary, dear. There's not much here, and it's cool. Let me have Hilde bring some more." The maid must have been within earshot. Marla never heard a summons, but in a moment she heard footsteps crossing from the door to the nearby table and back again.

Mary cleared her throat. "So, you're here, the piano is here, and Franz is here. Tell me who else came with you."

"Hermann Katzberg, Josef and Rudolf Tuchman, and Isaac Fremdling are the musicians. Hermann is an absolute wizard at harpsichord and organ, and does well with a Baroque flute. Josef plays viola d'amore, and his

brother Rudolf plays Baroque flute and has a good baritone voice. Isaac is a really good violinist in the German
style, and has a tenor voice that would have earned him
rock god status if he'd been born in the twentieth
century.

"Friedrich Braun came with us to see to the unpacking
and setting up of the piano, but he'll be returning to
Grantville as soon as possible. He has responsibilities in
the Bledsoe and Riebeck shop."

Mary looked over the rim of her cup, assessing the
young woman seated across from her. Her face was
drawn, with dark shadows under her eyes; her shoulders
slumped slightly from exhaustion. Nonetheless, her voice
was strong, her tone was calm, and she seemed composed. Either she was one of those people who bounced
back from injury quickly, or she was one who worked
through her pain. Either way, Mary liked what she had
seen of her so far.

"And where does Franz fit into this gallery of musicians?" she asked. She had her guesses, but she wanted
to hear what Marla said.

A small, dreamy smile appeared on Marla's face for
a moment, then she took another sip of coffee before
responding. "Musically, Franz is a work of salvage at the
moment. His left hand was crushed by a rival violinist
who was jealous of his skill."

Mary flinched a little. "That almost sounds like something out of the Pittsburgh docks and the mob."

"Oh, yes," Marla said. "That was my first thought also.
However, you know as well as anyone that musicians,
like actors, are typically passionate people. Sometimes

that passion takes a wrong turn. Anyway, Dr. Nichols wasn't able to offer any hope of surgical repair, but with some therapy Franz has regained enough use to hold an Italian style bow with his left hand. He's now in the process of learning to play again, only with reversed hands: the right doing the fingering and the left the bowing. He's frustrated at this stage . . . he knows what to do, but the muscles are still in early training and don't just automatically do what he wants them to do. But Isaac says that Franz was the best player in Mainz before the attack, and that he should regain that same level in short order."

"And personally?"

"Personally . . . " Marla drew the word out. "He's a passionate soul, with an incredible gentleness. He has very high standards for himself. And . . . " another long, drawn-out word, then a rush to "I love him."

"A love he obviously returns." Mary chuckled, recalling the scene when Marla sent him out to find out what had happened with her precious piano. "So, if it's not prying, do you intend to marry?"

"Franz won't hear of it until he can play in public again. He says he will not ask me until he can prove he can support us."

"I take it he's somewhat strong-willed?"

Marla burst out laughing. It took a moment for her to regain her composure. "That would be somewhat like calling water wet," she at length replied. "It's probably a good thing, too, as more than one of my friends have hinted that I'm a bit that way myself."

Mary smiled. "Actually, Franz did say much the same about you."

Marla laughed again. "I've always suspected it would take a strong will to both stand up to me and put up with me. Franz is the first man, up-time or down, that has managed to do that and interested me at the same time. My Aunt Susan says I'm obsessed at times. That's probably true, but it's usually about something musical, which as far as I'm concerned is worth being obsessed about."

The two women shared a look of understanding. Obsession about music was indeed a mindset they both understood very well. It boded well for their relationship.

Franz again knocked on the door to the Simpsons' house. He was a little taken aback when it was opened by Mrs. Simpson herself.

"Come in, Franz, come in. We've been having a lovely talk while we waited for you."

"Um, thank you." He stepped in, took his coat off and hung it on the same peg he had hung it on when he had first entered the house.

"Well?" Marla asked impatiently from her seat. He was encouraged to see even more color in her face than had been there when he left. "What's the verdict on the Steinway?"

He crossed over to her, bent down and kissed the top of her head. "The piano has been totally uncrated and reassembled in the Weaver's Guild hall. Friedrich has examined it with great care, and both he and Hermann are of the opinion that it has suffered no harm from its journeys. So, you may rest your mind about it, and therefore rest your body as well."

Marla sighed, and Franz watched as a certain tension drained out of her, leaving her almost limp in the embrace of the chair. Her blue eyes peered up at him through the curtain of her bangs, followed by one of those smiles that reminded him of just why he loved her. "Okay. I've had a nice long chat with Mary, but I think I'm ready to go to bed now. Help me up."

He reached down to take one arm just as Hilde the maid appeared at the other side of the chair; between them they raised Marla to her feet. He walked with them to the door that led to the stairway. Marla gave him a quick kiss, then started up the narrow stairs with Hilde supporting her.

"An unusual young woman," Franz heard from behind. He turned to face Mrs. Simpson.

"I believe that is what my friend Ingram would call an understatement," he said soberly.

Mary smiled. "No doubt."

"Frau Simpson . . . "

"Mary," she interjected.

"Mary, then . . . I thank you for arranging a place for my friends and me to stay, but I must tell you that a simple inn would have been more appropriate than the . . . Wettin household."

"Oh, that. Actually, my original plan was to rent some rooms in an inn, but Eleonore volunteered . . . insisted, actually. She said that now that she was a commoner, she wanted to meet some of these interesting people that before now would hardly open their mouths in her presence."

Franz was surprised into a laugh. "She may get her wish, then. Hermann will talk to anyone, and is almost impossible to stop once he begins."

"Good. I would so hate for her to be disappointed."
Mary's impish smile surprised Franz.

Saturday, October 16, 1633

The next day dawned with clear skies. The rain had
stopped in the middle of the night, and the clouds had
dissipated. Franz stepped out into the street with his
friends, smiling at Hermann's last joke with the maid
who closed the door of the Wettin house behind them.

"Right," Isaac said. "What do we do today?" They all
looked at Franz.

"You go to the guild hall. I will go to the Simpsons'
and look in on Marla, then join you."

They walked together past several houses, then separated to go their ways. Franz continued alone down the
busy streets until he arrived at the Simpsons' house. After
Gunther's revelation yesterday, Franz looked at the surroundings with new eyes, finding what Gunther had
assured him would be there: two young men, hard-edged
and hard-eyed, standing together under a streetlight
across the street from the admiral's house. He swallowed
nervously as he approached, but nodded to them and
said "Good morning." They said nothing, but did nod
in return.

Feeling somewhat encouraged, he crossed the street
and knocked on the Simpsons' door. Hilde opened it
with a smile. "Welcome." She stepped back to allow him
to enter, then took his coat.

"Good morning, Franz," he heard behind him. Mrs.
Simpson and Marla were seated in the same chairs they

had occupied when he left them yesterday. The only way he could tell that time had passed was that they were both wearing different clothing. Well, that and Marla looked normal again. Her eyes were smiling above her coffee cup as Mary reached for the pot to pour a cup for Franz. He took a seat as Mary handed the cup across to him.

"What's on the agenda today?" Mary asked.

Before Franz could respond, Marla said, "Practice at the Weavers' guild hall."

"Just a moment!" Franz interjected, not believing what he was hearing. "I do not believe that is a good idea, not after the way you felt yesterday, and the day before."

Marla carefully set her cup down on the table, clasped her hands together, and stared into Franz's frowning eyes. In a very calm tone of voice, she said, "I feel better than I have since we started the trip. It's not raining. I will bundle up and stay warm and dry. I will not push my limits. But I am going to the guild hall. The piano must be tuned, and I've got to check out the acoustics of the hall. Unless you plan on tying me to this chair, I am going." Her expressionless face told Franz that if he did, he would regret it.

Franz was astute enough to recognize a battle he could not win, so he gave in to the inevitable. "Mrs. Simpson . . . Mary," forestalling her correction, "would it be possible . . . "

Mary smiled as she said, "I've already arranged for a ride." Both women laughed at Franz's rueful expression. Franz muttered . . . under his breath, he thought.

"What was that?" Marla asked.

"Nothing."

"Franz . . ." with a rising tone of warning.

"I said, I feel conspired against."

Mary chuckled. "Poor man." Sobering, she continued, "She'll be fine, Franz. I would not willingly risk her, any more than you would."

And with that he had to be content.

Franz looked around as his foot touched the ground, seeking that which would previously have gone unnoticed. There, across the street, two more young men in the mold of those who waited outside the admiral's house. He turned to help the ladies down: first Mrs. Simpson, then Marla. Even after only one day in her presence, he had not a problem with thinking of Mary Simpson as the Dame of Magdeburg. Her charm and grace were the equal of the rumors and legends beginning to circulate about her. Marla, in her own right, young though she was, bid fair to shape into the same kind of woman. Already, he could see one or two little ways where she had been influenced by Mary.

Together they proceeded up the steps. Franz held open the outer door, then led the way into the ballroom. The sound of the piano poured out as he opened those doors. Marla smiled and pushed past him, hungry for her "baby." Mary followed in a more sedate manner.

Hermann was playing another piece from Bach's *Three Part Inventions*—and doing a good job of it, Franz thought, given that he had only been working on it for two weeks prior to the move to Magdeburg. He looked up from the keyboard. "Marla!" His obvious surprise resulted in a delighted tone of voice.

"Hi, Hermann." Marla plopped down beside him on the piano bench. "How does it sound?"

"The piano sounds fine," Hermann enthused. "This is the first time I have been able to play this one. It is much better than the pianos we heard at the school."

"Now you understand why I want it here. Move over." Marla bumped his hip. Hermann not only moved over, he got up and let her have the entire bench. She set her hands on the keys, paused for that instant that Franz had learned to recognize as her moment of focus, then began a piece that he didn't recognize. It was not polyphonic, but the chords were harmonious to his ear, so he knew it had to be an "early" piece from Marla's repertoire.

All the others gathered around the piano as Marla played: Franz, Mary Simpson, Johann and Rudolf and Friedrich. The piece was not lengthy, and before long she brought it to a rousing conclusion. Her audience burst into applause. Franz could tell from the startled expression on her face when she looked up that Marla had, as usual, focused on the music to the exclusion of everything around her.

"That, my dear," Mary said, "was simply lovely. I don't believe I've heard a piano transcription of Mozart's "Eine Kleine Nachtmusik" before. Did you produce it yourself?"

"No." Marla flushed slightly at the praise. "I would have, or Thomas Schwarzberg would have done it for me, but the Grantville High School band department has a band transcription of it. The condensed conductor's score actually is nothing more than a piano transcription. I borrowed it from the band a couple of years ago, and learned it for fun. I haven't played it for a while, so I'm pretty rusty."

"You should include that in your recital programme," the older woman remarked. "It should be well received by those who attend."

"I intend to," Marla responded.

Mary started to say something else, then visibly collected herself as Marla began playing a pattern of scales, beginning at the low end of the keyboard and rolling to the high end, pausing for a moment, then commencing again on the next highest pitch at the low end. She repeated this several times, until she had played every key on the piano at least once, and most several times. Finally, she stopped and played several widely separated keys individually, obviously listening carefully.

"Friedrich," she called out. "Where's the tuning kit?"

Friedrich was already digging it out of his bag, and in a moment handed it to her. He slid the music stand out of the piano frame above the keyboard and set it on a chair to one side as she unrolled the kit on the bench. Then he opened the lid up to its maximum height, standing to one side to allow Marla full access to the interior of the instrument.

Franz watched with Mary Simpson as Marla reached inside the piano with the tuning wrench. "Okay, how much did Ingram show you about tuning pianos?" Marla asked.

"Master Ingram said that I had learned the theory well, that what I needed now was the practice," Friedrich responded.

"Okay, practice away. First thing, the d2 is flat."

Marla and the journeyman instrument crafter labored to restore the piano to perfect tuning. Mary beckoned Franz to follow her to the rear of the room, where she turned to face him. "I understand why you and Friedrich are here, but why did Marla bring the others?"

"Hermann is to accompany her when she sings," Franz said.

Mary grimaced. "Of course, I should have realized that. She can't very well accompany herself, not with the art music I've asked her to sing. That explains Hermann; what about the rest?"

"Isaac she wishes to do a duet with, although she has not yet decided what to sing with him."

"Hmm, I may have a suggestion or two there, depending on what music she has brought with her. And the others?"

"I do not know. It was a late decision, made just before we left. She said something about Maestro Carissimi possibly having something for them to perform."

Mary's eyes widened. "Carissimi? Giacomo Carissimi?"

"Yes, I believe that is his name."

"She knows him?"

"Yes. We all do. He arrived in Grantville from Italy several weeks ago, along with an instrument crafter named Giro . . . Girolamo Zenti, I believe. He has had several long conversations with Marla, and even sat in on one or two of our seminar discussions. He is working now with Frau Elizabeth Jordan to learn the new music styles, much as we worked with Marla this summer."

"Oh, my." Mary was silent for long moments, staring at the wall beyond his shoulder.

"Do you know him?"

Mary sighed. "Know him? No, I don't. I do, however, know *of* him. I think it just finally sank in to me in a way that it never had before that I really am in the seventeenth century; that I will have a chance to meet some of the people that I have loved from afar and whose works I have listened to with joy and appreciation. Oh, my." She took a deep breath, and turned to focus on Franz with glittering eyes. "Yes, indeed, if she has an opportunity to do something by Maestro Carissimi, we should make every effort to include it."

"You must ask Marla," Franz said. "I have told you what I know."

Mary nodded, a determined look on her face as she stared in Marla's direction. After a moment, she looked to Franz again. "Weren't there more people studying with you?"

"Yes; Thomas Schwarzberg and Leopold Gruenwald. They were left in Grantville by their own desires." Mary looked at him with a quizzical expression. Franz continued, "Thomas stayed to copy music. He can notate anything he can hear, so he stayed to notate everything that is recorded in the records, tapes and CDs. It may well prove to be his life's work. And Leopold, although not as adept as Thomas, is also good at notation, so he will assist Thomas when he is not working with Master Wendell to learn the designs of up-time wind instruments. He is a crafter of horns in his own right, much as Friedrich and Herren Bledsoe and Riebeck are of things that sing from wood."

"So, after Friedrich leaves, Marla will have the core of your group with her, those who have learned from her and will perform with her?"

Franz turned to look at the others: Friedrich, who had his head inside the piano alongside Marla's as she explained something technical to him; Josef and Rudolf who waited patiently to one side, their fingers silently running patterns on their instruments; and Hermann, who was fidgeting in his chair—which was as patient as he knew how to wait—all of them somehow bound to Marla. He looked back at Mrs. Simpson. "Yes. These men will be with Marla forever. They have committed to her, to follow her lead, to be her hands and voices in this lifetime."

"And you, Franz," Mary asked, "what will you be to her?"

He looked down at Mary, who waited expectantly, then looked out at the sun and moon of his life where she laughed at something Friedrich said. "I will be her heart."

Wednesday, October 19, 1633

Franz threw the door to the tavern open and they all trooped in, exclaiming at how good it felt to be out of the weather. The wind was from the north that evening, and as dark closed in it felt as if it had blown straight down from the Swedish mountains, it was so frigid. Everyone but Franz had instrument cases tucked up under their arms as they blew on their fingers to try to warm them. His crippled left hand was aching savagely. He tucked it inside his coat under his arm to warm it as quickly as possible.

"Come on, guys," Marla said, eyes sparkling and cheeks reddened by the cold, "the host is waving us to the table by the stove." They made their way through the throng, Josef and Rudolf leading the way and parting the mass of people, followed by Marla and Franz, with Hermann and Isaac bringing up the rear. They all sat down on the benches and carefully set their instruments on the table.

"What will you have?" the barmaid near shouted to be heard over the roar of conversation.

"Coffee!" was the unanimous voice from every throat. She bobbed her head and scurried off to the kitchen, to return shortly with five cheap ceramic mugs and a large ceramic pot which she set on the table.

"Compliments of the master," she said, "to keep your throats wet tonight. He says whenever you are ready, begin. This lot will quiet down quickly enough." With another bob of her head, she dashed off to grab a circle of empty flagons being held up by a table whose occupants were loudly demanding beer.

The largesse was perhaps no great surprise, as the keeper of The Green Horse tavern had been delighted to find that players who had played in the famed Thuringen Gardens were in town. He had sought Franz out and asked if they would play in his humble establishment. When Franz polled the others, they were all ready for some fun, so they agreed to play one night in his tavern, on the condition that whatever funds were thrown their way by the patrons were theirs. The alacrity with which he agreed made it clear that he expected to make more than enough from the beer and wine and coffee that he would sell to those who came to hear them.

Franz grabbed for the pot as soon as their mugs were filled, letting the heat soak into his chilled and hurting hands. The blissful heat drove the ache from his fingers; as it did so, he mused on how the people who were touched by the Americans all adopted many of the American practices. Surprisingly—or perhaps not so surprisingly—the thing that everyone took up was the drinking of coffee. The Abrabanels were making a large fortune by importing it from Turkey.

He focused on the present again as Marla unloosened her scarf and unbuttoned her coat, took a big swig of the oh-so-popular coffee, then opened her flute case and began assembling the instrument. "Man!" she exclaimed. I forgot just how cold this thing can get." She began blowing into the open end, forcing air through it to warm it up.

Franz watched Marla closely. She was in high spirits tonight, with no evidence of the exhaustion, stress and pain that had drawn her down only days before. He worried, nonetheless, despite the assurances of both Marla and Mrs. Simpson that she was fine. It was foolish to do so, he knew, but nonetheless he did worry.

They spent several minutes warming their instruments: Rudolf rolling his baroque flute in his hands, letting the warmth of his flesh warm the wood before he blew into it; Isaac and Josef doing much the same thing as they ran their hands over the violin and viola d'amore. Hermann took the longest, holding the harp he had received from Ingram Bledsoe near the stove, then drawing it to himself to run his hands over the wood, then repeating the process until he was satisfied that it was warm. Finally, he ran his hands up and down the strings, then began the tuning process. Once he was satisfied, he looked over at the others, plucking a tone so they could tune to him.

Marla looked at them all and raised her eyebrows. "What will it be, boys?"

They looked at each other, then to Franz, who over the weeks had been proven to have the best skill for reading a crowd. He shrugged, then replied, "Brian Boru's March."

"Right," Marla smiled. She stood, and Josef, Rudolf and Isaac stood with her. Hermann stood long enough to shift a chair around to the center of their line to face the patrons. Franz moved the coffee pot to the top of the stove. No sense in letting it get cold while they performed.

Raising her flute to her lips, Marla counted, "One, two, ready, go!"

The strains of the music readily penetrated the fog of conversation, which died away almost immediately. The boisterous song soon had everyone in the tavern tapping the table or clapping their hands. Franz looked around, and no one was talking, no one was drinking; everyone, even the host and the barmaid, was caught up in the music.

The sound of the music triggered Franz's memory, taking him back to the day in early July when Marla had unveiled to their circle her mother's prized collection of Irish folk music, a mixture of old LPs and newer CDs with mostly Chieftains and Clancy Brothers albums. The down-timers had all fallen for the infectious melodies, rhythms and harmonies of the songs. Within a quarter hour they had all brought out their instruments and started trying to play along. They were all skilled at learning music from the hearing of it, so it hadn't taken them long to learn many of their favorites. Within a few weeks they were actually performing one night a week at the Thuringen Gardens, with Marla doing most of the singing and Isaac and Rudolf sometimes joining in. They would occasionally change a few of the words to fit them to Germany, but all in all the songs they sang adjusted well, and of course the instrumental music needed no translation. Whether they played the fast moving dances or the slow ballads, the music all seemed to strike a chord in their listeners; tonight appeared to be no exception.

They wrapped up the march with a flourish and the tavern rocked with applause. The players all grinned at each other as they sucked in air. Judging the mood of the crowd, Franz stepped up to the players and took Marla's flute. They all leaned in for his word. "Do 'Nell Flaherty's Drake' next." They nodded in response; he stepped back, giving them the downbeat. Isaac and Rudolf gave Marla an introduction with violin and flute, fast and bouncy like the Clancy Brothers and Tommy Makem version they had learned it from, and then she came in with the verse.

Oh, me name it is Nell, and the truth for to tell
I come from Cootehill which I'll never deny.
I had a fine drake and I'd die for his sake.
That me grandmother left me, and she goin' to die.
The dear little fellow, his legs they were yellow.
He could fly like a swallow or swim like a hake,
'Til some dirty savage to grease his white cabbage
Most wantonly murdered me beautiful drake.

Now his neck it was green, almost fit to be seen.
He was fit for a queen of the highest degree.
His body was white, and it would you delight.
He was plump, fat, and heavy and brisk as a bee.
He was wholesome and sound, he would weigh
    twenty pound,
And the universe round I would roam for his sake.
Bad luck to the robber, be he drunk or sober,
That murdered Nell Flaherty's beautiful drake.

Franz stood to one side near the stove, foot tapping to the beat of the rollicking song. He was as caught up in the music as the performers, and without conscious thought his hands were at waist level, directing the performance. He had seen Marcus Wendell direct the Grantville High School Band; he had seen various choir directors in Grantville leading their groups; during their seminar he had seen videos of men that Marla called great directors using their gifts to lift orchestras to unbelievable heights of artistry. Unbeknownst, unacknowledged, unperceived, the desire to be one like them—one who would gather the strands of single musicians and weave them into a unique tapestry—that desire was growing in him, and at unguarded moments his hands would make in miniature the movements he would make if he were a leader, not someone standing in the shadows.

Marla began the third verse, and smiles began appearing all over the common room as the tavern patrons began hearing the inventive curses of the robbed and deprived Nell.

May his spade never dig, may his sow never pig,
May each hair in his wig be well trashed with the flail.
May his door never latch, may his roof have no thatch,
May his chickens not hatch, may the rats eat his meal.
May every old fairy from Cork to Dun Laoghaire
Dip him snug and airy in river or lake,
That the eel and the trout they may dine on the snout
Of the monster that murdered Nell Flaherty's drake.

The smiles around the room had become chuckles.

May his pig never grunt, may his cat never hunt,
May a ghost ever haunt him the dead of the night.
May his hens never lay, may his horse never neigh,
May his coat fly away like an old paper kite
That the flies and the fleas may the wretch ever tease.
May the piercin' March breeze make him shiver
and shake.
May a lump of the stick raise the bumps fast and quick
On the monster that murdered Nell Flaherty's drake.

Franz could see Marla grinning as she sang, obviously enjoying how all the chuckles as quickly became guffaws. She glanced his way and winked, to which he smiled in reply. Her glance bounced back to the players; she nodded to them to bring it all together for the last verse.

Well, the only good news that I have to infuse
Is that old Paddy Hughes and young Anthony Blake,
Also Johnny Dwyer and Corney Maguire,
They each have a grandson of my darlin' drake.
Me treasure had dozens of nephews and cousins

And one I must get or me heart it will break,
For to set me mind easy or else I'll run crazy.
So ends the whole song of Nell Flaherty's drake.

The previous applause was now seen to be just a fore-taste of what the evening held, as the patrons now produced a volume of sound that had to be heard to be believed; cheers, yells, foot stomping and whistling to the point that the walls seemed to bulge and dislodged dust was floating down from the rafters. Marla dropped a mock curtsy, then flung her arms wide and took a bow, echoed by the rest of the players.

The noise abated a little when Marla beckoned Franz forward, and they all huddled together, eyes gleaming and breath coming hard but all of them quivering like a team of horses ready to run a race. "Now what?" Marla demanded of Franz.

He thought for a moment. "Do the fast version of 'Jug of Punch.' You sing it. Then let Rudolf sing 'Long Black Veil.' End with Isaac singing 'Rising of the Moon.'" Marla gathered the eyes of the players, and they all nodded as one. Franz gave them the count, stepping back as the music broke out again.

The three songs were performed in turn, with loud applause sounding after each. Finally, the players begged off, telling the crowd they needed a rest. Franz topped off the coffee mugs, and took the empty pot to the bar to ask for more. He had to push his way through the crowd that had gathered around Marla, then wend his way between the tables to reach the bar. He set the pot down, realizing as he did so that Gunther Achterhof was standing next to him. He started to say something, but was interrupted by sounds from the other end of the room.

Gunther straightened from his slouch against the bar as Franz Sylwester approached him. He gave him a slight nod in recognition. Franz seemed about to speak, when there was a sudden *Smack!* of hand meeting flesh, followed by a man's shout suddenly choked off. He spun to rake the room with a glance, immediately noting people pushing away from where Marla Linder stood facing an unkempt man. Grabbing Klaus, one of his confederates, by the arm, they plowed their way through the room, sending people reeling and tables and benches flying. Those who started to object took one look at him and hurriedly backed away. He could hear Franz following in their wake.

He noted as they neared the confrontation that Fraulein Linder had one hand at the man's throat, and that the man was standing stock-still, even rigid. Marla released her hold as soon as he and Klaus grabbed the man's arms, and the man immediately began choking and gasping, trying to grab his throat with the hands that Gunther and the other CoC man were restraining.

Marla grabbed his hair and tilted his head up, bringing his wide-eyed, fearful gaze to meet her narrowed, ice-cold blue eyes. Gunther could see the mark on his face where she had slapped him. "No one paws me," Marla hissed from a distance of inches. "Get out of my sight, and you'd better not ever let me see you again, or I'll shred you." Even to one as hardened as Gunther, her voice held unnerving menace.

Gunther released the arm that he held to another CoC man who arrived at that moment, just in time to grab Franz and prevent him from assaulting the slumping man, who by now was wheezing as he breathed. Marla stepped back, and a greasy smudge on the breast of her bright yellow sweater made it very clear what had happened. Gunther jerked his head at his fellows, and they hustled the man out the back door of the tavern. By main force he dragged Franz around to look him in the eye. "Tend to Fraulein Linder," he grated. "This one is mine." He dropped his hand from Franz's arm, but Marla placed a shaking hand on his chest as he started to follow out the back door.

"I know you," she said in a tone that, despite the tremor of her hand, was remarkably firm. "I remember seeing you in Grantville. Don't kill him." Her voice was so matter-of-fact that Gunther was slightly shocked. He stared at her, and she bore that gaze. Finally, he nodded. "Or maim him," she added. Angered, he started to move past her, only to have her step into his path and continue to steadily look into his eyes. Once again she bore his hot gaze, and once again he finally nodded.

Marla stepped out of his way and let Franz enfold her. Gunther now moved implacably toward the door. Those who were between him and it scrambled to be someplace else. He stepped out the door and closed it, then stood still until he was sure he could see well enough to walk without running into anything.

"Klaus," he called.

"Here."

Gunther walked toward the sound, rounded a cart that was standing in the alleyway, and there found Klaus and Reuel holding the attacker up against the rear of the cart. His breathing had eased some, so that he was no longer choking and wheezing, but he still coughed and hacked frequently. That such a piece of filth could—would—assault someone under his protection stoked the furnace of Gunther's ire to a level that would melt steel. He stopped in front of the drooping figure, grabbed his hair and slammed his head back against the cart, receiving a cry in response.

"I do not know you, and I know everyone in Magdeburg worth knowing. You are new to Magdeburg, are you not?" he snarled in the local German dialect. The man, whites of his eyes gleaming all around the irises, gulped and tried to nod. "Who are you?"

"Johann Gruber," the unkempt man slurred.

"What did you think to do in there?"

"I . . . I . . . "

"Spit it out, sow's get!"

"I thought she was a whore!" the man blurted. "She was dressed so strangely—indecently! Her hair was unbound in public. She was singing in a tavern! What was I to think?"

Gunther slammed his head back against the cart again. "If you had been thinking, you would have realized that no one was treating her like a whore, that everyone was respecting her and her companions. You would have had even the small enough amount of wisdom to ask questions." Wham! went the head against the cart one more time, leaving the man even woozier than he was when he was dragged out of the tavern.

When Gruber seemed to be able to focus again, Gunther said in a softer tone, "Have you heard of the Americans, in whatever midden you climbed out of?" Receiving a shaky nod in return, he said, "She is American." The man moaned, and sagged to the point that it was only the strength of Klaus and Reuel that kept him out of the reeking mud. "Yes, now wisdom arrives. If you had managed to harm her, they would have hunted you to the ends of the earth, they would have razed the town where you were born to the ground and sowed that ground with salt, they would have made your name so notorious that mothers would have used you as a bogey-man to frighten their children with."

Gunther stepped back. "You know of the Americans." His voice was hard again. "Do you also know of the Committees of Correspondence?" A shaky nod. "Do you know of Gunther Achterhof?" Again a nod. Leaning forward close enough to smell the foul breath of the frightened Gruber, he snarled, "I am Gunther, and that woman is under my protection. Tell me, why should I not kill you now, and leave the world a cleaner place?"

There was an acrid reek as the now thoroughly-panicked man's bladder released and he tried to struggle with those who pinioned his arms. Gunther let him struggle for a moment more, then stepped up and grabbed his hair again, yanking his head around to stare at him eye to eye. "I should kill you now . . ." he brought his large clasp knife out of his pocket, flicked it open and held it up in Gruber's vision, where he stared at it with dread fascination, " . . . but I will not. You are not worth cleaning your blood from my blade." Releasing him, he closed his knife and put it away.

"Even in her anger, Lady Marla," Gunther noted to himself in some surprise that he had started thinking of her that way, "had enough grace to command you be left alive and unmaimed." The object of his scorn and rage looked up, hope dawning in his eyes in the moonlight, until he saw the predatory smile on Gunther's face. "However, she said nothing about not punishing you."

The rock-hard maul of Gunther's fist drove into the pit of Gruber's stomach. Air whooped out of lungs, and Gunther watched in some satisfaction as he doubled over, retching. Long moments passed. Just as the wretch started to straighten a little, Gunther's boot crashed into his groin. Klaus and Reuel released him to drop to the mud. The three CoC men stared at him as he curled into an agonized ball, unable to do more than sob and gasp.

Gunther finally stirred. "Take him away from town, and leave him." His confederates looked at him in some surprise. He glowered at them, which produced its usual effect. They hastily dragged the moaning bundle of reeking cloth and limp body up and began marching it down the alley. Gunther watched until they turned the corner into the nearest street, then wiped his hands on his trousers and returned to the tavern.

Franz somehow put a damper on his anger as the door slammed behind the CoC man and turned to Marla, enfolding her in his arms. The others gathered around them, shaken, saying nothing, not touching, but emanating concern nonetheless. Marla was shaking slightly as she returned his embrace. "Shh, shh," he crooned. "It is all right. No reason to fear." He felt her shaking increase, and thought for a moment she was going to begin crying, until she pushed away from him and he saw that she was laughing. Laughing! Laughing with an angry icy glint to her eye, but laughing just the same. From the expressions he could see, their friends were as dumbstruck as he was.

"I'm not afraid," Marla finally explained. "I'm angry. No, I'm beyond anger—I'm furious." She pulled away from him, crossed her arms, and stared at the floor for long moments. She finally looked up with a crooked smile. "You might as well know, I guess. You would have found out sooner or later. When I was fourteen, I was nearly raped in the back seat of a school bus. If my brother hadn't missed me and come looking for me . . . well, it wouldn't have been good. He kicked the guy out of the bus, and then beat him to a pulp." She brooded for a time, staring at the floor. Franz didn't know what to say, so he decided that the course of wisdom was to say nothing and wait. Finally, Marla heaved a sigh. "Afterwards, I swore I wouldn't let that happen again, and learned a few things from Dan Frost and Frank Jackson. I hoped I would never need it, but . . . " another sigh, " . . . as Reverend Jones keeps saying, nowhere in the Bible does it say that life is fair." She turned to Franz with a fierce expression. "I wanted to hurt him. I wanted very much to hurt him very badly." Her voice took on a plaintive tone. "But, he hadn't actually hurt me, and he was ignorant. And what would it have accomplished, except to change the way you looked at me? I wouldn't chance that," her voice broke.

Franz once more took Marla in his arms. There were no words that he could say; all he could offer was the comfort of his presence. As his arms encircled her, her arms in turn went around him and delivered a ferocious hug. They stood thus for some time, sheltered by their friends.

They all turned as the rear door opened again.

Gunther found Marla and Franz standing near the door in a semi-circle of their friends. She had her hands in her jeans pockets, and his arm was around her shoulder. Her expression was calm . . . remote, even, but the fire in Franz's eyes was a match for that in Gunther's. Franz dropped his arm and took a step forward, saying with an understandable bitterness, "Is this how you protect her?"

Gunther felt a twist in his gut. He took a deep breath as Marla laid her hand on Franz's shoulder. "The fool was no one, an idiot who had just arrived in Magdeburg and had never seen American women. There was no real danger to Fraulein Linder. I regret that what happened, happened, but it will not happen again."

"You . . . " Franz began.

"Franz, enough," Marla interrupted. He turned his hot gaze on her, but she simply repeated, "Enough." Gunther watched as the anger drained, as the fire died away in Franz's eyes, leaving only a young man with worry and nascent grief on his face. She reached up to brush his hair back; he caught her hand and held it against his cheek for a moment.

"I couldn't stand it . . . " Franz murmured.

"I know."

They stood in a silent tableau for a moment, then Marla dropped her hand and turned to Gunther. She eyed him expectantly. "I won't see him again, will I." It wasn't a question.

Gunther smiled thinly. "No. He is being escorted out of town, alive and unmarked," he held up both hands, "but chastened, and with a clear understanding that he is no longer welcome in Magdeburg."

"Thank you," Marla said quietly.

Gunther hesitated, then finally asked the question that had been in the front of his mind ever since the whole scenario had begun. "Fraulein Linder, what . . . what did you do to him?"

She stepped up to him. "This." Swift as a serpent, her hand flashed to his throat. His eyes widened as he felt her thumb and middle finger snap into the little hollows on each side of his larynx and begin to squeeze. The strength in those fingers was undeniable. He couldn't talk; he struggled to breathe, he felt the cartilage begin to creak. Just as a flutter of panic began to make itself felt, she released her hold and stepped back.

Gunther rubbed his throat, coughed experimentally and decided that things were where they belonged. "Fraulein Linder . . . " he said as she started to turn away.

"Call me Marla, Gunther."

He wondered why the brief smile flashed across Franz's face, but continued on with, "Would you sing the song for us?"

Franz was almost astounded at the nerve of Gunther Achterhof. To ask Marla to sing after such a thing happening! He opened his mouth to let the man know that, regardless of who he was, he had no right to ask Marla to sing for him or anyone else right now. Before he could speak, he heard Marla say, "Yes."

"Marla!" Now Franz was truly shocked.

"It's okay, Franz," she said. "Tonight I need it just as much as they do." The level stare from her blue eyes and the firm tone told him that it would be fruitless to argue further, so he sighed and followed her and their friends back to their table.

During the summer, as their circle of friends had performed the Irish music at the Gardens and elsewhere, they noticed that the members of the Committee of Correspondence quickly developed a real affinity for the Irish songs of rebellion. "The Rising of the Moon" became one of their favorites, and they would roar the words right along with Marla or Isaac as they sang. But there was another song that they asked for, over and over again. It got to the point that they just began asking for "The Song." It was one of those for which Marla had adapted the lyrics. It wasn't one of the bouncy, catchy ones; in fact, it was rather grim. They would never sing along with it, but every time they heard it, the CoC people seemed to condense and become almost all edge. Now, as Marla, Isaac and Rudolf readied themselves, the people of Magdeburg were about to hear for the first time what seemed to have become the CoC's anthem.

Isaac led off with a haunting line on his violin, almost a quiet wail. The room grew deathly still. Marla opened her mouth, and began to sing.

I sat within the valley green,
I sat me with my true love.
My sad heart strove the two between,
The old love and the new love.
The old for her, the new
That made me think on Deutschland dearly.
While soft the wind blew down the glade
And shook the golden barley.

Despite the softness of her tone, Marla's voice was very intense. It reached throughout the room, filling every nook and cranny, and it seemed to cast a spell. All were still. No one moved. No one did more than barely breathe. All in the room were focused on the tall young woman singing with the flute, violin and harp underlying her voice, pouring her heart and her talent and all of her emotions into the song.

> 'Twas hard the woeful words to frame
> To break the ties that bound us.
> But harder still to bear the shame
> of foreign chains around us.
> And so I said, the mountain glen
> I'll meet at morning early.
> I'll join the bold united men,
> While soft winds shook the barley.

Earlier in the evening, Marla's voice had been warm, even inviting. Now, as she sang "The Song," it was just almost serene, with a purity of tone that was almost angelic, yet raising neck hairs all over the room. Franz shivered a little, knowing what was coming next.

> 'Twas sad I kissed away her tears,
> My fond arms round her flinging,
> When a foeman's shot burst on our ears
> From out the wild woods ringing.
> A bullet pierced my true love's side
> In life's young spring so early.
> And on my breast in blood she died,
> While soft winds shook the barley.

A note of loss and grief had crept into Marla's voice, and almost they could hear the keening for the dead. By the end of the verse she sounded so forlorn that, despite himself, despite knowing the song intimately, Franz felt tears welling up in response.

The first two lines of the last stanza were snarled, and several of the hearers jumped.

But blood for blood without remorse
I've taken at Oulart Hollow.

The second two lines were sung quietly again, almost meditatively, but again with a forlorn note.

I've lain my true love's clay cold corpse
Where I full soon must follow.

Marla was giving the finest performance of this song that Franz had ever heard; far surpassing the recorded version she had learned it from. The final lines were so poignant, and Marla invested them with so much grief, that his heart ached within him.

Around her grave I've wandered drear,
Noon, night, and morning early,
With breaking heart whene'er I hear
The wind that shakes the barley.

No one stirred. No applause was given. Finally, through the moisture in his eyes, Franz saw Gunther give Marla a salute and slip out of the tavern.

Friday, October 21, 1633

Marla hammered out the final chords of the "Revolutionary Etude," bringing it to a driving finish. She held the final chord for a long moment, then released the keys and sat back on the bench, smiling. "Well," she said to herself—or so she thought—"that wasn't too bad."

"I agree."

Gasping, she sat bolt upright and twisted on the bench, only to recognize Mary Simpson seated in a chair some distance behind her in the great room. "You startled me!"

Mary laughed. "Marla, my dear, I could have come in the door with clashing cymbals and you wouldn't have heard me. I don't think I've ever seen anyone focus like you do when you play."

"How long have you been here?"

"Let's see . . . I believe I came in during the middle of the Waltz in C# Minor, and after that I heard the 'Moonlight Sonata' and the "Revolutionary Etude." All of which, I might add, were performed very well."

Marla blushed a little. "Thank you."

The other woman stood, walked over to the piano and leaned against it. "So," she said, "have you decided on your program yet?"

"I think so . . . the instrumental part of it, anyway."

"And what are you considering?"

Marla began ticking off her fingers, beginning with the thumb. "For the flute, the first movement of the *Spring* concerto of Vivaldi's *The Seasons*."

"Good," Mary nodded.

"For the piano, Bach—either the Little Fugue in G or 'Jesu, Joy of Man's Desiring.' "

"Umm, I think maybe the *Jesu* would be the better choice, but I wouldn't argue with either one. What's next?"

"Piano, Mozart—first movement of 'Eine Kleine Nachtmusik,' " ticking off the index finger.

"The transcription I heard the other day? Excellent! Next?"

The middle finger was ticked for "Piano, Beethoven—first movement of the 'Moonlight Sonata.' "

Mary frowned. That frown caused Marla to tense a little. "I agree the program needs Beethoven," Mary said slowly, "but I'm not sure that's the best piece to use. It's beautiful, of course, and you did an excellent job of playing earlier, but I'm afraid it's too still, too placid for the audience you're going to have. You risk losing their attention with that one. Hmmm, do you know 'Für Elise'?"

"I have the music for it, but I haven't played it in quite some time." Marla attempted to hide her reluctance, but Mary noticed.

"Marla, I'm really not trying to be patronizing. You are the artist, not me, and you know best at this point what you can play." Mary straightened to her full height. "But, I know these people, and I'm telling you that 'Moonlight Sonata' would be a mistake for this program. Later, after you've raised their understanding of music, they will appreciate the elegance of it. Now, they would just consider it simple, and would tune it out. You would lose them, and probably not regain their attention. For your first recital, and the first program of the music we—sorry, not we, but you—have to offer, you really can't risk that. If you don't like 'Für Elise,' then find something comparable that you like that you can work up quickly."

The older woman stared steadily at Marla as she worked through everything that Mary had just told her. She didn't like anyone telling her what she could play, but Mary was right . . . she didn't know these people. And, truth to tell, since she had never performed a recital like this at all, she really didn't have any experience of her own to guide her. It took several moments before Marla came to the conclusion that Mary was the closest thing to a mentor she had right now. Mary's experience in the world of music and the arts, although not that of a performer, was so much wider than her own, particularly in the area of production. It would be at best foolish, and at worst suicidal to ignore her advice at this stage of her career.

Decision made, Marla gave one firm nod. "I can polish up 'Für Elise' fairly quickly."

Mary smiled. "Good. You won't be sorry for the change."

"For the final piano piece," Marla resumed her program list, "I considered something by Mendelssohn, one of the 'Songs Without Words,' perhaps, but I finally decided to do one of the Chopin pieces."

"Do you have a preference?"

Marla grinned. " 'Revolutionary Etude,' of course."

"Good choice," Mary replied, her own smile broadening.

Marla set her hands back on the keys and began doodling a little, feeling good about what they had just worked out, and likewise feeling good about how her relationship with Mary seemed to be developing. When she first arrived several days ago, she was somewhat uncertain about how to react to Mary Simpson. She had heard all the stories about the Simpsons, and even though they seemed to have changed, those stories had worried her a little. Too, arriving the way she did hadn't done anything to bolster her self-confidence, either. But Mary seemed willing to give her room and not dictate her every move. She could live with that, she decided.

Looking up, she said, "Tell me something . . ."

Mary raised her eyebrows. "All right."

"Why is the piano here? In the Weaver guild hall, I mean."

"Basically, politics," Mary responded with a laugh.

"Politics?" Even to her own ear, Marla sounded as confused as she felt.

"Not national politics, dear. Community politics, the kind I used to see in Pittsburgh all the time."

"Umm . . ."

"What happened," Mary explained, "was that word got around that I was bringing you and the piano to Magdeburg, and that you would be giving a concert. Well, that immediately started a spirited competition to see who would get to host you. Several of the guilds and even a couple of the wealthy burgomeisters made offers."

"So how did the weavers win?"

Mary grinned wickedly. "First of all, they had the nicest room. That gave them an advantage . . . although I didn't tell them that, of course. Second, they trumped everyone else by offering to pay for all the costs to relocate the piano and to support you and the others for six months. I didn't even have to prompt them; they gave that offer on their own initiative. Of course, I didn't tell them how much they overbid the others, either."

"Of course," Marla murmured, continuing with her doodling.

"It's a fair trade. We got what we needed to get you here and get you established, and they get a major prestige boost of the finest kind." Mary sat up straight, as if something had jabbed her. "Oh, by the way, dear, you may be sharing the billing. I've been trying to get Maestro Frescobaldi to come here from Florence."

"Italy?" Marla was astounded.

"Of course, Italy, dear. If we can bring him here and introduce him to our modern music, he could be an influential force in spreading the information and the techniques."

"Um, wow." Marla had moved from astounded to stunned. "I'm, uh . . . are you sure about that? I mean, about me being in the same recital as someone like Frescobaldi?"

"Of course, dear. You have the talent, and you have music that no one else can play or sing. Besides, it's not even definite yet that he can or will come. The Medicis may very well refuse him permission to leave their court."

Marla decided she had too much to do to worry about Frescobaldi right now. She began playing through part of the *Jesu* piece. After a few measures, she asked, "How long do I have to finish drawing up the vocal part of the program?"

"I'm leaving for Grantville soon, and I'll be gone for a while. I'd say until about November fifteenth. We have to have time to write and print the programs, if nothing else. Among other things, I'm working with Elizabeth Matowski to fund a performance of *The Nutcracker*."

"Elizabeth Matow . . . " Marla began, confused, but suddenly the light dawned. "Oh, you mean Bitty!"

"Bitty?" Mary was now confused in her own right.

"Oh, nobody calls her by her name. She's gone by Bitty for years."

"Is that short for Elizabeth?"

Marla laughed. "Nobody knows what it stands for. She won't say. But, she's pretty attached to that name. Somebody called her 'Bitsy' one day, and she tore into him and chewed him up one side and down the other.

"So, she's doing *Nutcracker* this year? That's great! I really missed seeing it the last couple of years."

"Let's say I've talked her into it," Mary said. "She's the best hope of bringing modern ballet to this time. I haven't actually met her yet, but from the letters I've received she doesn't seem to like me very much, though."

"I took dance from her for a few years as a kid, until I shot up six inches in the middle of sixth grade. I quit when I caught a good glimpse of myself in a mirror next to the other dancers. I looked like a pelican among ducks. Anyway, I know from experience that Bitty's a perfectionist and can definitely be prickly at times."

"I can deal with her not liking me." Mary's eyes had turned steely gray. "But she needs my help if she wants to preserve and spread ballet. She needs to work with me."

"Bitty's pretty sharp," Marla replied, still doodling on the piano, marveling a little at how she seemed to be somehow sidling into an inner circle. She doubted that Mary would say the things she'd just revealed to just anyone. "But she's not really very fond of people telling her how to stage her shows. I imagine that as long as you really listen to her, give her a little respect and let her handle the staging, she'll get along with you."

Mary absorbed that in silence, then nodded slowly. "All right." After a moment, she sat down in a nearby chair and continued, "Anyway, I'll probably be gone for about two weeks, so you'll have time to finalize the total program before I return. Do you have any thoughts?"

"There's an aria by Purcell I can do, and of course something from *The Messiah*. I was thinking something by Mozart, maybe from *The Magic Flute* or the *Requiem*."

"Can you do the 'Queen of the Night' aria from *The Magic Flute*?"

Marla squirmed a little. "Well," dragging the syllable out, "I've never performed it. My teacher was working it with me right before the Ring fell."

"I'll bow to your judgment, but if you can do it, that would create exactly the kind of effect we're looking for. What else?"

"Something Verdi or Puccini, don't know what yet."

" 'Un Bel Di,' perhaps?"

"That's one I'm thinking about."

"What about something from northern Europe?" Mary asked.

"Wagner, Mahler and Bruckner would be too over the top, I think."

Mary laughed. "Agreed. What about Schubert or Brahms, though?" Before Marla could answer, Mary's eyes kindled, and she exclaimed, "Schubert! What about 'Der Erlkönig'?"

"Umm, I don't know. Wouldn't that seem awfully pagan . . . I mean, given the times, and all?"

"No, no, no," Mary said quickly. "The audience for this performance will be the educated elite, the patrons, and they have all been steeped in the Greek and Roman myths. I don't think they would flinch at a literary treatment of one of their own."

"Okay." Marla was a little dubious, but she'd already decided to follow Mary's judgment in things like this. "I think I've got the music, but I've never sung it, so it will take some time to work it up. If I remember right, that's in a pretty low key. It might be under my range."

"Can you transpose it?"

"Sure, but it might sound funny."

"I've heard it done by a soprano. I believe it was Jessye Norman. It was very effective. See what you can do, please." Mary tapped her lips with a finger. "We don't have time for anything Russian. Wait . . . what about Rachmaninoff's 'Vocalise'?"

"I don't have the music."

"That's a pity. Well, it can't be helped, I suppose."

Marla didn't mention to Mary that there was at least one recording of the piece in Grantville and Thomas could notate it from the recording. She was afraid that what was supposed to be a recital was going to be a marathon as it was, without including a bunch of new music like the 'Vocalise.'

Mary set that disappointment behind her, and moved on. "What are your thoughts about twentieth-century choices?"

"I figured I'd select mostly Broadway songs," Marla said. "Partly because the Impressionist, post-Impressionist and Modernist stuff would be so dissonant to seventeenth-century ears, and partly because that's really the only kind of music I have from that time." She smiled. "Sort of making a virtue out of necessity. I haven't made any choices yet, though."

"Then the only thing I'll say now is to look at the strongly melodic composers: Sondheim, Lloyd Webber, maybe even some of the Disney composers." Marla felt her eyebrows raise, and Mary gave her light laugh again. "Oh, yes, there are some delightful little songs hidden in some of the Disney musicals. It's just a thought, though."

Marla shrugged. "I'll check it out."

She had been doodling all the while, and now her doodling led into a quiet rendition of "Amazing Grace." She played it several times through, varying the style each time. She held the final chord for several moments, letting the sound resonate. After it died away, she released the keys.

"Very nice," Mary commented. "I'm always amazed at how easily musicians can improvise."

"I'm not really very good at improvising," Marla replied. "I know that hymn well, so I know when and how to change it up. But if you hand me a new melody and tell me to improvise while I'm sight reading it, I'd be doing good to just put simple chords behind it the first few times through it. I need to improve, though, because it's considered one of the standards of musicianship in this era. Bach was well known for it, for example. If you want to hear someone who's really proficient at improvising, even by down-time standards, you should hear Maestro Carissimi some time. He's so good at it I can't even be jealous. He's awesome."

Mary took a deep breath. "Carissimi? Giacomo Carissimi? Composer of the oratorio *Jephtha*?"

"That's the one," Marla grinned.

"Franz told me he was in Grantville," Mary said. "I was stunned. I still am. I almost went to Grantville that day. The thought of meeting him just sends chill bumps up and down my spine." Marla found it a bit humorous that Mary sounded much like a school girl hoping to meet her favorite teen idol. There was a definite air of excitement about her, unlike her normal cool, collected grace. "Tell, me what is he like?"

"Well, he's very reserved, almost shy, but he seems to be a very nice man. He doesn't act like he's famous or anything. In fact, he seems to want to keep a low profile. His friend, Signor Girolamo Zenti, attracts a lot more attention. I had to read in the encyclopedia and some of the album notes to find out about him, or the him that would have been before the Ring fell." Marla paused for a moment . . . something about what she just said didn't sound right. "I mean . . . oh, never mind. Even without those write-ups, though, I would have known he was really talented, really good, just from the way he talks about music and from the way he took to the piano."

"He's learning piano, then?"

"Oh, yes. He's made connections with Elizabeth Jordan, my old voice teacher. She's a pretty good pianist in her own right, so she can show him all about it. Plus, she's got copies of all my notes from the seminars we did this summer, so I'm sure he'll be picking her brain about all of that, too. From what I could tell before we left, he was obsessed with learning as much as he could as quickly as he could."

The two women shared a smile as they both remembered their conversation about obsession on Marla's first day in Magdeburg.

"So, Franz said something about him writing a piece for you? For the recital, I assume," Mary said.

"Actually, no it's not." Mary looked surprised as Marla continued. "No, it seems that he has conceived of a new piece since the Battle of Wismar. He wants to write a lament, a formal eulogy piece, in memory of Hans Richter."

Mary was quiet for a very long moment, staring off in space.

"Mary?"

"Hmm? Oh, sorry, just thinking that through. Methinks I detect the fine hand of Mike Stearns in that. I could be wrong; it could be Don Francisco Nasi, but I'll wager that one or the other of them is involved in it." Mary saw Marla's confusion, and gave one of her light chuckles. "No, dear, I'm not disparaging them. Mike, probably more than anyone except my husband and Colonel Wood, knows the bitterness of the price paid to win that battle. But at the same time, it's entirely too convenient that a composer of Giacomo Carissimi's stature arrives in Grantville and just happens to want to write this piece at a time when it would have the most political benefit.

"Oh, I'm sure it will be a fabulous piece of music, and no doubt it will be a catharsis for everyone who hears it. Mike would push for it anyway, because he would think it the right thing to do, but he wouldn't be Mike Stearns if he didn't see the political advantage of it as well.

"So, does Maestro Carissimi have a title for it yet?"

"The last I heard, he was going to call it 'Lament for a Fallen Eagle,'" Marla said.

Mary gasped. "That is perfect. That is absolutely perfect. That will mean so much to Sharon Nichols and Gretchen and the family, and will speak so strongly to everyone in the country as well. Have you seen anything of it yet?"

"No," Marla smiled. "Right before we left, he had started writing the theme and was really feeling handicapped because there is no orchestra in Grantville."

"Oh, no," Mary laughed. "How did he take that?"

"Well, he tried for a little while to score it for band instruments. He figured out pretty quickly that wouldn't work, though. That was about the only time I saw him showing strong emotion during the little while I was around him. He threw his pencil down on the desk, grabbed the sheet of paper he was working on and tore it into little pieces. He muttered something in Italian that I think must have been pretty vulgar. At least, Signor Zenti looked awfully surprised at what he heard."

"So what is he going to do?"

"Well," Marla said, "he found out that about the only string players in Grantville are my friends Isaac and Josef, and that Rudolf, Thomas and Hermann can play flute. So, he told me that he would score it for that ensemble with piano right now, and rescore it later after he finds an orchestra."

"Something else we need to work on," Mary noted. "Not now, dear," in response to Marla's alarmed look. "Not until after the New Year, anyway," and she chuckled again at the resulting expression of relief. "So, will you be involved in the lament, other than providing the instrumental ensemble?"

"It's for solo voice with instruments," Marla said, "and he's asked me to sing the solo."

A pleased smile spread across Mary's face. "That's wonderful, Marla. Principal performer in a high-profile work by a major composer. This will help establish you just as much as your recital will. When does he think it will be performed?"

"Well, that's the tough part. He wants to do it before Christmas in Grantville."

"What?" Mary looked aghast. "But you're doing your recital here in Magdeburg on December fifteenth!"

"Tell me about it. I really want to do it, but there has to be some travel time and at least one rest day. And I—we—have to see the music soon."

"Yes, you do." Mary looked determined. "I will see to that."

"Thank you."

Mary leaned over and placed her hand over Marla's. "You will be a great success, my dear, both in your recital and in Maestro Carissimi's work as well. Believe that."

Marla watched as her new mentor picked up her coat and walked out of the room. She was still impressed at how much strength of purpose and will was enclosed in that small lady, and she was very glad to have her support.

Tuesday, November 16, 1633

"I can't wear that."

Franz winced a little at the sharp tone in Marla's voice. They were in Mary Simpson's parlor, gathered with Mary and a seamstress. It was Mary's first day back from her trip to Grantville. She had called the women together to address the question of what Marla would wear for her concert performance. Franz had quietly shadowed Marla, as was his wont. He could have told Mary that Marla would reject the down-time styles, but as the lone male in the room, he wisely chose the course of silence.

Affronted, the seamstress looked first at the young woman who had spoken, and then at Mary Simpson. Marla caught that glance, and before Mary could say anything, she continued, "I'm sorry, no offense, but it's just . . . too much. Too much fabric, too much bulk. I wouldn't be able to move freely. That outfit would restrict me in playing the flute and the piano."

The seamstress' daughter, who was modeling a clothing ensemble similar to what the seamstress wanted to prepare for Marla, did a slow turn, showing off her mother's fine work. Franz admired the quality of the tailoring; it was equal to anything he had ever seen in the prince-bishop's court in Mainz. But, somehow he doubted that he would ever see Marla wearing anything like it.

"Are you sure?" Mary asked.

"Yes," her young protégé answered firmly. "I mean, look at it: underskirts, overskirt, bodice, blouse, jacket, large sleeves, ruff collar. At least it's not an Elizabethan ruff, but still . . . " She laughed a little. "Mary, without shoes I'm four to six inches taller than most of the down-time women. What looks dainty on them would start to look ponderous by the time it's scaled up to my proportions, besides the fact it would make me so bulky I'd have trouble getting through doorways and sitting on chairs."

Franz nodded agreement from his seat by the stove.

"Not to mention," Marla frowned at the model as she concluded, "that after a few minutes of performing in that rig," the seamstress bristled a little—she wasn't sure what a 'rig' was, but it didn't sound complimentary—"I'd be sweating like a pig." Turning to her mentor, Marla said, "I understand why I can't wear my prom dress . . . bare arms and shoulders, and all that."

"That's right," Mary replied. "After that little episode at The Green Horse, you should understand the problem of down-time perceptions now."

Marla shrugged. Franz felt the flash of anger he felt every time he thought about what had happened a month ago. Marla had been able to put it out of her mind by the day after, but he still wanted to hurt someone . . . preferably the fool who had accosted Marla. His fists balled . . . or at least his right one did. The pain from his crippled left hand as it tried to close jerked him out of his mood. He forced himself to relax, rubbing the stiffened ring and little fingers on the crippled hand.

"I'm willing to accommodate perceptions." Marla had quieted. Perhaps she hadn't put that unpleasant event totally out of her mind after all. "But only to some extent, and definitely not if it interferes with my ability to perform." She stood, stretched her arms out, and performed her own slow rotation in front of the other women. "Mary, Frau Schneider, look at me. I am five feet nine and one-half inches tall in my bare feet, and I weigh somewhere around one hundred fifty pounds. I am not a small woman, and you can't dress me like I am. I may not know yet what will look good on me, but I'm very certain that what I've seen today will not work."

"Well, what do you want, dear?" Mary asked.

The young woman sat down again with a pensive look. "I don't know." There was a pause. "I just want to look . . . elegant." The momentary expression of longing that crossed her face tugged at Franz's heart.

Mary smiled her slight smile and reached into the large bag on the table near her. "Do you think you could wear something like this?" She pulled out a piece of paper with a bright splash of color on it.

Franz could see that it was the shiny paper that was found in some of the "magazines" that had come from up-time. He couldn't see more than that from where he was seated, but obviously it attracted Marla's attention. She took it from Mary's hand and focused on it. After a long moment, she nodded. "Yes, I could. We'd have to make sure I could raise my arms without binding, but I think . . . I think this would work. I like it."

"Good." Mary retrieved the page. "Frau Schneider," she beckoned the seamstress over, "can you make something like this?"

The down-time woman took the page, and her eyes widened a little as she took in the picture. After a moment, she said, "Yes, but . . . "

"But what?"

"Is this a dress? It looks more like a shift for bed wearing," with a slight frown.

Both Mary and Marla laughed, and Mary responded, "Yes, it is a dress. It's called an Empire style, and I had a little trouble finding a picture of one that I could bring back with me." She stood, and took the page back from the seamstress. "I suspected that Marla would not care for the styles currently in favor at the courts. She is right, you know. She is enough larger than most women here and now that she would look odd and out of place in court dress. But she is also right in her desire to look elegant. Here," Mary tapped the paper, "here is the solution: a dress that is somewhat fitted on the top, yet free to flow from the high waist; a dress that will allow her the freedom to move as she needs, yet will at the same time look elegant."

"But . . . but . . ." Frau Schneider sputtered, "it is so . . . so plain!"

Mary's smile returned. "Marla, stand up again, please." Turning to the seamstress, "Look at her, Frau Schneider. Imagine her dressed in that dress, in a deep, rich color. See her carriage, her grace. Imagine her walking in that dress." The down-time woman said nothing, but after a few moments began to nod. "Yes," Mary said, "she needs no ornamentation. In fact, anything more than the richness of the fabric would detract from her."

The seamstress tapped her finger on her lips slowly several times, then gave a firm nod. "Yes, I can do this. I will do this. And perhaps," she smiled a little, "perhaps we will see this become the new fashion." Franz could just visualize her rubbing her hands together in glee at the thought that she might become the leading name in Magdeburg court dress with this new creation. "Velvet in rich color, you said. What color do you desire?"

Mary looked to Marla, who said, "I don't care, as long as it's not olive green, yellow or pink."

Looking back to the seamstress, Mary asked, "What would you recommend?"

Frau Schneider walked over to where Marla stood and peered at her, looking at her skin, her hair, her eyes. The young woman bore the seamstress' scrutiny calmly. "I would say a deep blue."

Mary nodded. "Do you have enough on hand to make such a dress?"

"I know where I can buy it."

"Good. My contacts could not find a pattern that I could acquire. Can you make it from this picture? And can it be done in four weeks?"

Once again the seamstress looked affronted. "Of course I can, Frau Simpson. And I have a Higgins sewing machine." Franz observed as the expression on her face settled to one of satisfaction, almost glee. "It will take me longer to get the cloth than it will to sew it."

"Good. Then why don't you and Marla step into the next room so you can measure her."

The seamstress, her subject and her daughter all moved into the office. Franz remained where he was seated, deciding that he would be just a bit superfluous in the bustle that would be occurring in the other room.

"Franz," Mary said quietly. He looked up, to see her beckoning to him. Rising, he walked across the room to the chair Marla had just vacated, and sat just as Mary was removing some other items from the bag on the table.

"First of all," Mary handed him a large packet of paper, "this is the final version of the parts to Maestro Carissimi's 'Lament for a Fallen Eagle.' You can give it to Marla after the measurements are done. Tell her that he has decided on St. Stephen's Day, the day after Christmas, for the performance."

Franz grinned. "She will not be happy that it was not given to her last night when you returned."

"I know." Mary smiled back, "but I know her well enough now to know that if I *had* given it to her last night, I wouldn't have been able to get her here for this session, and in its own way this time with Frau Schneider is almost as important She may not think so, but it is. So, I prioritized her time a little bit for her. She won't stay mad long, not after she gets her hands on it."

Mary then handed a small box to him. "This is the other thing we talked about."

Franz opened it carefully. The sight of what was revealed caused a wave of pleasure and anticipation welled up in him, to the extent that he felt light-headed. He bowed slightly to Mary. "It is beautiful. Thank you."

"It was truly my pleasure. Do you know yet when it will happen?"

"Oh, yes," he breathed, "I do."

Thursday, December 15, 1633

Mary Simpson paused for a moment to look around. The great room at the Weavers' guild hall was beginning to fill. Those she had invited to the concert tonight were beginning to arrive, and as expected, were bringing others with them.

From where she stood she could see her husband, the admiral, and a few of his naval officers talking to some of the younger nobility. The events of the month of October had rung the status quo of Europe like a bell. Many young men of the lesser noble families were displaying a surprising ability to read the *Mene, Mene, Tekel, Upharsin* on the wall, and were seeking to enroll either in the newly mustering regiments or in the navy that was being built by John Simpson.

Beyond them stood Wilhelm Wettin (who, according to her sources, was becoming known as "The Great Commoner") and those men and *Hoch-Adel* present who were aligned with his growing movement, all deeply in conversation about some undoubtedly political topic. Fortunately, there were few in Magdeburg tonight who would contend with them, so hopefully this evening would be free of impassioned political debate.

To the other side of her she could see the group of women around the abbess of Quedlinberg, the core of her Magdeburg arts league. The names in that group were beginning to read like a Who's Who of many of the noble families in central Europe.

Yes, things were progressing nicely, and more were coming in the door at regular intervals. As she watched, a man entered who doffed his hat and cloak and handed them to a hovering guild apprentice, who bowed and scurried off to hang them in an impromptu cloak room. He was dressed well, in expensive forest green cut in an unfamiliar style, although not nearly as elaborately as the nobility in the room at the moment. The gentleman definitely knew how to make an entrance, striking a pose to shake his hair back and adjust his lace cuffs.

It took Mary a few moments to realize that she knew him, but as soon as she did she advanced across the floor.

"Signor Zenti, how good of you to come." She had met the redoubtable Italian in Grantville during her recent trip to confirm Bitty Matowski's production of *The Nutcracker* ballet, due to be staged in two more weeks. Her time with him and his—to her—more notable companion, the composer Maestro Giacomo Carissimi, had been very enjoyable. Girolamo Zenti was an outrageous flirt, to be sure, who managed to have her laughing and blushing at the same time, while Maestro Carissimi tsk'd at him. However, when the topics turned to music and instruments, even in his sometimes stilted English, mangled German, and the Tuscan dialect that was partly comprehensible to her twentieth-century Italian ear, he still managed to communicate intensity and passion about his work. All in all, she approved of Signor Zenti.

The Italian gave an elaborate bow as she reached him, then took her hand and raised it to his lips. "Signora Simpson, when I realized that I would in Magdeburg be at this time, I swore to attend. Maestro Giacomo drove me, reminding me that I would to Magdeburg go soon at any event, and begging me most piteously to hear Signorina Linder's concert tonight and plead with her to hear her practice of his 'Lament.' The poor man is almost prostrate with nerves. Chewing his mustache, chewing his pens, chewing his lace he is, waiting for her to return to Grantville so he can hear how she will sing his new work." Zenti chuckled. "It is *divertente* . . . how you say . . . humorous, to see him fret."

Mary laughed. "You are an awful man, Signor Zenti."

"*Si*, so I am told many times," he said equably, turning away as others came in the door and claimed her attention. She watched out of the corner of her eye as he headed for the buffet tables at the back of the room. Zenti collected a glass of wine, but was diverted from the food tables by a stack of programs. The program text was in German for the most part, listing the pieces to be played, the composers and the "dates" of composition. For the vocal selections, especially those from opera and theatre, there were brief paragraphs establishing the context of the song and the related story.

Just then, Amalie, landgravine of Hesse-Kessel entered, which gave her a swift sense of relief. With Amalie and the abbess on hand, the success of this evening's event was assured. They quickly clasped hands, and delivered the obligatory kiss to each other's cheeks. Then the landgravine released one hand, and turned to face the man following her, drawing Mary with her.

"Mary, may I present to you our guest, Signor Andrea Abati. Andrea, this is Frau Mary Simpson, of whom we have told you so much."

Mary felt her composure start to slide as she faced her friend's guest; and she was forced to grasp it quite firmly. If Signor Zenti had made a definite entrance earlier, this man trumped that in spades, posing as if he were an up-time model. Signor Abati presented quite a figure, and from the slight smile on his face he obviously knew it. Tall even by up-time standards, he was lean, with a face framed by thick, long, curly red hair, that from the way it floated when he moved his head was not a wig. And the face—heavens, the man was beautiful.

Signor Abati was obviously not one to keep a low profile. His sartorial selection for the evening was a statement designed to attract maximum attention. Starting at the ground, the shoes were the soberest part of his ensemble, being a gleaming black with large buckles that were obviously gold. The stockings on his well-formed calves were an almost gleaming white silk, while the *culottes* that ended below the knee were of bronze brocade. Overlaying the britches was a long waistcoat in white, which was elaborately embroidered in gold thread. This was, in turn, overlaid by a silver brocade coat which reached almost to his knees. Lace spilled, fountained even, from his collar and sleeve cuffs. Atop his head was a flat-topped, high-crowned blue hat, out of which sprang plumes. Mary saw an ostrich plume, a peacock feather and a third that she did not recognize. The final component was an ebony cane with an ornately carved ivory head on it, held casually to one side.

On someone else, Mary would have sworn that an uptime pimp had somehow been in Grantville when the Ring fell, only to find a new career as a fashion consultant for the tailor involved. Signor Abati, however, had such panache, and exuded such an aura of self-confidence, that on him it worked.

Mary shook her head slightly, then extended her hand to the Italian. Signor Abati gave an even more flourishing bow than his countryman had earlier. When he took her hand to kiss it, he looked up at her through thick eyelashes and she felt like a doe in headlights. She railed at herself for acting like she was sixteen, but the feel of his lips on her hand sent her heart racing nonetheless. Clearing her throat, she said, "I . . . I'm pleased to meet you Signor Abati."

"Enchanté, madame," he murmured in flawless French. His voice gave her another shock, for it was pitched higher than her own.

At that moment Landgrave Wilhelm stepped up and Mary forced herself to turn away from the Italian. After exchanging greetings, the landgrave suggested to his guest that they find the wine.

Mary turned to Amalie, and hissed, *"Who is that?"*

The landgravine gave a wicked little grin, and whispered, "He's from Rome. They call him *Il Prosperino*, and until recently he was *il gentilhuomo premiere* in that city, and the pope's favorite singer."

"Oh," Mary said, as the light dawned, "he's *castrato*."

"Mmm-hmm."

"Oh . . . my." Mary's thoughts whirled. "Well, what's he doing here?"

"He was invited to reside at the court of the elector of Brandenburg for a season, to sing for them. Both of his coach horses took lame near here, however, and he came to Magdeburg until they can be replaced or restored to health. Horses are in scarce supply, however," *for military reasons,* Mary thought, "and his are slow in healing, so it appears he will be our guest for some time." Amalie flashed her wicked little grin again, and murmured, "There are the most *interesting* rumors about him."

Recalling both her history and the effect *Il Prosperino* had had on her, Mary said faintly, "I can imagine."

Girolamo was headed for the buffet when he heard his name called in a soprano that seemed familiar but couldn't be placed.

"Signor Zenti! Signor Girolamo!"

He turned, a smile forming on his face, only to freeze when he saw someone who was one of the last people

he had expected to see in Magdeburg. *Il Prosperino!*
What was he doing here? He quickly made a bow.
"*Signor Abati. Signore stimatissimo ed illustre. Che sor-
presa meravigliosa il vedervi!*"

The other man bowed slightly, and laughed. "*Infine,
un viso civilizzata in questo incolto terreno culturale.*"

Girolamo caught a motion from the corner of his eye
as someone near them turned and frowned. He stepped
closer to his countryman. "*Attento, mio signore estimato.
Ci sono i presenti che capiscono l'italiano.*"

More laughter. "Shall we speak English, then?"

"*Si,* I mean, yes, esteemed sir."

Abati linked his arm through Girolamo's and they
walked together as they conversed. "Do call me Andrea,
and I shall call you Girolamo. We are almost brothers,
are we not, in this cold, almost barbarous country?"

"Yes . . . Andrea."

"See, that was not so hard, was it? By the way, I must
tell you that the harpsichord you made for the Holy
Father was excellent, perhaps the finest I have played."

"Thank you." They were walking slowly around the
perimeter of the room, with every eye on them. Girolamo
was still somewhat nervous, and could not bring himself
to say much yet, arm in arm with a man who was arguably
as famous as the pope . . . at least in Italy.

"So," Abati said in his cool soprano tone, "this music
we are to hear, will it be worth my while, or will I be as
bored tonight as I have been on every other night of
this trip?"

"I believe you will find it worthwhile," Girolamo said,
mustering his assurance.

"Of course Maestro Frescobaldi's works will be of interest, but what of this woman who will sing?" Doubt dripped from *Il Prosperino's* tones.

"Even so. Maestro Carissimi judges her accomplished enough to sing his newest work, a *lamento*."

Eyes wide, his companion stopped and said, "Maestro Carissimi is here? In Magdeburg?"

"No, he is in Grantville, where the *lamento* will be performed soon."

They resumed walking slowly. Abati said slowly, "I met *il Maestro* some time ago. He is a composer most gifted, and he writes such beautiful melodies. If he thinks that highly of her, then I will truly listen."

Marla peered out through a crack between the room dividers that screened off the end of the hall from the area where the guests were. Hermann had been playing music on the piano for some time, music from the downtime era. She could see the guests milling around and conversing, grazing from the buffet and soaking up wine. Hermann's music seemed to be providing dinner accompaniment. It still seemed strange to her that the concert would include food and drink, but Mary had explained to her that this was simply the way things were done here and now. Now that she thought of it, though, it really wasn't any different than singing in The Green Horse. If she could grab the attention of two-fisted drinkers in taverns, surely she could do it here.

She placed her hand over the gold cross hanging around her neck under the dress, remembering when Mrs. Simpson had given it to her earlier in the evening.

Marla was finishing dressing, using her mother's ebony combs to draw her long hair back from her face to let it cascade down behind her ears and down to the high waist of the Empire gown, when the older woman had entered the room carrying a small box. "Let me look at you, my dear." Marla had stood straight and turned slowly, coming around to face her mentor, who was wearing a big smile.

"Oh, Marla. You look exquisite. You only need a few touches." She had set the box down on a table, opened it, and showed it to Marla, who gasped. "I will loan you these tonight to provide just the right accent of elegance." She lifted out the pearl drop earrings and handed them to Marla, who received them very gingerly. "John gave these to me on our fifth wedding anniversary. He was stationed in Viet Nam for a while, and was able to buy these over there, even on a lieutenant's salary." As Marla had put them in her earlobes, Mary had lifted out the necklace and unfastened it. "This, too. Here, let me help you put this on." Marla remembered lifting her hair out of the way and bending down slightly so Mary could fasten the necklace around her neck.

Mary had turned back to the box and lifted out a thin gold chain with a crucifix hanging from it. "The pearls are for the audience. This one is for me. My mother gave this to me when I graduated from college. We—John and I—only had one son, and we . . . weren't on good terms with Tom when he left." Mary had looked slightly forlorn. "I know . . . hope . . . we will eventually reconcile, but I don't know when. In any event, this isn't something for a man, anyway."

Mary had looked her in the eyes. "I know you lost your mother when the Ring fell. In a way, this would be your senior recital, so let me give this to you in her place." As in a dream, Marla again lifted her hair and let Mary fasten the necklace around her neck. "Tuck it under your dress, dear. This will be our secret."

The two Italians had collected glasses of wine and continued to drift around the hall, conversing about this and that. It occurred to Girolamo that perhaps *Il Prosperino* was keeping him by himself for familiarity's sake. The northerners in this room would be a strange audience to him, which, as hard as it might be to believe, just might be causing a slight amount of uncertainty. Certainly, he was making no attempt to capitalize on the many swooning glances directed at him by many of the young—and even not-so-young—women in the room. Most unlike him, according to his reputation.

"So, my friend," his countryman said as they drew up behind the instrument being played by the very short German. "What is this . . . this Steen . . . way?"

"Steinway," Girolamo corrected.

Andrea grimaced, and said, "Steinway, then. It looks like as if it might be *un grandissimo* harpsichord, yes? But it sounds nothing like one."

"It is," Girolamo declared, "a piano, and it will revolutionize music."

"Oh, come now," the other scoffed. "Surely that is very strong language for such a thing."

"That is not just my judgment, sir, but that also of Maestro Carissimi."

"Is it indeed?" Andrea's attitude returned to thoughtfulness. "So then, what or who is this 'Steinway'?"

"It is the name of the family who built it. They were Germans originally . . . "

"Surely you jest," the other said with a smile. "Can anything excellent come out of Germany?"

Zenti chuckled at the Biblical allusion. "Andrea, from what the up-timers tell us, the future of music was almost dominated by Germans not long after our time. Composers, instrument makers, orchestras, it was all in their hands."

His companion stared at Girolamo with wide eyes. "I find that very hard to believe, but I must take your word for it. So, this Steinway was a German, then?"

"The family name was originally Steinweg, but after moving to America they changed it to Steinway."

"Did they invent this piano, then?"

"No, it was invented by a Tuscan."

"I knew it!"

Girolamo smiled at the enthusiasm for things Italian heard in the other's voice. "But it was this Steinway who took a number of innovations and created the great instrument you see before you. Even at the time when this so-called Ring of Fire occurred, for one hundred fifty years Steinway was the standard of excellence for pianos."

"And why do you know so much about them?"

"Because I will make pianos, and I will learn from the best. I just concluded the purchase of the only other Steinway in Grantville, one that is in need of renovation, for that express purpose."

Andrea sniffed. "I do not care much for their cabinet ornamentation. So plain," he said disparagingly. "Even your journeyman work was much better."

"There is a certain Spartan elegance to it. When it is so simple, it must be absolutely flawless. However, those who will come to me will want more, of course. I think you will find that I have not lost my skill. But of all people, Andrea," Girolamo said gently, "you should know that the quality of the gems on the hilt say nothing of the quality of the blade in the sheath. So it is here. I will learn from the best."

And with that, they began walking again, with Abati whispering improvised scurrilous doggerel in gutter Italian about various random individuals in the room, reducing Zenti to almost helpless laughter.

Marla returned to the present as Franz stepped up beside her, dropping her hand from where it had rested over the cross. She was still somewhat surprised by the gift from Mary—not the value of it, because it wasn't that much, but the personal-ness of it. She wondered at why it had been given, then shook her head to clear it.

"Is it time, yet?" she demanded of Franz.

"Almost," he replied. "I think I see Princess Kristina entering now."

Mary turned as the latest group entered the hall, and sighed in relief as she recognized Princess Kristina and Lady Ulrike. Finally. Now the concert could begin.

"Mrs. Simpson," from the princess.

"Princess Kristina." Mary bent and offered her hand. Having just spent a couple of weeks together on the round trip to Grantville, she and Kristina got along well. "I'm so glad you came tonight. I believe you will enjoy the music."

"Thank you, Mrs. Simpson," the young girl replied in her Swedish accented English.

Mary walked with them as they visited the buffet. She helped Kristina make her selections and collect a glass of apple cider, then escorted them to the chairs that had been set aside for them as the evening's most important guests. As she straightened and looked around, she could see Franz Sylwester standing against the side wall, watching her. Stepping away from the people who were slowly but not-so-subtly drifting to coalesce around the princess, she beckoned to him.

"Is she ready?"

"Past ready," Franz chuckled. "She dances as if she has ants in her stockings."

Mary laughed. "Are the others ready?"

"Yes. All are feeling some nervousness, perhaps, but excitement as well."

"How about you?"

Franz sobered. "I am ready to do my part. I hope to, ah, 'get it right,' as Marla says."

"And is tonight the night?"

The brightness of his smile almost blinded Mary. She waved her hand at him. "Go. Tell them to begin any time." He stepped back from her and slipped along the wall to disappear behind the room dividers.

Franz stepped in behind the room dividers, and walked over to where Marla and the others waited. They looked at him expectantly, and in Marla's case, impatiently. "Mary says to begin at any time." They stood and gathered their instruments.

"Isaac," Marla said, "give Hermann the high sign. We'll start as soon as he finishes the piece he's playing now." Turning to Franz, she accepted a quick hug and kiss on the forehead. "It's time."

Hermann stopped playing the piano background music. Most everyone in the hall looked in that direction for a moment as a screen was placed in front of the piano, followed by an ornately decorated harpsichord placed in front of the screen. There was a brief spatter of applause as Mary stepped forward to offer her hand to a somewhat pudgy man and lead him from his seat to the harpsichord.

"Princess," she bowed her head in that direction, "lords and ladies, friends, please lend your ears to the music of Maestro Girolamo Frescobaldi as he presents *toccatas*, *canzonas* and *ricercare* for your enjoyment." A slight amount of applause sounded as she returned to her seat by her husband.

The next hour or so was filled with music of the time, the contrapuntal works for which the good maestro was known. Mary watched the audience as much as she did the performer, and noted that although a good many of the people did pay him some attention, there were others who never once looked his direction.

The question of where Prime Minister Stearns was kept popping up in her mind. He had accepted her invitation, but as of yet still hadn't made an appearance. That wasn't like him. For all that he wasn't her favorite person on the face of the earth, he was unfailingly polite to her and would have made his excuses if something had arisen to prevent his coming. She kept wondering what had come up. After the third time through those thoughts, she firmly banished them to the back of her mind and spent the rest of the time listening to the music.

At length Maestro Frescobaldi's portion of the program came to a close. He stood and gave his bows, spoke to the princess for a moment after she motioned him over, then resumed his seat. The harpsichord meanwhile was removed. Then the screen was drawn aside to reveal the stark lines of the ebony Steinway, gleaming in the candlelight.

Mary's heart seemed to swell as she saw Marla leading the other players into view from behind the other screens. Tall in her royal blue Empire gown, Marla looked well from the audience, she decided. The richness of the velvet, with no ornament except the many small gold buttons lining the long sleeves; the high white collar framing her dark hair and face; the pearls—all combined into a picture of elegance that truly made Marla the focus of attention. The women in the hall all leaned toward each other and whispered behind fans and programs at the sight of the gown. Mary smiled. The seamstress would undoubtedly be receiving inquiries tomorrow.

The whispers redoubled as Marla raised her flute. No one in Magdeburg had seen a metal transverse flute before, and the Böhm keys just added to the mystery of what sound it was going to produce. Mary saw her give the slight dip of the head that gave the count to the others, and they began.

The first notes of the first movement of Vivaldi's *La Primavera* took flight, and everyone in the room stopped. The rapid notes as Marla played the solo part on the flute just mesmerized every listener. Mary looked over at Princess Kristina, who was staring at Marla, eyes gleaming, watching her fingers fly. The thin grouping of instruments behind the solo flute—violin, viola d'amore, Baroque flute and piano—sounded unusual to Mary, but she had to admit that they did justice to the piece.

It seemed like only moments passed, and suddenly it was done. A spattering of polite applause was offered. As the others filed out behind the room dividers, Franz came out and raised the piano lid, propping it to its most open position. He turned and took Marla's flute, then left.

There was a burst of conversation as the transition occurred, but as soon as Marla sat down it began to quiet. Mary was impressed that, by the time Marla began, the room was still again. She had anticipated that Marla would eventually become the focus of the audience's attention, but in the event it occurred much quicker than she had expected.

Franz slipped down the side wall of the hall, emerging from behind the room divider screens to watch this portion of the concert from the back. The piano pieces rolled smoothly, one to another. His heart lifted and soared with each, watching Marla; watching her every graceful move at the piano—never quite still, always moving, leaning forward, back, to one side or the other, hands lifting, floating across the keys.

The 'Little' Fugue in G minor, BWV578, by Johann Sebastian Bach, greatest scion of that incredible family of musicians, now never to be if the butterfly effect theory was correct. It was performed without flaw, and was received by a burst of spontaneous applause at its conclusion.

The first movement of the Eine Kleine Nachtmusik, K525, by Wolfgang Amadeus Mozart, perhaps the greatest German musician of the so-called Classical era. Again, performed flawlessly. The applause was greater this time, and the listeners flowed into a semi-circle around the performance area.

The Bagatelle in A minor, by Ludwig Beethoven, otherwise known as "Für Elise," a lilting composition that sounded deceptively simple but in fact required more than a modicum of skill to play well. At its conclusion, the princess clapped furiously, obviously taken with the beauty of the piece.

And finally, Etude No. 12 in C minor, from Opus 10, by Frederic Chopin, usually called the "Revolutionary Etude." Marla paused for a long moment, as she always did before she played this one. Someone coughed in the silence, and Franz jumped. Finally, she raised her hands and attacked (the only word Franz could use) the keyboard. As with the very first time he heard it, he was astounded by the rolling arpeggios, the percussive chords, how the music seemed to emerge from chaos. He tore his eyes from Marla, and looked around. Everyone was transfixed by her electric performance of the piece. When the final chords were hammered home, the room rocked with wild applause, which Franz joined for a moment before slipping back up the wall and behind the dividers.

The amazing young woman stood at the end of the piece, and despite being in a gown, gave a bow to acknowledge the applause. After she walked behind the screen, there was a moment of quiet, then conversation erupted all over the room. Everyone who had a program was pointing at it, everyone who did not was either looking for one or was gesticulating in the air. They all seemed to understand the term *Intermissio* which lay between the piano and the voice music in the program. Some few of them had headed for the wine table with alacrity, and a few more were picking up the remaining tidbits from the buffet.

Girolamo turned to *Il Prosperino*. He said nothing; merely raised an eyebrow, as if to say, "I told you so."

Andrea nodded in response, acknowledging the point. "How soon can you make me a piano?"

Girolamo shrugged. "Perhaps a year."

"Why so long?" in a surprised tone.

"First, I must finish refurbishing the one I purchased, which is dedicated to a special patron. Despite what I have already learned, I will learn more by doing, which is a slow process. While that is going on, I must locate an iron foundry that can cast parts according to my specifications. Even more critically, I must find a reliable source of relatively fine gauge steel wire. Then, and only then, will I be able to begin crafting my own pianos." He thought for a moment. "I have a facility in Grantville, but I believe I will relocate to Magdeburg."

"You will not return to Rome?" Andrea eyed him with even more surprise.

"No. Even if the Casati family were to forgive my putting a sword through a son's shoulder, everything I have learned in the last few months tells me that the future is here," he waved his arm around, "here among these Germans."

Andrea shook his head.

"I mean it," insisted Girolamo. "You think what you have seen and heard tonight will not change our music?"

Josef and Rudolf joined hands with the others and said, "Do well," then slipped out the way Franz had come in. Franz, Marla, Isaac and Hermann looked at each other, no one wanting to say anything. Finally Franz laughed. "To quote our good friend Ingram Bledsoe, 'Knock 'em dead.'"

Franz turned Marla to face him, looked into her gleaming eyes. "Continue as you have begun. You have won them over, now seal it." He kissed her hands. "Go. They await you." She squeezed his hands and turned to follow Hermann.

Franz and Isaac slipped back down the wall behind the dividers, to emerge at the rear of the room and join their friends. The applause that greeted Marla resounded around them. The four of them stood together at the back, not able to see very well because many of the patrons were standing, but listening none-theless.

Her butterflies were gone, Marla noticed. She was calm, now that she was finally getting to do what she had prepared all this time for, what she had always dreamed of. She turned her head to give a slight nod to Hermann. They began.

"Thy hand, Belinda . . . " The opening words of Dido's farewell recitative sounded in the room, and Mary closed her eyes and drank in the sound of that lovely voice. Henry Purcell's *Dido and Aeneas* had always been one of her favorite early operas, and the despairing recitative and aria where Dido realized that she had driven away her love and subsequently died never failed to grip her. It was a lovely choice by Marla, not just because it was from later in the seventeenth century and so would be easy for those present to relate to, but also because the classic story taken from Virgil's *Aeneid* was one that almost everyone in the room had heard before in many forms. Here was a fresh new form, and one of beauty, sung by one of the finest young sopranos she had ever heard.

"When I am laid, am laid in earth . . . " The aria began; Mary abandoned herself to the music, drifting with its rise and fall, until the final plaintive line, *"Remember me, but oh, forget my fate."*

The room was hushed. Someone at last broke the rapture and began to applaud. The room echoed with the sound for some time. Isaac and Rudolf nodded to the others before slipping back behind the screens to return to the head of the room. When the applause began to fade, they stepped out and joined Marla by the piano.

Hermann began an introduction, and soon Marla's voice was soaring again, this time with the beautiful melody of Mozart's "Laudate Dominum" from Vesperae Solennes de Confessore, K339. Mary remembered wondering if Marla knew what she was doing when the young woman told her that they were going to adapt this song, re-scoring the central section for a trio instead of a quartet. Now she didn't wonder, she just melted into the music and let that effortless soprano voice carry her along. Isaac's tenor and Rudolf's baritone added to the glory of it, but the solo ending, where Marla sang the final phrase, just was heavenly.

Once again the room was hushed. It took longer for someone to begin the applause this time, and it lasted longer. Marla, smiling, took a bow with both Isaac and Rudolf, and they exited.

The rest of the evening moved from one triumph to the next: "Rejoice Greatly, O Daughter of Zion" from Handel's *Messiah* was followed by "Senza Mamma" from Puccini's *Suor Angelica*. Each was received by great applause. Marla bowed, beaming.

Franz, knowing what was coming next, held his breath. If the audience would stumble over anything in the concert, it would be this piece. It had taken some little time to transpose it to a key that was at the same time low enough to retain some of the darkness of the original music, yet was high enough that Marla could sing it comfortably. They had finally achieved it two weeks ago, and Marla had diligently practiced it since then.

She opened her mouth, and sang.

"Wer reitet so spät durch Nacht und Wind?
Es ist der Vater mit seinem Kind;
Er hat den Knaben wohl in dem Arm,
Er faßt ihn sicher, er hält ihn warm."

Franz could almost feel the temperature in the room drop as the opening verse of Goethe's poetry mated with Schubert's music in *Der Erlkönig* was revealed. The story of the father and son's ride home continued to unroll; shivers chased one another up his spine, and the hair on his neck began to bristle. Once again, Marla was bringing to a performance an indefinable something that he never heard during rehearsals. It was as if being in front of an audience raised her to a plane where her voice was a tool in the hands of God. He looked over at Isaac, to see him with his arms wrapped around himself. From the look on his face, he was feeling it too.

The song progressed. In each succeeding verse, the child grew more and more panicked at the sight of the pursuing Erlking, and the worried father tried to calm him, assuring him he was safe. The tension in the great room was building, more and more.

The last verse arrived, and Franz braced himself for the ending. Marla arrived at the final line, and declaimed:

"In seinen Armen das Kind . . . ."

with a very pregnant pause, then

"war tot!"

Immediately applause broke out. Franz could see that this time it was led by none other than the very flamboyant gentleman standing with Signor Zenti. Whoever he was, he obviously liked that song, and to Franz's great relief was dragging everyone along with him. Marla was breathing deeply as she took her bow. Even after the applause died down she stood with her head down for several long breaths. Finally she straightened, smiled, and moved on to the penultimate section of the program.

Mary was almost wrung out at this point. Marla had so far delivered an absolutely bravura performance. She was so proud of the young woman, her protégé in part. In the afterglow of the intensity of the Schubert, she finally admitted to herself that perhaps she was living a little vicariously through her young friend, but perhaps even more her relationship with Marla had helped to fill the void in her heart caused when she and John—no, to be honest, mostly just she—had driven their son away.

Looking at her copy of the program to refresh her memory of what was next, Mary saw that Marla had filled the twentieth-century section of the concert with songs from three musicals. She didn't object—they were, after all, from three of the most memorable productions done in the last twenty years before the Ring fell, and the selections that Marla had chosen were among the strongest. It would be interesting, however, she thought to herself, tapping her finger against her lips, to see how some of them would be received.

Marla sailed through the next few songs, almost breezing through them. "Don't Cry for Me, Argentina" from Andrew Lloyd Webber's *Evita* led the way. Isaac then joined her to do the duet "All I Ask of You," also from a Lloyd Webber work, *The Phantom of the Opera*.

They then moved on to selections from *Les Miserables*, by Alain Boublil, Claude-Michel Schönberg and Herbert Kretzmer. Marla led off with Cosette's wistful "Castle on a Cloud." She then stepped back and took a rest while Isaac stepped forward and sang Valjean's pleading "Bring Him Home," which led to sustained applause, then followed it up with Marius' "Empty Chairs at Empty Tables." His pure tenor voice rang with sorrow, grief and anger throughout the song, and at the end generated applause almost approaching that offered to Marla. Finally, Rudolf stepped out from behind the screen, and joined them in performing "Do You Hear the People Sing." The rousing conclusion of the song led to another round of sustained applause.

◊   ◊   ◊

Franz moved to the wall as soon as the applause began, slipping behind the dividers until he reached the front of the room again. The final section of the program, entitled Christmas, was about to begin. Isaac and Rudolf each smiled and placed a hand on his shoulder for a moment as they moved past him on their way out. Once the applause began to wane, he took a deep breath, tugged on his jacket hem, picked up his violin and bow and checked that the newly-attached chin pad was still seated solidly. He softly tested the strings to see if the tuning had held, took another deep breath, and walked out to join Marla.

He took station at the end of the piano. She looked over from where she stood in front of the curve, melting his heart with one of her brilliant smiles, then nodded to Hermann to begin.

The introduction was short and soft, then Marla began to sing.

"Stille Nacht! Heilige Nacht!
Alles schläft; einsam wacht
Nur das traute heilige Paar.
Holder Knab' im lockigen Haar,
Schlafe in himmlischer Ruh!
Schlafe in himmlischer Ruh!"

Marla's voice was so soft and warm that Franz got lost in it and almost forgot to raise his violin to play. He gave a swift prayer that he would play well as she began the second verse, tucked the violin between his chin and right collar, positioned the bow in his left hand over the strings, and began to play a descant over her melody.

Franz was unaware of the picture he presented to the audience. Their other friends had dressed in attire that was normal for musicians of the day: knee breeches/ *culottes*, waistcoats, long coats with large sleeve cuffs over it all, embroidery with brass thread that in the evening's light looked to be gold, and much lace at sleeve and collar openings.

In contrast, Franz was dressed in long trousers, much like the styles worn by the up-timers, such as Admiral Simpson. They were black velvet, and looked very well indeed. He had wanted a coat out of the same material, but the black was so costly and so difficult to acquire that his jacket had instead been made out of the same royal blue velvet of which Marla's dress was made. And it was a jacket; rather short-waisted, instead of the long-tailed coat that was the rule here and now. Marla in her Empire dress and he in his trousers, jacket and short hair presented to the audience a glimpse of the future. The portrait was most striking.

The descant repeated over the third verse, then Marla dropped out for an interlude. Franz played the verse melody solo over Hermann's soft accompaniment. He poured his heart into the simple music, letting his violin sing.

Once the interlude was over, Marla sang the next two verses with Franz's descant, but when the final verse began, both he and Hermann ceased playing, and Marla sang *a capella.*

> *"Stille Nacht! Heilige Nacht!*
> *Hirten erst kundgemacht*
> *Durch der Engel Alleluja,*
> *Tönt es laut bei Ferne und Nah:*
> *Jesus der Retter ist da!*
> *Jesus der Retter ist da!"*

Marla held the last note for a moment longer than strictly called for, letting it resonate within the room. As it died away, the audience burst into applause. Franz gave a thankful prayer, and grinned in relief—he'd done it! He'd played his part, simple though it was, flawlessly. All of the challenges had been surpassed, all of the work had paid off, all of his fears had proved groundless. He now knew, without a doubt, he would once again be the musician he had been before the attack that crippled his left hand.

He looked to Marla and saw that brilliant smile again. She held out her hand to him. He stepped to her, joined hands, and they took a bow together. Then he stepped back once more and pointed to her, focusing everyone's attention on her, which let him escape. When he stepped behind the screen, Isaac, Josef and Rudolf all pounced on him, clapping his shoulder, pumping his hand, and hissing congratulations to him. He reveled in it for a moment, then hushed them as the applause out front began to die down. Gesturing to them that they should slip out again, he laid the violin and bow down, sat and leaned his head against the back of the wall. The final piece of the night was about to happen, and he didn't want to share that with anyone.

Hermann began the familiar introduction of the oh-so-beautiful Schubert song, and Franz was taken back in time twelve months, to last year's Christmas concert at the Methodist church in Grantville. This time, knowing what to expect, as soon as Marla began to sing, he was transported.

> "Ave Maria!
> Gratia plena, Maria,
> Gratia plena, Maria,
> Gratia plena.
> Ave, Ave!
> Dominus, Dominus tecum,
> Benedicta tu in mulieribus,
> Et benedictus,
> Et benedictus fructus ventris,
> Ventris tui, Jesus."

Hearing Marla sing, it was as if Franz was lifted out of his body. Even more than last year, he felt that he stood before the very throne of God, hearing what could only be described as the voice of an angel. Tears ran down his face. If this was what Mary had heard so many,

many years ago, then she was indeed blessed among women. After what seemed to be an eternity, the song came to an end as Marla sang the final *Ave Maria!* and Hermann finished the last few measures of accompaniment.

If the earlier hushes in the hall had been notable, what followed now was nothing less than remarkable. For the longest time, there was no sound: no applause, no movement, no coughing, no rustling—nothing. Franz began to worry and stood to put his eye against the crack between the dividers to see what was going on. Just as he did so, he saw one of the seated nobles stand to his feet and begin applauding. Within a moment, everyone in the room had followed suit. The storm of applause that followed seemed to have the walls of the hall bulging. He even thought he heard some muted cheering.

Franz stepped back and looked past the end of the screen, to see Marla giving bow after bow and motioning for Hermann to stand and take a bow. Recalling what his next responsibility was, Franz wiped his face and scrambled around behind the chair to find the long package that he had secreted there earlier. He unwrapped it and smiled at the bright colors. About to walk out from behind the screen, he stopped short and felt in the pocket of his jacket. Finding the expected lump, he squared his shoulders, and stepped out.

The applause seemed to be almost a physical force once he was out from behind the screen. He walked over to Marla, and as she turned to him he presented her with what appeared to be a long stemmed rose. She stared at it in amazement—December was not a month to expect roses, especially in Magdeburg—but reached out and took it anyway. Once her fingers touched it, she began to laugh, as Franz's little joke was revealed. Unable to find flowers, he had found a brass smith who had created him a rose in brass, which he had then enameled in the red and green of a true rose. She turned and lifted the "rose" above her head. The audience's laughter joined hers, even as they continued to applaud.

Mary watched, tears in her eyes, clapping and whistling for all she was worth as Marla acknowledged the applause of the elite audience. Her protégé's career was well-founded now, even assured, with this reception.

Just then Franz dropped to one knee, and Mary had to be very stern with herself to keep from laughing or cheering. The applause died away as everyone wondered what would occur next. Those behind the front rows craned to see. Franz took Marla's left hand in his, reached into his pocket and removed something that he slipped on her ring finger. Marla gasped, and would have dropped her "rose" if Hermann had not come up behind her and taken it from her. She pressed her right hand against her mouth, staring at the ring on her hand. Those in the front row were close enough to see the tears that began to roll down her flushed cheeks. Cheers erupted from the back of the room as she reached down and pulled Franz to his feet, only to then engulf him in a fierce embrace and a most passionate kiss, right there in front of the princess, who was grinning and clapping again.

"I think he got it right," Mary said to no one in particular.

Finally all the noise died down, and Marla and Franz slowly circled the room, accepting compliments and congratulations from all. Marla was bearing her "rose" as if it were a scepter, which it perhaps was on this evening of triumph. Mary was close enough to hear the conversation when two Italian gentlemen finally approached.

"Signora Linder," Girolamo Zenti began, obviously moved, "I have not the words in English to compliment you as you deserve. I do not have the words even in *l'Italiano* to say it. *Semplicemente magnifica. Belissima.*"

He stopped, obviously at a loss, only to be nudged by his companion. "Introduce me, lout," was hissed at him, and he jerked.

"*Perdonarme*, Signorina Linder," he said. "May I present to you Signor Andrea Abati of Rome, a most well known singer and famous musician, an acquaintance of both myself and Maestro Carissimi."

Abati elbowed him aside, almost rudely, only to say expansively, "Signorina, I congratulate you on your magnificent performance." Marla blinked at hearing a soprano as clear as her own coming from what appeared to be a man. "I have been singing for twenty-four years now as *un gentilhuomo*, and tonight I have heard that which, for the first time, made me wish that I had been born a woman. You were not, perhaps, perfect," Marla's eyes started to cloud over, and Franz began to bristle. The Italian hurried on to say, "But, only one of great experience, such as myself," theatrically laying a hand on his breast, "could possibly have noticed the tiny flaws." He took her hand in his, and smiled, "No, signorina, as I understand, this was your first concert such as this, and it was remarkable." He placed a hand over his breast again, and bowed to her. Marla's expression eased, and Franz stepped back.

"Now," Abati exclaimed, "Girolamo, you must help me find quarters here in Magdeburg. I will be staying for some time."

"But . . . but Andrea," the other man stuttered, "what of your trip to Brandenburg? What of the fees and acclaim you would earn?"

"Bah! Mere money, mere noise!" Abati drew himself up, flung a hand in Marla's direction. "Here, here is art! What is more, it is new art, art that I, *Il Prosperino*, will become a part of, will take to new heights. Here is new music I must learn, here are deserving pupils I can teach." He abandoned his theatrical posture, and laid a hand on Zenti's shoulder. "After all, Girolamo," he said in that disconcerting soprano tone, "you were the one who told me that the future of music was here in Germany. After tonight, I believe you, and I would be a part of it."

The two Italians made their farewells and walked off together, talking volubly and, on the part of Abati, gesturing flamboyantly.

Mary stepped up to the couple and took both their hands. "Well done, both of you."

"Thank you," Marla replied. She was beginning to droop a little as the adrenaline of the evening drained from her, but her smile was still the brilliant light that Franz loved. Franz said nothing, just nodded.

"Now," Mary said, "you have a taste of what the future could be. Do you still want it?"

Marla looked over at Franz. They both smiled and joined hands. "Now more than ever."

Ellis Island

Russ Rittgers

"Jeez, but it's cold out here," Wade Threlkeld said to Elizabeth Biermann, flapping his arms and stomping his feet next to the large bonfire that late January 1632 night. Their week-long assignment was to keep the fire in this mountain pass large so that all travelers coming to Grantville from outside would be attracted to it. Once there, they would be put into the old barn, fed and then held until one of the immigration medical staff could check them over. A few small bouts with typhus and now the entire community was wary of newcomers until they'd been cleared.

"*Ja*, but at least we have the fire," she confirmed, secure in her unbelievably warm army clothes and well-made insulated boots. Small and dark, her face was cold but her hands and feet stayed warm as long as she kept using them. The small family who'd come shortly after dark last night was only the third set of "immigrants" they'd seen this week.

"You know what this place is?" Wade asked.

"*Ja*. It is your Ellis Island. You tell me this every day," she grumbled. Ellis Island, the Gateway to America before the Ring of Fire. The Island of Tears as well because ten percent of the people who'd made it that far were sent back to their country of origin, mostly for medical reasons, Wade had told her. Fortunately, that didn't happen here. But they could be quarantined until their health cleared.

Elizabeth hadn't needed to worry about that. She'd been christened Elzhbieta Piwowska, one of the camp followers at the Battle of the Crapper six months earlier. When she'd gotten the opportunity to join the army, she had, changing her name to one which had about the same meaning and whose sound was comfortable in the mouth of Americans. She'd known and respected Gretchen, but Julie Sims was her role model. Vibrant, athletic and a dead shot.

Elizabeth had a lot of men she'd like to touch on the opposing side of a battlefield. Yes, reach out and touch a few mercenaries from a couple hundred yards away. Touching as in removing his brains from his head. Or better yet, a couple feet lower. She knew she'd never find the ones responsible for killing the rest of her family and raping her four years ago, but she'd take substitutes.

She'd very reluctantly become a camp follower to a different group of mercenaries. One of them had lost her in a card game to Adam a year ago. Of course, what was left of Adam was now fertilizing a field outside Bamburg, she thought with quiet satisfaction.

Father Mazzare said it was not healthy to dwell on the past. Nor was it healthy to plan your future around making someone else's death. So each time she went to confession, she told him of her sins and he gave her penance. She wouldn't think along those lines again until she next picked up her rifle. *Her smooth, sleek, steel-barreled rifle, capable of . . . Stop*, she thought. *You can't even remember their faces anymore.* A moment later she looked away from the fire and into the darkness, imagining looking down the sights from a concealed position at some oncoming mercenaries . . . *Line up the shot, breathe smoothly, slowly and squeeze . . .*

"Hey, Lizbeth," Wade interrupted her fantasy. "Where did you say that last family was from?"

Elizabeth wasn't out here on a mountain pass next to a huge fire because she was a good shot. She was here because she could speak four different German dialects as well as Polish. "From a town called Lositz. The Swedes, mercenaries, they claim, burned their town before Christmas and they've been traveling from town to town since then. When they heard there was food and jobs in Grantville, they took a chance and went through the mountains. As usual, they have nothing but needs," she bitterly commented, her mouth tight. It wasn't a new story. Only the point of origin and the destroying army had changed.

"Lighten up, Lizbeth. I haven't seen a single one coming through the pass who was a, a mercenary or b, someone who wanted to just sit on his butt. Lots of solid citizens in the making."

"Hmpf," she grumped. "Increase the fire," she told the younger soldier. That he'd actually do it came as a revelation four weeks ago. They were both privates, he a 1631 graduate from Grantville High, technically senior to her. She, well, she was three years older than him. Back in the old days . . . She shook her head and smiled as she watched him. America has it better.

Wade threw four more chunks of dry split wood on the fire. "Don't think we're going to get any more business tonight," he said, taking off his gloves to warm his hands directly on the fire.

Elizabeth walked away from the fire in the moonlight to the edge of the clearing and looked to the south at the white snow. Had there been a dark spot to the left of those trees earlier? *"Wade, komm hier!"*

"Papa, I'm cold," Drina complained, her six-year-old hands, feet and legs bundled in pieces of an old blanket sewn together. Her teeth were chattering as she followed her father and older brother on the trail they'd broken through the snow.

Three weeks ago her mother had died of illness in the village where they lived. It had taken Drina's papa two days to dig her grave. That night he told Joshua and her that the next day they were leaving the farm and going to find somewhere to live, somewhere the soldiers would not find them. Somewhere the memories would not hurt.

So, with all the possessions they could carry on their backs, the family began moving carefully. They rarely traveled by the day even if it was warmer, reasoning that soldiers would be able to see them from a distance and at night, they would see the soldiers' campfires and avoid them. But mostly they traveled the trails high in the Thuringian forest.

"We're all cold, Drina," her eleven-year-old brother briefly turned his head to say. Joshua wore an old coat of his father's covering his own clothing and like Drina, his hands were covered by mittens sewn together by his father two weeks ago. Also like her, he had outer trousers made from old woolen blankets.

"Quiet, you two," Papa said, breaking the trail in the snow between the trees. "There are real wolves out here who'd like nothing better than to eat you. Not to mention the human wolves who are even worse."

That was as much as Papa had said at one time while walking on the trail in the past two days, Drina thought. He was stumbling and was leaning on Joshua more and more often. They'd ground, boiled and eaten the last of their wheat a week ago. Before stopping each day, they set snares to catch rabbits and twice they had. They boiled it up with some grass and herbs in the small pot Papa carried. The last was three days ago and since then they had passed by two devastated villages.

Papa had gone down into the villages looking for food, coming back empty-handed the first time and with a freshly killed dog yesterday morning. "It's food," he said briefly, silencing any opposition. "It had been tied up. It was starving but still alive. Better than the pigs the wolves fed on." Drina didn't understand but Joshua shuddered.

"Did I tell you about Grantville?" Papa asked for the third time today, picking up Drina for a moment as Joshua took the lead. "I heard all about it when we were at that town a little over a week ago. The one where the bad man wanted to touch you, Drina."

He'd only put his hand on her shoulder but she'd cried out immediately. Papa turned quickly and hit the man with his shovel. She didn't know why the man had touched her but he shouldn't have. That's why they left that town.

"People in that town claimed that Grantville, no, it's not a French town, was populated by witches and wizards. Then I talked to a man from there who called himself an American. Grantville is filled with magic, he said, the good kind. Lights everywhere, machines that do the work of hundreds, all at your fingertips. Even carriages that didn't need horses. I asked about the streets of silver and he just laughed. Not silver, just black tar with stones in it. He said the people there are just like everyone else but each and every one went to school for ten or twelve years! They were all older than Joshua when they stopped, he said. Can you imagine? And it doesn't matter what your religion is, Catholic, Protestant or Jew, he said. All are equally welcome. That's where we're going."

Papa put Drina down again. "Come on, we've got to catch up with Joshua," he said, taking her hand. "Grantville can't be far now. Probably just on the other side of that pass."

Half an hour later Drina stumbled in the darkness and would have fallen if Papa hadn't grabbed her. "Just a little farther, darling. It's bound to be just over there. All we have to do is go up this pass and then down. Then you'll be warm and fed. Just a little farther," Papa said, breathing heavily in the cold mountain air.

Shortly after that, Papa stumbled and fell. "Papa!" Joshua looked back to see his father come slowly to his hands and knees, Drina standing next to him.

"Look, Papa," Joshua came back to him. "It's just over the hill. Not much farther now," he desperately urged. But Papa was slow to rise. The moon was out now and Joshua could see the hollows in his father's bearded cheeks. Suddenly he felt guilty for having taken that last piece of boiled dog. He knew it had been Papa's but he'd been so hungry.

"I'm exhausted, Joshua." Papa spoke slowly with great effort. "We'll stop here for the night. Build a back wall before we make a fire. It'll help hide the light from any soldiers. We'll sleep until afternoon and then go through the pass. Grantville has to be on the other side."

"But Papa, we don't have any food to eat," Joshua protested. "You'll just be weaker when you wake up."

"I'll be weaker but I'll be rested. So will your sister. We'll make it easily tomorrow," Papa answered, not really seeing him. "Go to the top of the pass and find Grantville. There will be lights, many bright lights, far more than any town or village you can imagine. The people, men and women will be happy to see us and we'll be safe. Go, Joshua and I'll keep your sister warm inside my arms."

Joshua knelt down, hugged and kissed his sister before rising and kissing his father on the cheeks. "I'll be back soon, I promise." His father hugged him and then turned to begin building a bank for shelter and to reflect the heat of the fire.

The boy looked toward the pass and, using the hoe as his hiking stick, steadily began moving forward.

"Found him passed out and he looks half-starved. Hope he doesn't have bad frostbite." Wade had carried the burden on his shoulder into the small cabin heated by a pot-bellied stove. He rolled the boy down onto one of the two bare cots. It wasn't the first time he'd brought in people unable to take the last few steps.

"This one looks much more than half-starved," Elizabeth grunted. "Here, let me see if he will take a little of this warm broth. Come on, open your lips and let this warm you up inside," she crooned in German, putting the spoon to his mouth. The boy's lips twitched and unconsciously sucked in the nourishment.

"Mama," he muttered.

"Not quite. But with a lot of rest and feeding up you'll probably live."

"Ever the optimist, aren't you, Lizbeth?" Wade looked over her shoulder at the boy.

The boy's eyes popped open. "Papa, Drina! Where are they?"

"Shit!" Elizabeth muttered in English. "He has family out there." Then switching to German, "This man behind me and I will find them and bring them here. Is it just the two of them or are more with you?"

"No, only two. Only Papa and Drina." He struggled to get up but Elizabeth stopped him with a hand on his thin chest. "We will find them and bring them here. You drink this broth and rest. We will bring them."

"Is Grantville?" the boy asked, looking around the small room.

"This is Grantville," Wade responded. "The city is not far. We will find your family. We will bring them here."

"Grantville." He sighed and laid back, relaxing into a sleep.

"If he was the strongest, God help his father and sister," Elizabeth said, quickly dipping broth from the kettle into an insulated flask. "We will follow his trail back. Put on snowshoes and grab some blankets."

"Teach your grandma to suck eggs," Wade muttered inaudibly as he strapped on snowshoes. Damn bossy women! Only reason he . . .

It was midmorning when the light shining through the single window in the small cabin hit Joshua's eyelids and woke him. Drina's small dark head was visible in the cot opposite his.

"Awake, are you?" Elizabeth's feet were propped up and her chair tipped back in the corner of the room where she'd been dozing. She'd kept watch outside alone from midnight until dawn while Wade slept. Now Wade was on watch. She pushed a chamber pot towards Joshua with her boot. "Use this or go outside. Doesn't matter much up here but down in the city, well, you'll see the difference."

"But where's Papa?"

Elizabeth sighed and shook her head. "He didn't make it. We found your sister wrapped in his arms and the blanket that should have gone around both of them was doubled across her. It was a very loving thing he did for her. Just for the record, what was his name?"

"Moses. Moses Amramsohn," Joshua answered and began sobbing.

Two days later, the sky was a bright blue and the morning sun reflected off the snow into Wade's eyes. He stood with his arms folded next to the much shorter Elizabeth as they watched Joshua and Drina walk with the medic down the hill. "The folks at the synagogue will take them in."

Wade took a breath and put his arm over her shoulders. "Going to America wasn't always easy," he slowly began. "Back when I was growing up you'd see reports of Haitians drowning, trying to cross a few miles of ocean to get to America. Chinese dying in cargo containers and Mexicans dying of thirst in the desert, all for the chance of a better life, mostly for their kids. The first generation of people coming in illegally generally had it really hard."

He lightly gripped Elizabeth's shoulder and she looked up at him. After a short pause she said, "Our reliefs are coming up this afternoon for their week at the fire. I want a long shower, clean clothes, food I do not have to make and four large beers. What do you think?"

Wade bent over, kissed her at the hairline and shook his head. "Two beers. You fall asleep after three."

Malungu Seed

Jonathan Cresswell-Jones

A telephone rang in the seventeenth century.

Nearly three years after his adopted town had changed times and changed a world, James Nichols heard an interruption, not a miracle. He laid aside a handful of Leahy Medical Center charts, reaching past his study's desk-clutter to the phone. "Yes?"

"Good morning, Herr Doctor, it's Margritte. There is a man here, a new arrival, who wishes to see you."

His Thuringian-born receptionist was cheerful, efficient, trilingual, and possessed of a voice that could melt men like taffy. Nichols' own German was serviceable and attractive—perhaps, to crows; he stayed with English.

"Margritte, I have rounds this afternoon at the center. I am working on a public health plan for next spring . . . " He suppressed the edge that wanted to creep into his voice. His heart knew that he was sitting in an empty house shuffling paper, while Melissa was a king's prisoner in London. In his own time, that distance meant an hour's flight; here, a month of storms and bandits.

"You know you must not call me—very much not call me at home—for every refugee and, and, *carpetbagger* that has a speech for me. That is what the bureaucracy is for. You must deal with it just as I do. You deal with it better than I do." He grabbed left-handed at a sliding chart, caught it.

"I apologize, Herr Doctor. But he wears the robes of a Jesuit, and this man . . . well, he looks like you. And so rarely have I seen a man who looks like you."

Nichols stared blankly at the chart he held. The white paper stood out sharply around the creased ebony skin of his thumb, cracked and rough from a surgeon's hygiene; as stark a contrast as his own color within this town, this province—this entire United States of Europe.

So rarely have I seen a man who looks like you.

"Herr Doctor?"

He thought of the half-hour walk to the center, its noisy offices, the urgent to-do lists: *Translate appendectomy procedure notes. Find paper clips. Stop bubonic plague.*

"Margritte," he said slowly, "you must *almost* never call me at home. Or bring anyone here to meet with me. I think this is one of the times you should do both." He set the chart down.

"To your house? Like a fine guest? He is only a traveler, Herr Doctor—a lay Jesuit, not a Father. He arrived
with no ceremony at all! That coachman with the beard
brought him in; Heinrich, that is, the fellow who married
my second cousin in the summer, after . . . "

Nichols let his gaze drift across the study—formerly a
living room, but the house wasn't large and his workload
and cobbled-together library had swamped it. Borrowed
books in a borrowed house; all that he'd once owned had
been left in twentieth-century Chicago when the world
changed. An ember popped in the fireplace, the only
sound in silence. His daughter's hand-copied paramedic
certificate hung over the mantel; Sharon was in Venice,
stagnant lethal Venice, as far away as Melissa in London.
Two travelers in foreign lands, with no safe home as
he had.

"There's room," he said softly. "Plenty of room."

At the second knock, Nichols cracked the door onto
freezing air and two backlit figures.

Margritte nodded. "Herr Doctor." Beside her genial
bulk, a taller, thinner man hunched in a tightly-wrapped
coarse robe, probably once black but faded now to a
scuffed brown lighter than Nichols' own complexion.
October sun was not kind to him; that complexion
showed chalky highlights where strong features shaped
sharp-cut shadows. The dark, bloodshot eyes seemed
calm enough, intently focused, but something in
them . . .

Nichols' greatest pride—when he had time for
pride—was that Grantville hadn't seen a refugee with
that look for a year; they'd done that much good, at least.

He'd seen thousands of eyes in 1631 and '32 with what he'd learned to call in his own time, in Vietnam, a thousand-yard stare. Not every wound hurt the body.

The traveler waited with stoic patience, robe ruffled in the wind. Nichols realized something belatedly. "I speak an inferior Latin," he said. "Physician's knowledge."

Hesitating a moment while he clearly parsed the words, the traveler inclined his head towards Nichols; a crucifix glinted in his robe at the motion. "*Guten tag, Herr Doctor,*" he said in a soft-accented rumble. "Matthias Mbandi, via Asuncion. *Sprechen sie Deutsch?*"

"Ah. Yes. Yes, I do." Nichols blinked. "Is that his?"

Margritte hefted the satchel. "Yes, Herr Doctor. I have checked it, there are only clothes and a bag of spices. Is there anything I may help you with here?"

Nichols knew from experience that Margritte's gifts included a love of gossiping over anyone not actually a patient. He couldn't help taking a harder look at the stranger, at Mbandi, checking shoulders and stance and hands; his own hands were chipped with marks much older than incessant scrubbing, older than his time in the Marines. Ten, fifteen years younger than himself, probably. Longer reach—but worn thinner than his robe. Mbandi returned the gaze without fear or challenge; Nichols eased to a smile, nodded, and glanced over. "No, thank you. I will see you at the center, and I will telephone if I need arrangements."

"Ah." Her eyes cut sideways to the thin stranger. "Well, if you are certain—"

Nichols' smile widened. The seventeenth century was a dangerous place at times, but assassins generally tried to blend *in*. "Here," he said, and took the satchel. "Now, please, at least one of us should be working. Thank you."

He gestured Mbandi inside and closed the door, plunging the hallway into dimness. "Through to that room," he said, hooking a hand toward the study. "Please, go to the fire, for the warmth. Ah, tea?"

"No, thank you," said Mbandi; but in the study, he stood against the mantel close enough to singe his robe. Another man's face might have dissolved into bliss. His did not.

Nichols dropped the satchel on his desk, then sat behind the cluttered surface, half-amused at doing so. *The doctor is IN.* He remembered early days as a physician, the occasional doubt or hostility, the whisper to the receptionist—*maybe someone else, ma'am, with you know, more experience?* He hardly needed to impress himself on a man who'd come—

"How far did you say? Asuncion. Is that in Spain?"

Mbandi looked up from clasped hands—for warmth, Nichols saw, not piety. "No, it is across the great Atlantic. Six days up the river Parana from Buenos Aires."

"Jesus H.—" Mindful of the robe, Nichols bit off the rest. "That is very, very far."

"It is. I crossed that ocean once before." He smiled as sharply as Nichols had earlier. "I liked it better this time. I could see."

In his mind, Nichols shoved aside the charts and papers. "You are a courier, then?"

"No, I carry no letters. Only, something far more important. Ah—" The traveler set himself in a formal stance. "Father Ruiz Montoya of Asuncion sends greetings to the famous Moorish physician of the United

States of Europe, the 'medical-doctor' James Nichols. It is his understanding that in your time, it is known what will succeed in ours, and what will fail. The work he has given his life to—" Mbandi hesitated in his clearly memorized speech "—the *reducciones*, the Jesuit missions, of Guaraya—the security and happiness of so many—this is now known to fail. The communal ways of living he practiced among the Guarani Indians, and that others are said to twist into such misery in later centuries, cannot survive. Their enemies will inevitably destroy them. And so the Company of Jesus has decided, with wise logic, to cease those ways. The Guarani missions will close and the fathers be recalled to where their efforts will bear fruit."

Something twisted in Mbandi's expression. "Father Montoya cannot convince the father general that this is wrong. Or that—that his enemies, the *paulistas*, raiders of the missions, can be stopped. Can, sometimes, be saved. Or that there is hope and will beyond logic.

"Therefore, he will depart from the Company, and remain with the Guarani to aid them as he might. He has only a few years before his body will fail, but his spirit will not. . . . Others are staying with him, choosing between their oaths and their dreams. His last hope, which failed him, he now wishes to pass freely to you."

Nichols concentrated on following the archaic German, and quashed the flicker of cynicism: No one gives anything for free, in this century or any other.

"Years ago, when word from your books first went through the Company, Father Montoya sent Father Gustav—" Mbandi smiled at that name "—to try to gain something which your time has shown to succeed. In the

Apolo region of the Viceroyalty of Peru, near the mines of Potosi, grows a certain tree whose bark has the highest property of curing fevers—"

"Quinine?" said Nichols, jerking upright in his chair. "You, you speaking are—" he floundered a moment "—are speaking of quinine?"

"Yes, what is, will be, called *cinchona roja*. The bark from which a true febrifuge can be made."

Nichols stared at the fat satchel. "Cinchona bark?" *Jesus H. Christ, there must be ten pounds of it.*

He looked back to Mbandi in astonishment, and new respect. There'd been solicitors enough before; Grantville, an alien pocket of future lore, drew them like a lodestone. Princes and courtiers, spies and merchants, and never a one of them could offer Nichols what he wanted. Clean your cities, inoculate your people. Stop the plagues and the dying. Even in the midst of what up-time records called the Thirty Years' War, humans couldn't kill each other as fast as pathogens could. And quinine worked, even if it didn't cure. The dose wasn't large, this would be enough to . . .

On the heels of surprise, dull realization settled in, a medical official's mindset trumping a doctor's. Not enough. Not for the coming summer. Malaria was widespread, even through much of Europe; it killed popes in Rome, kings in Spain, merchants in Venice—*Sharon!*— even Oliver Cromwell, supposedly, although perhaps now they'd never know. The Jesuit's Bark that could treat it traveled in small quantities like this—exotic, expensive, like the contents of the glass jar Balthazar Abrabanel kept under lock in his apothecary.

"No, not the bark," said Mbandi hastily. "Although there is a little. Father Montoya offers, offers . . . " He shrugged aside his recitation and took two hasty steps to the desk and his satchel, opened the buckles and dumped out an oilskin bag. Tugged at the lacings—

"Father Montoya offers *seeds*."

Nestled in the oilskin was a shifting mass as dark and fine as pepper.

"He has said that there are fifty thousand in this bag, and also in this other. Each seed may grow one tree, to provide bark for years. I am to be giving one bag to you, Herr Doctor, so that you may find your own places to plant them—not here, but in warm countries." He gave a belated shiver.

"Fifty thousand," marveled Nichols. He felt a shiver of his own. "And the other bag?"

"I will take that to Africa," said Mbandi with infinite calm. "I will go wherever I can, and wherever the soil is right, and the slope, the air and the rainfall—I will plant them, five in a cross, as the *cascarillos*, bark-hunters, learned from the fathers. And I will go on again. This is what Father Montoya has asked of me, and I will do it."

Nichols absorbed this for a few moments. It stunned him with its scope, but . . . He lifted a hand. "Who is this Montoya? You said he was the provincial, the senior Jesuit in the region? What is his interest in quinine—why was he there at all?"

"He is a great man," Mbandi said sincerely. "He founded the mission at Lareto more than twenty years ago. At first it was only to teach Christian ways to the Guarani, the Indians near the Parana River . . . ."

Nichols' patient questions—and an atlas from the shelf—pieced together the account. In what would become Uruguay and Argentina in Nichols' own time, a handful of Jesuit missions had themselves become pockets of communal society ever since 1609: Willingly organized, wisely ruled, and humane beyond anything else in this time, it seemed. Thousands of Guarani dwelt there without lords or kings; prospered; learned the catechism in their own tongue. "There was even an orchestra at San Mini," murmured Mbandi with wistful pride.

The coming of the up-timers changed all that in a year's time: both at the missions, and far away in Peru.

"Some books told of cinchona, the bark that cured fevers." Mbandi shrugged. "Who could tell what bark it was exactly? But all who heard came down upon the viceroyalty of Peru, hungry for bark worth a fortune for each quintal's weight." Government agents, adventurers, brigands, men who would be kings; a locust-swarm, seeking their feast. Many bark-cutters would have none of it; they claimed the cinchona as their own. Others fobbed off any bark as cinchona, and laughed at the joke with a pocketful of gold. All was chaos.

"And Father Montoya?"

Ruiz Montoya's great leap was to do what he had always done: to help those about him, and let them make their own choice. After a deadly flurry of attacks on the most vulnerable missions, those closest to Brazil, there was no choice but to retreat to the city of Asuncion; but Montoya spared an effort, and a man, to a new quest. He sent Father Gustav—Mbandi again seemed wistful at the name—to do what he could among the bark-cutters in Apolo. "While Father Montoya organized a desperate retreat of twelve thousand people—hundreds of miles down a river's falls and rapids, with *paulista* raiders snapping at their heels—Father Gustav befriended a *cascarillo* in dire straits, promised him sanctuary, and earned the gathered treasure of a secret hillside's *cinchona roja*. His name was Mamani, his loyalty unswerving, and he accompanied the Jesuit back to Asuncion with his great gift, determined to follow him forever.

"Father Gustav was my own guide to the faith for eleven years," explained Mbandi. "It was he who taught me German, and a little Latin like yours."

Father Montoya, rejoicing, sent this Mamani to look about Asuncion and the missions upriver, find a place where the cinchona might grow. He knew of the up-time texts that condemned the missions, and the debate at Rome as to their fate; his hope was that by offering a valuable crop, he might stave off the inevitable decision, even give the Guarani a prosperity all their own. His hope was soon destroyed. Cinchona would not grow at the missions.

"Too low—the land must be much higher. Too wet a soil, too thick a jungle." Mbandi shook his head slowly. "Upriver, far upriver, perhaps—but that is Brazil highlands, a few days' march from Sao Paulo, where the *paulista* bandits make their nest. No mission could survive there without guns and aid from Portugal and the Company, and no aid would come. In another time, it did, at Father Montoya's own appeal, and the missions lived another one hundred fifty years—but not in this time."

A lot of things won't happen this time, Nichols wished to say against this gentle accusation. *Did they tell you of the dictator with the mustache? Either one?* Instead he said, "These *paulistas*—they seem very . . ." Savage?

That was a disturbing word; he fumbled for another. "Angry. Fierce. Why—oh, no matter. You would not know."

"But I do," said Mbandi. "I was one of them myself. That is how I came to know Father Gustav, and was saved."

Nichols sat back carefully. "Okay," he muttered. "Ah . . . Mbandi, you will need to tell me something that I have been wanting to know of, to know, from when I saw you. How did you come to be in a Jesuit mission in—in Uruguay? Were you born in Brazil, or . . . "

"I was born in Ndongo, a kingdom in the Malanje highlands. That is perhaps ten days' march inland from Luanda, the colony town of Portugal. Less by river."

"In Africa? In . . . Hold on," muttered Nichols in distracted English, flipping the atlas' pages from one continent to another. "Ah . . . Luanda's still there . . . will still be there . . . Jesus!" He looked up. "You're *Angolan?*"

"Ngola means 'ruler' in the Kimbundu tongue." Mbandi smiled thinly. "The Portuguese called us all rulers, then? That is a bad way to treat one's king, how they treated us."

He spoke absently, his eyes on the open atlas, as they hadn't been before. Nichols turned the book about and slid it slightly across the desk. "Show me where?"

"I do not know these names." Mbandi peered down at Central Africa. "But the rivers . . . Here, the Lukala. My father fought a great battle there in his youth, when we gained independence from Kongo and a kingdom of our own. And the Kwanza—there I fought my battle, the year of our Lord 1619, against the Portuguese and their

Imbangala mercenaries. He won his battle, and I lost mine."

"You were a warrior?" asked Nichols neutrally.

Mbandi grinned. "A farmer, as he was. Even farmers fight when there is need. . . . My *soba* called us, and we came, and fought. And lost. He was killed, they say, along with many other *sobas*, and the city fell the next day; great Kabasa overrun and the kingdom lost with it, the king himself long fled. I was already marching west in a coffle."

Nichols set his face. "To a ship?"

"Yes. They baptized us there, at Luanda port, so that the ones who died aboard ship would find grace. I cannot say if that was a wrong thing . . . but the ship itself was a very wrong place, very hard, and some did die. I lived to see Brazil, and that too was a wrong place." He shivered again, glanced down, relaxed. "There are many strange names here."

"Yes." Nichols pointed. "English, French names for countries. Lines on a map, most of them . . . What happened to your city happened almost everywhere. The Belgians—here. The Germans—here. The French—here, here, and all through here. They brought—will bring—trade goods, and take away human beings, until all this—" He spanned a hand over the subcontinent "—is bled half to death."

"Yes. This is what Father Montoya wishes to stop."

Nichols blinked. "Stop the slave trade? Why does he want that?"

"Why should not any good man? But all things are one, to such a man as he is. He sees the links of them. The great chain of misery." Mbandi set his face in stillness. "I am such a link. In Brazil, I was angry when the work-drivers hurt me, afraid I might be killed. I fled into the jungle, full of my anger and fear, and nearly starved on the journey. To Sao Paolo, the *paulistas'* kingdom. I joined them. I did . . . many bad things, to prove myself, to survive. I did not care who suffered them."

A Chicago alley surfaced in Nichols' mind, jolt of a pistol butt gripped in his hand as he whipped a weeping juvie's face to blood; a boy no older than he was. *Blackstone, baby! You fuckin' well know Rangers own this turf!* He drew a breath. "Yes—I understand, I think. You hit back. Anyone will do, sometimes."

"We marched west. To Lareto and San Mini, the strange black-robes and their Guarani cattle. Good wealth to be taken . . . "

"Gold?"

"Guarani," said Mbandi bleakly. "For slaves. They fetched much money in Brazil . . . So many of us were Christian, though, that we did not harm the fathers—only taunted them, sometimes pricked them with our spears. They went on, unafraid. Father Gustav gave a sermon while we raided. I came to mock . . . and stayed, to hear. I could not run away from fear in the deepest jungle, but this man could stand against it, and calm others too. Our loot was nothing next to that . . . The following day I slipped away from the march back to Sao Paolo, and sought out Father Gustav. He blessed me and took me in." Mbandi touched a hand to his crucifix. "This is his own. After eleven years, it is a great gift, but not so great as what he gave me then. A new life, a good life."

"Different boot, same kick up the ass," muttered Nichols in English. He grinned momentarily. "Mine was a Marine high-top, and damn did it hurt . . . "

"But I was only one. There were thousands more taken from my homeland, from elsewhere, each year to Brazil, and each year more ran as I had." Mbandi beat his palm gently on the desktop. "Captive—slave—runaway—*paulista*. You see, then, the chain? Two years ago the *paulistas* came in great numbers, drove us downriver, smashed the missions, took many slaves. The Company of Jesus believes that they have defeated us forever. And so my journey here began."

He hesitated. "Father Montoya might have sent Father Gustav. He spoke Spanish and Latin very well, and a little English, and he . . . he had chosen to fight for the Guarani, like Father Montoya. But I am of the Malanje highlands. I know that ground, and the mountains farther east. I speak many Bantu dialects, some Kiswahili, and the Mandinga trade tongue. And . . . it was guessed that I might be of some interest to you, Herr Doctor."

Nichols grinned. "That was true."

"But . . . it was hard, to leave him there. Very hard. Perhaps in a few years more, he might have ordained me as a member of the Company. He was my confessor, my friend."

"And he had already taught you German, you said."

"Yes. Words come easily to me, since boyhood. I learned many dialects to speak with the different *kijiko* at the capital, when raising crops."

"What are *kijiko*?"

"King's laborers. We would say 'kinder,' I think."

"You use children to take in harvests?"

"No—not small child. Law-child, dependent. Captives from battle."

"POWs?"

Mbandi shrugged. "I do not know that word."

"I suppose you wouldn't . . . " Nichols tasted the next word, found it bitter, spoke it anyway. "Slaves?"

"No. That is what I was, in Brazil. My father would not treat another man like that, nor would I. Nor even the worst of our kings."

"But he owned men, you are saying. You owned men."

"The king's *tendala* did. I owned only their work." Mbandi spread his palms on the desktop. "Herr Doctor, you have not farmed? No? The beans do not grow themselves. It needs skill and work. He who has the decisions must have the, the . . . "

"Ownership?"

"The ownership, yes, for a plot larger than I may tend as my own."

"You can own the land, without owning the men!"

"No, we cannot. That is strange to me. Everywhere, here, there are barricades—fences," he said in puzzlement. "Holding in nothing but empty fields . . . Land is land. A man takes what no one else is using, grows what he needs. That, he owns. And what his *kijiko* grow, he owns through them . . . "

"Okay. Look." Nichols pushed back from the desk, crossed his arms. "Just tell me what you want, Mbandi, what you came here for."

"I have angered you," said the traveler slowly, straightening. "I did not wish to. As I said, I have done bad things, but only when others have hurt me. And it is Father Montoya's wishes I speak of."

"It doesn't matter. Hell, German POWs raised Allied crops during WWII . . . " Nichols realized he was muttering in English again. "So. No matter. Father Montoya wishes to stop the slave trade, you say. But quinine will make it easier for Europeans, Arabs, anyone to go into Africa and take them. In this time, diseases are weapons. You would disarm a continent."

"He has two ways of logic. Firstly . . . of numbers. We speak of young men here. Slave-takers—Portuguese or Imbangala, no matter—may only take whom they defeat. As the coastal states weaken, they will lose more battles like mine, and fight among themselves to survive. More defeats, more captives. More *kijiko* . . . Yet many more young men die from the fevers than die in fighting—even in Ndongo highlands—and many, many in Brazil, or the sugar islands. Fewer of us from Africa die when taken there, and so we are more of value as slaves. If quinine becomes common, cheap, then the fighters will not die, the workers will not die."

"I see," said Nichols. He rubbed at his chin, reflecting that malaria killed without regard to skin color —thousands of Europeans, but millions of Africans. No good having a guard dog that rips out your own throat. "There are other fevers quinine does not treat . . . but those may be reduced by good water, or proper treatment of wastes. So not the same . . . rate of replacement."

"Secondly, of men. For any man outside of Africa, to go there is a bad risk. Many die of fevers. So—if it is dangerous to go to Africa, then only dangerous men will go. Only the greatest wealth can draw them, and they value no one's life, even their own. If they risk so much, they want much; wealth that walks on its feet. With quinine, better men may go without the bad risk, and trade in kinder ways. We have much to trade: Hausa gold, fine steel from Sudan. Ivory, pepper, *Mandinga* cloth. In a few years, quinine . . . " He shrugged. "In Kabasa, we too had an orchestra. There will be others. We may trade in ways of life, not the taking of it."

Nichols nodded slowly. "Father Montoya is . . . wise. And what of you? Why do you do this—will you go home, then, to Ndongo? Settle there when you are done with the seeds?"

Mbandi looked away, to the far wall, and far past it. "I cannot go home. There has been word through the Company, from Luanda. A new king in Kabasa palace, set there by Portugal. The true king is long dead. His sister, Nzinga, fought on for years from islands in the Kalandongo River, gained allies, seized another land's throne. Now she is queen of Matamba, kingdom to the east, riding on spears back into Ndongo. There will be more *kijiko*. The saying is 'the victors eat the country.' No one will talk of seeds there, with killing to do and wealth that walks. I cannot go home." He shifted, looked down to Nichols. "I think it is the same with you, Herr Doctor? We have a Kimbundu word: *malungu*, a fellow-traveler on a ship that will never return. You and I, we are *malungu*. It is not the distance. Men may cross any distance. It is the changes . . . the *time*."

"Yes," said Nichols. He reached out and gently closed the atlas, smoothed the spine.

"I do this for Father Gustav." Mbandi blew out a hard breath. "This is his crucifix. This is his robe. You asked what I wanted. Only what Father Montoya wants—your help.

"I cannot make men grow these *cinchonas*. It needs years, nearly as many as a man's to grow of age. I cannot keep them growing after I move on, when another man may come and raise another crop; cannot ask a family to squat on a jungle slope and wait. People must live. . . . And it is dangerous in places. If there are Imbangala about, I must hire them as guards or face them as enemies."

"You need gold, then," said Nichols.

"Yes. Beads, if you have fine ones. Good iron nails. Horses."

"A fifteen-year supply of trade goods? That will take time," said Nichols. "Months, perhaps. Governments move slowly. No matter. There will be much to talk about while you wait."

Mbandi blinked. "But—No, Herr Doctor. There is very little time, and I have lost much of it already. Winter is colder each day. The harbors will freeze, the winter storms will close in. I must leave within ten days at most, or I will lose half a year; and I do not know how many years I have."

Nichols nodded slowly, thinking a moment of rats and fleas. "None of us do. . . . But if we cannot decide in that time?"

"Then I must leave without help, and do what I can."

"Very well. You must tell me exactly—" Nichols glanced aside at the thump of the door knocker. "Busy day. Excuse me." He rose, made his way to the front door, opened it.

"Good afternoon, Dr. Nichols."

Nichols recognized the creased face and well-pressed cassock immediately. "Hello, Father, I wasn't expecting you."

Father Kircher pursed his lips and made a *whooshing* sound. "No one expects the Grantish Inquisition," he cackled.

"Oh, for—" Nichols leaned against the wall for a moment to gather his strength. "Who showed you *that*?"

"Heinzerling, of course."

"Of course . . . Seriously, how did you know so fast?"

"Of your visitor?" Father Kircher smiled benevolently, shifted to German. "Ah, Herr Doctor, by that darling girl whom I shall one day steal away from your wearying service, and place in my own—that is, the Company's. At a higher wage, too."

"Margritte. Figures." Nichols stayed with stubborn English. "I'll double your offer, Father."

"Generous, but can you afford such?"

"Sure, I'll dock half her pay for gossiping. Come on, he's in here." Nichols gestured the Jesuit past him in the hallway, swung shut the door, and hurried after, brushing past Kircher into the study. "Mbandi! This is Father Kircher, one of our Jesuit priests. If you would . . . ."

He checked words and step alike as he caught sight of Mbandi's face: startlement, even fear, and then hardening, a man locking down his emotions. *Caught off guard, or just caught?* he thought an instant; then—"Father Kircher, this is Matthias Mbandi. He has just arrived from South America." Nichols knew Kircher well enough to afford Mbandi the courtesy of not saying, "claims to have just arrived." The Jesuit would frame the statement as such from logic if nothing else.

Mbandi lifted his chin slightly. "Good day, Father."

Kircher inclined his head. "It's considered an honor to welcome a procurator," he replied, adding with another nod to Nichols: "Ah, a Jesuit provincial representative, sent to report and negotiate in Rome . . . It's never been my privilege before."

"I have not come to report," said Mbandi. "To protest, perhaps. Or to testify . . . There will be no more procurators from Uruguay province. Nor a father-provincial to send them. Father Montoya may perhaps already be dead."

Kircher's smile dissolved. "What has happened?"

"Father Montoya has left the Company. There was a letter I was to have—" He shook his head. "No matter. You must believe me when I say that Father Montoya will have no further dealings with those who have abandoned him and his people. I thank you for the welcome, but I cannot accept it either. I, too, have renounced the Company. I will walk the world alone."

"If what you say—" Kircher paused, visibly shifting his thoughts from Jesuitical strategy to the human scale of a weary, wary man; Nichols warmed to him for it. "Matthias, many who study to become full Jesuits never succeed in their lifetimes, and some who do, fail in a task, and are punished—but there is no casting out. There is room in God's service for all. If you have come so far, in such urgency, then do not fear anything at the end of your journey. I am offering no punishments."

"Again, I thank you. But while I may yet fail in *my* task, I do not leave because of failure . . . not because of *my* failure, or Father Montoya's. Because of our abandonment. I will serve man, and God, upon my own, with more loyalty than I have seen *offered* to him and me. If you had seen—"

"Matthias! This is wrongful!"

"—if you had seen, when San Ignacio fell, when, when the *paulistas* began herding together their cattle—"

"*Mbandi*," broke in Nichols. "He does not know. You may tell him what you told me."

The traveler collected himself. "I—Of course. When we received the orders to withdraw . . . " He sketched the events much more bluntly than he had when speaking to Nichols, either from urgency or from no need to convince—or to sway. He finished, leaving three men standing silent in the room for a time, while the fire chuckled to them.

Kircher broke the silence first. "Your letters and your money were stolen. What was not?"

"The burden I will carry now."

"Cinchona seeds," said Nichols. "A large quantity."

"That would require a large effort . . . Did you gather them yourself, Mbandi?"

The traveler set his face. "That was Father Gustav's work, and Father Montoya's gift. To the United States of Europe, in hope of assistance. And to Africa, merely in hope."

Father Kircher visibly weighed his next words before he spoke them. "That is the act of a generous and good man. But it is also that of a provincial of the Company, serving its authority—and subject to it. As you state you were when you took up this burden."

"Do you claim the seeds for the Jesuits, then, Father?" said Nichols, keeping his own voice calm.

"No. That is not my place—and this man is your guest, Doctor. But I must raise the subject. In fact, there is a great deal to decide here, and you will agree that is more than may be judged by a medical official. Nor, thankfully, by myself."

"You intend to refer to the superior? Isn't he attending in Rome?"

"I believe this is a matter not for God, but for Caesar," said Kircher dryly. "President Piazza, in this case . . . Matthias, know that you are welcome at the Company dwelling. Please know that, always."

The traveler bowed silently; Kircher turned away and rustled from the room.

"He will appeal to the ruler here, then?" said Mbandi after the door had closed. "To this president?" At Nichols' nod, he hunched. "We should hurry, if you know a quicker way. The first to speak in a dispute is often the victor."

"With some men, yes." Nichols sighed. "Not this one. It will not be an . . . official meeting. And you are exhausted. You may rest here; I will summon Margritte to keep company with you."

"I should be there," said Mbandi.

"You will truly not speak with Father Kircher?"

"I have renounced the Company," repeated Mbandi, as though stating the obvious.

"Do you realize how this will appear to anyone judging a . . . dispute?"

The traveler shrugged. "Appearances are no concern to me."

"Trust me; it would be a concern to this president." Nichols deliberately sat at his desk again, and reached across it. "We have some little while. Would you like to see the atlas again?"

"Ed, it's phenomenal. There's a whole other Thirty Years' War going on in Angola!" Nichols turned in his pacing as he spoke. "1624 to 1658, civil war, raiding, treaties broken like pie crust. Nzinga becomes queen, eventually, and cuts some deals with the Portuguese. It doesn't end well. Nothing really did there . . . "

He turned again. Seated at the upstairs taproom's single table, Governor Ed Piazza watched him steadily. A mug of small beer rested beside him, untouched; the location had been chosen to make this meeting as unofficial as possible, not for the beverages. His slight slump wasn't inattention; a Croat musket-ball had smashed ribs and a shoulder blade, two years ago, as he defended the high school he'd once been principal of.

"But look what the Dutch did in Java! A pound of seeds that an English botanist got to them, and in a few years they had plantations of *cinchona*. Hundreds of thousands of trees. And there's places all over Africa with mountain rain forests. Zaire, Cameroon, Tanzania, Rwanda. You remember our Rwanda, Ed? Jesus, what if we could stop that four hundred years in advance? Or keep Leopold's butchers out of the Congo?"

Governor Piazza nodded. "It would be a hell of a thing to be able to do, yes." He was a small thin-faced man; smaller behind a coarse-planked table. Pain had whittled down his features during a convalescence extended by work. His lips were often pinched, as they were now—as they'd been when Nichols dug a flattened chunk of lead out of him, sharing half an ampoule of morphine with another casualty. He'd offered Piazza the bullet as a keepsake. *No, Doctor. Trophies are for sports.*

"And with our half, maybe we can beat the Dutch to Java. Or trade it to them for something. Who cares, as long as the stuff gets grown cheap enough? Montoya's a goddamn genius."

Piazza glanced to this right, where Father Kircher sat. "Jesuits have a reputation for being . . . thoughtful. No question there. But, James—in this time, a thoughtful man will give his courier a letter, to back him up and confirm the details. Parchment. Seals. Something official. Did this man bring a letter of some kind?"

Nichols' enthusiasm faded. "Well, no. He told me about that—Montoya wrote several letters for him to bring, but he got sick in Lisbon, and some bastard stole his purse. Money, letters, all gone, but they didn't think anything of a bag of seeds."

"I see. And, Father, you aren't yet able to confirm if he's even a Jesuit, that's correct?"

The priest quirked a smile. "You mean, a secret hand-shake? I'm afraid not. It will take some time to contact Rome and obtain the routine reports from that province."

"More than ten days, I'm guessing."

"Yes." Kircher turned a palm upward. "They might show his name, if nothing else. I am sure that if I spoke to him at length, it would become clear if he had been even a lay brother . . . but he declines."

Nichols shifted on his feet. "We've established why he does. I doubt he'll change his mind, either."

"Well, that's possible. I've known stubborn folk before." Perhaps it was coincidence that Piazza held Nichols' eye at that moment. "If his story is true, he'll *need* to be stubborn . . . But these letters bother me. He had them long enough to memorize—then at the last stop of the trip, they're gone."

"It is possible," said Kircher, "that—with no offense to you, Doctor—that this man calling himself Mbandi has intercepted a genuine courier, robbed him, and wishes to take a great gamble to gain great wealth."

Nichols frowned. *If they risk much, they want much.* "But then he would *have* the letters, the proof, anyway."

"Any such letter would describe the bearer in detail—appearance, scars, and so forth. Would this man have visible scars?"

Nichols nodded grimly. "I'd guarantee it."

"Then an imposter could not use them." Kircher sat back slightly, closing the logical loop.

"It'd be one hell of a coincidence that an imposter would be black, though. Maybe in South America it wouldn't, but to travel all the way here is a long way to go for any payoff."

"True enough . . ." Piazza tented his fingers. "Here's the thing, James. When I was in the State Department, we had one spice trader turn up who claimed he'd spotted Prester John's balloon over Ethiopia. He wanted one of our aircraft to fly there, to force it down so he could interrogate the crew and find the lost kingdom's riches. He'd split it evenly with us, of course—that was only fair, since we would provide the aircraft."

Nichols couldn't help a grin. "You sent Harry to talk to him, right?"

"Yeah. He bounced a few times on his way out."

"Not a real bright sales pitch. No balloons yet."

"Poetry travels, it seems." Piazza cracked a brief smile. "We tend to forget that while at first we only saw down-timers through our history books, now a lot of them only see us through our books, or a garbled version of them . . . James, there's a word I need to use. It's not a nice word."

Nichols tensed. "I've heard 'em all."

"Mountebank."

"Ouch." He tried to smile. "They got some nasty ones here. Yeah, I'll say it too—con man."

"A lot of people want our help, and a lot of them need it; some don't. When I was a principal, it was kids. In State they were princes; now they're traders. But some things never change, and a con man always tells you what he thinks you want to hear. James, by now half the world knows who you are, and has an idea what you want." Ed turned up one palm. "I suppose now's where you suggest that maybe I don't believe him because he's black?"

"I guess so," said Nichols dryly. "And then you say that I'm too eager to believe him because he's black." It was hard to argue with Piazza in some ways; he was too damn calm.

"Glad we got that out of the way, then. I think he's impressed the hell out of you, but not because of that."

"He said some things would have sounded better if he had lied, but with our books, we could check every-thing, so he didn't bother. Very, ah, Jesuitical."

"Yeah." Piazza sighed. "Were there battles at Kabasa in 1619? Yes, I think we can check that. Was a farmer named Mbandi captured by the Portuguese there? James, even history books about Europe don't name foot soldiers. We can't see that closely. Although, maybe . . . " He looked to Kircher; the priest shook his head.

"Okay, but are you suggesting he knows that? How could he know exactly what information we're missing?"

"Probably not," Piazza conceded. "But he can guess that we can't confirm the seeds either."

"Oh, shit. Why not?" Nichols blinked. "And how would he—"

"It sounds like everyone's blundering around Peru with no idea just what to look for. Therefore, *we* probably don't know. Because anyone who got the information about cinchona existing at all would not have stopped looking until they got everything of ours that they could."

"Ed, were *you* a Jesuit?"

"You'd be surprised how smart high school kids can be. Some were bigger than me, I had to outthink them . . . But, no, we can't verify these seeds. I've seen the crop species lists—even Stone's stuff. I'll check with Willie Ray at the Grange to be certain, but you said there's dozens of species even of this one kind of tree, and most are useless for quinine, right? It's just birdseed to us." Piazza added without smiling, "We could set up a greenhouse and plant samples. Might get a testable result in ten years."

"Great. I can be a gardener when I retire. Does it matter? What do we have to lose?"

"Reputation, for one. Mountebanks don't exactly keep low profiles. You've read Kipling? 'And Danny fell, and he fell . . . ' If this country of, ah . . . "

"Ndongo."

"Right, Ndongo, if it's in a state of civil war, we could be sending a rogue into it with enough wealth to seriously affect things. He could just be a failed bark-cutter who'd like to be a king, or make one—or break one. We're not about to start busting up Africa ourselves . . . Or he could be perfectly sincere—right now—but change his mind in six months."

"Or he could be straight up, and we could save millions of lives. Ed, I know the hurry looks suspicious, but I understand it. Time costs lives, a lot of them."

Father Kircher cleared his throat. "I agree. While I cannot speak for the father general, I do know that your people and ours share many goals, and I truly believe that if these seeds are to be used in this manner, this beneficence, then it will not divide us. But the risk is serious, and we must be certain. The goals of the long term take precedence."

"As they just did in South America?"

"I have given this some thought, Doctor. From the account, and reports I have seen, the upriver missions in Uruguay have become impossible to defend against slaving raids. In your time, support was given by the king of Portugal that helped to drive off the attacks, make the region safe for more than a century. Here, it will not be given."

"You could have *tried*," said Nichols.

"We did." Kircher smiled slightly at Nichols' surprise, and turned to the governor. "The will was the same as in your time, although with 'foresight' we moved a little faster . . . King Philip—or, more to the point, the conde de Olivares who 'advises' him—has refused any aid to a society that follows the laws of communism. He has read of this monstrous force of history, and it terrifies him." Kircher met Nichols' eye. "In your time, it was Father Montoya himself who made the successful appeal as procurator to Philip, some years from now. It would be a terrible irony if his own choice to leave the Company has deprived it of such a convincing voice."

"Never mind that. From the sound of it, nobody could persuade him. Was he really that frightened?"

"Every ruler is frightened, James," said Piazza. "But if they lose to us, they retire. If they lose to revolution, they'll get hanged. Or worse. Our histories are their horror stories . . . Father, since you can't get support, what is the Company's intention?"

"If we continue to develop the upriver missions," said Kircher relentlessly, "we will only stock the larder for hungry slave-raiders, by bringing together many Guarani where they may easily be attacked. And God is patient. We must be so as well. If, instead, we make efforts to resist the slave trade from outside—perhaps, in time, with Philip's help, and with that of the USE—we can do far more good in the long term." He folded his hands. "Father Montoya became too entangled in his own situation to understand this larger need."

"I can understand his take on it," rasped Nichols. "Look. I'm not a Jesuit either, and I don't care shit for politics. This is a way to fight disease, and I will be damned if I don't make use—"

Governor Piazza lifted a hand. "Okay, hold it. Didn't one private expedition already go off to another continent last year, looking for rubber and pitching malaria treatments on the side?"

Nichols blew out a hard breath. "Dieter was carrying artemisia. Different drug, different cultivation, different economics—if artemisinin production gears up here, it's not likely people in Africa can afford it, just like in our time. If we had an opportunity to make another cheap antibiotic, would you tell me to just be happy with chloramphenicol?"

"It works," said Pizza neutrally.

"Until something becomes resistant to it, yes. Monocultures are vulnerable. Ask Willie Ray."

Piazza nodded. Willie Ray had been a small farmer through much of the twentieth century—which meant that he'd lost a biological war that Cargill and Monsanto Inc. had won. "Point taken. But that bunch also gave us time to think it over properly. Ten days? I'm responsible to my council; there's no secret budget I can tap. Mike could, or Rebecca, but they're not here."

"No black funds. Huh. Kind of ironic." Nichols tried to match Piazza's coolness. "There's a lot at stake here. You've heard me rant on epidemics before, but this could be a big, big leverage against slavery in the New World—more than making nice with kings and counts. A lethal place means you send disposable people there—it's not cruelty, just, just fucking *economics*. Hell, we've got German people poor and desperate enough to emigrate to the West Indies and cut sugar cane for pay—if it's not a death sentence."

"I understand Mike's position on the slave trade very well," said Piazza. "It's already under way, but the big numbers aren't happening yet, and we can't project power very far. Yet. When we're ready, we are going to destroy it, though—no question. There aren't many

things we could feel good about exterminating, but this
is one . . . And I hardly need to ask your position, James."

"Ah. Well. It's not really that simple, for me."

Piazza showed actual surprise. "How can you say
that?"

"I'm a complicated man, Ed. Y'know, like Shaft."
Nichols grinned emptily as he finally hit a cultural reference that Father Kircher drew a blank upon. "I hate
disease. I hate pain and suffering and what human beings
do to each other when they're allowed to own people.
But who I am, *what* I am, it *isn't going to happen anymore*. I'm so glad, some ways, thinking that Sharon will
grow up where people who look like us don't get shot
forty-one times reaching for our wallets . . . but part of
what America was came from Africa. Good parts.
Mbandi won't be the first black Jesuit, but an American
would've been. Blood typing. Heh—blood, all right. One
hell of a lot of Purple Hearts, from Fort Wagner to the
Gulf. It *meant* something.

"The whole civil rights struggle that made Melissa
what she is—King, Malcolm X. Won't happen. Sojourner
Truth won't happen. Gospel. Jazz. Half the music of the
twentieth century won't. Who's gonna inspire Elvis, for
God's sake?"

"I could live without rap," offered Piazza.

"Don't dis yo' timeline . . . Hell, even the language
won't be the same. We'll all sound like ruddy Englishmen
or something." Nichols sobered. "It gets worse. Look
where they sent me as a Marine. Like you said, soon we
can 'project power.' I got projected into Khe Sanh
because we had a medical corps that could keep me from
catching the galloping crud. Everyone'll get quinine in a

while, and learn how to dig latrines properly. English redcoats in India? Richelieu's musketeers in China? The world won't play nice because we tell it to."

"I understand. But we may not always play nice ourselves. My apologies, Father, if I speak a little bluntly here?" Kircher nodded. "Well, this gift of seeds is . . . Generous isn't the word. It could be worth, what, billions in the long run. And Montoya may be a defecting Jesuit, but he's still thinking like one. That's one hell of a bribe, James, and if I take it, that will oblige Mike to honor it when he gets back—oblige the USE to do something, and you bet Montoya knows it. And that's a long way off to send anyone to do something, not just up some river in Europe . . .

"I'm an honest politician—have to stay bribed. I need to *know*, James, I need your final word on this."

Nichols swallowed. "How soon?"

"Can you get any information over the next ten days that you don't already have?"

" . . . No."

"Then very soon."

"I am sorry that he will not speak to me," said Father Kircher as he wrapped his cloak against the outside chill. "I suppose it is best if I do not accompany you back. You do understand, Doctor—the seeds are yours to make use of."

Nichols huffed out a cloud of breath. "You're sure of that?"

"I am certain of it. Are you certain of what to do with them?"

Kircher's eyes were mild, but it was an effort to meet them, and too great an effort to lie. "No."

"I believe you know your heart in the matter, though."

"I don't practice medicine with my heart, Father. There's no room for that. But to lose a year . . . " He trailed off, looking down the street at a running figure. It waved jerkily.

"Herr Doctor!"

"And to think *I* was about to run into her arms," murmured Kircher; then he stiffened. "Something is wrong."

Margritte all but staggered up to them. "Herr Doctor, the traveler! He is sick, he is very sick! You must come!"

"Shit." Nichols looked around, but no one was nearby enough to overhear. "Come on, and keep your voice down. Could—"

Father Kircher touched his arm, halting him. "I will come, if I may."

Nichols looked at him, hesitated, nodded. "Yeah, you already know. Hurry, then."

"James!"

He turned. Piazza stood in the doorway. "Don't run. People will see you."

"Ah. Right. Thanks, Ed—I'll call you when I find out what's going on."

Colder now than the air could make him, Nichols marched stiffly back to his house with Kircher and Margritte a step behind, nodding at the few passers-by; waved the others in, slammed the door.

"In here!" cried Margritte from the study. The atlas lay splayed on the desk; Mbandi sprawled in the armchair by the fire, shivering violently enough to see from across the room.

Nichols examined him with hasty care; dry skin, obvious chills. "He has not been sick of the stomach?"

"No, Herr Doctor."

Pulse fast and thready. No blue tinge under the fingernails—Wait. "You said you were ill in Lisbon. On the journey. You were ill again two weeks after that, weren't you?"

Mbandi nodded through the shivering. "It began this way, as well. The cold, such cold—then the heat. Dry, then wet."

Nichols counted backward for incubation. "About a month to cross the Atlantic . . . Buenos Aires, then. You were infected there by an insect bite, a mosquito. God damn it, you already *have* malaria!"

He choked off self-directed anger at missing the signs. The hell with thousand-yard stares; he'd not noticed the jaundiced yellow of the eyes themselves. "We cannot bring you to Leahy Center. They will see a strange man with a disease, and . . . " Belatedly realizing something, he turned.

Margritte had flattened herself against the wall, her face slumped white with shock. "Malaria," she said. "The air-fever, Jesus God in Heaven. I *touched* him, I touched his *belongings*."

Father Kircher gestured toward her. "Calm yourself—"

Nichols overrode him. "Margritte, listen. Listen, *please!* You have nothing to fear. This disease only moves from one person to another by the, ah, the bite of an insect that cannot live in cold air, or in clothing. It cannot hurt you. *Look.*" He reached and took a fistful of coarse brown robe, gripped it—tried not to think of typhus, or another parasite that any traveler might really be carrying. "He is badly sick, but he cannot make you sick, or anyone else. I promise you this." He stared at Margritte, holding her gaze.

"Very well, Herr Doctor." Margritte straightened, swallowed hard, then nodded. "If you say it is safe, then I know it is so."

Nichols glanced back to Kircher. The Jesuit met his eye, tilted his own head silently. Nichols could read the gesture easily enough: *Yes, the reputation works.*

"Good," he said absently. "Then you may care for him, here, to help me. Please put at least two pots of water on to boil . . . Father, if you could drag that couch over here." *Don't need to quarantine Mbandi, but we sure-hell need to quarantine any gossip.*

"Herr Doctor?" said Margritte on a rising note; but she smoothed her dress and strode into the hallway, only slightly veering her step around the traveler; the patient, now. Once her shock wore off and Margritte reclassified him as such, she'd be safe to return to her desk and its telephone.

"Is that necessary?" asked Kircher quietly as he crossed the room.

"No. It never is. Although usually it is the men who need to be kept occupied . . . " He turned to the traveler beside him. "We will make for you in comfort here, until you are again well. Do not be afraid. I do not have any way to treat the malaria itself, but there are powerful medicines to cool your fever, and we can give you water through a small tube, to . . . what is it?"

He followed Mbandi's eyes to the satchel on his desk. "Oh, no. That is not tested—"

"It is my only test left," hissed Mbandi through chattering teeth. "My only proof. No letters, no sig—signet ring, no Father Gustav to, to, to speak for me. Let this speak for me, then. It is the true *cinchona roja*; it will cure me."

"But if you are wrong, and I do not treat you as I should with my medicines, you could die." *Falciparium, by the recurrence period. Twenty percent mortality in healthy adults, let alone in him. Jesus.*

"All men die." Mbandi's eyes clenched shut. "Father Gustav will die, in my place, because Father Montoya sent me away instead. I know this. I cannot fail him."

"I took an oath . . . " whispered Nichols. Furniture groaned over the floor behind him, almost silencing his voice.

"All the fathers took oath as well. To the pope himself, in person, to obey his word. Those who saw what must be done, t-they broke it. I ask you, break yours this one time. Let me prove myself and my task. Please."

Nichols rose slowly, walked to his desk. He looked from the telephone to the satchel, and back; from the twentieth century to the seventeenth, aspirin and IVs to unknown quinine. The atlas was crumpled across Central Africa, he saw as he picked it up; sighed, and slammed it shut.

"Help me get him on the couch," he rasped to Kircher. "Then we need to grind up a handful of this bark he has brought, and make an infusion."

The dry chills lasted for five hours; the first infusion, cautiously gauged at thirty grains of an unknown powder's strength, did nothing. As the windows darkened,

Mbandi's shudders faded to lassitude—and his temperature began to rise.

"I don't know how long this crap takes to work," muttered Nichols, as Father Kircher poured another cup infused from sixty grains. "Or if it works at all." He slipped the thermometer from Mbandi's slack jaws. "One-oh-three and a bit. God damn it . . ."

"Keep trying," mumbled the traveler. His skin was as glossy and hot as a kettle. "Remember, I have lived through this before."

"Yes, and each time it's been tearing up your liver." Nichols had to steady his head as he drank. He'd doused the study lights long before; firelight and lamplight were gentler.

Two more hours. One-oh-four. Nichols picked up the phone, gripped it tightly; set it down. "Everything I do does harm," he muttered. "Always did. Come on, you fucking lunatic, you better be right or I'll kill you myself."

One-oh-five, and Mbandi began to babble snatches of words, his eyes no longer tracking. German. "Loreto, it's fallen." Spanish. *"Paulista, este non hombre—este perro."* Fragments of African dialects. His hands fretted at the blanket's edges, as though they could piece the words into sense. Sometimes, when he glimpsed Nichols' face above his own, he cried out in joy, spoke rapid tongues that sounded a continent away. *"Malanje—"*

Still the fever did not break. For another hour, Nichols sat slump-armed in the armchair, listening to garbled pain and joy and history. *Is this how they saw us, these glimpses? Prester John's balloon, all right.* But the fever did not break, did not break . . .

"A hundred and twenty grains, Father. This is the last try."

Kircher's thick fingers rasped the bark into powder, timeless in the firelight; steeped it into a glass of hot water. "It is no easy thing to clash with an oath, for some men," he said as the red tinge spread through the liquid. "I still believe—aside from my duty—that Father-Provincial Montoya was wrong in his choice. But I would not wish to have been in his place."

"Do you think I'm breaking mine? Because I'm afraid to decide?"

"I think," said Kircher slowly, "that man is making a very brave choice, and you are the instrument of it . . . and this too requires courage. You will know soon enough. Come, this is ready, is it not?"

Mbandi focused long enough to gulp the liquid, sighed "*Cinchona roja*, Mamani," and closed his eyes in sunken sockets.

Old in the ways of healing, Nichols took a meal in the kitchen, exchanged quiet words with an equally tired Kircher, and rested a while. He'd matched his strength against disease before, knew to husband it. In a weary predawn hour, he walked back into the dimness, the frail form on the couch; cradled the fire-hot head for the thermometer's test.

One-oh-three.

"Well," said Nichols softly. Beside him, Father Kircher murmured something—not English, not German, but Latin. He laid his own hand upon Mbandi's forehead a moment, and withdrew it. "Go, then," he said more strongly in German. "And may God go with you."

He turned away without another word.

Mbandi's eyes flickered, opened, fixed on Nichols' own. "*Malungu. Kamerade*," he said in a slur of German and—Kimbundu, was it? "*Malungu*, there is for us, no home behind. Only ahead. Seeds, across oceans. *Malungu* seeds."

Thin new-fallen snow crackled under Nichols' steps, frozen grass beneath. The knife-edged arc of the Ring of Fire had eroded to a gentle slope here, a good walk southeast of Grantville, a displaced circle knitting slowly with its surroundings. He looked back over fallow fields and thought of hoof prints leading west, toward Lisbon and a long voyage south. "Do you think it'll work?" he asked.

Ed Piazza shrugged inside his parka—carefully, when cold made the old wound ache. "Don't ask me now. I did this on your word, remember."

"Yeah. I don't doubt him—I might not be able to outthink a Jesuit, but I know he wasn't lying or faking, not half-cooked like that. Another hour and I'd have filled him with aspirin. Winter journeys are a bitch—must have triggered the relapse."

"Ah," said Piazza. "About that. I talked to Margritte for a while—"

"Hang on. I figured something out this morning. Amazing what sleep will do . . . Mbandi said that Father Gustav would 'die in his place.' " Nichols shortened his stride to climb the slope. "Let me play Jesuit for a second. Assume that the Jesuits got everything they could from us about their own history, and that Montoya gets a good part of that relayed to him as a provincial father. He knows he will ordain Mbandi in a few more years . . .

but he sees that in our history, no black Jesuit appears until Healy in 1850."

Piazza sighed. "I get it. If Mbandi died fighting at the missions before he was ordained, then he disappeared from history. Down in the grain, just another foot soldier who changed sides."

They both paused at the crest. "Right," said Nichols, trying not to puff. *I'm not old, just need four hundred years to catch my breath.* "Maybe that got to Montoya after a while. So he sent Mbandi away, broke the timeline—and somehow Mbandi found out, or figured it out. That's hard on a man—because you always feel relief first. Always." He stared at the horizon as he spoke, a thousand yards away; hearing the burr of a mortar fragment flying past his own ear, the impact into another man's flesh, the instant's thought: *Thank the Lord it was him and not me.*

"No wonder he tried so hard to convince me, then, is it? No letters, no proof. Just the sickness he was carrying himself, and the bark to cure it."

Piazza stuffed his hands in his coat pockets. "Well—as I said, I talked to Margritte, and she mentioned something that seemed peculiar. She was chatting with the coachman who'd driven Mbandi into town, and the coachman said this 'schwartzenjesuit' was riding on the roof the whole last day in; no coat, no robe, just shirt-sleeves. In that terrible cold! The guy said he could practically hear the Jesuit's teeth chattering over the noise of the coach wheels. Now, tell me what that was about."

Nichols closed his eyes for a moment, smiled. "Oh, I can tell you. He wanted to make sure." He shook his head ruefully, kicked a clot of frozen earth loose. "Damn!

You see? No letters, no backing from the Company—more likely the opposite—and everyone knows Jesuits are tricksy, right? How could we trust him? But nobody lies through a high fever—so he tried to bring one on, kick-start the 'quartan fever.' No logic games, just humanity. Not many'd take that sort of chance, just to save a year." His smile faded. "Of course, he knew that he doesn't have that many years, carrying falciparium. Not many like him around. Not many malungu. One less, now." *That leaves just about one.*

"I should get back," said Piazza. "You can freeze yourself like him if you want . . . But this 'malungu' thing. It sounded familiar, so I checked. Anyone told you about the Gowens, that family owned a farm a bit north of the Ring?"

"No. What's the point? I sure can't meet 'em now."

"They called themselves Melungeons—mixed-race, bit of everything; Indian, European . . . African. Angolan."

He nodded to Nichols' stare. "Yeah. That was the story, anyway. A lot of folks around here know it. When the Portuguese hit Angola, and started shipping people to Brazil, English privateers hit *them* along the way. Captured some slavers and took them into the Virginia colony to sell off."

"To sell," said Nichols flatly. "Not just the ships, then. The people got sold too."

"Into indentured labor, just like everyone else without money, white or black. But, James—after a few years, they were free. And no Jim Crow laws yet, no real racism until the eighteenth century. They bought land, married whomever they liked—they *settled*."

"Do you think it's true?"

"Maybe." Piazza shrugged. "Bob Gowen used to claim he was part Turk, for God's sake. We'll never know. Still . . . I think it was 1620," he added thoughtfully. "Ought to be raising the next generation about now. Sure sounds like African-Americans to me. If not them, it'll be someone else; even oceans don't hold out forever. Maybe some of those kids hear about a famous foreign 'Moorish physician' now and then, hey?"

"Well. That's . . . something." Nichols stared back toward Grantville's steam plumes. *Seeds, across oceans.*

Piazza shivered, stamped his feet. "C'mon, *malungu*, let's go home. We've got work to do."

Trials

Jay Robison

The young woman put her hands together in front of her chest, as if praying. The stone-faced prison guard wove the cords of the *sibille* around the thumbs of her joined hands. The guard held onto the whipcords, ready to tighten them.

She looked at the man who had caused her so much pain, both physical and emotional. He looked back. Was the sneer on his face real or imagined? She looked down again at her hands; it would be a small thing to endure if she could inflict pain in equal measure on the man whom she now confronted.

The judge asked her, "Is what you have said in your prior examination true?"

The cord tightened. Pain.

"It is true."

"Is the confirmation you have given here today the truth?"

Tighter now. More pain. The young woman steeled herself. She would be damned if she would cry out.

"It is true!"

The cord tightened yet again. The pain was nearly unbearable.

"It is true, it is true, it is true, everything I said!"

Artemisia Gentileschi awoke, sweating, to daylight and a concerned servant. She rubbed her thumbs, massaging away phantom pain and pushing the memory back down inside her mind. It took her a moment to realize where she was: in Rome, staying in the *palazzo* of Cassiano dal Pozzo, a friend and patron. She was sweating and didn't know if it was the June heat.

"Are you all right, Maestra Gentileschi?" the young woman asked. She held a bowl of water.

"I am fine. I will have breakfast after I get dressed."

The servant curtsied and left the water on a table. Artemisia rose from bed to wash her face. Her eyes fell on the letter lying on her bedside table and the news it contained. Her father, Orazio, was dead.

It had taken six months for the letter to come via agents of her patron, King Philip IV of Spain. His Most Catholic Majesty was currently an ally of England in the League of Ostend. Due to the war threatening to engulf half of Europe, communication with England was anything but quick. Six months for Artemisia to find out that her father had succumbed to plague.

Artemisia splashed cool water on her face, hoping to wash away her grief with the sweat. The sweat, at least, was cleansed. The grief remained, as well as the old memories it dredged up. She finished dressing, had breakfast, and a carriage took her to the Church of San Matteo, where Galileo's hearing was to be held.

Galileo was the reason she was even in Rome in the summer. He was an old friend, and it had pained her deeply that she had been unable to do anything for him. She was living in Naples, far from where he was being held; she had no money she could give him and no influence she could exert on his behalf. She had written him a few letters but wasn't sure if he'd ever gotten them; she'd had no response.

When Artemisia heard that Galileo was being brought to Rome to stand before the Holy Office—a *de facto* trial if not an official one—she decided the least she could do was to come to Rome and, if possible, be present in the church where the hearing would be held. She didn't know if Galileo would even know she was there, but at least there would be one friendly face among the spectators.

At least, she reflected as she stood in line with other noble parties, she would be able to sit in a pew rather than stand. Gian Lorenzo Bernini, the Holy Father's favorite sculptor, had made the arrangements. Artemisia couldn't help thinking, somewhat sourly, that it was another favor she owed the man. Almost two years before, he had made arrangements for her oldest daughter, Prudentia, to travel to Grantville in the company of Giulio Mazzarini. Gian Lorenzo would, Artemisia knew, collect on his favors in due time.

As the English might say, "In for a penny, in for a pound." For Artemisia, the benefits received from a favor had to outweigh the inevitable obligations to be incurred in asking for the favor. In this case the benefits were worth it. Because supporting Galileo was not the only reason Artemisia had for wanting to be present at the hearing. She wanted to see Father Lawrence Mazzare for herself. Prudentia had written many times of his kindness; the Grantville priest had helped make satisfactory living arrangements for her daughter, and he had never asked for anything in return. Artemisia hoped to meet the American priest and thank him personally if possible.

Finally, she was let into the church. Crowded as San Matteo's was, it was cooler than standing in the street. She looked around; everyone seemed to be whispering and pointing at a nobleman in very fancy *cavaliere* dress and the stout priest seated with him. They were sitting not far away. The whisperers were saying something about them being Polish, but to Artemisia—who'd dealt with several agents of King Charles of England—the *cavaliere* had the look of a Scotsman. Still, with as many mercenaries as were on the loose these days, who could tell? Artemisia was tempted to ask them herself, but they looked distracted.

Then the hearing started. Like every one else around her, Artemisia was completely unprepared for what happened next.

She came out of San Matteo's in shock, along with most of the other bystanders. The strange *cavaliere*, it turned out, was not Polish but (as she had suspected) a

Scotsman in the service of the United States of Europe. Artemisia, being long familiar with the politics of Rome, had no doubt that the implications of a Scots Calvinist being willing to exchange his life for the pope's would be a topic of endless conversation for the foreseeable future. The *cavaliere*—Lennox, his name was; he was an officer rather than a knight—had not, in fact, been killed. His cuirass had stopped the ball from the pistol of the Holy Father's would-be assassin. The truth was spectacular enough, but Artemisia had no doubt that before long, half of Rome would be claiming to have personally witnessed a legion of angels defending the pope against the demon servants of Lucifer (in human guise as heretical fanatics) while the Holy Father miraculously brought Captain Lennox back from the dead and made him see the folly of his Calvinist ways.

Artemisia herself could hardly get back to her rooms at dal Pozzo's quickly enough. The first order of business was to send a letter to Father Mazzare. She knew from what friends had told her where the American was staying; she wrote a brief note expressing to Father Mazzare her desire to meet him, in order to thank him personally for his kindness to Prudentia. As soon as a servant was dispatched to deliver the letter, Artemisia hurried to a room that had been set aside for her to work. She had to sketch.

She knew there would be hundreds, thousands, of depictions of what had just transpired at the Church of San Matteo. Works would be commissioned, and many more artists would complete works in hopes of selling them and getting noticed by the pope himself, other members of the Barberini family, or someone hoping to ingratiate himself with them.

The picture Artemisia began to sketch was different. For her the enduring image of the day's events would not be Lawrence Mazzare's eloquent defense of Galileo or Lennox's heroism, but a young man comforting his brother after the boy accidentally killed a man.

It was just as well Artemisia had work to occupy her. After the spectacular events surrounding Galileo's hearing, everyone in Rome wanted to meet Father—soon thereafter Cardinal—Lawrence Mazzare. Artemisia counted herself lucky that only a week later, she received an invitation from Cardinal Antonio Barberini the Younger to dine with himself and the brand-new cardinal-protector of the United States of Europe.

Artemisia made sure she was looking her best when she went to Palazzo Barberini. As soon as she was shown into the sitting room, she executed a smooth and practiced curtsy, kissing the rings of both cardinals.

"Your Eminence. Your Eminence."

Mazzare laughed. "I'm afraid, Maestra Gentileschi, that I'm not used to being called that yet. I'm not sure I ever will be. And I wanted to tell you what an honor it is to meet you. I've long been an admirer of your work and have been looking forward to this ever since I received your letter. Cardinal Barberini was kind enough to arrange it for me." Cardinal Mazzare spoke excellent, if oddly accented, Italian.

"And I am hoping to be able to discuss some business with you, Maestra, if you would not object," said Antonio the Younger.

"Of course I would not object, Your Eminence." She turned to Cardinal Mazzare. "I am still known, Your Eminence? Where you came from?"

Mazzare sipped his wine. "Not to the extent you deserve, alas. But I have a feeling that's going to change. And your daughter is becoming quite well-known in her own right. She's made quite an impression on Grantville, I can tell you."

Artemisia felt her cheeks warm at this compliment to herself and her daughter. She was sure she was blushing. "You do me too much honor, Your Eminence. I am grateful that you made arrangements for her, and though you have never asked for anything in return, I am your servant if you should ever need me. It was hard to send Prudentia away, but I felt it would be too good an opportunity for her to miss. I wanted her to be appreciated for who she was, not be looked on as an exotic animal in a menagerie."

From the looks on their faces, neither man seemed to know how to handle that remark. Artemisia regretted saying it. Now was not the time to bring up old hurts.

A model of tact, Cardinal Mazzare decided not to comment on that sentiment. "Tino Nobili and I have had our differences over the years, but he's one of the most generous men I know. And Prudentia has been a model of good behavior."

"In her letters, my daughter has spoken highly of Signor Nobili and his household. They have treated her like a member of the family. She also tells me," she said, with a significant look at Cardinal Mazzare, "that she has become quite enamored of a young man. A young soldier by the name of James Byron McDougal. Do you know him, Your Eminence?"

"Not as well as I'd like," Mazzare responded candidly. "Pete, Jabe's father, never grew up in a church. Zula, his mother, was raised Catholic and had her kids baptized, but she doesn't come to church very often now." The American cardinal looked rather sad at this. "Still, they're a well-regarded family in Grantville. Pete and Zula both are good parents and hard workers."

"But he's a soldier," said Artemisia with not a little scorn.

"In Grantville all the young men are expected to have some military training. The girls too, if they can pass the physical tests and wish to volunteer. They complete their training and for most of them, that's it. They're available as a reserve force if they're needed, but most of them go on to other things. Jabe has enlisted for a year, but I'm quite sure he doesn't plan to make a career in the military. You should also know," said Mazzare, with a significant look of his own, "that Pete McDougal is an old friend of Prime Minister Stearns. They used to work closely together."

Artemisia seemed mollified by this explanation. If the young man in question was well regarded, with good connections, perhaps she would not object to a match with her daughter—if one was proposed.

They were summoned to the dining room. The meal was served, and the conversation drifted into small talk. Cardinal Mazzare was fascinated by Artemisia's stories of her time in Florence, her opinions on the notoriously difficult Galileo, as well as her admiration of Caravaggio—another of the American cardinal's favorite painters. Antonio, for the most part, observed; Mazzare was turning out to be quite cultured for a man who, by his own admission, had been a priest in a small provincial town until fairly recently. After the meal, Antonio the Younger broached the topic that had been on his mind.

"Maestra," the pope's nephew said, "I should be most annoyed with you. If you'd wanted to send Prudentia to Grantville, you should have come to me, not Bernini."

"Gian Lorenzo is an old friend. I did not want to disturb Your Eminence with such trifles." Artemisia surprised herself by keeping a straight face while saying that.

"The fact is, Maestra, that I would much rather have you owing me a favor than owing Bernini one." The three laughed. Antonio continued, "I am hoping, and my family is hoping, that you would consent to accept our patronage once again."

"That will mean severing my ties with King Philip," she said.

"That miser isn't paying you half as much as you deserve. You know we are a generous family."

"And you have better taste," Artemisia said. The remark sparked more laughter. "You know, Your Eminence, that I would love nothing more to have the Barberini back as my patrons. I am hoping, however, to go to Grantville. Perhaps permanently."

"Why? Meaning no offense to my brother in Christ, but it is my understanding the artistic world in Grantville, and the USE as a whole, is practically nonexistent." Antonio didn't sound angry, merely curious.

Artemisia gathered her thoughts. In the past week she had been pondering this question a great deal. Bernini and dal Pozzo had asked the same thing when she'd sounded them out for advice; for that matter, it was a question she'd asked herself.

"Your Eminence, in the past few weeks, I received news from England. My father died about six months ago."

"I am sorry to hear Orazio has passed away," said Antonio with genuine feeling. Cardinal Mazzare added his sympathies. "I shall have a requiem mass said in his honor at our family chapel at Sant' Andrea della Valle. But what has that to do with your decision?"

"If you don't mind telling us," Mazzare added. From the look he gave to Antonio, Artemisia guessed that the American thought his fellow cardinal quite rude for pressing the matter.

"I do not mind, Your Eminence. It is a question I expected to be asked. I find myself tiring of the competition. I don't like Naples. It's crowded, dirty, and dangerous. I love Rome and will miss it, but I confess I rather enjoy the thought of being a preeminent artist up north. And I look forward to working where I will be appreciated for my skill as an artist, rather than treated as a curiosity."

"I appreciate your honesty, Maestra," said Antonio. "I must tell you that I have decided to direct considerable patronage to you."

"Would staying in Rome be a requirement?"

"What would you do if it was?"

Artemisia said nothing. The pope's nephew continued: "It is not. It is something my brother Taddeo might do, but not me. In any case, distance should not pose any great difficulties. The distance from London to Naples hasn't proved any great obstacle to your work for King

Charles, after all. And it is my understanding," said Antonio, with a sly smile at the American cardinal, "that my American brother seems to have a way of communicating rather quickly."

Cardinal Mazzare did not react to Antonio's last statement. He smiled at Artemisia and said, "If you wish, we—our delegation, that is—would be more than happy to have you travel to Grantville with Gerry and Ron Stone. In fact, I am quite certain it would set their father's and stepmother's minds at ease if you did."

After witnessing the pandemonium the Stone boys had been in the middle of last week, Artemisia wasn't quite sure she was up for the challenge. Still, she didn't see how she could gracefully refuse the offer. And it would be safer for her, in any event.

"I thank you, Your Eminence," she said. "I very much appreciate your kindness. Please let me know when the boys are ready to leave, so that I may make arrangements. I will need to collect my younger daughter and wrap up my affairs in Naples."

Cardinal Mazzare nodded.

"Maestra," said Antonio, "His Holiness has asked me to tell you that he wishes you to see him before your departure."

Artemisia had to fight down a brief flutter of excitement and anxiety. "Of course, Your Eminence. I am entirely at His Holiness's convenience."

It was a quiet night at the Club 250. Sherry Dobbs Murray was drinking alone. It was something she tried not to do too much, but tonight she couldn't help herself.

Things were going to hell with Ronnie, her husband, and it was either drown her sorrows or go crazy.

The problem with drowning your sorrows alone, thought Sherry, is that pretty soon you end up going crazy anyway. She had to go home sometime; it might as well be now. With luck Ronnie would be asleep or passed out. As Sherry left the Club 250, she saw a party leaving the Thuringen Gardens. She approached close enough to see what was going on. The only people she recognized were Pete McDougal's oldest boy and the Italian girl he'd been going around with the past few months.

That's when she saw the only unattached male in the group. He looked like a soldier—and a kraut. Normally, Sherry didn't have much use for krauts, but she couldn't deny the boy looked like a stud. Strong jaw, wide shoulders and a nice, tight ass. What more could a girl want? Sherry was lonely, drunk and horny; Ronnie had been hitting the sauce even harder than usual lately, which made him more useless than usual in bed.

Sherry wasn't what anyone would call beautiful. She knew she was sexy, though. The kraut stud gave her a second look. She was curvy, with auburn hair; men in this time liked a girl with meat on her bones. They eyed each other speculatively, and then Sherry joined the group. They went to Constantine and Danielle Nobili's house; apparently, most of them were getting sent to Rome for something or other, and it was a last chance to party with the wives and girlfriends. Jabe McDougal and his girl didn't join them. They made their apologies and left for the evening.

At the house, the conversation got louder and raunchier. The Revenooers Rue flowed freely. This stuff is almost as bad as tequila, Sherry thought, but it gets the job done. Dietrich, that was the kraut stud's name, was undressing her with his eyes, and Sherry was getting turned on.

They went somewhere private, but not before indulging in more moonshine. They were gone for about a half an hour, and all Sherry wanted to do by that point was go home.

Artemisia and Constantia Gentileschi arrived in Grantville, along with Gerry and Ron Stone, in October. In the livery stable at the edge of town, she found Prudentia waiting for her, along with a gangly, shy-looking young man. She hugged and kissed her oldest daughter, and then the two sisters had a joyous reunion.

"You look good, my daughter," Artemisia said. "I trust you have been working hard?"

"Yes, *Mama*."

"It is wonderful to meet you, Maestra Gentileschi," the young man stammered out in Italian.

Artemisia tried to look stern but couldn't quite manage it. "You must be young Giacomo."

"James, ma'am. Most people call me Jabe."

Artemisia's accent couldn't quite manage "Jabe;" for her, he would remain "Giacomo," "Gia'?" for short—the Italian version of "James" or "Jim." She was rather pleased that her daughter's suitor was easygoing enough to accept his new nickname. It was always a good sign when a man didn't take himself too seriously. She introduced him to her younger daughter, Constantia.

Jabe had hired a horse cart to take them into town. Prudentia explained that Signor Nobili offered a place for both of them.

"But, *Mama,* the house is rather crowded. I thought Constantia could stay with me, and you could stay at the Higgins Hotel. I know you like your quiet."

"Hotel?" The word was unfamiliar.

"It's like an inn, ma'am," said Jabe. "Larger than most inns, though. And much cleaner."

As soon as all passengers and baggage were stowed on the cart, they lurched off. Artemisia and Constantia were too tired for a full tour of Grantville, but Jabe and Prudentia pointed out some of the sights on the way to the hotel. Constantia pointed at the decorations on the street.

"Are you preparing for a celebration?" the ten-year-old asked in fair English.

"Yes," Jabe said. "Our president—well the president of Thuringia-Franconia, anyway, not the whole USE—our president, Ed Piazza, had Congress declare October 7 a holiday. State government offices will be closed and everything. There's also going to be lots of ceremonies and celebrations up in Magdeburg."

"It's in honor of the heroes of the Battle of Wismar. It's the first anniversary," Prudentia added.

"Officially, they're calling it 'Remembrance Day,'?" Jabe continued. "But most of us call it 'Hans Richter Day.' There's going to be lots of parties."

"I know you're tired of traveling, *Mama,* but we will need to leave for Magdeburg in a couple of days."

"One of Prudentia's paintings is being officially presented to Princess Kristina."

Her daughter blushed deeply. Jabe grinned wickedly, enjoying putting Prudentia on the spot.

Prudentia recovered quickly, though, and gave as good as she got. "Just wait till you see Jabe's documentary. It's being televised again." It was Jabe's turn to blush now. Artemisia was unfamiliar with "documentary" and "televised," but judging from the banter between her daughter and young Gia, she thought it might be wise to start raising money for a dowry.

Sherry knew she couldn't hide things from Ronnie much longer; if she didn't say something soon, her body would tell the tale for her. She was long past being "late," and was getting sick pretty much every day. If her husband wasn't drunk or hung over all the time, he'd have noticed something was up long before now, but even Ronnie wouldn't be clueless enough to miss a bulging belly. Better to tell him now and get it over with.

Ronnie's reaction was even worse than Sherry imagined it would be. He didn't hit her; that wasn't Ronnie's way. But the verbal abuse was worse than his fists would have been.

"You fucking kraut-loving slut! Whore! How much did he pay you, huh? Did that include popping out his fucking little kraut bastard kid? Whore! Stupid fucking whore! I bet you'd do your dad too if you had the chance!" From there Ronnie just got louder and less coherent. It was too much, even for the Club 250. They were kicked out, Ronnie calling her everything he could think of every step of the way.

Artemisia had had three days to recover from her trip. Constantia had been having fun tagging along with Prudentia, which kept her occupied. Jabe managed to get a day off from his work in the Grantville office of the Joint Armed Services Press Division to give her "the grand tour" and to help her get properly settled in. The first order of business was setting up a bank account. After that was done, Jabe engaged a local "real estate agent," Huddy Colburn, to find a short-term lease. It would give her time to decide what she needed for a house in Grantville.

At her audience with Pope Urban VIII, before she left Rome, Artemisia was given several commissions. Urban, after seeing her initial sketches for a painting of Frank Stone comforting his brother at San Matteo, told her he wanted the original when it was completed and directed her to paint a copy as a wedding gift for Frank and Giovanna Stone. In addition to that work, she would complete an altarpiece for Sant' Andrea della Valle, and there were frescoes to be painted in a USE church. The specific church would be left up to Cardinal Mazzare or his appointed agent, though the holy father made it clear that he expected to be kept informed as work progressed.

The practical upshot of all this was that Artemisia had two hundred *scudi*—about $10,000 in USE paper money—to sustain her and her household in Grantville for a few months, an advance on the commissions the pope had given her. She had a letter of credit for an additional twelve hundred *scudi* she could access once the altarpiece and painting were finished and work began on the frescoes. To show her appreciation for Jabe's efforts, Artemisia paid for dinner at the Thuringen Gardens.

When they left, the plan was to join Tino and Vivian Nobili for dessert at their house. It was a Saturday night, the Gardens was at its busiest and dessert with the Nobilis would be a chance for quiet conversation. As soon as they got outside, Artemisia noticed a couple arguing in front of a rather disreputable-looking establishment across the street from the Thuringen Gardens.

Jabe recognized the man's voice. "Ronnie Murray. He's a drunk and a bully." The scorn in the young man's voice surprised Artemisia; it didn't seem to fit with his nature, as she'd gotten to know him over the last few days. From the look on Prudentia's face, she was a little surprised as well.

"Let's go," Jabe urged. "He probably won't hit Sherry. Odds are he's so trashed he won't even remember this tomorrow." If not for Ronnie's choice of words, Artemisia might have agreed and kept on walking. However . . .

Ronnie's words echoed in her mind and became something else: "She was wild and leading a bad life . . . she was a whore, and her father didn't know how to remedy this . . . she told me her father wanted to use her exactly as if she were his wife . . . she flirted out of her window so much you'd have thought her house was a bordello."

These words flared inside Artemisia Gentileschi, erupting from a core of rage that remained at the center of her, even though it had been nearly a quarter-century since those lies had been directed against her in open court. Without being fully aware of what she was doing, Artemisia marched toward the argument. She spared only a quick glance back at Jabe; he was frozen, as if he couldn't decide what he should do.

Drunk and furious as Ronnie was, it took the brute a moment to realize she was even there. He tailed off in disbelief—he seemed shocked that someone had actually gotten involved.

"Monster! *Bastarde!* Leave her alone!"

Ronnie Murray found himself looking not at his cowering wife but at a very determined woman, a total stranger to him. Artemisia had never been petite but at forty-one the stockiness of middle age had long since set in; clearly she was not a tiny female inclined to back down against the likes of a cowardly bully. If looks could have killed, Artemisia's dark eyes, burning with fury, would have been deadly weapons.

"Mind your own goddamned business, bitch," Ronnie growled. "Or I'll give you what I'm gonna give her."

Eerily calm, Artemisia pulled out the knife she always carried with her, ever since . . . that day. Ladylike it was not, but she long ago determined that whoever tried to do to her what Agostino Tassi had done would pay. Dearly.

Fortunately for Ronnie two local constables chose that moment to arrive.

Marvin Tipton and Jürgen Neubert were technically off duty. Marvin had just received news that he was to be a grandfather, and Jürgen had insisted they have a drink together when their shift was done. When the disturbance call went out over the radio, Marvin told the dispatcher he and Jürgen would handle it, as they were already on their way to the Gardens. Marvin had to suppress a smile when he saw a woman holding a knife on Ronnie Murray.

"Okay, what's going on here?" Marvin asked.

He almost wished he hadn't asked the question. Ronnie started up with his rambling, drunken, profanity-laced version of events; Artemisia, reverting to her native language under stress, was trying to talk over Ronnie, ably backed by her two daughters. Jabe McDougal was trying to say what he had seen. Sherry Murray, Marvin noted, was the only one not saying anything.

"QUIET!" When everyone had fallen silent, Marvin continued: "Jürgen, why don't you take the ladies to the station in the cruiser? I'll find somewhere better to talk to Ronnie. Sergeant McDougal?" asked Marvin, turning to Jabe.

"Yes sir?"

"See the girls home. Where can I get hold of you?"

"I think I'll wait with Prudentia and her sister at the Nobilis' house, Officer Tipton," Jabe said.

"Good. I'll call you there when we're done." With that, Marvin led Ronnie back toward the Club 250, and Jürgen escorted Artemisia and Sherry to the patrol car.

Marvin caught up with Jürgen at the station about an hour later. The two women were nowhere to be seen. "They are at Leahy Medical Center. Herr Doktor Adams is examining Frau Murray," Jürgen said. "It seemed to me correct procedure after Frau Murray told me what happened. I told Herr Doktor we would meet him at the medical center after you returned."

"You can fill me in on the way, I guess. So much for a drink at the Gardens."

Jürgen gave Marvin the complete story, recounting his report. Sherry had broken down once they'd arrived at the station, and the whole story came pouring out, more to the woman with her than to Jürgen. A few nights before Ed Piazza's embassy departed for Rome, there had been a party.

As Marvin drove, Jürgen continued reading from Sherry's statement: "There was this young kraut—Marine, I think. He looked good. Ronnie hasn't . . . well, the kraut looked good, like I said. We were pretty smashed, we went off alone and things started getting kinda hot and heavy. I was into it, y'know, I was liking it. But when he started getting under my shirt, I started thinking what if Ronnie found out? And I told the guy I wanted to stop. But he wouldn't. He just kept on . . . he wouldn't stop." His partner looked at him, his face full of concern. "Marvin, she started crying then, and I could not get any more information, but it was clear she should go to the medical center."

"You were right. What about the Italian lady?"

Jürgen couldn't resist a wide smile. "Artemisia Gentileschi, famous artist; she's painted for kings. She said I had an interesting face, and she might want to sketch me!"

Somehow Marvin wasn't surprised that his partner knew who this Artemisia whoever was. Jürgen had a deep curiosity about the world, and Marvin knew for a fact he spent a lot of his free time in the library. He even took his cousin's family there on weekly outings. If Jürgen

Neubert were up-time, Marvin thought, he'd probably go on *Jeopardy!* and win a bunch of money.

"And what about you, Marvin? What of Herr Murray?" asked Jürgen.

"Well, I think I talked Ronnie into not pressing charges against Ms. Gentileschi." Judging from Jürgen's expression, Marvin figured he hadn't mangled the woman's name too badly "He could always change his mind, but I told him it was a waste of time."

"Frau Gentileschi did pull a knife on him. That is a violation." Jürgen was one of the most by-the-book officers Marvin had ever worked with.

"Maybe. But a judge or jury wouldn't convict. She wasn't even really threatening Ronnie with it; she was just making him think twice. Even Ronnie admitted as much."

They'd arrived at Leahy Medical Center. Jürgen parked the car, and the officers headed inside. Marvin paused before opening the door.

"Mark my words, Jürgen. If Sherry's story is even close to true, there's going to be a world of trouble."

"Well, Sherry's definitely pregnant," said Dr. Jeffrey Adams as he came into the office where Marvin and Jürgen were waiting for him. "Ten to twelve weeks, probably, based on when she thinks her last period was. Hard to tell exactly without doing an ultrasound, which I can't do."

"Was she violated, Herr Doktor?" asked Jürgen.

"She says she was. Medically? There's no way to tell, not now. If she'd gotten an exam right away, we might have been able to say, but nearly three months later?" He shrugged.

"She didn't mention any names, perhaps, Herr Doktor?"

He thought for a moment. "She wasn't sure. She said he was German. Definitely a Marine, attached to the Rome delegation. Thought his name was Dieter, Dittmar, something like that. She didn't remember for sure. Said she was pretty drunk at the time."

"That matches her official statement," said Marvin. "I was almost hoping she was lying. Damn. Damn, damn, damn. This is going to be a mess."

The constables—Marvin and Jürgen—took Artemisia and Sherry to the Higgins Hotel. It hadn't been easy for Artemisia to turn down Tino Nobili's offer to stay at his place, but with Constantia staying there and the grandchildren often there when Danielle needed a babysitter, the Nobili house was too crowded and noisy for her. The Higgins Hotel would do until Signor Colburn found suitable housing for her and her daughters.

By the standards of the day, the Higgins Hotel was luxurious, not to mention maybe the cleanest inn on the European continent. Artemisia thought it even put her rooms at Cassiano dal Pozzo's Roman *palazzo* to shame. There was a helpful staff that would deliver meals to the room upon request; all one needed to do was call them on a device known as a "telephone." Each room had two beds with freshly laundered sheets, a bathroom with running water, electric lighting (and what a marvel that was), something called a "hot plate" for heating water, a teapot and a selection of "Frau Tibelda" brand teas.

Artemisia selected a packet labeled "Frau Tibelda's Calming Chamomile" and started some water heating. She noticed the woman standing in the middle of the room, not doing or saying anything.

Artemisia indicated one of the beds. "That one's yours. You can sleep here as long as you need to."

The woman—Sherry—didn't move. "Why're you doing this? You don't know me."

Artemisia studied the teapot sitting atop the burner. "My name is Artemisia," she said, realizing the woman probably hadn't caught her name with all that had gone on. "Your man said some things that made me angry. No one should say that to someone they care about."

She sat down on the bed. "He's my husband. Ronnie."

Artemisia nodded. "May I ask you something?" Sherry merely shrugged. "Are you so sure that the child isn't your husband's?"

Sherry laughed bitterly. "Ronnie's been snipped." Artemisia looked at her questioningly. "So he don't have no kids. You know?"

Sherry had shut down mentally when Ronnie started laying into her, but she was finally starting to come back to herself. She realized that the woman now making tea for her was clearly a down-timer. Sherry was fuzzy on people's status, but she could tell this Italian woman's clothes were well-made. That probably meant she was important. Which left Sherry even more puzzled as to why this woman gave a damn about the likes of her. Be that as it may, this woman wouldn't know what a vasectomy was.

"He didn't seem like he'd been unmanned," Artemisia said seriously.

It took Sherry a moment to realize what Artemisia meant by "unmanned." When she did, she had her first good laugh in months. She laughed so hard she cried, and Artemisia couldn't help joining in. Sherry attempted to explain.

"No, nothing like that. They didn't cut off his balls. Though in Ronnie's case that might've been good. There's like a little tube thingie that runs to a man's thing. They close that off, and a guy can't have no kids. Ronnie didn't want 'em. Said one woman trapped him that way, and it wasn't going to happen again."

"I see. Your surgeons truly are skilled if they can do such a thing," said Artemisia. The water was now boiling; she turned off the hot plate and poured two cups. She set a strainer in each to let the tea steep. "That would be difficult, if a man knew for certain he couldn't have children."

"I've thought about getting rid of it. But . . . I don't know."

"Abortions are so easy to get here?" Artemisia asked, surprised.

"Doc Adams'll do them if you're not too far along. Or the Jew doctor, Becky Stearns' dad."

Artemisia couldn't help goggling a little. This woman—obviously lower class—could speak casually of going to a doctor of such renowned reputation as Balthazar Abrabanel? Artemisia didn't know Balthazar personally, but she was acquainted with several members of the Abrabanel clan's Italian branch, and they spoke highly of Balthazar's medical skills. Artemisia had suspected her daughter's reports of Grantville's wealth and radical notions of equality were exaggerated. Now she knew they weren't.

"*Dotto* Adams certainly seemed knowledgeable. And *Dotto* Abrabanel's skills are widely praised. An abortion from either one should be safe I would think."

A quick check of the tea showed it had steeped long enough. Artemisia gave a cup to Sherry and took a careful sip from her own. Sherry just held her tea, watching the steam rise off the cup.

"I've thought about it. But I'm thirty-four. I probably won't have a chance to have another one, especially if I end up trying to patch things up with Ronnie. I always thought I was okay with not having kids, but now . . ." Sherry trailed off.

"It's not an easy decision." Artemisia paused for a moment, as she decided whether or not to go on. "I have two daughters, you know."

"Well, I kinda figured the girl going with Jabe McDougal was yours."

"When I found myself expecting my younger daughter, Constantia, I was faced with a similar decision. I was pretty sure she was my husband's, but not certain. We had been living apart for several years by then but were trying to reconcile. He wasn't the only man sharing my bed at the time. In the end, I decided to have Constantia."

"That's not the only reason you're helping me," said Sherry rather sharply. It was almost as if she were issuing a challenge.

Artemisia was not offended. She smiled at Sherry. "You are quite right, Signora Murray. It is not. But that is a story best left for another time. Drink your tea, and then it will be time to sleep. You need your rest."

"You should call me Sherry. If we're going to be roomies, I don't want you calling me 'senyora.' "

"Of course."

"Can I ask you another question, Artemisia?" She nodded. "Did you ever regret it? Having your little girl, I mean?"

Artemisia smiled. "Not for one moment, Sherry. Not a single moment."

On Monday morning, September twenty-ninth—two days after the incident at the Club 250–the first order of business for Officers Tipton and Neubert was to pay a visit to Wes Jenkins. Head of the civilian administrative office in Fulda until recently, Wes had accepted an appointment to head up the State of Thuringia-Franconia Consular Service and had moved back to Grantville with his new wife, Clara. He had been at his post less than a month. Wes and Marvin chatted while one of staff looked for a list of Roman embassy personnel. Marvin briefly recounted the events of Saturday night. Wes groaned theatrically.

"You know, after everything that happened this summer, I was hoping I could just come back here, relax a little and enjoy married life. No rest for the weary, I guess."

"Are you?" asked Marvin.

"Am I what?"

"Enjoying married life?"

Wes couldn't resist a grin. "We're managing to enjoy it just fine."

"Well, congratulations, Wes. Really."

"Thanks. Congratulations yourself, by the way, on Sarah. Clara was telling me the news the other day—don't ask me where she heard about it. Maybe I'll join you at the Gardens."

"Sure. If I ever get the chance."

The assistant came in with a copy of the list and handed it to Marvin.

"Thanks. Thanks again, Wes. This is someone else's headache now."

"Thank goodness," Wes said. "Tonight at the Gardens, then?"

"Sure. As long as no Italian artists pull a knife on any white trash drunks, we're on."

A cart carrying the Gentileschis pulled up to the front gate of the Grantville Army base. They'd come to pick up Jabe on their way to the railroad station. They were due to leave for Halle on the afternoon train and from there travel to Magdeburg by riverboat. The girls waited while Artemisia went to get Jabe; she wanted to see where the young man worked. After the sentry placed a quick call to the press office, she was let through.

When she expressed doubts about Jabe being a soldier, Artemisia had assumed that the Americans, like everyone else, let their mercenaries run wild throughout the countryside or in garrison towns unless they were needed for battle. She saw how wrong she was. Even one such as her, not familiar on a personal basis with military procedure, could tell at a glance the people in this camp were orderly and disciplined. No one bothered her as she walked; in fact, one young man was kind enough to escort her to the press office when she got lost.

When Artemisia arrived at the press office, she found Jabe in the middle of a group as unruly as any Neapolitan mob she'd ever seen. He nodded when he saw her and began fighting his way toward her, handing out sheets of paper and shouting "No comment!" the whole way. When he finally reached her side, the young man looked as harried as a woman with three young children.

"You're a sight for sore eyes, Artemisia."

Artemisia understood the intended, if not the literal, meaning of the expression from the obvious relief in Jabe's voice.

"Do you have to deal with such savage behavior every day, Gia'?"

Jabe laughed. "No, thank goodness."

"Then what were you handing out that those people were eager for?"

"A press release. I'll tell you more about it later. It's about Sherry Murray, so it might end up concerning you anyway, at least partly."

Artemisia nodded. "If they want any information out of me, they had best be more polite about it."

Jabe chuckled. "If not, can I get you to pull a knife on them? Maybe it'll improve their manners."

They continued chatting on the way to the train station. Artemisia was nervous about traveling in such an outlandish device. Talking with Jabe was taking her mind off things, and after the scene she'd witnessed, she was interested in hearing more about his job.

"Most of the time things aren't that crazy," Jabe said. He went on to explain that Grantville itself had four newspapers: the *Times,* the *Free Press* (which published a German edition as the *Freie Presse*), the *Daily News* and a relatively new weekly, *Freiheit!*, which was published by the Grantville Freedom Arches and which hewed to the Committee of Correspondence line on the issues of the day.

That paper's opposite number was a weekly out of Rudolstadt called *Die Wochliche Krone*, known as *The Weekly Crown* to its English-speaking readership. *The Weekly Crown* was modeled on up-time news and commentary magazines and was firmly in the Crown Loyalist camp. Rudolstadt's newspaper, the *Rudolstadt Taggeblatt*—or *Rudolstadt Daily Times* (though it did well to come out three times a week)—was more neutral than the weekly, though it generally tended to be skeptical of Prime Minister Stearns and his policies. In addition, Jabe explained, the papers from Saalfeld, Suhl and occasionally Jena sent correspondents to the Grantville office, and there were freelancers who wrote dispatches for the Thurn und Taxis imperial couriers to distribute along their route. By the time he was done explaining all this, Artemisia was convinced that Jabe showed more bravery by facing these "journalists" than if he'd been fighting alongside the Swede in his military campaigns.

She could hardly believe it when they arrived in Magdeburg. For all her initial nervousness, Artemisia decided she quite liked traveling by rail. It was far faster and much more comfortable than carriage travel. She didn't even feel exhausted, as she usually did after even a relatively short carriage ride.

If Artemisia was happy to reach Magdeburg, her daughter was ecstatic. She'd never seen Prudentia so excited, and she couldn't blame her daughter. She remembered the first time she'd completed a commission for an important client. In the years since, she'd painted for people even more important than Grand Duke Cosimo II Medici, but even working for King Philip or the Holy Father didn't quite match the pride and excitement she'd felt when she'd delivered that first painting to His Grace. She knew Prudentia would be feeling the same thing when she presented her painting to Princess Kristina in just a few days. But even as Artemisia applauded her daughter in a ceremony at Hans Richter Square, she couldn't help wondering what was going on with Sherry.

Back in Grantville, the police went over the list supplied by Consular Affairs. There was only one person on the list with a name close to what Sherry thought her attacker's name was: Marine Lance Corporal Dietrich Linn. Marvin Tipton wasn't the only one who sensed this was trouble. Just because John Simpson's political campaign was in the past didn't mean that the divisions it attempted to exploit were completely forgotten. No one wanted anything to do with this case and kept trying pass the buck to a higher authority.

Police Chief Preston Richards didn't know for certain who had jurisdiction over military personnel. Grantville hadn't been near any military bases before the Ring of Fire, so it wasn't a problem the police department had ever had to deal with. He forwarded Neubert's and Tipton's report to Ed Piazza's office. Preston figured this was why Ed was president.

Ed viewed it as a matter for USE military command to handle and kicked it up to Magdeburg to General Torstensson and his staff. Torstensson's adjutant made inquiries and found that the civilian authorities had jurisdiction. Just to cover themselves, however, the general staff kicked the matter to the prime minister's office. By all reports, Mike had a fit and told Ed Piazza what needed to be done in no uncertain terms.

The Chief Justice of the State of Thuringia-Franconia poured two fingers of scotch for his father. He had a very big favor to ask, and he was dipping into his last bottle of eighteen-year-old Oban to "grease the wheels," so to speak. Chuck had gotten a taste for the brand on a trip to the Hebrides back before the Ring of Fire, and it became one of the former small-town lawyer's few indulgences.

"This must be serious, son," said Thomas Price Riddle. "I know how you've been hoarding this ever since the Ring of Fire." He sipped the scotch, smiling in appreciation.

Chuck locked the Oban away and sipped his own glass. "Alex and Julie have standing instructions for bringing some good stuff back with them. When I told Alex what I was ready to pay, he thought I was nuts."

"You're changing the subject, son," the older man said. "If this is some sticky legal problem you need your old man's help on, you didn't need to break into the secret stash. Not that I don't appreciate it."

"It is a sticky legal problem, Dad, but it's not your opinion I need. It's you." Chuck handed his father the memo.

Tom read it and frowned. "Judge in Extraordinary?"

"The official paperwork's on its way over from Ed's office even as we speak," said Chuck. "He wants you to preside over this trial." Chuck summarized the facts of the case for his father.

"But why me?" Thomas asked.

"Two reasons. The first is that Maurice Tito has more than he can handle on his docket as it is in the Grantville courts. This trial may take weeks, and everything else would grind to a halt." Chuck made a mental note to stay on the state congress's case about appointing more judges to help Maurice handle his increasing caseload. "Second, you're about the only person with a solid working knowledge of up-time military law."

"I thought you said this was being handled by the civilian authorities?"

"I did. But you never know what will be relevant these days. Ed said, and I agree, that the judge should have experience in military as well as civilian legal procedure."

"I should be defending the kid, not presiding over his trial!"

"You're expected to appoint a lawyer, and I'm sure you'll find a good one. And I'm also sure you'll school them in the basics of the Uniform Code of Military Justice, to the extent that it will be relevant to the case."

"That's irregular as hell, and you know it!" Thomas said. "Talk about conflict of interest! That's bad enough, but how can this kid get a fair trial if his lawyer only has a crash course in military law?"

Chuck sighed. He loved his father and respected him as a lawyer. But the old man could be real difficult sometimes.

"Corporal Linn's in Rome, and it's going to take at least a month for him to even get back here. Not ideal, but more than enough time for you to school trained lawyers in the relevant areas of law and make sure that the young man has a competent defense." Chuck took another sip of his scotch. "Besides, you'll have help. Maurice will be available to advise on an informal basis if you need him, and Jesse Wood will be observing the proceedings as well."

"I suppose I don't have a choice, do I?" Chuck shook his head. Tom continued, "Maurice should be running this circus, but I appreciate his help. But why Jesse? I'd have thought Admiral Simpson would have made more sense."

"For starters, Simpson can't be spared from Magdeburg. Jesse's about the only member of the general staff who still spends much time here in Grantville, and from what I understand, he won't be able to do much flying this time of year anyway. More than that, though, Jesse's very popular among the down-time Germans. His presence is a statement to our German citizens that one of their own is going to get a fair trial. That there won't be any railroading or lynch mobs."

"I'll need the file. And I'll need a printer to print up my copy of the UCMJ and the relevant case law, for everyone concerned."

"Done and done. The official file's on its way with your appointment paperwork, and my office will pay for the book printing."

The two men finished their scotch in silent salute. They shook hands, and Thomas left. Chuck knew that his father would want to get to work immediately.

Tom Riddle moved quickly to prepare for the coming trial. At Maurice Tito's suggestion, John Bradshaw, the junior assistant district attorney for Grantville, was appointed lead prosecutor for the case. John had fled England, one step ahead of King Charles's agents. His crime? In another universe—the universe in which Tom Riddle had been born—he had been Lord President of the trial that had found Charles guilty of tyranny and sentenced him to death by beheading.

"Cornelius Fricke is a fine lawyer," Maurice said of his senior ADA, "but he's busy enough right now. John's got one of the best legal minds I've ever come across, and the fact that he's neither an up-timer nor German can't hurt. It's time for him to have a high profile case, and there'll be no appearance of bias."

Tom's other mandate, to find a good defense lawyer for Dietrich Linn, ended up solving itself. Johann Selfisch, a junior partner in the Hardegg, Selfisch and Krapp law firm, contacted Tom and offered to take the case *pro bono*. Johann headed up his firm's Rudolstadt office and was a familiar figure in Grantville-area legal circles. He was notorious, in fact; the man had a mania for watching taped episodes of *Ally McBeal*, *The Practice* and the entire *Law & Order* family whenever business brought him to Grantville. He'd even watched most of the O.J. Simpson trial, though no up-timer would admit to having taped it. Johann Selfisch was enamored with the up-time concept of the "celebrity lawyer" and wanted badly to become one himself.

If Tom found that aspect of Selfisch's personality distasteful, he couldn't deny that the man was a competent attorney. More than competent, in fact. Johann Selfisch was quite good. If Dietrich Linn wanted another lawyer once he arrived in Grantville, that was his affair; until then, though, Tom couldn't turn down Selfisch's offer of representation. Not surprisingly, the man wasn't happy when Tom issued a gag order in the case.

"First of all, Sherry Murray's reputation is *not* going to be dragged through the mud!" he had told Selfisch when defense counsel argued against the order. "Second, I will not have Corporal Linn trying to flee if word of this gets out. He doesn't know why he's being called back—the warrant will be served when he arrives—but you know how quickly the couriers will spread the newspapers and dispatches. If he goes to ground, I will hold you responsible and do my damndest to see you're convicted as an accessory after the fact. Is that understood?" It was, but it didn't stop Selfisch from doing what a good defense attorney should: swamp the prosecution in paper. Nearly every single motion was denied, but that didn't stop him; John Bradshaw was heard to mutter darkly about preferring a cell in the Tower to dealing with Selfisch's innumerable motions.

The mood in town was getting ugly, and it only got worse by the end of October when Dietrich Linn arrived in Grantville and was formally arrested for the rape of Sherry Murray. Most people sympathized with Sherry; she was viewed as a fundamentally decent person, if unwise in her choice of men. But there was a vocal minority making a lot of noise about "dirty krauts raping our women," as well as a group who figured that if Sherry was going to get drunk and party with strange men, she shouldn't then cry rape. More than a few fistfights had broken out. The press coverage wasn't helping; even the relatively restrained Grantville papers were covering the so-called "trial of the century" from all possible angles.

Sherry clung to Artemisia for support. The two women formed an unlikely friendship, and when Artemisia moved out of the Higgins Hotel into more permanent lodgings, Sherry moved in with the Gentileschis. It wasn't as if Sherry was entirely alone; she was getting counseling from Henny DeVries. It wasn't as if her family was shunning her; Slater and Phyllis Dobbs blamed Ronnie for what happened more than they blamed her and supported Sherry's decision to have the baby.

Artemisia, though, always seemed to know the right things to say and when not to say anything at all. Most important to Sherry, though, was the fact that Artemisia always made time for her whenever Sherry needed her, no questions asked. She'd always suspected Artemisia had more reason for taking an interest in her than the Italian artist had said. But it wasn't until the eve of the trial that Sherry fully understood why this was.

The night before the trial was set to begin, Sherry's parents invited her to dinner. The pastor of her parents' church, Reverend Chalker, would be there too and wanted to say a prayer over her. Sherry had never been much into church, but at this point she would take all the help she could get.

Her parents didn't object when she insisted on bringing Artemisia with her. A month ago Sherry would have thought twice about bringing a famous artist to dinner at Dobbs Hollow. But as she got to know Artemisia, Sherry learned she was a lot closer to blue collar than Sherry would have thought. Her picture of what a "famous artist" was like was formed by that guy who'd painted soup cans—she couldn't remember his name—who was almost more famous for being famous than for being an artist. Artemisia, she found out, had only learned to read and write in her late teens and had very little formal education. She'd had to work hard to make a living, and she'd had a few patrons who were always trying to stiff her. In addition to being stuck-up rich snots, European nobility could also be a bunch of cheap S.O.B.s. If nothing else, Sherry knew, the fact that her self-appointed protector and new friend had pulled a knife on Ronnie would make Artemisia okay with Slater and Phyllis.

Dinner went well enough. Reverend Chalker said a blessing, and if he had any opinions about Artemisia crossing herself after the prayer, he kept them to himself. After they were finished, Sherry's father finally asked the question they all had been wondering about.

"Why are you doing this? Not that we're not grateful for the kindness you've shown Sherry, but why do you care?"

Sherry felt her friend take her hand and give it a squeeze. She'd gotten used to Artemisia being the strong one in their friendship, but now Sherry sensed that the comforter needed comforting.

"Your daughter asked me the same question the night we met, Signor Dobbs. I told her then that it was a story for another time."

"And now?"

"Now is the time."

It all came out, pouring out to these people who, with the exception of Sherry, were strangers. Sherry was amazed. She knew that Artemisia had great strength, kindness and compassion; she'd experienced that first-hand. But Sherry also sensed that her friend had a part of herself—a large part—that she kept closed off.

Now, though, Artemisia opened herself completely. She told them about growing up and following in her father's footsteps, how she tried to learn everything she could about painting from her father, his students and his friends. She told them about one of those friends, Agostino Tassi.

"He was friends with my father, and he became obsessed with me. It seemed like I couldn't go anywhere without seeing him. At church, at home, on the street—everywhere. It made me feel uneasy. But I will admit that a part of me, a small part, enjoyed the attention. He isn't a bad looking man, Tassi, and he has some talent."

Sherry felt Artemisia squeeze her hand even tighter. "What I didn't know is that he was working with a woman who I thought was my friend. Tuzia. She rented rooms from us. She let him into my bedroom. I was asleep when I heard him come in . . ."

Artemisia was never quite sure why she bared her soul to these people. She'd always intended to tell Sherry, but the other people were strangers to her. But she couldn't evade an honest answer to Signor Dobbs's direct question, and once she began telling the story, she couldn't stop.

In her mind, it was twenty-four years ago. She was facing not Sherry Murray, Slater and Phyllis Dobbs and Reverend Chalker, but a magistrate, his notary and other

Curia officials. She was swearing out her deposition all over again.

"He put his hands all over me. He put his knees between my legs . . . I felt a strong burning, and it hurt very much. I tried to scream as best I could. I scratched his face and pulled his hair. I even scratched him down there, but it didn't bother him at all. He continued to do his business."

For a time, all Artemisia could do was cry as she hadn't done in a quarter-century. Even the tears she'd shed when she got news of her father's death were a trickle in comparison with what flooded out now. But leaving her with those tears was a poison that had been corroding her soul all these years, and she wouldn't have stopped crying even if she had been capable.

It was inevitable that the trial of Dietrich Linn would become a circus. But Thomas Price Riddle at least kept it a small circus, rather than a huge, three ring, Barnum & Bailey affair. Riddle eased his gag order once Corporal Linn was in custody, and Johann Selfisch was in front of the press and on the radio at every opportunity, playing up his client's humble origins—he was the illegitimate son of a baker from Krefeld—and the Marine's spotless record. And while he stuck to the letter of Judge Riddle's order not to malign Sherry Murray, it didn't stop Selfisch from making veiled remarks about her reputation.

For Artemisia the trial was a revelation. Unlike her experience with the court officials from the Vatican, Sherry's trial was held in the open, for the public to attend. Judge Riddle did not allow testimony relating to

Sherry's past behavior. Artemisia knew Sherry did not have it easy, but no one—at least not in open court—was calling her a shameless flirt and a whore.

The trial took two weeks. John Bradshaw did his best to try a case that was anything but airtight. Sherry's claims were bolstered by the fact that she'd consistently told the same story since she came forward a few months ago. The nurse who had counseled her, Henny DeVries, testified that, in her expert opinion, Sherry had suffered psychological trauma.

The defense had good arguments of its own. Dr. Adams testified that by the time he actually examined Sherry, there was no way to tell whether nonconsensual sex had occurred. And although prosecutor Bradshaw had objected, Riddle allowed testimony from several witnesses at the party who stated that Sherry was quite drunk. By the time the case went to the jury, no one was willing to make a guess as to the verdict. Nearly everyone felt that it could go either way.

The evening the defense rested, Artemisia spent some time with Sherry at her parents' house. Sherry was splitting her time between Dobbs Hollow and Artemisia's townhouse in Grantville; Ronnie was telling her he wanted her back, she said, but she wasn't ready to move back in with her husband quite yet. Artemisia had come to feel great warmth for Slater and Phyllis, and Reverend Chalker too. It had been a long time—too long—since she had allowed herself to be that vulnerable in front of anyone.

That warmth was dispelled when she arrived home and found Jabe and Prudentia arguing. Her daughter had confessed to her that the two had had some problems talking to each other as their relationship had gotten more serious but that they'd mostly solved that problem. Perhaps, thought Artemisia as Jabe stalked off past her with barely a nod, this problem wasn't as solved as her daughter thought.

All she could get from Prudentia that night was that her daughter thought Jabe was being a pig because he thought Corporal Linn was innocent when clearly the man was guilty. She knew better than to try to reason with her daughter right then; she recognized the righteous anger and black-and-white view she herself had had when she was Prudentia's age.

As they waited for a verdict, Artemisia had Sherry read the dispatches Jabe and the Joint Armed Services Press Division had issued. Though she could speak English quite well now, Artemisia couldn't really read it. She was trying to learn, but it was very difficult. The releases were actually quite neutral; there was a lot about Linn being "innocent until proven guilty," which Sherry explained was a principle up-timers held particularly dear, but nothing which claimed the Marine corporal was innocent of the crime of which he was accused.

"It's pretty standard stuff," said Sherry with a shrug after she'd read the statements. "They're not attacking me; they're only saying the military will respect the verdict of the civilian court, and they want the trial to be fair."

"Which means my daughter is being a little ridiculous."

"She's a teenager," said Sherry with a snort. "It comes with the territory."

Indeed, after a few days went by with no sign of Jabe, Prudentia came to her in tears. Artemisia tried not to smile when her daughter asked her what she could do to apologize to her young man. Artemisia comforted her daughter and was glad she'd been talking to people who knew Jabe and his family over the past few months. Even as she dried her daughter's tears, she began mentally planning her wedding.

A week went by with no verdict. Just as Artemisia had predicted to herself, Jabe McDougal called one night after dinner. He carried some papers and a small box.

"Is Prudentia here?" he asked.

"She's painting right now. Do you wish to see her?"

"Um, maybe in a bit. If she wants to talk to me. But I want to talk to you first, alone."

"Of course, Gia." Artemisia knew why Jabe wanted to talk to her, but a part of her was enjoying his discomfort. *It is rather endearing,* she thought.

"I want to marry your daughter." He handed her the papers he'd brought with him. "Those are my discharge papers. As soon as the verdict comes in, I'm done with my military commitment. I don't quite know what kind of job I'm going to get, but I'm sure I'll find something. I've finally sold my book, so I've got some money from that to start us off. It's nothing special, just people talking about their memories of the Ring of Fire, but I hope it will do okay. And I know Prudentia has saved a lot from the paintings she's sold. We can probably get by till I find something."

She hugged Jabe. "Giacomo, I decided some time ago that I would agree to this—if Prudentia agrees, and I think she will. We will talk of your employment prospects after you've spoken to her."

Artemisia went to summon her oldest daughter and found that Constantia had already done so. Prudentia looked both anxious and hopeful as she left with Jabe. She was neither alarmed nor upset by the fact that Prudentia didn't come back until the next morning. Her brother would have had a fit, but "honor" was a lot of male foolishness. Artemisia knew Jabe was not one to make a false marriage pledge.

Prudentia could hardly contain herself, showing off the engagement token Gia had given her. If the diamond ring her daughter wore was any indication, her future son-in-law was either wealthier than he let on or very frugal. As soon as she saw it, she got an idea for a possible career for Jabe McDougal.

Two weeks went by with no verdict. Between her advancing pregnancy and the stress of waiting, Sherry felt tired and irritable all the time. She was at Artemisia's house when the call from the prosecutor's office finally came. They went to the courthouse as quickly as they could.

The jury trooped in, and the foreman (forewoman, in this case) handed a slip of paper to the bailiff, who in turn handed it to Judge Riddle. He nodded gravely and turned to address the jury.

"Madame Forewoman," he said, "are you quite certain you cannot come to an agreement?"

"Yes, *Euer Gn*—, I mean, Your Honor."

"And you swear that you have made your best faith efforts to reach a verdict?"

"Your honor, we are, I believe the correct expression is 'hopelessly deadlocked.' "

"Very well. Given the fact we have a hung jury I have no choice but to declare a mistrial. I would like to see counsel in chambers, along with the defendant and his accuser." Riddle banged his gavel.

Sherry brought Artemisia with her into Judge Riddle's chambers. No one questioned it; the Italian woman was by now Sherry's most visible supporter. They sat down in front of Judge Riddle.

"I had a feeling this might happen. I had the jury polled yesterday, and they were split down the middle. I'm getting too old for this, and I want to propose the following solution. Mr. Bradshaw, if you would please?"

In his quiet, Cheshire-accented voice, John Bradshaw offered a plea bargain: Corporal Linn would plead guilty to a Class A misdemeanor assault charge and be given a suspended sentence. In exchange, he would be put under bastardy bond; he would acknowledge Sherry's baby, assuming it was born alive; and he would continue to support the child financially until it turned eighteen. Finally, Corporal Linn would not be disciplined by the military for this incident.

"If you agree to this," Riddle said, "you will be held strictly to it. If you try to evade your obligations, young man, your sentence will be reinstated and you will serve every single day of it, I promise you."

Johann Selfisch conferred with his client. "We accept this offer, Your Honor."

"Is this acceptable to you, Ms. Murray?"

"I can't go through this again, Your Honor." Sherry said.

"Are you sure you want to give up so easily, Sherry?" Artemisia asked. "It doesn't seem like enough for what happened."

"It's more than I would get if another jury let him off the hook. I agree to this, Your Honor."

Sherry spent the next few days with her family. Artemisia understood; she had family things she needed to take care of as well. She had to speak to her daughter's fiancé about his future employment.

"Gia, I have a proposal for you. It may, I think, offer you a job you will find rewarding."

"Sure. What is it?"

"Lieutenant von Kessel spoke very highly of your skills in working with people and said that you have excellent manners. You always treat others with respect, even when they don't deserve it. He also told me that you are utterly reliable. He was quite sorry, in fact, that you did not plan to reenlist."

Jabe just flushed and stammered. Artemisia smiled and continued: "I have seen for myself that you are good at coordinating things. Prudentia and I will need someone reliable to represent our interests, meet with patrons and see that work is delivered and paid for. This is something family does, and you are now family. It would afford you the opportunity to meet important people and see a little of the world."

For just a brief moment Jabe looked trapped, but then he nodded. "I can do that. I think I'd like that. I haven't been anywhere much except Grantville and Magdeburg, except for a trip up to Luebeck a few months ago."

"It is settled then."

"Yeah, except . . . "

"Yes?"

"I'll need some help. And I just had a good idea."

◇   ◇   ◇

A part of Sherry didn't want to pick up the things she'd left at Artemisia's home. She hoped they would stay friends, but she expected now that the trial was over, just about everybody would forget her. She was surprised when she found not only Artemisia, but also her two daughters and Jabe McDougal waiting for her. She noticed the ring on Prudentia's finger.

"Congratulations," she said to the young woman. Atemisia's daughter glowed with happiness.

"You know you and the child are always welcome wherever I am,'" Artemesia said. "But I wish to offer you a job."

"What can I do for you? I can't even draw stick figures."

"I need . . . what is the term? . . . a personal assistant." Artemisia looked to Jabe and he nodded. "Someone I can trust. My soon-to-be son-in-law suggested you, and I can think of no one better. It won't pay well at first, but I think I can provide a living for you if you are willing to learn some needed skills. Please say yes."

Sherry found she couldn't say yes. She was too choked up. She could only nod.

"Good," said Artemisia, beaming with delight. "Your first job will be to help me plan a wedding."

The Chase

Iver P. Cooper

Grantville High School
July 1633

"Are you ready to play?" Gabrielle Ugolini asked, tennis racket in hand.

"Hang on a sec, my hands are cracking. Let me get some lotion." Heather Mason reached into her school daypack. One of the geeks at school had nicknamed it the "magic bag of holding" because there was enough stuff in it to fill a pocket universe. Her hand emerged, triumphantly, with a plastic bottle. The up-time lotion was long gone, but it had been carefully filled with Doctor Gribbleflotz's "Celestial Dew of Mount Sapo." She squeezed out a bit of "dew," and rubbed her hands together.

"Okay," she yelled across the net, "What's the holdup? Serve!"

The Barbie Consortium had staged yet another take-over. This time, it wasn't financial. There were three tennis courts at the high school, and they were playing on all of them. Hayley Fortney and Susan Logsden were playing singles on one, Judy Wendell and Vicky Emerson on the second. There was a doubles game on the final court, Heather and Gabrielle on one side, Millicent Anne Barnes and Kelsey Mason on the other. Kelsey wasn't actually a member of the Barbie Consortium, but she was Heather's older sister, and a good athlete.

◇   ◇   ◇

The main road was on an embankment, looking down at the tennis courts. William Cavendish, the third earl of Devonshire, stood there, watching the game. He was on his "grand tour" of Europe, a rite of passage for young British noblemen. He had traveled through France and Italy and across the Alps with his governor, Thomas Hobbes. On this fine summer morning, he was just three months shy of sixteen years of age.

"Geoffrey, what game are they playing?" Geoffrey Watson was one of the three lesser servants he had brought with him to Grantville.

"I couldn't say, sir."

"They're hitting the ball about with rackets. And there's a net to separate them. It's almost tennis. But there are no walls. It can't be tennis without playing shots off the walls and rooftops. And those balls—look how bouncy they are!"

"Fifteen-love!" shouted one of the girls.

William snapped his fingers. "This *is* some kind of tennis. No way the same crazy scoring system would appear, by chance, in an unrelated game."

William had been left to his own devices because he had interrupted Hobbes one time too many as the tutor tore through the Grantville Public Library. The last straw had been when William had brought Hobbes a comic book, saying, "Mister Hobbes, look at this, it has your name on it." Hobbes had taken a quick look at *The Complete Calvin and Hobbes* and then suggested that William go find the local *gymnasium* and converse with other gentlemen his age. With Geoffrey to watch over him, of course.

"Don't look now, but cute stranger at four o'clock," said Heather.

Gabrielle looked, of course, although she tried to turn her head as little as possible. "Since when are you interested in boys?"

Heather didn't deign to answer. "You think he's some kind of nobleman?"

"Duh? Dressed like that, he has to be. Guy next to him is obviously a servant."

"Perhaps he's a prince?"

"I hope not. Can't do much of a curtsey in tennis whites."

"He only has one servant. Maybe he's just a duke."

"With blond curls like those, even a mere earl would be acceptable."

"So, do we talk to him?"

Heather sighed. "No, he'd probably think we were forward."

"You could pretend to sprain your ankle."

"Real smart. Then I'd have to limp along the rest of the day, or he'd know I faked it. And why."

Millicent, waiting on the other side of the net, was dancing around, impatient. "Have you gotten tired of tennis?"

"Give us five minutes," Gabrielle shouted back. She turned back to Heather. "I suppose 'Hey! Don't I know you from somewhere?' would sound kinda lame."

"Ver-ree lame."

"Hey, I have the solution." Gabrielle turned and shouted, "John!" Gabrielle's brother John and Heather's older brother Derrick were nearby, playing one-on-one.

Heather was appalled. "But I don't want anyone to know."

"Everything's under control, Heather." Gabrielle raised her voice. "John, you moron, get your ass over here."

"Gabe, you made me miss the shot!"

"Big deal." She glared at him, arms akimbo.

"I'm coming. Jeesh." John walked over, while Derrick stayed behind, practicing layups.

"What's the problem, Gabe? Need a tennis lesson?"

"Stop dribbling the basketball with your head; it's affecting your brain. I need you to introduce yourself to that young man over there." She jerked her head, ever so slightly, in William's direction.

"Where is there?"

"I am not going to point, you idiot, I am trying to be subtle. S-U-uh-B-T-L-E. The one with the fancy doublet and the feathered cap. With the servant in black, behind him. Ask him if he is interested in sports, where he's from, how long he'll be in town, that kind of thing. Can you handle it?"

"Hey, you aren't interested in this guy, are you?"

"No, no, this is a public service announcement. Heather's making eyes at him. Or thinking about it."

"Heather?"

"Not a word to anyone about it, or I'll squash you like a bug."

"What about Kelsey? Or Derrick?"

"Definitely not Derrick."

Derrick had belatedly followed John. "What don't you want to tell me?"

The jig was up. "Keep your eyes where they are, but Heather's interested in that guy, the nobleman up on the road."

Derrick strained his peripheral vision. "Heather, you don't know anything about him. And you know what most of the down-timers think about girls."

"When I want you to protect me, I'll let you know. In the meantime, stay out of my life."

"But—"

"But would you like me to tell everyone about the swimming hole incident?"

Derrick blushed a deep red. "John, I'll wait for you at the basket." And off he ran.

"I hope you haven't done permanent damage to his psyche," John said. "Unless it will throw off his shooting."

"Well, what about the down-timer? We don't have all day."

"Get back to the game. I'll watch you play for a few minutes, then check him out. Is that S-U-B-T-L-E enough for you?"

Kelsey and Millicent were sitting on their side of the court, gabbing.

"What are you waiting for?" yelled Gabrielle. "Let's play!"

Heather tried two serves, both of which went into the net. It wasn't easy to keep her eyes on the ball and on the mysterious stranger at the same time.

After a few centuries had passed, John strolled over to William.

"New to Grantville?" They spoke for several minutes.

Heather was getting impatient. She waved Gabrielle over for further consultation. "I told him to introduce himself, not recite the Gettysburg Address."

"Just keep your mind on the game, okay? We're putting on a show for him, y'know."

At long last, John returned. "He's British, name's William Cavendish, he's the earl of Devonshire." Heather and Gabrielle laughed. "Have you girls gone nuts? What's so funny about Devonshire?" They laughed again.

"Anyway, he's done the grand tour through France and Italy and now he and his tutor are in beautiful downtown Grantville."

"Tell him that if he hasn't tired of Italian food, he can join us at the pizza parlor for lunch."

◊   ◊   ◊

Hobbes had given Geoffrey clear instructions. "Remember, you are supposed to keep Lord Devonshire out of trouble. No buying of supposedly ancient artifacts. No attempted descents into volcanoes. And most importantly, no playing chess with courtesans." All references to William's past escapades.

Well, there were no ancient artifacts here, just futuristic ones. There were no volcanoes, just chimneys here and there. And, while these ladies certainly were showing a lot of leg, Geoffrey was quite sure they weren't courtesans.

In fact, Geoffrey was pretty sure they were upper class. Whoever heard of servants wearing spotless white outfits, outdoors?

So there was no reason for intervention on Geoffrey's part, none at all.

Anyway, Geoffrey was enjoying the view.

Grantville Public Library
July 1633

"Excuse me, but the guard tells me that your name is Thomas Hobbes. Is that right?"

Hobbes frowned at the woman who had just accosted him. "Yes, I am. Mister Thomas Hobbes, a bachelor of Oxford University, and tutor to the third earl of Devonshire."

"Well, that's great. I read your book."

"My book? You mean my translation of Thucydides? I hadn't expected that anyone in Grantville would have heard of it."

"Thucydides?"

"Yes, Thucydides' *History of the Peloponnesian War*."

"No, no. *Leviathan*."

"*Leviathan*?"

"Oh, yes, I had to read it in school." She put her hand to her mouth. "I forgot. You might not have written it yet."

It had not even occurred to Hobbes that his name would be remembered, and his writings read, four centuries in the future.

"Is *Leviathan* about my contributions to geometry? Did I publish my method of squaring the circle? Am I a famous mathematician of your past?"

"Um, *Leviathan* is about politics. The 'Leviathan' is the government and, uh, that's all I remember."

That was even more of a surprise. Since he had not written anything about political philosophy yet.

"Is there anywhere I can find a copy of this *Leviathan*?" Hobbes was a firm believer in predestination, but this was getting ridiculous.

"We have a copy here, and there should be stuff about you in the encyclopedias."

"About me?"

"Just don't weird out when you read the date you died. The Ring of Fire changed history. And even little changes, like who was where on a particular day, can add up to become big ones. Anyway, gotta run."

Hobbes sighed. If the library lady knew about him, it was certain that others did, too. Half the down-timers in the Grantville Public Library were probably there as spies for someone else. Hobbes realized that he had best find out what the books of the future had to say about him.

As if he didn't already have enough to worry about. He had, as instructed, looked up various members of the Cavendish family. The entry for one of the William's uncles, the earl of Newcastle, mentioned that he had been a royalist commander during the English Civil War, and later a member of the privy council of Charles II.

This led to the discovery that in the original time line, in 1649, King Charles' head was chopped off. Hobbes' friend, the king's physician, William Harvey, had visited Grantville in early 1632, and Hobbes suspected that this bit of history was what had prompted Harvey's hasty return to London.

The encyclopedias also revealed that the Cavendishes were forced into exile during the era of parliamentary rule. So they, too, would want to know who became a roundhead, and who, a cavalier.

Surprisingly, during the Restoration, the unwed William's yet-to-be-born son had become a leader of the opposition to the pro-Catholic policies of Charles II and James II. Indeed, a leader of the Glorious Revolution that unseated the last Stuart king. Leading naturally to the question, did King Charles know that, and would it create a political problem for the Cavendish family?

All right, then, let's see what the Encyclopedia Britannica has to say about me.

When he finished reading, he sighed. He was happy enough with the conclusion: "he has gradually been

accorded recognition as one of the greatest English political thinkers." Hobbes was less happy to discover that,
"unfortunately, Hobbes antagonized both parties in the
current constitutional struggle."

The *Encyclopedia Americana* wasn't any more comforting: "he was suspected of atheism, and his attack
upon ecclesiastical authority enraged both Anglicans and
French Catholics. . . . As late as 1683 Hobbes' books
were publicly burned at Oxford."

Perhaps it was time to do some job hunting in Magdeburg?

Marcantonio's Pizza Parlor, Grantville
July 1633

John made the introductions as they walked over to the
pizza parlor. "Here in Grantville, we tend to go by first
names. I hope you don't mind. William, meet Gabrielle,
Heather, Millicent, Vicky, Judy, and Heather's brother
Derrick, and sister Kelsey. They're all nice, except for
my sister Gabrielle of course." She stuck out her tongue
at him.

"This is Marcantonio's. I hope you like their pizza."

William watched the cook slide a giant metal spatula
into a brick oven, and pull out a large round bread, covered with melted cheese and vegetables. "Is that the
pizza?"

John Ugolini frowned. "Yeah. Didn't you say you were
just in Italy? How come you don't know what pizza is?"

Gabrielle came to William's rescue. "John, you moron, we're in the seventeenth century, remember? The Italians haven't invented pizza yet. I thought everybody knew that."

They were seated at a large round table. Which meant that William could see all of them at one time. His rescuer, Gabrielle, had the classic Mediterranean look: brown eyes, olive skin, and coffee brown hair. Her tennis partner, Heather, had matching hair and eyes, but pale skin. Millicent, Kelsey and Vicky were blondes, and Judy was a redhead. Auburn, not coppery. Height-wise, Millicent was tiny, and Vicky taller than the two guys present, John and Derrick. Geoffrey had been offered a seat, but declined. But he was happily munching on a slice of pizza at a small table nearby.

Gabrielle nudged Heather. Heather said nothing.

"So, William, what did you think of our game of tennis?" asked Gabrielle.

"It was interesting to see how it differed from real tennis."

Vicky challenged this statement. "So what do we play, 'pretend' tennis?"

Gabrielle wasn't amused. "Oh, give him a break, Vicky."

William put his hand over his heart, turned to Vicky, and inclined his head. "Forgive my poor choice of words, mademoiselle." The girls tittered. "I suppose we can call it 'royal tennis.'

"Imagine putting half a cloister inside a high-walled building. A cloister's a garden, surrounded on all four sides by a roofed gallery.

"There is a cord strung between two poles, to separate the two teams. The players have rackets, with which they hit the ball, back and forth, across the line.

"The players make the game less predictable by serving the ball so that it bounces at least once on the penthouse to their left—"

"Wait. What penthouse?" asked Millicent.

"That's the sloped roof of the gallery."

"Monks with *Penthouses*, huh? What about *Playboys*?" said John.

"Shut up, idiot." Gabrielle looked at her friends. "Has anyone ever noticed that 'brother' is just one letter away from 'bother'?"

Heather nodded. "I always thought that the Russians were clever, because their word for 'brother' is *brat*." Derrick saluted her, and then converted the movement into a quick grab for her slice of pizza.

"Owww!" Heather had slapped Derrick's hand away. He held it up, bent at the wrist, and acted as if it had been maimed for life.

"Do I need to operate, Derrick?" said his other sister, Kelsey. She was in EMT training. "I recommend decapitation; then you won't notice the pain."

William grinned. His own brother, Charles, had been twelve when William left England. Such an endearing age. Decapitation, defenestration, and drowning had all appealed to William at one time or another.

"If, after the served ball comes down, it's volleyed back, or it bounces in a marked area on the receiver's side, it's a good serve. From then on, you can strike the ball so it bounces off a wall, to try to trick your opponent. You can try to hit a winning opening in the galleries.

And if the ball bounces twice on the server's side, or in the receiver's forecourt, or it lands in one of the other openings, it sets up a chase."

"What's that?"

"If a second bounce is anywhere on the server's side of the net, or in the front part of the receiver's side, a chase is marked at that position. Then, before the game ends, we play off the chase. We switch sides, and the new server, to win the point, either has to cause the ball to take its second bounce closer to the far wall than the mark, or get the ball into a winning opening."

"I guess that means you want to get distance on your shots."

"That's right. Otherwise, your opponent will just let the ball bounce a second time, close to the net, and then win an easy chase."

Vicky groaned. "I've heard enough about tennis. Anyone who wants to continue to talking about it—" She mimed swinging a tennis racket, two-handed. Her imaginary ball sailed out the window of the pizza parlor "—can go outside."

They told William about the twentieth century, the Ring of Fire, and the Croat raid. William spoke about his travels. The highlights, so far as the Americans were concerned, were that he had met Galileo and walked across the Alps.

William also described his home, Chatsworth Hall. Even though he was the earl of *Devon*shire, his estates were actually mostly in *Derby*shire. Chatsworth lay between the Derbyshire River and the moors, and it was a Tudor dwelling in the grand style: square turrets at the corners, a gateway (complete with a portcullis), a great hall worthy of the name, and an inner garden. It had already achieved some notoriety, he noted, as the elegant prison of Mary, Queen of Scots.

"Sounds a bit like Pemberley," Heather said. "Wait, let me find it." She rummaged in the infamous magic bag of holding for a moment, and emerged triumphantly with a well-thumbed copy of *Pride and Prejudice*.

"This is from a novel written in 1813 by Jane Austen. Hold on a moment." She skimmed it rapidly.

"Aha! Listen to this: 'the eye was instantly caught by Pemberley House, situated on the opposite side of a valley, into which the road with some abruptness wound. It was a large, handsome, stone building, standing well on rising ground, and backed by a ridge of high woody hills—and in front, a stream of some natural importance was swelled into greater, but without any artificial appearance.' And Pemberley was in Derbyshire!"

"Your 'Pemberley' does sound quite a bit like Chatsworth," William said.

"So that means—" Heather's eyes widened "—you're *Darcy*."

"Who's Darcy?"

"Uh, never mind." Heather fidgeted. "My Aunt Gayle's in England, now. She's with Miss Mailey, and Tom and Rita Simpson, and the rest of our embassy to King Charles."

"I hope to have the honor of meeting her and her colleagues, when I return to London. This Tom Simpson is the head of your delegation?"

Judy Wendell shook her head. "No, the official head is Rita Simpson, Mike's sister. Because Mike's President, and down-timers think he's some kind of king."

"And who, then, is the real head?"

"That would be Melissa Mailey."

William didn't comment. Vicky took issue with his silence. "You don't think a woman can handle the job?"

William held up his hands. "Please. It is only thirty years since the death of Queen Elizabeth. And if you ever met my lady mother . . . " He rolled his eyes.

"Sounds like my mother," said Millicent. "Always bossing me around."

"Where are you staying, William?" asked Heather.

"At the Higgins Hotel."

"Good for you," said Judy. "It shows you have excellent taste."

"Judy is at the Higgins, too." said Vicky.

William looked at Judy. "I thought you were a native of Grantville."

"I am," Judy said, "but my parents are working in Magdeburg, for the government. I stayed here since I wanted to finish high school. Delia Higgins is looking after me, so . . . the hotel is my home away from home."

John caught William's eye. "If I had known you could afford a room there, I would have made you pay for the whole pizza." Heather elbowed him.

"Do you know about our movies?" asked Judy.

"Movies? Some sort of race?" The up-timers laughed, and told him that movies were a form of entertainment, a bit like a play, but recorded and then looked at later, like a painting or a book. William wasn't sure he quite understood, but admitted he would like to see one.

Judy smiled. "We're all going to the Friday night movie at the Higgins Hotel. You should join us. Since you're a guest, you can get in for free."

"Yes, please do that, William," said Heather.

William was at the library, doing some research of his own.

"Hah!" The librarian shushed him.

William strode over to Hobbes' table. "Look at this. It says here that in 1638, Athanasius Kircher had himself lowered into the crater of Vesuvius. That's what I wanted to do, only you wouldn't let me. I could have done something that would have made me famous, like Kircher."

"It could also have made you dead, like poor Francis Bacon." Hobbes was referring to the infamous experiment in which Bacon, his mentor, had sought to prove that a chicken stuffed with snow would not decompose, and had instead contracted a fatal bronchitis.

Clearly, there was not a meeting of the minds here. William changed the subject. "There is a 'movie' being shown at the Higgins Hotel tonight. Are you going?"

"No, Lord Devonshire. I found out that one of the residents has a copy of an up-time book of great interest to me. But he is leaving town tomorrow, so I must either see him tonight, or wait several weeks until he returns.

"Enjoy this movie you speak of. Make sure you bring one of the servants with you; it would be beneath your dignity to go unattended."

William had somehow neglected to mention to Hobbes that he was meeting some young ladies at the Higgins Hotel movie theater. The hotel was brand-new, and only part of it was in operation.

The operational half was a mid-rise, which held shops, the hotel lobby, the restaurant, a lounge, and the movie theater. There was also a conference center, with both conference rooms and hospitality suites.

You passed through the lobby to enter the rectangular inner courtyard, which led to "the tower." This would be a "high-rise." Right now, it was still under construction. And the courtyard wouldn't be landscaped until the tower was done.

Still, the conference center was in business. Not only did people meet there, the hospitality suites were rented out at outrageous prices to visitors, like William, who wanted to make an impression. Once the tower was in operation, guests would stay there, instead.

The hotel also made money off the restaurant and the movie theater. The latter was equipped with a VCR and a large projection TV; the hotel charged admission and split the profits with the TV owner. Movie admission was free to hotel guests, but they had to sign in, so they could be accounted for.

Judy's informal guardian *in loco parentis*, Delia Higgins, owned the hotel. That meant Judy could see a movie pretty much whenever she wanted, which was usually at least once a week. Her fellow Barbie Consortium members often came, too. There weren't a lot of entertainment choices, after dark.

Vicky was the first to arrive. She sat next to Judy. Then Heather showed up.

Judy, who was watching the crowd, was the first to spot her. What she saw was so astounding, her brain had trouble processing what her eyes were telling her. "Heather's wearing a dress."

Vicky turned her head so quickly, it was amazing she didn't suffer whiplash. "You're right! She always wears pants. What's going on?"

"I think William is what's going on."

"Uh-huh. This will be an interesting evening."

It was. When William arrived, which was while Heather was off in the powder room, he sat down next to Judy. Heather came back, gave Judy a suspicious look, then hurriedly took a seat on William's other side. Gabrielle arrived, and sat next to Heather, and Millicent flanked Vicky. William looked like a sultan having a night out with his harem.

Judy squirmed a bit. She liked William, but she wasn't *interested* in William. Not like Heather. Who Judy was probably going to be hearing from, before the night was over.

It was obvious what Heather saw in William. He could pass, in the right clothing, for a rock-and-roll idol. He was reasonably well educated, for a seventeenth-century nobleman. He was athletic.

But, hey, what kind of long-term relationship could they have? The men of his class didn't marry for love; their marriages were more like corporate mergers.

Heather was usually practical. What was wrong with her?

Oh, that. Judy hoped not.

Sybill Johnson was very apologetic.

"I am sorry, Mister Hobbes. TJ isn't feeling well, you can't come in."

"Can you fetch me the book? It's Hibbert's *Cavaliers and Roundheads*. I'll take good care of it."

"His library is a mess, I don't know how he finds anything."

"Perhaps . . . you could just ask him, and then find it yourself?"

"I'm so sorry, but he's sleeping, and I'm not going to wake him up. But I'll ask him tomorrow, and you can pick up the book tomorrow night." She shut the door.

Hobbes decided he might as well see what a movie was like.

It wasn't easy spotting William in the darkened room. Hobbes hunched over so as not to block the view, and shuffled along until he found his charge. There he was.

Girls to the left of him. Girls to the right of him. A coincidence? Hobbes wasn't a big believer in coincidences.

William had obviously enjoyed more of a social life in Grantville than he had been letting on.

Hobbes decided that it was high time to get William away from his female admirers. Even if that meant forsaking the Grantville Public Library for a while.

As soon as the lights were turned on, Hobbes walked over. "Ladies, I am Mister Thomas Hobbes, Lord Devonshire's governor. Do you mind if I speak privately with him for a moment?"

Hobbes pulled William into a corner, then looked back. Sure enough, several of the girls were watching them. That confirmed Hobbes' suspicions. "Lord Devonshire, you remember how anxious you were to see Magdeburg? Now that it is an imperial city?"

"Yes . . . But I'm learning a lot here."

"I am sure you are. But you are destined for a political life, and that means you need to go where the emperor is. Magdeburg."

"I suppose a little visit might be nice."

"Actually, Lord Devonshire, I thought we might spend a month or so there."

William bit his lip.

Hobbes decided to sweeten the deal. "We'll see the Swedish Army at drill, and the Navy yard building new ships, and much else of interest. And Halle's on the way; we can play at the tennis court there."

William nodded, slowly. "That sounds good. When do we leave?"

"Next Friday. I need a few days to complete my research here." Hobbes didn't mention that his research would now include background checks on the girls sitting next to William.

"So, are you going to introduce me to these young ladies?"

After all the moviegoers had gone home, or to their hotel rooms, William went to the hotel lobby to use the telephone. He called Judy.

"William? What's up?"

"There's been a change of plans. Mister Hobbes says we're going to Madgeburg. Next Friday."

"That's pretty sudden."

"Yeah."

There was a long silence.

"Y'know, my parents are living in Madgeburg now. That's why I'm staying with Delia. She's a friend of the family. Mom and Dad usually come back once a month to visit me, but it might be fun to go see them instead.

"I could ask them if we could travel up with you and Mister Hobbes. If that's okay."

"That would be great! Uh, who's 'we'?"

"My girlfriends. I'm sure Heather would like to go; she's never been to Magdeburg. Perhaps some of our brothers. And I suppose we'd have to hire guards, or our parents would have conniptions."

William took a quick look across the lobby. No sign of his tutor. "Mister Hobbes told me that there's a real tennis court in Halle. That's on the way to Magdeburg. I could teach you all how to play."

"It's a date. I mean, that sounds like fun."

◊   ◊   ◊

Judy called Heather. "William's going to Magdeburg. For at least a month."

Heather started wailing.

"Take it easy. I have it all worked out," Judy said. "We'll travel along, let him show us his royal tennis in Halle, maybe do some sightseeing together in Magdeburg. It'll give you a chance to make more of an impression on him, and of course I'll get to see my folks."

"Thanks, Judy. Wait, you aren't interested in him yourself, are you?"

"Honestly, Heather, I have no ambition to be the 'Mistress of Pemberley.' Do you know how often I have to shoo off worthless young noblemen who hear that I'm rich?"

"But William isn't worthless."

Judy thought it just as well that Heather couldn't see her expression at the moment. "That's not what I meant."

"And I think he likes you."

"What do you want me to do, Heather? Walk around with a paper bag over my head? Come along, talk to him, play some tennis, and see how it goes."

"Okay. But what will our parents say? We can't go without adult supervision, that's for sure."

"Hmm. Mister Hobbes is going, he's perfect. If he can get William safely across France, Italy and the Alps, he can get us from Grantville to Magdeburg."

"And we can say it's like a social studies field trip, going with this great political philosopher."

Heather pondered this. "They might think that his loyalties are to William."

"Right. Like he and William are going to carry us to their castle, like in some Gothic novel. Well, that's what the guards are for. So Hobbes can't hit us over the head with a copy of *Leviathan*."

When there wasn't any military traffic, personal messages could be sent, via radio, between Grantville and Magdeburg.

Judy sent her parents a radiotelegram:

WOULD LIKE TO VISIT YOU IN MAGDEBURG STOP
IF LEAVE THIS FRIDAY, CAN TRAVEL WITH PARTY OF THOMAS HOBBES, FAMOUS BRITISH PHILOSOPHER STOP
WOULD LIKE TO INVITE VICKY, MILLICENT, GABRIELLE, JOHN, HEATHER, KELSEY AND DERRICK TO JOIN ME STOP

Judy hadn't mentioned Hayley or Susan, because she knew they couldn't go.

DO YOU HAVE PREFERENCE AS TO WHICH GUARDS TO HIRE? STOP

CAN YOU ARRANGE LODGING FOR FRIENDS? STOP

This was the sales technique known as the "assumed close," that is, the questions were about guards and lodging, not about whether to go at all.

She soon received a reply:

DELIA CHOOSE GUARDS STOP
FELLOW STUDENTS STAY HERE STOP
HOW OLD THOMAS HOBBES? STOP

How lame, thought Judy. She composed a reply and handed it to the radio operator.

FORTY-FIVE STOP
JEESH STOP
HOBBES PHILOSOPHER, INFLUENCED AMERICAN DECLARATION INDEPENDENCE STOP
  LIKE HAVING GUEST LECTURER IN SOCIAL STUDIES CLASS STOP

"Wait," Judy said. The operator handed the form back to her.

Is that a good reason for my parents to like the idea? Yes. Are they going to think it's my reason? No. So what will they do? They will keep hunting for my real motive. So what will satisfy their curiosity?

She thought a bit longer, and then scribbled an addendum:

HOBBES KNOWS WEALTHY ENGLISH FAMI-
LIES, POSSIBLE INVESTORS GRANTVILLE BUSI-
NESS OPPORTUNITIES STOP
TRIP CHANCE TO PICK HIS BRAINS STOP

There. That fitted in perfectly with her 'Judy the Bar-
racudy' rep. And it was true. Just not all the truth.

◊　　　◊　　　◊

They were at the train station, which was the old B&
O depot, waiting for the train to head out. William and
the girls were chattering a mile a minute. All of Judy's
invitees, save Millicent, had successfully reasoned, whee-
dled, screamed or otherwise buffaloed their parents into
agreeing to "the field trip."

Hobbes was not happy. The point of going to Magdeburg was to get away from the girls. Not to escort them
to the big city and teach them how to play royal tennis,
to boot.

Not that Hobbes had any problem with teaching
women. He had long been of the view that all humans
are naturally equal, which implied that women are equal
to men.

The problem was that if William got into any foreign
romantic entanglements, his mother Christian would
certainly blame Hobbes.

Upon interrogation, William had confessed that Judith
Wendell had invited him to the movie. And then invited
herself and her buddies along on this trip to Magdeburg.

It was small consolation that this Judith Wendell was,
in some respects, a suitable match. She was the daughter

of Fletcher Wendell, who was the "Secretary of the Treasury." As near as Hobbes could figure out, the equivalent British position was the "Chancellor of the Exchequer." The chancellor of the exchequer was almost always a nobleman; the present title holder was a baron, Francis Cottington. So it was safe to assume that this Fletcher Wendell was a nobleman, too.

Yes, yes, Hobbes had been told that the Americans didn't have a noble class. As a historian, Hobbes was familiar with several governments which were republican in name, but run by a small group of families. The Most Serene Republic, for example. Hobbes assumed that Grantville had a similar system.

The thought of William marrying Judy was amusing, in one respect. William had no idea how much Judy looked like William's mother Christian, when she was sixteen. Both pretty, redheaded wenches, accustomed to getting their own way.

The rail line from Grantville to Halle, when completed, would be almost ninety miles long. The track crossed "the ring," and then followed the west bank of the Saale as it leisurely wound its way through the forested limestone hills of Thuringia.

The train was powered by what the girls called a "pickup truck," and it drew three wooden cars on metal-topped wooden rails. The rails were not unfamiliar to Hobbes; there were similar structures serving a few British collieries. The "pickup truck," however, was a source of great amazement.

The train traveled at the astounding speed of ten miles per hour, without rest. William was quite excited, but

Hobbes caught the quickly concealed smiles on the part of the up-timers. *This is slow, by their standards*, he thought.

Their parties occupied much of one rail car. The five in the Cavendish party of course, Judy and some of her friends, and two hired guards. This amused Hobbes a bit. He suspected that they were present to protect the girls from William as much as from bandits. Whereas Hobbes was intent on protecting William from the girls.

The first stop was at Rudolstadt, just outside the Ring of Fire. About three hours later, they pulled into the station serving the university town of Jena. Some students came onboard their car. One, more courageous than the others, spoke briefly to Heather, who was sitting nearest to them. She spoke to the young scholar with great animation, but occasionally glanced at William. *To see if he is getting jealous?* Hobbes wondered.

An hour and a half later, they were in Naumburg. This was the end of the line for now, so they hired coaches and continued on to Halle, where they would spend the night.

They had reserved the following day for seeing the sights, and playing tennis. The next morning, they would board the barge to Magdeburg, another fifty-odd miles away. It would be slow, even though they were traveling with the current, but the girls weren't accustomed to riding long distances.

"This place is really gloomy looking," Vicky said. The walls and ceiling of the tennis court were painted a solid black. Nor did the flagstone floor do much to cheer up the look. "Is this a home for Goths?"

Hobbes looked puzzled. "The Goths? Well, they are a Germanic tribe, and we are in Germany, but I don't think they played tennis. At least, I don't recall any reference to it in Jordanes' *Getica*."

"She means, why all the black?" said Gabrielle.

"Oh. To make it easier to see the ball, which is white."

"Why not whitewash the walls, and use a black ball?"

"They do that in Spain, but nowhere else in Europe."

"They don't have very good architects here in Halle, do they?"

"Why do you say that?"

"There's a kink in that wall, the one without the penthouses."

"That's the *tambour*, the 'drum.' You see how at the kink, there's an angled face? If the ball hits that, it's 'pinball time.' "

William suggested that they watch others play first, then take their turn.

Two young gentlemen did some practice volleying, and then began the game in earnest. The server cried "*tenez!*," and his opponent responded "*Oui!*"

"So that's where tennis gets its name," said Heather. "But what does 'tenez' mean?"

William smiled. "It means, 'take this!' " The girls laughed.

They were seated in the *dedans*, the gallery behind the service side of the court. William had told them that it was one of the three winning openings. The first serve sailed up into the air, and skipped several times along the service penthouse. Were that not enough, it rounded the corner, striking the penthouse behind the receiver, before it finally landed. The ball was returned after the first bounce.

"Was that a good serve?"

"Oh, yes. The receiving player has to just wait patiently for it to come down. The Spanish even have a saying, *aun esta la pelota en el tejado*, 'the ball is still on the roof.' They say it when something is not yet decided."

Suddenly, the receiver swatted the ball over the net and into the main wall. It bounced off and flew straight toward the girls in the *dedans*. They flinched involuntarily, but the ball was caught by the net hung in front of them.

The impact rang a bell. "Fifteen-love," the marker intoned.

"So if this *dedans* is the winning opening for the receiver, where's the one for the server?"

"There are two, actually. If you look at the far wall, behind the receiver, you see that it's blank except for a small hole on our right."

"I see it."

"That's the grille. In the old monasteries, the monks went to that opening to talk to outsiders."

"To order a hamburger?" asked John.

Derrick offered John a high five. "Good one!"

Gabrielle tapped the side of her head with a finger. "I'm glad someone thinks John's funny."

"Besides the grille, the server can also score outright by placing a shot into the 'winning gallery.' That's the last of the eight openings under the service side penthouse, the farthest one from us."

"What happens if you hit the ball into one of the other seven?"

"That creates a chase, just as if you had a double bounce on the parallel part of the floor."

Eventually, the players finished their four-game set, waved to the spectators, and walked off.

William approached the marker, who happily accepted the fee for two hours of court time, and supplied William with rackets and balls. However, when the girls came onto the playing floor, he balked. Until William produced more money, which magically vanished into the marker's clothing.

Judy had watched the negotiation. "It's kinda annoying that you can't play this game without a referee to mark the chases."

William shrugged. "Before they used markers, there were many fights."

William had them first just hit the ball back and forth. They needed to get used to the balls and rackets, both different from the modern ones. He encouraged them to cut under the ball, so it would drop sharply at the end of its trajectory.

Then he had them try different kinds of serves. While this was going on, the master of the court, the ballmeister, arrived.

"What's going on here? Why are there women on my court?"

Their marker rose to the defense—of himself. "Women? Here?" He turned to Hobbes. "I am shocked, shocked, that you would bring women here. You dressed them in men's clothing to trick me. I am most disturbed."

"I'm willing to pay a suitable fee for the privilege of playing here with these gentlewomen," said William.

This offer didn't diminish the ballmeister's agitation. "This is a house for the royal game of tennis, not for the entertainment of doxies!"

William bristled. Hobbes carefully stepped on his foot. "I don't understand your objection, my dear ballmeister," said Hobbes. "Women play in Udine, the chief town of the Friuli. And in Ferrara."

"Well, let them go to Udine, or Ferrara, then, but they shall not, no, they shall not, play here." He shook his tennis racket in a threatening manner.

Hobbes decided to try a different tack. "They are the guests of this young gentleman, who is the earl of Devonshire. What you would call a count. That makes him one of the British *Hochadel*. Do you really wish to offend him?"

"You and he are welcome to play. Just not the women."

"I won't play if you won't allow my friends to play," William said. "And consider this: The father of one of the young ladies is the Secretary of the Treasury of the CPE, and a confidante of Gustavus Adolphus."

"I care not a fig. Get out, or I will have you dragged out."

William put his hand to his hip, reaching for the sword that wasn't there.

Judy saw the gesture. "It's too hot to play, anyway. Let's get some fresh air." She looked at the other girls. They took their cue, and agreed with her.

Once they were outside, of course, they were quick to vent their spleen. "I can't believe that in Halle, which gets so much business from Grantville, someone could be so obtuse."

"Don't forget that this kind of tennis isn't known to any up-timers, save us. The creep probably doesn't have much contact with people from Grantville."

Judy looked at William. "Are you disappointed? You said that tennis courts were rare in this part of Europe."

William shrugged. "As Vicky said, it was too gloomy in there. Don't worry about it."

"I wish there was a royal tennis court in Grantville. That would serve him right."

The barge ride down to Magdeburg was picturesque, Judy supposed. Meaning, boring after the first hour. With the day a balmy one, Judy dozed off. And found herself dreaming about William. More specifically, dreaming about kissing William.

She awoke with a guilty start, and saw Hobbes and William playing a game of chess, with Heather watching.

Good thing Heather doesn't have telepathic powers, Judy thought. *Or I might be swimming right now.*

Judy had thought that she just wanted a guy who was smart, and could make her laugh, she didn't care how handsome he was. Okay, now she had to admit, looking like a young Brad Pitt was a plus.

William had stood up for the girls in Halle, even though, let's face it, he'd never heard of women's lib. Of course, from what Judy had heard about his mom, he probably thought there was more of a need for men's lib. But still, Judy had been pleased by his actions.

And he did have, for lack of a better term, a curious turn of mind. Judy wouldn't have thought of descending by rope into Mount Vesuvius, that's for sure. Whether that was a good thing or a bad thing, Judy hadn't decided.

Okay, she admitted, maybe she was interested in William. And Heather had had a fair shot at him.

But Judy wasn't sixteen yet. And her parents had set sixteen as the rockbottom minimum dating age. Which Judy wouldn't reach until next year. By which time William would be back in England, for sure.

It wasn't the sort of thing Judy could renegotiate. If she tried, her older sister Sarah would side with her parents. Because Sarah had to wait.

At least it was an equal playing field. Heather was also fifteen and her parents would make her put off dating, too.

Of course, the definition of a "date" could be pretty elastic. Judy would just have to think about how to stretch it.

Imperial Palace, Magdeburg
July 1633

"A distinguished visitor? From England? Can't you fob him off on someone else? Isn't that what my staff is for? I have a war to win." Gustavus Adolphus was not really into the ceremonial aspects of royal office.

"If you insist, Your Imperial Majesty, but I think you should make the time. He is a young man, the earl of Devonshire. They are one of the wealthiest noble families in England, and he is at an impressionable age. If you will excuse my saying so, you do intend to inspire hero worship in such youths. That may come in handy when he is a bit older.

"And, sir, he is accompanied by a Mister Thomas Hobbes."

"That name sounds vaguely familiar."

"In the old time line, he became a famous political philosopher, a defender of monarchy. And yet his writings were influential in the development of the American political system."

"Yes, yes, I think someone showed me something about his book *Leviathan*. You think he could be useful to us?"

"He is quite a forceful writer."

"All right. Fifteen minutes."

Hobbes and William were ushered into the august presence of Gustavus Adolphus, Lion of the North, King of Sweden, Emperor of the Confederated Principalities of Europe, and Captain-General of the State of Thuringia-Franconia. Unfortunately for the royal schedule, the conversation drifted to the subject of tennis.

"Tennis, you say? I adore the game. I learned it when I traveled in France, as 'Captain Gars.'?"

"We played it in France and Italy," William said. "And, after we crossed the Alps, in Augsburg and Nurnberg."

"Nurnberg, yes. I was there last year, dealing with Wallenstein's army. Somehow never had the time to play tennis.

"Now, earlier in the war, when I was outside Ingolstadt, I wanted to play at the ballhouse there. With my officers."

"They wouldn't let you?" asked William.

"No. And I made them a very reasonable offer. I promised to leave my army outside, and to allow food carts to enter the city for the entire day."

Hobbes raised his eyebrows. "Oh. You wanted to play tennis in a city which you had under siege."

"That's right. It was very unchivalrous of them to refuse."

An hour later, Gustavus Adolphus was still rattling on about his tennis triumphs. His aide had to force him to go on to the next meeting.

Wendell Residence, Magdeburg
August 1633

"So, how was your trip?" asked Judy the Elder. "And would you like more salad?"

"No more, thank you," said Judy the Younger. She finished off the last leaf of lettuce and drank some weak beer. In Magdeburg, it was much safer than water. "The trip was fine, Mom. We even got to play a new kind of tennis in Halle."

"Who taught you?"

"We learned from Mister Hobbes. He's not just a philosopher, he plays tennis. Now that's something I bet Ms. Mailey didn't know.

"Anyway, we went to this gigantic tennis court, and they showed us how to play what they call 'royal tennis' in England. You play indoors, in kind of an enclosed monastery courtyard, and you serve onto a ten-foot-tall rooftop so it bounces on the other side, and then both players can bounce it off the walls, and there are goals you can sink the ball into to score a point, and—"

"Who's 'they'?"

"Hobbes and his student."

"Somehow, I don't remember your mentioning him traveling with a student."

"Oh, yes, that's how come Hobbes was in Grantville in the first place. He was guiding one of the Cavendishes around Europe."

Momma raised an eyebrow. "One of the male Cavendishes?"

Fletcher Wendell, who had been paying more attention to the food than to the conversation, heard the magic word "male" and came alert. But he let his wife continue to examine the defendant.

"Yes."

"A fellow middle-aged philosopher?"

"Not exactly. William is around my age. Actually, younger than me."

Fletcher finally intervened. "You do remember our dating rule, young lady."

"Oh yes. But we weren't alone at the tennis court, there were a half-dozen of my friends there. Plus Mister Hobbes, who's an adult, and William's servants. So it was an adult-supervised group activity. Not a date."

"Servants, plural? Just what is William's rank?"

"He's the earl of Devonshire. And very rich."

"I hope you aren't planning to take advantage of him." Fletcher reddened. "I mean, economically."

"I haven't anything to sell to him right now. We're still waiting for the printers to finish the brochures for our South Sea Trading Company."

"Very funny."

"Our slogan will be 'Send Your Money South.' "

Magdeburg
August 1633

Heather was not, she admitted to herself, the sort of person who let her emotions hang out. In fact, she looked down on those who did.

But when you were interested in a guy, all those inhibitions kind of got in the way.

She had traveled all the way from Grantville to Magdeburg, and she wasn't even sure that William knew that she liked him.

Anyway, she had been happy when Judy had excused herself to spend a quiet evening with her family. Judy was a great friend and all, but she was just a little too pretty for Heather's peace of mind. When William was around, that is.

So, she and Kelsey were walking arm and arm in the market square, with Derrick and William behind them. "You know what to do," she whispered to her sister.

"Oh, look at that," Kelsey said, pointing to one of the stalls. "Isn't that darling? Derrick, come with me. I think I might need your help."

"What?"

"Come . . . now."

That left Heather alone with William. She was searching for the right way to start, when he spoke up.

"So how long have you known Judy?"

Arrgh, she thought. "For years."

Her little tryst went rapidly downhill from there. He wanted to know all about Judy's likes and dislikes. And was she betrothed to anyone.

Arrgh.

Kelsey and Derrick emerged. Kelsey took one look at Heather, and her smile died stillborn.

"The weather has suddenly gotten chilly," Heather said. "I want to go back to the inn. Now."

By the end of the week, when it was time to head back to Grantville, Heather had more or less forgiven Judy. And even William. He probably wouldn't like doo-wop music, after all.

But she was thinking of a few new additions to the Trommler Records song collection. "I'm Henry the Eighth" was one. "Mad Dogs and Englishmen" was another.

Imperial Palace, Magdeburg
August 1633

Hobbes stared perplexedly at the paper in front of him. He had been assured that all applicants for positions with the CPE administration had to fill out this form.

Some of the questions were perfectly reasonable, others . . . less so.

But the most puzzling point of all was . . . why did they call it an SF-171?

Grantville
August 1633

Judy and Millicent were lying on the bed in Millicent's room. Millicent's mom had gone ballistic at the first mention of the possibility of a "field trip" to Magdeburg.

The two had a big argument, and Millicent had been grounded for the entire week that Judy and the others were away.

Judy had been worried that Millicent would hold this against her, but she didn't. Of course, Millicent insisted on a blow-by-blow account of the whole journey.

That completed, Judy said, "I've been thinking."

"About boys? Mister W, perhaps?"

"About tennis."

Millicent started warbling the love song from the *Titanic* movie. The DVD had been released some months before the Ring of Fire.

Judy slugged her with a pillow. "All right, about both," she admitted. "But I want to talk about tennis."

"So talk."

"It's getting harder and harder to find balls that are bouncy enough for twentieth-century tennis. Once we open the can, the balls lose their air within weeks. And even in the can, they're only good for two years or so."

"You're thinking about switching to royal tennis?"

"That's right."

"But we can't play in Halle, thanks to that jerk of a ballmeister. And constructing a matching tennis court in Grantville would be real expensive."

"It's a catch twenty-two. We could justify it if we had the players, but we won't have the players until we have the court. Still . . . tennis used to be a very posh sport. Just the thing to play at the Higgins Hotel."

"Yeah, but there's no way OPM would fund constructing a real tennis court there. Not until the hotel was in full operation and was getting enough down-time visitors who knew the game."

"Yeah." Judy puttered around a bit. "Wait. I was just thinking. About the back courtyard. It's much like a cloisters. And it isn't all that wide."

"You're right! And the walls have sloped roofs, to keep the snow off them."

"It would mean playing tennis like they did it a few centuries ago. I mean, back when they played in monasteries instead of customized courts. But it would be a way to work up interest in the game."

"And if enough people got interested, then maybe OPM would decide it was a good investment."

"William told me that there are almost two thousand tennis courts in Paris. And that when one of the indoor markets burnt down in 1590, it was replaced with a tennis court, because that was more profitable."

"We would need someone to teach the game. Someone that was willing to teach women to play."

"What about William, when he comes back?"

"Well, there would be a lot of snob appeal in having an earl as a teacher. But I don't think he knows how to make the balls and rackets. Perhaps Mister Hobbes, the seventeenth-century know-it-all, does?"

Judy had written to William: "So, if someone were to build a real tennis court in Grantville, what would be the right dimensions?"

When she got his response, she read it aloud to Millicent: "There are no two tennis courts which are exactly alike. They can have different dimensions, different winning openings, and so on."

She looked at Millicent. "That's crazy, don't you think?"

Millicent disagreed. "Crazier than baseball stadiums?"

When she had a chance, Judy stopped by the Grantville Public Library. The 1911 *Encyclopedia Britannica* had plenty to say about "royal tennis," including the typical dimensions of the various parts of the court.

Enough to show that the inner courtyard at the Higgins Hotel was an acceptable match. There would be compromises, of course. No main wall. And the grille side wasn't walled up. But she thought it might work. At least if any exposed windows were covered over. She didn't want to pay for broken glass.

She would ask William, when he got back from Magdeburg, to take a look.

Grantville
September 1633

"Hi, Heather!" William smiled at her. "I just got back last night. Took my time getting up this morning."

Heather picked up her books and hurried off. "Hey, what's the matter?" William said as she retreated.

Derrick Mason was on the other side of the street, and William waved to him. Derrick Mason turned his back.

What has gotten into these people? William thought. He walked over to the public library. Hobbes was already at a desk, with books piled in front of him. *Plus ça change, plus c'est la même chose.*

"Hello, Mister Hobbes."

"Good morning, Lord Devonshire."

"I haven't suddenly acquired leprosy, have I, Mister Hobbes?"

"What on Earth leads you to ask such a question?"

"My American friends haven't been very friendly today."

"Yes, I know why. I found out when I arrived at the library. Fortunately, the librarians didn't hold it against me."

"Hold what against you?"

"Against us. England, Spain and France have formed an alliance, the League of Ostend. The League defeated the Dutch Navy off Dunkirk."

"Good for them. The Dutch deserve it, after torturing our people on Amboina to make false confessions of treason."

"Indeed they do. But no one here believes that the League is arrayed against the Dutch alone. King Charles has transferred the American colonies to France. And the Grantville embassy in London has been imprisoned in the Tower. Do you know who is in that embassy?"

"Melissa Mailley, my friends' teacher."

"That's right. And Rita and Tom Simpson, Friedrich and Nelly Bruch, Darryl McCarthy, and Gayle Mason. All popular people here. I'd stay away from Thuringen Gardens for a few days, unless you have a taste for one-against-many bar brawls."

"So, are we prisoners, too?"

"Not yet, at least. But we do appear to be *persona non grata*, all of a sudden." Hobbes closed the book in front of him with a snap. "The attitude of the Americans is not our only problem."

"How so?"

"Your license from the Privy Council to 'go beyond the sea' says—" Hobbes changed the pitch of his voice to indicate that he was quoting from memory " '—do not haunt or resort onto the territories or dominions of any foreign prince not being with us in league or amity, nor wittingly keep company with any person or persons evil affected to our State.'

"If you stay, it could be interpreted as treason."

The coach was loaded to capacity. Hobbes and William had acquired so many curiosities in Grantville that if they put on another bag, the horses would just go on strike.

William was feeling sorry for himself. When he asked at the hotel desk that they connect him with Judy, they had told him, "she's out." Again and again. William suspected that she would be "out" until he left town.

William was leaning against the coach, waiting for Mister Hobbes to finish checking the hotel's arithmetic, when Judy appeared.

"Hi," he said.

"Hi, yourself."

William shifted from one foot to another. The silence grew.

"I know it's not your fault. I mean, the Treaty of Ostend. But people I know are going to end up fighting, and maybe dying, over this. Derrick and Kelsey Mason are in the military. And even civilians are at risk—we haven't forgotten the Croat Raid on Grantville."

"I know . . . But from what Mister Hobbes has taught me, history has a way of flipping things around. Enemies today, allies tomorrow."

"Yeah." Judy blinked, as though she was trying to hold back tears. "But it can be a long time in-between flips."

"Maybe . . . " William paused, wondering how to say it. "Maybe, someday . . . "

Judy gave him a little smile. "Yeah. Maybe someday. Write me, okay?"

"I will."

The coach was ready and the men were getting impatient. It was time to go. "Ah . . . " William wanted to say more but didn't have any words. "Ah . . . "

Judy leaned forward and gave him a quick kiss. "Maybe next time." She ran off, back into the hotel.

William watched the doors for a moment, but she didn't come back. Instead, Hobbes emerged. "Lord Devonshire, are you ready?"

"Yes, Mister Hobbes. It's time to go."

Hobbes and William stood on the docks of Hamburg. With the ports of Holland under blockade, Hamburg was busier than ever. The servants carried William's baggage, piece by piece, onto the ship that would take him home.

But Hobbes was not going home. He had told William everything that needed to be passed on to his family. It was far too sensitive to set on paper. While Hobbes didn't point it out, he knew that this knowledge would give William a kind of power he had never had before. Hobbes hoped that William would profit from it.

William would also give his mother an explanation of why Hobbes was staying behind. First, to continue his researches into up-time history that could affect Cavendish interests. Secondly, so that he could send word back home of any critical new developments.

Of course, Hobbes had other reasons, too. William knew them.

"Mister Hobbes, are you sure you are going to live in Grantville permanently?"

"The ball is still on the roof, Lord Devonshire."

Hobbes was quite sure that only the Americans would tolerate his views toward religion. While the Cavendishes might protect him from charges of heresy, such protection would probably come at the price of his remaining silent on any matter that could give offense to anyone.

Such silence was a price he had resolved not to pay.

Still, change might come to England, too. Perhaps sooner than the king, or even Doctor Harvey, expected.

William embraced him. "Goodbye, Mister Hobbes. I shan't forget all your lessons. And I will have your things sent to you."

"When you write to me, do not put my name anywhere on the letter. I would like to leave as vague as possible where I am and what I am doing."

"But how will the letter be delivered to you?"

"You must place some token upon it that the people in Grantville would understand, but the censors in England will not. A drawing of a whale to signify *Leviathan*, perhaps."

Hobbes paced. "Or perhaps not. The king may have sent agents to Grantville, to find every encyclopedia reference to Englishmen of our day, and the whale would surely point to me."

"Mister Hobbes, I promise to try to come up with something better. I have a long sea ride with nothing to do but think."

"Letter for you, Mister Hobbes."

"Thank you." Hobbes ripped it open the letter. It was from William. At least, Hobbes recognized the handwriting. The letter itself was unsigned. It thanked Hobbes for his efforts, and assured the unnamed recipient that he was to consider himself still on the family payroll. Without naming any particular family.

And there was a laundry list of gadgets to collect for William's uncles "if it wouldn't be too much trouble."

Carefully folded inside the main letter was a second one, addressed to Judy. Hobbes didn't open that one. Now that William was outside his custody, it was none of his business.

He decided that he would bring it by the Higgins Hotel and deliver it personally, as Judy might not otherwise realize who it had come from.

The next day, Hobbes spotted the postman as he walked down the street. Hobbes called out through his window. "That letter you gave me. How did you know it was for me?"

"It was obvious, Mister Hobbes." The postman waved and walked off.

Hobbes looked at the address side of the letter again, still puzzled. There was no name on it. No whale, for that matter. Just a drawing of a bipedal orange tiger, wearing a gown and a mortar board cap.

What could that refer to? Then Hobbes remembered the comic strip William had shown him, months before. Calvin . . . and Hobbes.

Eddie and the King's Daughter

K.D. Wentworth

King Christian IV nodded as the Danish court physician unbandaged what was left of Eddie Cantrell's leg. The monarch was a big, bluff man, narrow on the top and bottom, but wide in the middle. It was late at Rosenborg Castle, but, as Eddie had come to realize since his capture, the king kept idiosyncratic hours.

Lying on his narrow bed, Eddie flinched as his stump was revealed in the flickering candlelight, but the king's homely face took in the scarred flesh, the lack of both ankle and foot, with the utter aplomb of one who is whole himself and has never gotten in the way of an eighteen-pound roundshot in the heat of battle. "A very nice stump, Dr. Belk," he said in German. "Very nice, indeed. You have outdone yourself. Soon he can be fitted for a peg leg."

The doctor, who looked shriveled, as though he'd been freeze-dried at some point, waved a careless hand and replied testily, though Eddie couldn't understand more than a few words. Eddie's Danish was just barely coming along in the weeks since he'd been pulled out of the sea by the Danes, and the blasted doctor steadfastly refused to speak a single word of German to him. King Christian however spoke German like a native and seemed to prefer it. He even had a fair amount of English.

Eddie's room in Rosenborg castle was large and well furnished, with clean linens as well as a fireplace against Denmark's late autumn chill. He might have been an honored guest, but for the everpresent uniformed guard outside his room.

The doctor gestured at his truncated leg again, shrugged, then gathered the discarded bandages.

"What?" Eddie said. His fingers clawed at the bedclothes as he pushed himself up against the headboard. "Are you trying to tell me that it's going to grow back?" Despite of his gladness to be alive, even in this condition, he was tired of being treated like a stick of wood.

King Christian's forehead wrinkled. Fifty-six years old, he liked to dress in bright colors and sported a silly little goatee along with a single braid that stuck out of his dark hair. Tonight, as usual, he smelled of strong drink, but Eddie did not make the mistake of thinking him a fool. He just wished he could remember more of what the history books in Grantville said about Denmark in this era. Not that they'd said much, beyond some good articles in some of the encyclopedias. The problem was that given the rush with which Eddie and Hans Richter and Larry Wild had been sent up to Wismar to try to fend off the Danish fleet approaching it, there just hadn't been time to study anything that hadn't been directly tied to the task at hand. He'd read those encyclopedia articles, once, but simply couldn't remember much from them.

"They can do that?" the king said. "Your people from the future time?" His eyes, the pale-blue of winter ice, studied him shrewdly.

For a moment, Eddie was tempted to say yes. The more the king respected up-timers, the more leverage Eddie would have as a prisoner-of-war, but it just wasn't in him to tell a whopper that big at the moment. Lying took a lot of energy and he was fresh out. "No," he said, then tugged the red and blue quilt back over his stump so he wouldn't have to look at it. "We can't."

"Regrettable," the king said. "I would have liked to see that, but do not be downcast. You are mostly whole, just a little damaged, and it is not Our fault you attacked Our splendid navy in that tiny ship."

The battle flashed again inside Eddie's head—the roar of the Outlaw power boat, his foot exploding in raw, wrenching agony, blood everywhere—

He shuddered and threw an arm over his eyes as though he could blot out the memory. The grisly scene was embedded in his brain, though, and replayed endlessly. It didn't help that when he tried to sleep, he often saw Larry and Bjorn sliced to bloody ribbons by the same roundshot that had taken him out.

Christian patted his shoulder, but the man was so big, it felt more like a good-natured swat. "We have followed your Geneva Convention, and, by all appearances, your people set great store by you, even though you are only a lieutenant. Is your family highly placed?"

Eddie stared at the king's face, stifling an undignified snort at the thought of *his* old man being respected by anyone.

Christian didn't seem to notice. "Once negotiations are concluded, your people will most likely pay your ransom, and then you can go home to your family."

Eddie flopped back against his pillow. If Christian was pestering Mike Stearns for armaments or technology in return for Eddie's battered carcass, it just wasn't going to happen. He'd already come to terms with that.

He stared up at the fancy decorated ceiling. Besides, what good could he do the folks back in Grantville anyway? He couldn't see that anyone would have much use for a one-legged lieutenant.

"You rest now." The king turned away. "Tomorrow, I mean for you to tell my councilors about this Grantville so we can better understand how to defend against them. Your people are far too clever for my peace of mind."

Great, Eddie thought. Just great, icing on the cake, as his fellow Americans would have said. Now, on top of everything else that had happened to him, the Danes thought he should betray his country. Something to freaking look forward to. Too bad that roundshot hadn't been aimed just a hair higher.

He turned over and buried his face in his pillow as the door clicked shut.

Eddie awoke with a start to find a very pretty teenaged girl with long curly red-gold hair sitting on the stool beside his bed. She regarded him with unblinking blue eyes, her face very solemn for one so young. "Papà says you are feeling better," she said in flawless German.

His mouth sagged open and he could think of nothing to say. He'd kicked the bedclothes off in his sleep and suddenly realized she was leaning forward to examine his stump. Face burning, he covered it with the quilt.

"It is quite all right," the girl said. No more than fourteen or fifteen, she smoothed her skirts with utter aplomb. "I have seen such before. You are fortunate to be alive." The scent of roses drifted toward him.

It was still dark outside, so it had to be either very late or very early. The fire had burned down low in the grate. Shadows lay thick in the little room. Eddie struggled to sit up, clutching the quilts to his chest. "Who are you?"

"Anne Cathrine," she said as though that explained everything. Her hands were folded in her lap and a white lace shawl lay across her shoulders. She was dressed in a well-cut gown of dark-green, which was obviously far too expensive to belong to any sort of serving girl.

"I still don't understand," he said.

"Papà said you were feeling better when he came to tell us good night," she said again, this time speaking very slowly, as though he were brain-damaged, "so I thought I would visit you. I have never seen anyone from the future before."

He ran his fingers through his bedraggled ginger-colored hair, vainly attempting to restore some order. It had grown shaggy since his mishap at Wismar. "Who is your Papà?" Maybe the doctor or one of the court officials? he thought.

"Oh, he is the king." She cocked her head, studying him. "I thought everyone knew that."

His heart thudded and he became acutely aware that he hadn't washed in days. His scalp began to itch and he had to force his hands not to scratch. "Then you are a princess," he said.

"No, my official title is King's Daughter," Anne Cathrine said and picked at a bit on lint on her bodice with slim fingers. "The marriage with my mother was morganatic. Her rank was too far below his, so she was never queen and none of her children can inherit the crown." She sighed. "I did have a fiancé once, but Frantz drowned, swimming in the moat. Now Papà will marry me off to another nobleman, probably much older than me. Several have recently petitioned for my hand. I do not care for any of them."

"Gee, sounds like fun," he mumbled in English.

She leaned toward him, eyes bright. They were the same piercing pale blue of her father. "Is that American?" she asked. "If so, I should like to learn. I am very good with languages."

"Won't you get in trouble, if someone finds you here?" he said. "For that matter, won't they be angry with me?"

"Mamà was always very cross with us, so now that she's been exiled, Papà lets me do as I please," she said loftily. "At least until I am married. Then I suppose I will have to obey my husband."

"Well, he doesn't give me that kind of freedom," he said. Sweat pooled in the hollow of his back. "I think you had better go before someone finds you here."

"You are telling *me* to leave?" She blinked in surprise.

Eddie was no expert in royal protocol, but he didn't have trouble visualizing what folks would think if a jail-bait-aged princess, king's daughter, whatever, was caught hanging around with a disreputable prisoner—in his bedroom—unchaperoned.

"It's late," he said and turned his face to the wall. Jeez, he hadn't shaved in days either. Suddenly, he itched from head to toe, or at least the toes that he still had. "I am tired. I want to sleep."

Her skirts rustled. "Very well," she said. "I will go—for the sake of your health."

Footsteps, light and precise as a dance figure, crossed the floor. The door opened and closed. He rolled back over and stared at the empty room. Light flickered from the remnants of the fire in the grate and the scent of roses lingered in the air.

The next morning, he asked for hot water and a razor when the maid brought him the usual bowl of warm milk and thick slices of cinnamon bread for breakfast, then did his best to eat all of the food. Most mornings he hadn't bothered. The washing water, when it came in a basin, was tepid, the soap yellow and harsh.

He pulled off his nightshirt, then sat on the edge of his bed and sponged himself down, trying not to look at his stump. In the light flooding in through his window, he could count his ribs. He'd lost a lot of weight since being injured, and he hadn't exactly been sporting any extra pounds in this pre-junk-food world.

He sighed. What he wouldn't give for a bag of Doritos or an egg McMuffin or even one lousy bite of a Hershey bar.

The door creaked open and he made a grab for his lacy bed-shirt, which guys back in Grantville would have snickered at as a nightgown. "Who is it?"

"Anne Cathrine." Her expectant face peered around the edge.

He tugged the shirt over his head, but it caught on his ears. "Go away! I'm not dressed!" he said, struggling to get his arms in the sleeves.

"Good," she said and pushed the door inward. "I have brought new clothes."

"Jeez!" His face flushed. He thrust his right arm through the sleeve, then clutched the covers over his bare legs. "What is it with you people?" he burst out in English. "This isn't a damned bus station, you know!"

Anne Cathrine's arms were full of clothing. One red-gold eyebrow lifted. "Could you say that again in German?"

"It, um, wouldn't translate very well." He could feel his ears burning. "Don't you have a—" He wanted to say "keeper." "A servant to watch after you or something?"

"Yes." She stiffened. "Mistress Sehested, our governess, 'watches,' as you say, after us. Fortunately, she is busy at the moment with my younger sisters. She would most likely beat me if she knew I was here, so we will not tell her."

"But you're a princess," Eddie said, flustered. He dropped the blankets, then managed, finally, to get his left arm through the nightshirt sleeve. "I didn't think princesses were ever beaten. That just doesn't sound right."

"I have told you—I am king's daughter, not a true princess." Her eyes narrowed, as she sorted through the clothing items. "It is very clear you know nothing about court life."

"I didn't mean to offend."

"Anyway," she went on, setting her bundle on his bed, "I thought a man from the future should look distinguished when appearing before Papà's councilors." She had her father's height and would be at least as tall as Eddie, if he were standing. She wore a wine-colored gown this morning, and her red-gold hair had been carefully coifed into elaborate braids pinned about her head. Two bright circles of red appeared in her cheeks. "They are fussy men, most of them old, who never want to let Papà have his way and always they say we do not have enough money! You must impress them so they will back all his wonderful plans."

He looked at the little pile, topped by a pair of gleaming black boots. *Two* boots. His heart lurched. He wouldn't need but one.

A maid carrying a single crutch appeared in the doorway behind Anne Cathrine. "Oh," the girl said, "and you will need this too." She motioned the servant across the room. "Do you wish help in getting dressed?"

"No!" Eddie blurted and scooted back across the bed out of reach. "I do not!"

She gazed at him with those luminous pale-blue eyes as though he were a three-year-old who'd just spilled catsup on the carpet. "I can assure you that I was not offering to do it myself, Lieutenant Cantrell," she said. "I will, however, send for a manservant if you desire assistance."

"I can dress myself," Eddie said, wishing she would just go away. Was it really possible to die of embarrassment? "Been doing it for years," he added in English.

"They say it is different in Grantville," Anne Cathrine said in a breathtaking change of subject. "For women, that is. They say your women can choose whom they will marry."

"Yes," Eddie said cautiously. Sweat beaded on the back of his neck.

"I should like to see a place like that," Anne Cathrine said. Her fingers fiddled with the white lawn shirt she'd brought, aligning the seams as though it mattered. "Later, after you speak to Papà's councilors, I wish for you to tell me all about this Grantville, with its wonderful clockwork carriages and flying machines."

"Sure, sure," Eddie mumbled. "Just let me get dressed."

"Oh." She nodded. "Very well." She turned to the maid. "Put the crutch where he can reach it, Gudrun."

The maid, a tiny dark-haired girl no older than the king's daughter, scurried forward, leaned the crutch against Eddie's bed, curtsied, then fled. Anne Cathrine followed, skirts rustling, glancing wistfully at him over one shoulder. "Promise you will tell me about the future."

"Yes, whatever!" Eddie said.

The door closed and he collapsed back against his pillows, drenched in nervous sweat. Now he needed to take that darned bath all over again, and he could just bet the water was as cold as the December air outside his window.

He thought of Anne Cathrine's blue eyes, the exact shade of the winter sky, and her supple young figure, then sighed. Maybe a cold bath wouldn't be such a bad idea after all.

The trip down to the king's audience chamber was arduous. Unfortunately, his room was at the top of one of the castle's towers. Eddie hadn't tried walking with a crutch until now. He'd asked for one, for a pair of them, actually, weeks ago, but the doctor had refused, finally saying through a translator that he was too weak. Eddie suspected that the real reason for denying him had been that, with crutches, he would be mobile and harder to confine.

Unfortunately, using one wasn't as easy as he hoped. He had a number of narrow winding staircases to negotiate, and in the end, the male servant sent to fetch him had to practically carry him the last few yards. Eddie was soaked in sweat all over again, despite the day's chill.

Just as they reached the audience chamber, he heard voices inside, arguing in German. "We have lost too many ships already, both at Luebeck and Wismar," one of them was saying. "More warships will cost money that Your Majesty's treasury simply does not have!"

"These future people are very clever," the king's voice said. "Think of all the damage done by one roaring little boat and a single air machine. If we could use this prisoner to get access in trade to armaments built in such a style, we might just achieve the edge we need to hold off the Swedes. And if we have even one of these devices in hand, our artisans might then be able to build our own."

"They will never sell us any of these marvels," someone else said in a froggy bass. "They have allied themselves with that wretch Gustavus Adolphus!"

"They were hasty," the king said calmly. "Alliances can change."

"They have no reason to change!" another voice put in. "After our failure at Wismar, we will be lucky to just to keep what we have. Mark my words, the island of Bornholm is at extreme risk! The Swedes have had their eyes on it for years."

Eddie shook off the servant's arm, straightened his back as best he could, and hobbled through the door. King Christian looked up from his thronelike chair at the head of a vast gleaming wooden table. "You are here, Lieutenant Cantrell! Good!" he boomed with his customary good humor. "Now we can get started."

He recognized the king's heir, Prince Christian, a slight thirty-year-old, standing behind the king. The son had come up to the tower, accompanying the king, several times during Eddie's convalescence, but never spoken to him.

The other seats at the table were filled with eight richly dressed men, some old and some merely middle-aged. Only two were anywhere near as young as the prince, and they stared, one and all, at Eddie as though they had a burr under their saddle.

And there was no chair for *him*. He hobbled closer on the single crutch, feeling horribly unbalanced. The thought of tripping and putting any weight on that still-healing stump was terrifying. Black dots shivered behind his eyes like the blobs in a lava lamp, merging and merging until he could hardly see. The room seemed to be buzzing. He reeled, then felt strong hands easing him into a chair.

After a moment, his vision cleared and he realized the minister seated closest to the king had surrendered his place to Eddie and was now glaring at him from a few paces away. Embarrassed, he tried to get up, but Christian himself pushed Eddie back as the servants brought another chair for the displaced man.

"No, no," Christian said. The icy eyes were intent. "You have not much strength yet. Americans are not as hardy as Danes. I should have realized."

A servant wearing the black royal livery pressed a goblet of hot mulled wine into Eddie's trembling hands. "Drink!" Christian said heartily, then upended his own golden goblet and clanked it down on the table. Drops of red wine glistened in his beard as a manservant hastened forward to refill the empty cup.

Eddie's dad had been an alcoholic, so on the whole, he avoided the stuff, but he sipped the wine. It was deliciously hot and heady and burned all the way down. After a moment, he did feel a bit better. His heart stopped racing and his hands shook less.

"Now," Christian said, leaning toward Eddie. "Grantville. Tell us how to defeat your navy. How many more of those deadly little boats do you have? How many flying machines?"

The Outlaw power boat, now reduced to fiberglass splinters floating in Wismar Bay, had been a one-off, though Grantville had a few other power boats, none as big. They were building more planes back home, but he wasn't sure how that was going. Parts were of course limited to what had come back through the Ring of Fire with them, and anyway he'd been too busy helping with the construction of the ironclads in the Magdeburg shipyards.

He just wished he could be there when the first ironclad met Christian's navy and blew it out of the water.

"Lieutenant Cantrell!" Christian's florid face with its fussy goatee hovered inches from his nose. "Are you well enough to speak now?"

It would be easier to say no, to plead infirmity and retreat back to his bed, but, dammit, Eddie'd had enough of lying about, staring at the stupid ceiling. He was ready to do something, anything, even if it was just sparring wits with royalty.

"Yes, Your Majesty," he said and took another sip of the heady wine. "I am fine."

"The little boats that dash about in the water, then." The king gazed at him expectantly and Eddie noticed that, despite being bloodshot, those chill eyes were very intelligent. "How many?"

When he'd first been captured, he'd raised the issue of the Geneva Convention, refusing to give more than his name and rank, professing to have forgotten his serial number, though the truth was that he'd never been issued one. That had worked at the time, but now misinformation and misdirection might help Grantville more than his continued silence.

"Twenty," Eddie said off the top of his head and saw the councilors stiffen. A murmur ran through the room. "More or less. How long have I been here?"

"It has been two months since you were plucked out of the sea," Christian said and sat back in his gem-encrusted chair, thinking.

"Oh, then it's probably more," Eddie said and squirmed until he was sitting up straighter. Maybe if he told a big enough lie, they would think twice before attacking American and Swedish forces again. "We, um, build at least"—he was tempted to say "ten" but decided that would make it seem too implausible—"five or six a month."

"I . . . see." The king's tone was frankly disbelieving.

"We have over three thousand 'engines,' which we use to power machines like speed boats and airplanes, in Grantville," Eddie said. "I'm not sure how many have been allocated to the speed boat program, the airplane program, and other . . . projects. I'm just a lieutenant. They don't tell me everything."

"Three thousand?" echoed around the table. Chairs shifted uneasily. Startled glances were exchanged.

"We have calculating machines called 'computers' that help in their design," Eddie said. "And we have made some improvements lately in what we call 'software.' The new boats will be faster, and we should have a lot more of them."

"We have sent spies to Grantville," the king said, "and to the shipyards at Magdeburg. As far as we can tell, they are building very large ships with no sails at Magdeburg, nothing else. How can you explain that no one has seen any evidence of more deadly little boats anywhere?"

"They're . . . ah, in a building, hidden away," Eddie said. A drop of cold sweat rolled down his temple.

"Do you know this secret location?"

"Y-e-s," Eddie said, drawing the word out as he thought furiously.

"If we captured some of these 'engines,' " the king said, "could we build our own deadly little boats as well?"

"It wouldn't do you any good," Eddie said. "They require an energy source that you do not have, and anyway you would need what we would call a 'technician' to build, then service them." He gave the word in English.

The king pushed to his feet and loomed over Eddie. "Are you one of these 'technicians'?"

"No, I was just a 'pilot,'" Eddie said, "what I guess you would call a 'helmsman.'" The wine was potent, much stronger than any that he'd ever tried. He could feel it all the way down to his toes, even the ones that weren't there. He gazed morosely at his truncated leg, masked by the lame stocking they'd provided for him to wear under knee-length black trousers. He hoped the guys back in Grantville never got a gander at him dressed like this. "Or at least I was a pilot. Don't imagine I'd be good for much like this."

"You will mark for me a map!" Christian said. "Showing the location where these 'engines' of yours are built, so that we can send an expedition to acquire some for ourselves. And we will need to know more about this mysterious 'energy source.'"

"Sure, sure," Eddie said in English. "Whatever. It will be a waste of time, though. They will have moved the facility by now so that I can't give them away." The room was spinning again. The wine had gone to his head. He should have been more careful in his weakened condition. Well, what the hell. This was the best he'd felt since that terrible day in the bay. He upended the goblet and took another fortifying swig.

The king gave some commands in Danish that Eddie couldn't follow, then the ministers talked to one another in their native language.

At length, just when Eddie's eyelids were growing very heavy, Christian turned back to him and pushed a large map across the table. "Now, show us the location of these 'engines' at the time of your capture."

Eddie tried to make his eyes focus on the crude map of Grantville, with the high school and other major buildings indicated. "Right here," he said, trying not to slur his words. He stabbed his finger on the outskirts of town, pointing to the sketched-in square that he was pretty sure occupied the same space as Grantville's *Value Mart* in real life. It was a big retail building with a large area in the back for storage that wasn't accessible to customers. That might do the trick, unless the Danes could get a spy into the employees-only area.

An advisor made a careful X.

"And we will need at least one of your 'technicians,' " King Christian said, "who could construct and then operate one of these 'engines.' Give us a list of names."

A cold chill penetrated Eddie's increasingly hazy mind, then shivered down his back. He couldn't give them real names. Dimly, he was aware that he'd screwed up big-time. Jeez, couldn't he do anything right?

"Um, there's . . . " He tried to cudgel his useless brain to think. "Walt Disney and, ah, Harpo Marx. And Clint Eastwood. They're all pretty—you know—good at what they do."

One of the ministers scribbled down the names, asking Eddie for the details of the spelling. Christian looked satisfied, like an immense cat that had cornered a mouse. "It may not be necessary to actually infiltrate Grantville. Although ransom is usually paid in money, your king seems to value you highly for one of your rank. Perhaps he will be amenable to trading a 'technician' and one of these 'engines' along with its 'energy source' in order to ransom you."

Oh, yeah, Eddie thought as the room swooped around him in lazy circles, that was just so likely to happen.

Back in his room, once his head stopped spinning, Eddie was aghast at his stupidity. Eventually the king was going to find out there was no speed boat construction program. He'd think Eddie had made a fool out of him, and people who incurred the displeasure of monarchs didn't last long in this century. Outside, sleet rattled against the window and he shivered.

Lying on his bed, he folded his arms behind his head and wondered if they did that gruesome "draw and quarter" thing here in Denmark. In the movies, it always looked—

The door opened without preamble. Anne Cathrine peered in, then entered, wine-colored skirts rustling. "My papà was very pleased with your interview this morning."

Eddie struggled up into a sitting position. Even that was hard without two legs to push. "I'll bet," he muttered in English.

"He says, if you will give your parole, you may now have the freedom of the grounds." She stood before the fireplace, studying the guttering flames with a critical eye. "This is disgraceful. I will have it tended immediately."

"My 'parole,'" Eddie said. "What does that mean?"

"That you will not try to escape."

Eddie thought of trying to return to Grantville, one-legged, in the dead of winter, through hostile territory and without a single coin to his name. "Sure," he said, then added, "like I even had a prayer of getting away," in English.

"I so wish to learn your language!" She smiled and he saw that she had dimples. "They say you have books from the future in your city. If I knew this American tongue, I could perhaps read them one day." She pulled up a straight-backed chair and settled on it beside the bed. "It must be very wonderful, this future, with great clockwork birds you can ride through the sky."

"Airplanes," Eddie said and swung his foot over the side of the bed. "We call them airplanes."

Papà, it seemed, approved of Anne Cathrine learning English, or, as she termed it, American. Eddie suspected that she wasn't really supposed to spend time alone with him in his room, but so far no one had objected. Just to be on the safe side, though, he scheduled her language lessons down in the king's library.

Fortunately, she had tons of brothers and sisters so she wasn't exactly the center of attention. She'd explained to him that the king had fathered six children by his first marriage, including her half-brother, Prince Christian, who would inherit someday, and his younger brothers, the princes Frederik and Ulrik, also in line for the throne. Then there were twelve more children by Anne Cathrine's mother, Kirsten Munk, though several of those had been stillborn.

And now the king had a new mistress, some doe-eyed woman, not much older than Anne Cathrine, named Vibeke Kruse. The woman behaved abominably at every opportunity to all of Kirsten Munk's children, but especially to Anne Cathrine. The king, however, seemed infatuated with her.

Court politics were darned convoluted here at
Rosenborg, and Eddie didn't think he would ever get all
the pedigrees of the royal progeny straight. It was a little
like one of those television soap operas his mom had
used to watch, he decided, only a lot more complicated.

The ransom letter had been sent to Grantville. Eddie
wanted to beat his head against the wall every time he
thought about it. How could he have been such an idiot?
Even though he doubted it, still there might have been
some possibility folks back there could ransom him if he
hadn't set up an impossible situation.

The whole thing was insane anyway. When that letter
arrived, they were sure to think he'd lost his mind. And
maybe he had. Being shut up in this Danish nuthouse,
and one-legged on top of that, was enough to make anyone stir-crazy.

As near as he could tell, there was no such thing as a
wheelchair around here, and certainly nothing like
wheelchair access, even if there had been. The whole
castle was full of steps from one end to the other, and
most of them narrow winding ones at that. He was more
limited by his lack of mobility than he was by his status
as a prisoner-of-war.

At least Anne Cathrine was helping him with his Danish, so that every day he could understand just a little
more of what was said around him. And since he continued to communicate to everyone else only in German
and didn't let on that his command of Danish was
improving, he heard more than anyone realized.

King Christian was effusive every time he saw Eddie,
soliciting the American's opinion on where to build the
royal engine factory, how many Eddie thought they could

produce in the first year, and urging him to better explain this mysterious energy source. He also talked endlessly of Grantville's alliances, who was in charge, what sort of men they were, and how they had come to rely on that dastard Gustavus Adolphus. They could do better, Christian seemed to imply. Perhaps some of his fellow residents in Grantville might like to come and work for the Danes, sharing their advanced knowledge. Could Eddie inquire for such people, once he returned home?

Eddie did his best to answer without giving anything important away, working to create the impression that Grantville was a cohesive community with everyone pulling together for the common good. It was difficult, because the king seemed to see through everything he said and divine the truth of the matter, even when Eddie didn't think he was telling it.

One thing was for sure, the king drank even more as the winter progressed. Though he never appeared drunk, he always had a drinking bowl or goblet at hand. That made Eddie wary. Back home, before the Ring of Fire, his old man had known how to put it away too, and he'd been a mean, heavy-handed drunk, prone to smacking his family around.

One morning, when they met for Anne Cathrine's lesson, he asked her, as diplomatically as possible, if her father had always imbibed so much. She thought about it for a moment, her young forehead creased. "Yes, Papà is almost as fond of spirits as he is of young women," she said finally. "How would you say that in American?"

Anne Cathrine was wearing a gown of patterned blue silk today, which set off her eyes. Sometimes, when they were working together, he got lost in that pale gaze and couldn't remember what they were talking about.

"We would say 'he likes to tie one on almost as much as he likes to chase skirts,'" Eddie said.

"'Tie—one—on'?" Anne Cathrine repeated, her expression intent. Her accent was thick, but improving. She folded her hands on the table and leaned toward him. "I understand the reference to 'skirts,' but the tying part does not make sense. In what regard does 'drinking' involve 'tying'? Perhaps they do it differently in Grantville."

Before Eddie could answer, the king's elderly secretary, Anders Larsen, burst into the library. A great blob of a man tricked up in dark-red velvet, his eyes widened when he saw the two young people seated at one of the tables. "Lieutenant Cantrell! You are summoned to the king's chambers at once. A letter from Grantville has arrived."

"Wonderful!" Anne Cathrine handed Eddie his crutch, then bounded to her feet. "Now Papà will get one of your engines. Then we can build deadly little boats for our navy. We will be able to defend ourselves against wicked King Gustavus Adolphus, and you will go home to your family!"

"Not bloody likely," Eddie muttered in English, forgetting that the princess could understand a great deal of what he said these days.

She halted at the threshold and stared at him. "You think not?"

"I am not important enough for such a trade," he said, then felt a hot flush creep up his neck.

"But you were so brave in the battle," Anne Cathrine said. "Papà told me how you sank one of our ships all by yourself even after you were badly injured. Surely your king values you?"

Eddie ducked his head and followed Larsen's lumbering form to the door and then down all the steps to the first floor. He had a flash of that excruciating day, of the moment when he'd looked behind him and seen his friends bloodied and dead. Sweat broke out on his forehead. He shuddered. Brave. "Yeah, right," he mumbled.

The king looked up from a sheaf of papers when Eddie hobbled into his study. It was a sumptuous room, full of expensive woods, precious ceramic vases and burgundy velvet draperies. Even the blasted ceilings had fancy paintings on them, when you thought to look up, and the andirons in the massive fireplace appeared to be gold. He glanced out the windows and saw it was snowing again. As far as he could tell, that was what it did best in these parts.

"Sit! Sit!" Christian waved a careless hand at a stool and Eddie eased onto it gratefully, laying his crutch on the floor within reach.

The king's hair had its customary wispy little plait, called an "elflock," and a pearl earring gleamed in one ear. His clothing was black and red today, trimmed in black fur. It looked warm.

"I will read for you the letter," the king said and cleared his throat.

"Most gracious King Christian IV,

"We send you greetings. We are of course delighted that Lieutenant Cantrell, serial number 007, has recovered from his injuries sufficiently to be repatriated. We thank you for following the Geneva Convention and the excellent medical attention you have granted him.

"As for your offer to ransom him in exchange for one of our engines and a technician to instruct you in its use, we must regretfully decline. Our entire inventory of engines has been sent to His Majesty Gustavus Adolphus to aid in his preparation for defense in the coming year. None of the three men you mentioned are available, unfortunately. Herr Disney and Herr Marx are much too old to travel, and Herr Eastwood was killed in a duel recently.

"Is there not some other fee to liberate Lieutenant Cantrell that we might mutually agree upon? We send you this viewing instrument as a token of our good faith. It has come to you all the way from the future. Lieutenant Cantrell can instruct you in its use.

"Respectfully,

"Michael Stearns, Prime Minister, United States of Europe"

Prime Minister, Eddie thought, not President. And what was "the United States of Europe"? The last he knew, Grantville and the New United States had been part of the Confederated Principalities of Europe.

So things had changed, and apparently in a major way. He felt a sudden wave of homesickness.

Christian laid down the letter. "So." He frowned. "It seems Our enemy, Sweden, is to have its own fleet of fast little boats powered by these Grantville 'engines.'"

Sweat trickled down Eddie's spine. At least Stearns had understood and was playing along with his ruse. It was to their advantage for Christian to think they had tons of power boats in reserve.

"That does present a dilemma." The royal fingers fiddled with his lacy collar. "We shall have to give the matter careful thought." The king picked up something from the desk behind him and held it out to Eddie. "This is what came with the letter, some sort of far-seeing device, yes?"

It was a pair of binoculars, Boy Scout issue. Eddie'd had a pair of his own years ago. These had been shined up until the metal gleamed, but they were still undersized, obviously meant for a kid, and, by the battered look of them, had done time on any number of camping expeditions.

He took them from the king, turning them over reverently. "Well, Your Majesty," he said carefully, "Prime Minister Stearns certainly spared no expense. These are the finest binoculars I've ever seen."

"Binoculars?" Eddie had expected the Danish king to stumble over the English term, but he had no trouble with it. Belatedly, he realized the word was actually Latin in its origins and Christian, like most educated people in the seventeenth century, had a much better knowledge of the ancient language than any up-timer did.

The king examined the binoculars with interest. "Two telescopes combined, in other words. What is the advantage?"

"Come over to the window and I will show you." Eddie handed the binoculars back to the king and laboriously maneuvered upright on his one foot. He always felt so awkward these days. He'd never been particularly graceful before, but just walking without having to think about every single step seemed like it should have been such a pure joy. He wished he'd paid more attention to how great it was to be whole when he'd still had two feet.

Using his crutch, he hobbled over to the window. The study looked down on the a wide expanse of flower beds and trees, all now rather bare with winter almost arrived.

He put the binoculars to his eyes, made some adjustments, then smiled as the scene below came into focus. A horseman was riding toward the castle and he could even make out the auburn of the man's hair, the green of his jacket. This pair might be well worn, but they still worked just fine. He handed them back to the king. "Look toward the oncoming rider, your Majesty," he said. "If the view is not clear, turn this dial a little." He pointed at the top of the binoculars.

Christian gazed through the lenses, then inhaled explosively. "Magnificent!" he boomed, and Eddie could smell the beer on his breath. "I am familiar with telescopes, but their image is flat. This is like standing next to what you see!"

Eddie hobbled back to his stool and sat down, easing his stump out before him. Whenever he was standing, he was always terrified someone was going to bump into it or knock him into the furniture. Barely healed, it was still very tender.

The king's unsettling light-colored eyes regarded Eddie shrewdly, then he handed off the binoculars to his secretary. Christian reached for a bowl of beer on his desk, upended it and drank noisily. "If our positions were reversed, I would not send an 'engine' to my enemies either," he said, more to himself than anyone in the room. "These Grantville people are not fools." He stared moodily over Eddie's head.

The air crackled with uncertainty. The secretary glared at Eddie as if it were all his fault, while Eddie pictured himself relegated to the dungeon, clapped in irons, fed bread and water, and damned little of that.

Finally, the king sighed. "So what other secrets do these people from the future possess? If I am not to have an 'engine,' then what other wonders can your people provide?"

Eddie's head spun as though he'd drunk too much of that beer himself. What to ask for that wouldn't hurt the war effort? Automatic rifles? A truck? Radios? Down-timers were clever and often just needed a hint of the right direction in order to make use of future technology. He couldn't think of anything that wouldn't come back to bite them in the end.

"Your Majesty, they have rifles that can strike targets from a great distance," the secretary, Larsen, said. "One such weapon nearly killed Wallenstein at Alte Veste last year, and it is so light, they say it was even fired by a woman."

"A woman?" Christian dropped onto his thronelike chair and regarded Eddie. "Is this true, Lieutenant Cantrell?"

"It was Julie Sims. A young woman very gifted at shooting," Eddie said cautiously. "She used a special long-range rifle with sights that let you see faraway, like your gift."

Christian picked up the binoculars again, and turned them over, studying the glass lenses. "Then, perhaps our own gunsmiths could take this device apart and craft such sights."

Eddie was afraid he was right. The technology for grinding that grade of lenses was not out of reach for the tools of this era.

On the other hand, this could keep the Danes busy for a while. The longer King Christian's attention was diverted from attacking the United States of Europe, which included Grantville, the stronger they would be when that attack finally came. Once the ironclads were launched, everything would be different. "Yes, Your Majesty," he said, schooling his expression to polite encouragement.

"In the meantime," Christian said, "we shall write and require one of those rifles as your ransom." He cocked a dark eyebrow at Eddie. "Your life should be worth at least that much, do you not think?" He lounged back in his chair like a great bear, thinking. "They should send us one of your gunsmiths, too, to advise us. Who is the most accomplished among your firearms craftsmen?"

The secretary stared at him with expectant eyes, as did Anne Cathrine and the king. Eddie tried to think. Grantville wasn't going to send anyone here to take his place, no matter who he named. He gazed at his hands, scarred from the wounds he'd taken at the Bay of Wismar. "I think," he said slowly, "Elvis Presley would be your man."

"I shall miss you," Anne Cathrine said the next morning, when they met in the library for her American language lesson. "Once Herr Presley arrives and you are sent back to Grantville." Her eyes suddenly filled with tears. "I wish I could go with you and meet your women! It is so hard to believe that they do as they like!"

"That's how things were in the future," Eddie said, unsettled by her distress. Truth be told, if it weren't for the fact that he knew his claims were bogus and he wouldn't be leaving any time soon, he'd be unhappy himself at not seeing the girl again.

He pulled out a chair at the long table and eased onto it. "What's wrong? Has something happened?"

She dabbed at her eyes with a lacy handkerchief. "Forgive me, Lieutenant. I did not mean to behave so disgracefully. Perhaps we should cancel our lesson today."

She stood to leave and Eddie caught her hand in his before he thought. "No," he said, then flushed as his fingers closed around hers. "Tell me. What's wrong?"

Anne Cathrine sank back into her chair, her posture very straight. "It is that horrid man, Dinesen. He has asked my father for my hand in marriage."

"Dinesen?" Eddie tried to think. "You mean that balding guy with the chicken-neck and bad teeth?"

"He is one of Papà's closest advisors," she said. Her eyes, tinged with red, looked over his shoulder. "And he is not just a nobleman. He owns the largest shipyard in all Denmark. He builds some of Papà's ships and is quite rich."

"Your father hasn't said yes, has he?"

"No, but he will," Anne Cathrine said. "I have already lost one fiancé, though it was not my fault that the idiot bet my brothers that he could swim the moat." She sniffed. "Frantz was always a show-off. I liked him, though."

She stopped, though Eddie could tell she had more to say. "Also," she said finally, "my mother was not noble, and she behaved quite badly. Mistress Sehested, my governess, says that I am fortunate that someone such as Dinesen would have me."

Eddie leaned forward. "I don't understand. What did your mother do that was so bad?"

More tears brimmed in the girl's blue eyes. She lowered her voice and spoke slowly in English, evidently not wanting to be overheard. "She had a lot of . . . gentlemen friends, one in particular. A German cavalry officer. He was quite handsome, and I fear Mamà was . . . " She bit her lip, then switched back to German, evidently lacking the English vocabulary. "Indiscreet."

"Oh." Eddie sat back. His mind whirled. "That's a bummer, but what does it have to do with you, especially now that she's gone?"

"Mistress Sehested says I come from 'bad stock,' that I will be no better than Mamà was, like a 'cat in heat.' Already, she says, I spend far too much time with—" She broke off and her cheeks flushed.

"With me," Eddie finished for her. He felt his own cheeks warm. Anger surged through him and he struggled onto his remaining foot, supporting himself against the massive table. What he wouldn't give to punch Mistress Sehested right in the middle of her aristocratic snout!

"But you can't marry an old goat like Dinesen!" He almost lost his balance, then sat down again. "That would be utterly—bogus!"

Anne Cathrine's depthless blue eyes regarded him, then her nose crinkled and she was laughing through her tears. "An 'old goat,' yes!" she exclaimed in German.

"That is exactly what he looks like with that stringy little beard!"

"An 'old goat' you are fortunate to have, young lady," a female voice came from the threshold. "And you will not even have that much, if you are heard speaking in such an outrageous fashion."

Eddie turned to see Anne Cathrine's governess, Mistress Sehested, standing in the doorway. Still in her late twenties, she was regarded as a handsome woman throughout the court, though her expression was perpetually severe. Today, she was dressed in turquoise satin, and the cut was fine as any he'd seen in the palace. Her face was tight with anger.

"How can you even think of letting that man paw Anne Cathrine?" he demanded.

"She will do her duty," Mistress Sehested said, "as do we all. But I expect a commoner like you would know nothing about that."

Eddie's hand went to his stump, concealed in a baggy fold of hose. "Now, there you are wrong," he said, holding his head high. "I do know a bit about doing one's duty, however hard it gets."

The woman followed Eddie's gaze down to his truncated leg. "Any peasant can get in the way of a cannon ball. There's nothing noble about that." She stared at Eddie coldly. "Anne Cathrine, your presence is requested by your father." Then she left with a sweep of her full skirts.

"You should not anger her like that." Anne Cathrine's voice was only a whisper. Her fingers wrung the wet lace of her handkerchief. "She never forgets a slight, nor fails to remedy such."

"Neither do I," Eddie said, and was surprised at the steel in his own voice.

Three weeks later, the answer to the king's latest missive arrived from Grantville. Christian summoned him to the royal study.

Anne Cathrine was already present, head bowed, very subdued since the king had accepted Dinesen's petition for her hand in marriage. Her half-brothers, Princes Christian and Frederick, stood at the back of the room.

The King pulled the single sheet of creamy paper out of the envelope and read:

"Most gracious King Christian IV,

"We send you greeting, with renewed good wishes for your health and that of your family.

"Again, we are glad for word of Lieutenant Cantrell's continuing recovery. We hope to see him safe in Grantville in the near future.

"Upon receipt of your letter, we dispatched Herr Presley along with a long-range rifle, complete with telescopic sights, to Denmark, but word has reached us that he fell prey to bandits and the gun was lost. We have sent troops to recover the weapon, and rest assured that when it is found, we will send it promptly to you.

"In the meantime, please accept our regrets for the delay and tell Lieutenant Cantrell that his betrothed, Miss Marilyn Monroe, remains in good health.

"Respectfully,

"Michael Stearns, Prime Minister, United States of Europe"

An involuntary snort escaped Eddie. He tried to muffle it with a faked sneeze. Marilyn Monroe? Mike was really getting into the spirit of things.

"You are betrothed?" King Christian motioned him forward, so Eddie hobbled with his crutch across the inlaid wood floor. He was steadier now than he'd been even a week ago and moved with more assurance. The monarch's cold blue eyes studied him. "She is very beautiful, this Monroe woman?"

Eddie looked at his boot. "Some people think so," he said.

"Then We wish you joy," the king said, "when you return home."

"Uh, thanks," Eddie said.

Anne Cathrine gave him a strange look, then left in a flurry of rustling silk. Eddie's heart gave a lurch. She seemed upset.

"It is unfortunate about the rifle," Christian said, appearing not to notice. "I was looking forward to having it duplicated."

Balanced on his single foot, Eddie sighed. "Bandits have been a problem since we came here from the future." He moved several steps closer. "Have your craftsmen been able to reproduce the lenses from the binoculars yet?"

Christian scowled. "No. I have summoned a lens grinder from Amsterdam. Once he arrives, then We will see."

Mike Stearns had taken a calculated risk in sending the binoculars, Eddie thought. Just because the technology to make such things didn't exist here yet, that didn't mean people of this era weren't smart. With a good example of what could be accomplished, they would figure the process out.

As for himself, he wasn't fooled by that letter. No high-power rifle had been sent to Denmark. There were no bandits. Stearns was stalling. He had something in mind, some plan, even if it was just to put off Christian indefinitely while Gustavus Adolphus built up his forces and moved men and resources into place.

All Eddie could do to help was play along. He would never see Grantville again, never go home, but, so far, it seemed he was the only person in Denmark who knew it.

Anne Cathrine did not come for her language lesson the next day or the next. Finally Eddie sought her out in the apartments she shared with her sisters.

A young maid opened the door, then stared at Eddie, her mouth frozen in an "O."

"Please say that Lieutenant Edward Cantrell is here to see Anne Cathrine," he said in Danish, the words awkward on his tongue.

The door closed in his face and he was left teetering on his one foot and feeling stupid. Voices sounded from within, muffled and unintelligible. Finally, the door opened again. Anne Cathrine stood before him, stiff and proper, as though they hadn't spent hours and hours together.

She inclined her head. As always, her red-gold hair was beautifully braided, but her cheeks were pale, almost as though she'd been sick. Her gown was dark green and very formal with tons of laces and gold and velvet trim. "What's up, dude?" she said carefully in English.

Eddie had to stifle a laugh. "I was worried," he said in Danish. "You did not come for your lessons."

Mistress Sehested's voice spoke sharply behind her in the royal apartments. Anne Cathrine glanced over her shoulder, then edged out into the hallway and closed the heavy oak door. "I am very busy at the moment," she said. "I have fittings for my wedding dress and . . . " Her voice trailed off and she bit her lip.

"He's really going to make you do it, then," he said, "marry that old goat?"

"Dinesen is quite . . . zealous on the subject of our union." A tear trailed down her wan cheek. "He asked Papà to move up the wedding date, so I am afraid I have no more time for American lessons."

"You can't marry him!" Eddie said in English. "It just isn't right!"

"But you are to be married too," the girl said and brushed away her tears with the back of her hand. "To this Marilyn Monroe."

"Oh, that." Eddie glanced around, but they were alone in the shadowy hallway. He could hear the wind howling outside. "Prime Minister Stearns doesn't know it yet, but Marilyn and I are calling that off."

Her blue eyes widened. "You are breaking your betrothal?"

"She's, um, in love with someone else," Eddie said, "this guy named John Kennedy. I'm not going to stand in their way. We just haven't announced it yet. In Grantville, we consider it immoral to marry someone you don't love."

"But," she said softly, "what about duty?"

"The pursuit of happiness is a duty," he said. "Marriages made without love and respect don't last. Just look at your mother and father."

"But Papà did love her," Anne Cathrine said. "He was so unhappy when she turned away from him."

Eddie remembered his own mother, who had stayed with an alcoholic husband when good sense would have dictated otherwise. "I will never marry anyone I don't love, and who doesn't love me back," he said. "And neither should you."

"But I have to do as I am bid."

"Not if you lived in Grantville," he said. He thought of Sharon Nichols, Julie Mackay, and Melissa Mailey. They could all explain this so much better than he ever could. "I wish I could take you there."

"As do I." Her blue eyes shone with unshed tears.

Eddie thought for a moment. "Isn't there anything about this Dinesen that would make your father change his mind, some secret, perhaps?"

"He and Papà have been drinking companions for a long time," Anne Cathrine said. "His wife died in childbirth two years ago, and, when we are in the same room, he looks at me as though he could consume me like a hot apple pastry." She shuddered. "I barely know the man, and never wanted to."

"Then we'll have to make something up," Eddie said. "Leave it to me. I've always been good at whoppers. I had to be, growing up in my family."

" 'Whoppers?' " Her eyebrows rose in question.

"Lies," he said in German. He heard footsteps at the other end of the hall. "I'm going to rearrange the truth a little."

She patted at her skirts, smoothing nonexistent wrinkles with trembling hands. "Do you think it will make a difference?"

"I don't know," he said, "but we can at least give it our best shot."

Eddie lay in bed that night and cudgeled his brain for ideas. What would make the king dislike Dinesen so much that he would boot the wretch out of court, much less out of Anne Cathrine's life? He thought back through all the rumors about royal goings-on that he'd heard since being delivered here one-legged and half-dead in October. Anne Cathrine's mother had evidently carried on in a quite scandalous fashion with a German cavalry officer until, three years ago, Christian had banished her from Copenhagen. What if—?

He turned over and huddled beneath the warm quilts, a tiny germ of a plan forming in his mind. Maybe, for once, his dreams would be good.

"Okay," he told Anne Cathrine in the library the next day, "all you have to do is play along."

"But it is not true," Anne Cathrine said. She had dressed in wine-colored silk and it flattered her naturally fair complexion.

"Heck, three quarters of the things I hear every day here aren't true," Eddie said. He breathed in the scent of fine leather and old paper from the surrounding shelves and shelves of books. "That doesn't keep anyone from saying them."

She bit her lip and nodded. Her red-gold hair was coiled low on her neck today and pinned with a silver ornament. She looked so enticing, he found it hard to concentrate.

"Look, this may not work," he said. "I can't promise anything, but it's worth a try."

The flames crackled pleasantly in the fireplace, and they passed the time then conversing in English until a young apple-cheeked maid came in to remove the ashes. Eddie nodded at Anne Cathrine. "You saw Herr Dinesen go off into the stable with Vibeke Kruse?" he said in Danish, very softly, as though he didn't mean to be overheard.

"He had his arm around her waist!" Anne Cathrine glanced over her shoulder, then leaned closer. "He is my intended, so I am sure there was nothing improper going on, but it looked so—so—"

"Shocking?" he supplied.

"Dinesen would never dishonor my father," she said. "It just would not happen."

"Of course not," Eddie said. "He is the king. Everyone respects that."

Startled, the freckled maid dropped the brush with a clatter, then picked it back up and finished her task. Eddie winked at Anne Cathrine.

They abandoned the library and made their way down to the vast castle kitchens to snag some freshly baked cinnamon cakes. Several cooks were working on the king's midday meal, putting crusts on lamb pies. Anne Cathrine broke off a piece of hot cake and handed it to Eddie, who was balancing on his crutch.

"You must be wrong," he said. "Vibeke Kruse would not allow anyone to—"

Anne Cathrine edged closer. "His hand was, well, let us just say where a gentleman's hand would never be!"

Eddie took a bite of the delicious cake. The cinnamon melted in his mouth. "Did she slap him?"

"No," Anne Cathrine said softly. "She laughed!"

"This is a very bold man you are marrying," Eddie said, struggling with his newly acquired Danish. "He should give you interesting children."

"What kind of children do you think Vibeke Kruse will be having?" Anne Cathrine giggled. Obviously, Eddie thought, despite her initial misgivings, she'd warmed to this business like a trooper.

They left the kitchens under the staring eyes of the two cooks, who gave each other a meaningful glance over the young people's heads.

Anne Cathrine and Eddie made a circuit of the entire castle, gossiping in front of servants at every opportunity. The princess gave an Oscar-worthy performance each time, lamenting the lack of respect for her royal father and the unworthiness of her future bridegroom. When they had exhausted all inside possibilities for an audience, they put on warm cloaks and went out through the snow to the royal stable to chat in the hearing of grooms and stable boys.

The air was crisp and clean, filled with the salt tang of the nearby sea. Snow sifted down from a pewter sky, light and feathery. Eddie hadn't been outside much since his arrival, and it was pleasant to leave the castle, even on one leg. His stamina was improving, and even though he had to rest on a bale of hay after they reached the stable, he felt more like his old self than he had since the attack run in Wismar Bay.

Anne Cathrine stopped in front of a stall and stroked a sleek black mare's nose. "This is my horse," she said.

"Her name is Laila." She turned and looked at Eddie with those marvelous light-blue eyes. "When the weather is better, we could go riding. Then it would not matter about—" She colored, then pointedly turned her gaze away from Eddie's stump.

Eddie had never been much for horses, but he saw her point. On horseback, he wouldn't be lame like he was now. He could move about freely again. "I would like that," he said.

◊   ◊   ◊

They carried on with their plan for several days before they saw any results. Servant girls began to give Dinesen strange looks when he visited the castle, ducking their heads and making sure to remain out of reach. Vibeke Kruse's mood, always mercurial, darkened, and more than one of her maids was seen fleeing her chambers, weeping.

Eddie eavesdropped, whenever he had the opportunity. Most servants did not realize he'd learned much Danish, so they were much freer with their comments than they might otherwise have been.

"I heard he went right into her rooms late at night!" a footman said in passing to a middle-aged seamstress on her way to a fitting. "And he did not leave until the next morning!"

Eddie, hobbling past the pair in the hallway on his crutch, pretended not to understand.

"They say a child will be born in the summer," the seamstress said, clutching her bag of pins, thread, and needles. "And it will not resemble the king!"

"Last time, he sent the unfaithful wretch away," the footman said. "And he is not even married to this one."

"It is a bad business." The seamstress's long face creased. "When the king is angry, everyone suffers. We shall all have to keep out of the way."

Eddie rounded the corner before he could hear more, but smiled to himself. It was working.

King Christian sent for Eddie two days later. A male servant delivered the message, then escorted him from his little tower chamber down to the ornate Winter Room, as though he couldn't be trusted to show up. The servant, an older man named Jens, set a brisk pace and wouldn't look at Eddie.

When Eddie entered the richly appointed room, morning sun was streaming through the windows. Anne Cathrine was already there, standing beside the king's massive chair, along with Prince Christian, Dinesen, Vibeke Kruse and a whole raft of people Eddie didn't recognize. The room smelled strongly of spilled wine as though the king had already tied one on. Cold sweat prickled down Eddie's back. This had all the hallmarks of a set-up.

King Christian drank deeply from a golden goblet, then clanged it down on a side table. "My court has been rife with rumors for the last few days," he said in German. "Wicked rumors."

Eddie did his best to stand up straight, even on one foot, and meet Christian's ice-cold gaze.

"Fortunately, none of them could be substantiated," Christian said. "Yet, still it is troubling."

Busted. All the starch left Eddie's spine. He wanted to sink down on a stool and hold his head in his hands.

Not only had he gotten himself in deep, but he'd dragged Anne Cathrine in with him. Why hadn't he just kept his big mouth shut? He struggled to hold his head high.

"So I interview and ask questions," King Christian said. He glanced over at Vibeke Kruse who smiled back uncertainly. She was wearing a pale-gray dress cut scandalously low in the bodice. "The rumors say Dinesen has been indiscreet with my beloved Vibeke." He picked up the goblet again and pounded it in time with his words. "But this is not true!" Wine splattered the arm of his chair and floor. Servants hastened to wipe it up.

"Of course it is not, Your Majesty!" Dinesen started forward.

Christian held up a hand, his homely face creased in concentration. "But upon inquiry there were other things to be learned."

Dinesen paled. "Whatever you have heard, Majesty, rest assured I have not gone near—"

"There is the disturbing matter of the commissioning of four galleons by Gustavus Adolphus to replace his magnificent *Vasa*, which quite fortuitously sank in his own harbor a few years ago, praise be to God." King Christian took another long draft from his goblet, then held it out to be refilled. "Are We to suppose you have not 'gone near' that either?"

"But that—that—that—I—" Dinesen's mouth hung open.

"Was only business?" The king lurched to his feet. "You put money before loyalty to your monarch, and yet you expect the hand of my precious daughter in marriage?" His volume increased with each word until he was roaring. He dashed the remaining contents of the cup in Dinesen's face and red wine soaked into the linen of the shipbuilder's shirt. "From this moment on, Denmark will sell no ships to our sworn enemy, Sweden!" He turned to several uniformed guards waiting in the corner. "Take him away until I can investigate this further!"

They darted forward and seized Dinesen who was too horrified even to struggle. His face was as white as watered milk. "Your Majesty, please!"

King Christian turned to Anne Cathrine. "I had not thought to find you so like your mother, child," he murmured and touched her face with the tips of his fingers. "It seems you have something of her spirit after all."

"I am sorry, Papà," the girl said, catching his hand and pressing her cheek to it.

He glanced at the rest of the spectators and scowled. "Get out!"

Heart thumping, Eddie turned to go, too, but the king shook his head. "No, young scamp. You also will stay."

The room cleared, with Vibeke leaving last of all and giving both young people a venomous glare. The royal mistress's skirts swished through the door, then it closed behind her. Christian sighed. "Your mother was not all bad, you know, especially at the start." He upended his empty goblet, then gazed at it dolefully.

"She loved you then, Papà. I know she did." Anne Cathrine's voice was strained. She took the goblet and filled it again with dark-red wine from the bottle on the sideboard.

"Once," the king said. "But now is another day." He turned to Eddie. "My daughter tells me that you are not betrothed after all."

"No, sir," Eddie said. "Before I left Magdeburg, Marilyn Monroe's affections had settled upon another, and I released her from her promise. Prime Minister Stearns just is not aware of it yet."

"Very wise," the king said. "Once a woman's affections have altered, not all the tides in the world can turn them back." He picked at a ruby embedded on the arm of his lushly ornamented chair. "We received a new letter from Grantville. Perhaps you would care to read it?" He gestured at an envelope on the sideboard.

Anne Cathrine handed it to Eddie. He pulled the letter out, then read:

"Most gracious King Christian IV,

"We send you greetings. The gunsmith you requested, Herr Elvis Presley, is still missing and feared dead, though occasionally we do hear he has been sighted, so all may not be lost. In the meantime, perhaps we might make some other suitable arrangement to have Lieutenant Cantrell returned to us."

"Respectfully,

"Michael Stearns, Prime Minister, United States of Europe"

"I am not so foolish that I cannot recognize—what is that American expression my son Ulrik explained to me? Yes, 'stalling tactics.'?" Christian said. "So it seems you will be with us for some time yet. That being so, I suggest you consider your behavior more carefully in the future."

The king shook his head. "Vibeke now quite detests you, and with good reason. You behaved badly and will have to watch out for her. I must warn you that she is well skilled in repaying a wrong. On the other side—" He chuckled. "It does no harm for her to be aware how easily she could lose her position here at court, if she ever did choose to . . . " His fingers drummed on the arm of his throne. His pale eyes became icy. *"Misbehave."*

Eddie swayed, and the king waved a careless hand at him. "Sit! Sit, before you fall down and I have to call the royal surgeon to put you back together again. It was hard enough the first time."

Thankful, Eddie limped over to a straight-backed chair by the wall and sank onto it.

"Dinesen is a fool. I knew about the ships for a long time, of course. Business is business. A man must take profit where he can, but I discovered he has been bragging, telling everyone how splendid those other ships will be, better even than the ones he has built for Us, while taking his advancement through marriage to my daughter for granted. He has even been pestering me, seeking favors for his family. I have already grown quite weary of him, and the wedding has yet to take place!

"As for you, daughter." The king turned to Anne Cathrine. "Your willfulness has done you out of a bridegroom, and I have my doubts whether anyone else at court will be willing to take you on after this debacle. Do not think that everyone is as gullible as kitchen helpers and chambermaids."

Flushed, Anne Cathrine stared down and traced the red and gold patterns in the Turkish carpet with the toe of her slipper.

"Still, you are coming of an age when you will have to marry *someone*. I will need to give thought to the matter again."

The king took a long drink of wine, then wiped the residue out of his beard with the back of one hand.

"Now, on the chance that Prime Minister Stearns is telling the truth, we shall send soldiers after this Presley and Our missing long-range rifle." He turned to Eddie. "You will give the captain of my guard a complete description of the rascal's appearance. Especially useful will be anything distinctive about the man."

"Well," Eddie said, seeing a chance not to lie, exactly. "He's very fond of blue suede shoes."

Second Thoughts

Virginia DeMarce

Grantville
October 1634

Noelle Murphy rode into Grantville just before noon. It was well after dusk when she finished the in-box that had been waiting for her. People had started dropping things into it a month earlier, as soon as they found out she was coming back from Franconia. She looked at the note from her mother again. It wasn't very long and was dated right after Judge Tito had decided that Pat Fitzgerald had been married to Dennis Stull all along. Common-law, but married. It was certainly . . . different

. . . to find out that her parents were married to each other.

> *Since I'm living with Dennis now, I decided to stop paying rent on the trailer the end of this month and gave your key back to Huddy Colburn's office. We cleaned it out and moved the things that were in your bedroom over to his ma's house, so they'll be there when you get back. Most of the time, he's working in Erfurt. Love.*

It was a very "Mom" kind of note, Noelle thought. It brought up an interesting question. She got up and went down the hall to Tony Adducci's office. Normally, a field auditor in the Department of Economic Resources wouldn't just drop in on the Secretary of the Treasury of the State of Thuringia-Franconia, but he was, after all, her godfather. And it was after regular business hours.

"Tony?" she asked. "Ah. Mom's given up the trailer. Where am I supposed to sleep tonight?"

She handed him the note.

Tony looked at it for a while, thinking. "You're welcome to stay with us, of course. I can call Denise and have her put sheets and a blanket on the sofa. But . . ."

He dialed the phone. To his great gratitude and relief, someone picked up on the other end. Someone else who was working late. "Joe, is that you? Can you come over to my office for a few minutes?"

He and Noelle chatted, mostly about the Ram Rebellion. Then a man came in. Noelle looked up as he entered. Not tall, very thick in the neck and chest. He looked more like a bullfrog than anything else she could think of.

Tony got up. "Noelle, I'd, uh, like to introduce you to Joe Stull. He's, um . . ."

She stood up and held out her hand. "The Secretary of Transportation for the state. Dennis' brother. My . . . uncle. I'm . . . I'm glad to meet you, sir."

Tony looked acutely uncomfortable. "He's got a key to Juliann's house. Where your stuff is. He can take you over there, if you'd rather. It makes more sense, in a way, than having you on our sofa, because you'll be in town for a while and that's where they put your things. But you're welcome to stay with us, of course . . . " His voice trailed off.

Joe was shaking Noelle's hand, looking at her. The girl didn't much resemble a Stull. Luckily for her. Medium height, maybe five-four, more blonde than anything else. Broader in the shoulders than Pat Fitzgerald. That might be Dennis' contribution to the finished product or it might just be modern sports. Otherwise, he thought, this was Pat's daughter.

"Sure. I'd be glad to take you over there. Show you where it is. Just let me get my coat. There are extra keys on a pegboard in the kitchen, once we get there, so you can come and go. If that's what you want, just let me call Aura Lee over at city hall. We'll need to stop there and pick her up on the way. Since we live to the east, right at the edge of the Ring of Fire, I had our pickup converted to natural gas early on. There's a natural gas furnace in Ma's house, too, so the place will warm up quickly enough."

"That's very kind of you." Noelle voice was a little stiff. She looked at Tony. "That might be better, really. For me to go on over there. I don't have much luggage with me and I'd love to get into some clothes tomorrow that I haven't been wearing for the last several weeks."

"I hate leaving you on your own."

"That's okay. I've gotten pretty much used to being on my own," Noelle answered.

Joe cleared his throat. "I guess it was pretty much a shock to you to hear that Pat and Dennis, ah, got back together this fall."

She smiled at him. "Not as much as you might think." She paused a minute. "I know where the house is. Actually, I've been there."

Both men looked at her in surprise.

"After Mom rented the trailer here in Grantville—after she gave up the house in Fairmont because Maggy and Pauly and Patty were all on their own and we didn't need another room and we did need money if I was going to go to college—I'd . . . " Her voice trailed off a little. "Well, I'd wonder more about Dennis, sometimes, than I had in Fairmont. And what he had been like. Because, well, because he was . . . "

"Your father." Joe Stull nodded.

Noelle nodded. "And I'd never met him, of course. Because . . . "

"Because he left Pat before you were born." Joe didn't really believe in circumlocutions.

She nodded again. "So I heard that house was where his mother lived. It wasn't that far off the route I took when I walked down to the strip mall. I walked by it several times. And finally, one afternoon—it was the semester I didn't have any classes on Tuesday and Thursday afternoons and Mom was at work, of course—I just stopped in front of it. And walked up to the door and rang the bell. She came to the door and I said, 'Hi, I'm . . .' Then I didn't want to say 'Noelle Murphy,' so I just said, 'I'm Noelle.' And she asked me to come in, so I did."

To say that both men were surprised would have been an understatement.

Not that Joe was surprised that Juliann had never mentioned to any of them that Noelle had come. Ma had been able to keep her own counsel.

"Actually, I, ah, went several times. She said that first time that I was welcome to come back, so I did. I didn't think she'd say it unless she meant it."

Joe nodded. "If Ma said it, she meant it."

"And she was the only person who ever sort of explained it all to me. I mean, you know, when Mom took the older girls to see Paul and Maggie Murphy, I had to wait outside. They wouldn't let me in their house, but nobody really bothered to explain how come. Until Keenan told me it was because I was a 'fucking little bastard.' "

Tony looked down at the floor. "Damn Keenan."

"Well, I was about eight then. And he was a teenager. I was sitting in the car out front while Mom took Maggy and Pauly and Patty in to see them. Wondering why I was always left behind in the car. At least he gave me an answer, which was more than anyone else would. Mom sure never did."

Tony and Joe just looked at her again, Tony thinking that there were probably a lot of things none of the rest of them knew about that had gone into the making of Noelle. Reasons that had contributed to making her so unexpectedly . . . resilient . . . as a field agent, considering how young she was.

Noelle was looking at Joe again.

"Juliann said that Mom and Dennis, over the years, had hurt each other just about as bad as two people could. More than once. That Dennis hurt Mom when he wouldn't believe her about what was happening when he came back from Viet Nam and then again when he wouldn't stay with her unless she divorced Keenan's dad. And she hurt him when she married Francis in the first place and then again when she wouldn't divorce Francis after she got pregnant with me."

Joe nodded, looking at her carefully.

"But she said, too, that they couldn't have hurt each other so much if it hadn't been that they loved each other so much and for so long. That she didn't think they'd ever be able to stop loving each other. And that she still wouldn't be surprised if they got together again if they ever had an opening. So that's why it wasn't so much a shock to me, when Steve and Anita told me what had happened."

She paused and turned to Tony. "Thanks for your letter, by the way. I didn't get it for a long time. It kept following me around Franconia, from one place to another. It was weeks before it caught up. At that, it got to me before Mom's note did. And it explained a lot more than Mom's note did."

All Tony had written was a summary of what Pat had said as she sat on the floor of the funeral home. If Pat had written even less . . . "I don't really know what went

on between them the first time," he said a little uncomfortably. "I wasn't really old enough to know what was
going on."

"Juliann played me a song," Noelle looked at Joe. "She
had a lot of nice old 78s and a turntable that still played
them. I hope nobody got rid of those."

"They're all still there. We haven't done anything to
the house, yet."

Noelle bit her lip. "When you do . . . if you all wouldn't
mind, of course . . . do you suppose that I could have
that record she played for me? As a memento, sort of."

"I don't see why not. What was it?"

"It was on a collection of 'golden oldies' that she'd
ordered from a television advertisement." Noelle started
to hum.

I've got you under my skin.
I've got you deep in the heart of me.
So deep in my heart,
You're nearly a part of me.

"God damn it," Tony shouted, breaking the mood.

The other two looked at him, startled.

"A song with lyrics to match that one that Ron Koch
keeps throwing at me. I've always told him that country
music covers everything." He paused. "Never heard that
one, though."

Noelle shook her head. "Well, it isn't country music.
It's Cole Porter, I think. From some old Broadway musical. Way back in the 1930s."

"Hell," Tony looked disgusted. "Well, I guess a guy
can't have everything. It ought to be country music,
though. It's got the right spirit."

"It's not getting any earlier," Joe interrupted. "We'd better go pick up Aura Lee."

◊ ◊ ◊

Aura Lee looked at Joe. "We can't just leave Noelle in that house with nothing to eat. I don't really want pizza. We'd better stop at Cora's for carry-out." She turned to Noelle. "Billy Lee and our Juliann both have things at school this evening. They won't be finished until nine-thirty or so. That's why Joe and I were both working late. Let's stop for something and we'll eat with you after Joe unlocks the house."

"That's fine," Joe opened the door on the driver's side. "You two stay in the truck. I'll go in and get today's adventure in cuisine. Whatever it may be."

"Thanks," Noelle was grateful. Not only grateful for the company, but she had missed lunch. She had been sort of wondering what to do about supper and not looking forward to going out again by herself once Joe Stull had let her into Juliann's house and found her a key to use.

The house was dark when they pulled up. That was no surprise to her.

It was a surprise that after Joe opened the door, it was warm and there were lights on in the rec room at the back of the little hallway and sound from a television.

Joe paused. "Ah. We'll go on into the kitchen and get the table set. You might want to go on back there, Noelle. Dennis and Pat use the house when they're here rather than in Erfurt."

She walked down the hall, pulling off her hat and suspecting that she had been set up by Tony. She paused at the open doorway. Feeling a little betrayed, but maybe it was better that she hadn't been given a chance to duck it.

A man she couldn't remember ever seeing before was lying on the sofa, his feet up. Her mom was lying next to him, her head on his shoulder. The man was rubbing her mom's temples. She had her eyes closed.

"Excuse me." Noelle rested her hand on the doorframe. "I got Mom's note. The one that said my stuff was here. Joe let me in."

Pat's eyes popped open. She sat straight up on the sofa, folding her hands in her lap.

The man got up. Noelle looked at him. He was a couple of inches taller than Joe Stull—maybe about five-nine. Longer in the neck, not quite so burly in the chest. Gray hair, darker than her mom's shade of gray.

Noelle took a couple steps forward. "Joe and Aura Lee are here. In the kitchen. Aura Lee thought they should get carry-out."

The man grinned. "As long as I have known her, and that's over fifteen years now, Aura Lee has been hungry. We hadn't eaten yet, so that's fine." He held his hand out. "I'm Dennis Stull."

Noelle shook it. "I'm glad to meet you." She hoped that she meant it. Then she sat down and put her arm around Pat's shoulders. "It's all right, Mom. I'm not going to make any kind of a scene."

"Well, brother," Dennis put his feet up on the sofa. The women were washing dishes. "I have to say that you took something of a calculated risk."

"How so?"

"There have been quite a few evenings, when I wasn't quite so bushed as tonight, when I was lying there on the sofa watching the news and massaging various parts of Pat's anatomy that are less suitable for public viewing than her forehead."

"I don't think that Noelle is all that easily panicked. Given the reports we got on the way she handled things with von Bimbach and all that."

"Maybe not. But Pat is. I can tell that she's all upset, even this way, that Noelle walked in on us. Of course, she's way more upset about these hearings over at St. Mary's. She would just as soon have had them over before Noelle got back, I think. That's why I came down. I didn't want her sitting through those, all day, and then coming home to an empty house."

"Noelle would have found out everything anyway."

"Sure. But it's not quite the same thing."

"Noelle isn't going to be sitting there listening to the testimony," Joe pointed out. "She does have a full-time job."

"There's that." Dennis put his feet on the floor and leaned forward on his elbows. "Pat was a little worried by the letter that Noelle wrote her last summer, right after she found out about the shooting. The one that asked if Pat was sure that she knew what she was doing. She's afraid that Noelle doesn't approve of us."

Joe looked at Dennis. "Look, brother. That was nearly three months ago. It has to have been a good-sized shock to the girl when it happened and there's been a lot of water under the bridge since then. She's not made any fuss since she got back to Grantville. She didn't make any fuss this evening."

"That's what I'll remind Pat. But it won't help much. It's been pretty clear that quite a few of the wives of my employees up in Erfurt don't quite approve of us. And all of the discussion about bigamy isn't going to help much. The way most of them see it, either she was married to Francis and committed adultery with me or was married to me and committed adultery with Francis. Six of one and a half dozen of the other. Thank god for Amber Lee and Lorrie."

"What am I going to do about it?" Noelle asked.

"I can't see that it's such a problem," Bernadette Adducci answered.

"It is to me. Now that I know Mom wasn't ever married to Francis Murphy. After all the testimony at the hearings at St. Mary's. Even before the Ring of Fire, there were times that I felt awfully self-conscious about calling myself 'Murphy.' Several times, if I'd had the time and money and had been willing to go through all the hassle of changing my transcripts and stuff, I thought about going into court in Fairmont and asking to have it changed to 'Fitzgerald.' Now, with everything that's been going on, I guess that's not appropriate, either. And anyway . . . Well, I guess we can skip that."

"I can see your point," Tony looked at his wife. "What do you think, Denise?"

"Why not 'Stull'?" she asked.

Noelle shook her head. "Not unless they invite me. It's . . . Well, I don't want them to think that I'm pushy. It's not as if any of them in that family know me, really. I'd just like to get rid of 'Murphy.'?"

Tony scratched his ear. "Let me think about it a bit."

"You could always," Bernadette commented, "get married."

Noelle grinned at her. "Women are keeping their maiden names these days, unless they deliberately ask for a change, so that won't help automatically."

Bernadette shook her head. "Face it, honey. Becoming a nun won't, either. The new order isn't going the 'Sister Mary Anselm' route. If you ever do join up, you'll be stuck with 'Noelle Whoever-you-are' for the rest of your life."

"Even if I did marry and take my husband's name, I still wouldn't want Murphy for a maiden name. There's no one around I want to marry, though."

"Let me think about it a bit," Tony said again.

After Noelle left, Bernadette looked at the other two. "I know the pair of you think I'm being too hard-nosed with her. But did you hear that? 'There's no one around I want to marry, though.' Not, 'I don't want to marry, though.' That there isn't anyone around now is certainly no guarantee that there won't be. She's only twenty-three. I have no intention in the world of letting a situation develop where Noelle is in a religious order when 'anyone' comes along. No matter how firmly I have to put her off. Or how long."

Erfurt
October 1634

"You know what, Dennis?" Amber Lee Barnes looked up from the papers on her desk.

"What?"

"She's triple sharp, that girl of yours. Noelle. We spent all day on accounts. I'm taking her home for supper with me to hash over some more of it, if you and Pat are willing to spare her. I can get the guy downstairs to walk her over to her room when we're done."

"That's fine. Um. She and Pat are having a little trouble finding things to say to each other right now. And it's not as if I really know her."

"Are you going to claim her?" Amber Lee asked.

Dennis looked at her. "What do you mean by that?"

"She's still going by 'Murphy.' Don't you want her to be a Stull? As I said, she's triple sharp."

"I hadn't really thought about it."

"Maybe you ought to," Amber Lee advised.

"She frightens me a little."

"How?"

"When I first saw her standing there in the doorway at Ma's place, I thought she was another Pat. A little taller, a little sturdier, a shade less blonde, but Pat. Until she shook my hand and looked at me with those eyes. Not blue like Pat's. Dark gray. Not judging, exactly. Measuring. Assessing. Evaluating."

Amber Lee examined him. "She's yours, too. Have you ever looked at your eyes in the mirror? Are you going to claim her?"

"The day after the shooting, in the hospital, Joe was wondering if she would be willing to claim me after all these years."

"That's probably what she's evaluating," Amber Lee went back to her paperwork.

"I think we're done." Noelle closed the ledger she had been using. "At least, as done as we can get until we go through some more of the records tomorrow. Bolender, Bell, Cunningham. I knew that I was looking for those names. But with the peculiarities and discrepancies in these requisitions for machine parts, I keep thinking I should add a couple more. Barclay. Myers."

Amber Lee frowned. "Maybe I should talk to my mother about this. I have a feeling that Barclay and Myers have some kind of a family tie, but it escapes me. I don't know either of them, myself. Maybe you ought to ask Scott, too."

Noelle raised her eyebrows.

"Scott Blackwell, my ex. You must have met him when you were down in Franconia."

"Oh. Sure. But why would he know?"

"He and Stan Myers were both in the fire department. And in the National Guard together. So he may know what kind of a person he is. Or I can ask Dennis to do it, if you don't want to. I just feel a little odd about asking Scott myself, now that I've remarried."

"Yeah." Noelle tucked one foot underneath her, making her perch on the high three-legged stool a little precarious. She balanced by leaning one elbow on the podium desk that held the ledger.

"Not that we're on bad terms. We married in '93 and divorced five years later. Married because we were getting to that age and everyone said we were so well suited and every now and then we had sex, which was, errr, nice, because neither of us was having sex with anyone else. And we had known each other a long time and each of us knew that the other one didn't have herpes or genital warts or any of the other nasty STDs to which human flesh is heir. So my parents paid for us to get married with all the usual trimmings. Then after five years and no kids we realized that we bored each other so thoroughly that we could scarcely remember why we got married, so we divorced."

Noelle raised her eyebrows.

"Sorry to disillusion you, kid. Just having a lot in common really doesn't mean that a couple ought to get married. Scott and I tried to make it work. Counseling, various things that were supposed to put the zip back in a marriage like going out on dates, or having getaway weekends. We worked on communication. All that stuff. We bored each other just as much on a date or at a resort as we did at home. We didn't fight. He'd go and find a golf game or head for the library to do homework for his classes and I'd go to the gym and talk to the other aerobics instructors."

Noelle said, "I see." But she didn't.

"I heard he's married again. A German woman. All I know about her is that she works for Veronica Dreeson's schools. I hope he hasn't chosen someone else just because she seems to be suitable. Not again."

"I haven't met her, but she's pregnant, I know. Should be very close to term, by now."

"That's good. But, ah, Sterling still feels a little bad about it all because Scott had a couple years of college and he only has a GED, plus Scott's the top military administrator down in Würzburg and Sterling's just an ordinary soldier, so sometimes he starts worrying that he's a comedown for me. So I'd rather not ask Scott myself. Especially since Sterling's up north in Wismar and I'm here in Erfurt."

"Is he?" Noelle asked.

"Is who what?"

"Is Sterling a comedown?" Noelle asked.

"You don't beat around the bush, do you, honey?"

"Well, I sort of need to know. I expect they're going to send me back to Franconia. We haven't seen the last of this scam yet. So it's better if I figure out where the pitfalls are, if I'll be working with both of you—with you here and with Scott down in Würzburg."

Amber Lee looked at her. "Depends on how you look at it, I suppose. Economically, Sterling's something of a comedown from what I had when I was married to Scott, but not all that much. Scott wasn't a top military administrator back then. He was working as a security guard at night and going to college during the day. In any case, I hadn't been married to Scott for a couple of years before the Ring of Fire and I didn't have alimony or anything. I was self-supporting and not all that high-paid. Then when I got caught in the Ring of Fire, I joined the army as a private. Grantville didn't have much use for aerobics instructors in 1631. That's not high-paid, either."

Noelle nodded.

Amber Lee went on. "Sterling's not a comedown from a personal point of view, for sure. I was married to Scott for five years and never wanted to get pregnant. I was on the pill the whole time. Once I started sleeping with Sterling, I never even tried to get hold of birth control, whatever they have here down-time. I wanted to have a baby as soon as I could. By him. Whether he married me or not. He hadn't said anything about marriage in advance. But he hadn't said anything about birth control, either and he sure wasn't using anything, so I figured that I was playing fair enough. And when I told him, he thought about getting married right away. In fact, he said that he'd been trying to get me pregnant so that I might think about getting married to him. He couldn't believe that I would for any other reason."

Noelle giggled. "Let me not to the marriage of true minds admit impediments."

"What?"

"It's poetry. One of Shakespeare's sonnets. Whenever I'm in Grantville, I get Father Smithson at St. Mary's to read some Shakespeare out loud to me, so I can hear how it would have sounded at the Globe Theater."

"Poetry always left me cold. No matter how much of it they made me read in English class." Amber Lee smiled. "I just wish they'd send Sterling back so I'd have a chance at getting pregnant again. I'm thirty-four, so I don't want to put it off any longer than I have to. But, I suppose, since I'm still nursing the twins and they're only five months old, my chances wouldn't be all that good."

"Oh." Noelle looked at the playpen behind Amber Lee's desk. "They're so sweet. Jamie and Pel, that is. If you need a babysitter while I'm here in Erfurt . . . "

"I may take you up on that. But back to what you asked first, about whether Sterling is a 'comedown.' One thing to keep in mind is that the way you feel about a guy doesn't necessarily make sense to anyone else."

"That is one thing that I've never doubted. Considering the way Mom has run her life."

"Which sort of brings us back to your parents." Amber Lee twisted her braid around her index finger. "I scarcely know Pat. I only met her since Dennis brought her up to Erfurt after Maurice Tito dismissed the divorce case.

But you do know her—grew up with her. As for him . . . Actually, Dennis is a very good boss. One of the best I've ever had. Fair and really concerned about his employees. You might want to give him a chance, so to speak. You might get to like him."

"I'm trying." Noelle unwound her feet and stood up. "I'm trying."

"I'd rather," Noelle put her coffee cup down. "Rather have a place of my own than take up a room in Juliann's house, since you and Mom are using it whenever you're in Grantville. And I'm pretty sure that Mom would rather that I did. Have a place of my own, I mean. Uh. It seems to embarrass her a little having me there when the two of you have . . . ah . . . taken up with each other again. Even if you both spend most of the time here in Erfurt."

Dennis thought, a little reluctantly, that Noelle was probably right about that. Almost certainly right about that. In Erfurt, Noelle was staying in temporary employee housing, to Pat's obvious relief. His place only had one bedroom. It wasn't as if he had needed more than that before Pat came up, so he had let couples with children have the larger apartments.

"The Casa Verde apartments are nice," Noelle went on. "Not as fancy as Casa Blanca, but nice. Almost as new and a lot more affordable. So I'll rent an efficiency there as soon as I can get the money saved up. That's all I'll need when I spend so much time out of town. I just thought I ought to let you know that I don't intend to perch on your doorstep indefinitely."

"You do have money. Quite a bit of it, as a matter of fact."

Noelle looked at Dennis blankly.

"Part of it's in the bank in Grantville. Part of it's in real estate, though most of that was in Clarksburg and got left behind in the Ring of Fire. Part of it's invested in the business." He looked at his fingernails.

"Where did it come from?"

"Pat wouldn't take child support from me."

"Why on earth not?" Noelle exploded. "God knows, there were plenty of times we could have used it."

"She said that she didn't want to set up a situation where you were better off than the other girls." Dennis sighed. "I told her that would be fine. That she should just use the money for whatever she needed. For all of you. That she didn't have to spend it just on you. But . . ."

He shook his head. "It was just one more of those eternal head-banging arguments that we used to get into. She didn't want any of the privileges of being a wife, she said, unless she was carrying out the duties." He looked at Noelle with a kind of helpless frustration.

"Never mind. Yeah, I recognize the way Mom thinks. That a wife paid her husband to support her and the kids by letting him have sex whenever he wanted it. And then she apologized to God for having sex by having the kids and needing to change diapers for them and such. Going around in a circle. She learned that was how it was supposed to be. That's what they taught her when she was growing up. She never thought she deserved anything from you because, um, she never felt dutiful about you. You, uh, had maybe better ask Bernadette and Denise about that stuff, not me, if you want to find out more. All I know is what I wasn't supposed to overhear."

"So I just set it aside for you." Dennis thought he would ignore the rest of what she had just said, at least for the time being. "When you were getting ready to start college, when you were eighteen, I wanted to give it to you. So you could pick the school you wanted and not have to scrape and scrimp. But Pat got upset about the other girls again."

Noelle folded her hands on the table in front of her and closed her eyes, trying not to clench her fists. The money had been there. She could have gone to a four-year college for a four-year degree. She could have gone to WVU in Morgantown, like Jen Richards. Could have majored in what she was interested in, instead of making the hard calculations about what field would bring her a living wage as soon as possible. But then she would have probably been left up-time like Jen and Mom would have been here with no one, really. It was hard to count Keenan, and Aunt Suzanne had her own family and was busy. So did Denise. Even if Mom and Dennis had gotten back together, there would still have been a couple of years when Mom was alone.

"That's okay," she said. "Don't worry about it. But the others didn't want to go to college, anyway. Maggy's grades weren't good enough, to start with. They could have been, but she just didn't focus, and she was as happy as a clam working at the riding stables. Pauly got married right out of high school. She and Dillon bought a tow truck together and she drove it from his father's garage for Triple-A. Patty just wasn't interested. She made quite a bit of money waiting tables at the lounge, right away—more than a beginning teacher makes. And she liked to party."

"Anyway." Dennis came back to the topic at hand. "The money's there, in your name. If you'll come down to the bank with me one of these days, when we're both in Grantville, I'll have Coleman Walker put your signature on the account instead of mine. I'll take you to talk to Huddy Colburn so you can find out what's coming in from the real estate that's left in more detail. I've just been having him reinvest it in more when enough built up and checking the quarterly reports. I'll give you those. They already have your name on them and I can have him take mine off. And if you want to draw on the part that's in the business, just give me a couple of months' notice. There's more there, really. It's more profitable than drawing interest in the bank. But what's in the bank should be enough to cover just about anything reasonable that you need right away."

"Okay. Uh. Thanks a lot."

"You're welcome." Dennis didn't want to push things with the girl. He was just glad that he had been able to help her out with this.

When Noelle looked at the papers covering the bank account, she thought that there certainly was enough to cover anything she needed right away. Including the safety deposit and three months' advance rent on an apartment of her own. It was more money than she had ever expected to see at one time in her life.

Of course, that hadn't been much. Her financial expectations had been pretty modest.

Grantville
October 1634

"How did it go in Erfurt, Noelle?" Tony asked.

"I got to know Dennis a little better."

"Did you like him?" Denise asked. She put down saucers with fruit cobbler on the coffee table.

"I'm not sure. Juliann used to talk about him some, and his brothers. She said that he was different from Joe. That when storms came down, Dennis was like a tough old tree with deep roots growing into a cliff side. That he'd bend over before the wind and water and then, when the calm came, manage to stand up straight again. With some scars and gouges, the worse for wear, but stand up again and keep going."

"Interesting." Bernadette put down her cobbler. "What about Joe?"

"That he was like a flint boulder. He wouldn't bend in a storm. He'd just sit there and part the waters. Until they eroded the ground out from under him. Then he'd crash down the cliff and break into a thousand fragments." Noelle put down her empty saucer. "Thanks for having me over, but I really do have to go."

"It's odd." Tony sat down again after seeing her out the door. "When she first came back from Franconia, I was thinking to myself how unexpectedly resilient Noelle had been as a field agent, considering how young she still is. We've mostly still been thinking of her as Pat's. There may be more of Dennis in her than we thought. Maybe Juliann Stull spotted that. Of course, Juliann knew Dennis a lot better than any of us did."

"Noelle's not like Pat." Denise gathered up the cups to take them into the kitchen. "Don't be fooled by her looks. She's been feeling responsible for Pat for the last ten years. Totally responsible for her since Patty finished high school in '95 and moved out."

Bernadette picked up the forks and saucers. "If you ask me, the greatest kindness Dennis could do her is somehow convince her that he'll really take Pat's problems over now, for good, and cut her loose to live a life of her own without that constant worry."

"What do you think, Joe?" Aura Lee asked.

"Hard to tell. Noelle seems friendly enough. A little reserved, I guess, but that's not so surprising under the circumstances. That she's a little hesitant."

"Do you think that she might be a little more . . . forthcoming . . . maybe, with someone younger. Maybe if Eden talked to her?"

"We could try it, I guess. But Economic Resources keeps her pretty busy. She doesn't have a lot of time to socialize. They'll probably be sending her back to Franconia one of these days."

Aura Lee looked at him. "Doesn't that tell you that we ought to get a move on?"

Eden Stull decided to leave the dishes for the time being. Supper hadn't gone badly. But it hadn't gone particularly well, either. So far, she hadn't found any opening to bring up the question of whether Noelle would be willing to change her name to Stull. "I was there. When Francis Murphy shot Dennis, I mean. With the babies. My parents were really ticked off that he shot into the parlor of the funeral home with the five of us there. As if we ought to be immune to that sort of thing happening."

She stood up. "Help me get the kids to bed, will you? After that, if there are any questions you want answered, fire away. That's why I asked you over."

"I'm not sure you can answer my main question at all." Noelle got up too. "Considering that you weren't even born back when it was going on and Harlan was just a baby. Why did my mom fall in love with your husband's uncle, who's my father, to start with?"

"Well." Eden started to shoo her sons in the direction of the stairs. "That's a good one. You might as well ask why Julia fell for Tom. Those are Harlan's parents—they were left up-time. Or Aura Lee for Joe. Or why I went nuts over Harlan. Or, for that matter, why Blanche Leek fell for Ben—he's the guys' first cousin, son of Juliann's sister Lula. They're up in Magdeburg. I suppose you don't see any obvious reason or you wouldn't be asking."

"Well, I've never met Harlan or his father," Noelle stopped on the first step. "Or the Leeks. I don't think I ever even heard of the Leeks. And since Tom Stull was left up-time, I'm not likely to meet Harlan's father."

"They're no better looking than Joe and Dennis," Eden smiled. "In fact, Harlan looks more like Joe than he does like Dennis. When it comes to the rating scale, Dennis is the best of the lot. Lucky for you. No girl in her right mind would want to look like Joe or Harlan. It's just lucky that Little Juliann looks more like Aura Lee. I'm really happy that both my kids are boys. It doesn't seem to handicap the Stull boys."

"Okay," Noelle dropped a rubber ducky into the bathtub. "Where did you get the ducky? You didn't have kids before the Ring of Fire."

"It was Aura Lee's. She and Joe could have sold it for a bundle to the dealers who come through looking for up-time collectibles, but she gave it to me, instead. And I'm glad. I want my kids to have a rubber ducky. I know that when I finally get to go join Harlan, out of Grantville, we'll probably have a wood stove and a little round tin tub. I'll sort of miss central heating and a real bathroom, but the rubber ducky goes along. They can still have that and I want them to have that. I want them to have something from . . . from the real world, if you know what I mean."

"I know. It's odd what we miss." Noelle dipped her fingers into the crock of soft soap and dropped a dollop into the tub. "I miss bananas. That's what I used to have for breakfast. I'd just pick up a banana and run out the door. I've gotten used to a lot less sugar and a lot more fish, but I guess I'd just never imagined a world without bananas."

Eden pulled a couple of washcloths out from under the sink. "Anyway. Back to the Stulls. What really gets to the parents of their wives—at least, what got to my parents—is that they home in on us so early. And my parents didn't know the half of it. I was allowed to start dating when I was sixteen. And I had my first date with Harlan, who's ten years older. They didn't like it a bit."

"Well." Noelle thought a minute. "I mean, I can see why."

"What would really have made them mad," Eden grinned, "is that I'd known for almost three years that he'd call on my sixteenth birthday and ask me out."

"Good Lord!" Noelle exclaimed.

"I was in McDonald's one day, with a batch of other kids. I take after Mom in my looks. That is, I was as tall then as I am now and just as filled out. On top that is, at least when I'm not nursing. I got a bit more hips with the kids. I was leaning against the rail, waiting to order, when Harlan leaned on it from the other side, smiled at me, and asked me who I was. I told him, and who my parents were. He looked at the kids I was with and asked me how old I was. I told him that, too. Thirteen. And he said, 'I was afraid of something of the sort.' Then he asked, 'When are Nat and Twila going to let you date?' I said, 'when I'm sixteen.' He said, 'I'm Harlan Stull. Nat and Twila are in the phone book, so I'll call you then. When's your birthday?' And he did. Right in the middle of my birthday party. He asked me to the movies in Fairmont the next Saturday and I said that I'd go."

"That's . . . well, that's . . . " Noelle sputtered.

"Yeah, my parents thought so, too, when he called. So did the Mulroneys when Harlan's dad—Tom, that was—started dating Julia. Though that was just two years difference, not ten. They'd have married sooner than they did except that they were waiting for Julia's sister Barb to turn eighteen so she could marry John Nash without parental permission. And probably the Hudsons, when Joe started eyeing Aura Lee when she was fourteen and kissing her the next year. As for your parents, Dennis is more than four years older than Pat—closer to five years older. She may have run off to him on her eighteenth birthday, but she'd been waiting to run for a year, at least. Willing to run for two or maybe a little more.

"They just sort of . . . focus . . . on the girl they want when she's awfully young. Not putting pressure, exactly. Just moving in and occupying all the mental space she has available for thinking about guys. So he's the only guy she ever really thinks about. At least, that's the way it worked for me. I was so preoccupied with waiting for Harlan to call on my sixteenth birthday that I just more or less ignored all the other boys in town."

Eden grinned suddenly. "In a way, I think what makes the parents maddest is that they can't even call the guys pedophiles, because they actually do wait until the girl is of dating age to do something. Joe moved in on Aura Lee earliest, but even then . . . I suppose a person could say that she sort of provoked him occasionally, from everything I've heard."

Noelle frowned. "But why did it preoccupy you that much? After all . . . "

"Well, yeah. Probably if it had been anyone else who tried that trick, I'd have forgotten it in a couple of days. But it was Harlan, and if he called, then we'd have a date, and if we had a date, then some day he'd kiss me, and if he kissed me, then eventually . . . You can sort of see how the train of thought went. Trust me, it was plenty to keep me ignoring all the other guys. Of course, if he hadn't called, I'd have had to restructure my picture of my future life drastically. But he did, and like I said, I never doubted that he would. Honestly, the only thing on earth that my parents had against him was that he was ten years older.

"Plus the fact that I moved in with him on my eighteenth birthday, which was a year before I finished high school. But he wasn't on a 'barefoot and pregnant' kick.

He paid for me to finish a two-year degree in laboratory technology and then I worked two years before we got married. I guess we could have gotten married earlier, but there didn't seem to be any real reason to. For that matter, there wasn't any real reason in 1997 more than there had been for the last five and a half years, but we woke up one morning and decided it was time, so we did. We went to the courthouse and had a judge perform the ceremony with Joe and Aura Lee as witnesses and sent my parents a photocopy of the certificate.

"It didn't change the way we lived. I didn't get pregnant the first time until after the Ring of Fire and now I've got two kids. I predict I'll end up with a few more, because birth control down-time isn't what it might be. We've talked around all the angles and Harlan and I aren't likely to give up sex any time soon, thank you.

"Though having him over in Fulda really cuts down on the frequency. Once they get something going over there that doesn't mean that a lab technician is of six times more use to the world in Grantville than in Fulda, I'll be on the first freight wagon out of here. We're lucky that he's the budget officer, so he gets to come back more often than most of the guys in the administration there do. He'll be in town in a week or so. I'll have everyone over for dinner.

"The guys started to make a scrapbook about Juliann, after the visitation got shot up. Joe has it, I think. You'll have to ask him to let you look at it. They put in their favorite 'Ma' stories, so I'm not going to spoil things by telling you any of them."

"But Nat and Twila were with you at the visitation. So you must be getting along now?"

"Oh, that. When I finally had a baby, they couldn't resist. They showed up at the hospital nursery looking wistful, so Harlan told them to come on in and we all had a good cry together and made everything up. And we named the baby Nathan. On the theory that we were likely to have more, given the birth control situation, so we could name kids on down the line Tom for Harlan's dad and a Harlan Junior, maybe. Tom we've already got. He was born last May."

Noelle started to towel off the older boy. "If you ever need a babysitter when I'm in town . . . "

"My favorite story about Grandma for a scrapbook?" Harlan Stull asked. "God, it has to be the day that Eden moved in with me. June 11, 1992. It was a Thursday." He winked at his wife.

"I think I remember that one. The famous Lady God-iva of Grantville?" Joe grinned at him. "We were living in Fairmont then, but somebody called Aura Lee at work and the story that Eden had been streaking was waiting for me when I got home for supper."

Harlan grinned back. He had always considered his youngest uncle more of a cousin, considering their ages, and never gave him the 'uncle' title.

"One thing sort of led to another," Harlan turned to Noelle. He thought she was looking a little intimidated by her first family dinner with the entire world supply of Stulls all at once.

"Nat and Twila didn't really like it that I started dating Eden when she was sixteen. Considering that I was twenty-six. From the perspective of the parents of a girl, they might have had a point. Although I was very good.

Even by their standards. For the first six months or so, at least. I took her all sorts of neutral places, like to historical reenactments up at Prickett's Fort State Park, as if she really wanted to watch eighteenth-century gun-smiths at work, and to the district fair and stuff. Concentrating on Saturday afternoons. Sunday afternoons. Hiking and things like that. Roller skating. Co-ed volley-ball in the high school gym."

Eden interrupted. "Until I got a little pissed off and told him that I was perfectly willing to try to cram ten years' worth of growing up into two years or so, since it looked like I'd need to, but he had to give me a fair chance. Introduce me to his own friends and things."

Harlan shrugged. "Well, by that time, the people I'd gone to school with were mostly either married with a kid or two or doing things I didn't want to introduce Eden to, so my 'friends' list got remodeled. Pared down a lot in pretty much of a hurry."

Joe laughed. "Funny how that works."

"Anyhow, one thing led to another. Eden was born at 1:40 in the morning. She looked it up on her birth cer-tificate. So on June 10, I kept her out beyond her week-day curfew so I could stick an engagement ring on her finger at the very instant she turned eighteen in the early a.m. She didn't think Nat and Twila would be happy about it. The Davis household always had breakfast at 6:30 a.m. She asked me to be outside with the car by seven, because it might not go over very well. I called into work first thing in the morning and took the day off too, just in case. But I sure didn't expect what did happen."

"Which was?" Dennis asked. "Remember, Pat and Noelle don't know the story at all."

"Well, Eden came down to breakfast and served herself with toast and scrambled eggs. Nat started in on her about breaking curfew. She put her hand down on the table and showed them the ring. Itty bitty diamond on a very skinny platinum band. Nat told her to take it off. She refused and pointed out that she was of age. He said that either she took it off or he would throw her out. She said, 'then toss me down the steps.' He said that he had paid for everything she had and that none of it would be going with her."

"Oh." Noelle sounded a little surprised.

"Eden just looked at him. Then she got up from the table, went to their little half-bath downstairs, and stripped. Stripped everything, including her underwear and shoes. Took the bobby pins out of her hair. She even left her glasses behind. They were probably the single most expensive thing she had, given her prescription. Walked out the front door, down the steps, down the sidewalk, and got into my car just as bare as the day she was born, except for her engagement ring. With Twila screeching on the porch, by the time she closed the car door."

Dennis reached for the baked beans. "I was over in Clarksburg, then. But about that time of the morning someone called me, too. So I probably heard before Joe and Aura Lee did."

Harlan winked at Eden. "So we drove over to my place. She parted her hair in back so it would hang in front and sort of hunkered down on the seat while I ran in and got one of my shirts. It was a little later by then and more people were up and about in my neighborhood."

Eden tossed her head. "I'd have been willing to walk in just as I was. If that's what it took. But it was nice of him to get the shirt. I had a lot of hair—still do—but not anywhere near as much hair as Lady Godiva is supposed to have had and I really preferred not to show that many people how I was built."

"Ah." Harlan looked at the ceiling. "Having her there, so conveniently undressed, and having the day off, what with being engaged now and all, we spent the next three hours or so very pleasantly. We figured that the way Nat had behaved that morning sort of cancelled all the limits on our behavior that he had imposed in the way of dating rules. Somewhere in the middle of it, the police phoned. Eden talked to them, pointed out that she was eighteen, and told them that she was quite happy to be exactly where she was. When Ralph Onofrio asked where she was, she answered, 'in bed with Harlan,' which made the state of affairs pretty plain. Ralph must have figured out what had Nat and Twila in such a twist, because he just laughed."

Noelle was struggling with a desire to laugh, too. Or, maybe, a desire to cry a little.

"Then we began to think about slightly more practical things. Like getting her some clothes. Without her glasses, Eden couldn't even see to write down a list. I couldn't quite imagine myself over at the Bargain General buying clothes for her. Or trying to, even with a clerk to help me. And I thought that taking her there wearing one of my shirts and no shoes would sort of fuel the gossip that was bound to be going around. Plus, without glasses, she couldn't read the labels and I'd have had to read them out loud to her to get sizes. I could just see myself doing that."

"Yeah," Dennis was looking at the beans again. "I can just picture it."

"So I called Grandma. Mom and Dad were at work. Someone had already phoned her, of course. She came over and took a look at the two of us, Eden blinking at the world through a fog, so to speak, and trying to get the tangles out of her hair with a dinky little six-inch plastic pocket comb." Harlan paused and ran his hand over his scalp. "Well, working at the mine, I kept a crew-cut. It was a lot easier to keep clean. Why would I have wanted a brush? Grandma started to laugh so hard that I thought she would never stop. Eventually she did, though. Eden told her the sizes, I took her over to Bargain General, and she asked, 'How much can I spend?' I gave her five twenties. I'd stopped at the bank the day before, sort of expecting that I'd need some cash somewhere along the line. Grandma said that she'd probably never spent that much at once in her life and that she intended to have a good time. She got the practical stuff, toothbrush and hair brush and things. But then she picked out a couple of sets of pretty fancy underwear, a pair of jeans, a tee shirt, a pair of sandals. Said she expected I'd prefer it if she forgot about pajamas."

Joe laughed again. "Ma to the hilt."

"Then she looked at me and grinned. Asked, 'Do you *really* want to frost Nat and Twila?' By then, I sure did. 'You got any more money?' she asked. I gave her a couple more twenties. She said, 'Then take Eden to First Methodist with you Sunday,' and picked out a sort of rose colored tee with little frilly arms and a skirt with a background the same color and a little ruffle around the hem. And a headband that matched and a pair of little pink pearl earrings. And lipstick and nail polish."

Joe leaned back. "Whodathunkit? I'd scarcely have thought it of Ma."

"Well, I guess with three boys, you two and Dad, she never had a little girl to dress." Harlan grabbed the last of the beans before Dennis finished making up his mind about thirds. "She made the most of it. Then she ordered me to go by Nat and Twila's. She got out. I didn't think she should go up by herself, just in case Nat was still there, so I went with her. Charlene answered the door. Grandma said that they were certainly welcome to give the rest of Eden's things to the Goodwill if it suited them, but she did need her glasses and they wouldn't do anyone else much good if they threw them into the box at the Lions Club."

"Now *that* I would think of Ma," Dennis inserted into the conversation.

"Charlene went back inside, leaving us standing there on the porch. In about ten minutes, she came back with the glasses. In their case. I thanked her, and she said, 'Could you give me a lift downtown, please?' We did, of course. Didn't know it then, but when she got out at the library, she called Sam Haygood and stayed there until he came over and picked her up. And then they went over to the Davises at supper time and told Nat and Twila that they were getting engaged, too, which sort of distracted them from Eden for a while. A half hour or thereabouts, anyway. As long as Nat and Twila thought the two of them were just getting engaged. But the ten minutes of arguing about whether Eden could have her glasses had been the last straw for Charlene. She told them that she was moving in with Sam, too. Starting that night. They really brought out the big guns. Church of Christ members aren't supposed to behave like that."

Joe pushed his plate back. "Well, if Nat and Twila hadn't kept those girls on such a short leash, they wouldn't have reached the end of it so soon."

"There's that," Dennis admitted.

"Anyway, Grandma and I went back to my place and Eden got dressed. Right after she put her glasses on, she discovered that my refrigerator contained three slices of dried up pepperoni pizza and two cans of beer. She and Grandma took the car keys, extracted some more of my cash, and headed off to Stevenson's Supermarket. And that was when my life really started to change." Harlan grinned. "What with Twila being a home ec teacher and all, Eden had some really distinct views on what it was good for a person to eat. Most of them involving broccoli or fiber—or both. You win some, you lose some." He looked at his wife again. "Overall, though, having Eden move in was a winner."

"You'd better believe it," she answered.

"If you were living together anyway, why did you get married?" Noelle asked.

"We weren't just living together," Eden protested. "We were *engaged*. I wore the ring and all. Why did we decide to get married? The day we decided to—not the day we actually got married, because it took us a couple of weeks to pull things together and make sure Joe and Aura Lee could take time off from work to be our witnesses—was a little personal anniversary that we celebrated. Not when I moved in with him. That was in June. This was from November, a year and a half before that. When we started dating, Harlan kept taking me places that weren't exactly private."

"Harlan," Eden's husband said of himself, "had a pretty clear idea of how Nat and Twila would react if he deflowered their tenderly cherished virgin daughter. The age of consent might technically be sixteen, which she already was, but given that they weren't likely to see it that way, good old Harlan believed in playing it safe and waiting until the girl was altogether of age and at her own disposal. There were still a couple of years during which Nat Davis could have made dramatic paternal gestures and said things like, 'Never darken the door of our home again, you villain.' "

Eden picked up the story. "So there we were, up in the state park. There was a nature trail, about seven miles or so, and we picked that. It was a nice Sunday afternoon, sunny, not too cold, but not many people were out. Some, mostly families, but it wasn't crowded. We were about halfway along it, talking and holding hands. I kept feeling odder and odder. Finally I stopped. Harlan looked at me and I said, 'I feel really weird.' "

"So I looked at her closely and thought, 'Gee, thank you, Mother Nature. Not only do we have to deal with me wanting to have sex with Eden, now we've got to deal with Eden wanting to have sex with me. Not romantic feelings; plain old physical ones. And she doesn't even know what's bothering her. Time for a little instruction.' So I tugged her off the trail a few feet, backed up against a tree to have a little support, pulled her up against me, and started to kiss her the way I wanted to rather than the way I thought I ought to limit myself to."

"By the time we'd been leaning against the tree a while, kissing like that, with Harlan holding my hips against his, I figured out what the problem was. Which was a considerable relief. I had been starting to wonder if I was getting the flu or something, and I had tests in geometry and world history coming up on Monday."

"Flu?" Aura Lee asked.

"Well," Eden protested a little defensively, "It had been making me feel that wobbly. The health class at school told us something about the mechanics of it all but didn't say a word about the way a person feels while it is going on. At church they just warned us about places like the back seats of cars and the quarry. And the evils of dancing. They sure never said you could start feeling like that while you were hiking along a trail, wearing a down vest and boots, and listening to a guy tell you about improved standards and techniques for air quality measurement."

"About what?" Dennis sounded distinctly startled. "Harlan, you didn't! What a courtship!"

"Well, we had to talk about *something*. Other than the impact her bosom had on my testosterone, that is." Harlan put his arm around Eden's shoulders. "I was trying to minimize that train of thought about then. And it wasn't exactly courtship. That's when the male bird struts around displaying his plumage and the female tries to decide if she wants him. We had a done deal by that point. We were just working on procedures and implementation."

"It was interesting." The tone of Eden's voice was fiercely protective. "All the stuff Harlan told me about it was one of the reasons that I decided on lab technology when I went to choose a post-secondary course later on."

Dennis grinned at her.

"Anyway, we decided to get married on the seventh anniversary of the day Harlan explained to me the importance of being eighteen, as far as he was concerned. What he said made perfect sense. At the time, though, I wished that it didn't."

"I thought I might as well give her something to look forward to. I also told her that she'd get her engagement ring the instant she was of age and Nat and Twila didn't have to consent. Which she did."

"By the time we decided to go ahead and get married instead of just being engaged, I was twenty-three. Maybe that's why we waited so long. By then, it didn't upset most people so much that Harlan was ten years older. The people at the courthouse didn't ask any questions at all. They just issued the license and the judge married us off. Now that I'm coming up on thirty, it bothers them even less."

Eden stopped talking; then started again. "And I'm sure Noelle has found all of this very entertaining. But hadn't you all better get down to the business of why Aura Lee and I cooked this meal?"

Dennis, Joe, and Harlan glared at her. They would have worked up to the negotiations more gently. Taken an oblique approach.

Pat looked bewildered. The project was going to be a surprise for her, too.

Finally, Aura Lee sighed. Men! "Noelle, they'd like you to think about whether you really want to keep on using the name 'Murphy.' Or if you wouldn't maybe rather be a Stull."

"That could be a question, now that you've been exposed to us." Harlan grinned. "To the unexpurgated version, as they say."

◊   ◊   ◊

"What the hell are you doing?" Joe asked. "Rooting around in those cabinets? Come on to bed, Aura Lee. It's past midnight."

"I'm looking for the 1997 photo album."

"Why on earth?"

"I just wanted to check something." She closed one door and opened another. "Here they are, in this box. Someday, maybe, we'll get everything unpacked that we brought along when we moved into this house in 1998."

"Check away." Joe knew one thing. The auditor in Aura Lee would not leave her in peace. If she thought something needed to be checked, she would check it. Even if it was midnight and they had to get up as early as ever in the morning.

"I thought so."

"What?"

"Look. These pictures I took the day that Harlan and Eden got married. She was wearing the clothes that Harlan described this evening. The ones your ma bought for her to wear to church the Sunday after she moved in with him. At the time, I thought they weren't what I'd have expected her to pick. She looked pretty in them, but they were definitely a summer outfit and it was almost the end of November."

"Harlan?"

"Umm?"

"At dinner, when you were talking about those clothes your Grandma bought me, I sort of started thinking. You'll still be here in Grantville Sunday, won't you?"

"Yeah. 'Til Tuesday. Maybe longer if a few logjams in the budget discussions don't break up."

"I've gone to First Methodist ever since I went that first Sunday wearing the pink top and the ruffled skirt your grandma picked out. But I've never switched. It's probably time that I did. If it's okay with you, I'll call the Reverends Jones and set it up for this week."

Harlan sat up and looked her over. "You'll make a perfectly gorgeous Methodist."

"What do they think, really, of having the Stulls as members?"

He thought a minute. "Well, they say that everyone has a divine purpose in life. I guess having us in the congregation tends to take the minds of the ultra-righteous off whatever the Jenkinses are doing at the moment. In a way, that probably cuts the Reverends Jones a little more slack than they'd have otherwise."

Eden attacked him with tickling fingers and they both collapsed.

Joe Stull wandered into Tony Adducci's office first thing the next morning. "It was the damnedest thing. Aura Lee said that we wondered if Noelle would be willing to change her name to Stull. Pat crossed her arms on the table, put her head down, and started to sob her eyes out. Dennis picked her up and took her out into the hall. The rest of us stayed sitting there. I guess it was pretty obvious that we wondered what we had done to set her off."

"Ummhmmn," Tony answered.

"Then Noelle said, 'There's nothing wrong. She's crying because you want me, I think.' Then we all just stared at her."

Tony nodded. "How much of it did she tell you?"

"She said, 'There's no way you could know it, but this is the first time I've ever been invited to anyone's family dinner.' That's all."

Tony winced. "I told Carol Koch, a long time ago, that the Fitzgeralds were a bunch of uptight Irish Catholic Puritans. Except Denise, of course. It's not just that Patrick and Mary Liz Murphy wouldn't have her in their house. She's eaten with us and the kids, with Bernadette there sometimes. But she's never even been to Denise's parents' house. Or to Suzanne Trelli's. Because the Fitzgeralds, too, saw her as a child of adultery. So far, the facts that came out at St. Mary's haven't gotten them to change their minds. At least not as far as meeting her goes. That's one reason she keeps so busy at work, I think. And doesn't mind going to Franconia. Let me see if Denise can come downtown for lunch. You maybe ought to talk to her about this. Or maybe Aura Lee could talk to her."

That immediately struck both of them as a brilliant idea, freeing them of further immediate obligations in regard to understanding the female of the species and permitting them to get back to fulfilling their respective public duties.

"When we were retelling the Harlan and Eden episode of the Stull family history, I couldn't tell from her face whether she was going to laugh or cry." Aura Lee held out her mug so Cora could refill it.

"She probably didn't know either," Denise got a refill too. "She's never had a date, so the . . . freewheeling . . . approach to it all in Dennis' family may have boggled her mind. The first time she ever went to a party was the staff Christmas party at her job, December before the Ring of Fire happened. She didn't want to face it by herself, but she did, and came through it okay."

"Why no dates? Because of that nun idea she has?" Aura Lee frowned.

"No. The 'nun idea' came up since the Ring of Fire. No dates because she wasn't willing to put out the payback that guys over in Fairmont expected from a girl with her background. From what I've picked up as her godmother. Ah, that was confidential."

"Isn't that a bit overblown?"

"Not when you add Patty's reputation as a party girl on top of Dennis and Pat."

"Oh." Aura Lee decided not to comment on that.

"Noelle told me once that when she was young enough to have dreams, back when she was fifteen or sixteen, she dreamed that some day she would leave Fairmont and go someplace like Denver or Seattle, where no one had ever heard of her family, and meet a nice guy at mass one day. Someone who had grown up in an orphan asylum and done well. That they'd fall in love and when she told him about her family he would say that he didn't care and didn't have any relatives who cared, either, and they would get married and live there and Pat would go visit them, but she'd never have to come back to West Virginia again."

"That is as sad as hell," Aura Lee put her mug down. "Twenty-three and talking about when she was young enough to have dreams."

"She was more like nineteen, then," Denise answered. "Instead of Noelle's getting to go away, Pat brought her to Grantville in search of affordable housing. Where she was even more in the middle of it. Going to mass at St. Vincent's, where Pat's relatives never acknowledged she was there. She finally had to give up her pretty day-dreams completely when the Ring of Fire happened and she knew that she'd never be able to get away from people who knew about it all."

She sighed. "But it's one of the reasons that Berna-dette doesn't take the 'nun idea' all that seriously. It isn't that Noelle didn't date—doesn't date—because she was never interested in getting married some day. She just doesn't believe that she has any chance of it now. Not with a 'nice guy.' "

Aura Lee frowned. "If you look at the available pool, she may not have much of a chance. I can't think of anyone I'd recommend for her. Not since she takes being Catholic seriously. The nice unmarried men within a rea-sonable range of her age, like Jim Horton or Danny Tip-ton, Gene Woodsell, maybe, are either Protestants or don't go to church at all."

"The hell of it is, that neither can we. Tony and I've talked about it some, since we're her godparents. The

only Catholic guy anywhere her age who is anywhere
near worthy of her in the whole town is Lawrence Quinn,
but there's no spark there at all. Not on either side.
Bernadette won't have her, though. For the new order
they're planning, I mean. She says that Noelle's day-
dreams may have been of marrying a nice Catholic guy,
but Pat came up with Dennis, who didn't make any sense
for her at all. Which certainly didn't stop them. She's
sure Noelle doesn't have a religious vocation. Especially
since she gave us such an enthusiastic description of putting Eden's two little ones to bed."

"I hope it doesn't bother you, Denise, since you're
Catholic yourself and all." Aura Lee dropped a couple
of bills on the table to cover their coffee and a tip. "But
that's a big relief from our point of view, the Stulls being
Methodists. I'll mention that to Dennis and Joe, if you
don't mind."

Dennis Stull spread some apple butter on his pancake.
"If Pat won't give you answers, I will. At least to the best
of my ability. Where did I meet her? It was a square
dance. The fall of 1962. She was there with a bunch of
girls her own age from St. Vincent's. Maureen and The-
resa O'Meara, I remember. Pat Scanlon, the other Pat,
who married Joe Bonnaro. Jeannette Adducci. Two or
three more. I cut her out of the herd, so to speak, and
asked her to dance. She was so cute. Just unbelievably
cute. About five-two. Blonde ponytail. Blue eyes. Tiny
little waist. Every now and then, I'd return her to the
bunch, with good intentions of leaving her there, but
pretty soon I'd ask her to dance again.

"Then, at the end of the evening, we looked for the others and they were gone. So I told her that I'd give her a ride home. Which was all that I did. Got a stony glare from Mary Liz when I took her to the door, but since it was less than ten minutes after the dance closed down, she didn't have any real grounds for complaint. I told Mary Liz that she'd gotten separated from her friends."

"What happened to the others?"

"Pat found out later that they were ticked off because she was dancing more than any of the rest of them and deliberately went off and left her, sort of hoping she'd get in trouble. She was only fifteen. Didn't turn sixteen until the end of December. Kids that age do things like that. They were all supposed to be dancing with a bunch of boys from St. Vincent's, but the boys weren't that interested in dancing, yet, so the rest of them only got out on the floor a couple of times."

"And then you started dating her?" Noelle asked.

"By taking her home, I learned where she lived. I was twenty, then, in college. I was going on a combination of state scholarship and work study, commuting over to Fairmont. Not a frat boy, by any means. I finished two years of credits in December of '63 and then went into the army. Figured that I might as well. My grades were okay, but not outstanding. Better the second year than they had been the first, but not good enough to guarantee two more years of deferment. I'd have been willing to ask her out, fair and square, but she said that if I did, her parents would send her to a nunnery. Which, after I'd found out a bit about the Fitzgeralds, didn't seem as melodramatic as I thought when she said it the first time."

"It probably wasn't." Noelle picked up her toast and then put it down again, tucking one foot under her as she sat on the bench in the breakfast nook.

"So we sneaked around. There's really no other way to put it. The next summer, she'd go to the drive-in with friends, get out after she got there, and get in my car to cuddle up while the film ran. Things like that. The other kids knew, of course. And since we were sneaking, we spent more time in places that were private than in public. With about the results you would expect.

"I didn't push her into doing anything she didn't want to." He smiled. "Maybe I sometimes coaxed her into going ahead and doing something she did want to. Not before she wanted to, though. It was like that, between the two of us. I waited nearly a year for her to be ready enough that she would ignore her scruples. Not just about having sex outside of marriage, but about having sex outside of marriage with a Methodist who made it plain that he intended to use birth control. Those last two items bothered her a lot more than the first one."

Noelle pursed her lips. "Actually, I can see that. In a way."

"The easiest place for us to go was over to Ma's. It was only a few feet from the driveway to the kitchen door. Our pa was gone by then, so Ma was working two jobs. Tom and Julia had married in August of '62, so he was out of the house and I needed to be home to watch Joe as much as I could, to save Ma from having to pay a sitter. So we'd sit at the kitchen table and do homework, all three of us. Me for college, Pat for high school, and Joe for grade school. Which, I think, is why my grades went up the second year. Playing cards or monopoly with him, sometimes. We sure spent more time doing homework than we did making love. There usually wasn't much time between when we finally persuaded Joe to go to bed and when Pat had to meet curfew on week nights. Sometimes none. Lord, but he was a little night owl. She got to stay out later on Friday and Saturday, though."

"You're telling me that you . . . ? Right there?"

"Yeah, that's what I'm telling you. A couple of times, Ma got home before we came back out of my room. The first time, Pat just froze. I don't know what she expected. I introduced them to each other. Ma said, 'pleased to meet you.' Pat barely managed to nod. When we got into the car, she was trembling like a leaf. And I thought that if she was that afraid of her own parents, it must be some house to live in.

"Once I went into the army, we wrote. That had to be sneaked, too. Our go-between was Jeannette Adducci, Tony's aunt. She was the next-to-the youngest of ten, so her parents didn't watch her so closely that she couldn't mail Pat's letters for her or pick up mine to deliver to Pat. I'd rented a box at the post office in my name, so I addressed the letters to myself. And the end of that year, '64, when she turned eighteen, Pat picked up her courage and caught the bus for Leavenworth."

Dennis got up. "I should have married her then, but I couldn't bring myself to sign those promises to have any kids we had brought up Catholic. I'm sorry if that bothers you, since she brought you up Catholic, but it's the truth. And she didn't think that being married except by a priest was different from not being married at all. You pretty much know the rest of it by now."

"I suppose so." Noelle put the lid back on the butter dish.

"Except, maybe, that I loved her so much that it hurt. After I'd gotten to know her a little, not just look at her, she was so sweet. She still is. She can't stand the thought of hurting her worst enemy. That's what Bernadette says. That her sins have almost all been of omission rather than of commission, the way the Catholics put it. Not being able to bring herself to do what she needed to."

"She tried," Noelle picked up the butter and put it back in the refrigerator. "Most of the time, anyway."

Dennis looked down. "Sometimes, they weren't her sins. I sinned against her, too, the way the Lord's Prayer says. Not the sex thing. I don't regret that for a minute. More important things. When she did try, not having the person listen who should have listened. That first time she came over to Clarksburg, after I got back from 'Nam, I should have kept her there. Or if not the first time she came, the second. Or third, or fourth, or fifth, or sixth. I'll never get over blaming myself that I didn't. She tried to tell me what was going on. I let her down bad. I should never have let her go back to Grantville that spring of '68. I knew in my heart how much she was afraid of them.

"But I thought it would play out the way she promised the last time she left. That on the morning she was supposed to marry Francis, she would get in her car and go over to her classes in Fairmont and call me to say that everything was all right."

"Okay. I got the testimony from the hearing at St. Mary's. I know what happened then." Noelle turned around and looked at him, her gray eyes measuring. Evaluating. Assessing. "Were you as single-minded about Mom as Joe seems to be about Aura Lee or Harlan about Eden?"

Dennis looked back. Not a child. He was meeting this daughter as an adult. A daughter who would have to decide if she wanted to claim him.

"I would have been if I'd had the chance. I was while I was over in 'Nam and she was waiting. The way things turned out . . . While she was married to Francis, there were seven or eight years when I regularly saw, and slept with, a divorcee over in Clarksburg. Eventually she met a guy who was interested in marrying her, which was the end of that. After Pat wouldn't divorce Francis even though she was expecting you, I was so disillusioned that I slept around for a while. A couple of years. Until I figured out that there was nothing in it for me, so I stopped."

Noelle nodded.

"Nobody Pat ever knew. Nobody she ever heard of, I hope. I tried to make sure of that. Then I dated a couple of other women. Didn't live with either of them. Never wanted to. One moved to Indiana with a job transfer after four years. The other lasted quite a while. The Ring of Fire left her in Clarksburg. That's the chronicle of my misspent years. Abbreviated version more than unexpurgated, but the truth. Not that I'm particularly proud of what I did, either. Of the way I handled things. But if I'd spent all those years thinking about the fact that I couldn't have Pat, it would have driven me crazy."

"Thanks for being honest."

"You're welcome. I'd prefer that nobody ever rub her nose in that."

"Yeah. I guess I can understand where you're coming from. I'd never deliberately do anything to hurt Mom."

"Well," Dennis said a couple of days later. "You could think about it again. That is, since we're going to the bank and putting your name on the records, you could think about what name you want on the papers."

"Yeah. I'll do that. Well, not just think about it. Do it. I told Tony and Denise and Bernadette a couple of weeks ago that I had wanted to get rid of 'Murphy' for a long time. But I wouldn't have asked to use 'Stull' unless you all invited me. I didn't want to be pushy."

Dennis looked at her. It hadn't occurred to him that she might be a little afraid of offending them. Thinking that they were measuring and evaluating her. She always seemed so composed. Reserved. Collected.

"Joe said that you told him and Tony that you had talked to Ma a few times."

"Yeah. I did." She looked away. "I hope you don't mind."

"Not a bit."

"I don't know if Mom has said anything to you about it, but Patrick and Mary Liz Fitzgerald never let me in their house any more than the Murphys did. I never met them. Won't ever meet Patrick, since he's dead now. Probably won't ever meet Mary Liz, given the things she said about you and Mom at the hearing at St. Mary's."

"Pat never said anything."

"She wouldn't. But she thought she ought to take the other girls to see them sometimes. Not as often as she took them to Paul and Maggie's, though. Nowhere near. But maybe that was more so she could see Keenan at Paul and Maggie's." Noelle looked across the table at him. "She feels pretty bad about Keenan, you know."

"She hasn't said anything about that, either."

"She does. She thinks she let him down." Noelle took a sip of coffee. She didn't really like it; hadn't ever acquired a taste for it. But it was there in front of her and fiddling with the handle of the cup gave her something to do with her hands.

"But that's really why I never changed my name to Fitzgerald. I wanted to get rid of Murphy. I had wanted to get rid of Murphy for a long time. But even though it was Mom's maiden name, the Fitzgeralds didn't want me, either. The only ones who did were Denise and Suzanne and they go by their married names."

Dennis realized that she was working up to something, but he wasn't sure what. With employees, the best approach was just to keep his mouth shut and listen, so that was what he did next.

"So she—Juliann—was the only one of my grandparents I ever met."

"Oh."

"The first time I walked up to the door, I called her 'Mrs. Stull.' But she said that no one much called her that."

"Nope. Not even the garbage collector."

"So, for a long while, I didn't call her anything." Noelle started spinning the coffee cup slowly around in its saucer.

Dennis just stayed quiet.

"Toward the end, she asked me to call her 'Grandma.' Like Harlan does."

Dennis nodded.

"I wish I hadn't been off in Franconia for so long before she died."

"Things like that happen."

"Yeah."

"Did you?" Dennis asked.

"What?"

"Call her 'Grandma'?"

Noelle shook her head. "I just couldn't, quite. Maybe, eventually, I could have worked up to it. But not then. I called her Juliann."

"If that's easier for you. So far, you haven't called me anything."

"I could probably manage 'Dennis.' "

"That's better than nothing."

"Okay, then." Noelle shook his hand.

"Changing your name doesn't take a court order anymore. The judges are too busy with more important stuff." The clerk pointed her finger in the general direction of Central Funeral Home. "Just go over to the Bureau of Vital Statistics, tell them what you want, swear an affidavit that you aren't doing it for fraudulent purposes, get it notarized, file it, and Bob's your uncle. There are a couple of notaries working right there in the office."

"Noelle Brigitte Murphy?" the clerk asked in a flat voice.

"Yes," Noelle said.

"Changing to Noelle Brigitte Stull?" The clerk fished a form out from under the counter.

"Yes, that's right."

Noelle looked at Pat and Dennis. " 'Noelle' I can understand, since I was born at Christmas. But where did 'Brigitte' come from?"

Pat turned bright red. "It's for me. In a way. I hope the priest thought it was for a saint, but it's for me."

"How do you get 'Brigitte' from 'Patricia'?"

"Hey there," Jenny Maddox came out of the back office. "Hello, Pat, Dennis, Noelle. Focus. We have forms to fill out, I hear."

"Hi, Jenny," Pat said.

"Did I hear a question? Getting Brigitte from Pat?" Noelle nodded.

"This I know from my parents." Jenny looked mischievous. "Dad and Mom and Dennis were friends back then—he and Mom were in the same class in school."

"I guess there's no escaping my past," Dennis said.

Jenny barged on. "Noelle, did you ever hear of an actress called Brigitte Bardot?"

"No."

"Well, probably not. She'd stopped making movies long before you were born. Tell her the truth, Dennis," Jenny said.

Dennis looked a little uncomfortable. "When Pat was a teenager, when we were dating, I used to tease her by calling her Brigitte."

"Please," Pat said. "Don't ask." If anything, she turned redder. Her skin was very fair.

So Noelle didn't ask. But she did look the name up later. And blushed as red as Pat by the time she was done with the biographical sketch. Being named, even second-hand, for someone whose life history was summed up under the keywords "erotic French sex kitten" just didn't seem to be the proper image for a would-be nun.

"Um, Bernadette," she asked a couple of days later. "Did you ever hear of Brigitte Bardot?"

"Yep," Bernadette answered tersely.

"When we went in to do the name change. Ah, Dennis says that's what he called Mom when she was a teenager. Brigitte. She gave the name to me when I was baptized. For her. Because Patty was already named Patricia, I guess."

Bernadette looked at her. "Well, keep it in mind when you're thinking about whether or not you want to join a religious order."

"What do you mean?"

"You are Pat's daughter and he probably wasn't calling her that for no reason at all."

"Uh?"

"Look, Noelle." Bernadette tried to keep her voice kind rather than brusque. "Nowhere in all that testimony before Judge Tito and Tom Riddle or at the hearing over at St. Mary's did anybody so much as hint that Dennis and Pat waited until they were out in Leavenworth with his dime-store rings on her finger to start sleeping together."

"Oh." Noelle paused a moment. "Well, I guess that wouldn't have been likely. From what I've learned about Dennis' family so far. Actually, Dennis told me that they didn't wait that long. When I asked him about it. It would have embarrassed Mom if I asked her."

"I'm sure it would," Bernadette agreed. "And if you're even thinking about becoming a nun, Noelle, you might give some consideration to what she was doing then that would embarrass her so much if you asked her about it now."

And after that, Bernadette said to herself, *you'd better think again*.

The Austro-Hungarian Connection

Eric Flint

Chapter 1. The Track

Vienna, Austria
October 1634

Fortunately, that part of Janos Drugeth's mind that always remained calm and controlled, even in the fury of a battlefield, was still there to restrain his panic. Indeed, it found the panic itself unseemly.

You are a Hungarian cavalry officer in the service of the Austrian emperor, that part of his mind informed Janos sternly. *A breed noted for its valor.*

It was all Janos could do not to snarl "so what?" aloud. He was not facing the familiar terrors of war.

You are not even unaccustomed to this, the stern inner voice continued. *You have ridden in automobiles before. In Grantville. Several times. Just a few months ago.*

Janos' grip on the handrest of his door to the vehicle grew tighter still. He was sitting on what Americans called the "passenger side" of the automobile. They also sometimes referred to it as "riding shotgun," he'd been told, a phrase that didn't seem to make any more sense than many of the up-timers' expressions.

True. He had. Four times, in fact, with three different operators.

But, first, those vehicles had been driven by Americans very familiar with their operation. All three of them filled with the sobriety of age, to boot. Not a young Austrian emperor whose personal acquaintance with automobiles was this one, and no other. The cursed thing had just arrived in Vienna the month before, not long before Janos himself returned from his inspection of the frontier forts facing the Turks.

Second, two of the vehicles had been large and stately things, moving not much faster than a horse and stopping frequently. What the up-timers called "buses." The third had been a "pickup" filled with people in the open area in the back, which moved not much faster than the buses. And the fourth had been large and roomy, almost the size of a proper coach if much lower-built, whose operator had been an elderly woman.

None of them had been a so-called "sports car" driven by a maniacal down-time monarch. Nor had any of them been driven on a ridiculous oval-shaped course freshly prepared for the purpose at the command of the crazed king in question. Ferdinand called it a "race track." The term was English, and unfamiliar to Janos. But his command of the language was almost fluent now, and he could easily determine its inner logic. Its frightening inner logic.

The automobile skidded around another curve in the race track. The rear wheels lost their grip on the surface, just as Janos had known carts to do on slippery cobblestones during a rain or in mud. But the carts had been moving slowly, not at—his eyes locked on the "speedometer" and froze at the sight—sixty miles an hour. The phrase didn't have a precise meaning to Janos, but he knew that was far faster than he'd ever seen an American drive such a contraption. And even at slow speeds, such a mishap could easily cause a sturdy down-time cart to break a wheel or axle.

The slide continued, the vehicle now clearly out of control. Janos clenched his teeth, his grip on the armrest as tight as he'd ever gripped a sword hilt or a lance on a battlefield. Under his breath, he began muttering the same prayer that he always muttered when a cavalry charge he was leading neared the enemy and his own death might be upon him, commending his soul to the Virgin's care. "*Ave Maria, gratia plena, Dominus tecum . . .*"

Fortunately, the muttered words were covered up by Ferdinand's squeal of glee. Fortunately also, while Ferdinand might be portly, he was young and had good reflexes. He turned the round steering mechanism abruptly—in the direction of the slide, oddly—and within seconds the vehicle had resumed its steady and straightforward course. They were still going at an insane speed, but at least the king now had the automobile back under control. And apparently they'd broken neither a wheel nor an axle.

Ferdinand squealed his glee again. "Ha!" He glanced at Janos, grinning. "I learned that trick from Sanderlin. It's not like a horse-drawn carriage, you know. The worst thing you can do in a skid is apply the brakes. That means restraining the mechanical horses under the hood." His right hand released the control mechanism and his forefinger pointed to the smooth dark-blue metal expanse in front of the window. "That's the hood, by the way. It's hard to believe, but there are more than two hundred mechanical horses in there."

To Drugeth's relief, the king had slowed the vehicle considerably. Ferdinand glanced at him again, still grinning. "Congratulations, Janos. You're the first person who's ridden with me on the track who hasn't said a word. Screamed a word, usually—and in the case of my wife and sister, cursed me directly."

Drugeth tried to return the grin. The result, he suspected, was simply a rictus. "Perhaps they were not cavalry officers." He managed to relinquish his grip on the armrest and slap his chest. "And Hungarian, too! We are a bold breed."

Ferdinand chuckled—and, praise the saints, continued to let the automobile's speed decline. "The first, no. You are the only cavalry officer to ride with me. The second explanation, I'm afraid, doesn't withstand scrutiny. Your uncle Pal Nadasdy has ridden with me, and I can assure you the hisses and screeches of terror he produced were no less profound than any German's."

They were nearing the stablelike building that the king had ordered constructed at the center point of one of the two long stretches on the oval track. What Ferdinand called by the English term "the straightaways," another expression that was unfamiliar to Janos but whose inner logic was clear enough. Three men were emerging from the very large and open double doors, holding some sort of tools and wearing peculiar one-piece garments.

The distinctive clothing went by the English name of "jumpsuits" and would have been enough in themselves to identify the men. But Janos had excellent eyesight, and recognized them even at a distance. The one in the center was Ronald Sanderlin, Jr., the up-timer who'd sold the automobile to the Austrian king and had agreed to move to Vienna to maintain it for him. He'd brought his wife and two children with him, although Janos didn't know their names. Drugeth estimated his age at being somewhere in the mid-thirties, although such estimates were always tricky with Americans. You simply couldn't use the easy gauge of the condition of their teeth.

The older man standing to Sanderlin's left was his uncle Robert, who went by the nickname of "Bob." He was unmarried, and seemed to be extremely taciturn. At least, on admittedly short acquaintance, Janos had never heard the man say a word in either German or English.

The third man was the most interesting of the three, from Drugeth's viewpoint. His name was Andrew Jackson "Sonny" Fortney, Jr. He was also married and had also brought his wife and two children. He was supposed to be a close friend of Ron Sanderlin's—plausible enough, at first glance, since they were approximately the same age—and Sanderlin had insisted that he come along to Vienna as part of the "deal," as he called it. There was even, from the Austrian standpoint, he'd argued, the additional benefit that Fortney had experience working with train steam engines, which was not true of either Sanderlin himself or his uncle.

Sanderlin had been quite stubborn on the matter. Istvan Janoszi, Drugeth's agent, had finally agreed to include the third man in the bargain. But he'd sent a private message to Janos warning him that Fortney might well be a spy for the United States of Europe. The man was known to have been visited on occasion by the USE's fiendishly capable spymaster, Francisco Nasi, for one thing. And, for another, despite Sanderlin's fervent insistence that Sonny Fortney was his "good buddy," Istvan had not been able to uncover any evidence that the two men had spent any time together prior to the summer of this year—which was to say, right about the time the Austrian proposal to the Sanderlins would have come to the attention of the USE's political authorities.

The issue was of sufficient concern that Janos had even raised it with the emperor himself, the day after he arrived back in Vienna. But Ferdinand had dismissed the problem.

"Let's be realistic, Janos. There was no possible way to keep secret the fact that three Americans with mechanical experience were moving to Vienna—not to mention the two complete automobiles they brought with them. Ha! You should have seen the huge wagons and their teams when they lumbered into the city. They could barely fit in the streets, even after I ordered all obstructions removed."

The emperor drummed his fingers on the armrest of his chair for a moment, and then shrugged. "The enemy was bound to fit a spy into the mix, unless they were deaf, dumb and blind—and if there's any evidence that either Michael Stearns or his Jewish spymaster are incompetent, it's been impossible to find. So be it. Vienna is full of spies—but now, in exchange for allowing another, we've gotten our first significant access to American technology. I can live with that, easily enough. At least, this time, we probably know who the spy is to begin with. That'll make it easier to keep an eye on him."

Janos had his doubts, but . . . Technically speaking, although the USE and the Austro-Hungarian Empire were political enemies, the two nations were not actually at war. Furthermore, from what he could tell, he thought the USE's Prime Minister Stearns was trying to keep an open conflict from breaking out, at least for the moment. That would be almost impossible, of course, if—as everyone suspected would happen next year—the USE's emperor Gustav Adolf launched a war of conquest on Saxony and Brandenburg. In that event, Austria would most likely join the conflict.

For the time being, however, Stearns seemed content to let the death of Ferdinand II and the accession of his son to the Austrian throne serve as a reason to keep the peace. The new monarch's surprising decision to publicly renounce any claim to being the new Holy Roman Emperor and replace that with his new title of "Emperor of Austria-Hungary" had no doubt gone a long way toward that end. Contained within the formalities of the titles was the underlying reality, that Austria realized the days it could directly control—or try to control—all of the Germanies was at an end. Ferdinand III's public renunciation of the title of Holy Roman Emperor meant, for all practical purposes, that the Holy Roman Empire itself was now a thing of the past. Henceforth, presumably, Austria's interests and ambitions would be directed toward the east and the south, not the north and the west.

The Turks hadn't been pleased by that announcement, to say the least. But the enmity of the Ottoman Empire was more or less a given, no matter what Austria did. The Turks had plenty of spies in Vienna too, which was the reason Ferdinand had sent Janos Drugeth on an inspection tour of the Balkan fortifications, the day after he made the announcement—even though that had required Janos to be absent from the scene during the later stages of the technology transfer from Grantville that he had largely developed. The emperor's decision to send off one of his closest confidants on such a tour of the fortifications was a none-too-subtle way of letting the Turks know that Ferdinand realized they would be furious at his decision. And they could swallow it or not, as they chose.

The automobile was finally gliding to a stop, just in front of the three American mechanics who stood waiting. From the placid looks on their faces, it seemed they hadn't been much impressed by the ability of Austria's new emperor to move faster on land than any monarch in this history of this universe.

That was as good a way as any to distinguish up-time mechanics from down-time statesmen and soldiers—or down-time fishwives and farmers, for that matter. Anyone *else* who'd seen Ferdinand III racing around a track like that would know that a very different man sat on the Austrian throne from the former emperor, these days.

Assuming they hadn't figured it out already, which most of them would have, by now. In the first two months of his reign, Ferdinand III had forcefully carried through a major realignment of his empire in ways that his stolid father would never have imagined. The old man was probably "spinning in his grave," to use an American expression.

First, he'd pressured his father—on his deathbed, no less—to rescind the Edict of Restitution. At one stroke, at least in the legal realm, ending the major source of conflict with the Protestants of central Europe.

Second, within a week of his father's death, he'd renounced the title of Holy Roman Emperor—that was something of a hollow formality, since he hadn't had the title anyway—and replaced it with the new imperial title.

Third, and perhaps most important, he'd jettisoned his father's reluctance to even acknowledge the up-timers' technological superiority in favor of an aggressive policy of modernizing his realm. Ferdinand could move just as quickly on that front because, as the prince and heir, he'd set underway Drugeth's secret mission to Grantville. "Secret," not simply from the enemy, but from his own father. Had Ferdinand II learned of it, while he was still alive, he would have been even more furious than he was by his daughter Maria Anna's escapades.

Displaying better manners than Janos had seen displayed by most Americans in Grantville, two of the up-time mechanics opened the doors for the vehicle's occupants. Ron Sanderlin, on the emperor's side, and his uncle on Drugeth's.

"Nice recovery on that last turn, Your Majesty," said Ron, as he helped Ferdinand out of the seat.

"It worked splendidly! Just as you said!"

The older Sanderlin said nothing, as usual, and other than opening the door he made no effort to assist Janos out of the vehicle. Which was a bit unfortunate, since the contraption's bizarrely low construction made getting out of the seat a lot more difficult than clambering down from a carriage or dismounting from a horse. It didn't help any that Janos felt shaky and stiff at the same time.

Hungarian cavalry officer, he reminded himself. He decided that a straightforward lunge was probably the best way to do the business.

Somewhat to his surprise, that worked rather well. And now that he was on his feet, the properly stiff-legged stance of an officer in the presence of his monarch served nicely to keep his knees from wobbling.

Ferdinand III, Grand Duke of Austria, King of Hungary, and now Emperor of the Austro-Hungarian Empire, planted his hands on his hips and gave the newly constructed race track a gaze of approval.

"You were right, Ron," he announced. "We need to build up the banks of the track on the curves."

"Yup. Even at only sixty miles an hour, which is nothing for a 240Z, you almost spun out. Of course, it'll help a lot once we can replace that packed dirt with a solid surface. Tarmac, at least, although concrete would be better."

Ferdinand nodded. "We can manage that, I think, given a bit of time. We'll need to build spectator stands also."

He turned to Janos, smiling widely. "We'll call it the Vienna 500, I'm thinking. You watch! One of these days, it'll draw enough tourists to flood the city's coffers."

Janos Drugeth, Hungarian cavalry officer in the service of the Austrian emperor—a bold and daring breed, no one denied it—wondered what the "five hundred" part of that title meant.

But he kept silent. He was afraid to ask.

Chapter 2. The Emperor

A few hours later, in one of the emperor's private salons, Janos felt a similar terror. A greater one than he'd felt on the racetrack, in truth, albeit not one that was immediately perilous.

In the long run, though, what the new emperor was contemplating was likely to be far riskier than what he'd been doing a few hours earlier at the controls of an uptime vehicle.

"Driving," Janos recalled, was the term Ferdinand III and his American mechanics used to refer to that activity. They did not use the English term, just a derivative from the stout German equivalent verb *fahren.* In both languages, the verb had the additional connotation of half-forcing, half-cajoling someone or some animal to go somewhere they would not otherwise go.

In the afternoon, a young, portly, physically quite unprepossessing monarch had driven an automobile with flair. Tonight, he was proposing to drive an empire with the same flair. Indeed, in the full scope of his half-made plans, perhaps a fourth of an entire continent.

Slowly, Janos lowered the letter the emperor had asked him to read. The letter was a long one, and had been jointly signed by Ferdinand's oldest sister Maria Anna and her new husband. Don Fernando, that was—had been, rather, since he seemed to have dropped the honorific "Don" along with his former title of cardinal-infante. He was the younger brother of the king of Spain and a member of the Spanish branch of the far-flung and powerful Habsburg family.

Fernando I, King in the Netherlands, as he now styled himself, judging from the signature on the letter.

"Are you seriously considering this, Your Majesty?" Drugeth asked quietly. He resisted the temptation to glance at the two other men in the room. Whatever else, Janos knew, he had to be able to react to his monarch in this situation without being influenced by the attitude of others.

"Quite seriously, Janos. Be assured of that. Not that I feel bound by any of my sister and new brother-in-law's specific suggestions. They face a very different situation than I do, over there in the Low Countries. And while my sister is an exceptionally well-educated and intelligent woman, and was raised here, in the nature of things her knowledge of the Austrian empire was limited in many respects. Quite limited, in some. She has no close knowledge of military affairs, for instance." The new emperor chuckled, a bit heavily. "Of course, the same cannot be said of her new husband, who could legitimately lay claim to being the most accomplished military leader produced by the family in generations."

All that was true enough. Janos had encountered Maria Anna, and had been quite impressed by her forceful personality, as much the product of an acute mind as the self-confidence of a princess. What was even more true was that the situation in Austria and its possessions was quite different—radically different—from the one she now dealt with in her new domain.

There were but two or three languages in her new kingdom, for instance, and not too distantly related at that. Whereas in the Austrian empire, how many languages were spoken? And not by a handful of foreign émigrés or small groups in isolated pockets, either, but by entire regions and by powerful persons?

Janos didn't actually know, for sure. German and Italian, of course. Hungarian. A veritable host of Slavic dialects. Three very different groups of languages, with little similarities at all.

Maria Anna and her new husband only had to deal with a few religious strains, to name another difference. Catholicism and two brands of Calvinism. Some Jews. Almost no Lutherans. Whereas in the Austrian empire, although they'd been largely driven underground by the harsh policies of Ferdinand's rigidly Catholic father, there still lurked every variety of Protestantism, Christians who adhered to the Greek church, as many if not more Jews as there were in Holland—and, should the full scope of the successor's plans come to fruition, a great number of Muslims as well.

"*All* of the Balkans?" he asked, managing to keep any trace of quaver from his voice.

"Constantinople, too," said the emperor flatly. "The Turks have had it long enough."

Privately, Janos made a note to himself to try to limit the emperor's ambitions in that regard. He could see no real advantage to seizing the southern Balkans, beyond seizing territory for the sake of it. Especially given that the rest of the proposal was already so ambitious.

"Insanely" ambitious, one could almost say. Ferdinand proposed to overturn centuries of Austrian custom, social institutions and policies at the same time as he expanded Austrian power.

The older one of the other two men in the room cleared his throat. "I have read many of those same up-time history books, Your Majesty. I feel constrained to point out that, in essence, what you propose to do here in Austria is what another monarch in Russia would try to do at the end of this century."

"Yes. Peter the Great."

The man—Johann Jakob Khiesel, Count von Gottschee, who had served the Austrian dynasty as its principal spymaster for decades—cleared his throat again. "He failed, you know. In the long run, if not in his own time. His Romanov dynasty would be destroyed in two centuries—and, in great part, by the same forces he set loose."

The emperor nodded. "I'm aware of that. But simply because he failed does not mean that we shall. We have many advantages he did not possess. And please show me any alternative, Jakob? Given that those same histories make quite clear the fate of our own Habsburg dynasty. We were also destroyed, in that same conflagration they call the First World War."

Somewhere in Janos Drugeth's mind—perhaps his soul—he could feel the decision tipping. Pulled toward the emperor by Ferdinand's unthinking use of the pronoun "we," in a manner that made quite clear he was using it in the common form of a collective pronoun, rather than the royal We.

Although he'd only read some of the up-time accounts of the future history of Russia—which were fairly sparse, in any event—Janos was quite sure that Peter the Great had never done any such thing. The Russian Tsar had tried to transform his realm without ever once contemplating the need to transform himself and his dynasty.

That . . . might be enough.

Even if it weren't, Janos could not gainsay the emperor's other point. Drugeth had studied exhaustively every American account he could find—Austria had many spies in Grantville, and good ones, so he was sure they'd found most of them—and the accounts of the fall of the Austro-Hungarian Empire, and its likely causes, were clear enough. Insofar as anything was ever clear when it came to history.

If they continued as they had been, they were surely doomed. Not in their own lifetimes, probably, but so what? If a man had no greater ambition than to go through his life satisfying his personal wants and desires, ignoring what might happen to his descendants, Janos thought him to be a sorry sort of man. Not to mention a Catholic in name only.

The fourth man in the room put the thought to words. "I think we have no choice, Father. Like you, I can see all of the pitfalls and perils in the Netherlanders' proposal. But what choice do we have? And I will point out that if we have advantages that our counterparts in another universe did not have, we also have disadvantages." A thin smile came to the face of Georg Bartholomaeus Zwickl, the count's stepson and official heir. "They did not have to face Michael Stearns."

Stearns. Mentally, Janos rolled the harsh-sounding English name on his tongue. A former coal miner, now grown into a force that had struck Europe like Attila and the Huns a thousand years earlier. In his impact, at least, if not in his methods.

Janos had seen him, once, although only at a distance on the streets of Grantville. The man had been laughing at some remark made by his companion, the president of the USE's State of Thuringia-Franconia. That was Ed Piazza, whom Janos had met briefly and in person in the course of a casual social affair.

He'd liked Piazza's friendly and unassuming manner. Just as he'd liked the look on Stearns' face when he laughed, for that matter. Being fair, it was hard to imagine such a laugh ever issuing from the mouth of Attila.

Maybe . . .

He filed that possibility away. For the moment, and for the foreseeable future, Austria and the USE were enemies.

While silence filled the room for a time, Drugeth went back to scrutinizing the letter.

Very shrewd, many of those suggestions. Janos wondered who had actually originated them? For all their undoubted intelligence, he didn't think Maria Anna and Fernando would have thought of some of them. Being born and raised in royal families also created limits. They had—must have—at least one adviser who was capable of seeing beyond those limits.

"You have my full support, Your Majesty," he said. For the first time since he'd begun reading the letter, he looked directly at von Gottschee. The old man looked tired, more than anything else. As well he might, given that he'd served Austria's dynasty faithfully and well for so long—and now, almost at the age of seventy, he was being asked to undo much of what he had done.

Privately, Janos made another note. It was unrealistic to expect the count to do more than maintain Austria's spy network. Indeed, it might even be dangerous to try to force him to do more. Fortunately, Count von Gottschee had long been grooming his stepson to take his place. Janos got along quite well with Georg Bartholomaeus, who was in his late thirties.

Granted, their background and temperaments were quite different. For all his aptitude at the covert tasks Ferdinand had set him lately, Janos was still a Hungarian cavalry officer in the way he approached things. A soldier, not a spy, where Zwickl took to his stepfather's trade as if he'd been born to it. Still, he and Zwickl should manage to work together easily enough.

It might even be best to retire the count formally. Janos would raise that possibility with the emperor in private, at some later time. It would have to be done carefully, making sure that Johann Jakob was genuinely willing and did not resent being forced into retirement. Given the situation, there was probably no single individual who could do more damage to the dynasty, should his allegiances sour. Khiesel knew . . . almost everything.

Having made his decision, however, Janos was immediately confronted by his major and immediate quarrel with the proposal.

"So," Ferdinand III stated, clapping his hands together. "We're agreed on the basic points, then? First—which I've already had done—repudiate the Edict of Restitution, to as to restore peace in our relations with our Protestant subjects. Second, retake Bohemia. Third—simultaneously, I should say—press forward with the technology transfer from the USE so we can begin the modernization of our economy and our army. Fourth, prepare for an inevitable war with the Turks. Finally, and most important of all, begin the process of drawing all of our peoples and classes into support for our cause. That will necessarily require the introduction of a great deal of popular participation in the empire's political affairs, although we will strive to keep it under control."

That was at least one too many tasks, Janos thought. And he knew, for a certainty, the one that he thought should be eliminated.

For a moment, he hesitated. Then, bracing himself, spoke it aloud. "Your Majesty, I strongly advise you to seek peace with Wallenstein and a stabilization of the northern frontier, rather than trying to retake Bohemia. I believe Wallenstein has no further designs on our remaining territory, and would agree to such an offer."

He was fudging a little, there. Janos was fairly certain that Wallenstein's ambitions lay to the east, not the south, true enough. But those same ambitions would almost require obtaining at least a part of Royal Hungary, or Wallenstein would have no way to reach the east. Not unless he was prepared to launch a war of conquest on the Polish heartland, at any rate, which Drugeth thought unlikely.

He was willing to make the fudge, nonetheless, if he could keep the emperor from such a rash and unwise policy. The truth was, so long as Wallenstein satisfied himself with seizing only the northern portions of Royal Hungary, Janos didn't care. Those lands were mostly inhabited by Slavs, not Hungarians. From a military standpoint, they were more of a nuisance than anything else.

True, there was an awkward personal matter involved. His own family's estates were mostly located in that very area. It would be a pity to lose the lovely Renaissance-style residence that his father had built in Hommona. It was only twenty-five years old and had all the modern conveniences a man could wish for. But ceding a small portion of Austria's northernmost lands, even ones that included Hommona, was a small price to pay to get a stabilization of the northern borders.

The emperor would most likely find a way to compensate the Drugeth family for the loss, and what one architect had built another could build as well. But even if the emperor didn't, Janos would still argue in favor of ceding the northern portions of Royal Hungary. Being of the aristocracy, the way Janos viewed human relations, bound a man to his duties far more than to his privileges. What overrode all other considerations, certainly mere personal ones, was that fighting the immensely powerful Ottoman Empire over control of the Balkans was going to be a mighty challenge in itself. The last thing Austria needed was to be embroiled simultaneously in a war with Bohemia. Especially since Bohemia was allied to the USE, and they needed to make peace with the Swede also.

A heavy frown had formed on the emperor's brow. "Surely you're not serious, Janos? Wallenstein is a usurper and a traitor, whose claims to Bohemia are specious. Preposterous, rather!"

"Yes, they are, Your Majesty. But I feel compelled to point out that any war with the Turks will strain us to the utmost. I think it most unwise to get entangled with Bohemia also."

"Oh, that's nonsense, Janos. I don't propose to fight the Turks any time soon. We need Bohemia's resources. Surely, we can have it back in our hands within a year or two."

Surely we can't, Janos felt like snarling. He hadn't been present himself at the second battle of the White Mountain, since he'd been assigned to the Turkish border at the time. But he'd heard many accounts of it from his fellow officers who had been present. Granted, they were junior officers, who, as usual, were quick to criticize the failings of the top commanders in that battle. But the fact remained that while Austria might have won the battle with more capable commanders, it would still have been a savage affair. Nobody in their right mind dismissed Pappenheim lightly—not to mention that Wallenstein had proved himself to be one of Europe's most capable organizers of armies over a period of years. Any war with Bohemia, even a victorious war that resulted in a reconquest, would surely bleed Austria's armies badly. And that was the last thing they needed, if they intended to confront the Ottomans.

It was true that Bohemia had great resources, many of which were absent or scanty in the rest of the Austrian realm. But what good were resources that couldn't be obtained? By force, at any rate. If they established a stable peace with Wallenstein, Janos was fairly sure the Bohemians would be glad to provide those resources by way of trade—at a far smaller cost than the hideously expensive business of waging war.

Alas, one of the things those American future histories had contained was a clear record that Ferdinand III—still merely the king of Hungary, in that universe, since his father had lived a bit longer—had been, along with the cardinal-infante, the co-commander of the Habsburg army that had inflicted a massive defeat on the Swedes at Nordlingen in 1634.

That battle had not happened, in this universe, and never would. But the record had been enough to infuse Ferdinand with self-confidence in his abilities as a military leader which were simply premature in *this* universe. Janos didn't doubt that his new monarch indeed possessed a talent for military affairs. He was talented in many things. But "talent" and "experience" were not the same thing, in war perhaps more than in any sphere of human affairs.

"A year or two," the emperor repeated forcefully. "Watch and see if I'm not right."

Janos exchanged a glance with Zwickl. Some subtlety in Georg Bartholomaeus' expression made his attitude clear. *Let it go, Janos, at least for the moment. You're probably right, but you can't restrain him now.*

Drugeth decided he was right. As foolish and costly as it might be, Austria's new ruler would simply have to learn some things for himself.

And probably more than once, too. The thought would have been a gloomy one, perhaps, had Janos not been a soldier. He'd seen very few officers—and certainly not himself—who'd learned their brutal trade without making mistakes. It was just the way things were.

"I simply felt it necessary to advance my opinion, Your Majesty," he said, trying to sound obedient but not submissive. "That said, in this as in all things, you have my allegiance and support."

Ferdinand beamed. "Well, good. In any event, Janos, it's not something you're likely to be worrying about. Not directly, at least." Here, the emperor exchanged a meaningful look with Count von Gottschee. "Since you've done so well in Grantville, I propose to hand the entire operation to you. Which Johann Jakob tells me is on the eve of coming to fruition."

Janos wondered what the emperor meant by "coming to fruition." The work that Janos had set underway in Grantville some months earlier was intended to produce a slow and steady stream of technology transfer— including some personnel—from the USE to Austria. It was not the sort of project that ever "came to fruition," as such.

Ferdinand rose from his chair and waved his hand airily. "I have an audience I need to attend. The count will explain it to you. But you'd best start packing, Janos. You'll need to head out for Grantville on the morrow."

◊   ◊   ◊

After Johann Jakob Khiesel explained what had been happening in Grantville over the months since Janos had left for his inspection tour of the fortresses in the Balkans, Drugeth had to restrain himself from snarling again.

"In other words, in my absence, Henry Gage and Lion Gardiner—the benighted fools—allowed themselves to become cat's paws for a pack of American thieves."

Both Khiesel and his stepson looked startled. "But . . ." the count began.

"Don't you understand, Janos?" said Georg Bartholomaeus. "At one swoop, we will get a far greater transfer than anything we'd envisioned."

"And *then* what?" demanded Drugeth. He took a deep breath, reminding himself that neither the count nor his stepson had any personal acquaintance with Grantville or its up-time inhabitants. For them, as for most people in Europe, the Americans were a mysterious band of wizards. Drugeth had had the same impression himself, until the weeks he'd spent there had made the truth clear to him.

Grantville was a *town,* that's all. A town of people with knowledge and technical skills far advanced from any other in the world, true enough. But still simply a town—not of wizards, but of craftsmen. Simple folk, really, who understood in their bones something that most people who viewed them from a distance did not really understand at all. Their technical wizardry was the product of generations of skills compiled and passed on. Hard work lay at its root, not some sort of preposterous sorcery. There were no "secrets" in Grantville. No compendium of ultimate wisdom. No magic recipes, no magic spells, no magic wands—most of all, no sorcerer's grimoire that, once seized, opened all technical secrets to the possessor.

"What then?" he repeated. "By the very manner in which this escapade will take place—there is no way to avoid this—the Americans will surely put in place measures that make any further transfers ten times more difficult."

Finally, he did snarl. "Not to mention that we will have done the Americans the great favor of draining the worst sort of people from their midst, and planting them amongst us. For the love of God, these people are traitors and criminals. Who is to say they will not betray us in turn?"

For a moment, the memory of the three up-time mechanics whom he'd met at the race track earlier that day came to him. Janos was sure they knew far more than they were admitting, about matters that would be of direct benefit to Austria's power, not simply an emperor's whimsy. He knew, for instance, that while the three men insisted they were quite ignorant of all "aeronautical matters" that at least one of them, Ronald Sanderlin, had served for months as a mechanic at the USE's air force base in Wismar. He *had* to know how to construct at least the engine for a warplane, if not the plane itself.

But Sanderlin would keep that knowledge to himself, until and unless he became convinced that he could pass it on to Austrians without damaging his own nation. He was neither a traitor nor a thief.

Damnation! This was insane. They needed to make *peace* with the Swede and his Americans, not infuriate them. Just as they needed to forget the past and make peace with Wallenstein. The great foe of Austria was the Ottoman Empire—and would have been, even leaving aside the new emperor's determination to take the Balkans from them.

The two spymasters were still staring at him, obviously not understanding his concern. Spies and spymasters had their own limitations, he realized, produced by the very nature of their work. They dealt with criminals and traitors as a matter of course—which made sense, from the standpoint of spying, but made no sense at all from the standpoint of forging a new nation.

Janos made a note to remember that in the future. Always.

"Never mind," he said. "What's done is done. I'll be off to Grantville at first light."

Chapter 3. The Elf

Grantville, State of Thuringia-Franconia
November 1634

Noelle Murphy—Noelle Stull, now, having just changed her name legally—finished her report, and leaned back in her chair. Sitting at the desk in his office, Tony Adducci did the same. He looked to Carol Unruh, sitting in another chair facing the desk, at a diagonal from Noelle.

"Seems pretty complete to me, Carol. I'm not a lawyer, of course."

Noelle had to keep herself from smiling. "Not a lawyer" was putting it mildly. In point of fact, Tony Adducci's formal education extended to a high school diploma and two years at Fairmont State, from which he'd left to get a job in the mines without even picking up an AA degree. The main reason he'd been selected to be the secretary of the treasury for the New United States, not long after the Ring of Fire, was because he'd helped Frank Jackson keep the books for Mike Stearns' UMWA local. In those days—as was still the case, more often than not—Mike selected his administrators primarily because he thought they were solid men he could rely on, pedigrees and credentials be damned. And, in the case of posts like Tony's, knew that they were honest.

Noelle's suppressed smile would have been simply one of amusement, however, not derision. When all was said and done, Mike's crude method had worked pretty well. It had given the new government he'd been forced to set up in the midst of crisis and chaos a great deal of solidity and unity, however rough the edges might have been, and he'd simply shrugged off charges of "UMWA favoritism."

As the years had passed since the Ring of Fire, a number of those initial appointees had been gently eased out, when it turned out they simply weren't up to the job. But Tony had kept his post through all of the transformations— from the NUS as an independent principality, to its later status as a semi-independent principality within the Confederated Principalities of Europe, to its current (and hopefully final) manifestation as one of the provinces within the federal United States of Europe. Ed Piazza, who'd replaced Mike as the president of the SoTF after Mike became the prime minister of the USE and moved to Magdeburg, was no more inclined to replace Adducci than Stearns had been. He was capable, honest, and made up for his own lack of training by knowing how to use the skills of subordinates or associates who did have it.

Such as Carol Unruh, in fact, Ron Koch's wife although she'd kept her own name. Carol was the assistant director of the Department of Economic Resources, one of the branches of the Treasury Department. Her academic background might have been on the skimpy side for an equivalent position in the universe they'd come from. But by post-RoF Grantville standards, she was highly educated. She had a BA in mathematics and statistics and had taken graduate courses in the same subjects. She'd squeezed in the graduate courses on a part-time basis while she was bringing up her two children, but she'd always planned to go back full-time and finish her doctoral program once the kids were out of the house and she could really concentrate. Nobody much doubted she would have, either, except that the Ring of Fire had put paid to those plans as well as many others. Still, she was qualified enough to have been accepted as the University of Jena's instructor in statistics, whose male faculty was normally hostile to the idea of women teaching at the university level, outside of medicine and a few other special subjects.

"Oh, it's plenty good enough to put Horace Bolender behind bars," she said.

"*Keep* him behind bars," Tony growled. "Noelle and Eddie already got that much accomplished. The fucking bastard."

"He hasn't been convicted yet, Tony," Carol pointed out. "In fact, I think he's even going to manage to raise the bail money."

Again, Noelle had to fight to keep from smiling. Not at Tony's praise but at Carol's reaction. Unruh had the sort of prissy sense of duty that compelled her to add the caution—given that, in cold-blooded personal terms, she stood to benefit the most if Horace Bolender got convicted. Her title of "assistant" director was something of a formality these days. Bolender *had* been the director of the Department of Economic Resources, until Carol's suspicions and the investigative work by Noelle and Eddie Junker that those suspicions engendered had turned up plenty of evidence that the man had been using his post to feather his own nest.

Now, Carol was actually running the department, and everyone expected that it wouldn't be long before President Piazza made her the official director. Where a different sort of person in her position might have been pushing for a conviction, Unruh was being meticulously fair-minded and scrupulous.

That spoke well of her, of course, but Noelle still thought it was silly. She and Eddie had nailed the bastard, sure enough. It hadn't even been all that hard, once they started digging. Like untold thousands of officials before him, Bolender had been sloppy about his demands for kickbacks before he assigned contracts. That was due more to arrogance than actual stupidity, probably, but the end result was no different. It was easy for an up-time official to get careless on the subject of bribes, since most down-timers took bribing officials to be a routine cost of business.

He'd get a long, hard sentence, too. Bolender was not the first up-timer to have been caught breaking the law, but he was far and away the most prominent. Judge Tito was well known for his lack of leniency toward up-timers, because he was bound and determined to prove to the citizens of the SoTF—which had one million people in it all told—that the tiny percentage of them who were of American origin weren't going to be getting any special treatment or favors from the law.

Tony looked back at Noelle. "What else looks to be turning up? Besides Bolender and the Cunninghams and Norman Bell, I mean."

"Nothing definite, yet. But Eddie and I are still digging. We don't think we rooted it all out, by any means.

We're almost certain that Stan Myers' tip regarding Mickey Simmons is a good one."

"How about Myers himself?" asked Carol. "It wouldn't be the first time a crook tried to deflect suspicion by fingering somebody else."

Noelle shook her head. "Eddie and I don't think Stan's dirty. For one thing, because we just don't. Beyond that, Stan's in charge of the fire department's training program. He simply doesn't have access to the kind of temptation to ask for kickbacks that somebody like Bolender did. He's got a hard enough time, as it is, getting volunteers for the fire department, given all the other economic opportunities around."

Tony chuckled. "True enough. I can remember my dad complaining when he had to pass the dispatcher a five dollar bill to get work out of his union's hiring hall. Which was *not* the UMWA," he added self-righteously. "But those jobs paid well, so he thought it was worth the baksheesh. Most of the fire department posts are volunteer. Don't pay anything more than expenses."

Carol nodded. "I was just raising the possibility. I like Stan, myself, and I've never gotten any sense he was crooked. Mickey Simmons, though . . . " She made a face. "Well, I should keep personalities out of it, I suppose."

"He's a prick," stated Adducci. "He's always been a prick. Why the hell it took Lorraine so long to give him the heave-ho was always a mystery to me." He straightened up in his chair. "Just for the record. But I agree we should keep personalities out of it. There *is* such a thing as an honest assho—uh, butthead, here and there.

But I won't be surprised at all if Mickey turns out not to be one of them."

He mused for a moment, apparently lost in remembrances of things past. "He really is a Grade A prick. But let's move on to the rest. How about the down-timers, Carol? Any decision yet from the attorney general?"

"I just talked to Christoph yesterday. He feels in an awkward position, given that he's a down-timer himself, so he stressed that he'd defer to your judgment on the matter. Still, he thinks it would be a mistake to press charges against any of the down-timers, if their only involvement was having their arm twisted into paying the kickbacks. I'm inclined to agree."

Adducci grunted. "Yeah, so am I. Not that seventeenth-century Germans haven't got at least as fine-tuned a sense of lawyering as any West Virginian ever did. They knew damn good and well they were breaking the law too. Still, you have to make allowances for the chaos caused by fifteen years of war half-wrecking the Germanies. People slide into bad habits in situations like that. For us to run around hammering everybody probably wouldn't be a good idea. Still, this is it, folks. You also gotta watch out for being paternalistic about these things. Down-timers ain't children. Once these cases break and we start putting people in prison, let's make sure the message gets out to every businessman in the province who's thinking of cutting a deal beneath the table. Do it again, and we'll bust you, sure and certain."

Noelle thought their attitude was probably the right one to take, though she was even more inclined than they were not to err on the side of paternalistic tolerance. *It's just their traditional ways*, baloney. Her partner

Eddie Junker was a down-timer, and *he'd* never had any trouble recognizing that paying a kickback was just as illegal, if not perhaps as personally reprehensible, as demanding it in the first place.

That said, she was a little relieved. Her relations with Eddie had gotten awkward lately, and she was pretty sure she knew the reason. Now, with this decision having been made, she could see her way clear to straightening it out.

Adducci raised an admonishing finger. "But! That only applies to down-timers whose involvement was simply paying the kickback. Any of them who got more, what you might call enthusiastic and enterprising about the business, we'll go after them just like we are the up-timers."

For the third time in half an hour, Noelle had to fight to keep a smile from her face. *That* wouldn't be a problem for her, at least. Claus Junker might have been willing enough in the enthusiasm department, but when it came to "enterprise" it was just a fact that Eddie's father was a hopeless nincompoop. He bore about as much resemblance to a criminal mastermind as . . .

She tried to think of anyone she knew who could possibly be as inept as Claus Junker at the art of "making a deal." The only person she could come up with was her own mother.

She must have choked, or something.

"What's so funny, Noelle?" asked Carol.

"Ah . . . nothing. Just an idle thought."

Janos Drugeth's agents in Grantville, the Englishmen Henry Gage and Lion Gardiner, seemed bound and

determined to waste more time continuing the recrimi-
nations.

"In particular," said Gage with exasperation, "I told
you to stay away from the Barlow family!"

Gardiner scowled at him. "And I *did*—until I was
approached by Neil O'Connor, who is part of the affair
because *you* recruited his father Allen."

Gage looked defensive. "We need the O'Connors.
Between the father's knowledge of steam engines and
the son's experience working on aircraft, they'll be
invaluable. And we need Peter Barclay and his wife, too.
They both have experience in mechanical design."

"We *don't* need—"

Gage threw up his hands. "Of course we don't need
their crazy daughter! But the Barclays insisted that their
children had to be part of the bargain, or they wouldn't
agree." Sullenly, he added: "It's *not* my fault. It's certainly not my fault that the oldest girl Suzi Barclay lives
in a state of sin with Neil O'Connor, and she told *him,*
and he told his father, and—"

He broke off there. Gardiner picked it right up, now
with a sneer on his face.

"—and she also told her friend Caryn Barlow, who is
almost as crazy as she is—not surprising, being the
daughter of Jay Barlow—and she told her father and
there we were. In the soup."

"Enough," said Janos stolidly. Rubbing the back of
his neck, he looked around the small apartment his two
subordinates had been renting on the outskirts of
Grantville. At least they had enough sense to be packed
and ready to go. "This is pointless—and we have little
time remaining."

He gave Gardiner a cold eye. "Do restrain your indignation. It was you, after all, who recruited the Simmons fellow. Who has no skills I am aware of beyond embezzlement—and paltry skills at that, judging from the evidence."

It was Gardiner's turn to look defensive. "That wasn't *my* doing. The O'Connors insisted that their employee Timothy Kennedy should be included also. Seeing as he was very skilled in the steam work and was now disaffected from his wife—"

Seeing his chance, Gage interrupted with a sneer. "Who just happens to be the sister of Anita Masaniello, who just happens to be the wife of Steve Salatto, who just happens to be the American official in charge of administering Franconia."

Gardiner glared up. "As I recall, *you* thought recruiting Kennedy was a good idea at the time yourself. He seemed tight-lipped enough. How was I—or you—to know that he was good friends with Mickey Simmons and Simmons was up to his neck—"

"Enough!" growled Janos. He wiped his face tiredly. Part of his weariness was due to the rigors of the hard and fast journey he'd made from Vienna, much of which had been on horseback through forests and mountains to evade the USE's border patrols. Most of it, though, was simply weariness at the whole business.

He was still aggravated by Istvan's foolishness in having hired these two English adventurers as his direct agents in Grantville, as much as he was aggravated by the adventurers themselves. But, being fair to all parties, he also recognized that most of the problem was simply due to the nature of the work involved. This miserable business the Americans called "covert operations."

True, Gardiner and Gage were mercenary adventurers. On the other hand, they spoke fluent—now even idiomatic—English in a town of English speakers whose usage of the language was eccentric to begin with, by seventeenth-century standards. It was doubtful that any regular Austrian agents could have penetrated so deeply and quickly into the disaffected elements among the Americans. That was true even leaving aside the thugs who infested the so-called Club 250, who were automatically suspicious of any central Europeans. None of the thugs themselves were of any particular interest to Austria, which could recruit plenty of thugs of its own. But the Club 250 served as something of a liaison venue for other disaffected up-timers that Austria was interested in. Gage and Gardiner could go there easily. Between their excellent knowledge of the American idiom and the fact they were English—for reasons still somewhat murky to Drugeth, the American bigots who patronized the Club 250 made an exemption for Englishmen—the two of them could habituate the place where, if Janos went himself, he'd likely face a fracas.

True, also, many—no, most; perhaps all—of the Americans they were seeking to recruit were not what any sane man would consider upright and moral persons. At best, their guiding motives were nakedly mercenary. For some of them, such as Simmons, you could add a desire to escape apprehension by the SoTF's authorities for criminal activity. For others, like the O'Connors and their employee Timothy Kennedy, their extravagant and careless spending habits had led them to drive a seemingly prosperous business into a state of near-bankruptcy.

As for the "craziness" of the Suzi Barclay girl, a subject on which both Gage and Gardiner could expound at length, what was to be expected from the offspring of such parents?

He rubbed his face again. In the end, all the problems were simply inherent to the business itself. If a man insists on sticking his hand into a marsh looking for gold, he can hardly be surprised if he retrieves filth and leeches as well as the gold he was looking for.

And . . .

There was gold there, sure enough. Being fair to the two. Whatever the moral and mental characteristics of the up-timers whom Gage and Gardiner had recruited to move to Vienna and provide the Austrian empire with technological skills and advice, there was no question that they'd assembled an impressive group. Amongst them, there was extensive knowledge of American machining techniques, mechanical design, and steam engine design, not to mention the seemingly ubiquitous knowledge that American males had with regard to automobile engines. There was even a fair knowledge of aircraft principles, something which was in scant supply even among Americans.

Still, it was a mess. The original plan had been modified after the end of the war between the USE and the League of Ostend brought a period of peace. That, combined with the outcome of the Congress of Copenhagen and the decision of the SoTF to relocate its capital from Grantville to Bamberg, was producing a massive wave of emigration of Americans out of Grantville to other parts—and not all of them to somewhere else in the USE. It seemed as if every nation in Europe had launched a recruitment program here, even the French.

Most of those who chose to leave the USE, of course, went to either Prague or Copenhagen or the Netherlands. Bohemia and Denmark were allied to the USE; and, while the new kingdom in the Low Countries was not, it enjoyed quite friendly relations these days. Nowhere in Europe had the now-romantic figure of the Netherlands' new queen Maria Anna assumed such legendary proportions as it had in Grantville. "The Wheelbarrow Queen," they called her, often enough. Even the rambunctious and surly commoners of Magdeburg seemed inclined to favor the Netherlands, monarchy or not.

Janos had hopes that, eventually, that same romanticism might help relations between the USE and his own nation. Maria Anna was, after all, a daughter of the Habsburgs and one of the new emperor's two sisters. At one time—not more than a few months ago—an archduchess of Austria itself.

It was too early for that, of course. Everyone in the USE was expecting a new war to begin the coming spring, with Saxony and Brandenburg, and everyone was assuming—accurately, alas, unless Janos could persuade the emperor otherwise—that Austria would weigh in on the side of the USE's enemies. Still, Janos had hoped to keep tensions between Austria and the USE, especially its Americans, to a minimum. Sooner or later, he was sure Austria would have to seek peace with the USE, and he didn't want any more in the way of festering anger than was inevitable in the course of a war.

So, clearly and unequivocally, he'd told Istvan Janoszi to instruct his agents to keep any transfer of personnel and equipment from Grantville within the limits of the law, as the Americans saw it.

That hadn't seemed too difficult a project, at the time. The up-timers had sweeping notions on the subject of personal liberties, which included the right to emigrate and included the right to maintain personal property in the process. The key figures, the O'Connors and the Barclays, were in a position to do that. Simply move themselves and their businesses to Vienna. Impossible, of course, to move the actual physical plants, but they could certainly take with them all of their technical designs—"blueprints," those seemed to be called—and even much of the moveable equipment. Over time, if not immediately.

Unfortunately, what Janos hadn't foreseen was the inevitability of what followed. Like anything dragged out of a swamp, be it gold-colored or not, the Barlows and the O'Connors were *sticky*. They had relatives and friends, the relatives and friends had their own such—and among them, what a surprise, were some individuals whom no one in their right mind would want to encourage to move into his own country.

And so, a legal enterprise had become an illegal one. Not only were some of these people going to be fleeing the authorities of the USE, they were going to be taking goods and possessions with them that they had no legal right to take.

For a moment, Drugeth considered simply forbidding any such goods. But he dismissed the idea almost as soon as it came to him. First, because that was bound to produce a quarrel with the would-be emigrants, and there was no time left for such a quarrel. Second, even more simply, because Drugeth really had no way to know which goods were legal and which weren't, in the first place. Once the expedition got to the Austrian border, he had a large cavalry unit waiting to escort them all the rest of the way to Vienna. But from here to the border, he'd have only Gage and Gardiner to assist him in keeping control over the up-timers.

What was he to do? Insist on a search of the wagons, not even knowing what he was looking for?

It was just a mess, that's all. A marshy muck. But Janos had crossed marshes and swamps often enough, since he took the Austrian colors. Though he was only twenty-five years old, he had plenty of experience as a soldier. He figured he could manage this, well enough.

"Tomorrow morning, then," he said. "We start to leave as early as possible."

Chapter 4. The Biker

Three days later, in the evening, over the sandwiches they were having by way of a working meal on the folding table in Noelle's apartment, she finally nailed her partner.

"All right, Eddie, spill it. I got the word from Carol Unruh over lunch today. For what it's worth, she and Tony Adducci and Christoph Wieland officially decided that no charges would be pressed against any down-timer unless they were actively involved as one of the arm-twisters. Just paying the bribes, we'll let it go. This time, anyway."

Eddie Junker laid his half-eaten sandwich down on the plate, then stared at it for a moment, before sighing.

"It has been difficult. I've felt bad about it. Not saying anything to you, I mean."

"Yeah, I can see that. How deep was your father involved?"

Eddie shrugged, uncomfortably. "Not as deep as I'm sure he would have liked to have been. Dear God in Heaven, when will my father learn that he has the business sense of . . . of . . . "

"My mother," Noelle said crisply. For a moment, they both shared a laugh. Noelle's mother Pat was to good sense what a junkyard was to orderly. The woman wasn't stupid. She just didn't seem to have a clue how to separate abstractions from their application to the real world.

In her favor, though, Noelle thought but didn't say out loud, at least Pat wasn't greedy. Something which couldn't be said for Claus Junker.

"The point is, Eddie, nobody's going to go after your dad. But I'd like to know if there are any leads there."

Eddie used the time it took to finish the sandwich to compose his thoughts. Then: "I think so, yes. Do you know a man—an up-timer—by the name of Jay Barlow? And another one by the name of Allen O'Connor?"

Noelle stared at him for a moment. "Jay Barlow, yeah," she said abruptly. "He used to be a car dealer before the Ring of Fire, mostly used cars—and he was pretty much a poster boy for what people think of used car dealers."

Eddie frowned. "Which is . . . what?"

"Never mind. Crooked sleazeball is close enough. The kind of guy whose stock in trade was passing off lemons."

"I thought you said he sold automobiles."

"Never mind, like I said. Some other time I'll enhance your vocabulary of up-time slang. But right now I want to concentrate on the other guy. Allen O'Connor, you said?"

"Yes. I think he's actually the more important of the two, although my father's direct dealings were with Barlow."

Noelle chuckled. "Well, yeah, I can believe that. In the TO of organized crime, like any other enterprise I can think of, you'll find the Jay Barlows of the world pretty regularly enrolled under the rank of 'foot soldier.'"

"What's a 'TO'?"

"Table of Organization. Like I said, later for the vocabulary lesson."

She scratched the tip of her chin, forgetting for a moment her long-standing vow to eliminate that mannerism on account of it drew attention to her chin. She thought it was on the pointy side, which was especially unfortunate given the shape of her ears, which were also too damn close to being pointed. Add into the miserable bargain her too-slim figure, which she'd had since she was a kid, even before she started exercising regularly. She began that regimen after the scares she'd experienced in Franconia during the Ram Rebellion convinced her she'd better be in top physical condition.

All she needed, in her position, was for people to think she was some kind of elf.

Catching herself, she stopped. Then, tugged at her earlobe. Then, silently chided herself and brought the hand firmly down on the table. "O'Connor, on the other hand, has the potential to rise to higher levels. *Did* rise to higher levels, in fact, not long after the Ring of Fire, when he set up a steam engine business."

"So did Barlow," Eddie pointed out. "He's the partner and co-manager of the Grantville-Saalfeld Foundries and Metalworks—which is quite an important and profitable enterprise. More so than O'Connor's steam engine corporation, really."

Noelle sneered, forgetting momentarily her longstanding vow never to sneer on account of it made her look like an impudent elf. "Yeah, sure—but that's due to the *other* partner, Bart Kubiak, who's the brains of the outfit. I heard—never mind where—that the only reason Bart asked Jay to become his partner—and he doesn't have anything close to an equal share in the business, by the way, just a token amount—is because Billie

Jean Mase sweet-talked him into it and Bart wanted her to relocate to Saalfeld to be his office manager."

She shook her head. "There's another mixed-blessing character for you. By all accounts, Billie Jean is a cracker-jack office manager—"

"I thought those were a kind of cereal candy."

"What is it with your sudden obsession with learning every bit of American slang in one sitting? But whatever skills Billie Jean has in an office, she's a dumb blonde in the rest of her life."

Eddie was now eyeing Noelle's hair dubiously.

"Fine," she snapped. "It's sort-of blonde. It's just an expression. Some of the world's champion dumb blondes are brunettes and redheads. Trust me on this one, for just a moment. Who else but a dumb blonde would ever get hooked up with a guy like Jay Barlow? You can't even credit her with being a gold-digger, since she brings in most of the gold."

She raised the fingers of her left hand and began counting them off with the thumb and forefinger of her right hand, forgetting also her solemn vow not to draw attention to her fingers because they were too slender and nimble and, well, sorta elflike.

"First, he's a loser. Second, he's a sleazebag. Third—"

"I thought the term was sleazeball," Eddie complained.

Noelle contemplated strangling him. Then, simultaneously concluded her hands were far too delicate for the task—Eddie was on the heavily-built side—and remembered her vow not to display them. Hurriedly, she put her hands back in her lap.

"Third," she said forcefully, "he's thirteen years older than she is. Remembering my charitable Christian nature—"

Eddie was looking more dubious by the minute.

"—I will forego pointing out that his potbelly matches his age and then some. Fourth, he's lazy. Fifth—since after two months Bart Kubiak gave him the boot and told him to enjoy his piddly little share of the partnership back in Grantville where he'd be out of Bart's hair—he spends most of his waking hours lounging at the 250 Club, trying to pretend he's a tough biker even if the only part of 'biker' he has down pat is the boozing. Sixth—"

She broke off suddenly, and stared at the wall. Nothing there to look at, just getting an idea.

"What is it?" Eddie asked.

She started scratching her chin again, forgetting her solemn vow to work on her memory so it wouldn't resemble Swiss cheese. Just what she needed, having people think she was as flighty as an elf.

"I was just thinking, now that I think about it, that Jay Barlow is the mirror opposite of Buster Beasley. There's a guy who has 'tough biker' down pat every other way, except he finds most bikers pretty boring. So he doesn't hang out much at the 250 Club, true enough—but I'll bet he knows where all the bones are buried and whose skeleton is rattling which bike. He's honest, too. Well . . . allowing for a certain casual attitude toward mind-altering substances and stuff like that, but who cares? Those laws aren't in force anymore and even if they were you and I are working for the Treasury department, not the old DEA."

"I am now completely lost," said Eddie.

Noelle flashed him a grin, forgetting her solemn vow to suppress her quick way of smiling since she thought that was probably the silly way that elves smiled if elves existed which they didn't but too many damn people had heard of them and thought they probably did and she was suspect number one.

"I'll introduce you." She glanced at the clock on the wall. "It's only eight. He's probably still at his storage rental place."

She got up, grabbed her purse and shrugged into her coat, then headed for the door. Eddie followed. "If we're lucky, maybe his daughter Denise is there too. There's a real pip."

Outside, Eddie asked: "What is a 'pip'?"

Noelle did her best to explain, as they walked. She'd never realized before, just how hard it could be to explain a colloquial term like "a real pip." But, when she was done, Eddie nodded sagely.

"Ah. Sort of an American elf."

"There's no such thing as an elf," Noelle snapped.

She thought his ensuing silence had a dubious flavor, too.

"Forget Simmons," said Buster Beasley. With the booted foot he had planted on an overturned crate, he kept rocking back and forth on his chair. Given that it wasn't a rocking chair, just a beat-up old wooden kitchen chair, and given Buster's heft, Noelle wondered how much longer it would last.

"Simmons is a clown," he continued. The light cast into the office of Buster's rental storage operation from a single naked light bulb in the ceiling threw his face into deep shadows, making him look more like a prophet than the middle-aged, long-haired, heavily-bearded and burly ex-biker that he was. If you ignored the muscular arms exposed by the cutaway denim jacket, anyway. Noelle was familiar with the lives of many of the saints and the Old Testament prophets, and she was quite sure not one of them had had a *Born to Raise Hell* tattoo on their shoulder, with or without a dagger through it.

"He can manage to slice bread on his own, I suppose, but anything more complicated would stump him for sure. The only reason he got that job heading up the training program for the Department of Transportation was because his ex-wife Lorraine talked her twin sister Lauren into getting it for him, even though she'd dumped the bum years ago."

Buster's fifteen-year-old daughter Denise was perched on an upended crate not far away, as was Eddie. Noelle had been given the one stool in the office to sit on. She'd have preferred a crate herself, actually, since the stool looked to be as rickety as the one and only chair in the office that was getting a workout from Buster.

"I don't get it, Dad," Denise said. The girl's expression was one of intense curiosity, which seemed to fit her face quite nicely. She shook her head a little, causing her long dark hair to ripple. "I mean, sure, I like Lorraine. Who doesn't? But where'd she get the pull to land an ex-husband—not even the guy she's married to now—a job that good?"

Denise didn't seem to think there was anything odd about her father calling another man a bum and clown. This, despite the fact that Buster's office furniture consisted of upside-down crates and stools, a cheap metal cabinet that looked like an antique except no antique shop would have bothered trying to restore anything that badly stained and covered with rust spots, and a desk—Noelle was still trying not to grin at the thing—that was actually the bed of a junkyard pickup truck that Buster must have cut out with a torch and provided with legs made out of parts from the frames of old motorcycles. He ran a welding business on the side and was quite good at it. Good enough, in fact, that if he'd concentrated on that business he could have become very prosperous. But Buster valued his free time a lot more than he did money.

Noelle wasn't surprised by Denise's respect for her father, quite evident despite the relaxed and informal ease of their relationship. Buster Beasley, like Tom Stone, was one of those people who managed to live outside the normal boundaries of social custom without being considered a hopeless screwball. Screwball, maybe, hopeless—no. They were just too effective at managing their lives, each in their own way. In Buster's case, of course, the tattoos helped stifle vocal criticism, especially combined with the seventeen-inch biceps displayed by the cut-out jacket. Not to mention the scars.

Despite her appearance, which she'd inherited from her mother—slender and very attractive, where Buster was neither—Denise was a chip off the old block. She was just a few weeks shy of her sixteenth birthday. Most girls her age would have been either egotistical or confused by her good looks, and the effect it had on boys. Denise was neither. She took it for granted, didn't seem to care in the least—she certainly didn't pick her girlfriends based on *their* looks—and God help the overeager high school boy who didn't take "no" seriously.

Denise was the only girl Noelle knew who'd been hauled in front of the high-school vice-principal for punching a kid out. Fortunately, there weren't too many boys stupid enough to harass Buster Beasley's daughter.

Buster gave his daughter a grin. "How many times have I told you not to underestimate networking skills?"

Denise snorted. "Coming from you!"

He shrugged. "I didn't say I was good at it, I just told you not to underestimate them. In this case, sure, Lorraine doesn't have any direct clout worth talking about. But—"

He held up his thumb. "Her twin sister Lauren owns and runs the town's best restaurant, along with her husband Calvin." He raised his forefinger alongside the thumb. "If there's a power-that-be in Grantville that doesn't hang out there, I don't know who it is." The middle finger came up to join them. "For sure and certain, Joe Stull—remember him? he's the secretary of Transportation—eats lunch there practically every day."

Buster brought up the ring finger, somehow managing not to haul the little finger along with it. He was a very well-coordinated man, despite the graying beard and the muscle. "Moving right along, since Lauren and Calvin Tyler's daughter Rachel has all the sense when it comes to men that Lorraine doesn't, she married that Scot cavalryman Edward Graham, who—he ain't no dummy, either—immediately left the Swedish colors and wrangled himself a partnership in the restaurant with his new in-laws. And—"

Finally, the little finger came up. "That damn Scotsman could charm a rattlesnake, which Joe Stull ain't—and Graham makes it a point to be the waiter any time a bigshot shows up."

Denise was looking a little cross-eyed by now. For that matter, Noelle thought she might be herself.

The fingers started closing back down, one at a time, gracefully despite their heft. "So Lorraine talked to Lauren and she talked to Graham and Graham put in a word with Joe Stull, and I guess Joe must have been having one of his rare off days because he agreed to hire the clown. And that's how it happened."

Throughout, he hadn't varied in the slightest the metronome regularity of his chair-rocking. Now, he looked back to Noelle. "So, like I said, forget Simmons." He gestured with his thumb to the tattoo on his shoulder. "If Mickey had a tattoo, it'd read *Born to be a Small-Time Loser*. No, the people you want to start looking at are the Barclays."

Noelle frowned. "Pete Barclay? The guy who works for Dave Marcantonio?"

"Yup. Him and his wife Marina. She works there too, y'know." He finally ceased the chair-rocking and stood up. Then, picked up a big black flashlight perched on a shelf, one of those long, heavy Maglites favored by cops because they could double as a club in a pinch. Buster was holding it the way cops did, too, with the lamp cupped in his hand and the shaft perched on his shoulder, ready to swing forward if need be. So far as Noelle knew, Buster Beasley hadn't been in a brawl in years. But he'd been notorious for brawling in his younger years—if not for starting fights, certainly for ending them—and he clearly still had the ingrained habits.

The big ex-biker headed for the door, not bothering to put on a coat to fend off the autumn chill outside. "Come on. Let me show you something."

A minute later, they were staring into one of Buster's storage sheds. It was one of the big ones down by the end.

"There is nothing in it," said Eddie, puzzled.

"Not today, sure enough. But if you'd looked into it three mornings ago, you would have found it packed full. The Barclays showed up right when I opened, along with Allen and Neil O'Connor—I think most of the stuff belonged to them, actually, even though the Barclays are the ones who paid the rent—and cleaned it all out. They had three wagons for the purposes. Well-built wagons, driven by some down-timers I don't know. The guy who seemed to be in charge was a real dandy, dressed to the hilt. Fancy plumed hat, the whole works."

Noelle hissed. "The *O'Connors*? But . . ."

There seemed to be a thin smile on Buster's face. Between the beard and the darkness, though, it was hard to tell.

"But they have a successful business here? I wouldn't be too sure of that, the way they go through money like it was water. I can tell you this much, for sure. Since the Barclays rented this shed six months ago, they've been steadily filling it up with mechanical equipment— smallish stuff, of course, no big machines—tools, blue- prints, diagrams, you name it. I'm pretty sure some of it was swiped from Marcantonio's machine shop, although I couldn't swear to it."

"Oh, wow," said Denise. "Dad, the fuckers are *defecting*."

"That's my guess. Got no idea where to, though."

Noelle's lips were tight. "You know, Buster, you *could* have maybe said something about this earlier."

He swiveled to face her. Whatever smile might have been on his face was gone now. "Said something to who? The so-called 'authorities'? Meaning no offense, Ms. Murphy—"

"It's Stull, now. I changed it."

"Good for you," said Denise. "I kinda like your mother, but her ex-husband—the guy who was supposed to be your dad and wasn't—is a complete shithead."

Clearly enough, whatever parental instruction Buster had felt it necessary to give his daughter had never included "proper language for a young lady." Noelle couldn't really fault Buster for that, though. He made a lot better father in everything essential than Francis Murphy had, she didn't doubt that in the least.

"Yeah, good for you," echoed Buster. "Your real dad Dennis is an okay guy, in my book. But like I was saying, Ms. Stull, I mind my own business. I'm as likely to go to the cops as I am to eat tofu for breakfast. I got along with Dan Frost well enough, once him and me straightened out a few issues. But I've generally got as much use for cops as I do for cockroaches. Especially since, in this case, I can't see where they were doing anything illegal anyway except for maybe some petty theft from Dave's machine shop."

He gave his daughter a stern look. "How is it 'defecting' when we're not at war with anybody any longer? People got a right to live wherever they want, you know—and take their property with them. You really oughta watch your language, young lady."

Noelle barked a laugh. For his part, Eddie gave Buster a wary look.

"We're not actually policemen," he said. "No powers of arrest. We're just investigators."

Buster shrugged. "Like the guy said in that Muppet movie. Authorities is authorities."

"He didn't say that," Denise protested. "He said—"

"Do *you* want to help them?" demanded her father, gesturing with a thumb at Noelle and Eddie.

"Yeah, sure. I don't care what you say, Dad. Those fuckers are defecting. Buncha traitors."

"Then quit arguing with me about movie dialogue and get a move on." He turned back to Noelle and Eddie, smiling again. "If you want to catch them, you'd better plan on starting at dawn. They'll have three days' head start on you, wherever they're going."

"You have no idea?"

"Not a clue. Like I said—"

"You mind your own business. I heard you." Noelle tried not to sound too snappish and testy. Despite his appearance, Buster was generally an easy-going sort of fellow. Still. Aggravating a large ex-biker on his own property in the middle of the night when he was carrying an eighteen-inch flashlight in his hand did not strike Noelle as falling into the category of "good idea."

Eddie was scratching his head. "We'll need to alert the police, first. Then, we'll have to figure out which way they went."

Denise grinned. "I'll find that out for you. Me and my bike. I'll get started as soon as it's light enough to see anything."

"Ain't she a pip?" said her father, admiringly.

Chapter 5. The Nature of Plans

Near Grantville, State of Thuringia-Franconia

"Fucking idiots, what they are," pronounced Denise. She finished the beer she'd ordered at Stephan Wurmbrand's roadside tavern just outside Grantville on the road to Rudolstadt and almost slammed the glass back on the bar. She glared around the room, as if defying any of its habituees to challenge either her use of language or her judgment of police chiefs and cavalry officers.

No challenge came forth, except from Lannie Yost, perched on a nearby stool. Owlishly, he peered at her empty glass. "Ain't you a little young to be drinking that stuff?"

Denise gaped at him. So did several of the other barflies in the place. In their case, because they were downtime Germans who thought the notion of anyone being under age to drink beer was silly—one of those up-time fetishes they'd thought must have died a natural death by now, three and a half years after the Ring of Fire. In Denise's case, because her father was Buster Beasley and *she* thought—so did Buster, actually—that she was practically abstemious when it came to substance abuse.

She was also gaping because she was outraged, of course.

"You! Lannie Yost, you're pie-eyed half the time! So-called test pilot. You got some nerve—"

"Hey, Denise, take it easy! I wasn't trying to pick no fight."

That wouldn't normally have done him any good at all, except he added hurriedly: "You got the right of it when it comes to Captain Knefler, that's for sure. Guy couldn't find his ass with both hands in broad daylight."

"That jackass. I *told* him I found their trail, leading south from Rudolstadt. But, noooo. Mr. Military Genius insisted they must have used those rafts the one guy—the one in charge, whoever he is—bought in Jena."

By now, the news had spread all over the area, including some of the details. "The rafts *were* gone," one of the down-timers pointed out. He was sitting with a friend at a table nearby.

Denise sniffed. "Big deal. All the guy in charge—and I think he's got more brains in his little toe than Knefler does—had to do was hire a few men to pole the rafts downriver. There's day laborers hanging around all over the place, in Jena. Probably told them they needed to pick up something in Halle and take it down to Magdeburg. Off goes whichever idiot came in pursuit—his name's Knefler, did I mention that? It's spelled 'k-n' like in numbskull—while the guy with the brains keeps heading up the Saale valley. Hasn't it struck any of you geniuses yet that Mr.-Whoever is good at this? Why would he have been wearing such a flamboyant outfit just to buy some cargo rafts—if he hadn't been trying to draw attention to himself?"

She was pretty proud of that deductive logic. Maybe she oughta become a detective when she grew up. Finished growing up. Which she was practically there. She'd bet Minnie would partner with her.

On the other hand, she'd neglected to mention that
Mr.-Whoever-He-Was had been wearing the same outfit
when he arrived at her father's storage place to load
the wagons. Obviously, just to make sure every idiot in
Grantville connected Obvious Dot A to Blatant Dot B.
The Grantville police chief and Captain Numbskull had
squeezed that information out of her, despite her misgivings about what they'd do with it, but she saw no reason
to weaken her case by divulging it to these layabouts.

Lannie took a swallow from his own beer. "You think?"

"Sure. What sort of lunatic would make his escape
further into the USE?"

The same down-timer wasn't ready to let it go. "Not
so foolish, that. Before he gets to Halle, he can offload
the rafts and make his way into Saxony. Probably he's
working for John George."

Denise opened her mouth. Then, decided it wasn't
worth the effort to get into an argument with somebody
who was obviously not playing with a full deck.

Right. Sure. That made sense. In six months, the elector of Saxony was staring in the face an all-out invasion
by Gustav Adolf. Fat lot of good some tech transfer
would do him at *this* stage of the game. Except give
Gustav Adolf another Cassius Belly. Or whatever the
name was of that ancient Roman guy who'd caused a war.

Denise might be willing to concede that John George
was that stupid. But none of the up-timer traitors were
that dumb, except maybe Jay Barlow and Mickey Simmons. Even Suzi Barclay wasn't that dumb, just nuts.
No, wherever the lousy defectors were going, it was
someplace they figured could hold off the USE, at least
for a while. That meant Austria, probably—that had been
Noelle's guess—or maybe Bavaria.

Lannie finished his beer and stood up. The motion was just a little bit too exaggerated to be that of a completely sober man. Which, given Lannie, was no surprise. He wasn't actually drunk, just in his more-normal-than-not state of a pleasant buzz. Lannie's alcoholism wasn't so bad that he couldn't get by in life, with his rare skills. Jesse Wood hadn't been willing to accept him in the air force, but the Kellys used him for their test pilot.

"Okay, then," he said. "Give me a ride back to Grantville on your bike, kid. I'll nail the bastards for you."

Denise frowned. "What are you talking about?"

He slapped his chest. "When the cavalry falls down on the job, you gotta call in the air force. One of the planes at the facility—that's the *Dauntless*—is finished and ready to go."

Denise stopped laughing after a while. Then, shrugged. "Sure, why not? I'll take you there. I'm warning you, though. Those hands of yours better not move around any while you're holding onto me."

Lannie looked aggrieved. "Hey, there's no call for that. Besides, I ain't crazy enough to piss off your dad."

Denise squinted at him. "You start groping, and my dad will be the least of your worries."

The Saale Valley, south of Saalfeld

"It has to be them," Noelle pronounced.

Eddie sighed and wiped his face. His whole body ached, from spending three days in the saddle. Especially his thighs. "No, actually, it doesn't. They passed through Saalfeld yesterday evening, in bad lighting, and the guards we talked to didn't recognize anybody. Just three wagons, which they didn't give more than a cursory inspection if they gave them any at all, because they most likely got bribed. Those are not exactly elite troops in that garrison, now that nobody's worried any longer about another raid deep into the Thueringerwald. Even if they weren't been bribed, they probably wouldn't have bothered to check the wagons anyway. You have any idea how many times heavily loaded wagons pass through Saalfeld?"

"It has to be them," Noelle repeated stubbornly. She swiveled in the saddle, the slight carefulness of the motion making it clear she wasn't feeling any too spry herself. "We should have gotten reinforcements by now. I guess Denise couldn't get anybody to take her seriously. Maybe I should have—"

"*You* weren't going to stay behind, since *you* can't resist the thrill of the chase. *I* couldn't stay behind, because somebody has to look after you. That left Denise—and we practically had to sit on her to get her to agree."

He wiped his face again. "And, yes, they probably didn't take her seriously. Given that she would have had to report to Captain Knefler, him now being the commander of the Grantville garrison, and Knefler is a jackass." He smiled. "Probably, after ten seconds or so, Denise started denouncing him. She's a real pip, that one."

Noelle eyed him suspiciously. "She's only sixteen years old. Not even that."

"All the more reason they wouldn't take her seriously."

"That's *not* what I was referring to. I was referring to the possibility of other men taking her too seriously."

"Don't be ridiculous."

The Saale Valley, near Hof

"Stop complaining," Janos said. He gave the wagon a cold, experienced eye. "The likelihood of having an axle break was very high, given the route we've taken and the speed we've made."

"And that's another thing," complained Billie Jean Mase. "You've been wearing everybody out."

Janos didn't bother replying to that accusation. In point of fact, while the pace he'd set had been hard by the standards of a commercial caravan, it was nothing compared to the pace Hungarian cavalrymen and their supply trains were accustomed to while on campaign. He was feeling perfectly well rested, himself. Granted, he'd been in a saddle, but Gage and Gardiner had been driving two of the three wagons and they were holding up well also.

Of the three drivers, the one in the worst shape was Mickey Simmons. He'd gotten the assignment because he'd boasted of the wagoneering skills he'd developed as a result of being the coordinator of training for the transportation department. Naturally, within less than four days he'd broken an axle.

"There's no time for this," Janos said curtly. He glanced up at the sun. "We'll camp here. We have perhaps three hours of daylight left to sort through the wagons, jettison whatever is least important, and repack the two surviving wagons."

Needless to say—he didn't think he'd ever met such self-indulgent people; they were even worse than Austrian noblemen—the Americans set up a round of protests and complaint. The gist of which was *we need all of it*.

He gave them no more than a minute before cutting the nonsense short.

"We have no means of repairing the axle. Nor can we seek the assistance of a wainwright in Hof, because there is a USE garrison there. By now, the alert will have reached them. Like most such garrisons, they will not exert themselves to search the surrounding countryside—but if we show up in the town itself, which is quite small, they will be almost certain to spot us."

He gave the assembled up-timers perhaps five seconds of a stony stare to see if any were stupid enough to argue those points.

None were, apparently. He revised his estimate of their common sense. Higher than carrots, after all.

"That leaves two options. The first is that we unload the contents of the broken wagon and pile them onto the two others."

"Yeah, that's what I was figuring," said Jay Barlow.

Sadly, the level of common sense did not attain that of rabbits.

Janos half-turned and pointed southeast toward a low range of mountains. "By tomorrow, we have to be well into the Fichtelgebirge. That terrain is considerably worse than we've been passing through, and the roads are worse yet. We are certain to break another axle, or a wheel, with overloaded wagons—and these are already dangerously burdened as it is. I leave aside the fact that we are now into late autumn. The weather has been good, so far, for which we can be thankful. But who knows when the weather might turn?"

The Americans squinted at the mountains. "We gotta go up *there*?" whined Peter Barclay's wife Marina. By now, Janos had come to recognize her as a champion whiner. She almost put his great-aunt Orsolya in the shade. Not quite.

"Why?" demanded her husband.

Janos shook his head. "This close to Bayreuth, we can't stay in the lowlands or we run the risk of being spotted by a cavalry troop. Even in the Fichtelgebirge, there may be an occasional patrol. Once we enter it, we can take only a few days—no more—to reach Cheb by following the Eger."

The Barclays' daughter Suzi frowned. She was a bizarre-looking creature, who would have been an attractive young woman if it hadn't been for the short cropped hair dyed a truly hideous color, five earrings in her left ear and three on the right, two metal studs through her right eyebrow—and, capping it all, a tattoo of flames done in black ink reaching from the wrist of her right arm to the top of the right side of her neck. The woman was so attached to the grotesque decoration that she insisted on wearing a sleeveless vest instead of a coat, despite the November temperatures.

"That can't be right," she said. "I know somebody from Cheb, one of the girls—well, never mind that, but she's Bohemian."

"That is hardly surprising, since Cheb is in Bohemia. It's an old fortress town that guards the western approaches. Good for us, in this instance, since the garrison is a mercenary company and its commander has been well bribed. We'll abandon these wagons in Cheb and replace them with several smaller ones, much better designed for travel in the mountains. We'll even have a cavalry escort while we pass down part of the Bohemian Forest until we reenter the USE near Kötzting. There, we will follow the Regen down to Regensburg, where we will exchange the wagons—that has also been arranged—for a barge that will take us down the Danube into Austria."

He'd already explained this to the leaders of the uptimers, the older Barclays and O'Connor and his son. But it seemed they either hadn't paid attention or hadn't considered all the implications.

"Hey, wait a minute," said Allan O'Connor. "We're coming *back* into the USE? What the hell for? I know my geography, dammit. Once we're across into Bohemia, let's just stay there until we get to Austria."

Janos stared at him. "Indeed. As a geographical proposition, that is certainly feasible. Follow the rivers down to Pizen. From there we could take a good road to Ceské Budejovice, the largest town in southern Bohemia. From there, of course, it is a short distance to Austria—and along a very good road, given the long and constant intercourse between Vienna and Prague."

O'Connor nodded. "Yeah, that's what I was thinking."

No rabbit had ever been this stupid, for a certainly. "You have missed the news, then. Of the war between Bohemia and Austria. Which has been going on for a year and a half, now."

The up-timers frowned at him. They looked like a pack of confused rabbits. All except Suzi Barclay, who just looked like a crazed rabbit.

Janos grit his teeth, reminding himself that he needed to remain on the best possible terms with these—these—people.

"Not a good idea," he said thinly. "The reason I could bribe the commander of the Cheb garrison is because no one expects hostilities to erupt between the USE and Bohemia, so that frontier post was given to a man who was competent enough but needed no further qualifications. Such as . . . what you might call a rigorous sense of duty. At Pizen and České Budějovice, on the other hand, we would be dealing with Pappenheim's Black Cuirassiers."

The up-timers seemed to draw back a little.

"Ah. I see you have heard of them. Yes. We do not wish to have dealings with the Black Cuirassiers."

Enough! Still more time had been wasted. He pointed stiffly to the broken wagon. "So let us begin unloading it. Now. And discard from the other two wagons whatever is not essential."

Chapter 6. The Mess

High Street Mansion, Seat of Government for the State of Thuringia-Franconia
President's Office
Grantville, State of Thuringia-Franconia

After Grantville's police chief finished his report, Ed Piazza, president of the State of Thuringia-Franconia, half-turned his swivel chair and looked out of the window in his office. That was the first time he'd so much as glanced outside since he showed up for work this morning. His schedule had been jam-packed even before this latest crisis hit.

The weather was still good, he saw. Clear, with not a cloud in the sky. Very crisp, of course, the way such days in November were, but not yet bitterly cold the way it would become in January and February.

Well, not "crisis," exactly, he mused. He and Mike Stearns had long known that there was no way to keep the USE's enemies from getting their hands on American technical knowledge—nor from suborning some of the Americans themselves. Among the thirty-five hundred people who'd come from up-time through the Ring of Fire, there was bound to be the usual percentage who were excessively greedy and not burdened with much in the way of a conscience. That was even leaving aside the ones—there were a lot of those, now—who'd accepted legitimate offers to relocate elsewhere. You couldn't keep people from emigrating, after all; not, at least, without building some sort of Godforsaken version of a Berlin Wall, which neither he nor Mike had wanted any part of.

Some people were surprised, even astonished, at the number of Americans who were leaving Grantville these days. They'd assumed that long familiarity, habits, family ties—not to mention modern indoor plumbing—would keep almost everyone from straying. But that was unrealistic. West Virginians, especially northern West Virginians, had been accustomed to moving around a lot, since the area was economically depressed except when the mines were working full bore. Most families had at least one person, in the past, who'd moved to one of the industrial cities to make a living. Often they came back, when things at home picked up, but sometimes they didn't.

And those had been relocations just to get decent-paying but usually hard jobs in a steel mill or auto assembly plant. Today, anyone with any skills was being offered salaries that were the down-time equivalent of the kind of money top-drawer technical and business consultants made back up-time. Often enough, with lots of perks and benefits attached. And since the prospective employers were rich—many of them noblemen, sometimes royalty—even the problem of leaving modern plumbing behind wasn't so bad. It wasn't as if the upper classes of the seventeenth century were medieval barons living in stone piles, after all. They already had indoor plumbing, however rudimentary it might be by late twentieth-century American standards. And it would get better quickly, too, since the people offering the jobs had a keen desire themselves to get better facilities. Anyone in Grantville who had significant plumbing skills and experience practically had a *carte blanche* to go anywhere in Europe.

To add pressure to pull, most up-timers after the Ring of Fire had lost what they'd had in the way of safety net back up-time. Which, for working class people like most of the town's inhabitants, had never been all that munificent in the first place.

Social Security was gone. Company pensions were gone, except for a few companies headquartered in Grantville who'd been able to maintain them. Medicare was gone. That might not directly affect young people, right away, but most people in Grantville were part of families, often extended families. They had parents and grandparents and other elderly relatives who were in a tight situation, sometimes a desperate one—and now, Baron Whoozit or Merchant Moneybags or City Patrician Whazzisname was waving a small fortune under their noses, if they'd just relocate to wherever and apply their skills.

So, since the end of the Baltic war—the decision to move the SoTF's capital to Bamberg had been a prod, too—a great migration was underway. "Great," at least, in per capita terms if not absolute numbers. Some people were even starting to call it the "American Diaspora." What had been a trickle, in the first three years after the Ring of Fire, was now a small flood. By the time it was over, Ed wouldn't be surprised if half of Grantville's residents wound up living somewhere else, at least for a time.

Most of them were staying in the USE, true enough. But the number who were accepting positions in other countries was not inconsiderable, especially countries that had good relations with the USE like Bohemia, Venice, the Netherlands, and the Scandinavian nations now united within the Union of Kalmar. Some had gone to France and Austria. A few, even farther afield, to eastern Europe, Russia, Spain and Portugal, southern Italy—even the New World.

In fact, Ed was a little puzzled by the fact this batch of emigrants had chosen to break the law by stealing things that didn't belong to them. Why? There was no legal barrier, as such, to moving to Austria, if that's where they went. The Sanderlins and Sonny Fortney had moved to Vienna not long ago, perfectly openly and aboveboard. They'd even hauled two complete automobiles with them.

Carol Unruh's suspicion, which she'd voiced two days earlier, was that at least some of them were going to wind up implicated in the legal fall-out from the Bolender arrest. She'd probably turn out to be right. But, whatever the reason, the immediate effect—and the thing that made it a problem for Ed—was that it transformed what would have otherwise have been a simple emigration into "defection" and even "treason."

What a stupid mess.

The worst thing about this episode with the Barclays and the O'Connors—assuming for the moment that they got away with it—wasn't actually the tech transfer itself. True, among the whole group of them, they had quite a bit of technical knowledge and skills, not to mention the stuff they'd taken or stolen. But it was hardly as if there was any one "secret" that was equivalent to a magic wand. One of the USE's enemies, probably Austria, would get a major boost to whatever modernization program they'd set underway. That was hardly enough, by itself, to transform them overnight into an industrial powerhouse—which was something of a double-edged sword in any event, for Europe's royal houses and aristocracy.

No, insofar as the affair constituted a crisis, it was a political one, not a military or technical one. Among the still-murky set of possible outcomes, one outcome was a certainty. Wilhelm Wettin and his Crown Loyalist party would pull out the stops to make as much political hay of it as they could. Wilhelm himself would keep within the limits of using the episode to argue that it showed Americans were nothing special, so what difference did it make if Mike Stearns' party had the support of most of them? A large number of the Crown Loyalists would go a lot farther than that, though, arguing that the whole affair cast suspicion on American loyalty in general.

And there were some elements within the CLs who'd take it to the hoop. It was well-known that reactionary elements were infiltrating that loosely-defined and none-too-disciplined party, now that nation-wide elections would be taking place within a few months. Some of them were outright extremists. They'd trot out their usual anti-Catholic diatribes, of course, given the high percentage of Catholics in the defecting group—even if most of them were lapsed Catholics. They'd probably also fire up the anti-Semitic propaganda, ignoring the fact that none of the defectors were Jewish or had any connection to Jews beyond purely casual ones. Logic was hardly the strong suit of that particular current within the politics of the Germanies.

Ed managed a chuckle, then, remembering one wood-cut illustration of himself in a pamphlet put out by one of the reactionary outfits. The Knights of Barbarossa, if he remembered right. The thing had been quite charming, in its own way. The horns and the cloven hoofs and the forked tail were standard fare. Generic, really. But he'd thought the addition of a grotesquely "Jewish" hooked nose was a nice touch, given his rather puglike features. Not to mention showing him sacrificing a presumably gentile baby in some sort of religious rite, and never mind that he and his wife were lifelong Catholics and attended mass regularly.

He swiveled the chair back, to face Preston Richards and Carol Unruh, the two other people in the room. "What if Noelle's right, Press? And have we gotten any word from her since she left?"

"Nothing," said Carol Unruh, answering his second question. "Not a peep. We don't know where she is, really, except 'somewhere south of Rudolstadt.'"

The police chief grunted. "She hasn't passed through Saalfeld—or, if she did, she didn't stop for anything. We're in radio contact with the authorities there." His expression grew sour. "Not that it's likely to do any good. The garrisons in all the towns in the area are small and entirely mercenary, since—"

Ed waved that aside. "Yeah, Press, I know. Since the emperor is keeping most of the regular army units in the north because he wants them in position to attack Saxony and Brandenburg in a few months—and he's sending the ones he can spare down to reinforce the troops facing Bavaria and Bernhard. So we make do with what we can get. No point pissing and moaning about it all over again.

I take it they haven't gotten off their butts and started scouring the countryside?"

" 'Scouring,' " Carol jeered. "Their idea of 'scouring the countryside' is trotting a few miles out of town to the nearest watering hole, getting plastered, and reporting that they saw no signs of suspicious activity or suspicious persons passing through. Two or three days worth of getting soused later." Her expression grew more solemn. "I'm mostly worried about Noelle, Ed. She could get hurt, or even killed. I mean, you know what she's like."

Indeed, he did, having read the detailed report of her activities the previous summer and fall in Franconia, during the Ram Rebellion. Ed's wife Annabelle had once described Noelle Murphy—now Noelle Stull—as Grantville's distaff version of Clark Kent, absent the glasses. Primly-mannered maybe-I'll-become-a-nun young woman, zips into the phone booth, out comes Super-Ingénue. She'd even blown a torturer's head half off, when he attacked her partner Eddie Junker. Since Noelle couldn't shoot straight, she'd done so by the simple method of shoving the barrel of the gun under his chin and pulling the trigger.

Timid, she was not, appearances to the contrary.

"We'll just have to hope for the best," he said. "Captain Knefler took practically the whole garrison with him up to Halle. That just leaves the police force, which is under-strength to begin with, the way Grantville keeps growing."

Richards gave Carol an apologetic glance. "I did send a couple of officers over to Rudolstadt, and they were able to get the garrison commander there to detach three of his soldiers to accompany them. No more than three men, though, and no farther south than Hof, without the count's okay. I radioed Magdeburg to see if I could reach him, but it seems Ludwig Guenther and his wife are out of the city visiting relatives at the moment."

That was too bad. The count of Schwarzburg-Rudolstadt was a capable and conscientious man, and maintained good relations with Grantville. If he or his wife Emelie had been in residence at their castle in Rudolstadt, they'd have sent out the whole garrison to search for Noelle and Eddie—and the defectors, too, if Noelle was right and they were in the vicinity. It wasn't a big garrison, but it was a good one. Mercenaries, true, but a well-trained and disciplined company that had been in the service of the count for a long time, not a contractor's slapdash outfit.

The problem was that the State of Thuringia-Franconia—at least, the area around Grantville—simply didn't have much any longer in the way of military forces. In the months after the Croat raid on Grantville and its high school, more than two years earlier, the town had fairly bristled for a while with cavalry patrols, freshly built fortifications, sentinel outpost, the works. But two years was a long time in the war conditions of Europe. Soon enough, it became obvious that there was no immediate military threat to Grantville any longer. The key development had been Wallenstein switching sides in 1633. The same man who'd launched the Croat raid was now allied with the USE—and, given the number of Americans living in Prague today, some of them very closely connected to the new king, there was simply no way Wallenstein could organize and launch a secret attack even if he wanted to.

So that ended the threat from Bohemia, which was the most pressing one. Who else could launch a raid on Grantville? The Austrians would have to fight their way through Bohemia first—and Wallenstein had beaten their army at the second battle of the White Mountain. The Bavarians were in no position to do anything more than try to hold their ground. That had been obvious even before Gustav Adolf's general Banér seized their fortress of Ingolstadt, which left the Bavarians without a bridgehead north of the Danube.

The Saxons were the only real possibility, and that was negligible. John George, the elector, had a full scale invasion coming and he knew it perfectly well. He was concentrating entirely on readying Saxony's defenses, not wasting energy on raids that would simply chew up his army. Holk's mercenary forces were really the only ones he had available for something like that, anyway. Holk would have to fight his way through sizeable forces—USE regulars, too—stationed in Halle, in order to reach Grantville or any of the towns in the Thuringian basin. Nobody thought he could manage that, and if he even tried he'd leave Saxony's frontier with Bohemia open to an attack by Wallenstein. There was no way the elector of Saxony would countenance such a thing. He'd hired Holk and his army in the first place, despite their unsavory reputation, in order to help protect his southern flank.

Who else? A few hysterics shrieked about the "French menace," pointing with alarm to Turenne's daring raid on the Wietze oil fields during the Baltic war, but that was downright laughable. Given the political tensions in France after the war, there was no way Richelieu was going to send his best general haring off on a long-distance raid. Even if he did, so what? Only somebody who was geographically-challenged and completely ignorant of logistics could possibly think that a raid from France to Grantville was anything like a raid into Brunswick. That Turenne was an exceptionally gifted military commander had been proven in this universe, as well as being attested to by the historical records of another. That did not make him a magician, who could fight his way through the entire USE. It was three hundred miles from the French frontier to Grantville, even as the crow flies. At least half again that far, the way an army would have to travel.

No, aside from the mundane and everyday risks of living in a boom town, Grantville was about as safe as any place in Europe, these days. So, beginning in the fall of 1633, the military forces that had once protected it carefully had been almost completely drained away. They were needed elsewhere. The regular cavalry patrols were a thing of the past, the sentinel posts had been abandoned completely, and the outlying fortresses had no more than a handful of men detached from the small garrisons maintained in the towns of the basin—who were really there to keep order and double as a police force, more than serve as an actual military defense.

"We haven't got a pot to piss in, is what it amounts to," he said.

"Not for something like this, Mr. President," agreed the police chief.

Carol looked fierce. "If those bastards so much as hurt Noelle and Eddie, I don't care what Mike says. I'm for firing up the war against Austria. Or whoever it is."

There'd be a lot of that sentiment, Ed knew, if Noelle and Eddie came to harm. Granted, assuming Austria was behind the affair, most people would hold a grudge about the mass defection in any event. But most of the grudge would be aimed at the defectors themselves, not the Austrians. It wouldn't be the sort of thing that would set off any real war fever. Noelle and Eddie getting killed or badly injured would be a different kettle of fish altogether.

Ed contemplated the problem, for a few seconds. As a practical proposition, of course, launching any sort of immediate campaign against Austria was a non-starter. But "immediate" meant next year. The year after that . . .

He shook his head slightly. That was pointless speculation, right now. They still didn't even know what was really happening.

"I guess that's it then, for the moment." He straightened up in his chair. "Unless Denise Beasley—there's a real pip, for you—shows up with some more information."

Press Richards grinned. "Don't think that's too likely. I got no idea what she's up to now. The last I saw of her she was racing off on her bike, giving me and Knefler the finger. Most of her spleen wasn't really aimed at me, since Denise knows I haven't got the resources to do what she wanted. But she probably has me lumped in with 'the fathead' for the time being."

Carol's mouth made a little O. "Did she *really* call Captain Knefler a 'fathead'? I mean, to his face?"

"Oh, yeah." Solemnly, Press shook his head. "Wasn't all she called him, I'm deeply sorry to report. Girl's got a real potty mouth, when she cuts it loose. She also called him a fuckwad and an asshole and a motherfucking moron."

"She's not even sixteen!"

"She's Buster's kid," Ed grunted. "That's got to add a decade or so, at least in the lack-of-respect-for-your-betters department. Thank God I'm no longer the high school principal. She's not my headache, these days."

Richards and Unruh both looked at him.

"Well, she isn't," Ed insisted. Hoping it was true.

Chapter 7. The Wild Blue Yonder

Kelly Aviation Facility
Near Grantville, State of Thuringia-Franconia

Denise stared at the object that was the center of the proposal Lannie had just advanced.

"No fucking way," she pronounced.

Yost shook his head lugubriously. "You really oughta watch your—"

"Don't fucking start on me, Lannie. Just don't." She pointed an accusing finger at the aircraft. "There is no fucking—or flibbertyjerking, if that makes you happier—way in hell I'm getting into that thing."

Lannie frowned. "What does 'flibbertyjerking' mean? And what's the matter, anyway? It flies. It flies just fine. I've taken it up plenty of times." After a two-second pause he added, "Well, maybe three times."

Denise scowled at him. "You said yourself. It's a *prototype*, remember?"

"Well, sure, but . . . "

He let that trail off into nothing. The truth was, except for being a boozer, Lannie wasn't a bad guy. And he did have the virtue of being a very loyal sort of person, even if Denise thought he had to be half-nuts to give his loyalty to Bob and Kay Kelly.

Kay was a harridan, and Bob was . . . Well. Impractical. Not hard to get along with, but the kind of guy who simply couldn't control his enthusiasms and seemed to have the attention span of a six-year-old.

She looked around the big hangar. There were no fewer than four planes in evidence, all of them in various stages of construction—or deconstruction, in the case of two—and every one of them bore the label "prototype." It seemed like every time Bob Kelly got close to finishing a plane he decided there was something not quite right about it and he needed to redesign it. Again. The slogan of his company might as well be *The Perfect is the Enemy of the Good Enough—and We Can Prove it to You.*

The only reason he hadn't gone bankrupt three times over, since the Ring of Fire, was because of his wife. For reasons Denise couldn't begin to fathom, Kay Kelly seemed to have a veritable genius for drumming up investors and squeezing money out of the government.

"I'm *not* getting into it," she repeated.

Alas, some trace of uncertainty must have been in her voice. The third party present detected it and pounced immediately. That was Keenan Murphy, the mechanic who was the only other person in the facility that day. The Kellys had gone up to Magdeburg to lobby the government for more funds, and apparently the office manager had decided to take the day off.

"C'mon, Denise," said Keenan. "We gotta help Noelle. I mean, she's my *sister.*"

Denise almost snapped back, "half-sister," but she restrained herself. First, because Keenan was giving her such a sad-eyed, woebegone look; second, because he was a sad-sack, woebegone kind of guy; but, mostly, because whether or not Keenan Murphy was a loser he was another one who had an exaggerated, irrational sense of loyalty.

As did Denise herself, and she knew it. In her own personal scale of things, the way she judged people, that counted for a lot.

She stared at the plane again, trying to imagine herself in it *up there*—what? maybe a mile high?—with a souse for a pilot and a low-achiever for a . . .

"Hey, wait a minute." She glared at the two of them. "I thought you said Keenan didn't know how to fly."

"He don't," said Lannie. "He's the bombardier. He'll ride in the back." He pointed toward the rear of the cockpit. Now that she looked more closely, Denise could see that there was a third seat there, behind the two side-by-side seats in front.

Her eyes widened. "You have *got* to be kidding. You want *me* to be the copilot? I don't know fuck-all about flying!"

Keenan Murphy shook his head. "Naw, not that. We need you to be the navigator. I can't see well enough, back there, and Lannie . . . well . . . "

Yost gave him a pained look. Keenan shrugged. "Sorry, Lannie, but it's just a fact. You get lost easy."

"Oh, swell," said Denise. She ran fingers through her dark hair, starting to wind it up into a bun. No, hell with that. She'd just put it in a pony tail, like she did riding the bike.

"Gimme a rubber band," she commanded. With a sneer: "I'm sure you got plenty around here, for engine parts."

"Hey, there's no call for—"

"Leave it, Lannie," said Keenan, chuckling. "I'll find you one, Denise. It might not be real clean, though."

She looked around the hangar again. Bob Kelly followed the Big Bang theory of design and manufacture. Out of chaos, creation—and, clearly enough, they were still a lot closer to chaos. The area was completely unlike her dad's weld shop, which was as neat and well kept as he wasn't.

"Never mind," she said, heading for the hangar door. "My bike's right outside. I got some in the saddlebags."

The Saale river, south of Halle

"I ought to have you arrested!" shouted Captain Knefler.

"For *what?*" demanded the burly boatman. Clearly, he was not a man easily intimidated by a mere show of official outrage. Not here, at least, while he was still within Thuringia-Franconia. In some provinces of the USE, not to mention the districts under direct imperial administration, he might have been more circumspect. But the laws concerning personal liberties were strict in the SoTF—and, perhaps more importantly, were strictly enforced by the authorities.

The *real* authorities, which did not include any cavalry captain who thought he could throw his weight around.

"You are part of a treasonous plot!" screeched Knefler.

Watching the scene, standing behind the captain where Knefler couldn't see him, Sergeant Reimers flashed a grin at the two soldiers with him. None of them had any use for their commanding officer. This was entertaining.

"Oh, what a pile of horseshit," jeered the boatman. He waved a thick hand at the three rafts now drawn up to the river bank. "Your evidence, please?"

No evidence there, since the rafts were quite empty, except for some parcels of food and a few personal belongings. Unless something had been dumped overboard, the crude vessels obviously hadn't carried anything down from Jena except the boatmen themselves and their travel necessities.

Reimers' amusement faded a bit. To be sure, there was no chance the boatmen had jettisoned anything, since they couldn't have spotted the cavalry troop coming up from Grantville until it was almost upon them. Whereupon, Knefler had ordered them—with the threat of his soldiers' leveled carbines, no less—to bring the rafts immediately ashore.

Still, the captain was furious enough—he was certainly thick-witted enough—to order his men to start dredging the river for miles upstream. As useless as such a task might be, given their small numbers and lack of equipment.

The problem was that while Knefler was thick-witted, he was not a complete dimwit. He knew perfectly well that he now faced a major embarrassment. Probably not something that would get him cashiered, more was the pity. But certainly something that would not enhance his prospects for promotion.

The young American girl had told him the culprits had fled to the south, in language that was still a delight to recall. But Knefler had dismissed her arguments and insisted on following his own reasoning.

Knefler was now wasting time glaring at the empty rafts. "I need no material evidence," he insisted. "There is the evidence of your actions. Why, if it were not part of a treasonous plot, did you leave Jena before dawn?"

He tried a sneer himself. "Of course, I am no boatman. But I doubt such is standard practice."

"Because our employer *paid* us to do so," said the boatmen. "A bonus, he said, to make sure we got to Halle in time to pick up—"

"Nonsense! Nonsense! You did it so there would be no witnesses! Nobody who could tell me that the rafts were empty!"

The boatman planted his hands on his hips and squinted up at the tall, almost-skeletal officer. "In other words, you were outsmarted. Not by me and my boys—we are innocent parties only accidentally involved—but by the man you're chasing. Not so?"

Knefler glared down at him. "You will have to answer for your actions. Prove your innocence."

The boatman's sneer was magnificent. "To the contrary, Your Mightyship. This is Thuringia-Franconia, or have you forgotten? *You* have to demonstrate my guilt, not the other way around."

Knefler was so angry he started waving his arms. "Even the silly fucking Americ—ah, the up-timers— accept such a thing as circumstantial evidence."

"Fine. There is the circumstantial evidence that we were hired to take rafts down the river to Halle to pick up a consignment of goods for early delivery to Magdeburg. Said deed being committed in Gerhard Pfrommer's tavern on the waterfront in Jena, by a man unknown to anyone there who approached Gerhard asking for reliable boatmen and was pointed to us at a nearby table."

The sneer didn't waver once. "Said table, I might add, being right in the middle of the tavern—crowded, it was, that time of evening—so that any number of people heard the whole thing. He paid for the rafts, in addition to our labor. Bought them from Rudi Schaefer, also at the tavern, in a discussion also overheard by plenty of people. Good rates for the rafts and good pay for us, too, with a bonus for an early departure."

He took his right hand from his hip and gestured at the rafts. "So, we did. Why in the world would we refuse? I could show you the money. Still have almost all of it."

He made no movement to do so, of course. Even in Thuringia-Franconia, no sensible workman would gratuitously show money to an officer.

Stymied, Knefler went back to glaring at the rafts. "Describe the man who hired you," he commanded.

"Again?" The boatman's squint now verged on sheer melodrama. "Perhaps you should add more rosemary to your diet. It's good for the memory, they say."

"Describe the man again!" screeched Knefler.

Shrugging, the boatman did so. The description was identical to the one he'd given when he first came ashore. A handsome man, a bit taller than average, broad-shouldered, appeared to be well-built. Wasn't armed with a sword but carried himself like a nobleman. Long dark hair, dark brown eyes, a complexion that was not quite dark enough to be called swarthy but came close. Olive, you might call it. Maybe he was an Italian.

He wore fancy apparel, the most noticeable of which items were a red coat, expensive boots, and a feathered cap. The feathers were very large. You couldn't miss the fellow in a snowstorm. He spoke German—old-style, not Amideutsch—with something of an accent, at least to the boatman's ear. No, he had no idea what accent it was. There were dozens of German dialects, even among native speakers of the tongue. How was he to know? The man paid in good silver, which was a lingua franca accepted anywhere.

Finally, Knefler released the boatmen. He gave up trying to force them to return to Jena when their leader pointed out that he would then be taking responsibility for reimbursing Rudi Schaefer for the price the rafts would bring in Magdeburg. That being, of course, standard business practice for the disposal of rafts, and well-established in law.

So, off the boatmen went, as cheery as could be. And why not? They'd been well paid to do nothing more strenuous than guide empty rafts following the current downriver. As work went, about as easy as it gets.

After they pushed off, Knefler snarled to Reimers: "First thing I'll do when we get back is teach that little whore a lesson. She'll learn the price for cursing an officer."

One of the soldiers cleared his throat. "Ah . . . Captain. I don't think—"

"Silence, Corporal Maurer!" bellowed the sergeant. "The captain gave you no leave to speak."

Maurer was suitably abashed, and shut up. Knefler sniffed at him and went for his horse.

About an hour later, on the ride back to Jena, Maurer drew his horse alongside Reimers. "Sergeant, you know who that girl *was*?" he asked quietly, after looking ahead to see that Captain Knefler was too far away to hear them.

Reimers smiled. "Denise Beasley. The daughter of Buster Beasley."

The poor fellow seemed confused. "But . . . if you knew that . . . remember the time . . . "

"This is why you are a mere corporal and I am a lofty sergeant," said Reimers. He nodded toward the captain in front of the little column. "Do *you* want the shithead for a garrison commander?"

The expression on Corporal Maurer's face was answer enough.

Reimers' ensuing chuckle had very little humor in it. "Sadly, the current fuck-up is probably not enough to get him discharged. But we can hope that his temper is still high when we get back to Grantville, so the idiot goes to chastise the daughter and discovers the father in the way. If we're lucky, we might even get to watch what happens."

It took Maurer a few seconds—he was pretty dull-witted himself, truth be told—but then he started smiling.

"Oh."

Kelly Aviation Facility
Near Grantville, State of Thuringia-Franconia

The take-off wasn't too bad, actually. Lannie would have been in the air force except Jesse Wood didn't want any part of his drinking habits. But he did know how to fly, as such.

Denise suspected that "as such" probably didn't cover all that a pilot needed. But it was a done deal now, so there was no point fretting over it.

"That way," she said, pointing. "It's called 'southeast.'"

"You don't gotta be so sarcastic."

Fortunately, she'd thought to make sure they had a map before they took off. Lannie and Keenan, naturally, hadn't thought of that. Apparently, they thought Denise could navigate by feminine instinct or something—which was a laugh, since feminine instinct when it came to directions was just to ask somebody, and who was she going to ask up here? A fucking bird?

The map was on the grimy side, like most things in Kelly Aviation. At that, it was better than the seat she was sitting on.

Printed across the top of the map, the ink a little smeared, was a notice that read: *Property of Kelly Aviation. Unauthorized Use Will Be Prosecuted.*

"How'd you talk Bob into letting you use the plane whenever you wanted?"

"Well," said Lannie.

Behind her, Keenan cleared his throat. "It's an emergency, you know."

"Oh, perfect," said Denise. "The first recorded instance since the Ring of Fire of plane-stealing. I betcha that's a hanging offense."

Lannie looked smug. "Nope. I checked once. Seems nobody's ever thought to getting around to making it a crime yet."

"See, Denise?" added Keenan. "Nothing to worry about."

They even seemed to believe their own bullshit. Amazing. Did the jack-offs really think that somewhere in the books there wasn't a provision for prosecuting *Grand Theft, Whatever We Overlooked?*

But . . .

This was kinda fun, actually. Except for having to help Keenan attach the two bombs underneath. The bombs weren't all that big, just fifty-pounders, but they were still a little scary. What had been even scarier was watching Keenan do it. He belonged to the what-the-hell-it's-close-enough school of craftsmanship. Fine for chopping onions; probably a losing proposition over the long haul for munitions-handling.

Still and all, it was done. Denise couldn't remember a time she'd ever worried about water under a bridge. Now that she'd almost reached the ripe age of sixteen—her birthday was coming up on December 11–she was pleased to see no signs of advancing decrepitude.

Chapter 8. The Cuirass

Near the Fichtelgebirge, on the edge of the Saale valley

Janos Drugeth was trying to keep his temper under control. Despite his demands—he'd stopped just short of threatening his charges with violence—the up-timers had wasted so much time arguing over which items could be left behind that there had been no way to resume the journey until the next morning. And *then,* the idiots had wasted half the morning continuing the quarrel before they finally had the two intact wagons reloaded.

But, at least they were on the move again. Luckily, the USE garrison at Hof seemed to be sluggish even by the standards of small town garrisons. There'd been no sign at all that they were searching the countryside. They'd be a small unit, anyway, not more than half a dozen men with a sergeant in command. Perhaps just a corporal. As was the rule with sleepy garrisons in a region not threatened directly by war, they were mostly a police force and would spend half their time lounging in taverns by day and conducting desultory patrols of the town in the evening. The only time they'd venture into the countryside would be in response to a specific complaint or request.

It was even possible that they didn't have a radio. The up-time communication devices were spreading widely, at least in Thuringia-Franconia, but from what Janos understood of their operation—"reception" seemed to be the key issue—the sort of simple radios the Hof garrison would most likely possess might not be able to get messages sent across the Thueringerwald. Not reliably, at least.

So, hopefully, the delay would not cause any problems.

At the edge of the forest, on a small rise, he paused to let the wagons go by. Then, drawing out an eyeglass, scanned the area behind them.

Nothing, so far as he could tell.

He was about to put the eyeglass away when his lingering animosity caused him to bring it back up and study the wagon they'd left behind, the way a man might foolishly scratch an itch, knowing he'd do better to leave it alone. It was still quite visible, being less than half a mile distant.

The only good thing was that at least they'd left the road by then and been making their way across a large meadow toward the forest when the wagon axle broke. Janos had ridden back to the road while the up-timers squabbled to see if the wagon was visible from there. The terrain was flat, but there was enough in the way of trees and shrubbery and tall grass to hide it from the sight of anyone just passing along the road—at least, to anyone on foot the way most travelers on that small country road would be. Someone on horseback would be able to spot it, if they were scanning the area.

Other than that . . .

What a mess. He'd tried to get the up-timers to repack the wagon with the goods they were leaving behind, so that if someone should happen to come across it they might assume the owners had just gone off to get assistance. If so, they'd either go about their business or—better still—they'd plunder the unguarded wagon. In the latter eventuality, of course, they'd hardly bring the attention of the authorities to their own thievery.

But, no. Careless in this as in seemingly all things, the up-timers had simply strewn the goods about. Anyone who came across it now would assume that foul play had transpired.

Nothing for it, though. Sighing, he started to put the eyeglass away. Then, catching a glimpse of motion in the corner of his eye, looked back again.

Two horsemen were approaching the wagon. Not locals, either, since each of them was leading a pack horse.

He brought the glass back up. But even before he looked through it, he could see the flashing gleams coming from one of the riders. That had to be armor, reflecting the sun.

"What the hell are you doing?" asked Noelle.

Eddie shook his head and finished untying the cuirass from his pack horse. "You said it yourself, remember? 'That's got to be them!' Very excited, you were."

He started putting on the cuirass. "Do us both a favor and hand me the helmet."

When she just kept staring at him, Eddie looked up at her. "Think, Noelle. These are 'villains,' remember? Not likely to surrender simply because we yell 'stop, thief!'?"

She stared back in the direction they'd spotted the wagon. Then, put her hand on the pistol holstered to her hip. "I thought . . . ."

"Have to do everything myself," Eddie grumbled. Now that he'd gotten on the cuirass, he took the helmet from the pack. "I remind you of two things. First, you can't shoot straight. Second, while I can—"

He finished strapping the helmet on and started clambering back onto his horse. An awkward business, that was, wearing the damn cuirass. Eddie was trained in the use of arms and armor, but only to the extent that the son of a wealthy merchant would be. He was no experienced cavalryman.

"While I can," he continued, now drawing the rifle from its saddle holster, "you will perhaps recall that due to Carol Unruh's penny-pinching, the only up-time weapon I was allotted was this pitiful thing."

Noelle studied the rifle. "It's a perfectly good Winchester lever action rifle." A bit righteously: "Model 94. They say it's a classic."

"A 'classic,' indeed." Eddie chuckled. "The gun was manufactured almost half a century before the Ring of Fire. Still, I'll allow that it's a sturdy weapon. But it's only a .30–30, it has no more than six cartridges in the magazine, and while—unlike you—I can hit something at a respectable range, I'm hardly what you'd call a Wild Bill Hitchcock."

"Hickok," she corrected. "Hitchcock was the guy who made the movies." She looked back in the direction of the wagon. There still didn't seem to be anyone moving about, over there. "You really think . . ."

He shrugged, planting the butt of the rifle on his hip and taking up the reins. "I have no idea how they will react. What I do know is that if they see a man in armor demanding that they cease and desist all nefarious activity, they are perhaps a bit more likely to do so. I'd just as soon avoid another gunfight at the Okie Corral, if we can.

" 'OK,' she corrected. 'Okies' are sorta like hillbillies.''

"And *will* you desist the language lesson?" he grumbled. "Now. Shall we about be it?"

Noelle hesitated, for a moment. She considered riding back to Hof and trying—

No, that was pointless. When they'd arrived in Hof early this morning, the garrison had still been asleep. Sleeping off a hangover, to be precise. All except the corporal in charge, who'd still been drinking. They'd be as useless as tits on a bull for hours, yet—and the traitors were almost into the Fichtelgebirge. Noelle was pretty sure there was no way she and Eddie would be able to get the garrison to go into the forest. That meant trying to get help from the soldiers at Saalfeld, and that was at least thirty miles away. By the time they got there, convinced the garrison commander to muster his unit, and got back, at least two days would have passed. More likely three, unless the garrison commander at Saalfeld was a lot more energetic and efficient than most such.

Two days, maybe three. Given that much lead time, it was unlikely they'd ever find the defectors. The Fichtelgebirge and the Bohemian Forest it was part of wasn't a tall range of mountains, but it was heavily wooded. Mostly evergreens, too, so they wouldn't get any advantage from the trees having shed their leaves. Assuming the man in charge, whoever he was, knew what he was doing—and there was no evidence so far that he didn't—he'd almost certainly be able to shake off their pursuit. There was enough commercial and personal traffic back and forth across the forest between Bohemia and Franconia that there would be a network of small roads—well, more like trails, really, but well-handled wagons could make their way through them. After the passage of two or three days, especially if the weather turned bad, it was unlikely they could figure out which specific route the defectors had taken.

"It's now or never, I guess." She started her horse into the meadow. "I'll do the talking. You just look fierce and militaristic and really mean and not too smart. The kind of guy who shoots first and lets God sort out the bodies, and doesn't much care if He gets it right or not."

"There!" hollered Denise, pointing across Lannie's chest out of the window on his side of the plane. "It's them!"

He looked over and spotted the wagon immediately. "Yup. Gotta be. Keenan, you get ready to unload when I tell you."

"Both bombs?"

"Better save one in case we miss the first time."

Denise wondered if they actually had the legal right to bomb somebody, without even giving them a warning. No way to shout "stop, thief!" of course, from an airplane doing better than a hundred miles an hour.

"Why don't we just call in their position on the radio?" she asked. "That way . . . you know. We could ask somebody up top how they want us to handle it."

"Well," said Lannie.

Behind her, Keenan cleared his throat. "The radio don't exactly work. Bob took some of the parts out of it so's we could—"

"Never mind," she said, exasperated more with herself than anyone else. She should have known better than to get into the plane without double-checking that all the details were up to snuff.

She'd once hitched a ride with Keenan Murphy into Fairmont, just a few weeks before the Ring of Fire. First, the tire had gone flat. Then, after borrowing a jack from a helpful driver passing by, which Keenan needed to borrow because he'd somehow or other lost his own jack, he discovered the spare was flat. Then, after the still-helpful passerby drove him to a nearby gas station where he could get the tire fixed, they'd continued the drive to Fairmont until he ran out of gas. Turned out the fuel gauge didn't work and Keenan had lost track of the last time he'd filled up the tank. She'd wound up walking the last three miles into town.

As for Lannie—

But there was no point in sour ruminations. Besides, what the hell. She had expansive opinions on the subject of "citizen's arrest." Why should the lousy cops get special privileges? If she'd heard her dad say it once, she'd heard him say it a million times.

"Now," commanded Janos. While Gage and Gardiner got off the wagons and untied their horses, he looked down from the saddle at the up-timers gawking up at him.

"Wait here," he said curtly.

"I got a gun!" protested Jay Barlow. As if that needed to be proven, he drew it from the holster at his hip. "Way better than that ancient piece of shit you're carrying, too."

Janos looked at the weapon Barlow was brandishing. It was what the up-timers referred to as a "six-shooter," a type of revolver, which the man had drawn from one of those holsters Janos had seen in the so-called "western movies." The ones slung low, for the "quick draw," tied down to the thigh.

Naturally, it was pearl-handled.

With his soldier's interest in weaponry, Janos had made inquiries during his weeks in Grantville. The man named Paul Santee had been particularly helpful on the subject of up-time firearms. On one occasion, when Janos had asked about "six-shooters," Santee had explained the careful distinctions to be made between serious revolvers and the sort of "Wild West bullshit pieces" that some of the town's more histrionic characters favored.

As for the wheellock Janos carried—he had two of them, actually, one in each saddle holster—the weapons were quite good and he was quite good with them.

"Wait here," he repeated firmly. The last thing he wanted was someone like Barlow involved. Janos still hoped the problem could be handled without violence. Barlow was the sort of man who would lose control in a confrontation—and then miss what he shot at.

Gage and Gardiner were ready. Both of them, from their long stay in Grantville, with up-time firearms. The weapons called "pump-action shotguns," which were much favored by soldiers. They'd be loaded with solid slugs, not pellets.

"Let's go," he said.

"Abandoned," Eddie pronounced. Given the broken axle and the goods strewn around the wagon, Noelle thought that as redundant a statement as she'd ever heard.

She didn't tease Eddie about it, though. She knew he'd really said it just to steel himself for the inevitable. They'd have to continue the pursuit into the forest.

Feeling more than a little nervous, she studied the terrain ahead of them. The Fichtelgebirge was not only a low range of mountains, it was an old one. Erosion had worn its peaks down to round forms, with not much rock showing. As a barrier to travel it wasn't remotely comparable to the Rocky Mountains, much less the Sierra Nevadas. It was more like the sort of terrain in most of Appalachia that Indians and early white settlers had never had too much trouble passing through.

But as ambush country, it did just fine, thank you.

Hearing a familiar and quite unexpected sound, she twisted in her saddle and looked up behind her.

Eddie had already spotted it. "Look!" he shouted, pointing toward the oncoming aircraft. "The Air Force has arrived!"

Her sense of relief was brief. She couldn't really see what good a warplane would be in the situation. There couldn't be more than one plane available. In fact, she'd thought the air force had all of their few craft stationed in Magdeburg or points north. Jesse Wood must have detached one of them to Grantville when he got news of the defection.

One plane would be almost useless trying to spot a small party in the forest, and even if it did spot the defectors it couldn't maintain the patrol for very long before it had to go back to refuel. By the time it returned, they'd have vanished again.

As the plane got closer, what little sense of relief remained went away altogether.

"That's not a warplane," she said. "It's got to be one of the Kellys'."

Eddie squinted at the oncoming aircraft. "You are sure? I didn't think any of theirs were operational yet."

Noelle shook her head. "Define 'operational.' Nobody ever said Bob Kelly didn't know how to build airplanes. The problem is he doesn't know when to quit. At any given time, he's got at least one plane able to fly—until he starts tinkering with it again."

The aircraft was heading straight for them, no longer more than a hundred yards off the ground. By now it was quite close enough to recognize the details of its construction. The USE's air force had a grand total of two—count 'em, two—models of aircraft. The Belles and the Gustavs. Even someone like Noelle, who'd never been able to distinguish one model of automobile from another unless she could see the logo or it was something obvious like a VW bug, could tell the difference between either one of them and the oncoming plane.

"No, it's one of the Kellys'. Couldn't tell you which model, except it'll have a name like 'Fearless' or 'Invincible' or something equally bombastic, but it's one of theirs."

Eddie was still squinting at it. "You're *positive*?"

"Yes, I'm posi—"

"The reason I ask," he interrupted, pointing his finger at the plane, "is because it's carrying bombs."

"Huh?" Noelle squinted herself. Her eyesight wasn't bad, but it wasn't as good as Eddie's. Still, now that she looked for it—the plane was close, and coming pretty fast—she could see two objects suspended underneath the fuselage.

Those *did* look like bombs, sure enough.

And now that she thought about it, the oncoming plane's trajectory . . .

"Let's get out of here!" she yelled. "They're going to bomb us!"

Chapter 9. The Bomb

"Bombs away!" shouted Lannie. Way too soon, in Denise's judgment.

Fortunately, Keenan objected. "Hey, make up your mind! You said only one—"

"Drop it!" Denise hollered, when she gauged the time was right. Lannie might have buck fever, but she didn't. Not with Buster for a dad, teaching her to hunt.

"It's off!" said Keenan.

By now, the plane had swept by, over the wagon and the two enemy cavalrymen guarding it.

Well, one cavalryman, anyway. The other one might have been a civilian. They'd been moving too fast for Denise to get a good look at them.

Lannie brought the plane around. As soon as they could see the effect of the bomb, he shouted gleefully. "Yeeee-*haaaaa*! Dead nuts, guys!"

Sure enough, the wagon had been hit by the bomb. If not directly, close enough. Denise wasn't sure, from the quick glimpse she'd gotten as they went over it, but she thought the wagon had already been busted. It had seemed to be tilted over to one side, as if a wheel or an axle had broken, and she thought some of its cargo was on the ground.

Now, though, it was in pieces. And something was burning.

One of the cavalrymen was down, too. His horse was thrashing on the ground, and the rider was lying nearby.

Dead, wounded, unconscious, it was impossible to tell. The other cavalryman—well, maybe cavalryman—was dismounting to tend to his partner.

Denise frowned. There was something about the way that second cavalryman moved. . . .

"Fly back around," she commanded.

Keenan, even from his poor vantage point in the cramped bombadier's seat in the back, with its little windows, had been able to see the results too. "Jeez, Denise. I don't know as we gotta be bloodthirsty about this."

"Fly back around!" she snapped. "I just want to get a better look. And slow down, Lannie."

"Don't want to stall it out," he warned.

"Yeah, fine. So don't stall it out. Slow down and get lower."

"Backseat driver," he muttered. But he did as commanded.

"Wait," said Janos, holding out a hand. They were now sheltered beneath a large tree, not more than two hundred yards from what was left of the wagon. As soon as Janos had spotted the plane, he'd led them under the branches. Hopefully, they'd be out of sight.

"What a piece of luck," said Gage. "They bombed their own people."

Janos wasn't surprised, really. He knew from experience how easy it was for soldiers to kill and wound their own, in combat. In some battles, in bad weather or rough terrain, as many as a third of the casualties were caused by the soldiers' own comrades.

He'd never thought about it before, but he could see where that danger would be even worse with aircraft involved. At the speed and height it had maintained when it carried out the attack, the plane's operators couldn't have seen any details of their "enemy."

"What should we do?" asked Gardiner.

"Wait," Janos repeated. "The plane is coming back around. If we move out from under the tree, they might spot us."

That was the obvious reason not to move, and he left it at that. Still more, he wanted to see what would happen next.

Gardiner put up a mild objection. "That bomb was loud, when it went off. The garrison might come to investigate."

His tone was doubtful, though. Janos thought there was hardly any chance the explosion would alert the soldiers at Hof. Hof was miles away and while the sound might have carried the distance, it would have been indistinct. Thunder, perhaps. Of course, if the USE warplane kept dropping bombs, the situation would probably change. People would investigate an ongoing disturbance, where they would usually shrug off a single instance.

But Janos knew the plane couldn't be carrying very many bombs. By now, months after the Baltic War, Austria had very good intelligence on the capabilities of the up-time aircraft, and Janos had read all of the reports. Even the best of the enemy's warplanes, the one they called the "Gustav," was severely limited in its ordnance.

And this was no Gustav. Janos had seen one of them, on the ground at the Grantville airfield. Nor was it one of the other type of warplane, the one they called the

"Belle." He'd seen those on several occasions, both on the ground and in the air.

Drugeth didn't know which type of airplane this was, but it couldn't have capabilities that were any better. In fact, if he was right in his guess about the object he could see under the craft's body, it had only had two bombs to begin with. He'd seen the bomb they'd dropped, although he hadn't spotted where it came from. But he was pretty sure it must have been the companion of the object he could see now.

As they came over the wagon again, moving as slowly as Lannie dared, they weren't going any faster than a car breaking the speed limit on an interstate highway. And Lannie had the plane not more than forty feet off the ground.

So, since he also obeyed Denise when she told him to fly on the side where she could see what was happening, she got a very good look at the second cavalryman when he looked up as they passed by. Glaring in fury and shaking his fist at them.

Except it wasn't a cavalryman and it wasn't a he.

"Jesus H. Christ!" Denise exploded. "We just bombed Noelle and Eddie!"

"Huh?" said Lannie, his mouth gaping.

"Well, shit!" screeched Keenan from the back. "Well, shit!"

"I'll kill 'em," Noelle hissed, as she went back to tending Eddie. Luckily—by now, she'd unfastened the cuirass—he didn't seem to have been wounded by the bomb itself or any of the splinters it had sent flying from the wagon when it exploded. At least, she couldn't see any blood anywhere, that she thought was any of Eddie's own. He did have some blood on one of his trouser legs, but she was pretty sure that came from his horse. One of the splinters or maybe a part of the bomb casing had torn a huge wound in the horse's belly. It had thrown Eddie when it fell to the ground. Kicked him in the head, too, in the course of thrashing about afterward, judging from the condition of his helmet.

At least, she didn't think that big a dent in a sturdy helmet could have been caused by his fall. The meadow had hardly any rocks in it.

Eddie's eyes were open, but he seemed dazed. Might have a concussion. And a broken left arm, from the looks of things.

Gingerly, she started unfastening his sleeve. Eddie moaned a little, but she got it peeled back enough to check its condition.

A broken forearm, sure enough. Noelle had broken her own forearm as a kid, falling out of a tree. She could remember insisting to her mother all the way to the hospital that the arm wasn't really broken. Just bent a little, that's all.

But it wasn't a compound fracture, and the break was obviously well below the elbow. Give it a few weeks, properly splinted, and it would heal as good as new.

The relief allowed her fury to resurge. She looked up, tracking the plane from its sound, so she could shake her fist at them again. The stupid bastards!

But when she spotted the plane, the gesture turned into a frantic wave.

"You stupid bastards! *Watch out!*"

The cramped interior of the cockpit seemed like bedlam to Denise.

"Jesus, Lannie, you bombed my sister! You bombed my sister!" Keenan kept screeching, in blithe disregard for the fact that he'd been the one who'd actually released the weapon.

Naturally, Lannie's response was to shift the blame himself. "She told me to do it! She told me to do it!" was his contribution.

"Shut up, both of you!" was Denise's own, trying to settle them down.

In retrospect, she'd admit to her best friend Minnie—nobody else—that she probably should have kept concentrating on the "navigating" side of the business.

Eventually, it did occur to her that she ought to see where they were going.

"*Lannie!*" she screeched.

"Fascinating," murmured Janos. He'd always wondered how fragile the devices were. Now, seeing one of the plane's wings partly-shredded by its impact with a mere tree limb—a large tree, granted—his longstanding guess was confirmed.

As was his determination to remain a cavalryman. Say what you would about the stupid beasts, horses were rather sturdy. Nor did they move at ridiculous speeds, nor did they keep a rider more than a few feet from the ground.

"Jesus, Lannie, you wrecked the plane! You wrecked the plane!" was Keenan's current contribution, even more useless than the last.

"Shut the fuck up!" Denise hollered. "Just concentrate, Lannie. You can do it."

Fortunately, Lannie had left off his own shouting. Now that he was in a crisis, his pilot's instincts had taken over.

"We're going in, guys," he said. "Can't do anything else."

Even to Denise, it was obvious from the damage suffered by the wing on her side that he was right. "You can do it, Lannie," she said calmly. "And we got a big wide meadow here."

Lannie's grin was as thin as a grin could get, but she was relieved to see it. "Just better hope we don't hit a gopher hole. Got no way to retract the landing gear."

"There aren't any gophers in Europe," she said, in as reassuring a tone as she could manage.

"Yeah, that's right," chimed in Keenan from the back. "No ground hogs, neither." Thankfully, he'd left off the screeching.

Denise saw no reason to voice aloud her firm conviction that there were probable umpteen thousand things that could produce holes in a meadow. All but two of which *did* exist in Europe.

They'd be coming down in a few seconds. Lannie did have the plane more or less under control. Hopefully it'd be a crash landing they could walk away from, if nothing caught fire or—

"Drop the other bomb, Keenan!"

"Huh?"

"Drop the fucking bomb!"

"Oh. Yeah."

Watching, Janos didn't wonder for more than an instant why the up-timers had committed the seemingly pointless act of bombing an empty patch of meadow. Judging from the way the first bomb had exploded, the device had been detonated by a contact fuse, probably armed by the act of releasing it. Not the sort of thing any sane man wants to be sitting atop when he tries to crash an aircraft as gently as possible.

The plane came down. And confirmed once again Janos' long-standing conviction that plans and schemes and plots are just naturally prone to crashing.

"Oh, hell," said Noelle. At first, she'd thought that the plane had come down safely. Almost as if it were landing on a proper airfield. Then—one of the wheels must have hit an unseen obstruction—she saw the still undamaged wing dip sharply and strike the ground. The plane skewed around, tipped up on its nose—*please God, don't let that propeller come apart in pieces and chew anybody up*—and seemed to balance precariously for a moment.

Then it looked as if the plane just more or less disintegrated into its component parts. The newly-damaged wing broke off, the fuselage tipped and rolled, and the plane flopped down on its side. Most of the other wing broke off, as did part of the tail assembly when it hit.

Still . . .

There was no explosion. No flames. People had walked away from car crashes worse than that.

"Just wait for me, Eddie," she said. "And don't move. Your arm's busted."

She got on her horse and headed for the crash site.

Janos pointed to the enemy cavalryman still on the ground by the remains of the wagon.

"Gardiner, see to him. Keep him under guard, that's all. Do him no harm unless he attacks you. Gage, follow me."

He set off after the other cavalryman, toward the downed plane.

"What are we going to do?" asked Gage, loud enough to be heard over the sound of the cantering horses.

"Seize them and take them with us, any who survived. What else can we do? I don't think this is a reconnaissance patrol from a larger force following them. They wouldn't have sent just two men for that purpose. I'm not certain, but I think these are operating alone. If we let any of them go—and there's at least one of them in good condition—they'll take the alarm to Hof. Two bomb explosions, a crashed warcraft, even the sorriest garrison in Creation will react to that."

Gage was silent for a moment. Then, as Janos expected, he raised the other obvious alternative.

"We could kill them."

"Oh, splendid," said Janos. "Just what Austria needs. Half our army is facing Wallenstein on the north, most of the rest is facing the Turks to the south—and we ignite a new war by committing a pointless massacre."

"It was a thought," said Gage mildly. "Probably not a good one, I admit."

Drugeth's irritation with the Englishman was only momentary. He'd considered that solution himself. But he still had hopes they could complete this adventure without the sort of drastic measures that would trigger off an explosive reaction from the USE.

Firmly, he ignored his own hard-gained wisdom on the subjects of plans and their likely outcomes.

Chapter 10. The Sword

By the time Denise got done hauling Lannie out of the wreck, she was exhausted. Getting Keenan out hadn't been too bad, even though he'd been in the cramped rear of the cockpit. But Keenan had just been dazed and bruised, not pinned by some of the equipment that had been broken loose and all but completely unconscious.

Denise was strong for a girl her age and build, but the fact remained that the age was almost-sixteen and while the build was great for making girls jealous and boys drool—not that she appreciated either one—it wasn't that good for frantically trying to free a normal-sized man from wreckage and haul him out by bodily force. Not for the first time in her life, she wished she'd inherited more of her dad's bulk and muscle and less of her mother's appearance.

But, finally, it was done. Probably hadn't taken more than a few minutes, actually. With the last of her strength, she lowered Lannie onto the ground and half-spilled herself out of the fuselage. Fortunately, the meadow was pretty soft ground. On her hands and knees, she saw that Keenan was sitting up and holding his head. He was groaning a little, but so far as she could tell he didn't really seem to be hurt.

In the corner of her eye, she caught sight of a pair of legs. Looking over, she saw Noelle, with a very strained expression on her face.

"Hey, look," she said defensively, "I'm sorry. We didn't know it was you."

Belatedly, she realized that Noelle wasn't actually looking at her. She was looking over Denise's head at something off to the side.

Denise swiveled, flopping onto her side in the process, and propped herself up on one elbow.

"Oh, great."

The *something* Noelle had been staring out turned out to be two men, with two horses not far away behind them.

Both down-timers, obviously. Neither of them was smiling—hey, no kidding—so she couldn't see their teeth. That was usually the simplest indication, especially with a man somewhere in middle age like the one holding the very nasty looking and oh-so-very-up-time pump action shotgun, if not the younger one who was standing a little closer with a sword in his hand.

But it didn't matter. Leaving aside the clothes they were wearing and the hair styles, she would have known just looking at the way the young one held the sword. She didn't know any up-timer who held a sword like that. Maybe somebody like Harry Lefferts did, by now, with all of his escapades. But Denise hadn't seen much of Harry in a long time, and on the few occasions she had seen him Harry had been carousing in one of Grantville's taverns with the wine, women and song that seemed to accompany him like pilot fish did a shark. The wine and women, with complete ease, the singing a whole lot less so since Harry had a nice natural voice and could even carry a tune but somewhere along the way had picked up the silly conviction that he was one of those old-style Irish tenors who could make nasal sound good but he couldn't.

Her thoughts were veering all over the place, she realized, and she commanded them back to attention.

Concentrate on the fucking sword, idiot.

The damn thing didn't look any better when she did. This wasn't one of those fancy swords that a lot of downtime noblemen and wannabe noblemen carried about when they were trying to look impressive. Pretty, lots of decorations—even jewels, if they were rich enough—and looking as if they'd seen as much actual use as the kind of fancy china that people kept in a cabinet and didn't eat off of except once in a blue moon.

No, this sword looked like her mother's favorite kitchen knife, allowing for a drastic increase in size. Solid, plain, sharp as a razor and so often honed that the blade wasn't a completely straight line anymore. And the bastard was holding it just the way her mother did, too—or the way her dad held a welding torch or a tool he was using to work on one of his bikes.

Casually. The way no up-timer except maybe a few wild-ass screwballs like Harry could *possibly* hold a sword. The man wasn't flourishing it, wasn't brandishing it—didn't, really, even seem more than vaguely aware that he had it in his hand in the first place. A weapon so familiar and comfortable that it was just any other tool, used more by instinct than conscious thought.

Some tools chopped onions, some tools chopped metal, and this one wasn't any different except it chopped off heads and limbs and from the look of the miserable son-of-a-bitch any part of a human body he felt like chopping off.

She tore her eyes away from the sword and looked higher up, at the man's face. For a moment—one wild moment—she almost burst into laughter.

He looked for all the world like a rock star!

Dammit, it was true. Good-looking, in that sort of older-than-he-really-was way that indicated either dissipation or too much familiarity with the wicked ways of men—music recording executives in the case of rock stars; probably not in this guy's—and judging from the easy athleticism of his stance he didn't seem dissipated in the least, so scratch that theory.

Long, curly, dark hair. Flowing fucking locks, fer chrissake. A flaring mustache and a neatly trimmed full beard that'd looked silly on almost anybody except genu-ine rock stars and guys who could hold a sword like that.

Just to complete the picture, soulful brown eyes. The kind of eyes with which rock stars sang to the world of their sorrow at the faithlessness of women and guys like this bastard looked down upon the corpses they left behind.

"Well, fuck," she said. "Just what it needed to make the day complete."

In German, she added: "And who are you?"

The swordsman had been staring back at Noelle the whole time Denise had been assessing him. Now he looked down at her.

"My name is Janos Drugeth. From the family with the estates in Humenné. Homonna, as we Hungarians would call it. I am a cavalry officer in the service of the Austrian emperor."

Hungarian. Denise didn't know much about Hungarians, but she knew they liked to call themselves "Magyars" because they were descended from a tribe of nomadic conquerors. Like some biker gangs liked to call themselves "the Huns."

Perfect. Just perfect.

To her surprise, he added: "We may speak in English, if you prefer."

His English was good, too, if heavily accented.

Noelle stood very straight. "My name is Noelle Stull. I am an official for the USE government. Well, the State of Thuringia-Franconia. And I—me and my partner, Eddie Junker, over there—"

She pointed toward the demolished wagon, some distance away. "—are in pursuit of the criminals whom we believed to have been in possession of that vehicle. Please either assist us in that task or, at the very least, do not impede us in our duty."

Bold as brass. Mentally, Denise doffed her hat in salute. Not that she ever wore a hat.

The Drugeth fellow gave Noelle a sorrowful smile. "I will not dispute your characterization of the individuals in question. But I am afraid I cannot respond as you wish to either of your requests. Not only may I not assist you, I am afraid I shall have to detain you myself."

He slid the sword back into its scabbard. The motion was swift, easy, practiced. He hadn't even looked at the sword and scabbard as he did it, just letting his left thumb and forefinger guide the blade into the opening. The fact that he'd chosen to sheathe the weapon while explaining what he was going to do just emphasized his complete confidence that nobody would think to dispute the matter.

Which . . .

In point of fact, nobody would. Sure as hell not Denise. That sword could come out just as quickly and smoothly as it went in. And leaving that aside, the other guy still had the shotgun in his hands and didn't seem to be in the least inclined to emulate his leader's example and put it away. True, he didn't have the barrel pointed at anybody, but it was obvious he could in a split-second. That was just good gun-handling, not carelessness.

He didn't look like a rock star, either. More like a record producer. Shoot you as quick as he'd shell out payola or cheat singers out of their royalties.

To Denise's alarm, she saw that Noelle's hand had moved to the vicinity of her holster.

That was crazy. First, that was no quick-draw holster. It was a safe-and-sound holster with a flap, and the flap was buckled. By the time Noelle got the pistol out, the older guy with the shotgun could kill them all. Assuming the Hungarian nomad-cum-rock-star hadn't sliced them up already.

And even if Noelle had been a quick-draw whizzeroo, so fucking what? The pistol was a dinky little .32 caliber and her marksmanship was something of a legend, in Grantville. The anti-Julie Sims. There were two schools of thought on the subject. The optimists insisted Noelle could hit the side of a barn. The other view was that she could only do it if she were inside the barn to begin with.

"Uh, Noelle . . . "

Fortunately, Noelle reconsidered. Her hand moved away. "This is an outrage!" she snapped. "You are on USE soil here, not Austrian. You have no right—"

"Please," said Drugeth, holding up his hand. "You are wasting our time, and I believe you know it perfectly well. Although there have been no open hostilities in some time, Austria and the USE are enemies. I have been given the task of escorting the individuals in question to Vienna, and I intend to complete it successfully."

Noelle glared at him. "And you won't stop at outright abduction."

"Hardly 'abduction,' I think." He shrugged. Like the dark eyes, the gesture was sorrowful. Not really-sad sorrowful, just what you might call philosophically sorrowful. Exactly the same way, Denise imagined, the guy contemplated the bodies of his foes after he sliced them up.

"I will set you free, unharmed, as soon as we have reached a place where I can be confident you cannot bring troops in time to prevent our escape. If you will give me your parole, I shall not even disarm you. And please do not delay the matter any further. I point out"—here, he nodded toward Lannie and Keenan, and then toward the wagon—"that you have injured persons in your party, who should get medical attention. And I will also point out that none of the injuries were caused by me and my men."

Noelle shifted the glare to Denise.

"Hey, look, I *said* I was sorry. And he's right, Noelle."

For a moment, she even thought Noelle might start cussing. But she didn't, of course.

By the time they got back to the wagon, Keenan and Denise propping up Lannie along the way—he turned

out to be okay except for a sprained ankle—Eddie Junker
was up and moving.

Well. Sitting up and fiddling uselessly with his busted
arm. There was another shotgun-toting sidekick of Drugeth's there, watching Eddie carefully but making no
effort to assist him. Drugeth had probably told him to
do that, and by now it was clear enough that anybody
who worked for Drugeth followed orders.

"Cut it out, Eddie," said Noelle crossly, kneeling next
to him. "It's broken. Denise, give me a hand."

"Why me?"

"Because you broke it, that's why."

"I don't know squat about setting a broken arm. Have
Keenan do it."

Noelle looked at Keenan. Keenan looked alarmed. "I
hate the sight of blood."

"There's no blood," Denise pointed out.

"I hate the sight of suffering. I'm not going to be any
good at this."

"Enough," said the Drugeth fellow. He motioned
Keenan toward Eddie. "All you have to do is help hold
him down. You ladies as well. This will be painful, for
a time."

Eddie looked alarmed. More by the sight of Drugeth
approaching him with that sword on his hip than anything else, Denise thought.

"It doesn't need to be amputated!" he protested.

"Of course not," said Drugeth calmly. "Now do your
best not to thrash around. Hold him, everyone."

Drugeth set the arm just as swiftly and smoothly as
he'd sheathed the sword. It seemed like *zip-zip-zip* and

it was done. By then, his shotgun-toting cohorts had found a couple of pieces of wood broken off from the wagon that would serve as a temporary splint, along with one of Suzi Barclay's flamboyant costumes that, sliced up, would serve to bind them.

One of the cohorts did the slicing, not Drugeth, using a simple knife he had in a scabbard. Clearly enough, the Hungarian's sword did not come out for any work less lofty than hacking flesh, still on the bone and twitching.

By now, Drugeth didn't remind Denise of a rock star at all. Just a good-looking nomad barbarian, who'd never once lost that serenely-sorrowful expression even while Eddie had been screaming bloody murder. And who'd obviously set more than one broken limb in his day; which, given that he wasn't old enough to have seen all that many days, would indicate the days themselves had not been spent in the pursuit of serenity.

"It's done," he said, coming back up to his feet. "Good enough for the time being, at least. It's a clean break, so it should heal well."

Eddie was gasping, his heavy face pale and sweating. "You—you—" he said weakly, apparently searching for suitably vile cognomens to heap upon Drugeth. Then, he tightened his jaws. Then, looked up and nodded. "Thank you."

That was classy, Denise thought. She hadn't known Eddie was that solid. Of course, she barely knew the guy.

Drugeth nodded in return. "Let us be off then. Gage, retrieve that rifle over there." He indicated a spot not far away. Denise hadn't seen it until Drugeth pointed at the thing, but she recognized an up-time lever action rifle. Must have been Eddie's.

"Then," the Hungarian continued, "you ride ahead and make sure the party we are escorting is ready to go when we arrive. Gardiner, you ride alongside Ms. Stull. Ms. Stull, I would appreciate it if you'd lead my horse."

He even said it that way, too. "Miz," not "Miss." This guy knew Americans, somehow, even down to the subtle quirks of what you called career girls like Noelle.

"For the rest of us," Drugeth continued, "I recommend walking, since we have injured persons."

It was all done very courteously, but Denise didn't miss the fact that Drugeth's dispositions also meant he had all the USE loyalists under control. If Noelle tried to ride off, Cohort Gardiner could go in pursuit. He wasn't encumbered by having to lead another horse, and Denise didn't doubt for an instant he could ride better than Noelle as well as shoot better than she could.

And by remaining on foot, Drugeth was there—with the damn sword—in case any of the others decided to try something tricky that might throw off a horseman for a time. Like . . .

Who knows? Finding a hole dug by something bigger than a gopher—they had badgers in Europe—and trying to hide in it. Not likely, but Drugeth didn't seem like a guy who'd leave much to chance.

Eddie's horse was still thrashing a little. Cohort Gardiner went over and looked down at the poor animal, then looked at Drugeth.

The Hungarian officer nodded. *Clickety-BOOM,* and the horse was out of its misery.

As they headed toward the forest, moving slowly because of Eddie and Lannie, Denise decided things weren't so bad. Perhaps oddly, the fact that Drugeth's cohorts seemed just as familiar and relaxed in their use of up-time shotguns as Drugeth himself did with a sword, was somehow reassuring.

Whatever else they were, enemies of the USE or not, they obviously weren't wild-eyed desperadoes. Everything about them was experienced, controlled, disciplined—or self-disciplined, in the case of Drugeth.

True, that same control might lead to a quick, relaxed, practiced and easy execution squad too. But if they'd wanted to do that, they would have done it already. And would a man planning to kill her in a few minutes have bothered to give Noelle a courteous helping hand getting onto her horse? Denise didn't think so.

Besides, her assessment of Drugeth had shifted yet again. From rock star to nomad barbarian, it had tentatively come to rest on a label she was generally skeptical about but seemed accurate enough in this instance. Every now and then—not often—you did run across a down-time nobleman who actually lived up to the name instead of being a puffed-up thug with delusions of grandeur.

Drugeth had told them he would release them once his expedition got far enough away from any chance of pursuit. Okay, he hadn't officially "given his word." But Denise was pretty sure that the genuine articles when it came to noblemen didn't bother with silly flippery like solemn vows, except on formal occasions. He'd said what he would do, and so he would. To do otherwise would be a transgression of a code he took seriously.

Good enough, she decided, for a day that included bombing your own guys. Jesus, it'd take her *years* to live that down. Even Minnie would make fun of her, when she found out.

But when they reached the small clearing where the defectors had been waiting, things immediately got tense.

Unfortunately, even sober, Jay Barlow was nobody's idea of a nobleman—and he'd apparently spent the time since Drugeth left him with the others getting half-plastered. Him and Mickey Simmons. There was another prize for you.

"That's the fucking bitch!" he shouted, when he spotted Noelle. He thrust a half-empty bottle into Mickey's hand and took several steps forward. To make things perfect, he had his hand dramatically positioned to yank out the silly cowboy gun on his hip. He looked like something out of Grade D western.

Drugeth moved up in front of him. "Enough, Barlow. Get back on the wagon. Now. We have to be moving."

"Fuck that!" Barlow pointed the forefinger of his right hand accusingly at Noelle. Unfortunately, he was left-handed and his left hand was now gripping the gun butt. "She's the one went after Horace! I say we shoot her now and good riddance."

Matching deed to word, he yanked the gun out of the holster.

Keenan squawked. Denise probably did too. She wasn't sure, because whatever she'd been about to say was stifled in her throat by Drugeth's sword.

Blurring like an arc. Barlow's gun and the hand holding it went sailing off somewhere. Barlow stared at the stump, gushing blood. His expression seemed one of amazement, not pain.

But it was Drugeth's expression that mostly registered on Denise. The Hungarian seemed to be in some sort of weird brown study. Just standing there, the sword in his hand, point down, dripping a little blood from the tip, while he contemplated Jay Barlow.

He shifted deftly to the side, the sword blurred again, and a fountain of blood gushed out of Barlow's neck. His whole throat looked to have been cut, from one ear to the other.

Paralyzed by shock, Denise realized that Drugeth had just been calculating whether to keep Barlow alive or not. The decision having come up negative, he'd shifted to the side so he wouldn't get blood all over himself.

And he didn't, not a drop. Barlow collapsed to his knees and then to the ground. He was effectively already dead.

Mickey Simmons was shouting, and clawing for something in the wagon. A gun, Denise assumed.

"Kill him," said Drugeth. Quietly, almost conversationally.

Gage and Gardiner's shotguns seemed to go off simultaneously. The heavy slugs hammered Simmons into the side of the wagon. He collapsed to the ground.

A lot of the American defectors were making noise now. Billie Jean Mase came running up to Drugeth, screaming at him. For a moment, Denise expected to see her throat sliced in half, too. But Drugeth simply planted a boot in her belly and that was that. She went down, gasping for air.

"Silence," said Drugeth. Not hollering, exactly, but the word carried like nobody's business. "You will all be silent."

That shut them up. Including Denise. Which was a good thing, or she might have giggled hysterically, because—well—there *was* something insanely amusing about the scene, if she ignored the gore. It was like watching a bunch of rabbits suddenly realize they'd pissed off a bobcat. Or a cougar.

Drugeth drew out a handkerchief and cleaned off the blade, then slid the sword back into the scabbard. Throughout, he did not take his eyes once off the defectors clustered around the two wagons in the clearing.

"I told Ms. Stull and her companions that they would be released unharmed once we were far enough from pursuit. So I spoke, and so it will be. And I am no longer inclined to tolerate any obstruction or dispute. I am in command, not you. You will obey me in all things, until we reach Vienna."

He waited a few seconds, to see if any protest would be made.

None was. What a shocker.

"And now, we must dig two graves. Mr. O'Connor, perhaps there is some tool in the wagon that might serve."

"We didn't bring any shovels," said Allen O'Connor uncertainly. His voice was a little shaky, maybe, but not much. He certainly didn't seem stricken by grief. Leaving aside the shock of the sudden blood-letting, Denise didn't think many of the defectors—leaving aside the cretin Billie Jean and Caryn Barlow—had any serious personal attachment to the two dead men. Simmons' wife was a down-timer, a widow he'd married the year before. But she wasn't in the group. Mickey must have decided to abandon her when he defected.

And the baby they'd had a few months ago. And his two step-children by his wife's first marriage.

The shithead.

Qualifying that, the now-dead shithead. And good riddance.

O'Connor's son Neil started digging amongst the goods piled in the wagon. "I'll find something."

Marina Barclay swallowed. "Are you sure, Mr. Drugeth? I mean, you were saying we needed to move as soon as . . ."

Her voice trailed off, as it must have dawned on her that she was perilously close to "obstruction and dispute." Nervously, she eyed the sword.

But either Drugeth was inclined to be lenient toward women—Billie Jean, still gasping for breath, supported that theory—or he was simply not given to bloodshed for the sake of it. That theory was supported by everything else Denise had seen.

Including his next words.

"They are not animals, to be left to scavengers. Time presses, yes, but God created time also. Everything we do is watched by Him."

Noelle got off her horse, holding a small spade that she'd retrieved from her saddlebag. "Let's get started," she said. "Officer Drugeth is right." She seemed quite calm, although with Noelle you never knew. She was the kind of person who clamped down her emotions under stress. She didn't so much as glance at Drugeth.

Less than half a minute later, having found a good spot, she started digging. Drugeth came up and offered to replace her. But, still without looking at him, she shook her head.

"You can spell me when I get tired. This'll take a while."

Denise started digging alongside her—more like just breaking up the ground—with a heavy stick she found in the woods. Meanwhile, the two male O'Connors and Tim Kennedy dug the other grave, with some tools they'd found in the wagon and a spade that Gardiner had in his own saddlebags.

When Noelle did relinquish the shovel to Drugeth, maybe half an hour later, she finally looked at him.

"What *is* your rank?"

He was back to that sad-eyed sorrowful-look business. "It is quite complicated, and depends mostly on the situation. For now, 'captain' will do."

She nodded, still with no expression. "Why did you kill him, Captain Drugeth? You'd already disarmed him."

"Literally," muttered Denise; again, having to fight off a semi-hysterical giggle.

"I am not certain," was the soft reply. "I fear some of it was simply ingrained reflex, although I strove to contain it. First, because it would have been a struggle to keep him alive on the journey, with such a wound, and would inevitably have slowed us down. Second, because I decided if I didn't kill one of them now, I would have to kill one of them later. Perhaps more. They are undisciplined people, prone to emotional outbursts. That was bad enough before you appeared to make it worse. Clearly, they have an animus against you."

He took a long breath. "And, finally, because he was not essential to my mission. Not even important, really. Neither was Simmons."

The two of them stared at each other.

"Just like that?" she asked abruptly.

"At the time, yes. Just like that. In the time to come, of course, it will be different. I will spend many hours of my life thinking about the deed. And praying that I did not transgress His boundaries."

Noelle looked away, for a few seconds. "Yes," she said. "I understand."

She handed him the shovel and climbed out of the shallow pit. "I will give you my parole, Captain Drugeth."

"The others?"

"Eddie will too. So will Lannie and Keenan, probably, but I wouldn't believe Lannie or Keenan if they told me the sun rose in the east. It's not that they're dishonest. Just . . . forgetful."

He smiled. "Much like several of my cousins."

Now, he looked at Denise.

"You can take her word for anything," said Noelle. "If you don't mind it coming with vulgar qualifiers."

Denise scowled. "Well, thank you very much."

Drugeth just looked at her, saying nothing.

After a while, Denise shrugged. "Sure, why not? You've got my fucking word I'll be a good little girl."

He stroked his mustache. "Qualifiers, indeed," he said mildly. "Do I need to insist on qualifying the terms? No attempt to escape. No attempt to overwhelm us by force."

He even said that last with a straight face. "That sort of thing?"

Denise thought about it. "Nah," she said. "I hate all that legal dotting-the-I's and crossing-the-T's bullshit. But I'm okay with the spirit of stuff."

He studied her for a bit longer. Denise was primed to strip his hide if he started nattering about her potty mouth. Or asked her if her father knew the sort of language she used, when who the hell did he think she'd learned it from in the first place?

But all he said was, "I believe that will do quite nicely."

By nightfall, they were well into the Fichtelgebirge. They made camp just before nightfall.

Three camps, really, separated by a few yards from each other. One for the defectors, one for Drugeth and his two cohorts, one for Denise, Noelle, Eddie, Lannie and Keenan.

After they ate, Lannie and Eddie fell asleep. Between their injuries and the rigors of walking or riding a wagon along mountain trails for several hours, they were exhausted.

Denise and Noelle and Keenan stayed awake a while longer, mostly just staring into the little fire they'd made. All three of the camps had fires going. Drugeth had given permission to make them. He didn't seem too concerned they'd be spotted, given the thick woods around them.

And who'd spot them anyway? The ever-vigilant and non-existing USE park rangers? Overflying aircraft, when they'd already crashed the only one in Grantville that could get off the ground, and Jesse Wood only let even the air force guys fly at night in extreme emergencies?

But Denise's sarcastic thoughts were just her way of coming to a decision.

"I've decided," she finally pronounced. "Drugeth's okay."

"Scary son-of-a-bitch," Keenan grunted. "But. Yeah. He's okay, I guess. What do you think, Noelle?"

But Noelle said nothing. Denise wasn't even sure she'd heard them talking. She seemed completely preoccupied by the sight of the flames.

Chapter 11. The Prayer

Two days later, after they'd made camp for the evening, Janos was approached by the Barclay couple and Allen O'Connor. They were the leaders of the up-time defectors, insofar as such a group could be said to have leaders.

The day before, Janos had heard Denise Beasley refer to them sarcastically as a "motley crew." The term being new to him, he'd asked for a translation. He'd found her explanation quite charming, especially the qualifiers that seemed to be inseparable from the girl's vocabulary. Even more amusing had been her pugnacious attitude. Clearly, she seemed to be expecting him at any moment to begin chastising her for her language.

Indeed, he was sometimes tempted to do so, when she lapsed into blasphemy. But he'd already learned from his weeks in Grantville that Americans had a casual attitude toward blasphemy, just as the rumors said they did. And despite his piety, Janos was skeptical—had been since he was a boy—that the way so many priests lumped all sins into unvarying categories was actually a reflection of God's will. Janos did not presume to understand the Lord's purpose in all things, and blasphemy was certainly listed as a transgression in the Ten Commandments. Still, he doubted that the Creator who had forged the sun and the moon made no distinction at all between blasphemy and murder.

As for the girl's profanity, he simply found it artful. Growing up as the scion of a Hungarian noble family in the countryside, he'd learned profanity from high-born father and low-born milkmaid alike. His were not a prissy folk. Janos himself avoided profanity, as a rule, but that was simply an expression of his austere personality. He didn't paint or write poetry, either. But he could still appreciate the skill and talent involved in all three of the arts.

Had Janos' father still been alive and been there, he might have had caustic remarks to say about the girl's language. But the old man would have criticized her for the sloppiness of the form, not the nature of the content. When it came to profanity, Janos' father had been a devotee of formal structure; Denise Beasley, of what the up-timers called free verse.

Jarring stuff, free verse, at first glance. But in the hands of a skilled poet, it could be effective. Janos had read some poems by an up-timer named e. e. cummings—he'd refused to capitalize even his name—and found them quite good. He'd even had a copy made of some of them to give to his uncle, Pal Nadasdy.

"We just wanted to tell you that Billie Jean's settling down," said Barclay. "We were a little worried there, for a while."

Janos nodded. He'd been somewhat concerned himself. Caryn Barlow seemed almost indifferent to the death of her father, but that wasn't particularly surprising. Their relationship had obviously not been close. In fact, it had seemed to verge on outright hostility. She'd joined the group because of her friendship with Suzi Barclay, not because of her father's involvement.

The Mase woman, on the other hand, was an odd one. Clearly intelligent, in most things, even quite intelligent.

But it had been hard to analyze her attachment to such a man as Jay Barlow as being anything other than sheer stupidity. It was not simply that the man had been unpleasant, since that was true of many husbands and paramours. He'd been feckless and improvident as well.

Marina Barclay shook her head. "There's a history of abuse, there. I think it's got her all twisted up."

Janos couldn't quite follow the idiom. "Excuse me?"

"Billie Jean's father . . . Well. It was pretty bad. God knows why that got transferred over to an asshole like Barlow, but I think that's what happened."

"Ah." That was somewhat clearer. It was certainly as clear as Janos wanted it to be. Up-timers set great store by what they called "psychology." They claimed it was almost a science. Janos was dubious, but supposed it couldn't be any worse than the astrology which so many down-timers used to guide their way through life.

"The point is," said O'Connor, "we don't think she'll be a problem anymore. Now that she's cried herself out, we think she's actually kind of relieved. That was a bad situation."

Marina's expression darkened. "He beat her, sometimes, when he got drunk."

Janos looked from her, to her husband, to O'Connor. "Does she have possession of a weapon? A gun, I mean." He was not concerned, of course, that she might have a knife.

"No," said Peter Barclay firmly. "We took that away from her right away. We didn't . . . uh . . ."

Janos was tempted to scowl, but didn't. *We didn't want her taking a shot at you because you'd slaughter all of us.*

As if he himself couldn't make distinctions! They were truly annoying, sometimes, in the way they insulted without even realizing they did so.

Barclay's wife immediately demonstrated the talent anew. "And, uh, thanks for not killing her at the time."

Janos kept his face expressionless, since he knew there was no intentional insult involved. True, there might come a time in his old age—assuming he lived that long, which was unlikely—when he would be forced to kill an unarmed woman who attacked him. But to do such a thing now, when he was twenty-five, an experienced cavalry officer, and one of the best swordsmen in the Austrian empire? She might as well have thanked him for not being a coward.

There was such a difference between them, and the ones he had captured. Eddie Junker he understood almost immediately. A few exchanges over the past two days had been enough for the purpose. A sturdy young fellow, from a good down-time family. Lutheran, true, not Catholic. But Janos did not particularly hold that against him, since Junker retained the other virtues of the station he'd been born into. Loyal, quietly courageous, dependable, solicitous of his mistress' well-being.

In their own manner, the same was true of Lannie Yost and Keenan Murphy. A bit hapless in some ways, those two, as their actions with the plane demonstrated. But Janos had learned while still in his teens that some retainers could fumble at things, and one overlooked their failings for their virtues. The position of a nobleman was simply a transient charge given by God; gone in an instant, measured against eternity. In that, as in so many things, Father Drexel's *School of Patience* was a superb guide.

Young Denise had seemed a bit outside Janos' experience, at first. But eventually he'd realized that was because the fluid class relations of Americans always blurred one's view of them until you understood where to look. Ignore class, and she was not so strange at all. Neither was the Suzi Barclay creature, for that matter. Wild young noblewomen were not common in Hungary, and even less so in Austria. But they were hardly unheard of. What mattered was the way they shaped themselves as time went by. Some wound up quite well, as Janos thought Denise was likely to manage. Others were . . . hopeless. A nuisance to their families at all times, perhaps never more so than when they reached old age and the obnoxious wretches had to be cared for.

Mostly, he was intrigued by Noelle Stull. Such a perceptive one, she was. He was quite sure that it would never occur to the Barclays or O'Connor to ask him the question she had. Where they would thank him for not killing a woman, when the reason was obvious, she'd wondered why he had decided to kill a man. Even more, what he thought the cost would be.

She was attractive, too, in a way that some young Hungarian noblewomen were and a few Austrian ones. Pretty in a subdued sort of way; slender; far more athletic than most such. He wondered what she'd look like in formal court costume.

He was a little jarred when he realized the direction his thoughts were heading. Just so, a few times in the past, had he gauged a possible marital prospect. In one instance, an assessment that led to his marriage to his now-deceased wife Anna Jakusith de Orbova.

Anna had died a year and a half earlier. This was the first instance since that horrible time when he'd even thought of another woman in those terms.

The thought was preposterous on the face of it, of course.

He realized his silence was making the Barclays and O'Connor uncomfortable. They'd assume he was thinking about them; possibly, even contemplating harsh measures.

"I am pleased to hear she is settling her nerves. Please see to it, though, that she remains unarmed. Just in case."

They nodded.

"Are there any other problems I should know about?"

"Uh, no," said O'Connor. "Everybody else is fine."

Janos wasn't surprised. Barlow and Simmons had wound up attached to the group through happenstance. They were not and never had been part of the inner circles. Nor liked, for that matter.

Truth be told, the episode's outcome had been much as Janos hoped it would. The rest of the up-timers had been far easier to handle since the killings. That would improve their chances of reaching Austria safely.

Marina Barclay looked uncertain. "I guess I should tell you that Billie Jean's threatening to complain to the authorities—the Austrian authorities, I mean—once we get to Vienna. She says she'll press charges against you. Take it all the way up to the emperor, if need be."

"She will certainly have the right to do so, under Austrian law. Even the right to appeal to the emperor, although he rarely takes such appeals under consideration."

Now, all of them looked uncertain. After a few seconds, Marina's husband finally got around to asking.

"Do you, uh . . . know the emperor? Personally, I mean?"

"Oh, yes. We have been close friends since we were boys."

They stared at him, then started to turn away. Moved by a sudden impulse, Janos cleared his throat.

"Excuse me. If you would satisfy my curiosity? Noelle Stull. What is her family background?"

The three of them looked at each other. By whatever silent communication passed, Peter Barclay assumed the role of spokesman.

"Her family is, uh . . . Well. Strange. There are several families involved, actually. The Murphys and the Stulls and the Fitzpatricks."

The tale that followed was intricate; complex; even tortuous at points. More than it needed to be, really. It was clear that the up-timers assumed he would find almost all of it incomprehensible.

When they finished, he nodded. "I believe I understand the gist of it. Noelle's true father, Dennis Stull, was betrothed to her mother, Pat Fitzgerald—in their own eyes, at least. Then her family, largely for religious reasons, forced her into a marriage with Francis Murphy. By whom"—he glanced over at the five USE loyalists, readying their camp—"she gave birth to Keenan, over there. During the years that passed, meanwhile, her once-betrothed remained unmarried. Eventually, Pat—Murphy, now, not Fitzgerald, as is your American custom—abandoned her legal husband and went to live with Dennis Stull for many years. By whom she had her daughter Noelle, although the fiction was publicly maintained for over two decades that Noelle was Francis Murphy's daughter. Until it all—'blew up,' was the term you used?—because Francis Murphy was outraged that his long-estranged wife attended the funeral of her lover's mother when she had refused to attend the funeral of his father. So, in a drunken fury, he attempted to murder her at the funeral."

"Well, sort of," said Marina. "Stupid bastard shot into the funeral parlor from outside. The only solid hit he got was on the corpse in the casket. His own son Keenan was the one wrestled him down, and kept him from anything worse."

"The whole thing was a comic opera, really," added her husband, "although it wouldn't have been if Francis had been sober enough to shoot straight. As it is, the only thing they wound up charging him with was attempted murder and desecrating a corpse."

Janos stroked his mustache. "A reasonable legal decision. The latter is certainly a charming one."

The Barclays and O'Connor didn't seem to think it was the least bit charming. "That was Judge Maurice Tito. He wasn't anywhere nearly as prone to be lenient to poor Horace Bolender. Threw the whole damn book at him, the self-righteous bastard."

Janos decided not to pursue that. It was the common characteristic of thieves to believe that one of their own was roughly handled by the law, where favoritism was shown to others.

In truth, there was some substance to the charge. By their own account, the flamboyant conclusion to the long and complex family saga they'd narrated was the product of emotion and unreason, not cold-blooded and premeditated criminal intent. Austrian judges—certainly Hungarian ones—were prone to gauging the two differently also. As was Janos himself, for that matter.

"This must all seem weird to you," said Marina, smiling.

Janos shook his head. "It all sounds quite familiar, actually. I can think of several similar episodes involving Hungarian noble families. Rather mild escapades, actually, compared to other things that have been done by such. When we reach the Danube and can finally relax a bit, remind me to tell you the history of Countess Erzsebet Bathory. She is—was—my maternal grandmother. A Calvinist, true, not a Catholic. But I do not believe a fair man can ascribe cause to effect in this instance. My parents converted to Catholicism when I was two years old, and I was raised in the church. But one of her sons, my uncle Pal Nadasdy, has stubbornly remained a Calvinist to this day, unmoved by all of Ferdinand II's many proffered carrots and occasional brandished stick. Yet I have rarely met a more respectable man."

◇   ◇   ◇

After they left, Janos stood there staring into the fire, mulling on the problem for a while. The up-timers, as usual, had not understood his question. They categorized families by their deeds, as if noble families did not typically have more outlandish members and histories than most peasant families; simply because they had more power, if for no other reason.

So. It was still probably a preposterous idea to entertain, for many political reasons. But if he persisted in contemplating the matter—which he very well might; he was an introspective man, and knew himself rather well by now—then, sooner or later, he would have to face the problem squarely.

It was a thorny one, given that he was Hungarian. In many of the Germanies, by now—elsewhere too in the western countries, he thought—the theory had taken hold that Americans as a class belonged to the noble ranks. At the very least, stood outside the class categories altogether. Hungarians and Austrians thought that nonsense, by and large, although Janos was fairly sure their resolve would start crumbling as time went by.

As such resolve always did, given realities and the passage of enough time. His own august family could trace its origins back to Naples. Three centuries earlier, they had come to Hungary in the entourage of Charles Robert of Anjou, when he assumed the throne of Hungary as King Charles I. Family tradition insisted they'd been a highly-respected family in the Italian aristocracy. Perhaps it was even true. Given Italy, though, that was always suspect. That was a land steeped in commerce, quite unlike rural Hungary. Everything was for sale, including titles.

But even if it were true, what then? Trace it back still farther, if you could, and what would you find? No Christian family in Europe could claim, as did some Jewish ones, to be able to trace themselves back to the lords spoken of in the Bible. And who had made them lords, except the Lord Himself? Who had also made the Ring of Fire, through which came the man whom many Germans now called their prince. And whose soldiers had, just a few months earlier at Ahrensbök, shoved the title down the throats of haughty French noble generals.

But that took a lot of time, as a rule. Probably more than Janos would encompass in that span of his life that mattered. Soon enough, he would have to marry again. His little boy Györgÿ needed a mother, and given his position in the empire he really should produce more heirs in case misfortune took his son as it had taken his wife. For which latter purpose, unfortunately, if not the first, a morganatic marriage would probably not be suitable.

So. He flashed a quick grin at the fire he was staring into. A problem, then. Complex; complicated; even tortuous at points.

Janos enjoyed solving problems. He also took vows seriously, although he seldom made them formal ones. At the age of twelve, after he realized the full scope of his responsibilities, he had made a solemn vow that while he would be a faithful son of Hungary, he would not—would *not*—agree to marry a dullard. Be her rank never so high, or her station never more suitable.

He'd kept that pledge to himself when he married Anna Jakusith. The all-too-short time he'd shared his life with her had confirmed the wisdom of his youngster's vow. As a purely personal matter, and leaving aside the needs of state, he'd far rather remain a widower for the rest of his life than marry the sort of woman who, every morning and every nightfall, only made him think regretfully of the woman who was no longer there. He would remember Anna always, of course, so long as he lived, as he remembered her in his prayers every day. But he wanted a wife who could forge a place of her own in his life and affections.

"You're *kidding*," hissed Denise. Quickly, almost surreptitiously, she glanced at Drugeth. The way he was just standing there, not moving at all while he studied whatever the hell he found so fascinating in a campfire, matched Keenan's depiction perfectly. The expressionless, handsome, brooding face, half in shadows, the easy stance—*everything*. She could picture him just like that, standing in a castle in Transylvania. Which was part of Hungary, now that she thought about it. Well, parts of it were, anyway.

"Oh, wow." She took her eyes away from Janos, lest she draw his attention somehow. She didn't really believe in supernatural powers, but you could never be sure.

"Yup," said Keenan. "That's the whole story. I got it from Gardiner and Gage an hour ago, while we were out foraging for wood. Janos Drugeth is a *vampire*."

Noelle sniffed. "Keenan, I am quite certain that neither Gage nor Gardiner said any such thing."

"Well, sure. Not in so many words. But what else could we be talking about? I mean, I've even *heard* of his grandma. The Blood Countess. She's almost as famous as Dracula himself. The one who sucked all those virgins dry of their blood so her complexion wouldn't get bad. *Dozens* of virgins."

Noelle sniffed again. "There are so many errors in what you just said that I don't know where to begin.

For starters, she didn't 'suck the blood' out of anybody. She—uh . . . "

Denise had heard the story, too. "That's quibbling, Noelle. So she drained them dry with a knife and bathed in the blood. Big fucking difference. And it's a fact—well, that's what I heard, anyway—that when they caught her they didn't try to execute her 'cause they couldn't. So they walled her up in a room until she died of old age."

"Why didn't they drive a wooden stake through her heart?" Lannie asked plaintively. "That's supposed to work."

"There are no such things as vampires!" Noelle hissed. But Denise figured the reason she hissed it instead of shouting it was because Noelle was just as concerned as anyone else not to draw Drugeth's attention.

Denise glanced quickly at Janos again. He was still in that brown study he seemed to fall into about twenty times a day. Not surprising, really. Denise figured if she were a vampire she'd probably spend a lot of time contemplating the whichness of what herself.

How fucking exciting could it get? A *vampire*.

Well. Close enough, anyway.

Eventually, Noelle gave up. Even Eddie seemed dubious of her arguments.

Superstitious dolts!

She avoided looking at Drugeth for the rest of the evening, she was so exasperated.

But she found that she couldn't stop thinking about him, even after she rolled into her blankets, and that was even more exasperating.

The problem, she finally admitted to herself, was that while she absolutely did not—*Did. Not.*—believe in vampires, she also had to admit something else.

She doted on vampire stories. She owned every one of Anne Rice's books that had come out before the Ring of Fire, and had read none of them less than twice. Her copy of Bram Stoker's original novel was dog-eared.

She'd even once, in college, gotten into a ferocious all-night-long argument with three other female students over the subject of which actor's Dracula had been the best. Stupid mindless twits had been all ga-ga and gushing over effete fops like Bela Lugosi and Christopher Lee.

Even at that age, Noelle knew the truth. A *real* vampire—which didn't exist, of course—would be like the Dracula portrayed by Jack Palance. Medieval rulers, commanders of armies, swordsmen, guys with muscles as well as fangs. Not layabouts loafing in a castle somewhere.

Interesting guys. Exciting guys.

And just how deep, anyway, was she going to wallow in this idiotic fantasy?

She was a sane, sensible, rational modern woman. An official of the SoTF government. And *he* was an enemy soldier.

Period.

"Boy, do you look bedraggled," was Denise's greeting the next morning.

"I didn't sleep well," Noelle said grumpily.

Denise grinned at her. "You gotta admit, the guy's fascinating as all hell. If he weren't too old for me, I'd be checking him out myself."

That evening they reached a village in one of the many little valleys in the Fichtelgebirge. It was a Catholic village, with a small church.

The village was too small for a tavern, so they camped just outside it. After the camp was made, Janos went to the church.

Noelle followed him, after waiting a few minutes. *Not* because she was following him, but simply because she felt the need herself.

When she entered, he was in one of the pews, praying. She was quite certain he was praying for the souls of the two men he'd slain, a few days earlier. For his own, too, of course. But mostly theirs. There was still much about Janos Drugeth that was a mystery to her, but not everything. One of the prayers she'd be making here, as she had so many times since it happened, would be a prayer for the soul of the torturer she'd killed in Franconia last year. And for her own, for having done it.

So much for the idiots and their crap about vampires.

Even as quietly as Noelle was moving, he heard her come in. Being honest, the man really did seem to have preternatural senses. He turned his head and gazed at her for a while, his face as expressionless as it usually was.

Noelle did her best to ignore the scrutiny. She dipped her fingers in the basin, made the sign of the cross, and went to a pew some distance away from Drugeth. As far distant as she could get, in fact, allowing for the tiny size of the church.

She concentrated on her own prayers, and was pleased that she managed that pretty well. At least until the end, when she found herself fumbling because she was waiting for Drugeth to leave. There was no way she was going to leave with him.

Finally, he left. She waited perhaps five minutes before leaving herself.

Not that it did her any good. She discovered him waiting for her outside.

It would be silly to avoid him. So, she came up and nodded a greeting.

"I am told you are a devout Catholic," he said. "Have even contemplated taking holy vows."

"Ah . . ." She looked away, caught off balance by the unexpected question. "Yes, sort of. It's something I've thought about for years, off and on. Even though everybody who knows me says I'd make a lousy nun. Well, not that, exactly. They think I'd wind up very unhappy with the choice."

He said nothing. She was pretty sure that was because he didn't want to seem as if he were crowding her.

"What do you think?" she asked suddenly. And then found herself caught even more off balance by her own question—*what are you doing, you ninny?*—than she had been by his.

"I think that decision, unlike many others, is one that only the person involved can make. We are all—those of us who are Catholic, for a certainty—obliged to follow the teachings of the church involving matters of conscience. But not even the church presumes to tell a man or a woman if they should take holy vows."

He smiled, in that gentle, half-melancholy and half-irenic way he had. "I grant you, for noble families and royal ones more so, that decision is often tightly circumscribed, even sometimes forced outright. Still, I will hold to the principle."

"You have no opinion?"

"I would not put in that way. Let us say I do not presume to advise. That is not quite the same thing as having no opinion."

He seemed on the verge of adding something. His lips even started to part open. But, then, he closed them firmly and just shook his head.

"I should speak no further on the matter. May I escort you back to the camp?"

Silly to refuse that offer, as well, so she nodded.

They said nothing on the way. By the time they reached the camp, though, Noelle was in a quiet fury.

Not at him, but herself. A decision she hadn't been able to make for years had somehow gotten made in that short walk of no more than two hundred yards. She knew it as surely as she knew anything.

Damn her impudent soul, Denise was waiting for her with that same aggravating grin.

"Yeah, right. Enemy of the state. Is he as cute in church as everywhere else?"

"Vampire, remember?" Noelle half-snarled at her. "As if a vampire would enter holy ground!"

Denise's grin didn't so much as flicker. "You're dodging the question. Nice try."

"What he is, is the most exasperating man I've ever met."

"Wow." Denise shook her head, the grin vanishing completely. "You've got it bad, girl."

Chapter 12. The Date

The Bohemian Border, near Cheb

A little after noon, three and a half days later, Drugeth called a halt and ordered a rest. The last stretch before they reached Cheb was going to be very difficult, and they couldn't afford to lose the last wagon due to someone's fatigue. The other one had broken a wheel two days earlier, and they'd lost two hours repacking the surviving wagon with the items that were too bulky or heavy to be loaded on pack horses. By then, fortunately, they had several of those. Foreseeing the likelihood that at least one of the wagons would not survive the trek across the Fichtelgebirge, Janos had purchased pack animals at any of the small villages they'd passed through which had one they were willing to sell.

They needed to stop, anyway, because it was time to release Noelle Stull and her companions. By now, Janos was sure that Noelle had figured out that his escape route was taking them into Bohemia. He wasn't concerned about that, in itself, because by the time she could return to a town that had a radio with which she could alert the USE authorities, his expedition would have long since left Cheb and would probably already be reentering the USE farther south. The main thing was that he didn't want her to realize that Austria had suborned the commander of the Cheb garrison.

Partly that was a matter of simple straight-dealing. Honesty among thieves, perhaps. But just as the up-timers had a witty saw that "an honest cop is one who stays bribed," it was equally true in the gray world Janos now spent more of his time in than he liked, that the man who bribes the cop is obliged not to carelessly betray him afterward.

Mostly, though, it was cold-blooded calculation. The future was impossible to predict, and Janos still hoped he could persuade the emperor to make peace with Wallenstein. But he'd probably not be successful in his effort, and the war with Bohemia would heat up again. In that event, as unlikely as it might be given the geography—but who could say where the winds of war might blow?—it could be highly advantageous to Austria to have the commander of the Cheb garrison on its payroll. Even if the man objected to flagrant treason, he could be blackmailed into ceding the fortress with the threat of exposure.

Janos was feeling a little guilty, actually, allowing Noelle and her group to come this far. If one of them had a good enough knowledge of geography, they might be able to deduce that Cheb was his destination. He should have set them free the day before, in retrospect. Without horses—which he certainly wouldn't give them, even if he had any to spare—they probably still couldn't have gotten out of the Fichtelgebirge in time to cause any damage to his project.

But . . . he'd stalled, since there were so many "mights" and "probablies" involved on both sides of the equation. Looking back on it, he'd allowed himself to be influenced by a purely personal factor. He was reluctant to part company with Noelle Stull; it was as simple as that.

As the days had passed, his interest had deepened. He'd never thought about it before, but he'd come to realize that spending several days with a woman in a forced march, under considerable tension and strain—conflicting and complex ones, too—was as good a way as any to get a measure of her.

Which he had, at least to the extent possible in the few days they'd spent together.

Noelle was as perceptive as his dead wife had been, when it came to navigating difficult political waters. Demonstrated, in Anna's case, by her ability to work a compromise between the Catholic church and the many Orthodox inhabitants on their domains, which satisfied everyone well enough and kept the peace. In Noelle's case, by the way she maintained a workable relationship between her own captured party and the defectors. There was no love lost there, and she'd refused—quite firmly—to allow her people to be used in any of the labor directly connected to the defection. They'd taken no part, for instance, in the strenuous labor needed to repack the wagons again. But, that line drawn, she'd not been foolishly obstreperous about anything else.

So. Principles combined with flexibility where needed. A combination much rarer than one might think.

She also knew how to maintain authority over her own charges: smoothly, easily, and without either bullying them or ceding anything important. No easy task, that, given the nature of the people involved. Not a problem with Eddie Junker, of course. Although Janos was sure that Noelle would insist that Eddie was her "partner," as well as a close friend, the fact remained that the relationship was one of mistress and subordinate. Something which he was equally sure Junker himself understood—but was good-natured about because of the light hand of the mistress herself.

Lannie and Keenan, on the other hand, while they had the habits and temperament of subordinates by virtue of their origins and history, had not had a previous relationship with her, other than a family one in the case of the Murphy fellow. More than once—many more times than once—Janos had seen how awkwardly a new commander handled such a situation. In contrast to Anna, who had swept into her new position as the mistress of the estates at Homonna with complete ease. Within a short time, as the Americans would put it, she had the servants in the large household—even many of the peasants nearby—"eating out of her hand."

Noelle had even managed to keep Denise Beasley under control, for a wonder. And had done it, not by the harsh disciplinary methods a less perceptive person would have tried—and which would have succeeded poorly, if at all—but because she had the art of persuading a young, bright and rebellious girl that she was more in the way of a trusted older sister and a confidant than a substitute mother. It had been quite deftly done, and the fact that Noelle herself would no doubt be indignant if he suggested she was being manipulative, did not change the reality. The up-timers seemed to feel that "being manipulative" was a negative trait, even an evil one, but that was just one of their many superstitions. The ability to get other people to do what needed to be done was simply a valuable skill, that's all—especially for the wife of an important figure in a major realm.

Finally, there was her athleticism and quite evident good health. Anna had been less athletic than the average noblewoman, which, in and of itself, had not much bothered Janos. He was not one of those idle aristocrats who spent half their waking hours on the hunt, and wanted a wife who could ride with him. Where Janos was most likely to be riding at a full gallop was on a battlefield, where no wife could go or was wanted to go.

Unfortunately, Anna had been sickly, not simply sedentary. Had been since she was a girl. Janos had known that when he married her, but had chosen to overlook the problem in favor of her many other virtues. Having lost one wife after a short marriage, however, he had no desire to repeat the experience. That had been anguish such as he'd never felt in his life, and never wanted to again.

True, Noelle was not as physically attractive as Anna had been. The woman was pretty, where Anna had been a real beauty. But that did not concern Janos. First, because it was a matter of flesh, and thus trivial. Second, because it was always transient, as was the nature of fleshly things. Finally, because given time it would be irrelevant in any event. The Americans could wallow in their romanticism, as they called it, but that was another of their odd superstitions. A good marriage produced affection and physical desire as naturally and inevitably as trees grew. Love was simply the fruit, which they confused with the seed.

There remained, of course, all the immense obstacles of a political nature. Which might indeed be too great to overcome. But he'd decided the matter was worth raising with the emperor. He'd need his permission to pursue the matter, anyway. Beyond that, Ferdinand was one of his closest friends and a man whose advice was often shrewd, sometimes uncannily so.

"I'm telling you, Noelle, you oughta ask him out on a date. Or finagle him into asking you out, if you're still hung up on proper gender roles on account of you're such an ancient."

"Why don't pharmacists develop the most useful drug of all?" Noelle grumbled. "The label would read: 'Eliminates shit-eating grins. Especially effective on teenagers.'?"

Denise ignored that, of course. "Me, if I want to go out on a date with some guy—not often, but it does happen—I just tell him when I'm going to pick up with my bike."

"He's an *enemy,* in case you've forgotten."

Denise waved her hand. "Wars come, wars go. True love remains."

"You are insufferable, sometimes. And shut up, will you? He's heading our way."

A few minutes later, after Janos explained that they'd be parting company, Denise's silly idea became a moot one as well.

Which made it all the more alarming, to Noelle, that she felt such a sharp anxiety at the news. Denise, at least, had the excuse of being sixteen years old. What was hers?

Firmly, she told herself she was simply worried about the practical aspects of the situation.

"I think it's outrageous, Captain Drugeth, that you are abandoning us without even a single horse."

He gave her that damned soulful smile that did annoying things to the primitive and ancient parts of her brainstem.

"First, Ms. Stull, it is rather absurd to use the term 'abandoning' when I am simply doing what you would have done yourself several days ago had you not given me your parole. Second, you don't need a horse to travel. Lannie Yost's ankle has healed and Eddie Junker's broken arm does not impede him from walking. Third, this is hardly a wilderness or a desert which must be crossed swiftly on pain of death. I am not, I remind you, depriving you of money with which you can buy food and shelter from any of the villages in the area. I am even allowing you to keep Eddie Junker's rifle and its ammunition, should you need to hunt for sustenance. Something for which, I can assure you, Austria's gunmakers would curse me if they found out."

Noelle sneered. Tried to, anyway. "You know perfectly well it's an antique."

He shrugged. "All the better, actually, from the standpoint of a down-time gunmaker using it for a model. As *you* know perfectly well, the USE's now-famous SRG is patterned after an even more antiquated design."

Which was true, of course. So Noelle fell back to glaring silently, feeling as if she were all of fourteen years old. Drugeth's conditions for releasing them were perfectly rational. Even somewhat generous, in fact. Her anger was just the way the underlying anxiety was working its way to the surface.

Why didn't the stupid pharmacists develop a drug that would anesthetize those useless brainstem parts?

Probably because we've been tested over and over again by evolution, and passed with flying colors, came the unwanted reply.

Out of the tension and confusion of the moment, like a thesis and antithesis struggling, came the synthesis.

"Very well!" she snapped. Her eyes became slitted. "But I warn you, Captain Drugeth. You haven't seen the last of me!"

"I look forward to that with great anticipation."

And off he went.

Denise shook her head. "Well, that's about the weirdest way I ever heard anybody make a date, but sure enough. It's a date."

"Shut. Up."

Chapter 13. The Map

High Street Mansion, Seat of Government for the
State of Thuringia-Franconia
President's Office
Grantville, State of Thuringia-Franconia

"You should fire that whole garrison at Saalfeld," Noelle said testily. "For sure, get rid of that useless commander. I swear to you, Ed, if they'd been willing to get off their butts as soon as we arrived, I might have still caught the bastards."

"Not likely, Noelle. By then, they'd have been well into Bohemia—and there's the tiny little problem that while our relations with Wallenstein are good, they aren't so good that he'd take kindly to us sending a military unit into his territory without his permission. And getting that permission would have taken at least another week."

He shrugged. "Besides, it wouldn't do any good. The SoTF doesn't have the kind of money it would take to throw top wages at mercenary units to make sure we get good ones for mere garrison duty far from the war zones. If we fired Captain Stamm and his company, anyone we got to replace them wouldn't be any better in the raring-to-go department, and would probably be a lot worse in what matters, which is doing a decent job of keeping the peace locally without gouging the residents more than they think is reasonable."

He came out of his relaxed slouch and folded his hands on the desk. "Relax, will you? I know you're like a bulldog when you set your teeth into something, but this is really not worth the amount of sweat you're putting into it. Look, you did your best, and the baddies got away. It happens. That said, it was not the crime of the century, the only people who got killed were baddies themselves—I almost wish I'd seen that; I really detested Jay Barlow—and the military impact of the tech transfer will be minor in the short run and probably not even that significant in the long run."

Noelle eyed him skeptically. "I notice you didn't say anything about the political impact."

Ed shrugged again. "So the Crown Loyalists are trying to make hay out of it. Big deal. That's the nature of politics, Noelle. You win some, you lose some, and when you do lose the other guy points with alarm and swears to the electorate that the sky is falling. I've talked to Mike about it, and I can assure you he's not losing any sleep over the affair. Neither am I. Neither should you."

Noelle sighed. "I *hate* giving up on something I started."

After a moment, she managed a smile. "At least Eddie's arm looks to be healing okay. The doctor told him it should be as good as new in a few more weeks. So I guess—I feel bad about it, even if it wasn't my fault—that the only real casualty on our side is that Lannie and Keenan are out of a job."

"No, they aren't. Didn't you hear? Kay Kelly had a conniption, of course, and demanded that her husband fire the two bums. I guess she was even making noises about filing criminal charges. But you know Bob. Hell of a nice guy, even if it does take him a month to screw in a lightbulb because he's got to redesign it to his satisfaction first. So he just plain refused, on the grounds that they meant well. And don't let anybody tell you that he doesn't wear the pants in that family, even if Kay could teach graduate courses in henpecking."

"That she could," said Noelle, grimacing. "I'll make it a point—even more than usual—to steer clear of her over the next few weeks."

"Unless you go to Magdeburg, you won't have to," Ed said. "She left yesterday, once she realized Bob wasn't going to budge."

"What? She's going to try to get the federal government to press charges?"

"Oh, hell no." Ed shook his head, smiling. "I don't like the woman, but nobody ever said she let any moss grow. She went up to Magdeburg to lobby the government to put in an order for the *Dauntless* line. Now that it's been field-tested and proved it could carry out a successful bomb run. Not the *plane's* fault the dummies piloting it bombed the wrong guys, after all."

"You're kidding!"

"Nope. One of her arguing points—you know how quick she is to level accusations of favoritism—is that that's more than Mike Stearns, playing his usual favorites game, ever asked Hal and Jesse to prove with *their* planes. Which he commissioned on nothing better than a prayer and a promise."

Noelle couldn't herself from laughing. "She's got brass, I'll say that for her."

The laughter finally broke her sour mood. She gathered up her stuff and rose. "Well, okay. I guess you're right. And what I do know is that you're busy. So I'll get out of your hair. Besides, I'd better see if I can put in a word for Denise before her parents skin her alive."

But when she got to the Beasleys' place, one of those big double-sized trailers called "mobile homes" in blithe disregard for the cinder blocks it was actually sitting on instead of wheels, she discovered her mission was unnecessary. Denise's mother Christin had thrown a fit, sure enough. But Buster had taken it all in stride.

There were some advantages, it seemed, to having a father with an ex-biker's views on parenting.

"What the hell, Noelle, it's like I told my wife." He placed a large, affectionate hand on his daughter's shoulder. "It's not like she got pregnant or strung out on dope or started working for a pimp or even got in trouble with the cops. For that matter, her new tattoo she got yesterday's sorta reasonable."

Noelle eyed the tattoo on Denise's shoulder, easily visible because she was just wearing a tank top inside the warm trailer. That was the tattoo she'd gotten at the age of fourteen. A death's head with the logo *Watch it, buddy.* Completely tasteless, in Noelle's opinion, although she'd allow it might cause high school boys to think twice.

Buster had thought that tattoo was reasonable, too, she remembered—and without the "sorta" qualifier. She didn't want to think—

"I love it!" exclaimed Denise. "Here, I'll show you."

With no further ado, she yanked up the tank top, exposing her slim midriff.

"Oh, dear God," was all Noelle could think to say.

It was a lot better from an artistic standpoint, certainly. The tattoo artist had quite a bit of skill.

Still.

The central image, right on the girl's belly, was that of a sexpot wearing a flying jacket—not that any flying jacket would expose that much bosom—pants that looked painted on, and spike-heeled boots. She was sitting with her legs crossed—lounging, rather—and holding a bomb in one hand, with a sputtering fuse.

Smiling seductively, of course.

That was bad enough. The logo was worse.

Above the image: *You can land here*

Below it: *If you don't crash*

Denise frowned. "You don't like it?"

"Well . . ."

Huffily, the girl dropped the hem of the tank top. "Just 'cause *you* can't keep from beating around the bush. How's Eddie doing?"

"Fine," said Noelle. Warily: "Why do you ask?"

"He's cute." She jerked a thumb at Buster. "My dad even says he's okay. I thought I might drop by on him later."

"You stay away from Eddie!"

"I bet *he'll* like the tattoo."

Noelle hurried away to warn Eddie of an impending visitation by a one-girl Mongol horde.

Alas, Eddie seemed unconcerned. "What's the problem? I like Denise. A lot, in fact."

"She's wild. And she's much too young for you."

"Don't be silly, Noelle. Denise is a bit wild, I suppose—although nothing like my cousin Kaethe—but she's not actually foolish. And I'm certainly not."

That last was true enough. Noelle started to feel relieved until she saw that Eddie's gaze seemed more than a little unfocused. As if he were contemplating in his mind's eye a certain tattoo that she had, perhaps unfortunately, described in great detail.

However the visit turned out—and Noelle wasn't *really* worried, since Eddie was to deliberation what a cow was to munching grass—he seemed his usual self when she visited him the next morning. He had a large map of the SoTF and the surrounding territories spread out across his table, and was studying it intently.

"What are you doing?" she asked.

"Just indulging in my curiosity. I'm as tenacious as you are, you know. I just don't have your compulsion to act on it at all costs." He lifted his eyes from the map. "Any more news from Bohemia?"

Noelle flopped onto the nearby armchair. "Nothing. Well, not 'nothing.' Wallenstein is certainly taking seriously the incursion of an Austrian expedition into his territory, even a small one. He and Pappenheim have the Black Cuirassiers scouring the whole area. But . . . nothing. Not a sign of them. We just got another lack-of-progress report on the radio an hour ago."

Eddie nodded. "I'm not surprised. I've been thinking about it, and considering the terrain. It finally dawned on me that Drugeth probably didn't stay in Bohemia for very long."

Noelle sat up straight. "What?"

"Come here. I can show you better on the map." Noelle was there in a heartbeat. Eddie's finger started tracing a route through the Fichtelgebirge. "He can cut

back across here, near this little town called Kötzting.
From there, he can just follow the Regen down to
Regensburg, and from there it's an easy barge-ride into
Austria."

"But . . . We have a *garrison* at Regensburg. A great
damn big one, too, and real soldiers."

"Indeed so. Because they have been assigned, no matter the cost, to keep the enemy from crossing the Danube by seizing the bridge there. Regensburg anchors
our left flank against Bavaria. Not likely, therefore—is
it?—that they'll be much concerned with anything else.
And there are no troops to the north until you reach
Amberg. A lot of military traffic between Amberg and
Regensburg, of course, but they'd be going along"—he
pointed to a river just west of the Regen—"the Naab.
Not the Regen."

Noelle stared at the map, while Eddie continued. "See
what I mean? He doesn't have to worry about anything
except the short time he'd be passing through Regensburg itself."

"But . . . Damnation, the garrison at Regensburg was
warned to look for them."

"Noelle, be serious. Yes. The garrison at Regensburg—
along with a dozen others—received an alert over the
radio to keep an eye out for the possibility that a party
of up-time defectors might be passing through. Maybe.
At a time unknown. In wagons. Possibly with pack
horses."

He tapped the spot indicating Regensburg. "First,
they would have paid no attention to it. Even if they did,
they'd be looking for 'up-timers' on wagons or horses.
Given Janos Drugeth, what do you think the likelihood

is that, by now, he hasn't obtained river transport and doesn't have the defectors outfitted as a party of down-time merchants?"

His eyes narrowed, as if he were gauging something. "If I'm right, he's already on the Regen. Should be passing through Regensburg today or tomorrow."

Given Janos Drugeth . . .

"That son-of-a-bitch!" Noelle yelped. Out the door she went.

After Eddie closed the door and sat back down at the table, he shook his head.

"Denise was right. She's got it bad."

Chapter 14. The Bridge

High Street Mansion, Seat of Government for the
State of Thuringia-Franconia
President's Office
Grantville, State of Thuringia-Franconia

"I'm afraid Mr. Piazza left for Bamberg this morning, Ms. Stull. He won't be in radio contact again until this evening, at the earliest. Carol Unruh went with him." The secretary folded her hands, in that inimitable and unmistakable way that they must spend a whole semester teaching people how to do in Executive Assistant College.

"I Am Afraid There Is Nothing I Can Do."

In caps. Noelle went out the door.

Municipal Complex
Police Department
Grantville, State of Thuringia-Franconia

"Gimme a break, Noelle," said Preston Richards. Grantville's police chief scowled at an assignment chart on the wall of his office. "You got any idea how stretched thin I am? No, I don't have any cops I can detach from duty on what sounds like a wild goose chase. And how would they get there in time anyway?"

Before she could keep arguing, he raised his hand. "I'll send another radio message to the garrison at Regensburg. But that's it. And I doubt very much that'll do any good. Word came yesterday that the Bavarians are moving more troops into the area."

No caps, but it didn't matter. Press Richards had a baccalaureate from Stubborn Like a Mule College. Graduated *magna cum laude*.

Noelle went out the door.

Regensburg
The Upper Palatinate, *under USE imperial administration*

"Idiots," snarled Colonel Moritz Kreisler. "We've got at least three Bavarian regiments moving around just the other side of the Danube"—he pointed an accusing finger at the river, as if it were the guilty party—"and they want me to disrupt my disposition of forces in order to hunt down some fucking *thieves*?"

"I'm just passing on the message, sir," said the radio operator apologetically. "How should I respond?"

Kreisler took a deep breath, controlling his temper. He reminded himself that whatever the legal formalities might be, a message from any figure of authority in Grantville—even a miserable be-damned police chief—had to be handled diplomatically.

"Tell them we received the message." With an effort: "No, thank them for sending us the warning. Assure them we will do everything possible. Emphasize 'possible.'"

After the radio operator left, Kreisler went over to the window of his office and looked down on the Danube passing almost directly below.

They might be using a barge or other rivercraft.

"Oh, marvelous," he muttered, between teeth that were almost clenched. Just at a glance, he could see five such vessels on the river. Four of them were piled high with goods, and two of those were carrying a number of passengers as well. Did the cretins think that merchants and farmers and I-need-to-see-my-poor-uncle-before-he-dies suspended their activity because of a war?

Still, he should do something, just for the record. "Lieutenant Müller!" he bellowed.

His orderly appeared almost instantly.

"Send word to whatever squads are monitoring the river traffic—no, one squad should be enough; and make sure it's a squad right inside the city—I do *not* want the men watching the river up and down stream to be in the least bit distracted—to keep an eye out for a large party of American traitors—accompanied by a Hungarian officer; probably two or three other soldiers—who might attempt to pass through Regensburg on their way to Austria."

Lieutenant Müller was a little cross-eyed. "Yes, sir. Ah . . ."

"How should I know what 'American traitors' look like?" the colonel said testily. "Try to spot excellent teeth combined with a shifty expression. But if I were you, I'd concentrate on the Hungarian officer. You know what *those* look like, don't you?"

Müller practically sighed with relief. "Yes, sir. Of course."

"All right, boys, you heard him," said Corporal Brenner. "Keep an eye out for one of those Hungarian dandies. Can't be hard, since they're even more vain than Austrian noblemen."

As usual, Private Sandler looked confused. Sighing, the sergeant planted a large forefinger on the top of his helmet. "Just look for the plume, Jochen."

Kelly Aviation Facility
Near Grantville, State of Thuringia-Franconia

"Please, Bob. It's the only chance that's left."

Noelle felt like an idiot. Princess Leia, in a movie. *Please, Obi-Wan Kenobi. You're our only hope.*

Bob Kelly shook his head. "But . . . the authorities . . ."

"There *are* no authorities. Not in town that I can reach in time who have the clout to get anything done. But if I get there myself . . . ."

Bob looked from her to one of the planes in the hangar. The one that looked as if they'd been working on it round the clock. Noelle had figured they might be, with Kay up in Magdeburg doing the full court lobbyist's press.

"Well . . . . The *Dauntless II* is ready to fly, sure enough. But we haven't got it fitted with the bomb attachments yet. The best you could do would be to toss a grenade out the window."

Noelle set her teeth. "Bob, I am *not* planning to bomb anybody."

He peered at her nearsightedly, over the half-moon glasses he favored. He looked for all the world like a chubby middle-aged elf. Not one of the Tolkien-type heroic and dramatic elves, either. One of the Santa's-helpers elves. Exactly what Noelle was afraid she'd look like at that age if she let her figure go and didn't pay attention to her solemn vows to eliminate all elflike mannerisms.

"Then how do you plan to accomplish anything once you do get there?" he asked.

Good question. But Noelle was not to be thwarted.

"I'll simply summon the garrison to its duty. With an official from Grantville on the scene who's directly involved in the matter, I'm sure that'll be sufficient."

Which was a laugh, from Noelle's past experience with military commanders. They swore by Chain of Command the way other people swore by the Father, the Son and the Holy Ghost.

But she'd deal with that when she got there. First, she had to get there. By nightfall—and it was already two o'clock in the afternoon, in late November. They just had enough time.

Fortunately, Lannie piped up. "They do have a landing strip in Regensburg now, boss. Been operational for a month."

Kelly rubbed his jaw. "Kay'll have a fit, when she hears about it."

"Why?" Noelle tried to look as self-assured as she possibly could. She was pretty good at that, actually. "It'll just be another test of the capabilities of the Dauntless line."

She even said "Dauntless" without a waver.

"Well . . ."

But it was enough, she could tell. Bob Kelly had been smarting for years over the constant jokes about his unfinished planes.

"Yeah, sure. What the hell. The weather's clear and Regensburg's only a hundred and fifty miles away. Be there before sundown, easy. Lannie, take her there. Keenan, you go with them."

Unfortunately, Noelle didn't think to ask about the condition of the radio until they were half an hour into the flight.

"Well," said Lannie.

From the rear seat, Keenan's hand appeared over her shoulder, clutching a map. "I remembered to bring this, though."

Naturally, it was the wrong map.

"Never mind," she said, after checking to make sure—you just never knew with these guys—that the plane did have a functioning compass. "Just head south until we reach the Danube. Then follow it."

"Which way?"

Not. To. Be. Thwarted.

"I'll figure it out when the time comes."

She did, too. It wasn't even hard, since Noelle had a good knowledge of geography and she knew Regensburg was at the crest of a large northerly bend in the Danube. Between that and the compass, she could figure out where they were.

A bit too far to the east, as it happened. Here, the river was coursing southeast.

She pointed upstream. "Thataway."

Regensburg
The Upper Palatinate, under USE imperial administration

Sure enough, the airfield was in good shape. Lannie brought the plane down as smoothly as you could ask for.

The soldiers guarding the field, of course, were practically jumping up and down with fury.

No one had informed them! They should have been notified of the flight plan by the radio!

But at least they weren't suspicious. Everyone knew that practically every country in Europe had started aircraft projects. But except for a handful of commercial craft operating out of the USE or the Netherlands, all the airplanes in existence were still in the USE's air force.

Besides, she'd brought a magic wand.

Documents. Official Documents. Testifying that she was indeed an official for the State of Thuringia-Franconia and never mind exactly what her powers were and where her jurisdiction began and ended.

They even let her take one of the unit's horses to ride into town and summon the garrison to its duty.

"I am afraid that Colonel Kreisler has gone out of the city, checking some new reconnaissance reports. He is not expected to return until tomorrow at the earliest."

Lieutenant Müller clasped his hands behind his back. Allowing for variations, it was the well-known and detestable gesture. As were the capital letters.

"I Am Afraid There Is Nothing I Can Do."

Down at the river, on the great bridge that spanned the Danube, she considered whether she might prevail on one of the squads of soldiers below . . .

What a laugh.

Besides, now that she was here and could see it herself, she really couldn't blame the soldiers for their attitude. The Bavarians were in the area, after all, with sizeable forces. The USE's troops were concentrating on protecting the bridge and spotting any attempt to ferry large numbers of soldiers across the river.

True, there was *already* a small fleet of boats on the river—six of them that she could see, just on this side of the bridge looking upstream—but they weren't clustered the way landing craft would be. Just some of the many commercial craft that plied one of Europe's major waterways day in and day out, and had been doing so for centuries.

She glanced at a small barge just passing below the bridge. This one, for instance, looked to be carrying mostly—

"*You son-of-a-bitch!*" she screeched.

She raced over to the downstream side of the bridge, clawing at the flap of her holster. By the time she got the pistol out and steadied her nerves enough to check that the clip was in and the safety was off, the barge had reappeared.

Janos was standing at the very stern, looking up at her. Wide-eyed, as if in fear or astonishment.

Well, no. Not fear. Wide-eyed with astonishment.

Not for long, though. Suddenly he broke into a smile—a genuine grin; the first she'd ever seen on his face—and doffed his battered-looking cap. The sort any boatman might wear, although the flourishing bow that followed had obviously been learned in palaces.

She pointed the gun right at him, remembering to use the two-handed grip that was her only chance of hitting anything. He replaced the cap on his head, but otherwise just kept standing there, looking at her. His face had no expression, now.

He was maybe twenty yards away. Well, thirty or forty, allowing for the height of the bridge.

She'd probably miss. Worse, she might miss him and accidentally hit somebody else. There were kids playing on the river bank. Way off to the side, sure, but she'd heard all the Annie Oakley jokes people made about her. It wasn't likely, but she *might* hit one of the kids. Or hit a piece of metal on the barge that caused a ricochet that hit one of the kids.

She wondered if Janos had heard the jokes. He might very well have, in fact, as smoothly as he could finagle information from people.

That was probably why he wasn't making any attempt to take cover.

Well, no. She knew as surely as she knew anything that even if she'd been as good a shot as the real Annie Oakley, Janos Drugeth would have done exactly what he was doing.

She even knew why. A Hungarian nobleman's valor was only part of it. Two days after the encounter in the church, she'd told him about the torturer in Franconia. And the hours she spent in prayer because of it. They understood each other quite well, in some ways.

There was no way she was going to pull the trigger, and she knew it, and he knew it, and he knew she knew he knew it, and . . .

"You are the most exasperating man!"

She leaned way over the rail of the bridge, clasped the gun tightly in both hands, pointed the barrel straight below her, and emptied the entire clip. She even had enough presence of mind to make sure another barge wasn't passing through before she did it.

And she didn't miss the water, either. Not once. Hit the Danube every time, dead nuts.

She felt a lot better, then. She even used the gun to give Janos a little salute as the barge made its way down toward Austria. She didn't stop looking at him until it passed out of sight. And he didn't stop looking at her.

Then she giggled. "I guess Denise was right. Maybe I should get a tattoo."

When the others finally emerged from the shelter they'd taken behind the goods piled on the barge, Allen O'Connor came up to Janos, still standing in the stern.

"You got balls, I'll give you that. I told you the woman was crazy."

Janos said nothing. If a man couldn't recognize a sign from God, right in front of his face, what was the point of explaining it to him?

O'Connor shook his head. "No telling what she'll do. You ought to warn the emperor about her."

"Oh, yes. I most certainly shall."

Chapter 15. The Motto

High Street Mansion, Seat of Government for the
State of Thuringia-Franconia
President's Office
Grantville, State of Thuringia-Franconia
December 1634

"As long as the Regensburg authorities drop the serious charges," said Ed Piazza, "we won't contest the rest. We don't actually want to let people get the notion that officials of the SoTF can fire a gun anytime and anywhere they please."

Josua Mai, one of the down-timers who served the SoTF as legal advisers, seemed hesitant. "Ah . . . Mr. President. I'm afraid that the charge of fishing without license and with equipment not approved by the fisherman's guild *is* a serious charge, in Regensburg. The fine is quite heavy."

"Is there any jail time, too?"

"Not if the fine is paid. Otherwise . . . " He grimaced.

Ed nodded. "So we'll pay the fine. It's not as if we're actually broke. Not even close, in fact."

The lawyer looked as if he might argue the matter. Despite his good humor, Ed was not in the mood for legal quibbling. "We'll pay it," he said firmly. "Noelle's gone way past her pay grade plenty of times, what she's been willing to tackle. The least we can do is return the favor. End of discussion."

He sat up straight, just to emphasize the point. "Any spin-off problems I need to deal with?"

Mai looked at his notes. "Well, Grantville will need a new garrison commander, but that's not something you need to deal with, Mr. President."

"I thought it was decided not to fire Knefler. Not that I'd mind it if he quit. Sure, he screwed up, but you can't fire officers just for making one mistake."

"Ah . . . the problem is of a different nature. It seems that shortly after he returned to Grantville he assaulted Denise Beasley with a quirt. Tried to, at least. According to the report I received from Chief Richards, the girl was actually doing a fair job of defending herself with—ah—" He rummaged in the notes and drew forth another sheet. "Seemingly, every loose object you might find in a roadside tavern, short of a full-size table."

Ed chuckled. "Boy, can I picture that. Girl's got a hell of an arm. Star pitcher for the girl's baseball team until she lost interest." Then, he scowled ferociously. "But what I want to know is why we *didn't* fire Knefler for that."

The lawyer was still examining the report. "He will be discharged for it, Mr. President. After he gets out of the hospital. His injuries were quite severe. A number of bruises and a split lip inflicted by the girl—Chief Richards says she gave as good as she got—and then . . . " He cleared his throat. "Well. The father arrived. And was apparently in a very foul temper even before Knefler drew his sword. Tried to draw his sword, rather."

Both Ed and Carol winced. "Oh, Lord," she said.

After the lawyer left, Carol Unruh shook her head. "What was Noelle thinking? She's usually such a responsible person."

Ed leaned back, clasping his hands behind his head. After the news came of Noelle's arrest, he'd finally taken the time to visit Denise Beasley and get her version of the whole Noelle vs. Captain Drugeth Affair.

The full, complete, unabridged—nay, annotated and footnoted—Denise Beasley version.

"Domestic violence can be a terrible thing," he intoned solemnly.

Carol frowned at him. "What's that supposed to mean?"

"I don't know, actually. But it'll sure be interesting to find out."

The day after she got back to Grantville, Noelle did get a tattoo. She'd always secretly harbored a desire for one, she just hadn't seen any way she could pull it off. But she figured three days in the squalid jail Regensburg maintained for women—God only knew what the men's jail was like—gave her the needed credentials.

Denise guided her to the tattoo parlor. Offered tons of advice, too, but Noelle ignored almost all of it.

The design was entirely her own. A death's head—much more refined than Denise's, of course; ladylike, topped by a jaunty little feathered cap—with crossed pistols below and the logo above: *I Shot The Danube*.

The one and only piece of advice she took from Denise concerned the placement of the tattoo.

"Me, I put it on my shoulder, where all the pimply twits in high school could see it. You, on the other hand, got a lot more focused target. So put it way down on your hip, over toward the ass, where nobody will ever see it—"

The grin was as an impudent as ever. "Except."

Vienna, Austria

"Interesting idea," said Emperor Ferdinand III. He got up and went to the window in his palace, looking over the gardens. "Yes, I think so."

"Many suppositions, first," Janos cautioned.

"Oh, yes. And probably as many problems afterward, assuming it unfolds. But many opportunities also. And you sometimes forget—even you, Janos—who I am."

"Your Majesty?"

The emperor turned away from the window. "Majesty, now, yes. Go back five hundred years and I would have been a mere count in Switzerland or Swabia. Five hundred years before that, who knows? Certainly not a 'majesty.' The most ancient figure known in my line is a Carolingian. A nobleman, family tradition insists—but I can't help think that his cognomen of 'Guntram the Rich' casts some doubt on the matter."

He resumed his seat. "What I am ultimately, Janos, is a *Habsburg*. Something which I never forget. And what is our unofficial motto?"

Understanding, finally, Janos nodded. "*Bella gerunt alii, tu, felix Austria, nubes.* 'Let others wage war; you, happy Austria, marry.'"

"Precisely so. A guiding principle which has stood us in good stead for centuries. So why should we abandon it now?" Ferdinand made a small waving gesture. "At worst, you already have an heir. But I do not think it would come to that. The distinction between noble and morganatic marriages is already fraying. I have no objections to fraying it still more. In fact, I'm inclined in that direction."

So, that was that. Simply a problem, now.

"It wouldn't be anything quick, anyway," Janos mused.

The emperor chuckled again. "Not given the political situation."

Janos smiled. "I was actually thinking of the lady in question. The last time I saw her, she was shooting at me."

Ferdinand just gazed at him, looking very placid. He'd gotten the entire story by now.

"Well, not exactly that," Janos allowed. "Still, it was a dramatic gesture, you have to admit."

"When are you going to stop—what is that American expression—ah, yes, 'beating around the bush'—and ask my advice as well as my permission?" The emperor of Austria-Hungary spread his arms. "Here you are, alone, in the very seat of wisdom when it comes to such matters. If it weren't beneath my dignity, I could double the Habsburg fortune—count the Spanish bullion fleets in it, too—by starting one of those American businesses . . . what are they called?"

"Marriage counseling."

"Yes, that one."

Janos hesitated. Despite the jocularity, the fact the emperor made the offer meant he took the matter very seriously indeed.

"I would deeply appreciate it, Your Majesty."

"For this—we're in private, after all—you'd best call me Ferdinand. Very well, my old friend. Start with a rose."

"Excuse me?"

"A rose, Janos. *Always* start with a rose. Then add something with just that perfect personal touch. And keep the accompanying note brief. Very brief. Lest, by your silly long-windedness, you make the recipient feel like someone hunted, instead of a weary traveler seeing an open door, spilling light to invite them in."

Grantville, State of Thuringia-Franconia January 1635

Denise studied the three items spread out on Noelle's table, which had arrived that morning in a package.

There had been no return address, but that was hardly necessary.

"Gorgeous," she pronounced, after completing her examination of the first item. "Of course, you gotta subtract a few points since he probably got it from the imperial gardens. Still, that is one hell of a rose."

Next, she passed judgment on the note. All it said was: *Should we happen to meet again.*

"Way cool. Way, way, cool."

Finally, the third item, which she picked up and admired. "And this is just fucking perfect. Wonder where he got it?"

Noelle peered at the thing, not sure whether she should smile or frown or . . . what.

"By now, I'd imagine those could be found in lots of places in Europe. Certainly Vienna."

"Still. He even got the right caliber. And .32 caliber rounds are scarcer than you think. Most people want a heftier handgun."

Denise folded her hands on the table. "So. No point packing yet, of course, since we'll probably be at war again in a few months. Still, it's never too early to start putting together some nice luggage."

Noelle scowled at her. "I can't for the life of me remember why I asked you to come here and give me your opinion."

" 'Cause it's the wisest opinion you can get. I got the advantage of the perspective of my years."

"All sixteen of them!"

"And barely sixteen at that," agreed Denise. "Exactly my point. When you figure what we got here are two people from about as two different places as you can imagine—we're talking centuries, girl, not just piddly geography—then what you got amounts to a couple of teenagers. D'you wonder why they call it 'sweet sixteen'?"

Noelle tried to remember how she'd looked at the world at the age of sixteen. "Well. No."

Denise smiled jeeringly, as only she could. "Never knew, I bet. Being a pious Catholic girl instead of a biker's kid. The reason's simple. It's because by the time you reach sixteen—at least, if you aren't dumb as a rock, which I'm not—you've figured out the basics and you're pretty much free and clear."

Her forefinger pointed to the rose. "That means he's got the hots, simple as that—but nicely expressed. Not a spot of drool on it."

The finger moved to the note: "That, the invitation. No, call it the ball's now in your court. Very classy guy. Understands that you play a game with somebody, not against them. Won't never be no backseat groping with this cool dude. Not ever."

She plucked the cartridge from the table and stood it upright, then planted her forefinger on the tip. "And just to make sure you understand, that's your insurance policy."

"Oh, nonsense!" exclaimed Noelle. "I didn't even try to hit him when I had the chance."

"Remedial Romance class, come to order. *He knows that*, you dummy. But he also knows you could have." She squinted at Noelle. "Well. Could have tried, anyway. The point is, he knew you had a choice."

With a little clipping motion, the forefinger knocked over the cartridge and sent it rolling over to the rose, where it nestled against the stem. "So the reason the cartridge came with it is so you'd know he knows you still have a choice. Like I said. Very classy guy. Best opening moves I ever seen in my life."

"All of sixteen years," Noelle tried again. Even to her, it sounded feeble.

Denise looked serious, for a change. "The last three of which—no, closer to four—have been a very concentrated educational experience. I've been good-looking since I was twelve, and every kid in school knew my dad was a biker. Sure, he scared 'em some, but they'd also heard all the rumors about biker chicks. You figure it out. I had to learn real quick and learn my lessons well."

Noelle looked from the rose to the note to the cartridge. Then back again.

The truth was, the girl's opinion *did* look shrewd.

"So what do you think I should do?" A bit crossly. "Now, I mean. Not in the maybe-never time after the maybe-war."

Denise got up and grabbed the tote bag she used instead of a purse. The one with the severed serpent and the *Don't Tread On Me* logo that Noelle would have assumed she'd picked up at a patriotic souvenir shop before the Ring of Fire except for what was on the other side. A dragon eating a knight, with the logo *I Love Hard Metal*.

"Come on. We're hitting the malls."

Noelle got her purse. "There aren't any malls in Grantville."

"That's the first thing. You gotta stretch your poetic license."

Noelle flatly refused to buy the specific item Denise recommended. No way in God's green earth was she going to send *that* book to Janos Drugeth. But she did allow that the general category was suitable. Even if the postage would be a little steep.

And she decided the girl's final advice was probably good, too.

"*Of course* you put on a return address." Denise slapped her forehead. "Jeez, Louise. You don't know anything. *He* didn't, because *he* was serving. Ball might have gone out of bounds, so he left you a graceful way to just pretend you didn't know where it came from."

She started more-or-less dragging Noelle toward the postal service. "But *you* decided to hit it back. So now

we got a volley going. Can't do that without return
addresses. Face it, girl. The game is afoot!"

Vienna, Austria
February 1635

"Oh, splendid," said Ferdinand, positively beaming. He
turned another page of the beautifully bound volume.
"I've always been very fond of Father Drexel's writings,
myself. So is my sister, Maria Anna."

So was Janos himself, for that matter. But he was still
puzzled by the gift.

Seeing the slight frown on his face, the emperor
clucked his tongue. "Amazing, really. You're so shrewd
on the fields of politics and battle."

He held up the book. "First, it reminds you of your
piety. Whatever else, you are both devout Catholics. The
most solid foundation there is, no?"

Well, that was certainly true.

The emperor turned the book, so Janos could see the
title. "But there's the woman's subtle touch. I will even
say, her wisdom. *The School of Patience.* Which you both
will surely need."

Janos nodded. "Yes, now I see. The war, most likely.
Then, even afterward, a difficult political situation."

Ferdinand set the book down on the table next to his
chair and threw up his hands. "I have allowed a dolt into
my chambers! No, Janos. You will need patience for a
lifetime." He slapped the book. "And that offer, my
friend, *that* is the gift."

"Oh." After a moment, finally understanding, he smiled. "It's going well, then?"

Ferdinand was actually rubbing his hands. "Yes, indeed. Happy Austria. Again."

The following is an excerpt from:

1636
THE DEVIL'S OPERA

ERIC FLINT
DAVID CARRICO

Available from Baen Books
October 2013
hardcover

Chapter 1

Simon came out to the river at least once a week, usually in the predawn light, and walked the bank of the Elbe looking for anything he might scavenge and use or sell. Today the sun was just barely visible over the eastern bank of the river, and the dawn light had not yet dropped down to the shadowed eddy under the willow tree. There was something large floating in the water.

He stared down at the floating corpse. It wasn't the first one he'd ever seen in his young life. It wasn't even the first one he'd seen in the river. But it was the first one he'd seen that he might be able to get something from, if he could only get to it. He edged down to where the water lapped on the bank where he stood, and for a moment crouched as if he was going to reach out and draw the body ashore. That moment passed, though, for as the light brightened he saw that there was no way he could reach the corpse without wading out into the water, which he was loath to do since he couldn't swim.

The boy glanced around. There were no stout sticks nearby, so he had nothing at hand that he could maybe use to draw the body closer. He frowned. There might not be much in the man's pockets, but anything would be more than he had.

His head jerked up at the sound of other voices coming nearer. No help for it now. He'd have to hope the men coming this way would give him something.

"Hai! This way. There's a deader in the water by the tree."

A moment later two of the local fisherman came bustling up. "Och, so there is," the older of the two said. "Third one this year. Well, in you go, Fritz."

"Me?" the younger man replied. "Make him do it." He pointed at Simon, then ducked as the older man made to cuff his ear.

"And a right fool I'd be to send a lad with only one working arm out into even still water."

The young man whined, "Why is it always me that has to go in the water after the deaders?"

"For I am your father, and I say so," the older man replied. "Now get in there afore I knock you in."

The younger man muttered, but he kicked off his shoes and stepped into the water, hissing as the chill moved up his legs. The boy shivered in sympathy as he watched, glad it wasn't him getting wet in the winter breeze. Three strides had the corpse within reach, and Fritz drew it to the bank by one arm.

"Fresh one, this," the older man grunted as he rifled the dead man's pockets with practiced hands. "Ah, here's something." He lifted up something and showed his son. "One of them new clasp knives like Old Barnabas bought." The boy watched with envy as the blade was folded out and then back again. It disappeared into the older man's coat. "Help me turn him over, Fritz."

They flipped the corpse onto its back. The dawn light fell on the face of the corpse, and men and boy stepped back at the sight of the bruises and cuts. "*Scheisse*," the old fisherman said. "This one's no drowning." He shook himself and returning to rifling the clothing, feeling for pockets. "No money, not even a Halle pfennig. His coat's worn worse than yours. His shoes...aye, they might do. Off with them now, and run them to your ma and tell her to set them near the fire to dry."

Simon almost laughed to see the younger man struggling with the corpse to get the shoes off. "Ach, you worthless toad," the older man shoved the young one out of the way and had the shoes off in a moment. "Now get with you, and I'd best not beat you back to the boat."

He turned back to the boy. "Now, you, lad." He looked at him with narrowed eyes. "Seen you about before, I have. Simon, isn't it? Go find a watchman, one of these newfangled *Polizei*, and tell him that Johann the fisher has found a deader in the river. Say nothing to him about the knife and shoes, and tonight there will be a bowl of fish soup for you, and maybe a bit of bread to go with it. Fair enough?"

Simon didn't think it was fair, but he gave a nod anyway, knowing that it was the best he would get. The older man returned the nod, and Simon turned to scramble back up the bank to find a city watchman.

Chapter 2

Otto Gericke looked out the small diamond-shaped panes in his office window at the sprawl of the exurb of Magdeburg, what some had taken to calling Greater Magdeburg. When Gustavus Adolphus had chosen Magdeburg to become the capitol of his new continental realm, what had been a city of perhaps half a square mile within its fortified walls had quickly mushroomed into a metropolis that, if it wasn't in the same league as Paris or London as far as size, bid fair to grow into that league in the not-too-distant-future. And as the up-timers put it, it was Otto's baby...or his headache, depending on which up-timer you talked to. He was mayor of Greater Magdeburg, appointed so by Gustavus Adolphus, who had then scurried off to war without giving him much more instruction than "Clean up this mess, and build me a capitol to be proud of." Certainly there was no provision for a city council for Greater Magdeburg to share the work, or for an election of a replacement. Which meant that everything of any consequence, and most items of little consequence, ended up on Otto's desk. He had started mentally labeling days as "baby" or "headache," and when he had shared that thought with up-timers like Jere Haygood, all they had done was laugh.

Looking at his clock, Otto decided that he'd best get back to work. He had just settled back into his chair when the door to his office opened and an elderly man was ushered in by his secretary.

"Thank you, Albrecht," Otto said. "See to it that we are not disturbed, if you would." The secretary nodded and closed the door as he stepped out.

Otto stepped around his desk and embraced the man in turn. "Papa Jacob. It is good to see you." He smiled. "Even if you did catch me somewhat *deshabille*." He indicated his jacket on the coat tree and his rolled-up shirt sleeves.

Jacob Alemann, Otto's father-in-law, stumped over to a chair obviously prepared for him, sat down and lifted his foot onto the waiting stool. He leaned back with a sigh, holding his cane with loose fingers.

"I see the gout still troubles you," Otto commented as he walked to a sideboard and busied himself with a wine decanter. "Have you not read what the Grantville doctors are saying about gout?"

"I have, and what is worse, my wife has. And I am, with reluctance, willing to moderate my eating, but I will not give up my daily regimen of wine. After all, it was Saint Paul who said, 'Take a little wine for thy stomach's sake,' and who am I to disregard the instruction of an apostle and saint?"

Otto returned to offer a glass of wine to the older man. "With all due respect, Jacob, I somehow doubt that the good saint had in mind the quantities of wine that you drink."

Alemann chuckled, then took a sip of the wine. His eyebrows climbed his forehead, and he looked at the glass with respect. "Where did you get Hungarian wine around here?"

The destruction of the war so far had caused devastation in much of the farmlands of the central Germanies.

The wineries in particular had been hit hard. Not much had been produced for several years, and the quality of what had been bottled was noticeably lacking.

"Wallenstein, actually," Otto responded, settling into his chair behind the desk. He grinned at the frown that crossed his father-in-law's face. "He felt he owed Michael Stearns somewhat, so as a favor he shipped a small portion of the Bohemian royal wine cellars to Michael. Rebecca Abrabanel was kind enough to provide a small share of that to me. A small share of a small portion, to be sure, but I understand that the Bohemian wine cellars were, umm, significant, so there were more than a few bottles." He chuckled as he swirled the wine in his own glass.

"Indeed," Alemann said, lifting his glass again. "Small recompense for the damage Wallenstein's dog Pappenheim did to Magdeburg, but I suppose we should be thankful for small blessings, no matter the source."

Otto thought that was a remarkably temperate statement from one who had been in Magdeburg before the sack and resulting destruction done by Pappenheim's troops several years before when he served under Tilly. Most survivors' comments concerning the erstwhile Austrian army field commander began with the scatological and descended quickly to the infernal and blasphemous. The fact that Pappenheim was now firmly ensconced in Wallenstein's court, and Wallenstein was now at least nominally allied with the USE and Gustavus Adolphus, had little effect on the depth of rancor that the survivors of the sack of Magdeburg had for him.

"Enough of unpleasant topics," Alemann declared. "Why did you ask to meet with me, Otto?"

"Jacob, you are still a member of the *Schöffenstuhl*, correct?"

Gericke was referring to the senior jurisprudence

body for the *Magdeburger Recht* association, the group
of cities in central Europe which had been granted laws
and rights by their sovereigns that were drawn from
the laws and charter of Magdeburg itself. It had been
located in Magdeburg, and until the sack had functioned
as what the Grantvillers would have called an appellate
court for cases that their own courts could not address
or whose decisions needed ratification.

"Yah, you know that I am, but that means nothing
now, Otto." Alemann shook his head. "All of our files,
all of our books, all of our documents were destroyed
in the sack, except for a handful that I managed to
snatch up in the face of the flames. Centuries of work,
centuries of civilization, centuries of wisdom, now nothing
but ash at Pappenheim's hand." From his expression,
he would convert the soldier to a like condition if it
were in his power. His mouth worked as if he desired
to spit, but he refrained.

"But you and some of your fellow jurists still live."
Otto leaned forward, his expression very intense. "Your
names still carry weight. People still respect your wisdom, especially people in this part of the USE. Maybe
not so much over in the west or by the Rhineland, but
definitely in Saxony, Brandenburg, Thuringia-Franconia,
and even into Bohemia, Poland, and the Ukraine."

"And if that is so?" Alemann shook his head again. "It
is a dying reputation, Otto. What use is it to talk of it?"

"Ah, Jacob. Perhaps the wine has affected more than
your foot," Otto said with a small smile. "Your position
and authority as jurists has never been recalled or
revoked. And Magdeburg the city needs you. I need you."

"Say on," Alemann replied.

"You want work to do. I can give you that work."

Otto watched his father-in-law rock back in his

chair with a bit of a stunned look. He rallied quickly, however. "Oh, come now, Otto. We are in no position of authority."

"You may not now be, perhaps," Otto conceded, "but you do occupy a position of undoubted moral authority. And I can give you proper legal standing."

"How will you accomplish that?" Alemann looked at Otto in some surprise.

"Magdeburg is an imperial city in the USE, you know that. We are independent of the province of Magdeburg, yes?" Otto spoke incisively. "That means we should have an independent magistracy and judiciary as well. I've been making do, but we need the *Schöffenstuhl* to resume, to serve as the senior judiciary for the city, including as what the up-timers call an appellate court. Some of the matters that are coming before me and the other magistrates," he shook his own head, "should be coming to you. So take on this work as the reconvened *Schöffenstuhl*, and I will then empanel you as part of the city governance. You will have good work to do, and it will take a fair amount of work off my shoulders."

"And paper out of your office, no doubt," Alemann retorted, looking at the files stacked on various tables and cabinets.

"A side benefit." Otto waved a hand airily.

"And you have this authority?"

Alemann was sounding interested, Otto thought to himself. That was a good sign. He chuckled, then held up a hand as his father-in-law frowned at him.

"I think you will find, Jacob, that within the boundaries of Magdeburg, Imperial Province and Free City of the United States of Europe, my authority is limited only by the will of the emperor himself. He never got around to giving the new city a charter or giving me much of a job description before his injury, and until he or his heir or Parliament does..." Otto shrugged.

Before Alemann could respond to that thought, there came an interruption. Albrecht opened the door from the outer office and stuck his head in.

"Excuse me, Herr Gericke, but your stepfather is here and wishes to see you."

"By all means, let him in, Albrecht." Otto stood hurriedly and moved out from behind his desk just in time to embrace the man who almost charged past the secretary. "Papa Christoff, it is good to see you!"

"And you as well, son."

Christoff Schultze was a lean man who was active beyond his years, as the thump he gave to Otto's shoulder bore witness. He had married Otto's mother after the death of her second husband, and had never treated Otto with anything other than care and consideration. Love may not have come into play between them, but certainly affection had, and it showed in their greetings.

"Please, be seated."

Otto gestured to the other chair in front of his desk, and returned to the sideboard to quickly pour another glass of wine for his stepfather.

"Aah," Schultze sighed after taking his first sip. "I do like a glass of good wine. I only wish I had time to properly savor this one."

"Then I take it you are here on some official matter?" Otto asked.

"Indeed," Schultze replied. "Ludwig sent me."

That would be *Fürst* Ludwig von Anhalt-Cöthen, Otto thought to himself, Gustav Adolph's appointed administrator for the archbishopric's properties, owned by the *Erzstift* of Magdeburg, which in turn was now owned by Gustavus Adolphus.

"And how is *Fürst* Ludwig these days?" Otto asked, wondering just what errand could have forced the good *Fürst* to send his chief lieutenant.

Schultze's response was very sober. "Concerned. Very concerned."

"And who isn't?" Alemann responded dryly. "The news from Berlin is not good, and Chancellor Oxenstierna's actions do little to inspire one to confidence." Otto nodded in agreement.

A darker tone entered Schultze's voice. "Indeed. You know of Gustav Adolph's condition." Schultze was not asking a question—it was wellknown that the emperor's head injury received in battle with the Poles and the resulting wandering wits that Dr. Nichols called "aphasia" had for all intents and purposes rendered him *non compos mentis*. "I assume you also know of what Oxenstierna is attempting."

Both Otto and Alemann started to reply. Otto waved his hand at his father-in-law, who nodded and said, "Every child above the age of three in Magdeburg understands what the Swedish chancellor is attempting. He desires to roll back, make null, the many changes that Gustavus has made in the governance of the USE, or at least the ones that changed the social order and the religious tolerance—or should I say, lack of tolerance?"

The older man looked over to Otto, who picked up the thread. "He and his allies have some kind of hold on Prime Minister Wettin, what the up-timers would call leverage, and between that and Oxenstierna's position as chancellor of Sweden, they look to control the government of the USE. I believe they have misread the tenor of the times, but I am deathly afraid that we will all pay for their mistakes before they go down."

Schultze nodded. "Your judgment, Otto, is much the

same as *Fürst* Ludwig's. And his situation as administrator of the property formerly owned by the Archbishopric of Magdeburg is a bit complicated. On the one hand," Schultze held out his left hand, "his authority comes from Gustav Adolph; he gave an oath to the king of Sweden before he became emperor, and therefore he might be considered to be under the chancellor's authority as he acts as regent for Princess Kristina during her father's incapacitation. On the other hand," he held out his right hand, "he detests Oxenstierna, so he would dearly love to tell him to, ah, 'take a flying leap,' as one of the Grant-villers described it. Even for a Swede, the chancellor is overbearingly arrogant. On yet another hand..." Otto smiled as he saw his stepfather struggle for a moment over which hand to hold up again, only to drop them both back into his lap, "Wilhelm Wettin, the prime minister, is his nephew. And although he loves his nephew and would ordinarily support him just on that cause, he is very much concerned that Wettin has made some ill-advised decisions in recent months. So he has a great desire to be very cautious as to what he does."

"I can see that," murmured Otto, who nonetheless wished that the *Fürst* would be more direct. And his earlier feeling was proven correct—this was going to be a headache day. He propped his head on his hands, massaging his temples.

"So, he is delaying responding to demands from the chancellor and his nephew, while he sent me hurrying from Halle to meet with you here. I had planned to ask Otto to bring you here, Jacob," Schultze focused his gaze on Alemann, "so the coincidence of finding you here at the moment simply speeds my errand. Jacob, I need you to reconvene the *Schöffenstuhl*."

Otto burst out laughing as his father-in-law's jaw

dropped. A moment later Alemann pointed a long finger in Otto's direction.

"You put him up to this, didn't you? Confess it!"

Still laughing, Otto raised both hands to the level of his shoulders. He finally choked back the hilarity enough to speak.

"Before the throne of heaven and all its angels, Jacob, I did no such thing. I had no idea that Papa Christoff would even be here today."

He turned to his confused stepfather.

"You see, I just told Jacob I need him to bring the *Schöffenstuhl* back into being in the service of the city of Magdeburg."

Both of them started chuckling as Alemann directed a dark look first at one of them, then the other.

"Oh, leave off, Jacob," Schultze finally said, waving his empty hand in the air. "There is no collusion here."

"Well enough," Alemann said, shifting his foot on its stool. "And if that be so, then what brings you here seeking the *Schöffenstuhl*?"

"What the *Fürst* would ask of the *Schöffenstuhl* is an opinion, a judgment, as to whether under USE law, custom, and practice, the chancellor of Sweden can serve as regent for Gustav's heir for the USE in the absence of a specific appointment by Gustav."

For the second time in less than an hour, Otto saw his father-in-law taken aback. He could see the objection in Alemann's eyes, and spoke up before the older man could.

"Authority," Otto said. The eyes of both the other men shifted to him. "As we discussed, Jacob; you already possess the moral authority, and I will give you the legal standing and authority."

He could see the words really sink in this time. Alemann responded with a slow nod.

"Such a judgment could have great effect, you know," Schultze observed in a quiet tone.

"And what if we were to rule in favor of the chancellor?" Alemann demanded.

Schultze shrugged. "Ludwig is willing to take that chance. And in truth, if you ruled that way, it would allow him to support family, which for a man of his lineage is always an important consideration." He paused for a moment. "But I do not think that is the ruling he truly wants. As much as he finds many of the recent changes distasteful, Ludwig is fearful of what will result from Oxenstierna's machinations."

"And why do you not send this request to the *Reichskammergericht*, or rather, the USE Supreme Court as it is called now?"

"Time, Jacob," Schultze responded. "We need an opinion soon, and if we send our request to Wetzlar, who knows how long it will take those 'learned men' to respond?" It was evident from the sarcasm in his voice that he did not have a high opinion of the Supreme Court.

Otto thought about the matter for a moment, then looked to his father-in-law. "Jacob, do it. You know you want to."

Alemann snorted, then turned to Schultze. "Have it your way, Christoff. Let *Fürst* Ludwig have the petition and brief drawn up and sent to us. I will convene my fellows, and we will deliberate; perhaps even consult with someone like Master Thomas Price Riddle from Grantville, or Doctor Grotius at Jena. I will even endeavor to conduct the deliberations at a pace somewhat faster than deliberate." He smiled at his little joke.

"And you, Otto," Alemann looked back to his son-in-law, "if you would have us do this, then find us space. The rebuilt *Rathaus* in Old Magdeburg will not contain us. And it is most likely that those members serving on this year's council will not allow us to use it anyway, once they hear of what we are doing, Brandenburg sympathizers that they mostly are."

There was a tinge of distaste in the way he said "Old Magdeburg." The term was commonly used to refer to the half-a-square-mile within the fortifications that was the original city. Despite its near-total destruction in the course of the sack of Magdeburg by Tilly's army, the still-official status of Old Magdeburg enabled its authorities to maintain a legal façade for their behavior. Obstreperous behavior, so far as both Alemann and Otto were concerned.

Schultze pulled a folded document from an inside pocket of his coat. Otto began chuckling as the document was unfolded and seals dangled from the bottom of it. "Here," Schultze said, "one petition and attached brief, duly executed and sealed by the petitioner."

"The *Fürst* anticipated me, I see," Alemann said with a wry grin.

All three men sobered quickly. "Yes, he did," Schultze replied. "And his last words to me were 'Tell them to hurry. The time when I will need this is fast approaching.' Ludwig is not one to jump at shadows, you know. If he feels fear, then should we all."

With that thought Otto had to agree.

Chapter 3

Gotthilf Hoch, detective sergeant in the Magdeburg *Polizei*, walked out the front door of his family's home in the *Altstadt*, the oldest part of Magdeburg. The early morning air was cold, even for December. He remembered hearing that the up-timers from Grantville sometimes said this was the "Little Ice Age." On days like today, when his breath fogged in front of him and the hairs in his nose tingled when he breathed in, he could believe it. The old pagan stories about Fimbulwinter were easy to accept right now.

He pulled his hat down over his ears and pushed his gloved hands into his coat pockets, then started off down the street. Just his luck, when he wanted a cab, there wasn't one to be seen.

When he reached the Gustavstrasse, he turned right and headed for Hans Richter square, where he turned right again and headed for the nearest bridge across *Der Grosse Graben*, the moat that encircled the *Altstadt*, which was usually called The Big Ditch. He passed through the gate in the rebuilt city wall, which triggered his usual musing about the fact that the walls had been rebuilt. He'd never seen much sense in all that time and effort being spent on that task, but the city council of Old Magdeburg had insisted on it, saying that the contracts they had signed years ago to allow people to seek protection in times of war and siege required it. From what

Gotthilf could see, all it did was emphasize a boundary between the old city and the new. Which, come to think of it, may have been what the city council was intending all along.

Gotthilf looked over the railing of the bridge at the water moving sluggishly through the moat. Dark water; it looked very cold. He shivered and moved on, feet crunching in the gravel after he stepped off the bridge.

Only the busiest streets in the exurb of Greater Magdeburg were graveled. Most of them were bare dirt. One thing that Gotthilf did appreciate from the cold was that the ground was frozen most of the time, reducing mud to solid. He still had to watch his step, because an ankle turned in a frozen rut could hurt like crazy, but at least he didn't have to scrape the muck and mire off his boots like he did in the spring and fall.

There were more people on the streets now, as the sun rose higher in the eastern sky behind him. The bakers had been up for hours, of course, and he swung by one to grab a fresh roll for breakfast, since he hadn't felt up to facing his mother across a table that morning. He munched on that as he walked, watching everyone walking by.

Construction workers of every stripe were moving briskly about; carpenters, masons, and general laborers were in demand for the new hospital expansion, as well as several other projects in the city, not to mention the navy yard. Several women were out selling broadsheets and newspapers, including the shrill-voiced hawk-faced young woman who handed out Committee of Correspondence broadsheets in that part of town.

But still no cabs. He shook his head. Never a cab when you wanted one.

A hand landed on Gotthilf's shoulder, startling him.

He looked up to see his partner, Byron Chieske, settling into place alongside him.

Gotthilf had to look up at Byron. In truth, he had to look up at most adults. He wasn't very tall; not that he was a dwarf, or anything like that. Nor was he thin or spindly. He was a solid chunk of young man; he just wasn't very tall.

Byron, on the other hand, was tall, even for an up-timer. He stood a bit over six feet, was well-muscled, and had large square hands. His clean-shaven face was a bit craggy in feature, but not of a nature that would be called ugly.

"Yo, Gotthilf," Byron said. "Ready for the meeting with the captain this morning?" The captain would be Bill Reilly, another up-timer. Byron was a lieutenant. The two of them had been seconded in early 1635 to the Magdeburg city watch to lead in transforming that organization from what amounted to a group of gossips, busybodies, and bullies to an actual police force on the model of an up-time city police group. They had both been involved in police and security work up-time; they both had at least some education and training in the work; and they had both been in an MP detachment from the State of Thuringia-Franconia army that was stationed in Magdeburg at the time, so they had been available.

"As ready as I'm going to be," Gotthilf muttered, "considering we have nothing of worth to report."

"Yeah, Bill may chew on us a bit," Byron conceded as they walked down the street toward the station building. "But he knows we can't make bricks without straw. No information, no leads, no results."

Gotthilf snorted. Byron looked at him with his trademark raised eyebrow, and the down-timer snorted again, before saying, "You know, for someone who professes to not darken the door of a church, you certainly know your way around Biblical allusions."

Byron chuckled. "Oh, I spent a lot of my childhood in Sunday School, Gotthilf. I may have drifted away from it some as an adult, but a lot of it stuck." He shoved his hands in his coat pockets, and grinned down at his partner.

Gotthilf grinned back at Byron, who seemed to be in a garrulous mood this morning—by the up-timer's standards, anyway. Byron was ordinarily one who wouldn't say two words where one would do, and wouldn't say one where a gesture or facial expression would serve instead. So to get five sentences out of him in as many minutes bordered on being voluble.

As they stepped on down the street, Gotthilf's mind recalled their first meeting, ten months ago. He had trouble now even remembering why he had joined the watch; something to do with wanting to do something to prove to his father he was more than just a routine clerk, if he recalled rightly. He had been smarting from another comparison to his brother Nikolaus, studying law at Jena. Not that his father was impressed with the city watch, either, as it turned out.

On the day that he met Byron, Gotthilf was the youngest member of the city watch, the newest, and possibly the angriest. He hadn't really wanted to be paired with the lieutenant, and he wasn't of a mind that the over-tall up-timer had anything to teach him or anything to bring to the city watch. But their first case—one involving the murder of a young girl and a young blind lad involved in petty thievery—had opened his eyes to what the Polizei could do.

So now, even at his young age of twenty-three, Gotthilf was an ardent supporter of the captain and the lieutenant, having quit his clerking position and thrown himself into the job. He was now one of three detective sergeants on the force, partnered with Byron, and still one of the youngest men in the *Polizei*.

And that and a pfennig will get me a cup of coffee at Walcha's Coffee House, he gibed at himself.

The two men walked into the station house, hung their coats on pegs in the hallway, and headed for their desks. They flipped through the papers and folders lying there, then looked at each other.

"See the captain?" Gotthilf asked.

"Yep," Byron responded.

They headed for Reilly's office on the second floor. Byron took the lead.

"Chieske, Hoch." The captain set down his pencil, folded his hands on top of the document he was reading, and nodded toward a couple of chairs a bit to the side of his desk. "Have a seat. Any progress on that floater case?"

"The one the riverfront watch pulled out of the water a few days ago who looked like he'd been run through a meat tenderizer before he got dumped in the river?"

"That's the one. The floating corpse who was identified as . . ." Reilly picked up a different document from his desk. ". . . one Joseph Delt, common laborer." His eyebrows arched.

"Officially, nothing to say," Gotthilf began.

Reilly nodded. "And unofficially?"

"Nothing," Byron responded with a shrug before Gotthilf could speak.

The captain steepled his hands in front of his face. "Why? Or why not?"

"No leads, Captain," Chieske responded.

"Make some. Start flipping over rocks and talking

to bugs and snakes, if you have to, but get me some results, and soon. You know as well as I do what's going on here, Byron. It's not as if American history wasn't full of it."

Seeing Sergeant Hoch's quizzical expression, the police chief elaborated. "Magdeburg's a boom town full of immigrants, with more coming in every day. We had a lot of cities like that in America back up-time. It went on for centuries. Certain things always came with the phenomenon, and one of them was the rise of criminal gangs. I'll bet you any sum you want—don't take me up on it, I'll clean you out—that what we're seeing here is one or more crime bosses trying to establish themselves in the city. These men being killed are the ones who were too stubborn, too stupid—or just couldn't learn—to keep their mouths shut."

He leaned back in his seat. "There's no way to completely stop it from happening, but we need to at least keep it under control. Because if we don't and it gets out of hand, sooner or later the city's Committee of Correspondence will decide it has to crack down on the criminals. I don't want that, Mayor Gericke doesn't want that, you don't want that—hell, the Fourth of July Party and even the CoC itself doesn't want it. But it'll happen, sure as hell."

Gotthilf made a face. The leader of Magdeburg's Committee of Correspondence was a man named Gunther Achterhof. Like most people in today's Magdeburg, he was an immigrant. He'd arrived from Brandenburg with his younger sister, the two of them being the only survivors of a family ravaged by the mercenary armies that had passed through the region.

Gunther had also arrived with a sack full of the ears and noses of stray mercenary soldiers he'd killed along the way. He was an honest man, but one whose concept of justice was as razor sharp as the knife he'd used to kill and mutilate those soldiers. If he unleashed the CoC's armed squads on the city's criminal element, they'd certainly bring order to the streets—but they'd also shred any semblance of due process and reasonable legality in the doing.

As it stood, there was already a fair amount of tension between the CoC and the city's fledgling police force. If these kinds of killings continued with no one apprehended, the CoC's existing skepticism concerning the value of a duly-appointed police force would just be confirmed.

"You got it, Captain," Byron said.

"Go on," Reilly waved a hand. "Go encourage the good citizens of Magdeburg to be good citizens."

Gotthilf followed Byron up the hall, down the stairs and out the main entrance of the building, grabbing their coats on the way. He caught up with his partner outside, waving for their driver to bring up the light horse-drawn cart they used for transportation.

"So what are we going to do?" Gotthilf asked as the cart pulled up.

"Dig some more," Byron replied tersely. Gotthilf followed his partner onto the cart, and they left to begin digging.

The city of Magdeburg in the year 1635 was unique throughout Europe—throughout the world, actually. There was no place like it.

On the one hand, it was old. The city name originally meant "Mighty Fortress," and historical records indicated that it was founded in the year 805 by none other than the Emperor Charlemagne. Histories of the Germanies, whether contemporary or from the up-time library in Grantville, mentioned the city often. It had many connections with Holy Roman Emperors over the years. It became the See of the Archbishop of Magdeburg in 968, and its first patent and charter was given in 1035. It was even one of the easternmost members of the Hanseatic League. And Martin Luther had spent time there, beginning in 1524, which perhaps explained the subsequent dogged Protestantism of the city.

On the other hand, Magdeburg was new. The city had been besieged by the army of the Holy Roman Empire from November 1630 until May 20, 1631. The siege culminated in the Sack of Magdeburg, in which over 20,000 residents were massacred. Over ninety percent of the city was destroyed by fire, and what little wasn't burned was ransacked, looted, plundered, and pillaged. Magdeburg was devastated; prostrate.

Then came the Ring of Fire, with the arrival of Grantville, West Virginia, from the future. And everything changed.

Gustavus Adolphus, king of Sweden and champion of the Protestant cause, connected with the up-timers from Grantville, and set in motion a train of events that gave birth—or rebirth, if you prefer—to the modern Magdeburg of 1635.

Pre-Ring of Fire Magdeburg was small, by up-timer standards. The area within the city walls was about half a square mile. It was shaped something like a right triangle, with the long side of the triangle running parallel to the river Elbe, and the hypotenuse side running from northeast to southwest. The normal population of the city had been about 25,000 people. That boosted to nearly 35,000 during the siege, as everyone from the surrounding regions who had a contracted right for shelter and sanctuary moved into the city when the HRE army approached.

Magdeburg in 1635 was a very different creature. Gustavus Adolphus, now proclaimed emperor, had decreed that the city would be the capitol of what became the United States of Europe. Otto Gericke was appointed mayor of the city, and was given imperial instruction to make Magdeburg a capitol city of which the emperor could be proud. And things just kind of mushroomed from there.

Instigated by the up-timers, north of the city were the naval yards, where the iron-clad and timber-clad ships of the USE Navy had been constructed. There wouldn't be any more ironclads in the foreseeable future, and the timberclad construction had slowed down considerably. But the yard was still working and its work force was still fully employed. The navy yard's machine tools and facilities were being turned into the USE's major weapons manufacturing center and were now working around the clock. In theory, that was to provide the army fighting the Poles with the weapons they needed. But nobody was oblivious to the fact that those same weapons could easily be used to defend Magdeburg itself, in the event the current crisis turned into an all-out civil war.

South of the city was the coal gas plant, surrounded by a constellation of factories that were powered by the plant's output. All of these operations drew hungry unemployed and underemployed men from all over the Germanies. So, since early 1634, the city had become home to a horde of navy men, factory workers and skilled craftsmen. Inevitably, construction workers had followed to provide homes for the work force and facilities for the employers. All this gave Magdeburg a certain flavor, a "blue-collar" spirit, as some of the Grantvillers called it, which was certainly fostered by the Committees of Correspondence. It also made for interesting times.

But workers, and their families, need places to sleep, and food to eat, so rooming houses and bakeries and such began to grow up to the west of the old city. And it turned out that the big businesses along the river side needed smaller businesses to make things for them, so various workshops began to appear in the western districts.

By late 1635, Greater Magdeburg occupied several square miles along the riverside and to the west. No one had a good estimate as to how many people lived in the new city because of the constant influx of new residents, but the Committees of Correspondence had recently told the mayor that they thought it was approaching one hundred thousand. Germans, Swedes, Dutch, Poles, Hungarians, Bohemians, even the odd Austrian, Bavarian, or Romanian could be found in the city streets or swinging a hammer at the Navy yard.

A population of that size would naturally have a leavening of rough-edged men. Hard men, one might call them, who would be more inclined to follow the ways of Cain than of Abel. Mayor Gericke realized in late 1634 that the city watch of the old city was not able to deal with the influx of these men, so in early 1635 he requisitioned a couple of Grantvillers with police experience from the up-timer units contributed to the USE army to try to mold the city watch into something that could provide up-time style civic protection and police services to the whole city.

The city watch had never been held in high esteem, so there was a certain reservation on the part of many of the citizens and residents to take issues to them. The well-to-do patricians and burghers of Old Magdeburg could afford to utilize the courts. The workers of Greater Magdeburg couldn't afford a lawyer, most times, so their recourses were three: take it to the Committees of Correspondence, if the matter was one that the CoC was interested in; handle it themselves or with the aid of their friends; or take it to the newly formed *Polizei*.

Such was Greater Magdeburg in December 1635: newly born, vibrant, alive, with a spirit like no other city in the world, and sometimes an edge to it that could leave you bleeding.

Such was the city Gotthilf thought of as his own. Such was the city that he and his partner watched over.

Chapter 4

Mary Simpson stood as her guests entered the room.

"Good morning, Representative Abrabanel, President Piazza."

When Rebecca Abrabanel had asked to visit, Mary had suspected that the resulting conversations would involve politics to some extent. After all, given that Rebecca was a member of the USE parliament from Magdeburg, that her husband was the former (and first) prime minister of the USE, and that she was one of the leaders of the Fourth of July political party, it would be difficult to find something to discuss with her that *didn't* involve politics in some manner. And seeing Rebecca accompanied by Ed Piazza, President of Thuringia-Franconia, up-timer, and also a leader of the Fourth of July party, simply confirmed her suspicions.

"Mary," Ed said, holding out his hand. She grasped it, glad that he was a seasoned enough politician to know the difference between a firm grip and a crushing one, even—or especially—for someone as small as she was.

Ed released her hand, and she turned to Rebecca, who offered her hand in turn. "Ed, Rebecca, it's good to see you," Mary said as she shook hands with the other woman. "You know Lady Beth, of course." Lady Beth Haygood, the up-timer who was head of the Duchess Elizabeth Sofie Secondary School for Girls in Magdeburg and also happened to be one of Mary's lieutenants, stepped forward from where she stood before her chair for another round of handshakes.

"Please, be seated," Mary said, motioning to the nearby chairs. They settled in as Mary motioned to Hilde, who was hovering nearby, to present the coffee tray. Mary poured the cups and handed them around, then settled back with her own, grateful that it was strong and hot enough to fight the chill from the outside weather. Like many people who were both short and slight, she seemed to suffer more from cold than larger folks. Thinking back to winters in Pittsburgh, she shivered a bit, and took another sip.

"One of the reasons I like to come to your parlor," Ed said with a smile. "You do serve a good cup of coffee."

Lady Beth nodded in agreement.

"Thank you," Mary said. "Don Francisco finally made connections for us with a supplier of the best beans, and Hilde has learned the best ways to roast and grind them, so I'll admit to enjoying my own coffee."

"Walcha's Coffee House isn't bad," Lady Beth observed. "A lot of the teachers go there."

The conversation continued on that line for a couple of minutes, until Mary brought it to a close after there was a brief lull. "To see both of the leading lights of the Fourth of July Party sitting in my parlor puts me in mind of the days when the Pittsburgh politicos would come around looking for a favor." She smiled at them over her cup.

Rebecca set her cup down on a side table, and leaned forward a bit in her chair, expression becoming more intent.

"Mary, I want to thank you and Lady Beth for agreeing to meet with us on such short notice. And you are correct; we do have something important to ask of you."

Mary took another sip of coffee to feel the warmth

slide down her throat. She had had some contact with
the senator in the past, of course. How could she not?
Rebecca Abrabanel was not only a government figure in
Magdeburg, but was also the wife of Michael Stearns,
who'd been the prime minister of the USE during the
time when Mary had become the leading social light
of Magdeburg. They weren't close friends, not by any
standard, but there was a solid respect between the
two women.

"Rebecca, if you and Ed need to bring something up
with us, then, given the times, we'd best be available
to you. So what's up?"

Mary almost expected Ed Piazza to take the lead, since
he was an up-timer and would be perfectly comfortable
speaking to another up-timer. Her estimation of the
senator went up when she continued as she had begun.

"We need your help," the other woman began. "With
everything that's going on with Gustavus Adolphus and
Oxenstierna, it's pretty obvious that the chancellor is
trying to draw what Ed calls the center of gravity from
Magdeburg to Berlin."

Ed continued, "It's like this, Mary. If Oxenstierna
gets everyone to start thinking that Berlin is the center
of power and all things governmental..."

"Then he's gone a long way toward becoming the
de facto government," Mary completed the thought,
"regardless of the legalities involved."

"Right." Both Rebecca and Ed sat back in their seats.

"I'm neither a politician nor a political theorist," Mary
said, "so I'm not much help in the political arena." Ed
Piazza snorted at that, but Mary ignored him. "You must
want something from me, though, or we wouldn't be
having this little chat."

Rebecca resumed with, "Mike told me that you once

said you wanted Magdeburg to glitter. Well, right now we want, or rather, we need you to make Magdeburg glitter like it never has before. We want every newspaper in the empire and all the surrounding countries to be filled with news about Magdeburg. We want Magdeburg to be so present and so prominent that Berlin seems like a country village beside it."

Mary set her cup aside and steepled her fingers beneath her nose. After a moment, she looked up. "Unofficial propaganda, huh? By downplaying Berlin, you downplay the chancellor and his cronies."

"Exactly!" Ed barked with a grin.

Mary frowned. "I can see that. But you realize I can't be overtly political in this—in anything. I *am* the Admiral's wife, after all." They all heard the capital letter as she pronounced her husband's title.

Admiral Simpson's stand of neutrality in the chaos swirling in northern Germany was widely known. Everyone over the age of twelve had their opinions as to whether or not it was a wise or prudent position for him to have taken, but no one doubted that he meant what he said.

"Caesar's wife," Lady Beth inserted in support of her leader.

"Who must be without reproach, yes," Rebecca said. "We are not asking for coordination and collusion. Simply that you do those things you would ordinarily do, but as prominently and loudly and, ah, 'splashily' as you can, if there is such a word."

"There is now," Mary replied with a smile. She sipped her coffee while she thought on everything that had been said, and much that hadn't.

Naturally, she was tempted to ask for some funding. The arts *always* needed more money, and squeezing the powers-that-be for it was something Mary Simpson had done for so long—first in Pittsburgh, in another universe; now here in Magdeburg—that it was almost second nature to her.

But it would be a bad idea, in the long run. As much as she'd love to add an additional revenue stream to the Arts Council, she needed to maintain a public image of political neutrality. She could afford to let that image get strained, but not get broken outright.

No, this was something that would just have to be done for its own sake. When her cup was empty, she set it down on its saucer on the table before her and looked to her guests.

"No cooperation, no collusion, no conspiring. We will do what we think is best, and you will find out about it through normal channels."

Rebecca looked at Ed. He nodded.

"Agreed."

"Then I think we have an understanding," Mary said. "Keep an eye on the papers."

When her guests left, Mary accompanied them to the door. Just before the door closed behind them, she heard Ed Piazza exclaim, "Not political, hah!"

She was still smiling when she returned to Lady Beth in the parlor. Mary looked over at her friend and lieutenant as she refreshed their coffee. "What do you think?"

Lady Beth had a notepad open and was already reviewing notes. "Salons, concerts, recitals, parades, feast celebrations, we can do lots of things. There are at least a couple of news reporter types in town that we can probably work with for articles, maybe more."

Mary nodded. "We need to commission some musical

works from the local composers, but at least one of them needs to be based on King Arthur. The theme of the wounded king who would return to his people in their time of trouble would just absolutely resonate with most of the folks."

Lady Beth frowned. "It might be better to use Barbarossa as the subject, since he was a German emperor and his legend has many of the same elements—especially the theme of the sleeping ruler who will someday return to save his nation."

"It's a possibility," Mary said, "but... The problem is that I can't see the legend serving well as the story for an opera. So Emperor Barbarossa is sleeping with his knights somewhere under—what mountain was it?"

"There are variations. Some say Kyffhäuser, in Thuringia; others say it's Mount Untersberg in Bavaria."

Mary shook her head. "How do you do an opera based on a bunch of sleeping men? And what's probably still worse from a dramatic standpoint is that there would be no suitable female roles in such an opera. Well, I suppose..."

She made a face. Lady Beth laughed. "Yes, a bit difficult! The only woman anywhere in the Barbarossa legend is his wife Beatrice, who was insulted by the Milanese. And the emperor took his revenge by forcing the authorities of the city to eat figs coming out of the hind end of a donkey. How in the world would you stage *that*?—much less put it to song!"

Both women chuckled. Then Mary said: "No, best we stick with the Arthur legend."

"Great idea," Lady Beth said enthusiastically. She rubbed her hands together. "Get a couple of memorable songs out of it to put on the radio and send out the sheet music, and it could weld people together like nothing else. Only make it better than *Camelot*. I never could stand that show," she muttered. "Julie Andrews—*pfaugh!*"

"And I know just the people to pull it off," Mary said. "How soon can we get Amber Higham and Heinrich Schütz over here? What's the use of having a theater director and a great composer among your friends if you don't put them to use?"

—end excerpt—

from *1636: The Devil's Opera*
available in hardcover,
October 2013, from Baen Books

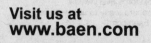